JOHN GRIESEMER

SIGNAL & NOISE

A NOVEL

THE INTERNATIONAL BESTSELLER

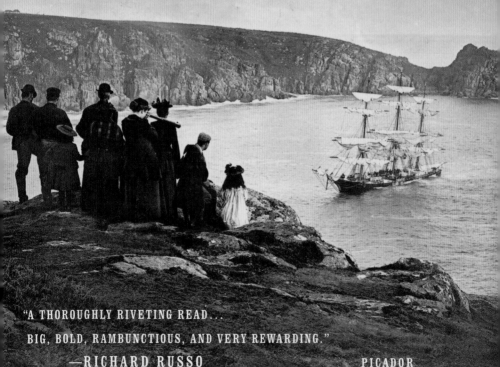

"A THOROUGHLY RIVETING READ...
BIG, BOLD, RAMBUNCTIOUS, AND VERY REWARDING."
—RICHARD RUSSO

PICADOR

Additional Acclaim for John Griesemer's *Signal & Noise*

"Ambition, failure, triumph, love, betrayal, farce, and spirit conjuring—these are some of the subjects powerfully animated in this grand novel. John Griesemer is a masterful writer. In *Signal & Noise,* he has turned the clamor of history into a beautiful symphony."

—Joanna Scott, author of *Arrogance*

"Griesemer packs his vision of history with imaginative verve . . . an operatic tale rife with intrigue but permeated by the conflict between the proud stride of ambition and the frequent abjectness of reality. Griesemer builds powerful momentum here. . . . [He] shows that ambition can also commingle with emotion."

—*The Denver Post*

"Massive, structurally complex, ambitious . . . Griesemer brilliantly draws us into the lives of these characters and the era in which they lived. . . . A first-rate historical novel, *Signal & Noise* offers readers open passage on a captivating and remarkable voyage."

—*The Oregonian*

"What could have been a dry story about the laying of the first transatlantic cable comes to life with the human drama behind the massive project."

—*USA Today*

"A rollicksome good read . . . At 593 pages, it reads like a breeze. And if you want substance, Griesemer supplies that as well. . . . Griesemer captures this world with élan . . . recalls *Ragtime,* with its mix of historical figures and fictional characters, set against a momentous backdrop. I can hardly wait for the movie."

—*San Antonio Express-News*

"Epic . . . boasts a cast of engineers, artists, seamen, and spiritualists."

—*Newsday*

"[A] breakthrough . . . It's a hefty, energetic depiction of the mid-nineteenth century. . . . Griesemer has written a historical novel in which, for once, the characters don't sound like moderns in fancy dress, and the fascinating history doesn't detract from the fiction."

—*Chicago Tribune*

ALSO BY JOHN GRIESEMER

No One Thinks of Greenland

SIGNAL & NOISE

JOHN GRIESEMER

PICADOR NE

For Ida and Sam

www.picadorusa.com

Picador® is a U.S. registered trademark and is used by St. Martin's Press under license from Pan Books Limited.

For information on Picador Reading Group Guides, as well as ordering, please contact the Trade Marketing department at St. Martin's Press.
Phone: 1-800-221-7945 extension 763
Fax: 212-677-7456
E-mail: trademarketing@stmartins.com

The author salutes Simon McBurney and Theatre Complicté's production of *Mnemonic* for stagecraft crucial to Chapter 20. Thanks, also, to the libraries and their staffs at Dartmouth College and the Thayer School of Engineering. Thanks and high regards especially to Josh Kendall, Frances Coady, and Bill Clegg; and, as ever, to Faith Catlin.

Design by Phil Mazzone

Library of Congress Cataloging-in-Publication Data

Griesemer, John.
    Signal & noise / John Griesemer.
        p. cm.
    ISBN 0-312-30082-4 (hc)
    ISBN 0-312-42334-9 (pbk)
      Cables, Submarine—Atlantic—Fiction. 2. Americans—England—Fiction.
    ᵉⁿ—Death—Fiction. 4. London (England)—Fiction.
      ᵗˢ—Fiction. 6. Engineers—Fiction. 7. Telegraph—Fiction.
          ⁿ. I. Title: Signal and noise. II. Title.

          ᵖ3

                                                2003042938

      ᵗⁱᵒⁿ: April 2004

CONTENTS

vii

CONTENTS

BOOK THREE

BOOK FOUR

CONTENTS

PROLOGUE

THE ISLE OF DOGS

London, November 1857

Never was there such a ship. From the marshes where it rests parallel to the river, the hull rises above the advancing crowd like a black, iron cliff. It forms an escarpment that blocks the people's view of the Thames for what appears to be miles. The masts have yet to be constructed, and this only seems to extend the vessel's length farther for all who have come to behold it on this grim, wet day.

Once launched, the ship will be triple the length of anything afloat. But there has been much talk that this nautical folly never will float, that it will founder in its first go with heavy weather in the Atlantic, or perhaps, more thrilling for the multitude making its way toward the shipyard, the monster will fall apart this very day at its own launch.

A slanting rain descends upon the Thames. The rain may soon turn to sleet; it's cold enough. The American engineer, Chester Ludlow, trapped in a brougham, resigns himself to his driver's insistence that they can get no closer to the launch because of the crowd. So Chester steps down to a road muddy and choked with jostling, excited pedestrians all headed in unison beneath a bobbing canopy of umbrellas. The air buzzes with expectation and freezing rain. Men, women, and children babble, laugh, and trip through the muck as if they were on a June picnic.

The crowd stretches out from the City, passes the West India Docks, then crosses the bridge over the canal to congeal along the West Ferry Road with its mean little terraces of cottages and public houses between the marshes and the shore. Every lane and path is jammed with people. Coachmen and teamsters try to turn their horses and vehicles around, but the crowd makes it impossible; some drivers just abandon their cabs and wagons where they stand, tether their dripping animals to whatever stunted poplar, fence post, or stile they can find, then join the masses heading toward the shipyard.

Through the moving river of people, Chester spies a small hummock—probably an overgrown midden—behind a public house. Perhaps, Chester thinks, he can get away from the crush and see better from there. He has been feeling ill since yesterday. New England Yankee though he is, he is unaccustomed to the surpassing dankness of London weather. Chester aches generally and senses in the prickling of his skull the beginnings of a fever.

He angles toward the pub, a cottage that slants in the soft soil of the marshes as if—and he shouldn't think of this, not today—as if it were a ship beginning to sink. Chester trots through the mud, past a bleating and squawking brass band, then cuts alongside the building, and mounts the small rise. From there he can see the massive black hull in all its enormity and the thousands of people heading across the marshes toward the ship as though it were an ark waiting to take them all aboard.

Inside the crowded, lopsided cottage pub, a newspaper sketch artist orders another pint—his second of the morning—finds a dry page in a notebook that is already filling with quick, deft drawings of the crowd and the scene outside, slugs the page "3 Nov. 1857" and writes, "Men and women of all classes are joined together in one amicable pilgrimage to the East, for on this day, at some hour unknown, the 'Gr East'n' (or 'L'vi'thn' or whatever it is to be called) is to be launched at Millwall on the Isle of Dogs. . . . For two years, London and, we may add, the people of England have been kept in expectation, and their excitement and determination to be present at any cost are not to be wondered at when we consider what a splendid chance presents itself for a fearful catastrophe."

There are no empty tables in the place, so the publican thumps the pint down on the crooked windowsill by the sketch artist and looks down his nose at the notebook as he takes payment.

"Writing memories of the great day for your grandchildren?" he asks.

"Yes," the sketch artist says. "That's it."

"You look too young to be a grandfather."

"Well, I suppose then I'm merely preparing for the future."

"Two more shillings and you can see the future from an upstairs room. Avoid the soaking you're sure to get out there." He nods toward the window, its rippled panes steamed by the many bodies, the tobacco smoke and the soaked garments that suffuse the room with an atmosphere almost thick and wet enough to slurp like a stew. Even with the hubbub of the taproom, the sketch artist can hear loud thumping and singing from the floor above. There must be a crowd up there jamming every window facing the river.

He smiles to say no to the publican's offer, but the man is already gone, having sized up the sketch artist's unlikely ability to pay for anything more than a pint by the worn look of his cuffs. The sketch artist feels his insides shrink amid the din of the laughing men and women; the fact is he *isn't* too young to be a grandfather—or at just fifty, very nearly isn't—but he has never married, lives alone, has risen no higher than a drawing master at Miss Orford's Academy and a beat reporter and artist on any of the papers where he's worked on and off for the past thirty years. He is feeling suddenly pathetic and dispirited in the happy throng that crowds around him, that moves past in a slithery blur beyond the glass, that chatters and slips in the mud and whoops under umbrellas carried by gentlemen with ladies on their arms and children in tow on the lanes and roads that cross the marshy peninsula, all flowing, pressing toward the event of their lives, an event the sketch artist, his name Jack Trace, has been chronicling intermittently for the past three years since the keel laying: the launch of the greatest ship ever built.

Down in the shipyard, the Little Giant is apoplectic. Not only has his letter been ignored, it has been flouted, and he, Isambard Kingdom Brunel, has been betrayed. His board of directors has sold tickets!

He had written to Mr. Yates: "I must have sole possession of the whole of the premises on the day of the launch, no men, even of our own, still less strangers, in any part of the yard except those regularly assigned their respective duties, and everybody must be completely under my control."

He had written all this, and yet the board has thrown the gate open to any fee-paying customer who cares to wander in.

Now there are hordes of inquisitive, noisome, and noisy sightseers all around the ways and even clambering about the launching cradles under the hull. There are bands playing. Vendors hawk ales, pies, Union Jacks, roasted potatoes, and scraps of oilcloth for protection against the rain, scraps that look suspiciously to Brunel, stomping lividly through the mud, as if they've been pilfered from an equipment shed in his own yard.

Brunel is looking for Mr. Yates, the board secretary and agent of his betrayal. Brunel wants to find the bastard Yates himself. Isambard Kingdom Brunel has built the world's fastest railroad, the world's longest tunnel, the world's finest bridges, and now, at the hour of his greatest achievement—the launching of the world's largest ship—he is so furious, he is having trouble seeing.

As he pounds through the muck near one of the checking drums, shouldering his way past men, women, and children, he notices that he is looking down at his boots as if he were staring at them through two narrow tubes.

To steady himself, he jerks his head up to look at his creation, his "Great Babe," as he calls it. Even today, with the launch impending, he and the board have not yet settled on a name for the ship. There has been too much else to do in preparation.

From where Brunel stands on the ground amidships, he can see the hull stretch for nearly four hundred feet in either direction. He is close enough so that the structure rises almost over him. It always leaves Brunel vertiginous when he sees the hull from so low and so close. It gives him a tingling in his privates, as if fear and exhilaration have become corporeal and hang like a plumb bob between his legs. He gets the same feeling standing on one of his great bridges, looking down. But here he is looking up and feeling that whirling in the loins, the tug at his scrotum, the desire to leap into space, then the simultaneous awe and horror at the thought of it. Oh, he loves this ship.

Brunel had dreamed of a vessel that could carry enough coal to sail to the goldfields of Australia and back without stopping for fuel, and he had been the first to calculate that the longer a ship is, the more efficiently it can carry great cargoes through the water. Conventional wooden sailing ships cannot be built longer than about two hundred feet, but the *Great Eastern,* which is the name the giant is called most often, will be more than three times that length. Brunel has used the principles of bridge truss construction on the hull. The ship has two giant, fifty-eight-foot paddle wheels amidships and a twenty-four-foot propeller that Brunel likes to claim could power all of Manchester's cotton mills. The iron plates of the hull each weigh seven hundred pounds. There will be accommodations for four thousand passengers in five shipboard hotels. It is Brunel's grandest vision, and now this rapacious swarm of humanity threatens to ruin it all. As he keeps staring up at the hull, he can feel the masses jostling him. He cannot bear to look at them. Eyes up, he stiffens his shoulders. He will not move.

High above Brunel a single, errant line dangles from the ship's rail, left by some workman, no doubt, in the confusion and press of the impending launch. The line hangs free in space, and to Brunel it's the image of ease: it bears no weight; it pulls no load. It merely swings there, dancing in slow undulations with the drizzle as the river breeze makes the line and the rain sway together, and the ellipses they inscribe soothe Brunel's eyes, widen his vision, relax him.

"Sir?"

Brunel turns. He is looking at the buttons on the waistcoat of one of his assistants. Brunel stands only five feet four inches tall. He steps back and snaps his head up toward the young man who speaks.

"Sir, the syndicate asked me to deliver this list of names to you for your consideration?"

The man has the hesitant, rolling accent from the Midlands that makes almost every statement come out sounding like a question. It annoys Brunel, a Londoner. He should have the man fired. He shall have the man fired. After the launch.

"The list, sir? They don't like the name *Great Eastern*?"

"And why not?"

"Two adjectives? Great? Eastern? They don't find it to be suitable for a ship?"

"I'll give them two sodding, bleeding adjectives. Where is Yates?" Brunel begins stomping around in a circle, hands on hips, coattails flared. His vision is tunneling again.

"Secretary Yates?"

"Yes, dammit. Where is he?"

"I don't know?"

Brunel wheels right and sloshes away toward the bow of the ship. The board had ordered a private viewing gallery built on the shore at that end of the yard for friends and visiting dignitaries. Maybe Yates is among them.

"Sir, aren't you going to even read the list of names?"

"No!"

"But what should they christen the ship?"

"Tell them to christen it *Tom Thumb* if they like!"

"Sir?"

"And you're fired!" Brunel shouts, almost at a shriek, half in the hope that he can fracture the narrowing aperture of his sight by force.

But he fails. He nearly takes off the top of his own head when he runs into a cable stretched about five feet off the ground in his path. He picks his stovepipe hat—meant to add height to his diminutive stature—out of the mud. He slaps it back on his head, the hat soiled with gobbets of slime. The crowd swallows him. Back near the checking drum, the assistant sighs and looks up at the swaying rope and imagines the Little Giant hanging from it by the neck until dead.

Still on the hummock, Chester Ludlow looks up at the people waving handkerchiefs from the upper windows of the cottage. At this distance, in the rain, the building looks even more like a sinking ship, her passengers signaling for rescue from her topmost deck.

Chester is able to see past the dark, brick buildings of an oil manufactory across the road. He can make out the river. Beyond that, he can see nothing. The scaffolds and masts of the Surrey Docks across the Thames and the edge of London, which he might be able to see on a clear day up at the end of Limehouse Reach, are lost to him in the mist. The river seems to be seeping out from under one cold, gray wall and, downstream, back in under another. But directly offshore he can see perhaps a hundred boats clustering around the anchored winch barges with more craft steaming and rowing and paddling out of the mist toward the massive, dark hulk on the near riverbank.

The road beyond the cottage is more crowded now than when Chester left the carriage. He wonders how close he'll get to the launch, if he should even attempt to go down there. He has been told that as an engineer with the Atlantic cable project, he'd be permitted to attend the event from the dignitaries' dais. He has a letter, but the invitation expressly says the launch will be closed to the public. The Little Giant had sent out orders that everything must be conducted in complete silence so that commands from the engineers could be heard by the winch operators and by the men on the hydraulic screws and by the mass of workers. The ship weighs nearly twelve thousand tons. The launch will be a feat of engineering nearly as staggering as the building of the ship itself.

Chester cannot believe the size of the crowd. Something must have changed since he received his invitation. This is anything but an event closed to the public. He heard from his carriage driver that the ship's owners have sold thousands of tickets to the launch during the past three days.

The mass of sightseers is thickening near the yard gates. People are pressing against the plank fencing like a tide against a seawall.

There is an urgency stirring here. He can feel the crowd's hunger reaching all the way into his constricted chest, wanting to pull him forward, pull him down to the gates, to get close to that looming iron wall. It's a need to attend an event of import. Why else would so many people turn out on so horrid a day? It is ceremonial, maybe sacramental. The newspapers have been beating the drum for months—years, really, if you go back to when the keel was laid or further, to when the plans were announced and the syndicate formed.

Chester Ludlow has followed the *Great Eastern*'s progress with a professional's interest. He has been in England for several weeks now to help the Atlantic cable project recover from its failure of last summer. The cable was to be the great, shining achievement of the age, the connection between peoples, the harbinger of a new era for mankind. But more than three hundred miles off the coast of Valentia, Ireland, last July, the cable snapped as it unspooled from its ship, the *Niagara,* and now it lies in a disappointing tangle on the bottom of the ocean.

Chester's old professor from the University of Glasgow, William Thomson, is on the cable project's board of directors. He summoned Chester to come help. Chester had his doubts. His wife was not well. But, Thomson had written, it was Chester's engineering brilliance that the cable needed. Chester had the theoretical knowledge and, more important, the technical ability to improvise, and that was what the project required most. Besides, he had done work on American lines up near the St. Lawrence. He had experience.

Still, Chester wasn't sure about Franny. With her indisposition, she was becoming something she'd never been to him . . . a burden. But perhaps he needed a respite. "Please come," Thomson implored. Chester decided he would. He sailed from Boston.

"You are the one to figure out a way to keep the damned cable from breaking of its own weight," Thomson had said when Chester arrived, and now Chester thinks he has accomplished just that. He's designed a paying-out mechanism that can allow for variations in a ship's speed and the ocean's depth. He came upon the idea while touring a British prison and watching the inmates toil at a windlass on which the guards could regulate the resistance to lessen or increase the inmates' travail.

The paying-out mechanism has tested well. The cable company will use it next summer. The board toasted Chester and offered him a position as an engineer.

"Take it, my boy," Thomson urged. "This is a project of great moment."

Chester knew his professor was right. This would be an ascendant step. It might even urge Franny out of her lassitude. He would return to America with the good news in time for Christmas. It occurred to him that as he was now to be part of one of the world's greatest engineering marvels, he should stop to visit another one before he left England: the launch of the *Great Eastern*.

He starts walking off the hummock and through the muck toward the shipyard. His ailment, a cold or grippe, irritates him and puts all the commotion at a remove.

From the cottage window the revelers wave and laugh. By the catcalls and profanity, by the pairings of men and women in the windows, it is obvious that it is a bawdy house.

As there is no hope of getting another pint in the crowded tavern—the publican now concerning himself only with tables of large parties, not solitary drinkers—Jack Trace pockets his notebook and heads out into the flow of people and the rain. Bands play beneath awnings and makeshift tents. Most of the musicians are well drunk, and little of what they play is in tune or in time. Two bands stand in the middle of the road and blare directly at each other, forcing pedestrians to walk through a gauntlet of noise.

Closer to the gates of the yard, scores of hucksters have erected booths. Food vendors sell apples, potatoes, and ginger cakes. There is even a hokeypokey stall selling ice cream on this, a November day. A performing dog dances on the head of a man who must weigh twenty-five stone and has clothed himself in a black robe with a sign reading GREAT EASTERN II. At another booth a young man is bellowing for people to come see his six-legged sheep.

Jack makes a couple of notes: "The half aqueous world of the Isle of Dogs has been transformed into a kind of carnival of rain and noise and human and animal wonders, all in the shadow of a ship that towers over the trees outside the yard as if something Miltonic is kept in there." Now that he is looking at it again, he realizes he's had dreams about the ship on and off for months. It has weighed upon his mind. "An iron nightmare," someone has written. *Whence and what are thou, execrable shape?*

Jack Trace has written about the ship, about Brunel—the Little Giant— and about the preposterousness of this construction. Nevertheless, here Trace is, drawn inevitably back to the thing itself. It must matter to witness this launch. A greater weight man hath never moved. A greater ship man hath never built. There might be something for the ages here in this launch. The failure of the cable last summer was a disappointment. Perhaps this is to be the signal event of the age—"Of our Age for all the Ages." He writes that down, crosses it out, then circles it. By the time he has performed this little redaction in his notebook, the page is soaked.

Near the six-legged sheep's tent, the barker is no longer trying to attract the crowd but is fending off an irate man with a dark beard.

"*Sheisse.*"

"Go on. Go on."

"It's dead, everyone!" the bearded man shouts. His accent is thick. He has turned from the barker to the crowd. "Don't go in there, nobody," he bellows. "The sheep is dead!"

"Go on. Go on. Ruin everybody's fun," the barker yells.

"I did not pay to see a dead sheep!"

"You paid to see a six-legged sheep, and that's what you got!"

"That sheep is not even born!"

"Did it have six legs or not?"

"*Ja!* Six legs. In a jar!"

The barker by now has leapt from his box and is down among the crowd, heading toward the bearded man, who keeps shouting, "He sells looks at an unborn animal in a jar of fluid. Pickled! Beware, you people."

"You're the one pickled, you kraut," the barker shouts.

The crowd is amused. Trace finds himself in the circumference of a circle opening up space for the two men. He is nearest the bearded man, who does indeed smell of alcohol.

"Don't buy from this man!" the bearded fellow shouts.

Some people in the crowd clap. Everyone is smiling as if this were a staged argument, part of a music hall Punch-and-Judy olio for them to enjoy before the headliners. Far from herding their children away from the altercation, mothers are pushing young ones toward the edge of the circle for a better view.

"Don't buy!"

"Hear! Hear!" someone shouts.

"Shut up, Heinz!" someone else yells.

The barker by this time has reached the bearded man and, with both hands outstretched, pushes at his shoulders with a flicking motion. More goading cheers from the crowd. Trace notices a volley of cannon fire from somewhere out on the river. The report comes as a flapping sound muffled by the blanket of low clouds overhead. But Trace and the crowd are too interested in the flaring tempers near at hand to pay the distant guns any mind. Trace does glance above the trees to check the dark hull of the ship. It hasn't moved.

And in that moment, the bearded man comes flying backward into his arms. A cheer goes up from the crowd. Trace drops to his knees in the mud with the unconscious fellow. The barker has already turned back toward his booth. One blow has felled the heckler.

The last smatter of applause blends with the splashes and sucking of shoes in the mud. Trace becomes acutely aware of the rain. It trickles down his collar. He can smell the drink on the bearded man's breath, the oniony smell of his armpits. The man has taken a hit in the left eye. It is beginning to swell. Rain splatters his face. He opens his good eye.

"*Danke,*" he mutters, and begins the struggle to get up. His feet slip and pedal in the muck. Trace barely keeps his balance, but eventually they both are standing.

"I heard a cannon fire, I think," says the man. "Or was it the report of the scoundrel's fist on my jaw?"

"Cannon," says Trace. "Are you all right?"

"*Ja.* If they are firing, perhaps the boat is launching. I better go. I thank you." He straightens up into the exaggerated perpendicular of an inebriate and starts to turn toward the gate, but immediately slips back into Trace's arms.

"I'll help you," Trace says. "At least until you're steady."

"*Danke.*"

"You're from Germany?"

"*Ja.*"

"Your name is Heinz?"

The man shakes his head. "Marx."

Trace holds the man by the arm; Marx presses a handkerchief soaked in puddle water to his eye. To get to the shipyard gate, they must walk past the barker, who is back to his shouting. Marx tries to keep his shoulders hunched and his face averted. The barker espies him immediately and begins to taunt. "Heinz! Look over here. Hey, everybody! Come see the one-eyed kraut-eater!"

Marx grumbles. He picks up his pace and fairly pulls Trace along with him through the gate.

Brunel finds Yates about to ascend the steps of the viewing stand. He reaches for the secretary's elbow, misses, and has to call his name. Yates, two steps up, turns. Brunel's chest tightens as he shouts, "Yates!"

"Sir?" The man appears utterly unperturbed, placid even. He is staring down at Brunel as if it were Brunel who has the explaining to do, as if Brunel should account for being so wroth.

"What is the meaning of this, Yates?"

"Sir?"

"*This!*" And he gestures wildly at the milling crowd, the mass of people threading around the drums, the cables, the chains, the planking and scaffolding as if they were attractions on a carnival midway.

"Ah. The people."

"Are you an idiot, Yates? Is that what I am looking at? An idiot? Please disabuse me of this notion. Please find some way to convince me you are not an idiot—"

"Sir, if you—"

"—or maybe it were better I believe that you are an idiot. I could abide that. I made an error in judgment. I have been working, lo, these three years with an idiot, but at least my project gave some poor unfortunate fool a modicum of employment he might otherwise never have had. Surely that would be preferable to the knowledge that I worked alongside a traitor, a blackguard who would resort to treachery, who would sell tickets! Yates, you sold tickets!"

"I did, sir."

"Why? Why, in the name of God, *why?*" Brunel pounds the railing that leads up to the reviewing stand. He can see a couple of top hats and a lady's bonnet above the bunting. He doesn't care who hears him yelling now. "*Why?* Did I not write you, expressly forbidding any strangers in the yard for the launch? Did I not require total and complete silence for the launch? Did I not say that success or failure of the launch requires this? Did I not? *Yates?*"

"You did, sir. But you did not explain how the syndicate is to make back the three million it has invested in the ship."

"We've got to get the damn thing in the water for that!"

"And in doing so, sir, the syndicate thinks it meet to try to recoup, sooner rather than, as you would have it, later, some of its investment in a small way by capitalizing on the excitement around the event. Excitement, sir, which you, in no small way, have helped foment."

"So you sold tickets."

"Three thousand, sir, in advance. More at the gate."

It is enough to make Brunel double over with rage. There are twenty times three thousand already in the shipyard, with easily that many visible on the roads outside. He imagines long lines stretched all the way back to London Bridge. The bands have by now set up and are playing inside the fences. An organ-grinder walks by with a shrieking monkey that bares its teeth and takes a swipe at Brunel's stovepipe hat. Children have begun crying. Brunel hears laughter drift down from the reviewing stand. A tap-ster muscles past him with a keg on his shoulders. Brunel is muttering to himself, hands on knees, staring at the mud through the two portals of his constricted vision.

"Sir?"

"Yates," Brunel gasps. He flutters his hand toward where he thinks Yates must be, signaling him to come closer. Brunel stays bent over. The mud is gaining a clarity such as Brunel has never noticed before. It seems he can make out every rivulet, every tiny pool that reflects the gray light of the sky. If Yates had not grasped Brunel's elbow, Brunel might have let himself fall face first into the ooze.

"Yates," Brunel says in a small voice. "I must be calm. The ship depends upon it."

"Sir?" Yates asks, his normally saturnine voice taking on a tone of concern, "are you not well?"

"Yates, you *are* a fool," Brunel says in a near whisper as he straightens up. His sight has narrowed to mere pinholes.

Brunel turns his head as if it were a searchlight, casting its insensate rays on the crowd, the yard, the rain, the massive black hulk above them.

"You are a fool," Brunel says again, almost sweetly, "but you are all I have. You followed orders, I take it."

"If you mean the tickets, yes, sir. The syndicate ordered me to sell–"

Brunel motions for him to stop. The little man begins walking unsteadily away from the reviewing stand. Yates follows him.

"You know, Yates, I keep a diary."

"Do you, sir?"

"Yes. I write in it every day. Or night. At home. Or by the light of the lamp when I sleep in the engineers' shanty. A little entry. A reflection or two on the tensile strength of the iron, on how the weather is affecting the speed of construction, how the ship looks, my hopes for it, how much I love my son, my wife. Little things such as might calm me or steady me or steel my resolve against adversity; things, too, that might prove of interest for posterity if all of this comes to anything."

"It will, sir."

Crowds are pressing around them as they walk against the flow of people pushing closer to the ship. Most spectators ignore them, mesmerized as they are by the preponderance of the hull against the sky.

Brunel speaks again. "I wrote in the diary recently that I am a man not above self-conceit and a love of glory."

Yates looks down at Brunel, offering a flat, uncomfortable smile, waiting for more.

"Not above self-conceit and a love of glory, Yates. Not above them. Now it seems I am buried by them."

"We don't know that, sir. The launch may still go off all right."

"No thanks to you, Yates."

Yates tries to speak, but several people have recognized Brunel, probably from his likeness in the papers. The people are now pointing at him. The hat and Brunel's short stature give him away. The onlookers break into polite applause that is muffled by gloves and the necessity of holding on to umbrellas.

Brunel looks away from Yates and brightens. He stops for a moment and nods to those clapping. Other passersby join in. Brunel doffs his stovepipe. The clapping turns to applause that begins to spread back in a radiating wave from where Brunel and Yates stand. Brunel smiles and nods and sweeps his hat back and forth. Then he points up toward the looming wall of iron. Huzzahs skip toward him from somewhere in the crowd. He and Yates are now the center of an ovation. Brunel steps in front of Yates, downstage of him, as it were, and raises both his hands in a salute. He looks up and squints into the rain. The dignitaries on the reviewing stand are on their feet, the men with their paunches pressed against the bunting, the women smiling, all applauding, pointing at the ship, extending their clapping hands toward Brunel to serve him up their praise.

Brunel waves. He smiles. He snarls out of the side of his mouth, "I should kill you, Yates."

Yates, bowing deeply, utters to the mud, "Yes, sir."

Achy and aguish, Chester Ludlow stands near the ship's prow. He has made his way through the rain and the crowd, down the road, through the defile of hawkers and barkers, past a fight near one of the stalls, into the shipyard itself. His feet are soaked, and his boots are fretting his heels. His toes are cold. He is feverish. He wants now only to move farther forward, and so he follows the path of least resistance, stepping toward wherever there is an opening in the crowd. Quite without foreknowledge, he ends up at the stem of the ship.

He looks up. That such a massive thing will move seems absurd; that it will float seems mad. Each side of the hull meets here at the bow in a vertical edge that must tower eighty feet above the crowd.

A bass drum thumps somewhere.

There is a low platform with bunting and flags near the bow. A young girl and a group of men are on the stand. She must be the daughter of one of the dignitaries. A man is addressing the crowd. Chester can understand only an occasional word; the noise of the shuffling, sloshing people makes hearing the entire speech impossible, but the man seems to be saying something about christening the ship.

*   *   *

Marx and Trace are practically beneath the hull. It is dry under there, Marx insists, and less crowded. Workmen are trying to make their way through the throng. They bear sledgehammers. Some of the workers seem put out by the crowd, others are caught up in the spirit of the event.

Marx, still tipsy, reaches out to pat the men on their shoulders as they march past.

"You do the work of the ages with those tools," he says. "They are your symbol. They are *our* symbol."

"It's a bleedin' hammer," a large Irishman says, and makes to push Marx, who hops back and smacks his head on the iron hull. The laborers laugh and duck away under the timbers as if they were descending into a mine.

Marx's eyes are watering from the pain. Trace winces in sympathy. He has hobbled around the mobbed yard with this bearded man who is exuberant in his enthusiasm for so large a ship but who is also sputteringly disdainful of the men who own it.

"It will take an ocean of tears and sweat to sail this thing," Marx has said. "And who accounts for that?"

Sledgehammers begin to swing at the chocks holding the cradles.

"Perhaps we should get out from under here" is Trace's reply.

It is a little before half past twelve. Brunel has ascended alone to the control platform on a thirty-foot tower in the middle of the yard. He puts his finger to his lips as if to hush the crowd. This the onlookers take as a sign of modesty, so they clap all the louder; more people are joining in the fun now. Brunel raises his hands and pats down the air. The crowd realizes it can play a game of one-upmanship, so the people begin to cheer as they applaud. Now Brunel jams his fists onto his hips, his legs apart; he scowls at the sea of faces. Everywhere he looks, heads are upturned, laughing, enjoying him. The damn ship seems to be floating on the faces. In a quick, violent swipe, he makes a slashing, throat-cutting motion across his neck. The horde erupts in a roar. Somewhere they begin singing "For He's a Jolly Good Fellow."

Brunel can do nothing but wait it out. Fuming, he steps back from the rail, back to where no one can see him. He shouts down to Dixon, the foreman on the level below him, to tell him to signal when the wedges are free from the cradles. Dixon waves in the affirmative, but Brunel can't be sure if Dixon means he'll do as Brunel bids or if the wedges are already out.

This is exactly the kind of ambiguity Brunel can ill afford. He tries to steady himself. He must have clarity. His eyesight is all right. He's been sweating, but he doesn't feel chilled, despite the rain. He suddenly finds himself thinking of the sketches he first made of the ship. Not the blueprints—the sketches. *There* was clarity. Pen scratching on vellum. A thread of ink laid out on the paper. The long lines of the hull. Proportions that thrilled him, aspect ratios that almost gave him the same vertigo he later would feel when he stood beneath the hull. A dizziness begotten of his own mind. A love of glory. As he drew the length of the ship in each sketch, he almost had to will the pen to keep going toward the end of the page: She will be *this* long. She will travel *this* far.

Dixon is calling now. The hammering has stopped. The wedges are away; the cradles are free. Brunel tells Dixon to give the orders to slack off on the checking cables. Dixon, a short, red-haired man with a face the color of a blister, gives a quick nod. He shouts fore and aft. The crowd's heads pivot. Umbrellas swing and slant; hands reach up to slap them down.

Close enough now to the platform, Chester can see the young girl, the daughter of one of the directors. She must be about seven years old and is standing amid the phalanx of dignitaries. She has a bright blue wool overcoat on with silver buttons and a hood to keep off the rain. One of the men has a gloved hand upon her shoulder. She looks out over the crowd with an expression of contained astonishment. She seems ready to burst into tears or laughter. Chester thinks of Betty, his own daughter, who would have been nearly this girl's age.

A man on the end of the line crosses to the little girl and gives her a bottle of champagne wrapped in a purple towel.

"Drink it up, lass!" a drunk shouts. She does not hear him.

Chester begins to feel light-headed, as if he could slip and fall right there in the mud without even taking a step. He wants to think it's his fever making him feel this way, but he knows it is the sight of the little girl, the thought of Betty.

He becomes terribly aware of all the wet cloth around him: the suits, the dresses, the hats, the capes, the damp wool, the tons of soaked fabric weighing down. How heavy it all must be. And the smell. It coats the inside of his skull. The odors of mud and bodies under fabric, the worsted, the linens, the flannel. The little girl must be uncomfortable. She seems so small up there. The prow towers over her like Death, black and pointed.

The men on the rostrum turn their backs to the crowd and step toward the ship, flanking the child. With the men all around her, the little girl raises the bottle. Chester sees Betty. She is there. The black wall. No mistaking this. She stands poised with the bottle, ready to strike. Chester raises his hand toward her. *No,* he thinks.

She says, "I christen thee *Leviathan,*" and Chester lets out a cry.

"No!"

She smashes the bottle on the ship.

Applause. Nearby faces look quizzically at Chester as their clapping hands work together and apart, together and apart. What do you mean, *No?*

Chester stammers. The spinning stops. "She named it *Leviathan,*" he says. "It is supposed to be the *Great Eastern.* She gave it the wrong name."

"She named it *Leviathan,*" someone says.

"I tell you that's wrong," says Chester.

"Looks right enough to me. If that's not a leviathan, I don't know what in hell's name is."

Chester thinks it strange: everyone has been calling the ship the *Great Eastern* for months. Now it has a different name. It's bad luck to change a ship's name. Unaccountably, this saddens him, and he takes a couple of steps backward, nodding, wanting no further encounters, trying to piece together what has just happened, what he has just said.

The little girl stands with the men on either side of her. They all look up at the overhanging prow.

It is to be launched sideways into the Thames. Customarily, a ship is launched stern first into the water, but with the *Leviathan* that would be impossible. With a stern-first launch, the ship would likely span the river, grounding its stern on the far shoals in Deptford and leaving its bow stuck here in Millwall. It would become a bridge across a river, not a ship. It would be a joke.

So, the vessel rests parallel to the water on two cradles, each one 120 feet wide and built on a crisscross lattice of twelve-by-twelve timbers. The ship has 240 feet to slide down to the low-tide line.

Chains with links weighing seventy-two pounds apiece go out to barges anchored in the river and back to steam winches on the shore. This tackling will keep the *Leviathan* sliding toward the water. Nine-foot-diameter checking drums are at the head of each slipway to hold the ship back from sliding too fast. Four eighty-ton manual winches are mounted on barges amidships to aid in the launch. Fore and aft, there are two hydraulic rams to give the ship its initial push.

The crowd grows quieter than it has been all morning. There have been momentary remissions in the din, as when the cannons fired or the director's daughter christened the ship, and there has been enough concord among the throng for sustained applause, as when the champagne bottle broke or when a young man climbed up a scaffold and hung a Union Jack over their heads. But now, with the purposeful thumps of the sledgehammers having come to a halt, something else is happening.

Bands and hurdy-gurdies and solo musicians squeak and honk and wheeze out of their march and waltz tempos, through discord, and into silence. The noiselessness is grand, vaulted, as if the whole crowd has just stepped into a great cathedral. A baby's cry rises from somewhere; then, just as quickly, it flutters back into silence. The rain, for the first time in hours, is audible.

People crane their necks to see what is happening. Thousands of feet are on tiptoe in the mud. Children raise upturned hands, fingers opening and closing. People sway back and forth as they stretch for a view. No one knows quite where to look. *What is happening? What is happening?* the women are all whispering to their men, who only hold their breath.

On the starboard side of the ship, the side facing the water, a workman receives Dixon's relay signal and waves a white flag. Chester can see this because he has worked his way from the christening stand, down along the rails and ties of the forward ways, to the water's edge. He can smell the fetid dankness of the Thames. Before it had been a vague estuarine twinge that came and went on the rainy breezes: a hint he was close to the tide. Now it carries a stench. In the water, brown lumps eddy near a piling. Excrement. Chester's boots, his feet numb inside, crack small mussel-shells attached to the spar he stands upon. He slips a little on some seaweed, a filamentary green slime, and recovers only to feel a stab of pain in his back. The cold has begun to make him ache.

Out on the downriver barge, its captain orders a signal given: message received. Deckhands on each barge wave white flags back to the shore.

The captain has just been joking with his boatswain that they probably have the best seats in the house. The *Leviathan*'s bulk stretches before them; they can see the entire ship at a glance. The captain, his right arm missing from action in the Crimea, waves his left hand to his men to take up the slack on chains attached to the ship. They begin cranking on the winch handles, their backs bobbing up and down in the dirty weather.

The boatswain points out a pair of men running over and under the rails below the ship. Somehow they have strayed directly into the path of the launch. They are scrambling. Each of them falls at least twice, sometimes pulling the other down with him. They rise to run again.

"Those two better hurry," the captain says.

"This ain't the launch the Little Giant rehearsed," the mate grunts.

Marx panics. He and Trace have stumbled out onto the shoreline side of the ship, the empty negative to the ship's landward side. The massiveness of the iron, the hodgepodge of equipment, timbers, and workmen below the hull had them confused, and now they've ended up in the launch's path. Nevertheless, it looks easier to make it to safety on the river side than to thread their way back through the maze under the hull. So they run and slip and slide over the iron rails, over the pilings, around the bulkheads and coffers, through mud, sea life, shells, garbage, and sewage. Trace curses all the way.

"We're going to miss the launch!" Marx keeps shouting.

"We're going to be *under* the bloody launch!" Trace shouts back.

A groaning has begun as they scramble, frightening them even more.

"I'm going to die!" Marx shouts.

"Run!" Trace yells.

There is a woeful, echoing sound that is so consuming, it seems to come from within their lungs, devouring the very air they need to breathe to keep running. It's a hundred yards on, safety, as they leap over the timbers and weave and fall and rise; and then fifty, the heads and shoulders of the crowd now visible, the two men stumbling, the horrible groans seeming to radiate out of their heaving chests; and then it is only a few yards more, and the cheers of sailors on the barge are audible on the shore.

And they make it. They duck under the last rail and thrust their way into the crowd that pulls back to give them room. Two ragged, muddy men, panting, their hands on their knees, their open mouths lapping for air. Now they can truly hear the groaning. Marx thinks it is Trace having some sort of attack. Trace thinks it is Marx.

It is the ship. Brunel has given the signal for the winches to pull hard. The engineers have signaled to one another with whistle blasts. Dixon is down below, waving the flag back and forth, back and forth.

"Enough!" Brunel says.

"Enough tension?" Dixon shouts, his mouth a black, toothless hole in the blister face.

"No! Enough flag waving!"

"Sorry, sir."

Brunel feels a gust of relief, evanescent, a moment of control. But then it is back to worry.

The steam winches grind fore and aft, and the chain links clank through the machinery. The chains rise out of the river as they come back from the barges to the shore, their catenary curves dripping water, shuddering with a tension that makes them seem to be alive, showing a tendinous strain that makes everyone in the crowd who can see it grimace in apprehension.

The noise of the stress on the hull has become a steady, drumlike roll. It is the alimentary rumblings of a starved beast the size of a city. Chester tries to shift and see if he can discern any movement of the ship, but the crowd has pressed around him now right down to the water's edge. He can only just make out the prow against the sky. The rain clouds shuttle along toward the east, making the ship seem to move sideways down toward the river, but Chester can tell the launch has yet to begin. People would be cheering if the ship were truly moving.

Marx and Trace are near the dignitaries' observation platform. Trace looks up at the bunting and the canopy. He can see an occasional tweed-sleeved arm reach out beyond the railing and point toward the ship. Once, a lady's gloved hand waves to someone. Marx hacks out half a dozen crackling chest coughs.

The ship is groaning. Or is it Marx? Trace wishes he could ascend those stairs to the platform to sit dry among the rich, the dignified, the idle. Instead, he is down here in the mud, waiting with a crazy, consumptive German for an iron mountain to move. Trace looks at his companion. Marx is just straightening up from his coughing fit. He clutches at Trace's arm but doesn't look at him. He throws his head back and looks at the ship. His eyes are fiery, charged by the excitement. Marx now begins talking about the workers, about the triumph of the age, about this engineering marvel and the scurrilous dogs that manipulated the labor that built it. *Talking or babbling?* Trace thinks at first, but then he begins to feel a stirring intellectual heat coming off this man. If he shifts his mind a little, Trace can believe Marx is making sense in a strange, mad way.

The drumrolling noise coming from inside the ship is almost circuslike, as if meant to build suspense before the big climax. But this is a huge noise, much bigger than any number of circus timpani could make. It forces Brunel to squint. His vision is blackening down again. But not out of anger now. Now it is dread. They have been waiting for nearly ten minutes for something to happen. The chains have stimulated these rumblings coming from within the hull, and there's no telling how much more strain the links can endure. Brunel has an image of a chain breaking and whipping back like an enormous flail, winnowing the crowd, cutting a swath through a meadow of human flesh. From his command tower, he can see the infernal mass of people begin again to bustle and rock impatiently. Nothing is happening. The ship isn't moving. It's just making noise. This is not what they came for.

The rain continues. A band strikes up a waltz. Down on the dignitaries' stand, several of the gentlemen and ladies are standing to stretch their legs.

Brunel leans out and tells Dixon to signal the hydraulic rams. He can hear the popping flutter of Dixon's yellow flag as it waves back and forth. Brunel knows that yellow flags are flying on the far side of the ship to let the captain of the barges know what is about to happen.

"Yellow flag, sir," the boatswain says.

The captain steps out of the barge's shanty into the rain. He has to use his left hand to pull the slicker back up onto his diminished right shoulder.

"Alert the crew."

The boatswain calls fore and aft, "Yellow flag!" The barge crewmen all stand still to watch.

Down among the pilings and timbers onshore, the greased pistons of the rams press against the bow and stern of the ship. A shrill whistle goes up from the steam engine on the forward ram. The crowd cheers spontaneously and congeals in a tighter mass around the ways.

Chester feels the people begin to push him toward the ship. He tries to resist, but he slips off the timbers again. By all rights he should have fallen into the foul turd-muck of the riverbank, but the crowd is now so thick, he is kept upright and regains his balance as the mass sweeps him along. The reek of the Thames, the smell of sodden wool, perfume, tobacco, alcohol, sweat, breath, coal smoke, all the exhalations fill his head. He thinks he will shout, "No!" again at any moment.

Then there is a new noise all around him. A howl, really, and not from the crowd. He realizes the ground beneath him is trembling. The bow of the ship is moving, now making a raging screech as its huge cradle grates downward on the rails.

On the barges, several crewmen scream, not warning shouts but high-pitched shrieks. The captain himself gasps as he sees the prow of the ship seem to wobble and swerve. He points to the bow and utters, "She moves!" but instantly realizes that he mumbled the words too softly to be heard and that he wasn't pointing at all. He only thought he was. It was his missing right arm he believed he was raising toward the ship.

Onshore, amidships, a winch crew has been standing on the housing and pilings around their mechanism. An Irish laborer, Thomas Donovan, who isn't manning the winch but who has ducked away from his hawser crew because he thought the checking drum would be the best spot to view the launch, climbs up on a winch handle.

The winch crew has been endeavoring to see over the heads of the

crowd around them. They see the bow swing down toward the river suddenly, and the huge ship shrugs, opening up an appreciable wedge of sky
and horizon that had been walled off just a moment ago. Then, just as
suddenly, the ship stops. Still, the crowd has let loose a roar. The men on
the drum know from experience the ship shouldn't move this way. They
are about to jump off the drum.

But they never make the move. The ground by the stern shivers as
now the rear cradle lets loose and begins to grate its way down the rails.
The scream of galling metal echoes everywhere. People on the reviewing
stand rise to their feet, hands covering ears. Brunel is up in his command
tower, waving his arms wildly. The stern is sliding. The checking drums
pay out cable in an instantaneous, furious burst; this sets the winch handles
whirling like scythe blades, and Thomas Donovan is left floating in the air
as the handle he once stood upon drops out from under him and the men
near him fall away from the machine. The next handle comes whirling
around and smashes Donovan just above the knees and upends him in
midair. The next handle catches him in the groin, and he folds around the
wooden grip. The winch spins Donovan through the rotation, and just
before he reaches the top of the arc, he flies free.

Chester Ludlow sees a black, tattered shape spinning through the sky
above the treetops. It is hard to miss because, from Chester's angle, it is
near the silhouette of the towering bow. Chester thinks for a moment it is
something being thrown off the hull, a banner perhaps, an exuberant workman's coat. It is too big for a bird, he thinks; it is difficult to tell how large
the thing is or how far away.

Donovan's body spins upward above the crowd. Countless people fail
to even notice the flying shape; those who do only stare at it in stupefaction.
Is it the wind, or just the opposition of forces involved with flight that
makes his arms flutter so? He is on his back in the air; his face is toward
the sky.

Brunel sees it. The body is even higher than Brunel in his command
tower. Brunel, as ever, must look up.

Donovan begins to fall.

Now most of the crowd near the bow see it, and people clutch at one
another, pull one another away from where they perceive the body will

land. People are screaming. The body grows larger, spinning half a turn as it approaches. Marx see it and swears in German. Trace says nothing as the body falls.

Donovan lands near the reviewing stand, having been hurled nearly a quarter of the length of the ship. In the instant before he hits, a woman throws her umbrella up as she leaps backward. The umbrella and Donovan meet for a peculiar moment, and then Donovan lands on top of it, in the muck, face up, the umbrella shaft protruding from his chest. Both his legs are torn open like shucked ears of maize; blood and fat and gristle flop in a puddle. Donovan's face is left twisted in a garish look of shock and pain. Marx and Trace are a few feet away. A woman shrieks for help. She says the word over and over.

The ship is no longer moving.

The barge captain has ordered his boatswain ashore to tell Brunel that his crew is too panicky to be of use. The deckhands keep their jittery eyes glued to the huge wall of iron that appears ready to topple over on them at any moment. The boatswain does not head toward shore. He rows off downriver into the fog.

Into the circle of mud left by the horror-struck crowd, Marx strides boldly toward Donovan. Trace will think later how Marx made the move against the tide of the masses who were still recoiling from the impact of the dead body.

Marx is already there. His coat is off. He places it over the body, around the umbrella shaft. Not over the face, though. Another man, a handsome blond fellow with gold-rimmed spectacles, moves purposefully in and feels for a pulse. He shakes his head. Now the men gently pull the coat over the dead man's face.

On the tower, Brunel has shouted to Dixon to have the crew chiefs check the cradles, check the cables, try to see what is wrong.

But he already knows he won't be launching his Great Babe. This is not the day. The idiotic crowds. The technical problems. And now this corpse falling from the sky.

The rain has become heavier. As if waiting for this folly to play itself out, the clouds have opened up.

Chester, upon seeing the dead man land in the crowd, felt his fever sweep away. The impulse to help, to act decisively, rushed in, clearing away his

malaise. He ran to the body and assisted a bearded fellow who was kneeling in the mud, doing what he could. There was nothing to do.

So Chester carried the body, still impaled, with the bearded man and
some others to a wagon behind the reviewing stand. He arranged with the
teamster to take the body away once the crowd dispersed. He paid the
driver, not sure how much of the British money to proffer, not sure of
the denominations even after all these weeks in the country. He is ready
now to go home.

He looks back at the huge ship. The bearded fellow has disappeared.
The sound of the downpour nearly surpasses the noise of the crowd. Chester's head feels clear now, shocked by the sight of the slain worker, yes,
but purged, too, by the rush to help, invigorated by the familiar impulse
to accomplish something rather than merely look on. It was that same
impulse that brought him here to England in the first place, to accomplish
something with the cable; it will bring him back.

He can hear voices, thousands of them, *tens* of thousands, going at
once. The sound is like barking, the struggling of frustration and disappointment working out of a hundred thousand throats. The crowd is congealing and flowing around certain points: near the winches, below the
dignitaries' stand; filling the gap where the dead man landed, moving toward the exits. Some people recognize Chester as one of the fellows who
tended to the fallen corpse. They nod and point and smile as if they know
him.

Brunel can see the crowd, too, moving below his tower. He feels the
structure tremble. Dixon's boiled face looks up questioningly. Brunel tells
him to wave the red flag, the signal calling off the launch. Dixon unfurls
the cloth. The flag pops as it whips back and forth over the heads of the
crowd.

Trace has lost Marx. He last saw him tending to the body that had
flown through the air. Trace is under the dignitaries' stand, out of the rain,
wiping his mouth with a handkerchief. The sight of the dead man has
made him ill. The flesh, the unnatural twisting of the limbs. The rictus of
the dead man's face.

He hears the footsteps of the dignitaries above him. He thinks of the
tavern and its roistering upper rooms. If he had stayed there and gone
upstairs, he could be warm and dry and full of cakes and ale now, perhaps
even in the company of a gay and willing woman.

Wet bunting from the reviewing stand hangs down around him, so he is in a dim, curtained box that is holding in the stench of his own vomit. He pauses before stepping back out to face the rain, the crowd, the disorienting mass of the crippled ship. He pulls his pad out of his pocket and takes pen in hand to write: "Our nation, our glorious age, seem to have fallen short of our grandiose schemes of late. . . . We were to make the oceans disappear and unite the world, first with our telegraph cable, then with the greatest of all ships. But the oceans roll on: the Atlantic cable is dead, and now *Leviathan* will not budge."

BOOK ONE

OTIS LUDLOW'S JOURNAL

Ireland, 1866

Foilhommerum Bay

The storm begins again. One storm is so much like another here. Perhaps it is a different storm. Perhaps the same. This Irish coast mixes its foul weathers into volleys of rain, lowering clouds, and dark, dark nights.

I have spent winters in Siberia, lived in the jungles of Malaya, and I think I should prefer anything to this early spring on the western coast of Ireland.

I have been here for nigh half a year, tending the telegraph house. I shoo away the curious locals; I warn ignorant fishermen against anchoring near the crossing. I watch for signals from the wire. I am the fragmented cable's amanuensis. It is a form of solitary confinement well suited to my condition. My brother told me it would be for the best. It is. It is. It is.

And at least I have my wire.

Well, I call it "my wire." It is neither. Neither mine nor a wire. It is, if anyone's, Chester's, and it is properly called a cable. Wires are bare, a single filament most often strung from poles. Wires sing in high winds and gales. Cables lie on the bottom of the sea. This cable lies under the Atlantic. It has seven strands of copper at its core. It is sheathed in four layers of gutta-percha. It has a layer of hemp, then it has ten charcoal iron reinforcing strands around that. Withal, it is only slightly more than an inch thick.

This cable ends in a broken stump on the ocean bottom 1,250 miles from where I sit. Messages still come through it.

My brother succeeded once. 1858. President Buchanan and Queen Victoria exchanged pleasantries. All day just to transmit a few sentences. Only to end in failure.

Nothing if not valiant, my brother. Chester survived the War Between the States. (I was in Siberia.) Last year he failed again with the cable. (I swam from the great ship and was saved.) Come summer he will be trying once more.

And here I shall sit, in a darkened room, watching a minuscule ray of light projected by a tiny foil mirror on a screen in Professor Thomson's galvanometer.

There are messages sent along this broken cable. From where, however, I do not know. They come in bursts of lucidity amid otherwise indecipherable ravings. I record it all.

The galvanometer is a wondrous little torture device. Professor Thomson invented it. I like the story that the professor, whilst in his laboratory contemplating a mechanism to read the weak signals sent along the submarine cable, was twirling his monocle from the end of its ribbon. The lens spun in a beam of sunlight. The worthy professor saw the reflected beam dance around his room. Light . . . reflection . . . inspiration. Professor Thomson used the cable's minuscule electrical impulses to spin a tiny mirror reflecting lamplight.

Now we poor graphers are lashed to our galvanometers as we watch that light dance across the gradiant as the pulses come and go. We record the dance; we decode the signals.

But this severed cable's meaningful signals are few and far between. I keep waiting for more.

The storm continues. I hear the waters.

Our father disappeared when I was fresh back from my first voyage to the Pacific. I found him. My brother was down in Cambridge. It was just as well. It was enough that one of us had to endure the Old Man's depredations. Our father reappeared floating face up in Nancy Brook, near Crawford Notch, not far from Mount Washington in New Hampshire.

Sometimes, I think, he speaks to me. Our father who art in water.

The telegraph house is in a sheltered cove here in Foilhommerum Bay. The cable rises out of the sea, crosses the stone beach, traverses a small stretch of grass, and enters the house. Here, in a perpetually darkened room on the seaward side of the building, the cable is attached to the galvanometer.

We graphers have had our worst fights in the little darkened room. The silent, dim, tiny fluttering of the light demands a debilitating degree of attention.

Pulses—erratic, random twitches of electricity—still come along the cable. This is my purpose. This is my reason. It is necessary to record the signals to keep an accurate account of the condition of the wire. We are able to take measurements and assure the syndicate that the cable is still intact all the way out to the stump end that lies on the bottom of the Atlantic.

It can drive a grapher mad. After Christmas, they sent more men. No one lasted but Roger Buttrey. He and I came to blows over, I think, his cat. Something about it soiling the stair landing. In no time, Buttrey and I were on the floor, rolling around, punching each other. Furniture crashed about us. The cat, I remember, howled. We stopped only when we began to pitch toward the table holding the galvanometer. We knew we could destroy each other, even the entire building, but we must never harm the galvanometer.

We stopped, frozen, just as we smacked against the table. Between our heaving breaths we listened for a crash.

But there was nothing. We relaxed our grips on each other and slowly rose to our knees, faces surfacing above the edge of the tabletop to where the galvanometer sat. We looked at the screen. The tiny light fluttered across the polarity line.

We are both adepts; we could read the code as easily as if it were printed in flowing script:

> *WRUCKST SLLLVOVSKQ MRWEF*
> *HOLY RNGI RKSDDDD*
> *HOLY HOLY HOLY*

"Holy," I whispered.

"That's it," Buttrey said. "I quit."

I looked at him.

"I'm leaving." He got up and brushed off his trousers. "Gone. Done."

"Buttrey!" I called. But he was out of the room.

Light streamed in from the outer chamber through the door Buttrey had left open. A few drops of blood—his or mine—stained the floor.

I kneeled, looking into the galvanometer again to see what further signals the ocean was transmitting. Holy . . . Holy Holy Holy.

But nothing more came through. It had gone back to gibberish. Meaning was twisted and bound beyond comprehension within gnarled letters. This is the pain of decoding. I couldn't endure it. I fell on my face on the signal room floor.

Buttrey did not contact the syndicate about his departure. Nor shall I.

With Buttrey gone, I am assured a long period of solitude. A time for me and my signals. A time to ponder the interstices between meaninglessness and the flashes of the comprehensible. The entire ocean speaks through the cable. Its storms and magnetisms beat out a message. We have given meaning to certain patterns, but who is to say there aren't patterns in the rest of what flickers through the light?

The storm continues. Or a new storm comes.

I have seen so much in my life. I have sailed the globe. I know what froth and inspiration and rage the ocean is capable of. I know aimless calms and towering gales. Imagine a probe capable of reading all those moods. That is our broken cable.

I found my father in Nancy Brook. Nancy Brook flows into the Saco River. The Saco flows into the Atlantic. So you see how things go.

I will record the signals and the noise from the cable. I will leave them—my brother, the syndicate, anyone—with the messages. Holy. They will discover that their severed cable is a cord that attaches them to a greater world.

CHAPTER I

AT THE THEATER

New York, December 1857

Checking the House

If there was a more desirable woman than his wife in the theater that night, Chester Ludlow didn't see her. The glow from the cold and the flicker of light from the melting snow crystals still shone on Franny's face as they looked for their seats in the crowded auditorium. The entire audience sparked and buzzed with anticipation. No one seemed to mind as Franny and Chester made their way along the row, excusing themselves and shuffling between knees and seat backs. Some of the people smiled at the couple. Perhaps they recognized her. Then, too, perhaps they recognized him.

As he straightened his waistcoat before he sat down, Chester faced away from the stage's huge curtain and stole one last look toward the back of the house and up to the few rows visible in the mezzanine. It was a reflexive survey, something he'd been doing quite without thinking ever since reaching manhood. He wanted to see if a face caught him; if here amid a large and random gathering, there was a woman who attracted him. It mattered little whether he would ever speak to this woman, although in his bachelor days, he would have striven mightily to make the opportunity happen. It was enough to know that near him was the commingling of

33

qualities in face, carriage, bosom, hair—the aggregate of attractors—that could set his desire chanting. And even if that chant were only a distant, low pulse, Chester felt comforted, in a tantalized way, that he was in a room, on a street, in a crowd, with someone who drew him toward her. The theater was a wonderful place to have it happen.

The incline of the room, slanting upward from the front rows toward the back of the house, made Chester feel as if he were back on the ship. He'd just crossed the Atlantic. He felt he should lean into the slant as he had into the slope of the deck on that rolling ship. It was a sea of faces before him. Jewels sparkled like spray; cuffs and collars flashed like white-caps on waves; soft necks and throats and shoulders swirled like foam.

But he did not see a face that caught his eye. Instead he felt a tug on his sleeve.

He looked down. And there was the face that caught him: Franny's. She looked so happy.

Chester had recently arrived from London, where he'd begun his du-ties as cable engineer, where he'd designed the checking mechanism that everyone assured him would be the key to the project's success. He had stayed long enough to see the failed launching of the *Leviathan* and had returned to America to find his name and picture in the newspapers as the man who "will shrink the Atlantic." His star was on the rise. People oc-casionally pointed at him on the street.

Once in New York, he had wired Franny, encouraging her to come down from Maine. Just being back in America had made his cold disappear. He felt buoyant. The rendezvous was his idea: spend the holidays in New York. Something, he hoped, that might bring her out of her mood, the one he'd left her in, the one she seemed to be making them both live under for going on three years now. And the plan was working. She looked so happy. No mention of Betty. He had engineered a success.

He and Franny had walked through the falling snow all the way from their hotel, lingering to admire the Christmas ribbons and yew boughs hanging from the gaslights in Gramercy. They had even held hands and, when they realized they were late, ran laughing across Broadway, dodging the hansom cabs and barouches that were converging on the theaters. Such gaiety was almost out of mind for them of late.

"Dear . . . Sit down." She smiled.

Chester felt himself flush, and he sank into his seat. Franny's hand settled on his wool sleeve.

"Checking the house?" she whispered.

She gave him that coquettish, downturned smile that made dimples appear in her cheeks. It made him think—always had made him think—that he could do things that made himself irresistibly amusing to her.

"You looked like an old stage manager, counting heads," she said. "Peeking out from the peephole, getting an idea what the take is."

"Did I?"

Tiny beads of snowmelt still shone in her hair. A sea creature, he suddenly thought. A siren risen out of the groundswell of the audience, her voice floating to him from somewhere amid the waves. It was difficult for him not to be thinking of the sea, of ships, even here in the theater, gazing into his wife's brown eyes.

"Yes," she said. "You always like to do that. I've noticed."

He could feel himself flush again. "I didn't know I did."

"Or are you hoping someone will recognize you? Like a young actor, looking for a compliment from someone who's seen your latest performance."

"I think I prefer hearing more about your knowledge of old stage managers," Chester said, "than of young actors."

"I care only about the performance of a young engineer," she said. She raised a gloved hand to brush, ever so slightly, his cheek.

He took a deep breath. The smell of perfume in the hollows of flesh, of tobacco smoke still trapped in whiskers, the scent of cordials and whiskey on whispers that buzzed all around him, filled his head. He wished the show would begin.

"Aren't they late?" he asked, and nodded toward the crimson and gold curtain glowing in the gaslight. He had come with Franny to see *Camille,* the French play that was causing a sensation in New York.

"Probably because of Mademoiselle Heron," Franny whispered. " 'La Heron' is known for making an audience wait."

Franny squeezed Chester's hand. He turned and nuzzled her ear, pressing his lips against her skin, smelling her perfume, the last of the moisture in her hair. The one woman in the crowd who aroused his ardor was right there, next to him, his wife.

"My imp," he whispered to her, feeling his lips graze the velvet folds of her ear. It was all he could do to keep his tongue in his mouth. Someone coughed behind them, probably scandalized. Chester pulled away from

Franny. She shone with a victor's smile. Her husband was in her thrall. This was like the old days.

The lights began to go down. The ushers were moving from sconce to sconce, lowering the gas. Franny sat straighter in her seat. Chester could see the smile vanish from her face. She was alert, focusing her attention now on the stage and the towering red curtain. He could almost feel her pulse quicken in his own chest. She had had a career on the stage, and she still felt a thrill, she said, right before a play was to start. She knew what was going on beyond the glowing curtain in these final moments.

"It's about to begin," she whispered. Again, Chester thought of them on a ship. They were in a trough between waves, just before the ship was to begin a long surging rise toward the wave's crest, from which they would be able to see for miles.

"It's about to begin," Franny repeated softly as the curtain started to rise.

The Actress and the Engineer

Chester had met Frances Piermont ten years before, while he was studying metallurgy and mathematics in Glasgow under William Thomson and she was recovering from what the doctors had called incipient phthisis—the beginnings of consumption. They had met on a North Sea packet sailing from Bergen, Norway, back to England. Chester had been on holiday, a fortnight's walking tour above the fjords near Aurland. Franny had been at a sanatorium outside Bergen, recuperating. She had collapsed onstage in London. They had first told her it was pneumonia, then revised their diagnosis. The doctors had said her case was mild; her constitution had been strong, and her cure could be complete. But, they'd also said, she should give up the theater; the life of an actress was—how to put it?—too *extreme* for her now somewhat compromised health.

She had told all this to Chester as they sailed toward Newcastle. He had approached her while she stood at the windward rail of the ship as they cleared the last of the outlying islands off Bergen's harbor. Chester's student friends were on the quarterdeck, smiling and looking on eagerly for signs of his progress. He was the only one of them who'd had the courage to speak to the beautiful young woman gazing toward the snowcapped Norwegian mountains that were falling off to the stern.

One of the students had recognized Franny as the American actress who had made a stir two years before in London as Isabella in a production of *Measure for Measure*. It was seen as an act of cheek: a little-known American performing the role in London no less. But her managers knew what they were doing. Franny had won over the audiences and critics with what was often referred to as her "flash."

"It is in the eyes where her proficiency resides," a freelancer had written for the *Mail and Sun*. The writer had garnished his review with a flattering sketch, "taken from this reviewer's notebook."

"Her technique is serviceable," he had written, "and her countenance pleasing—she of rosy cheek and well-formed arm, erect carriage and agile movement: all of it hinting at the forthrightness and heartiness of her New World homeland perhaps more than of the Viennese nunneries, prisons, and halls of the play—but her eyes tell stories perhaps even the Bard himself would have stopped his pen to hear. What is this power? Reader, you must see for yourself."

Chester had never seen the reviews, had never heard of her brief London triumph. It was when he stood close to her on the deck of the westbound packet that he learned about the "proficiency" of those dark and inviting eyes.

He and Franny talked very nearly through the whole crossing. Chester's fellow students went from amusement at his success to disgruntlement. He had thrown them completely over for this *actress*. Such an old story.

For her part, Franny was intrigued with the blond, bespectacled engineer. He held her gaze; he talked of things other than the theater, of which he confessed to know little. He was working with electricity and telegraphs, metals and mechanics. He tried to explain to her about something he called periodic oscillations by using the sea waves all around them as examples, but he was only able to make her laugh. She could feel even the most trivial things they said take on a burnished glow. She knew even before the sun went down off the starboard bow that she was falling in love.

They talked through the night, never going belowdecks. This abashed Chester's friends and caused no small amusement among the sailors. Chester had fetched blankets for himself and Franny, and they wrapped themselves up and sat on the forward cargo hatch, near the mast. When dawn came, Franny was asleep on Chester's shoulder. As the sun rose and the rigging was singing around them, Tynemouth hove into view.

Chester further irked his friends by purchasing a train ticket to Liverpool, Franny's point of departure for America. They rode together and made plans. He would finish his studies within a year and return to her. They would write. He would court her through the mail. This they did. They were married a year and a day after meeting on that North Sea packet. Three years later Betty was born. Four years after that, having suffered occasional, undiagnosable maladies—not unlike fits or seizures—the little girl fell from the bluffs near Willing Mind, the home on the coast of Maine Franny and Chester had inherited from Franny's father. Betty died on the rocks by the sea below the house. And then began the years that had closed hard around the couple. Until—for Chester—he received the call to work on the cable, and until—for Franny—this brief moment, this night of snow and gaslight and theater, a temporary stay of the darkness.

A New Kind of Show

Chester hadn't told Franny that he might be called away during the play. He had even forgotten about it himself. As the curtain went up, he found himself swept up in Franny's and the audience's excitement. They had gotten seats, after all, for Dumas's *Camille*. Reputed to be autobiographical, the play's subject was the fall of a renowned Parisian courtesan. Laura Keene had done a production in London. Barnum's American Museum was even doing a version. But this was *Camille* with Matilda Heron.

A couple of minutes into the play, Mademoiselle Heron made her entrance. The theater exploded with applause. The force and suddenness of the ovation made Chester's breath catch. He sat up straighter in his seat. The cheering subsided only after it was obvious the actors weren't waiting any longer and had resumed performing the play.

Heron's voice surfaced out of the noise as she spoke her lines to the actor playing Varville: "My dear friend, if I were to listen to all the people who are in love with me, I should have no time for dinner."

Laughter. As the audience was settling in to the show, Chester noticed, with a twinge of disappointment, that Mademoiselle Heron was, he thought, almost unattractive. Dark browed, thin, angular. Surprisingly mannish, he would have said. He'd hoped, from all he'd heard and read about her, that he'd be able to sit there in his seat and be seduced watching an alluring actress in a provocative play.

Instead, he turned to look at Franny. Her face blushed with light from the stage. He could see a tiny pulse in her neck. Her chin rose elegantly above her throat. The voices coming from the stage seemed far away. He always had such trouble concentrating on plays. He kept seeing people moving around in a box with only three walls. Absorption into the story was almost impossible for Chester; his mind would always wander. But Franny was the perfect audience: rapt, quick to gasp or cry out, she'd mutter imprecations at villains, sigh for the lovers. Even when reading a book at home in bed, she'd interrupt the silence of an evening with her exclamations.

"I wish Mr. Dickens were here to listen to you," he'd say as they lay together, him reading aloud to her.

And she'd roll over, smiling, those eyes teasing, her hands reaching for him under the covers. "I don't," she'd say.

But that was in former times. He recalled all this, there in the theater, and the play began to fade away.

It was the shifting of people around him that brought Chester back. Someone was tapping his shoulder. He turned to his right and saw a line of faces looking toward him. At the far end, a man, bent low in the aisle, was signaling Chester to come. Chester recognized the man.

He clasped Franny's hand and whispered that he had to go.

"Go?" she asked. "Why?"

"Spude."

He saw a tightening below the glow of her skin.

"I'll be back here soon," he said. "I promise."

He hunched and shoved and apologized his way down the row and soon was out of the theater, walking hastily through the snow with the man.

"He knows I'm at the theater with my wife?" Chester asked.

"He knows."

The man walked ahead on the cobbles into the darkness. Though he had a limp that sprang his stride, his head seemed gimballed on his shoulders and remained steady while the rest of him flapped and swiped along down an alleyway. The man kept up such a pace that Chester was hard-pressed to stay with him as they dodged through a warehouse district, avoiding snow piles and slushy pools of horse stale left from the day's commerce. They traveled down an unlit street still near the theater but that seemed distant and deep in a darker night than the one Chester had walked through hand in hand with Franny less than an hour ago. The snow had stopped. In the slits visible between the crowded buildings, Chester could make out a violet and brown night sky. Somewhere a bell chimed.

It occurred to Chester how preposterous, perhaps even sinister, it was that he was being taken to a man of J. Beaumol Spude's stature through a place like this. As he hurried behind the limping man—Spude's manservant, Agon Bailey—Chester kept thinking that they would round a corner into a brighter and more accommodating neighborhood or that there would be a carriage waiting to convey them to Spude's office.

"He knows I can't very well leave my wife alone in a theater."

"He knows it."

"He knows I can't spend much time with him."

The man stopped and turned. "Sir, when has Mr. Spude ever spent much time with you?"

Almost before Chester could register that this might have been a supercilious insult and not just a statement of fact, the man turned again and opened the door to a three-story brick building wedged between two taller warehouses. There was a light burning on the top floor above the entrance; otherwise, every building on the block was dark. They entered and began to climb the groaning stairs.

They were in a disused manufactory somewhere east of the Bowery. Bailey had produced a candle to illuminate the stairs, a couple of which were missing treads and risers and provided a view to the flight below. Leprous plaster exposed lath in large holes. A window was out on the second floor, and Chester could hear the disconsolate cooing of pigeons awakened by his and Bailey's footfalls.

"Sorry about the difficult going, sir." Bailey had a pinched smile on his face calculated to subvert any pretense of sincerity. "And that Herr Lindt's studio is on the top floor. A street-level atelier somewhere near Gramercy would have been far more convenient and commodious."

"Indeed," Chester muttered, neither knowing who Herr Lindt was nor wanting to ask.

At the top landing, Bailey knocked three times, then waited. He seemed to Chester to be counting the seconds. Chester reached into his overcoat and withdrew his pocket watch.

"My wife," Chester whispered. "There'll be an intermission—"

Bailey raised his hand for silence. He still seemed to be counting the seconds; his lips moved perceptibly. Then he blew out the candle, and the hall was completely dark. In a moment, though, Chester heard a whirring and hiss as if machinery was starting up somewhere and gas was escaping through valves. Then, at his feet, he saw a blade of brilliant white light slice out from under the door. At that moment, Bailey threw open the door and the music began.

It was a duet. A player piano and an organ. A sort of martial music. A little off-key, a little raucous, but celebratory. A fanfare.

Chester felt a hand, Bailey's probably, on his back, pushing him into the room. The interior was long and wide, bare, with a rough wooden floor and Corinthian columns supporting the high ceiling. To his right were lights. Perhaps half a dozen brilliant limelights, hissing with their exhaust smoke venting from their tops and gathering against the pressed tin panels of the ceiling, their Fresnel lenses focused on the opposite end of the room.

The hand turned Chester to face away from the lights before they blinded him. There, at the far end of the room, perhaps fifty feet away, so vivid and detailed as to seem viewed through a window, was the harbor of Liverpool.

Though framed by curtains and brilliantly lit, it was not a model, not a picture, not exactly a stage set, either. Chester thought he was peering into a giant stereoscope. Ships crowded into what appeared to be the Prince's Dock. There was the forest of masts and rigging set against a mottled gray sky. Along the quays were the ranges of iron sheds. Closer were the bollards and cleats and coiled hawsers, crates and bales strewn about in the foreground, just as is so common on the wharves. If the music weren't so loud, Chester was sure he would be able to hear the shouts and songs of the sailors, hear the cry of gulls wheeling overhead. It all appeared so real.

After his first moment of surprise, Chester began to discern what was part of an intricately painted backdrop and what were actual props and scenery. But differentiating between them was no easy task. That was the marvel of the thing. Then, everything began to move. The ship, the entire fleet berthed in the Prince's Dock, the hawsers in the foreground, all of it, began an effortless glide to the right, disappearing behind a curtain. And as the machinery smoothly moved the scene away, a cloud swept across the stage, first appearing as a harbor fog, then as something else—a mist perhaps. As this mist began to clear, another scene precipitated out of the vapor. The organ and the piano began to thrum, more in a drumming counterpoint now than in melodic concert. Trees took shape and drooped and crowded around the stage. Huts and shanties appeared huddled in the middle distance. Steam seemed to exhale from forested mountains in the distance. A small illuminated sign, stage right, said this was the jungle of Malaya and the central yard of a gutta-percha plantation.

And this time, the scene did not pause but kept rolling toward the curtain. Smoothly, the lights grew amber, then nearly violet. The crepuscular glow subdued the scenery change, and when the stage was illuminated again, they were in the wireworks at Greenwich. Chester felt he could walk right into the scene. Light seemed to filter down from the skylights in the long twining shed just as it had when Chester went there recently to monitor the cable's manufacture. Cable samples and splicing tools hung from the foreman's station downstage.

The lights suddenly went dark. The piano dropped out as the organ rumbled a suspenseful drumroll in the lower register while on the upper keys a hornpipe tootled. Tiny bits of phosphorescence streaked across the stage, replicating miniature fireworks. When the lights came up a few moments later, there appeared a rugged coastline. A frigate lay at anchor on the horizon. A crowd of people waved hats and flags—the Union Jack and the Stars and Stripes. It must have been the launch of last year's cable-laying expedition. Dignitaries, sailors, common folk, were all helping to carry the cable at the water's edge. Score upon score of sailboats, dinghies, coracles, and rowboats dotted the harbor.

Then, this time without a light change, the scene rolled away, to be replaced by the painted figure of a man standing at the stern of a ship, looking off toward the horizon, at dusk. No, Chester realized, it would be dawn. The view was to the east. The cable was visible going through the checking apparatus—a reasonable likeness of the new one Chester had designed. The man watching all this was painted two and a half, maybe three times the size of a normal human. He was hatless. His hair was windblown. His collar was turned up against a stiff breeze Chester himself could almost feel as he looked at the scene. The man seemed sculpted by the dawn light that threw a stunning golden path across the sea in the ship's wake. The man, Chester could tell, was he.

The music stopped, and the lights went out.

As he stood blinking in the dark, his ears ringing, Chester heard applause, but from only one pair of hands.

"Bravo, Joachim!" called a voice from the darkness. A chair scraped somewhere. A rude organ chord honked; someone must have hit the keyboard as the bellows drained.

Chester could hear movement, but he still could not see anyone. From behind him, back where the lights were, came a thwump and a hiss as one limelight came back on; it trained to one side of the stage, where Chester saw, for the first time, a lectern.

A flushed, pear-shaped man in a frock coat stood there beaming and applauding with hands upraised: J. Beaumol Spude.

"And this, Ludlow, is where you come in." He gestured toward the image painted on the huge scrim. "Like it?"

"I am impressed," Chester said.

"The hell you are!" Spude bellowed. "You're aghast! I saw you."

"Very well, aghast."

Spude walked over and threw an arm around Chester's shoulders. "An engineer capable of laying a goddamned cable across the Atlantic. It's nice to see you stunned by someone else's mechanical wizardry once in a while. You aren't the only genius on the planet. Nevertheless, I'm glad you're our genius. Good to see you again, my boy."

Chester felt uneasy. He wasn't sure if it was Spude's jovial deprecations that put him on edge or if it was the lingering disorientation of being plucked from his wife's side in the theater. There was something, too, about the charm of the scenes, their substance and the way they'd materialized before his eyes. It was magical. He almost felt himself wanting to beg for more, the way a child might after being yanked away from a circus sideshow.

A man came out from behind the curtain to the left of the now dim and inert stage. He was mustached, with a head of tight, dark curls. He wore a long, taupe smock, spattered with paint and burn holes.

Spude removed his arm from Chester's shoulders and motioned for the fellow, who was advancing anyway.

"Meet the man behind the miracle, Ludlow. Meet Herr Joachim Lindt, the premier panorama artist, stage designer, miniaturist, gargantuist, me-chanical wizard of illusionary arts throughout all Europe and Asia."

Lindt bowed and extended his hand. Chester shook it.

Spude took both men by the elbow and led them down the room toward the stage.

"We call it the Phantasmagorium. And you have seen only the begin-ning, Ludlow. Literally. We slapped together this demonstrator for you to see and for us to work out the kinks." Spude had them stop before the display. There was a conveyor belt, about knee high, in front of them. The foreground props and scenery moved along this track, synchronized, Ches-ter surmised, with the movement of the scrim and the lighting effects. The scrim on which the enlarged portrait of Chester was painted was startlingly exact, even at close range, as if it were a gigantic, colored daguerreotype.

"You are looking at the latest in staged entertainment, Ludlow. There have been panoramas before. There have been tableaux vivants. But there has never been the Phantasmagorium. Lindt is preparing a kinetic pano-rama, now hear this, nearly *half a mile long*," Spude said. "Music. Properties. Even sound effects. And with it all, we will tell the story of the Atlantic cable. You've seen the beginning. Liverpool, where the ships set out. Ma-laya, where the gutta-percha is harvested. We will have the wireworks at Greenwich. The creation of the magic cord. Mr. Morse's tests of the two thousand miles of wire. We will have the loading on. The celebration for the departure from Valentia, Ireland. The bands. The crowds. The Irish in their rags and tatters. We even have you, Ludlow," and here Spude pointed emphatically at the picture. "*You* standing at the taffrail, looking back toward shore, clouds towering overhead, the sea spray on your cheeks. It's all here. Painted by Lindt, engineered by Lindt, built by Lindt. Art and science. It rolls out, unfolding the story in all its heart-swelling pageantry, as you tell it to the prospective investors. There'll be no stopping them as they dive for their pocketbooks."

Spude had left them behind. He was nearly standing in the panorama, his back to them, his voice echoing around the room. Lindt stood to Ches-ter's right, his hands clasped behind his back. He was looking up at some of the cables and pulleys visible above the scrim. Half listening to Spude, Lindt appeared to Chester to be calculating new mechanical advantages or friction reductions. Chester knew the look. Engineers often glaze over when the money men perorate.

Spude was fingering one of the ratlines that swooped up toward an imaginary masthead on the cable ship. J. Beaumol Spude had the build and stature of a parlor stove. His unruly silver hair curled from his head like chromium filigree. His appetite for the entrepreneurial was an unchecked blaze, and his face glowed with the heat. He had sunk—literally, for the first, failed cable was on the bottom of the ocean—thousands into the project, and yet he wanted to go for more.

In the few months he had known Spude, Chester had come to realize that what Spude wanted was acceptance. Among the cable syndicate, Spude was the outsider. The westerner, the Missourian, almost a southerner. His money was in beef, but he was trying to work his way into telegraphy and into the New York syndicate that was staking so much on the cable: Cyrus Field, Peter Cooper, those fellows who were inclined to accept Spude's money for their project but who kept him at arm's length socially.

"This is the story of the cable?" Chester asked.

"The story *thus far*."

Chester noticed that Lindt had come out of his computational cloud and was now looking at him, but sidelong, hands still clasped behind his smock. Spude's man Bailey had moved out from the shadows, too. Chester had the feeling they were closing in.

"You mentioned something," Chester said, "about me. Me telling the investors? Is that what you said? Me telling the investors? Me telling the investors what?"

"The story. This story!" Spude exclaimed. "A lecture tour with the Phantasmagorium."

Chester shook his head. "But I—"

"You are perfect for the job. Handsome. Fair-haired. Well spoken. Experienced with a firsthand knowledge of the enterprise. An engineer. Short of an Edwin Booth, who would be better?"

"I'm not a lecturer," Chester blurted. "I'm not a showman. You've already said it: I'm an engineer."

Spude smiled a stagy, indulgent smile; he looked to Lindt and Bailey. "He doesn't want it," he told them in a near singsong. "He's not a showman. He's an engineer." Then Spude sighed. He put his arm around Chester's shoulders again; he had to stretch up to do it.

"It's yours," he said.

"But—"

Spude shook his head, put a finger to Chester's lips to hush him. "Yours," Spude whispered.

Chester tightened his jaw, looked at Bailey and Lindt quickly through narrowed eyes, then tried to move out from under Spude's grip.

But Spude held fast.

"You see, Ludlow, we have a problem. This should be obvious to you. The cable is on the bottom of the ocean. Lindt here is preparing a final panel of the cable story with a depiction of you, plus members of the syndicate, plus noble and common folk from England and Ireland and the Continent, all bestriding the ocean, pulling the cable toward America, reaching out for the shore of the New World, straining to touch, to connect, to achieve victory, the spark . . . there, there . . . almost within reach. Borrowing a little from da Vinci. Right, Joachim?"

"Michelangelo," Lindt said; his voice had the broadness of a German accent.

"Of course," Spude said. "*The Creation.* God and Adam." Spude pointed his two index fingers together. "The ceiling of the, the . . ."

"Sistine Chapel," Lindt said.

"The point is," Spude went on, turning both his index fingers on Chester, "we need you. I put this little money-raising juggernaut together. I bankrolled Herr Lindt here to come up with the production. And I submitted you as the spokesman. They loved it."

"They?"

"Field. Cooper. All the fellows."

"They loved it?"

Spude nodded, folded his hands in front of his belly, and gave an innocent, helpless smirk. "In fact, they insisted."

Chester stepped away and scratched his head. He wondered how long he'd been away from Franny. Was she growing concerned?

"Your plan is for me to travel around with this . . . show and raise money for the cable project?"

"Have you looked at the books recently, Ludlow?"

Chester shook his head.

"Have you *ever* looked at the books?"

Spude waited for an answer, but Chester didn't budge. Of course he'd never looked at the books. He'd been with the project for only a matter of weeks, and for much of that he was in London.

"Well, no mind. The simple fact is there's not enough money, Ludlow. You want our cable project to succeed, you must go forth and spend your time in the wilderness. Telling our story. Bringing the efficacy of our vision—its setback notwithstanding—to the people with the means to make it happen."

"Like a patent-medicine showman?"

Lindt coughed. Spude reared back in shock, exaggerated shock. He pointed at the panorama. "You equate this marvel, this wedding of art and engineering, with dancing dogs or fraudulent mesmerism proffered as a come-on to sell tinctures and elixirs?"

"The thought occurs—"

"Of course you don't. I know. I know. You're shy. You're modest. You work with your mind and your hands. You've never seen yourself as an exhibitionist. You don't feature yourself in front of an audience. Believe me, Ludlow, you have the stuff. And you must use it. We are counting on it. Put simply, if you don't, then you are no longer with us."

The air sucked out of the room. Chester stood breathless a moment, almost enjoying the heady disorientation. What surprised him was not the news that his job was already on the block. He knew going into it that the cable project was a wild-eyed, anything-can-happen venture. He had expected difficulties, strains, pressures coming to bear, but what surprised him was Spude's threatening him: Spude the outsider; Spude, the man Chester knew the others considered a near buffoon whose only asset was his wealth and his drive. Spude had contrived a fund-raising gimmick that the others supported, perhaps out of desperation or maybe as part of a plan to sidetrack the Missouri meat magnate. And now Spude was forcing Chester to do his bidding.

"This is what Cooper and Field want?" he said softly.

Spude nodded. "They thought my idea brilliant. Said so themselves. They knew you might resist, but I told them to make it a quid pro whatever with your staying on. They said fine to that."

Chester stared up at the scrim. His huge portrait on the darkened canvas, towering, looking off into the painted dawn, now seemed to be a mere blotch of colors, infuriating, bleeding together in his eyes.

"You're not going to be doing this from the back of a wagon in one-horse towns," Spude said consolingly. "That's not where the money is. You'll be in fancy halls, ballrooms, opera houses, theaters. This show will be a technical marvel, as I think you've witnessed. It will be a sensation. *You* will be a sensation. You'll meet powerful men, beautiful women. You'll be helping us. And yourself."

"When would I start?"

"Right after the holidays. You'll be done in time to set sail from Valentia with the new cable next summer."

"My wife," Chester murmured.

"She can go with you," Spude said. "That is, if you think she wouldn't, how should I say this, be in the way." He clapped Chester on the back.

"No," Chester said. "I mean, my wife, right now. She's at the theater. *Camille* . . ."

"Ah!" Spude said; he pulled out his pocket watch. "You must be getting back. So. We're in agreement? You'll do it?"

Again, Spude squeezed Chester to him by the shoulders; this time, though, it was as an embrace. "A sensation, Ludlow. *You!*"

Chester nodded.

"He'll do it, Lindt! Bravo to us all!"

Chester was looking at the floor, seeing only a dusty chaos of lines, the seams between the worn planks; he could hear the percussive claps of Spude's applause and then Lindt's. From across the room he could hear Bailey's hands applauding in a slower, more reticent rhythm. And then something else . . . a soft, gloved clapping and the sound of approaching steps on the floorboards. He looked up to see a woman.

"Ooof!" Spude exclaimed. "How could I forget? A thousand apologies, Lindt. Ludlow, the music you heard upon entering? The music you will hear as part of your presentation? Allow me to introduce its composer and performer, Katerina Kovolik, Frau Lindt."

She held out her hand. Her eyes were blue; her frame slight, but she moved directly, with agility, around some staging planks lying in her path. Her hair was pulled back in a kind of knot or bun behind her head; it was impossible for Chester to know which because she had approached him straight on, never turning her head or shifting her gaze, not to Spude, not to her husband, not to any of the obstacles on the floor. She smiled an open-mouthed smile as if she were about to say something but was holding back, waiting for Chester to speak.

He took her hand. "Pleased," he murmured.

She closed her mouth, looked down, and nodded. He had been taken aback by her entrance and her beauty, so she seemed to be adopting a similar, if more demure, semblance of abashment. He had the feeling she could have met him with bravado if he had responded to their introduction with bonhomie, with reserve if he had shown coolness, with a riposte if he had shown wit; she could have, he thought, matched him at anything.

Spude told Bailey to convey Chester back to the theater by carriage, then to give Chester a ride to his hotel. They would work out the details of the tour later.

"Have a lovely holiday," Spude said once they were down on the dark street and Chester was in the carriage. Spude closed the door and peered through the carriage window. "And be prepared to travel. Do this now, my boy, and by summer's end you will be able to telegraph the queen. By next Christmas, you'll be a rich man. By century's end, we'll all be in the history books."

As the carriage jerked forward, Chester bumped his head on the window. He was turned around in his seat, looking at the building. Spude was at the curb, waving.

Now as Chester moved away, a brightness fell from the upper reaches of the street, illuminating the snow, which had begun to fall again. The limelights, back on in the loft, threw a pale brilliance out into the night and onto the stonework parapets of the buildings across the street. Shadows moved across the loft windows. Then Chester heard music under the sound of the horse's hooves and the carriage wheels on the snow-caked cobbles. She was playing. The melody was obscured by the distance and the snow, but Chester could make out a tempo even inside the carriage. It was a waltz. He strained to hear more, but the carriage tilted, bearing him away around a corner.

Secret Selves

Everyone at the theater was in tears. The show was letting out as Chester alighted from the carriage and told Bailey to wait. He sought Franny in the crowd. Women were covering their faces with handkerchiefs as men led them gingerly down the steps into the gaslit snow. The men themselves were using their free hands to wipe at the corners of their own eyes or to blow their noses. Two or three outright wails went up from the crowd, and they provoked a brief keening from segments of the throng. The grief seemed contagious. Cabmen, who must have seen this spectacle before, seemed more solicitous than usual seeking fares and helping people into their carriages. Everywhere there was a murmuring and moaning, with more intense waves of it moving around the congregation.

Chester spotted Franny near the east end of the portico, leaning against a column. He shouldered his way to her.

"You missed it," she said through swallows and catch-breaths. She must have been sobbing before he got there.

"My dearest—"

She held on to his sleeve for support.

"I have a carriage," he said, but she didn't seem to hear.

"She died," Franny said, and crumpled into Chester's shoulder. He had to bend his knees to keep his balance and support her. He got them walking again.

"Well, we *knew* that, didn't we? We went to the play knowing she'd die. I mean, after all, it's the *tragedy* of *Camille.*"

Franny's brimming eyes shot him a hard glance; then she shook her head, dismissing what she'd heard. Chester knew instantly this was the wrong approach, but he was impatient with all these people spilling out onto the street with their ostentatious grief for something imaginary. He had his own problems, his own news; he had wanted to meet a relaxed and reflective Franny, one who had been pleasantly stimulated by an evening of theater and would be able to hear and accept with equanimity the news of his coming departure, not a Franny who was near to apoplexy over the fictional death of a French courtesan.

He tried to be patient. He got her comfortable in the carriage and told Bailey which hotel.

"You missed it," Franny said quietly, her head on his shoulder as the carriage picked up speed now that it was away from the pedestrian glut outside the theater.

"I know, my dear. And I'm sorry."

"What did Spude want?"

"Plans. He wanted to talk about plans for the project."

"Spude," she said, drawing the word out to savor the disdain the sound could afford her. "What a ridiculous time to do business. I hope it was worth it."

"I do, too."

Franny nuzzled down more against Chester's sleeve. Her woe was subsiding into fatigue.

"She died of what I recovered from."

"Yes, my dear."

"It was a brilliant performance."

"I'm sorry I missed it."

"In a way," Franny said, sitting up a little now, "I'm glad I was able to see it alone."

"Really?"

"Yes. You aren't angry I said that, are you?"

"No, my love, I'm not angry."

"Sometimes it's best to be alone in a theater, or with a book, or listening to music. Alone with your secret self. Have you ever felt that?"

"Yes, my love. I have."

They said nothing more until the carriage reached the hotel, where, with only the most perfunctory of conversation, they made ready for bed.

CHAPTER II

UNDER THE THAMES

London, December 1857

A Launch at Last

The tunnel had seen better days. On the cut stone walls the gaslights were leaving soot smudges like large, black exclamation points that rose up and curved with the arc of the ceiling. Years ago they would have been scrubbed away daily. On the entrance arch, people had carved their initials and chipped away souvenir pieces of stone. There were dates and names, hearts and skulls, figures and scribbles, all in a jumbled runic mess, and just below the keystone were the words, written in gaudy red and yellow chalk,

THE THAMES SUBFLUVIAL

LADIES' AID SOCIETY

WELCOMES YOU!!!

Jack Trace stood drunk and alone, pondering these signs. He was in the rotunda of the Wapping entrance to the Thames Tunnel. He had come because he thought a little obeisance was in order here. A little visit to the first Brunel triumph. Overhead, a mile or so downriver, Brunel's latest achievement, the *Leviathan*—or the *Great Eastern,* as it was increasingly being called—was afloat at last. Trace had been to the launch. He had gotten drunk at the launch. He had been out on Captain Harrison's barge, and they'd both gotten drunk. Harrison had said the stump of his amputated arm—the one he'd come to call his Crimean arm—bothered him; Trace said watching another goddamned *Leviathan* launch bothered *him.* So, with a mutual desire to avoid further sufferance, they agreed liquor would be their anodyne of choice and proceeded to imbibe from the bottle the captain kept in the barge shanty.

Trace had been to a dozen—was it a dozen? well, nearly a dozen— attempts by Isambard Kingdom Brunel to launch the *Leviathan* since that first disastrous try back in November when thousands of spectators crushed into the shipyard, when a dockworker had been flayed and flung over the crowd by a runaway winch, and when the ship that was to be Brunel's surpassing contribution to the empire's technological mastery never moved.

Trace had become something of an authority in London's newspaper world on the subject of the *Leviathan*'s travails. Brunel had come to recognize Trace's hulking form around the yard and to dread the pen-and-ink drawings that Trace would use to embellish his reports. With every failure, Trace would denigrate Brunel a little more. First there were pictures of Brunel as a valiant seaman trying to pull the massive ship into the river, then sketches of Brunel as a humuncular alpinist attempting to scale the "Great Iron Cliff" or of Brunel as a sad clown in a stovepipe hat, sitting in the mud on the banks of the Thames, the *Leviathan* behind him covered with spiderwebs and vines. Before today's launch, Trace had drawn the ship as a landlocked sideshow with ramps and walkways leading up its sides and banners proclaiming THE *LEVIATHAN* CASINO—OPEN EVERY NIGHT—NO ATTRACTION MORE THAN 2P.!!! It was a cartoon of Boschian profusion, with crowds crawling all over the shabby, beached ship and signs advertising talking dogs, footraces, dancing bears, the Christy Minstrels, General Tom Thumb, and even a Wild Man of Borneo. When Brunel saw the drawing in the *Evening Despatch*, he declared that if Trace ever set foot in the Millwall shipyard again, Brunel's workers had license to brain the reporter with any wrench, brick, timber, hammer, or fist available.

In the end, it was just another combination of hydraulic jacks, winches, and chains that got the ship afloat. Brunel had at last worked out all the flaws. The *Leviathan* inched its way down the rails and eased into the Thames like an enormous matron entering the chilly waters at Brighton.

"Something of a letdown, I'd say," Captain Harrison had muttered as he'd passed the whiskey bottle to Trace out on the barge. They could hear the smattering of applause coming from the shore. Trace had counted only fifty spectators watching the event. Harrison was supposed to fire a cannon announcing the launch of the world's largest ship, but he forgot. Trace reached for his book to draw a couple of sketches but lost the inspiration and took another drink instead.

There was something off about the day. It was a melancholia, Trace thought, borne of the ridiculousness they all felt at the ship's prospects. She was too big, too clumsy, and, now it was obvious, too costly to be any good to anyone. Trace had calculated it cost Brunel five thousand pounds for every foot the ship moved from its cradles into the water.

When the barge began to rock slightly from the waves set in motion by the *Leviathan*, Trace and Harrison were leaning against the barge gunwale, letting the whiskey ring in their heads. It was a warm winter's day and the river was beginning again to smell of sewage.

"I'm not one to complain," Harrison said, "but with that ship in the water at last and with the Little Giant out of money, I'm in all likelihood out of a job. For all his faults, he was good enough to hire a one-armed barge skipper."

"For all his faults, he kept me drawing all these weeks," Trace said.

"A toast," Harrison said, looking up from the water, and they raised their cups to the black cliff before them.

"To the Little Giant."

"Hear, hear."

Crewmen on the barge's deck were waving their caps, not exultantly but with an air of resignation and relief that an unavailing job was at last done. There was barely a breeze that afternoon, and the pennants strung along the rails of the *Leviathan* hung like tatters.

A New Invention Overhead

Trace had gotten good and drunk after the launch. Harrison gave him the remainder of the whiskey and put him on a smack that transported him upriver and let him off at Wapping Stairs. He didn't want to go home to his room. He didn't want to write the story of the launch or attempt to draft some pictures of the event. Instead, he wandered about until dusk, unsure of where to go, unsure of why he felt so bereft. It was Christmastide. He stood dumbly before a wall with posters for carol sings and a reading by Mr. Dickens. He walked on. He stopped for a couple of pints at a pub south of Commercial Road, then meandered some more. All in all, not a good season for Jack Trace. He'd had one or two middling Christmases growing up; ones he'd spent with families who took in orphans for the holidays, but mostly it was a grim time—with a few extra candles and sprigs of holly about the dormitory at the Bonewald Residence School for Boys—a time that for him heralded only the commencement of another winter.

Then, as it was growing dark, he got the idea to visit the tunnel. Maybe to do some sketching. Maybe to visit another of Brunel's handiworks as a way of saying farewell to the man's whole bloody endeavor. Or maybe just for the other things possible in the tunnel, in the dark.

Trace lurched down the pedestrian stairs to the floor of the entrance rotunda. The large, circular shaft, perhaps fifty feet across, reminded him of pictures he'd seen of the Pantheon in Rome. The rotunda had smooth marble walls adorned with columns and stone molding; a lavender, dusky light sifted down through the fan of glass panels in the circular ceiling. When he reached the bottom, where the purple twilight failed to penetrate, Trace stood woozily in dim yellow gaslight. Before him was the tunnel portal.

Brunel's father, Marc, the preeminent engineer of his day, had started construction on the Thames Tunnel some thirty years previous. Isambard Brunel finished the project, and it launched his career. But the tunnel, open since 1843, had begun its life as a major metropolitan attraction, drawing a million pedestrians in its first three months of operation. There had been numerous stalls and barrows set up inside. People would pay handsomely to buy shaving mugs or tea services embossed with PURCHASED IN THE THAMES TUNNEL. It had been a subterranean—subfluvial—bazaar of the grandest sort. Ladies and gentlemen would promenade under the river from Wapping to Rotherhithe and back again, marveling at the construction, with its embellishments of arches and floral stonework. The strollers would stop to make purchases at the stalls, all the while thrilling themselves with the notion that they were underwater and that the river was amassed, chockablock with ships and boats, its flood tide weighing down mightily, flowing onward, just above their heads. But the tunnel had fallen on hard times in the fifteen years since.

From out of the entryway, where he'd probably played music most of the day, came an elderly man carrying his hurdy-gurdy. He nodded quickly to Trace and passed by. His shoes crunched on the stone steps leading up to the street and echoed around the circular chamber. The gaslights flickered. The smell of urine, exhaling from the tunnel or from the drainage grate at his feet, met Trace's nostrils; he felt his stomach heave, then settle. From somewhere down the passage came the sound of a person whistling. A lonely and desolate sound, conjuring up in Trace's bleary thoughts the paradoxical image of spaciousness while coming, as it did, from inside a constricted stone artery beneath a river. The acoustics of the curved walls set the tune to bouncing around Trace's head. He tried to settle himself by looking down the tunnel, to focus into the dark eye itself, the exclamation points of soot.

Nothing was moving in there. There seemed to be no sound now that the whistling had stopped. Trace had an urge to get out of there, get back up to ground level, but a stronger urge pulled him toward the portal and beneath the river. He walked forward and glanced up at the Ladies' Aid sign as he passed under the arch. Did Brunel even know about this? Trace felt a stab of despondency when he thought of Brunel, who, even if he was ailing and astride a monstrous floating folly, had in his life gone from this tunnel on to serial triumphs, building masterworks of the age, while he, Jack Trace, had come to this pass: he was an oafish, aging bachelor, who, though he'd pulled himself up and out of the workhouse as a boy and had used his talent and his orphan's annuity to obtain a seat at the St. John's Wood Art School, never went on to the Royal Academy and ended up a sketch artist for newspapers, a part-time drawing master at Miss Orford's, seeking relief here, in a man-made cave, under a foul-smelling river.

There were people in the tunnel; it had only seemed that the place was empty. Trace knew you could find them any time of the day or night, but you had to be careful. Particularly at night. Which was coming on, he seemed to remember, as he staggered on deeper into the passage. Night.

He had walked far enough to be under the river when he heard the hum of commerce. Or of congress, he thought. He braced himself and walked farther, feeling as if he were sliding on rails down a hill, moving as ponderously as the *Leviathan* had that afternoon on her way into the river. He wanted to forget that ship. He felt for the whiskey bottle, pulled it out, and checked it by holding it up to a lamp. A mere thimbleful left. He sucked it down, then placed the bottle neatly against the wall. It wouldn't do to smash a bottle in Brunel's edifice, although others had, he could see.

The Ladies collected in the deepest part of the conduit, the section directly below the center of the Thames. This afforded them the greatest time for warning if the Metropolitan Police made a sweep from either end. The Ladies and their gentlemen could pull themselves together, bustle out of the alcoves and tabernacles that lined the artery, stroll arm in arm toward ground level, offer a "Lovely evening, innit?" to the police, and neatly avoid arrest.

Trace saw the first sentry standing near a lamp about twenty yards away, an emaciated one-legged woman in a shawl and tied hat. She had long ago sunk below the Trade to now wash up begging and standing lookout for the Ladies.

"Lovely evening, innit?"

Trace nodded and colored. "Lovely," he said as he shuffled by.

The light in this section of the tunnel became dimmer. Only every fourth or fifth lamp was lit. Trace saw movement. Shadowy figures shifted about in the tenebrous chamber. It was hard to tell what were the echoes of whispers to others and what were bids to him alone. He walked on in a daze. The early evening work had begun in the alcoves. The rustle of fabric. A cough. A laugh. A cane clattering to the stone floor. Crooning somewhere. The Cockney growl of a client getting rough. The weeping of a baby-talking gentleman begging not to be punished. The slap of a spanking. Another Boschian cartoon began to form in the darkness in Trace's mind: *Brunel's Subfluvial Casino of Eros . . . No One Leaves Unsatisfied!*

Trace chose a woman, perhaps a girl by the sound of her voice, who said her name was Maddy.

"Short for Madeline," she said.

"Of course," Trace muttered. He gave her all the money he had.

"Not enough for a full go," she said as she counted the coins. It was too dark for her to see how much Trace had put in her palm; she did the counting by feel. "But we can get you something of value for your cash."

She took him by the arm and led him deeper into the tunnel.

"We ever met?" she asked. As they passed a gaslight, he could see she had a scar running from her lower right eyelid to her cheek. It made her eye droop a little and gave it a constant appraising cast, as if she wouldn't believe Trace no matter what he said.

"No."

"Oh, well. Thought we might a' done."

Trace's heart was pounding. Once he'd found himself heading for the tunnel, he had approached the endeavor with grim resolution, as if it were a compulsory obligation, an answer to a summons that went back years; but now, in the final moments, he was beginning to feel skittish . . . as he always did at times like this.

"Here's a spot, sir," Maddy whispered, and pulled him into an empty alcove along the stone wall. Trace felt his foot slip a little in a pool of something wet. Urine perhaps . . . or worse. From its first days, the tunnel floor always had a reputation for being remarkably dry—another Brunel engineering triumph. Trace shuffled a little to rub his shoe clean. Was the other scraping sound he heard the scuttle of rats' feet? No, it was Maddy hoisting her skirts.

"Care for a look? 'S free."

"Ah—"

"Care for help?" and she reached over to undo his trousers. "This is what you can afford, and . . . oooooo, wha's this?"

"Just a book."

"A book, is it? And here I was thinking it was *ye-ew*. So, what kind of book are we reading tonight?" She rubbed against his thigh, fingers working his buttons dexterously.

"Not reading. They're drawings."

"Drawings? Whose drawings?"

She had her hands—both of them—on him now.

"My drawings."

"*Your* drawings? Well, maybe you'll show me your drawings. I'd love to see your drawings. Will you show me your drawings?"

"Maybe, maybe I will."

"Maybe you will? Only *maybe?* Say, maybe you'll draw Maddy? Maybe you'd like to put me in your book. I could do that for you. Be your model. Wha' you say?"

Trace was losing his balance. He tilted back to feel the pocked surface of the tunnel wall support him. It was near dark in the alcove, the closest gaslight was in the main artery. Maddy was backlit and stood out as a warping shadow, one that seemed to grow, sucking the very air away and making him weak and powerless. Her hands were working him now, almost furiously.

"Maybe—" he repeated when everything began to spin, and he felt his knees begin to buckle and his groin ache pleasurably.

Then suddenly Maddy stopped and yanked her hands out of his trousers.

"Hello—?" Trace's voice popped out of his throat, half bark, half plea.
"Shhhh!"

Maddy was standing, hands waving, telling him to hold, wait, listen. "Hear it?"

"Hear what?"
"That!"

Trace held his breath. His head was spinning, but there was a sound. A distant noise; a metallic, spiraling rasp that twisted downward into the tunnel. It was clearly coming toward them.

"I hear it," Trace said.

"Course you do," she whispered and pointed to the sound, moving her finger in the shadows from one side of the tunnel to the space above their heads. With her other hand, she grabbed at Trace's trousers and pulled him into the main passage.

"What is it?" he asked.

"Ship."

Trace noticed now that other Ladies of the Tunnel were there too, gathering, with their gentlemen in various stages of dishabille. One elderly fellow wore a horse's bridle, and his Lady sat astride him. They were all listening to the noise.

"It's a ship?" Trace asked.

"Innit now?" whispered Maddy, nodding. "A steamship with one of those *things* on it . . . ," and she made a spiraling motion with her hand.

"A propeller?" Trace said.

" 'At's it."

"You can hear that down here?"

"Right over our heads, she is," Maddy said, pointing toward the ceiling. "Close."

The grinding noise was indeed close. It was as if insects were buzzing down toward them through the passage. The sound put Trace on edge, but when he looked, Maddy appeared enthralled with the noise, amazed. Her scarred eye held a tear at its corner. In the dim light of the tunnel, Trace noticed all the other Ladies were similarly captivated. The men either looked determined to ignore the interruption and keep pumping or, if they were listening, seemed confused.

"I love it," Maddy said. " 'At's progress, it is. Progress. Ships with what-you-call-'em going right over our heads. Don' happen out on the streets now, does it?"

"I suppose not," Trace said.

"Course not. How could it?" and Maddy let loose with a loud laugh that echoed around the tunnel and brought a chorus of *shhh*es from the other Ladies.

The grinding was twisting away as the ship bore downriver, twisting away into the spaces of darkness in the tunnel. Maddy pulled Trace back into the alcove.

"They call 'em screws, you know," she said. "Them propel-things. Screws."

"Do they?" Trace didn't know what to make of all this. "I mean, yes, I know they do." Her hands were back in his trousers, starting their work again from the beginning.

"Someday all the ships'll have them."

Trace's flesh was quickening again.

"I have a nice little surprise for you, Mr. Artiste," Maddy said. "The full go. No extra charge. House rules. We do it every time one of those new ships goes overhead. Brings luck. What goes around"—and she made that spiraling motion with her hands on Trace—"comes around."

Trace shuddered; he was almost . . . relieved.

"Compliments of the Ladies' Aid Society," Maddy said.

She took one hand out of Trace's trousers, pulled her skirts up, and stepped on a stone that put her at the perfect height for him. She raised her left leg and fit herself onto him. "Course, we can't be offering this forever, but for now . . . a screw begets a screw."

The sketchbook fell to the floor. The sound of the steamship had ground away into nothingness. There was only the noise of his and Maddy's exertions in Trace's ears. He felt the pressure rising. Relief would be coming soon. With his left hand he steadied himself and gripped the dry stone of Brunel's tunnel; with his right hand he clutched Maddy's ass.

He closed his eyes, and out of the swirl and sea waves behind his lids, he saw a picture form. Its grandeur, coming fast upon him, made him gasp. As it took shape, he recognized himself. He was in an enormous, beautiful drawing, done in his own hand, complex and profound, unfolding in all directions. In this picture engineering marvels abounded. Steam engines. Smokeless locomotives. Wires. Beautiful bridges. Telegraph cables anyone could use. Aerogondolas. Outside the drawing, Maddy flexed, relaxed, and flexed her thighs, encircling him. He was under the river that flowed through the middle of the capital of the empire, just upstream from the largest ship in the world. And in his picture, he was not a figure on the periphery; no, in the picture, he was at the center of it all.

"Progress," he groaned.

CHAPTER III

AT WILLING MIND

Maine, January 1858

Betty's Walk

Everywhere there was a blueness and cold of such intensity, it was as if the world itself had been asphyxiated. The cloudless sky was a cerulean glass bell placed over Casco Bay. The sea was calm, almost indigo, with a few ripples here and there from a strangled breeze. There were ruffles of foam made by the tiny waves at the shoreline, and they took on the same whiteness as the snow that blanketed the rocks and the marshes to the west. And yet all held an undertone of that frigid blueness. The snow rang with it. The spruce trees on the bluffs beyond the house were nearly black with it. And on this day, almost two weeks after Christmas, Franny Ludlow wore a blue coat for her morning walk on the path through the heather toward the cliffs.

Franny knew that Chester did not care for her walking along the cliffs. Even with a new guardrail it was still dangerous. One could slip and fall, just as a four-year-old girl might. Franny secretly called it Betty's Walk. Chester would have been even more concerned if he knew that; he would have indulged her and perhaps not criticized her name for the path, but privately he would have been filled with a dread that Franny had gone too far in her grief, which should now be passing.

And it was passing, for the most part. Franny could now put the weight of Betty's death in a small corner of her mind and let life go on. It pleased her that she had this control. It was the obverse of the skills she had developed as an actress: summoning and letting emotions fly on demand in the service of drama; here she was subduing and confining feelings for equilibrium. But only in public. Alone, or often with Chester, her mood could be stolid and dark.

She made it to the bluff at the top of the path that led down to the rocks. She turned her back on the sea and the morning sun and faced Willing Mind, the rambling, gray-shingled house her father, the Boston architect Augustus Piermont, had built here on the Maine coast and that she and Chester now owned. Franny had spent all the summers of her childhood at Willing Mind. She'd had her doubts about it as a year-round residence, but Chester, with his engineer's prowess and drive, had supervised insulating and tightening the structure, and by judiciously closing off various upper and little-used rooms in the winter, it had become a snug home even during the coldest months. Chester had applied his engineering skills to all sorts of household embellishments: a dumbwaiter for Mrs. Tyler, the housekeeper, to convey meals to the second floor when Franny was indisposed; a two-person, narrow-gauge funicular that went from the bluffs down to the beach; a carousel—now dismantled—for Betty; an experimental furnace and bellows system to circulate warm air through the house in winter. After Betty's accident they had thought about leaving, repairing perhaps to Gramercy Park in New York, but it was Franny who said no, they must make a go of staying: it was home; Betty was buried on the property; they must stay with her.

Back at the house, smoke curled from all four of the chimneys. Gilbert Tyler, the lobsterman from down the road who doubled as the Ludlows' caretaker, had lit all the fires in anticipation of the arrival. (He was chary of Chester's furnace invention and preferred fires.) Chester was in the study, going over the lecture notes he'd been sent by Spude. "The troupe," as Franny called it, had sent word they'd pulled in to Portland by train the night before and would be arriving at Willing Mind by wagon later that day.

Franny was not sure how she felt about this venture, about the whole idea of "the tour," as Chester described it. The plan was not to tour in America but to cross the Atlantic to England.

"The economy is better over there," Chester had told her. "We'll go where the money is."

Franny was curious about the Phantasmagorium. Chester had told her what he'd seen the night he'd left her watching *Camille*. They were bringing the final version of the show to Willing Mind. Spude was coming, as were the Lindts, the couple whom Chester said had executed the show's design. Spude had wanted a secret, out-of-the-way place for rehearsals. Chester had suggested his estate, not thinking that its remoteness would appeal to Spude. "Perfect!" Spude had said. "We can work undetected. We'll be there by Twelfth Night." And so they were, to the day.

Franny hunched a little in the cold brightness. There was a letter in her left pocket and she felt it with her gloved hand. She'd kept the letter there since its arrival two days ago. She had not shown it to Chester. He'd seemed too distracted, too concerned about the approach of Spude and the others. She wanted, she thought, to protect him. She wanted, for once, to be a bulwark.

It was from Otis, Chester's older brother. It was posted from the Sandwich Islands, where Otis said he would be recuperating for a few weeks before setting out for America. He was returning earlier than expected from the cable syndicate's gutta-percha holdings in Malaya. Otis gave no indication as to what necessitated his recuperation. The letter was typically cryptic. It was also atypically effusive about his longing to be home again. As touching as it might have been for someone to read that, Franny's first thought was that Willing Mind was *not* his home. He had always been, would always be, a visitor here.

Franny could see the sail of Tyler's lobster boat out on the water. The white triangle luffed in the light breeze, and the old man had begun to row from one lobster pot to the next. The pots' buoys were indiscernible to Franny at that distance, but she knew by heart where they were. She'd seen Tyler make the rounds of his traps for years; she'd even gone out with him upon occasion when she was a little girl, and had watched him pull the slatted traps up from the sea bottom. She stood on the bluff and could make out the old man bending over the gunwale. She watched until she saw the flash of the wet oar blades in the weak winter sun and saw the boat move on, and somehow that gave her the feeling it was all right to descend the path to the water.

Chester Prepares

Chester paced before his study's window facing the sea. Sunlight splashed up from a broad shield of reflected brilliance lying upon the water. The room clattered with the light, but the thought of pulling the curtains was intolerable. Chester's mind was jangling, but it would be worse to shut himself in and see that throbbing glow press on the drapes.

Chester was trying to prepare his speech, but having a bad go of it. He had read through the manuscript that Spude had sent him—the speech, the lecture, whatever it was—which he would deliver to the moneyed heads of Britain. He had tried saying the speech aloud, but hearing his own voice in that sun-beseiged room made him uneasy, and he began to pace. Maybe he should move to the back of the house; maybe he should read the speech again in silence; maybe he shouldn't read it all.

He had seen Franny walking down the path toward the bluffs. He assumed she would be taking the route around the rim of the lawn, back to the marshes and thence to the house. Or perhaps she would walk over to the little funicular—the "gravity railroad"—he'd built to convey passengers from the far end of the property down to the sandy beach. But when he noticed she had disappeared, he realized she must have descended the steep path to the rocks.

Chester stood with his forehead to the glass. He was abstractedly pondering Franny's mood, but it was Frau Lindt who came to mind. He noted with analytical interest how much he'd thought of her since that first meeting in the Manhattan loft nearly a month ago. It vexed him. He kept seeing her lips parting in a smile as she approached him; he kept feeling that strange sensation he'd initially had that he was meeting someone who was formidable in ways he could not articulate.

Betty's Rock

Franny stood by the rock. It wasn't a singular act of morbidity that brought her here, despite what Chester might fear. She had just wanted to think. She'd made it down the path with little trouble. Gil Tyler kept it clear. Besides, everyone agreed, it hadn't been dangerous footing that had killed Betty. She'd had an attack. Otis said he'd recognized it from across the lawn. He knew what it was because he'd had them himself. So had his father. It ran in the family.

The water gurgled and swirled around the rock; the seaweed barely gave off its fetid odor as the cold was keeping all smells locked away. The cliff pulled in here from the ocean and cupped the sun's meager heat, so the little cove felt warmer than any place Franny had been since she'd left the house.

This was the rock onto which Betty had fallen. Franny touched the hard granite and the tiny, abrasive disks of the thousands of barnacles that clung to the boulder. The rock felt warm. She spread her arms farther apart on the boulder and lowered her head. She curved her whole frame around the rock; with her boot tips in the eddying water, she lay spread-eagled upon the rough surface. She lay there and let herself think of Betty.

They had been grand mal seizures, and they had been frightening when they occurred, especially when the child was an infant. Strangely, it was Otis who had put her mind more at ease about them; Otis, who seemed difficult and enigmatic in what Franny thought was his calculated way. Otis told her about how the seizures might feel to Betty, what she might be seeing, what it was like when they were over. When Otis talked about the malady with Franny, the effect was calming. It intrigued her how reassured she'd felt by Otis, who, with his sudden appearances, his wanderings, his mysteriousness, had usually set her on edge.

Franny closed her eyes tightly; she felt the grittiness of the rock on her cheek. The tide soughed and gurgled around her. She couldn't help herself; she saw her daughter spinning, falling through the air, approaching the rock. She heard a thud.

Gil Tyler was a few yards offshore in the little cove, pulling up a trap. He hadn't seen Franny until she bolted up and cried out.

"Mrs. Ludlow"—he called her that now; it had always been "Miss Piermont" when she was a girl—"you all right?"

Franny nodded. "Fine." She gulped some air. She blinked, felt her heart still galloping. Tyler kept looking at her, his gaze steady as his boat rocked. She took a couple of deep breaths; she smiled and pulled herself up off the rock. To diffuse the moment, she asked the old man the question she'd been asking him for years, knowing she'd receive the same answer.

"How's luck?" Franny called.

"Luck's still lookin' for me," Tyler said. Then, as if to prove it, the pot he pulled up was empty. The timing was so perfect, even Tyler had to smile at the vacant trap. "She's got a whole ocean to work. Same as me." He baited the trap and threw it back in.

"You'll find each other," Franny called.

"Same as I found you?"

"Same as."

It was a call and response they'd been doing ever since she was a little girl. It delighted old Tyler. Franny could see his face, and the sight made her almost happy.

The Arrival

Seven wagons came up the lane from the Freeport Road. Seven! Or to be precise, six wagons and a coach. With that kind of an entourage leaving Portland, there wouldn't be any secrecy about the rehearsals. Spude must have chartered two or three freight cars to get the equipment up from New York; a score of men must have helped load the wagons at the Portland train station. And now the procession was pulling up the drive.

Old Tyler's wife, Edwina, who was Chester and Franny's cook and housekeeper at Willing Mind, had knocked meekly at the door to the study, where Chester had been standing with his head still to the glass window. She'd said it looked as if an army were approaching.

"More like the circus," Chester mumbled as he pulled on a coat and proceeded to the front porch to greet the arrivals.

Spude was already coming up the steps by the time Chester made it to the door. Spude's tread made the porch's cold boards creak and bang under his feet.

"Beautiful, Ludlow. A lovely place. The rock-bound coast of Maine. I love it." Spude pumped Chester's arm.

"You had an uneventful trip, I hope," Chester said.

"Now, why would you say that? It was *full* of events. Lively discussions on the train. Fine cigars. Excellent meals. A card game in which I must say I did nicely. Some lovely ladies with whom an old widower could pass the time. You who are about to travel, Ludlow, and cause a sensation and raise untold thousands of pounds sterling for us should not be aspiring to 'uneventful' trips."

Chester mustered a smile. "Yes, well. I'm glad you're here. We'll make sure you have an eventful stay," and he felt the broad slap of Spude's hand on his back.

Chester had half his attention focused beyond Spude's shoulder to the carriage, where he could see Herr Lindt climb down and talk to Agon Bailey, who was unstrapping luggage from the roof.

"I've hired some men from the village to help set up," Spude was saying, "and I've made arrangements for the chef and some of the staff at the Casco Hotel, I believe it was, to arrive here later with a meal for this evening. I hope that wasn't presumptuous of me. My intention was to relieve your housekeepers of the burden."

"That was very kind," Chester said. He was breaking away from Spude and descending the steps to greet the Lindts.

She stepped down from the carriage, her husband offering her his hand. She didn't seem fazed by exposure to the harsh, coastal chill or the bright sunlight. They seemed to elevate her, make her more erect and imposing. Her pale blue eyes shone with an adamantine glitter. Chester took her hand and offered a slight bow.

"We are glad to be here," Herr Lindt said. He wore a green Tyrolean hat with a narrow brim and a brushlike feather. It gave his face a pointed, feral look. His wife did not speak.

"I—we—are glad to have you," Chester said, making his eyes move from one Lindt to the other.

Franny Sees a Guest

Franny was lying on her back on the rock when she heard the voices. She had been dozing. She must have been. What else could account for her feeling of dislocation? She had seen old Tyler row away, she remembered that. She had felt a moment of happiness, of relief really, then fatigue had swept over her and she'd lowered herself again to the rock and had lain with her face up toward the sun. But the sun was at a different angle now, higher in the sky—afternoon, she would have guessed. So time must have passed.

She'd had thoughts of leaving Willing Mind. Or of having already left. She was unsure if they were thoughts or one of those half dreams that flicker through an uneasy, light sleep. It was surprising how warm the day had become down in the cove. She lay on her back, and shielded her eyes to look up toward the bluff.

She could make out her husband against the sky, talking to a woman. A fair-haired woman who held her hat to her head against the breeze up there. Chester was sweeping his hand back and forth as he described something out to sea. Was he telling the woman about the cable project, the distances and depths he must span and plumb to be a success? Or was he explaining to her how Gil Tyler caught lobsters in these waters? Franny looked to see if Gil was visible. He wasn't. When she turned back to look at the cliff, she could see the woman lean slightly toward Chester as he talked. She touched his arm and laughed. He smiled. Then the woman left, and Chester stood a moment, gazing out to sea. The guests must be here.

Supper and What Went Before

At supper Spude proposed a toast to the triumph of the project—not the cable project, but the Phantasmagorium. "One thing at a time," he said, addressing his own raised glass. He sat at the head of the table, an honor he had assumed more than been granted, but as he had arranged for the entire meal, he was, at least for the duration of the dinner, more host than guest in the Ludlows' home. He had forgone lobster and had ordered meat (Spude, after all, had made a fortune in beef) and potatoes ("We must have some Aroostook County *pommes de terre*," Spude had said, and so they did); they had squash, baked beans, wine, and apple pie ("A real Down East repast," Spude had said).

Chester sat opposite Spude at the foot of the table. The Lindts sat along one side, and Franny had the other side to herself. Chester was pleased to see how radiant his wife seemed. From the start of the meal she'd engaged the Lindts and Spude in conversation and banter. Spude was charmed, and the Lindts were made comfortable. Franny had seemed so subdued of late, but here Chester saw in her eyes some of the lambent glamour that had once made her famous on the stage.

From their arrival, the Lindts had been hard for Chester to plumb. Just moments after alighting from the coach, Herr Lindt had begun to supervise the men unloading the wagons into the barn. He had stood for the barest of cordialities and introductions, then he'd hastened immediately to work. Spude had gone off to his room to freshen up. Frau Lindt had also. But Herr Lindt was hard at it. Chester decided he should go out to the barn to help. He hadn't been able to find Franny, and he was peeved that she'd wandered off just before the guests had arrived. Additionally, he figured that helping Lindt, a fellow engineer, was a good way to start things off on the right foot.

He squeezed by two men carrying a long roll of canvas through the barn door. Chester had seen to it that the large woodstove was fired up, so there was a bit of warmth in the building.

"It's better than nothing," Lindt had said when Chester found him blowing on his fingers and hopping from foot to foot in the cold. "If the Phantasmagorium works under these conditions, it will work anywhere."

Then he turned and went back to directing the workmen. Chester was left standing near the stove, where he untied a few ropes binding some of the crates. Eventually Frau Lindt came into the barn through the large door, blinking from the sudden absence of sunlight.

"Did Mrs. Tyler take care of you?" Chester asked.

Frau Lindt must have still been barn-blind because she jumped and gasped at the sound of Chester's voice so close to her. They both betrayed an awkward surprise when they realized her hand was clutching his sleeve.

"Yes. Everything is satisfactory," Frau Lindt said, blushing as she withdrew her hand. She cast a quick glance at her husband, who was bent over a costume trunk; then she smiled at Chester. "More than satisfactory. There is a splendid view from the room."

They watched Herr Lindt directing a couple of workmen affixing blocks and tackle to a crossbeam above the barn floor.

"For suspending the panorama," Herr Lindt called when he noticed Chester observing, the first bit of spontaneous intercourse from the man. He nodded curtly to his wife, and she waved a gloved hand. Herr Lindt then turned and ordered the men to tie off their lines.

Frau Lindt had stepped away and was looking out the door of the barn toward the house. Chester joined her.

"Your home," she said. "It has a name. 'Willing Mind.' Why?"

"My wife's father built the place. He was an architect. Son of a parson. The name comes from an old Scottish hymn," and Chester startled himself by actually singing,

"Though soon I part
This vale unkind,
Thy light my eyes shall see.
With eager heart
And willing mind
I built a life for Thee."

For a moment work stopped in the barn. Even Herr Lindt had looked up from his schematic. Then, just as suddenly, he turned and told the men, "The stage will go here. Please open the proper crates. Note they are marked."

Chester leaned toward Frau Lindt. "It went something like that," he muttered, flushing badly.

Frau Lindt smiled. "I haven't met your wife," she said. "I should like to."

"Yes. Of course. We'll find her. I can show you around."

"Please do," she said.

"*Ja,*" said Herr Lindt dismissively. He'd moved close enough to hear the end of their conversation. "Please do." As if to get them both out of his hair.

And they went, Chester disoriented and overwhelmingly relieved to be out of the barn and in the cold sunlight.

"So, Herr Lindt," Franny said that night at the dinner table, "this theatrical device you've brought here . . . Why are my husband's services required? He's not even an actor by trade. Why take him from me?"

"I can answer that," Spude said.

Franny turned in her seat. "I'm sure you can," she said.

Chester straightened, now on guard; he sensed a change in Franny's mood.

"And I shall." Spude kept his smile, but it was clear he, too, was on guard. "Your husband is vital to the success of the transatlantic cable. All the artistry in the world—and I will say this: that Frau and Herr Lindt's artistry is equal to or surpasses any in the world—all their artistry in this endeavor cannot stand alone without authority. And *that* your husband has. He is the man who had the engineering wherewithal to get us unstuck. He can take us to the end. Nay, to the beginning, to the beginning of . . . the *dawn* of . . . the Age of the Planetary Telegraph."

Spude leaned forward over his dinner; in each fist he clutched a utensil. He was speaking to Franny, but his flush and the force of his message drew them all in.

"I see," Franny said. "And is that where we are? At the dawn of the Age of the Planetary Telegraph? If so, I must remember to wake up and greet the dawn."

Spude smiled to Chester down the table. The Lindts seemed united, for the first time since their arrival, in their fascination.

"It may mean little to you, Mrs. Ludlow," Spude said soothingly. "You are an artiste. An artiste who specializes in communicating with your audience directly, in person, in the same room, through gesture, articulation, and thespian oratory. *Our* humble art, on the other hand, is not a dweller in gilded monuments to amusement with crimson curtains lit by gas lamps; ours is not caparisoned in sumptuous costumes, painted in alluring colors, festooned with oil and tempera canvas flats. No, our stage is a humble thread of metal stretched beneath the dark and cold ocean wave; ours is a cord lying on the frigid and muddy bottom of the sea. Our art manifests itself in the tiny galvanic flickers of light in a squalid, cramped, and dark room; a flicker with no more nuance or affection than on or off, positive or negative, left or right, dot or dash, yes or no. But that binary essence is about to join continents, Mrs. Ludlow, unite nations and unseat tyrants through the spread of truth; it will permit monarchs to converse with presidents, mother with son, lover with beloved, you with me, no matter where on earth either of us may dwell; we shall converse as intimately or as grandly as we might right here, sitting face-to-face, that is, sitting with my old, saddlebagged phiz gazing into your lovely, bewitching, utterly charming countenance."

Spude bowed his head, putting it so low as to almost insert his nose into the mound of orange winter squash on his plate.

The table was silent.

"Quite," said Franny after a moment. "And are the words my husband is to so authoritatively utter during the presentation anything like the ones you have just offered us?"

"Well, I wrote them," Spude said. He smiled at Chester. "I'm sure your husband can embellish them in any way he might wish."

"Embellishment, I should say, is hardly what is called for," Franny said. "Nevertheless, thank you for your delightful explication. Would anyone care for coffee with their dessert?"

In designing Willing Mind, Franny's father had dispensed with the usual smoking or billiard room. He had only one large parlor that stretched the length of the main floor. He did not read, play snooker, or socialize enough to feel he needed a place to which he might escape after a meal with the men to pull on cigars, sip brandy, and laugh rumblingly. So, when Chester, Franny, the Lindts, and Spude adjourned after an awkward and more or less silent dessert, they all had to repair to the main room, the men to stand near the fireplace, the women to sit down near the piano.

Spude passed out a round of cigars, Chester lit everyone's, and after a few puffs, Lindt proclaimed, "We are ready. The equipment is set up. We may commence work in the morning. If it is warm enough."

"I will outfit you with anoraks and leggings if it is not," Spude said.

"I will have Tyler stoke the stove and keep it running throughout the night," Chester said. He glanced down to the other end of the room. Franny and Frau Lindt were thumbing through piano scores. They both laughed at something. Chester was at a loss to fathom Franny's moods. One moment she would be morose, as when she walked out that morning onto the bluffs and disappeared well into the afternoon; another moment she would be goading, as she was at the end of supper; or there were moments like the beginning of the meal or the present one, when she could charm laughter and intimacies out of her guests.

"Ludlow," Spude said. He, too, was glancing down toward the women. "What have you thought about bringing your wife along on the tour?"

"We have discussed it," Chester said.

"And?"

"She is considering it."

Spude nodded and let a cloud of cigar smoke slough upward across his face. "Has she been hectoring you about going?"

"Hectoring?" Chester said with slight heat in his voice.

"Bad choice of words," Spude said. "Perhaps it came to me because she seems to be a woman of such . . . spine."

Lindt smiled, watching Chester closely. For the first time, Chester had the feeling that Lindt and Spude had been talking about him and Franny behind his back and that the two men were far more equals in this venture than he was.

"I mean to say," Spude went on, "has she resented your going or worried about your going or asked you *not* to go."

"Nothing of the kind," Chester said. "She knows the importance of my work. Besides, she was an actress once herself. She knows the necessities of touring."

Chester couldn't shake the feeling that the men were examining him, that they were considering his marriage to Franny, and that they might be thinking that something about it, or about him, was a liability. He bridled at the notion. Again, here was Spude, the parvenu in this project, grilling *him*, Ludlow, the chief American engineer. And this Lindt. Who was he? An Austrian carriage mechanic, for all Chester knew. Married to a surpassingly beautiful woman, true, but couldn't *that* union be called into question?

When they had left the barn for their walk that afternoon, Chester had half hoped they wouldn't find Franny. He was distracted by the prospect of walking alone with Frau Lindt. They strolled across the carriageway between the house and the barn, the sound of their feet going from the crackle of the gravel to soft crunches as their shoes broke through the crust of the snow on the yard. The ground rose up toward the bluffs, and at that angle, all that was visible to the strollers was the utterly blue sky.

"Your husband is devoted to his work," Chester had said. "I don't know him, but he spared barely a minute for himself before he set about opening the crates."

There was a pause before Frau Lindt spoke. "He *is* brilliant," she said with a sigh of finality, as if she had come to the end of a long argument that somehow Chester had missed. Then she added, "But there is something of the clockmaker about him. Whirling little parts. Tight, whirling little parts." And she meshed her gloved fingers as if they were fidgety gears.

"He is under a lot of pressure?" Chester asked. "I can see that Spude can be ruthless even if you're working *with* him."

"Pressure? Yes . . . Pressure . . ." She let the thought trail away as if she were talking to herself. Was it pressure *she* felt, too? Chester wondered. Or pressure she was exerting? The two Lindts had seemed barely able to countenance each other's presence back in the barn.

"Will that make it difficult traveling with him? You *are* traveling with him, with us?"

"Yes, I am. And we shall manage, Mr. Ludlow. We *all* shall manage."

As they walked, Chester tried to steal looks at Frau Lindt. She had a broad face with pale blue eyes set almost too close together. It was a paradoxical combination resulting in such beauty. A face any broader, eyes any closer or bluer would have been excessive and unbecoming. As things were, her features bespoke a strength and a wistfulness, especially when she was looking away and preoccupied.

They walked farther and began to make their way through a growth of heather, threading along the random lanes between the clumps of low plants. It was as if they were strolling through a maze in a cultivated garden, their progress to the sea cliff indefinitely confounded as their route twisted and turned.

"After we first met in New York," she said, "Herr Spude could not say enough good about your abilities and how you are indispensable to the project."

"That's kind of him," Chester said.

"He made you seem like the colossus who will bestride the ocean and tie the continents together with your telegraph."

Chester laughed. "How could I live up to that kind of billing?"

"You could succeed," Frau Lindt said.

The remark brought Chester to a halt. Frau Lindt had said it so simply and with such clarity that he had to stop. He saw immediately she knew she would draw him up short, had planned it, had pleased herself in it.

"We failed once," he said, looking at her directly. "There are several hundred miles of useless cable out there under that ocean right now."

Frau Lindt shook her head, her eyes closed. When she looked at him again, it was not long enough to indulge him or to see him register surprise as she said, "That was before they had *you*. You know what you desire. You will succeed, and I shall enjoy watching you do it."

Then she turned and began walking again.

They reached the peak of the bluff. The ocean spread out before them. Light reflected off the wavelets but now angled out toward the east as the sun had passed its zenith.

Chester stepped up beside Frau Lindt, who stood back a little from the brink. She seemed uneasy with the height, and this gave Chester a renewed sense of command. The breeze caught her hat, and she had to hold it to her head. Chester began to point out landmarks. He had her look to the south and try to discern the observatory tower on Munjoy Hill in Portland. He showed her shipping lanes and the schooners at anchor in the roadstead beyond the harbor. He pointed out some islands to the north, doing it even as he knew he was becoming tedious with his disquisition as to why, because of the prevailing winds and currents, when sailing north up the coast of Maine one refers to it as sailing "down," as in "Down East."

"Are you cold?" he asked.

"A little," she said, "but it is beautiful out here. You are fortunate to have such a home. You said it is your wife's family's?"

"It is ours now," Chester said, almost saying, "mine."

He had wanted to impress her. Instantly he felt as if this was the wrong way to do it.

Gesturing toward the water, he said, "That's the ocean we have to work with. I feel uneasy, yes. I wonder how we will ever succeed."

She reached out and placed a gloved hand on his forearm. It was the same place she had clutched him when he'd frightened her in the barn; now, though, it was a touch somehow light and firm.

"You've said as much already," she told him.

Her touch, rather than unsettling him, gave him confidence. He was able to smile. "I know. Notice I did not say *if* we'll succeed. Just *how*."

"Show me back to the house," she said abruptly, but with an expression of satisfaction, as if they'd just sealed a compact and to say more would be superfluous. She turned to go first, even though she'd asked him to escort her. These contradictions about her were so unsettling, so compelling. Chester felt himself sliding as surely as if he had taken a few steps backward and dropped off the cliff. He even imagined the rush of air and the exhilaration of the descent.

Then, with sudden dread, he realized he was indulging this flirtation— for that is what he knew it was becoming—on the ground, or near it anyway, where his daughter had died. The thought left him dizzy. Frau Lindt was entering the heather thicket, moving gracefully over the snow. He wanted to tell her all that had been racing through his mind: the craving he had for her, the shame of what he'd imagined, the sadness he barely realized even at times like this, the loss, the things he knew—just *knew*—she would understand.

But he couldn't do it; it would be unconscionable. So instead, he turned away to take one last look out to sea and cast his eyes down over the edge of the cliff to the rocks.

Chester nearly cried aloud when he looked down and saw the body sprawled there, the blue coat spread out on the granite, the kelp-choked waves swirling gently around the boulder.

It was Franny. She was on her back on the very rock where Betty had died, and she, too, was dead. Chester was about to scream when he realized that, no, Franny was conscious, was all right, was even smiling. She raised herself up on her elbows and waved to him, to him who was so nonplussed, so utterly confounded by the sight of his smiling wife that he could do nothing but turn on his heels and stride away, crashing through the heather, away from the cliff and back to the house, which Frau Lindt had just entered on her own.

With his haunches to the fire, Spude was telling Chester and Herr Lindt about the gambling clubs of London. He had picked one of them to be the first venue for the Phantasmagorium's British premiere. The men were almost done with their cigars. Spude, in describing London, had begun to slip into what he thought were Britishisms.

"The clubs are large and opulent. Perfect for us. The Brits have gone positively dotty over gaming," he said, "so I thought it would be the proper place for us to appeal to that passion. Not bad, say what?"

He wanted to tell Spude he sounded like an idiot, but Chester turned toward the hearth and flicked his cigar ash into the fire. He was about to suggest they all retire for the night when he heard music coming from the piano. He looked up from the dwindling flames to see that the other men had also turned and that he had a view, framed by their shoulders, of Frau Lindt playing. Franny was standing in the curve of the instrument, hands folded, looking almost smug, as if it had been a small victory of hers to coax the maestra to play. As Chester watched, though, he saw Franny's gaze transform. He saw in her face the expression of someone watching something very dear be drawn away. He didn't know what this meant; it vaguely troubled him. He felt a rising desperation in his breast until he realized what Frau Lindt was playing. The shock pulled him away from any thoughts of Franny. He knew the music was played for him. Frau Lindt's back was to him; she had no sheet music before her; she was playing from memory, embellishing as she went along, but always coming back to that same, simple strain: the hymn that Chester had sung for her that afternoon in the barn.

Rehearsing

Sudden warm weather made the rehearsals go pleasantly. The coast of Maine was blessed that year with a January thaw of salutary mildness. The snow softened, the days were sunny, there was a blue haze in the air such as usually comes only in the spring. On breaks from work, the company would step out, blinking, from the barn into the sunlight and could, if active, remain outside without coats or wraps for as long as Spude, the taskmaster, would let them.

Spude, for all his bluster and bombast, kept the company hewed to a tight schedule. This seriousness in Spude lent an air of professionalism to the proceedings. There was little time for socializing. Chester stole occasional glances at Frau Lindt but tantalized himself more with the astringent of toiling alongside her. They ate, slept, worked, and rarely spoke. Franny, for her part, seemed to enjoy watching the proceedings.

They ran through the program several times the first couple of days, stopping for adjustments, halting to instruct the local lobstermen hired to perform and work the lights and props and backstage mechanics. Spude was paying the fishermen handsomely for their services, for their lost time and their uncaught fish, so they were willing apprentices.

Chester practiced the text Spude had prepared, memorizing great chunks of the prose. He personalized the speeches occasionally, telling a story or two he'd heard about the first cable expedition and the preparations leading up to it but avoiding any direct references to the mission's failure. He'd redact technical data where Spude's text spun off into inaccurate fantasy and gross, insupportable exaggeration. The cable syndicate was, after all, sending them out to ask for money, and Chester, as an engineer, believed you had to back up your claims with good science. Spude, on the other hand, forthrightly allowed as to how the whole Phantasmagorium had a bit of the carnival show about it, that the cable syndicate understood this, and that the wealthy people they would petition would *assume* they're sought for their money and *expect* to be entertainingly hoodwinked as they're being cadged.

Franny sometimes went to sit near the barn door and watch as the show would unfold or—more literally—unroll from one side of the building to the other. Word of the Phantasmagorium was spreading, for on days when Spude had scheduled a run-through, wives and children and neighbors of the men working for Spude would show up. At first, Chester didn't want them in the barn, but Spude prevailed.

"An audience will give us the reactions we need," he said. "I'm sure Mrs. Ludlow, a veteran of the stage, knows the value to performers of an audience's reaction."

Franny, sitting in the shadows, near the door, turned her head.

"I know she knows, Spude," Chester said. "But Mrs. Ludlow isn't performing. *I* am. In fact, I'm not performing. I'm lecturing. In fact, I'm not lecturing. I'm *begging*."

They had long since given up taking their arguments seriously. These were the motions they went through before a single line in the script was cut, a fact was clarified, or, as in this case, the spectators were allowed to stay. Because, in fine, Chester rather enjoyed the audience. He was becoming adept at "working the crowd," as Spude put it, and the power and impressiveness of the Phantasmagorium were undeniable. Their show, as it came together, was a spectacle to behold, and Chester, in spite of himself, was becoming increasingly proud of it.

The barn grows dark. A bit of light seeps in through some of the boards unjoined by seasons of cold and shrinkage, but for the most part, the room is plunged into a softened darkness. The audience of locals and Franny, sitting on benches and bundled in overcoats, murmurs. The woodstove thrums in the rear. The stage is a broad expanse of blank white canvas framed by red curtains and crisscrossed by two swords of sunlight spearing down from cracks high in the hayloft. The bellows of the organ wheeze softly in readiness for the first notes. A prop clatters to the floor somewhere backstage. Then . . .

A spotlight shutters on, and a bright white glare focuses down on the podium at stage left. Chester Ludlow is there in a well-tailored morning coat and cravat. He has learned not to blink when the limelight flashes into his eyes. He is composed, handsome, commanding. The locals, after a slight gasp at the brilliance of the artificial light and the stunning figure before them, applaud. Franny smiles. Her husband has always cut such a striking figure. Brilliant as he is to look upon, he could have been an actor. No wonder Spude and Field and the rest of the syndicate want him to do this. They will have their money before Easter.

In a quick, self-effacing moment of nerves, Chester adjusts his gold-rimmed spectacles. They glint in the spotlight. Then he speaks: "Since the dawn of time, man has sought to communicate with his fellow man. . . ."

From somewhere in the darkened barn comes the sound of a primitive drumbeat, then a horn blowing, then the sound of a town crier (one of the lobstermen) calling, "Hear ye! Hear ye!" of a poet (another lobsterman) asking, "Shall I compayah thee to a summah's day?" of another voice (a child's, scripted, not a squirming malcontent in the audience) mewling, "Mama! Mama!" and of a statesman declaring, "When, in the course of human events . . ." Chester has paused for this montage of sounds, but now continues:

" 'In the beginning was the Word.' And ever since the beginning we, as supreme among God's creatures, have tried to use our own words to communicate, to enlighten, to court, to condemn, to trade, to pray, to do the thousand upon thousand things we as humans have done to make ourselves the civilized—and not-so-civilized—beings we are today. We have triumphed over greater and greater distances, to speak our poetry, to bind our covenants, to plan our attacks, ratify our trades, pledge our troth, bring ourselves closer to that godly state of truth and enlightened knowledge. . . ."

And here Chester gestures sweepingly toward the stage on his right, where the lights come up on a tableau vivant, bringing gasps of appreciation from the audience. There, on various levels and planes crowded together in a composite of humanity, are savages executing smoke signals from a hilltop, a bewigged patriot signing a piece of magisterial parchment, a lover tucking a billet-doux into her bosom with a sigh, a Roman senator silently proclaiming an edict perhaps to be heard on the far banks of the Tigris or Euphrates, a pair of corpulent merchants shaking hands—over and over again—a family sitting by a crackling fire, reading a Bible, a white-gowned child holding her arms out to the audience as if beseeching an unseen mother; and all of it so strikingly real, so wonderfully varied, so still and yet so animated with a real-seeming fire in the hearth and smoke puffing upward from the savages' clifftop redoubt, that the audience can do nothing but stare in silence.

It is the triumphant first chords on the organ played by Frau Lindt that break the spell and bring the crowd out of its trance to cheer at the wonder of the spectacle and at their recognition of relatives and friends onstage.

Even Franny can't resist applauding. There is something wonderfully mawkish about it, yet something undeniably appealing, for Herr Lindt has truly done marvels with stagecraft and lighting. It is the most lifelike painting or the most painterly live tableau Franny has ever seen.

And then, to everyone's shock and delight, it all begins to move. Silently, gliding smoothly as if feather-light and floating on channels of whale oil, the whole scene begins to slide stage left and out of sight behind the curtains. Lights change, dimming, a spot focusing once more solely on Chester; the music becomes staccato and a loud, rapid rat-tat-tatting fills the barn. Chester must nearly shout to be heard, but it befits rising excitement, his zealous conjuring:

"Yet nothing has so stirred our hopes or so stimulated our wonder as the invention, ladies and gentlemen, of the telegraph. . . ."

And here, gliding out from stage right is a stark, little room, dignified by its simplicity, wherein sits a young clerk, in shirtsleeves and an eyeshade, at a rough, wooden table, hunched over a telegraph key. The scene is illuminated by a kerosene lantern. It is a depiction of a faithful servant of progress, keeping his solitary vigil at some frontier outpost, connected to civilization by a gleaming wire and a wondrous clattering code.

"The twin impediments of time and distance have been rendered mere trifles by this marvel. We can, in moments it would seem, speak across vast distances, verily, across entire continents. And we are about to span the sea itself. It can be done. We have the wherewithal, we have the technical means. We have nearly done it already."

Chester pauses. He looks out at his audience. Then he continues:

"It all begins, ladies and gentlemen, in the steaming jungles. . . ."

And the story unfolds with the tableaux rolling through, with the music shifting from ominous thrumming to proud marches to rhapsodic flights, the lights changing colors and intensity with every scene; the effect of it all dumbfounding and entrancing and delighting the audience. There are the scenes in the jungle and the gutta-percha plantation; the depictions of the cable construction; the complex mechanisms for paying out the cable; the loading on; the voyage out from the Irish coast; the illustration of Chester, the master engineer, supervising it all; and there is the finale: the depiction of President Buchanan, smiling as he reads a message sent all the way from England—all the way from across the stage—by an unsmiling but nonetheless pleased Queen Victoria. The scene metamorphoses as the entire cast of costumed lobstermen comes onstage and the music swells, and the pageantry becomes Spude's vision of Michelangelo's *The Creation* with Englishmen and Americans, lowly and highborn, plain and grand, city dandy and rowdy pioneer, rough and smooth, rich and poor, reaching out in a magnificent scene of hands across the sea with ocean waves rolling below them, clouds scudding overhead, and a brilliant sunset aglow behind them, Union Jack and Old Glory flying, music swelling, and Chester asking the crowd to give, to give, to *invest*, for the betterment of mankind, for the furtherance of knowledge, for their own well-being now and the better life of their children in the world to come.

And when the performance was over, and the locals had all gone home, Spude having thanked each and every one for his help, Franny looked around the barn and found on the last bench a simple knitted fisherman's cap, and in it were coins, mostly pennies, left there by the audience, a contribution from the lobstermen's kith and kin for the completion of the cable, an offering of $2.58 and one whalebone button.

Otis Enters

He walked from Portland. He was blind in one eye, and although he had learned to discern depth and distance years ago, somehow being here in his native country had unsettled his vision. He wasn't able to compensate for the loss. His "eclipsed eye," as he called it, cast a shadow over his world. Wagons coming from behind that he'd heard approach were suddenly grazing his shoulder; a pastured horse that hadn't seemed to be there before suddenly sprung to life; the poor, begging sot who'd accosted him on Water Street in Portland soon after he'd disembarked the schooner and who'd also had a glass eye, the same color as his, startled him. So he tried to rid himself of his disorientation by setting his good eye on something distant, something solid that would not surprise him and would confirm that he was home.

That morning before lighting out on foot from Portland, he'd climbed the observatory tower. He didn't spend a moment looking out over Casco Bay and back toward the shining ocean. He wished to see only one thing. He pressed his face to the west windows, his glass eye nearly clicking against the cold pane. And there it was, the mountain: a broad pyramid of white some seventy miles away above the blue-gray horizon. It was the "Chrystall Hill" sea captains had espied two hundred years ago from far out in the Atlantic.

Mount Washington had, through all his travails, become a kind of lodestar for Otis. It was the pivot and pinnacle of his universe. He had grown up in its shadow. Otis and Chester's father had died in its watershed—literally—and he, Otis Ludlow, had spent his life traveling in ever widening concentric circles away from it. In his experiments with transetheric travel, he had used the mountain as a fixed point from which to radiate his spirit. After his sessions, the *manang mansau* would ask him where he thought he'd gone or what he'd thought he'd seen. He never told the shaman of the mountain. He lacked the words. How could one explain snow to a Dayak priest, or make a mountain of pure rock with no trees, with barely any vegetation at all, comprehensible to a man raised in a jungle? Except once; once, he did try to explain the mountain to his teacher, and the old man shocked him by nodding and closing his eyes and saying, "Yes, yes, and *cold,* too," as if he of the steaming jungle could know what that meant, as if he had been there himself and felt the lacerating wind and had nearly died in it.

Coming down from the observatory, Otis began his walk from Portland, through Falmouth and Yarmouth and farther. So taken was he by being on his native soil that he walked through the night, past Freeport, thence to the east and south again down the long peninsula at the end of which lay Willing Mind.

Franny Decides

"I shan't be going with you." Franny spoke as soon as she came upon Chester in the kitchen. He stood alone at the woodstove, warming milk for a cup mixed with nutmeg before bed. The others had all retired after Spude had held what he called a "briefing" in the great room before the fire. They could be heard moving about now on the floor above, murmuring softly. One of them was climbing quickly up the back stairs, probably returning from the privy.

Chester stirred the milk with a spoon, making soft scraping noises in the saucepan. He nodded almost imperceptibly. He seemed flushed, in a sweat, as if he'd just caught his breath.

Franny still had her blue coat on. She had been out for another walk while the group met. The weather had turned cold again; the moon was full, and she had gone out to the bluffs. Instead of spending her time looking out at the silvery moon path on the water or at the few stars able to prevail over the moonlight, instead of walking to gaze down on Betty's rock, Franny stood amid the heather thicket and looked back at the house. She loved the place: the long, consistent solidity of it, the rhythms in its design. Her father had built it, and with its gambrel roof and rank of dormers it seemed more barnlike than the barn itself. In the moonlight it was at its most substantial. In the sun, the gray shakes, weathered as they were, looked soft as flannel, and on the ever so common foggy days, the house seemed almost transparent. But at night it was dark and large and like a sleeping bear curled around the pocket of light glowing from the lamps and fire in the great room. Franny could see through the French doors to where Spude was gesturing, his hands waving, his wide body bobbing before the sofa where the Lindts sat. Chester stood to one side, his hand resting on the upholstery near Frau Lindt's shoulder.

The little company. Franny had watched for two weeks as Spude's troupe coalesced. She marveled at how Chester had transformed himself so thoroughly. He had been awkward, resistant at first, but gradually, as she audited rehearsals, she saw the change. He became adept, then confident, then commanding. Even she couldn't take her eyes off him. It was what she'd always seen in him, but somehow up there on a stage by dint of artifice and authority he was absolutely magnetic.

It wasn't Spude's prose or even the Lindts' genius that had moved the locals to dig spontaneously into their purses and come up with the few coins. It was Chester. With him, success was assured.

Chester stuck his finger in the milk to test its temperature. He licked the milk away. Franny could almost taste the sweetness as she watched him. He hadn't answered her declaration.

"I thought you'd gone to bed," he said finally.

"No," she answered. "Did you hear what I just told you?"

"Yes," he said, looking into the milk as a ring of fizzing bubbles formed at the edge of the pan. "You're not going to England. And what will you be doing?"

"Staying here. Caring for this place."

"Frances"—Chester now looked at her—"that's not necessary. The Tylers can do that. They have before."

But Franny shook her head. "I shan't be going." She realized she had no reasons prepared for this decision, but she knew it was irrevocable; it would be up to her to learn what the consequences would be.

Chester moved the saucepan off the stove. He stepped over to her and held both her shoulders in his hands. "I *want* you to go with us," he said. "I insist upon it."

Again, dodging his gaze, she shook her head. He looked at her quizzically. He dropped his hands and paced before the woodstove. "Franny, we've worked so well together. You're my helpmate. And I've always *needed* you so."

That surprised her. When had he needed her? Not that he couldn't be dear and speak frankly with her, not that they didn't feel a passion for each other; it was just that *now*, well, something had come over her. And he had pulled away. How could she explain that to him? Even she had trouble understanding what it was, this weight. All she could do was say again she wasn't going. Chester didn't speak, didn't turn.

Then she noticed, on the counter, a tortoiseshell comb. It was not one of hers. Suddenly she heard again in her mind the footsteps going up the back stairs. It hadn't been someone returning from the privy; it had been Frau Lindt after leaving Chester in the kitchen.

Then Chester spoke, "I shall miss you."

He turned.

Franny looked up before he caught her looking at the comb.

"And I shall miss you," she said. "I feel as if I already do."

They spoke no more about it, as the next two days were filled with the business of departure.

Departure and Approach

Eight wagons and two single broughams left Willing Mind on an overcast evening in late January. An extra wagon had been added to the entourage to accommodate Chester Ludlow's possessions and the new properties and scenery the Phantasmagorium had acquired during the final rehearsals. The next morning the troupe would be sailing for London from Portland. They would have to travel south all night to make the morning departure. Spude had arranged for a bark to be diverted from Boston on its way to England with a shipment of spruce lath. They reserved enough room for the Phantasmagorium and its company. The troupe would be in England inside of three weeks if all went well, sailing some of the way above the dead cable that lay on the ocean floor, or as Spude kept reminding them, above the route of the *new* cable.

Chester and Spude rode in one carriage, the Lindts in the other. The plan had been that Franny would accompany them to dockside in Portland to see them off. She would visit some friends, do some shopping, then return to Willing Mind.

But when the evening for departure came, she said she was too ill to rise. So she bade farewell to Chester from her bed. He left her after kissing her brow, holding her hand, and sitting at her bedside in the iron light of dusk.

He spent the ride in silence whenever Spude dozed in the seat opposite, and he grunted, nodded, or mustered smiles whenever Spude was awake and talking about the coming trip. The Lindts sat in near silence as well, bundled in blankets, looking out the seaward side of their coach into a black night. It was a somber way to start an adventure. An apprehensiveness to which only Spude was immune had settled over the party. Chester thought of Frau Lindt in the carriage behind. They had hardly shared three words in the days since he had kissed her late at night in the kitchen after Spude's briefing, kissed her moments before Franny walked in. They had hardly shared three words, but she had been receptive to the kiss, even more than receptive.

Franny needed to rest, and he was restless. Perhaps this tour was for the best. He settled into his seat under a red wool blanket. Spude was waking again; that meant more talk.

As the coaches pitched and yawed and the wagons creaked their way through the dark, Franny slept in her bed in a room facing the sea. She had clutched the tortoiseshell hair comb until its teeth had drawn a row of tiny blood drops from her palm. The effort and the pain released her from the weight that had been bearing down for days. She was able to rest finally; it mattered not at all that the little wounds dripped stains onto the clean sheets; she was able to sleep at last.

It was the next morning that Otis Ludlow climbed the observatory stairs, moving carefully; it was the next morning that the wagons clattered down Commercial Street to Custom House Wharf, where a bark and its crew waited anxiously to sail for England. When Otis reached the top floor, he never saw his brother's ship hoist sail behind him in the mouth of Fore

River and beat windward toward the sea. He stared in the other direction, out toward the White Mountains and that high, wide triangle of ice and rock on the horizon, stared for a good hour before descending and setting out for his two-day walk north.

CHAPTER IV

AN EXPLOSION

London, Spring 1858

A Disastrous Maiden Voyage

If he hadn't tried to avoid the whore, he might have been killed. Though if he hadn't sought her in the first place under the river those months ago, he wouldn't later have recognized her on the ship, wouldn't have felt the embarrassment, wouldn't have felt the excessive modesty and the need to get away when she came up behind him in broad daylight on the bow deck, where a few minutes later door-sized pieces of the ship's funnel would come winging forward like frenzied birds of prey, leaving a gaping hole from which steam screeched to drown out the cries of the dying and panicked passengers.

Brunel had grown too ill to prevent Trace from receiving permission to sail on the maiden voyage of the *Great Eastern*. That was what the *Leviathan* was now called. Popular opinion had won out over the syndicate, and the huge vessel entered the British Registry as the *Great Eastern*.

Meanwhile, the Little Giant had shrunk in stature and in the board's estimation. Brunel could barely walk. His frame was hunched, his face pale. He coughed incessantly. He was unable to raise a penny. The vessel sat for months, with outfitting work progressing slowly, and Brunel spent days lying on his cot in the engineers' shanty down in the shipyard, calculating what he thought were necessary equations to get the vessel launched, even though it was already afloat and berthed at a dock nearby.

The ship was nicknamed the "Great Iron Cliff." Trace had written a couple of stories about it, once visiting the hull at quayside on New Year's Day to do a story with a "forlorn giant awaits the New Year" theme. A wet snow fell across the Isle of Dogs. It was a scene of cold abjection, and it suited Trace's mood. Rather than doing a caricature of the ship, he drew a realistic pen-and-ink rendering with the snow mantling the bollards and hawsers and a lone watchman walking down the quay in the foreground. He sat working until his fingers went numb under the eaves of the engineers' shanty. He never knew it, but Brunel was lying not three feet away, inside the shanty, near the coal stove, dazed and calculating. No editor ever bought the picture, though Trace was as proud of it as anything he'd ever done.

When the syndicate finally scraped together the money and spring was in the air and the ship was ready for a shakedown cruise, the editors perked up and Trace had two offers to cover the story. The *Evening Despatch* obtained a press pass for him, and four days before the cruise he went to the syndicate's dockside office to see about his papers.

The place was in an uproar. At first Trace thought it was just over-enthusiastic preparations for the long-awaited—*desperately* awaited—cruise. In the hallway outside the office in the dockside warehouse were cases of champagne, bolt upon bolt of bunting, a makeshift indoor dovecote holding 250 birds for release when the ship cast off, cheese wheels, and crates of biscuits, oranges, and firecrackers for the celebration. For an organization so strapped for funds, Trace thought, the syndicate was preparing to throw a sizable party. He was walking among the foodstuffs when a crowd of frantic workers came roaring toward him down the hall. They were shouting and trying to squeeze through the narrow passage.

Two large men leading the crowd yelled at him to make way; he squeezed in next to the dovecote and heard the birds fluttering in alarm, bits of plumage flying upward. When the crowd of men—some obviously from the docks, others clerks and office functionaries—was abreast of Trace, he could see they were bearing someone on a stretcher. Trace peered over the shoulders of the litter bearers to see Brunel, pale, mouth open, unconscious.

When the crowd passed, a distraught clerk told Trace that Brunel had collapsed on the ship.

"We had to help him up to the deck," the clerk said. "He'd come to make an inspection before the shakedown. He never should have done it. He looked around, let out a groan, and fell flat, out cold."

Trace stepped over to a dusty window on the stair landing and saw the men load Brunel into a lumber wagon down in the yard. A teamster whipped the horses, and the wagon tore out of the cobbled warehouse enclosure. That evening the papers had the news that Brunel had been felled by a stroke. Trace had sold the *Despatch* his first-person account plus a drawing of the clerks and stevedores bearing their fallen leader, an engraving done in the heroic style of West's *Death of General Wolfe*. He had twenty bids for the piece. Brunel's fall had raised Trace, for the moment, to a respectable height above the Fleet Street hurly-burly.

The doves flew, the bands played, the sun shone down warmly on the sailing. The *Great Eastern* bore a manifest of close to a thousand dignitaries, gentry, members of the royal family, syndicate backers, and gentlemen of the press for its cruise down the Thames estuary and into the English Channel.

The ship's size was staggering. Trace had never seen anything like it— and he had been to the yard countless times while the hulk was under construction. But being on the deck, out in the mouth of the river, was like standing atop a piece of the continent as it broke loose from the mainland and proceeded to glide seaward.

After the ship had navigated the tricky point at Blackwell, an officer released a dozen carrier pigeons to spread the news back to a waiting city. A steam whistle blast sent the birds on their way.

Trace strolled around the main deck, dubbed "Oxford Street" by the sailors, marveled when he gazed over the side rail at how far above the water he stood, listened as Petronius Durning, a spokesman for the syndicate, lamented in a speech to all gathered on the afterdeck that Brunel couldn't be there.

"He is the right man for our nation," Durning said. "This wondrous ship proves it! Here's to his speedy recovery." And the crowd cheered.

While Trace did a few sketches of the dignitaries, a couple of the Fleet Street boys recognized him. He doffed his hat, the notoriety pleasing him. He smiled at a scowling daguerreotype artist who was having difficulty with his equipment owing to the vibrations of the vessel's steam engines. The daguerreotypist was running back and forth between the camera on its tripod and his subject, a portly gentleman posed regally at the ship's rail.

"Oh, come *on*, man," the gentleman was saying to the frustrated artist, who was now under the black cloth, using the hem of his smock to brush a piece of coal ash from the ground glass.

"To *hell* with it!" the gentleman said, and brusquely walked away, leaving the daguerreotypist shouting under his hood for him to "Please, sir, move to your left more! I can't see you!"

When the daguereotypist popped out from under the shroud and saw his subject gone, he clapped together his tripod and shouted at Trace, "Well, go ahead and *sketch* the haughty bastard then."

Trace just laughed, the first time he'd felt jolly in weeks. Flags on the six masts fluttered against the blue sky. As there was no craft afloat with as many masts, there was no nautical terminology for them. The sailors named them after the days of the week: Monday through Saturday. Trace asked a crewman why no Sunday.

"That would be a day of rest, and there's none of them at sea, sir," the sailor said, and went back to coiling a line.

Trace began to whistle as he drew. Magnificent cauliflowers of black coal smoke poured forth from the five funnels. Gentlemen promenaded arm in arm with their ladies around the deck ("Four laps to the mile," another crewman had told Trace), and a string orchestra played in the grand saloon below.

Trace watched a chevron of mallards fly in fright before the towering prow of the ship as it plowed into open water. He strolled along the port side and gazed into the creamy marble foam stirred up by the massive side wheel as it churned the ship into the Channel. He thought about going below to see what he might find to eat; he thought perhaps he should get back to work and do more sketching; he thought of just standing at the rail and tilting his white winter face up to the spring sunlight. He was just too intoxicated by the salt air and the foam, the festive atmosphere and the beautiful weather, the very miracle that the *Great Eastern* was actually afloat and moving and that he was on it. He had a momentary image of that picture he'd seen in his mind's eye, the picture of the magic empire with him at its hub. Perhaps if it were real and he were in it, he would feel something like this. He was sorry for poor Brunel, lying abed somewhere in London, missing the first steps of his Great Babe.

"Why, it's Mr. Sketch-man."

Trace turned away from the rail toward the deck. Before him stood Maddy, giggling. She looked respectable, more or less, with a layer of pancake subduing the scar on her face, and wearing an overly large cotton dress and worsted jacket and carrying a threadbare parasol.

"A friend got me on," she said, anticipating his question. "*Another* friend. Besides you. Lovely day for a sail, eh?" She spun the parasol and gazed with affected wistfulness at the sky. "Maybe *now* the big artist will draw Maddy? I seen you got your book. And your little pencil. Never go anywhere without that now, do you?"

"Excuse me, madam?"

" 'Excuse me, madam?' " She giggled again.

"I'm sorry," Trace said. "It's just that I'm a little . . . *surprised* to see you."

"Now why is that? It's a lovely day. I thought I'd take the sea air. And you might like to know there's a lot more of us on board than the big muckety-mucks and their wives and the C of E would care to admit."

"Of *us?*"

"Of my ilk," Maddy said, twirling the parasol.

Later, it would occur to Trace that he had become so flustered before the whore because when he saw her, he was face-to-face, once again, with an inspiration. He had avoided thinking of her in the past months—a queasy shame came over him whenever he did—but he couldn't chase away the idea she'd inspired. It was the picture. The one that had come to him during their congress. In recent weeks he would wake from a sleep and see one of the complicated machines, one of the impossibly cantilevered gantries that had been in that picture of a whirligig utopia. It was the *feeling* of seeing it all that he wanted back desperately. He knew he was embellishing it every time he thought of it, but he couldn't keep his mind away. It had become a real work in his mind; it *existed*. He began to feel compelled to paint it for himself.

But that prospect frightened him. He was a sketch artist, not a—what?—a visionary muralist. Still, he wanted to see that place again in its entirety, that place he only half ironically called Progress, that place he had first encountered in the tunnel, in this whore.

But for now, the abashed Jack Trace could think of nothing to do but tip his hat, offer the appearance of cordiality, and end the conversation quickly. He bade Maddy adieu and fled along the deck, past where the photographer's subject—the man with the muttonchops—was holding forth for a dozen or so gentlemen. He was telling them something about the electrical forces needed to move a telegraph signal under the breadth of the Atlantic.

A reporter from the *Mail* saw Trace and slapped him on the back. "Seasick already, Jack? Looking a little, shall we say, *unsettled*."

Trace couldn't get away fast enough. He had just ducked behind the main cabin and looked with relief toward the broad semiellipse of the stern deck towering over the Channel. This was the moment, he later realized, when his life was saved. This was when, having fled the length of the ship, he heard the explosion.

It was a preternaturally low thud. It seemed to come from all around him: an enveloping, singular moment of percussion, big and immediately ominous. He knew something was dreadfully wrong.

A faulty steam valve in the forward funnel had backed up and blown. The explosion ripped downward, buckling the deck and sending beams crashing to the floor of the grand saloon. One beam burst through the floor and protruded into a companionway on the deck below, where it struck the head of a porter and drove him to the floor, dead. It was a neat job compared with what the explosion wrought on deck.

At the moment of the enveloping thump, Trace instinctively turned toward the bow. There, plates from the stack flew out from the buckling funnel. He could see the wings of iron wheeling and skimming through the air over the blue and white water, pieces of clothing flying with them. Guy wires affixed to the forward funnel snapped and made huge, spiraling loops in the air as they flew outward then slapped into the ship's wake. A mammoth jet of steam blasted upward from the funnel. All around passengers began to scream.

Trace started running toward the bow, jostled by a crowd of panicked people heading in the opposite direction. More or less amidships, he fell when his feet tangled in a deck chair, and he skidded along the varnished planks, his palms burning from the abrasion. He sat for a moment, dazed and flicking the hot pain from his hands. A confusion of running legs pounded all around him. He began to scramble up, and as he did he realized for the first time he'd been running, by reflex, *toward* the trouble; he was running toward where he'd last seen Maddy.

A deckhand blocked his way.

"Far enough, please, sir," the man said, holding up his hands to Trace's chest.

Three other deckhands joined him, men in navy sweaters and tasseled caps emblazoned with S.S. GREAT EASTERN in gold on the bands. All four men were smaller than Trace, but they had the look of accelerated blood in their eyes; they were near panic themselves and could trip into violence with the least provocation.

"I . . . I want to help," Trace said.

"Help enough, sir. Stay. Please." The man was looking past Trace toward others who might be gathering behind him.

Trace pushed his chest a little at the sailor's hands. He shifted left, then right. Other passengers were moving up behind him now.

"No help needed, sir," the sailor said.

Trace could hear angry and pleading voices around him: people calling for help, people screaming to be let through to find a son, to look for a friend, to see what happened; people—men and women—howling. The sailors had now locked arms and were spanning the space between the rail and the superstructure, preventing access to the foredeck.

"Push through the bloody bastards," someone yelled from behind.

Trace could see crewmen running frantically around on the foredeck, trying to avoid the massive jet of steam, crouching over a body or two visible, waving for more help, aiding what passengers they could.

"I'm press," Trace yelled over the noise. "I'm with the press." He groped for his papers.

"Push through the bastards, I say!" came the voice again, and the crowd behind Trace began to surge against his back, pressing him harder into the sailors' linked arms.

Then a stout boatswain shorter even than the other four sailors appeared behind them with a shotgun. He aimed it skyward and jerked the trigger. The sound was swallowed by the din, but the puff of smoke from the muzzle was unmistakable.

"Stop this bloody shit *now!*" he bellowed. *"Get the hell back, you bastards, or I'll shoot to kill!"*

He trained the weapon on the crowd, sweeping the muzzle across the chests of Trace and the others in the front. His obscenities, as much as the gun, stopped them. In the pause that ensued, Trace noticed that the ship's engines were not throbbing through the deck. The crowd was not shouting. The steam roar and cries from the bow seemed suddenly distant, a replica of what they were moments ago.

"Now!" the boatswain shouted again, and Trace felt the pressure on his back relent. The crowd was receding.

"Please," Trace said to the sailor before him.

"Forget it, mate."

"Press?" A weak little plea.

The sailor shook his head. He then stole a quick look behind him, beyond the boatswain, who still had his weapon trained on Trace. The chaos forward was being enacted now behind a scrim of white steam, a pantomime of silhouettes in poses of distress and rescue.

"Press," the sailor said to the boatswain holding the gun.

"This ship's had enough trouble with the press now, ain't we?" the boatswain said. Then to Trace, "You'd be the first I'd shoot."

Trace relented and backed away. He ducked through the crowd, clambered up some sponson stairs that took him across the top of the main cabin, around the Wednesday mast, where he made his way down, and forward on the starboard side. Here the crew wasn't as mobilized, and he was able to slip around the steam clouds and work toward the crater in the foredeck.

Iron bulkhead plates were curled like wilted flower petals. A hole big enough to swallow a London mail coach yawned before Trace. Crewmen ran about, frantically screaming and pointing into the chasm. Trace could see right down into the saloon, with its carved teak sofas and chairs with claret upholstery. The maroon carpet was in shreds; the silk portieres billowed in the fire and ash that belched from deeper within the ship. The blast had gone all the way down to the stokehole. Cinders and flames spewing from the boilers were visible from the deck. Myriad bits of sky were reflected in the thousand pieces of gilded mirror that lay shattered on the carpet below.

In no time, it seemed, the crew had donkey pumps going, spraying the flames with seawater. More steam billowed up from the beleaguered ship, which now looked as if it were manufacturing its own thunderheads.

Crewmen pushed Trace back from the opening. Across the crater, he could see the boatswain with the shotgun gesturing angrily and pointing his way. He knew it was time for retreat. He quickly made for the cordon of sailors keeping other passengers back, and he ducked under the sailors' linked arms. He scuttled hunched over, wiggling through the crowd until he nearly rammed his nose into two pillars of bloody flesh. He shot upright to stand light-headed and face-to-face with a stoker, skin blackened, clothes torn, eyes glazed. Two more sailors emerged from a nearby companionway like a pair of sleepwalkers. One still carried his shovel, his skin welded to the handle. The first of them had his thigh flesh burned in holes clear down to his femur. It was a wonder he could walk at all, let alone make it up from the hold. He patted Trace on the shoulder.

"And who may ye be?" he rasped.

Women nearby began to scream.

"Help here!" Trace shouted to the blockade of sailors. "Help!"

A couple of the crewmen rushed over and bundled the staggering men back into the companionway, off to somewhere invisible to the eyes of the passengers.

The crew now herded the people with renewed adamancy, yelling even at the women, shoving any and all who resisted or objected. They succeeded in forcing the entire passenger population back to the stern half of the ship.

Trace had no choice but to pace about on the afterdeck with the other passengers as the great ship slowly turned north and made its way to the harbor at the Bill of Portland. The steam clouds began to subside.

Soon stewards came aft serving tea, and officers spread out through the milling throng, telling the shocked and dazed crowd that everything was under control, the ship was fine, the hurt were being cared for, no one of royal or gentle blood was injured, three physicians were on board, and the vessel would be docking soon; they would all be transported back to London by rail.

The crew repeated this for what seemed like hours but offered nothing more. Trace slumped against a ventilator funnel and began to notice the scorching in his palms from his fall. He licked his hands. A steward with a gleaming salver came by and gave him a teacup of champagne.

"It was for first-class only, but considering the situation . . ."

Trace raised the cup to him.

"Cheers," he said.

The steward glanced around, grabbed a cup himself, and downed it.

"Bloody cheers it is, sir," he said, giving Trace another cup and disappearing into the crowd.

Trace took the cool liquid and poured it over his fiery hands. He then did the only thing he could do at such a time—he drew.

His sketches appeared in five of London's largest newspapers the next day. Pictures of the stack blowing, panicked figures running, the funnel toppling toward the deck, the gaping hole open all the way down to the furnace hemorrhaging fire, a scene of the crew at dockside in Portland Bill bearing the injured down a gangway.

Trace, sleepless after working all night on the train, had raced from paper to paper on Fleet Street, peddling his drawings. Within an hour he had made more money than he had in any single month of his professional life.

The papers played up the curse of the *Great Eastern:* months of delays, numerous failed launches, astronomical costs, now a disastrous maiden voyage. Then six days later, they all ran the story that Isambard Kingdom Brunel, the empire's preeminent civil engineer and creator of the *Great Eastern*, had died when he heard the news of the explosion. Picking up on Durning's invocation the day of the voyage, the *Morning Chronicle* said in its obituary, "Brunel was the right man for the nation, but unfortunately, he was not the right man for the shareholders."

The *Chronicle* summed him up: "They must stoop who would gather gold, and Brunel could never stoop."

The news of the explosion had killed him, the papers all agreed; he'd died of a broken heart.

At every stop on Fleet Street, after every sale of his sketches, Trace had asked the editors if he could see a list of the injured or dead from the disaster. He scoured the names then and as the lists were revised in the papers for days afterward. The toll varied. Some accounts said five dead, some as many as ten. Trace never saw a list naming Maddy. But then, he reasoned, it was unlikely she'd used her own name or that her existence would have even been acknowledged, hers and the others of her ilk who had been aboard the *Great Eastern* for her maiden voyage.

CHAPTER V

THE PHANTASMAGORIUM SHOW

London, Spring 1858

"Du und Ich"

Joachim Lindt had a set regimen of thrusts and bends and snaps and squats with which he greeted every dawn. He took exercise wherever he went. In hotels he would ask upon arriving to have two dressing screens installed in his room: one for his wife, one for him. Hoteliers might smirk at this as some kind of strange Austro-Hungarian prudery, but Lindt actually did it out of courtesy to Katerina. Frau Lindt hated the exercises. She thought them clownish: her husband in his underthings, twisting and whipping at the waist, flicking his arms eight times left, eight times right; four left, four right; two, two; one, one; then the same for his legs. He was like a cuckoo-clock figure gone mad, a marionette left to hang out in a gale. She would roll over in bed and groan.

He knew she didn't like the exertions, so he hid them—by hiding himself—behind a dressing screen. He probably would have stopped them altogether if he could have known how revoltingly silly they seemed to his wife, but he had come to believe they were necessary. They had become a charm, a ritual: his huffing breath had become an incantation, all to ward off something that, as he grew older, seemed to show around the edges of his life the way storms would sometimes limn the Karwendel before breaking over the peaks onto the valleys.

This was a most unmechanistic way of looking at things, he knew. But for all his expertise in things mechanical, he firmly believed the body was not a machine. To see it as such was too simplistic an explanation, and Joachim Lindt knew a marvel when he saw one. True, the body needed care like a machine, and it needed fuel, but Joachim Lindt believed firmly that the body's parts were more likely to wear out from idleness than from overuse. And exertion did something for the mind, too; exertion kept those storms behind the mountains; exertion kept peaceful the well-groomed valleys where Lindt's thoughts lived and toiled and built their intricate mechanisms. He needed to take his exercise every morning, he believed, or he would go mad.

So to spare his wife, he asked for a dressing screen wherever they stayed, or he brought along, at no small expense, the screen from their flat in Innsbruck. It was the dressing screen his mother had cherished when he was growing up first in Barcelona, then back in Vienna. It had been brought from Japan and purchased in Madrid by Joachim's father, Baron Heribert Lindt, the emperor's emissary to Spain, and given to his new wife, Isabella, before Joachim was born. When he was a child, Joachimito would lie on the floor for hours looking into the triptych painted on the fabric. He would lie there alone or while his mother hummed and rustled as she dressed behind the screen. He loved staring into the pictures. The painting showed a grand scene of a Japanese battle—or perhaps it was an entire war—with thousands of tiny soldiers painted across a landscape that ranged from cloud-capped jagged mountaintops pouring forth raging cataracts and a rain of arrows from archers hidden among the crags and pine trees, down into a broad, expansive plain where most of the battalions of minute cavalry warriors raged with their sail-like battle streamers flying from poles attached to their armor and swarms of infantrymen fought hand to hand; finally it proceeded to the sea, where bluff-lined junks engaged in flaming naval combat.

Joachim Lindt had grown up with this screen, had grown up, he might say, inside it, talking to the men, climbing the rocks, moving invincibly through their rain of arrows, sailing on the junks, leading charges across the plain, aiding the wounded, sitting around the campfires, pointing out weaknesses in the defenses to the generals, and sometimes climbing around to the quiet side of the tallest mountain on the right triptych and leaning against a boulder, sitting beneath a sighing pine and looking out into the distance, a distance that went right off the picture and into the world where his mother moved through light and shadow and dressed and hummed and rustled in her silks and brocades and once or twice wept softly before her husband left them for good. Joachim would stare harder into the picture then, lose himself all the more in the intricate painting that, no matter how closely he examined it, never seemed to lose its mimetic power, never became mere strokes of ink on a stretched bolt of cloth. The picture held him, and even though it was of war, it kept him safe. It was one of the inspirations, he was sure, that led him to create so perfect a marvel as the Phantasmagorium. That screen had enabled him to avoid the world, even when he heard the weeping beyond the pictures.

But now he pumped and flexed and stretched behind the triptych. His wife was just getting over her seasickness from the crossing. She looked at the room through one eye. Spude hadn't done too badly by them. The chamber was decent; she and Joachim had been in worse. She rather liked this one: small but snug; a view out on a little army of chimney pots and, of course, gray skies. There was room enough for a sofa and an ottoman by the door, and there was a round table large enough for Joachim and her to take breakfast on, if she could stand the English idea of breakfast— yesterday it had been baked beans and a rasher of bacon. And there was room as well for the dressing screens. Joachim grunted back there behind the paintings of the ant battle as if he were some fuming god of war beneath the earth, urging the soldiers on.

It didn't bother Katerina so much today. She even felt a shiver of bemused affection for her tight, muscled husband who began each day in this manner. Maybe it was the first sign of relief from the queasiness she'd felt for nearly two weeks on the Atlantic, or maybe it was a welcome distraction from the uneasiness she felt about the tour.

For Frau Lindt, there was something unsettling about the whole venture. The fustian Spude was comical to a degree, but he offended her. Spude was from the American West—or the Midwest, as he said it was now being called—but she shouldn't hold that against him. Yes, he was overly garrulous, overbearing really, but he was a species of American, and his bombast was to be expected, enjoyed perhaps, for its novelty.

Maybe it wasn't Spude. Maybe it was the enterprise. Despite her declamations to Chester about his success, maybe it was the air of humbug about them all that bothered her. She was skeptical that a telegraph cable could be laid beneath the length of the Atlantic. The details of such an enterprise were beyond her; it seemed as impossible as flying to the moon. True, there had been telegraph lines strung across countries, even across the English Channel and the Black Sea, but these were somehow comprehensible wonders. There were hot air balloons that flew, too; they just didn't fly all the way to the moon.

"Bitte?" asked Joachim from behind the screen. He stopped twisting for a moment.

"Nichts," Katerina said quickly, almost breathlessly. She could feel her heart pound against the mattress. Had she been speaking as she lay there half asleep? And speaking in English at that? She was thinking of the telegraph, yes, but had she actually said anything?

Joachim was back to his exercises. Katerina shifted in the bed. She knew why she'd been thinking of the telegraph. It was the reason she'd been distracted for weeks; the reason she'd found herself unsettled . . . disturbed. It was Ludlow. *He* made this project unsettling for her; he made her *life* unsettling.

Spude had said it that night at dinner back in that barn of a house in Maine: Chester Ludlow had the authority. She and her husband had the artistry, but Chester Ludlow had the *authority*.

She whispered the word. This time she knew she was speaking it: Joachim never heard her. He was still behind the screen: *ein, zwei, drei, vier . . .*

He has, she thought—and being careful to only think it—*authority over my heart*. She felt a flush bloom all over her, and she curled into a ball under the covers in girlish embarrassment. She shuddered, then stretched out again, suddenly languorous. Such quick changes. *Authority over my heart*, indeed. *She* had authority, too, in this thing, whatever it was. She had enjoyed keeping Chester Ludlow off balance whenever they were together. She could see him blush, then try to compute his way through his calculus of infatuation to stay ahead of her, to surprise her, to shock. He was clever, she thought, but unschooled . . . or out of practice.

There had been that kiss in the kitchen, though. Now, *that* had caught them both unguarded. He had seen her approaching the back stairs. He had stepped toward her, about to say something, brow knitted. She had thought she instigated the kiss, but now she was no longer sure. In an instant his face had drained of all consideration, and she knew in that moment they looked upon each other with identical countenances. They kissed, and she pressed herself—or was she impelled?—toward him. She thought of them there under the yellow light of the oil lamp, the black windows, the butcher-block table where she placed a steadying hand, the table's knife-gashed hieroglyphs under her flexed fingertips. Their arms then enfolding each other for a moment until the door slammed from the outside, and she, barely comprehending how, was up the stairs and running away.

For days she and Ludlow avoided each other. For the entire journey across the Atlantic, they had only the slightest of contact, owing mainly to her seasickness. He sent inquiries as to her health by way of Joachim. She never knew what Joachim told him. She knew Joachim harbored resentment, but was it professional, or did he suspect something? Perhaps it was only because Ludlow was an engineer, too. An engineer on a project that would unite continents, span half the globe, and change history, whereas Joachim had merely perfected a mechanical toy.

Her husband was toweling himself over by the washstand. He had his wool trousers on, but his shirt off. His suspenders crisscrossed his bare back.

She was thinking of Ludlow, lost in her thoughts, feeling the heat of them, while she blankly stared at her husband's back in the dawn light of London. When she became aware of what she was looking at, she felt pity. Joachim—tight, strict, driven little Joachimito—married to her. She was a trial for him, she knew. It was her appetite, her experience. Ludlow wasn't the first. But he was the one *now*. She pictured the blond American engineer. She'd never seen him without his spectacles, those glinting delicate things that framed his features. She imagined his face softer without them. She imagined herself removing those spectacles.

Again she noticed her husband: dark hair, olive skin, still shirtless. He had tiptoed over to her dressing screen. She had left her clothes in heaps back there. From the bed, she could see far enough around the screen to watch him poke some of her clothes with his bare foot as if he were sorting through some intriguing flotsam on a beach.

She whispered to her husband. He froze, but she called to him as if she were unaware of what he'd been doing, as if she were unaware even of his whereabouts; she called as if she were rising out of slumber, rising hungry for him. She said his name and bade him come.

"Ich?" he whispered.

"*Ja,*" she said. "*Du.*"

He glided across the room toward her.

"*Du und ich,*" she whispered as if to convince herself it was just the two of them who were to be involved in what was about to follow. "*Du und ich.*"

"*A Surgeon of Everything*"

Dr. Edward Orange Wildman Whitehouse of Brighton, England, the British "electrician-projector" of the Atlantic Telegraph Company, proponent of the five-foot induction coil, the man ready to ram two thousand volts of electricity down the length of a cable spanning the Atlantic Ocean, was not a practical man. Nor was Dr. E. O. Wildman Whitehouse a scientific man. He fell into neither the practical nor the scientific camp, and thus, Dr. Whitehouse was a vulnerable man.

Dr. Whitehouse was the Atlantic Telegraph Company's sole hope, if only the company knew it. They didn't need Professor Thomson—that estimable Scotsman up in Glasgow—and his doubt-filled projections. Not if the company planned to raise money. And Wildman Whitehouse knew the company was desperate to raise money. He'd read about the catastrophic collapse of the Ohio Life Insurance and Trust Company that had pulled an enormous amount of capital down with it last year. Money was tight in America, and thus the cable would need British pounds and a British engineer to raise them. The Americans, bless their bumptious hearts, were bringing over some kind of circus show to solicit funds. That's how desperate they were. Shameful. Wildman Whitehouse might have been a vigorous self-promoter himself, but he would never be a circus act.

Wildman Whitehouse was the first to admit he was a "dabbler" in electricity. He had called himself as much in his first speech at the Mathematical and Physical Section of the British Association in Glasgow three years before. He asked to be pardoned for presuming to invade the territory of the natural philosophers; he was interested only in the applications to which his measurements might lead. He held no university chair in physical science, nor had he ever worked on a submarine cable. He never dealt in formulae, nor had he ever gone out and laid cable. He had no theorem named for him, nor had he, like some veteran cable layers, ever knelt down and tested for the flow of current in a wire by touching it with his tongue.

No, E. O. Wildman Whitehouse prided himself on working alone, on hewing to *exact* measurements made by tools of his own invention. And felicitously, Whitehouse's measurements confirmed precisely what the cable investors wanted to hear: just when evidence was mounting that it might be impractical (if not impossible) to transmit a signal under the Atlantic, Whitehouse's measurements were proving that it was possible, perhaps even easy. On the strength of these reports, the cable syndicate made him its chief British electrician. And so, in a twinkling, he went all the way from the comfort and satisfactions of a respectable medical practice in a seaside resort town on the English Channel to the heights of his country's engineering academy and entrepreneurial adventure. And yet he was running into resistance. Always resistance.

The Scotsman, Professor William Thomson of the University of Glasgow, was telling people that Whitehouse was wrong. Thomson and his former student, the American Chester Ludlow, had come up with that infernal Law of Squares. The law stated that the longer a cable, the more its signals slow down, pile up, jumble together, and become meaningless noise on the receiving end. A signal's speed decreases with the square of a cable's length.

The only way around the Law of Squares, according to Thomson and Ludlow, was to thicken the cable. A thicker cable, a lower voltage transmission, and more delicate receiving instruments were what was needed. So they said.

The Law of Squares wasn't what the investors wanted to hear. Besides, Wildman Whitehouse and his instruments had come up with the opposite conclusion: keep the wire thin and boost the power of the signals. That should make the investors happy: no need to manufacture cable to new specifications, plus Wildman Whitehouse had the generators and the induction coils—his own patented inventions—ready to go.

Whitehouse had never met Ludlow. He had corresponded with him once Chester had been appointed Whitehouse's American counterpart, and Whitehouse rather liked the man's respectful tone from the letters he'd written, wrongheaded though they may have been about the science of the endeavor. And so, when the Phantasmagorium Show arrived in London, Wildman Whitehouse went up to town to meet the American. The encounter, urged by Spude and the board, was intended to clarify any empirical differences and to keep the cable project moving. If word got out that the American and the British chief electrician-projectors were at odds, money would again grow scarce, Phantasmagorium or no Phantasmagorium.

Whitehouse took the night coach up from Brighton and arrived at Ludlow's hotel shortly after breakfast. He was struck by the stature of the American. The man met him at the door with a vigorous, forthright handshake. Whitehouse liked that; it made him feel as if already Ludlow were taking him seriously.

For his part, Chester had presumed the doctor would be larger. A man of greater bluster and age, perhaps more like Spude. Instead, Whitehouse was shorter than Chester and seemed only slightly older but with graying muttonchops and strands of black hair pulled tight over a balding crown, and while not rotund, he wore his breeches and waistcoat tight over a paunch that projected before him like a small, padded fender. His nasal voice, combined with his accent, sounded to Chester like the call of jays around a bird feeder. His manner was decidedly formal, perhaps judgmental, thought Chester, who remembered also what Professor Thomson had written: Whitehouse was brilliant, but "like other men of our age and profession, alas, too often more concerned with their stature than with their study, with praise more than with their practica."

Chester, in recalling those words, had wondered fleetingly if there might have been in them a veiled admonition to him as well. He decided against it: Professor Thomson had praised Chester's work, and Chester had kept a rein on his ambition; Whitehouse, not Chester, was the errant intelligence Thomson said they should watch.

Whitehouse arrived with a portmanteau and two pasteboard tubes of documents. He carried them up to Chester's rooms, utilizing the footman only to show him the way. He had outfitted himself in a bright red cravat. He thought it bespoke a forcefulness that would compensate for his lack of formal training in the face of this Glasgow-schooled American. His wife had selected his whitest linen shirt, so he knew when he stood at Ludlow's hotel door that he presented a formidable picture: a stark black coat, pure white shirt, bright red neckwear, flaring gray sideburns—a visionary laden with tenable documents.

"I know your wife, sir," Whitehouse said.

Chester raised his eyebrows as he shook Whitehouse's hand.

"I mean to say I saw her once. I know her *work*," Whitehouse said.

Chester was trying to ascertain if this talk about Franny's former profession might approach insult. He was ever alert for mention of her as an
actress coming with a slight leer or hint of condescension.

But Whitehouse seemed genuinely impressed.

"I saw her *twice*, actually. *Measure for Measure*," the doctor said. "Once
with my wife and once, I blush to say, alone. I returned for a second look
because I was so smitten with her. May I say I held her 'as a thing enskyed
and sainted'? Truly. But soon enough my schoolboy crush was trumped
by the power of her artistry. Sir, she was luminous. Precise. Passionate.
Wonderful. You are a lucky man. An inspiration she was. How is she? Is
she here?"

"She's fine, I suppose," said Chester. "I cannot say with certainty, for
she is not here. She remained in America."

"Ah," said Whitehouse, dropping his shoulders. "Pity. Please give her
my regards."

Chester nodded, then noticed that the footman hadn't been dismissed
and was still waiting at the door. Chester told the man to bring them coffee,
and Whitehouse proceeded to bustle about, spreading his papers on the
table, the sofa, the bed, the chairs, the dresser, and in a small semicircle
on the floor, talking all the while.

"Now, Ludlow, let me be forthright, as the occasion dictates nothing
less. I expect the same from you. Free license, yes? We must speak openly.
Let us begin. We differ in our outlooks. You see the cable, as presently
proposed, facing great difficulty in transporting signals. You see us facing
trouble with the so-called retardation of signals. Well enough. That *is* the
problem. How then to achieve strong, clear, individuated pulses of electricity down a lengthy, say it, *transoceanic* cable?"

Whitehouse by now had the charts and graphs arrayed almost to his
satisfaction. He moved one sheet from the table to a footstool, adjusted its
angle, then looked up to smile at Chester, who by this time was almost
enjoying Whitehouse's opening maneuvers of besotted encomiums for
Franny and the elaborate preparation of his diagrams and test results.

Chester told himself he had to be careful, though. He had it all over
this fellow, this surgeon, when it came to qualifications and study, but even
at a quick glance it was easy to see Whitehouse had done an impressive
battery of tests. Still, Chester was the man who had to represent Professor
Thomson's calculations. He must not let Whitehouse run away with the
meeting.

"Just what are you a surgeon of back there in Brighton?" Chester asked.

Whitehouse stopped, openmouthed for an instant, surprised by the American's question, lacking as it was in context. He drew a breath; he perceived a flanking move.

"A 'surgeon of' . . .?" he asked with his best pasty smile of condescension.

"Of the heart? Of the bones?" Chester said. "The gut? Of the brain?"

"Why *all* of them, Mr. Ludlow. When needed. I'm a surgeon of everything. Are you in need of a surgeon?"

"No." Chester laughed, a little too jovially. "Why, no. I was just curious."

"Yes. Well. Thank you for your curiosity. May I return to our discussion of the cable problem?"

"Please." Chester nodded, deciding he would drop the guise of hearty American naïveté. It had jostled the Englishman, but the jostling had brought out a patronizing tone, and Chester knew in the long run that would be bootless for them both.

"Now," said Whitehouse, and he began to pace back and forth across the small, fringed Persian carpet in the center of the room, staying on the rug as if he were constrained to a minuscule desert isle. "I know that you and Professor Thomson are proponents of the use of battery currents for signal transmission. I know that Professor Thomson is pressing to come up with some sort of receiving instrument sensitive enough to record the slight signals that batteries are capable of sending. But he hasn't produced such an instrument as of yet. Therefore, I come to you with this evidence"— and he made a complete revolution in the center of the rug, sweeping his hand toward the whole room and its array of papers and charts—"to urge you and the good professor—but mostly you, as you are the chief American engineer; my counterpart, as it were, in the New World—to urge you to consider and to accept, nay, to *approve* our using stronger signals."

"Stronger signals sent," Chester said, arms folded, chin cupped in his left hand, "by means of an induction coil of your own making."

Whitehouse shrugged. "Just so. You could test my data by building one yourself. Here are the plans." He stepped over to the sofa and proffered a sheath of schematics. "Mine, however, is ready to go."

Chester didn't move.

"And to record the signals?" he asked.

"I have an apparatus," said Whitehouse, and going to his portmanteau, he pulled out a small device on a polished wooden pedestal. It looked like a miniature freight scale. "This," he said, "is my magneto-electrometer."

Whitehouse placed it on the table. Now a palpably intense interest emanated from Chester; Whitehouse could feel it, and he knew the tide was turning. Theorems, data, diplomas, and national differences aside, there was nothing that could so move an engineer as a new device placed right before his eyes.

"Fascinating," Chester said, lightly touching the lever arm.

Whitehouse shot his cuffs and stationed himself squarely above the device, forcing Chester to step back from the table and assume the role of audience or customer.

"The current to be measured goes through the electromagnet here and pulls down on the lever here and lifts—or fails to lift—the weight here," Whitehouse said, hovering over the machine, darting his fingers in and out to point at each element of the apparatus. He employed the lightsome flourishes of a magician.

"I measure what I call the 'value,' or the strength, of the current by how much weight it can lift. Properly calibrated, this little machine or larger ones like it measure values over a range from a thousandth of an ounce to nearly a hundred pounds. Our telegraph operators will merely record the movements of the lever."

He picked up a stack of papers from a chair by the window. "It's all here." And he thrust the hefty stack into Chester's hands.

Chester said, "But what about an ordinary measurement with an ordinary galvanometer?" Professor Thomson had been working with galvanometers, had even been trying to perfect an extra-sensitive one.

"An ordinary needle galvanometer is too flighty," Whitehouse said, trying to hold his agitation in check. "If I may be so poetic as to use an image, sir."

Whitehouse leaned forward, hands resting on the table on either side of the magneto-electrometer. "A needle galvanometer is too feminine to stand up to the rigors of a strong current. It is of no value whatsoever. The needle jerks backward and forward in a most hysterical and passionate way. Even the most patient observer can make neither head nor tail of its bewildering movements. This, however . . . this apparatus handles the electric pulses in a staid and businesslike way, quietly lifting its weight on the end of the arm in a steadfast manner, giving you the exact value of the current in the cable."

"A most manly device," Chester said.

"Precisely, sir."

Whitehouse could see he had the American on the line. He played him for the next two hours by taking him through selected calculations and tests as outlined in his notebooks. The footman returned with the coffee, but both men ignored it and let it go cold on the table. They were too busy going through the papers.

Eventually, late in the morning, Chester looked up from the data. He spoke almost wearily, wondering if he could build up the necessary steam. "As you know, Doctor, Professor Thomson and I have been working on the Law of Squares. Professor Thomson's conclusions—"

Whitehouse held up his hands and nodded. "If I may be so presumptuous, I think I know the direction you're heading. Perhaps I can save us some time. Forgive me if I'm overstepping my bounds. I only want to expedite things for us, for it is we—you and I—who are the engineers here, the engineers of the Atlantic Telegraph Company. Professor Thomson, with all due respect to his wisdom, has done far fewer experiments on actual telegraph cables than I. His theorems, like his laws, are most noteworthy, but as yet they are all on paper. This little machine and its brethren designed to record messages have been tested by me on actual cables of varying lengths—it's all right here in these records and in these over here and here in these—and they *work*. I cannot stand on my reputation as a theoretician. I have none. I cannot stand before you as a practical man with years of cable-laying experience on the high seas. I have never been on a cable-laying ship. I can stand before you only as a man interested in progress, who sees this project as one of great beneficence and profit for mankind. I stand before you as one who, like yourself, wants the project to succeed. I stand before you as a man who has done the tests, made the measurements, and now offers the data that prove we can do it."

Wildman Whitehouse had his hands clasped before him, his head bowed almost penitentially.

"Well," Chester said. "I'll have to study the research further—"

"Of course," Whitehouse said, looking up smartly.

"But I *am* favorably impressed."

Whitehouse smiled. He stepped toward Chester, then gestured for

Chester to accompany him to the window, to step away from all the piles of paper, the schematics, the magneto apparatus.

"Ludlow, I'm sure I'm not the first to say this. In fact, I'm sure I'm only repeating something you yourself have long realized. I probably woke up to the fact long after you, on your side of the Atlantic, had pondered this."

They stood now side by side, looking out at the city. They could see over the jumble of rooftops to where the round dome of St. Paul's rose just above the skyline appearing there like—Chester was shocked he'd thought of it—a breast. He had a flashing impression of Frau Lindt. He wondered where she was this morning.

"The fact is this, Ludlow. We stand to make a lot from this project. And I don't mean money. No, no, no. We *shall* make money. That's obvious. But I'm talking about our reputations. I cannot but feel we are standing before something enormous, wondrous, something that could transform the age and all who live in it. We could herald something wholly new—the binding of continents, the rapid flow of information. Information is everywhere, Ludlow. It's not just in epistles or books or telegraphs. It's paintings, it's formulae, it's music, it's the score of a tennis match, the price of stock, the meaning beneath the meaning of sweet nothings whispered in lovers' ears, it's thought, it's concept, it's feeling, it's the protoplasm of all culture, it's anything we experience that isn't death. And who knows? Maybe death is a form of information we have yet to decode. The point is, Ludlow, we—you and I—stand at the brink. When the cable succeeds, the information will flow, like a huge wave, Ludlow, and we shall be riding the crest of it, with all civilization looking up to us."

"That sounds a little . . . *grand*," Chester murmured.

"Grandiose is what you're thinking." Whitehouse also spoke quietly. They were hushed, as if keeping a confidence from the whole city that spread before them.

"True enough."

"But," said Whitehouse, "you had the same thoughts yourself. Didn't you? Yes?"

Chester nodded almost imperceptibly.

"I *knew* it when I met you," Whitehouse said. "You and I have much in common."

"A penchant for delusional thinking?" Chester said.

"A visionary is called deluded only when he runs afoul of misfortune.

We have here in these data the means to avoid running afoul. The telegraph will work, and we will become men of consequence."

"Good," Chester said softly. He thought of what Frau Lindt had said to him on the bluffs back at Willing Mind. She was going to watch him succeed, she'd said, and she'd enjoy it.

"Hell," Chester said, "I might as well enjoy it, too."

"Pardon me?" Whitehouse said.

But Chester had spun away and was gathering up the papers. "I'll want to go over these, convey my impressions to Professor Thomson, but for the moment, and barring any unforeseen complication, it's safe to say we're in agreement. Let's use your devices."

"Excellent. This will go over most happily with the investors, both present and future."

The words jogged Chester; he pulled out his pocket watch. "You remind me," he said. "I am due for a rehearsal."

Whitehouse cocked his head inquiringly.

"I have found a second calling—as an actor. You've seen the bills posted about for the Phantasmagorium?"

"Of course," said Whitehouse. "You are part of the show?"

"A principal role," said Chester. "We open in three days. At the Bardolph."

"Ah. I see. The Bardolph."

"You'll be coming?"

"Well, I suppose I must. At some point. I mean, yes, of course. I'm honored."

"I know, I know—the Bardolph's not actually a theater. But you've heard of it? It's a gaming club."

"Yes. Certainly," Whitehouse said, blinking, smiling, trying to appear jovial. "Gaming. I know it well. The club, that is."

Whitehouse's palms immediately began to sweat, and he had to surreptitiously wipe them on his trousers before he shook hands with Ludlow and bade him farewell at the door.

Success at the Bardolph

J. Beaumol Spude could not have been happier. If the first night was any indication, the Phantasmagorium was going to break even and then some by the end of the week. They cleared £30.15 at the opening alone, with four times that much in notes of hand.

Spude prided himself on how well he'd orchestrated the fund-raising campaign. He could barely contain his pride in the letter he wrote to Field, Cooper, and the others in New York letting them know how capital a start he was off to in London.

"Choosing to present the Phantasmagorium at a gambling club was a masterstroke, if I may say so," he wrote, then continued:

> The British are positively dotty over gaming. They will bet on anything: faro, dice, vingt-et-un; a game of écarté at the Bardolph Club will have forty or fifty spectators betting on the players; a table of drinkers will wager on whom the waiter will serve first, on whether a gentleman or a lady will be next to walk through the front door (I once saw a whole table lose at this when a spaniel entered on a leash ahead of a baroness), on whose plate of food would a fly first alight, on who could make a barmaid blush and who could make her cry. In this atmosphere of frenzied wagering, all I had to do, I reckoned, was play to the Englishman's sporting impulses: I rewrote some of the script and had our man Ludlow "punch up" the riskiness of the cable project. "It is a gamble," his speech now reads. "It is not for the faint of heart, not for weak-kneed seamen nor for tentative financiers. We need brave people who are wholeheartedly in the game." The language works.

The Phantasmagorium company, to a person, was agog at how well the language worked. Within days—hours, it seemed—the show was becoming the talk of London. Joachim Lindt's mechanical wizardry, his wife's musical virtuosity, the magnificent pageant of the submarine telegraph's story, were drawing capacity audiences from the first night onward.

True enough, the Bardolph was too far on the outskirts to be considered one of the most desirable clubs of Mayfair, but the establishment served the Phantasmagorium company well. Lit by a galaxy of gaslights on the grand salon's colonnade, the walls were painted with trompe l'oeil columns, receding into infinity as if the room were a chamber in a vast acropolis devoted to pleasure. The ceiling was a fresco bordered with the sculpted foliage of grapes and corn and showing a youthful Apollo driving his sun chariot across the sky. The lights all had milky spheres of glass over them, softening the gas glare and creating the atmosphere of a moonlit garden in Arcadia. The floor was tessellated marble, white and blue-green, giving it the appearance of a rippled lake across which patrons could walk to their tables, where underfoot were thick, almost mossy, Persian rugs mimicking parterres of orchids and serpentine vines found only in sub-equatorial jungles. From everywhere came the buzz of social intercourse, the tintinnabulation of flatware and china, the affectless incantations of the croupiers, and the edgy din of bets made, raised, and called.

For the Phantasmagorium Show, Spude had the room transformed. The furniture was removed, chairs lined, and at the end opposite the grand staircase, the stage set. Spude had hired a score of London actors by spending several days and nights patrolling from Drury Lane to Wardour Street and asking at stage doors if anyone knew of any "blokes" or "chums" who might be interested in working for "an American theatrical and telegraphic enterprise."

The troupe he assembled had none of the naive devotion of the lobstermen at Willing Mind (at least three of the actors proved to be embittered drunks who were fired after a fistfight broke out over accusations of upstaging), but they nevertheless were interested and curious enough about the workings of the Phantasmagorium, were excited enough to be part of the spectacle, and were moved enough by Spude's sense of mission that they pulled together into a more than serviceable ensemble.

For all the excitement surrounding the show, for all the attention paid to the stagecraft marvels of the Lindts' Phantasmagorium, to the smoke, the music, the sounds, the lights, the procession of scenes; for all the capacity crowds of glittering gentility and titled wealth that flocked to the Bardolph; for all the standing ovations that greeted the climax and the final bows, it was not lost on Spude that Chester Ludlow had become the center of the evening.

Spude had seen it coming. He received his first inkling from the attitude of the actors toward Chester. During the rehearsals in an unused sawmill off Tottenham Court Road, they would sometimes look over from their tableaux to watch Chester deliver his speeches. He had the capacity to distract, to inspire curiosity. People heeded him. They wanted to approach him. Spude heard one of the actors whisper, "He's a natural, he is," after one particularly stirring rendition of the "In the beginning was the Word" speech. (Spude had to tell the actors to stay attentive to their tribal drums, their smoke signals, all their pantomimic duties; they must not, he barked, "break character." "This character's about to break me, guv," groaned one of the "redskins" on his knees by the signal fire.)

Chester, Spude could see, had an effortless way of becoming the center of attention. It was a graceful, quiet acquisition of power—not a usurpation, really, but more just a willingness by the cast to defer to Chester over anyone else, Spude included. They knew Chester was the chief American engineer. Though he hadn't designed or written the show, he had designed and overseen some of what the show was *about*. They knew he had designed a new paying-out mechanism that would prevent the cable from snapping. They knew he had been elevated to American co-electrician-projector. All this added to his authority, but the cast also responded to his bearing. Chester Ludlow was tall, blond, graceful, and gracious. He would take the time to answer the question of the smallest bit player out in the alley during a rehearsal break, and soon several, half a dozen, a full dozen actors would be gathered around him.

Far from being jealous over this tilt of power, Spude watched it with eagerness. He hoped it would redound well for his project.

It did. From opening night forward, Spude noticed how amid the excitement and enthusiasm after the show—as donors were lining up to sign notes and inquire about buying shares—Chester would be equally surrounded, more often by the ladies, who were taking a surprising and heretofore undeclared interest in the mechanics of telegraphy; they all seemed to want to learn more about the finer points of the science from the company's chief American engineer. Nor was it only women who seemed drawn to Chester; the men gathered, too, attentive and convivial, enjoying Chester's amiability, his attractiveness, his—Spude searched for a word for it—*biomagnetism.*

But Spude also noticed how Chester comported himself through the initial excitement of the Phantasmagorium Show's opening. He was a sterling ambassador for the cable venture. He spoke well and enthusiastically about the project. The investors couldn't have asked for more. And yet it was obvious, if one knew the man more that slightly, that Chester Ludlow was distracted. Perhaps it was being away from his wife; perhaps there was something wrong back home with the woman; perhaps . . . But then, Spude didn't know Ludlow well enough to be sure what was wrong, just that something was a little off.

A Meeting at the Bardolph

The Bardolph had more than one floor of opulence. A marble staircase led up to a collection of smaller salons, lounges, and apartments with varying degrees of privacy. Some were furnished for gambling, some for socializing, some for dining, some for more intimate purposes.

The proprietors of the Bardolph, quickly seeing what a boon the Phantasmagorium had become, cordially threw open their doors to the company, giving all members of the cast the run of the establishment. The actors were obliged to remain in costume following each night's performance as a novelty and amusement for the patrons. This was a small price to pay for the privilege of gaming and dining the night away. Spude had to act as proctor for the troupe, however, and often spent until nearly dawn making sure his charges were all reasonably decorous and safely off in cabs before sunup, with strict orders to be back for half-hour call at seven-thirty the next evening.

"Damn," he said to Chester near the end of the first week. "It's like trying to herd squirrels. Ludlow, the next time I come up with an idea that involves *anything* to do with actors, you have permission to shoot me in the head."

A waiter had just presented Spude with the liquor bill for the previous night's festivities. Spude and Chester were in the grand salon after a packed performance. The Bardolph's staff had swiftly rearranged the chairs, brought back the tables, and fanned the stage smoke out the tall casement windows into the rainy night. In no time the Phantasmagorium theater had been transformed back into a gaming club, and a soiree had begun. A quartet played behind the potted palms near the stage, waiters circulated among the crowd, and people were lining up to talk with Chester and Spude.

This was their routine after each show. Chester took questions about the cable expedition; Spude took orders for stock options and signed notes for company expenses.

"Lord, what now?" Spude grumbled.

Across the room an Indian brave and a sailor had begun a loud and inebriated rendition of "If You Can't Forgive Her, I Certainly Shall." The majordomo, a stern man dressed in white with snowy hair and whiskers and stationed at a mahogany podium near the door, was signaling to Spude that his actors' antics would soon disrupt the flow of wagering and investing.

"Good Christ Almighty," Spude said in a sideways stage whisper to Chester. "The curtain just came down. How could they be soused already?" And he dispatched himself across the room like a cannonball fired at low range, adroitly taking each actor by the elbow and whisking them into the foyer. The song clipped off in mid-chorus with a little yelp from each singer, and in no time the room returned to its ambient hum.

The majordomo saluted Chester with a smile and a nod showing respect for Spude's managerial dexterity. Chester smiled and turned back to the three ladies to whom he'd been explaining the principles of a paying-out device for laying submarine cable.

"It was an ill-designed device on the last expedition that caused the trouble," he said. The ladies nodded. "There was too much tension on the cable as the sea swells rose and raised the ship. The cable going out over the stern tightened with each swell and slackened with each trough, until a large enough swell came along and the cable snapped." The ladies blinked. "But I've come up with a new design that I think will work." The ladies smiled. "It's based on a mechanism in use in your prisons." The ladies' eyes widened. "The jockey brake. It regulates the amount of labor needed on a crank or a windlass to fit a prisoner's strength for forced labor. We'll use it to regulate the amount of pressure on the cable. So . . . out of punishment comes reward. Of course, it's your convicts' punishment and our reward."

The ladies laughed. Chester joined in, basking in the warmth of their appreciation.

Spude returned to pull Chester away.

"You could've charmed them with a parts inventory, Ludlow." Spude slapped him on the back. "That's why you've got this job."

"My *job* is chief American engineer and electrician-projector," Chester said. "*This* . . . this is something else."

"It's a damned success is what it is. I only hope you can get that wire from here to Newfoundland with half the mastery you show as a matinee idol."

Chester made to ignore him and ordered a glass of port from a passing waiter, then he began scanning the crowd. Spude guessed why.

"She was saying farewell to her husband at the door as I was hailing a cab for our two potted thespians," Spude said. "He left. She stayed." And immediately Spude pushed off toward a clutch of naval line officers who wanted to praise the Black Sea telegraph in the Crimea and to sign on as Atlantic telegraph investors.

When the waiter returned with Chester's wine, Chester was gone.

He found her in the smallest and least populous of the gaming rooms on the second floor. She was sitting on a chair near a pilaster between two French windows. She looked lustrous. She always did, he thought, after a performance. It was the exertion of playing both the pianoforte and the pipe organ during the show, as well as directing the percussionist Spude had hired to accompany her, the vigor of her performance, her absorption in it. She bloomed each night when she came out to take her bow, and the bloom stayed. She had gentlemen congratulating and praising her after each show. Even her husband had to contend with an admiring public, chiefly military men and gentlemen who fancied themselves conversant in matters of mechanical engineering. They were always asking for a tour of the backstage traps and catwalks, the running mechanisms, and the lighting system. Joachim would stiffly oblige, sometimes feigning a near complete lack of knowledge of English to avoid revealing too many trade secrets of his wondrous device.

Tonight, though, for the moment, Joachim was gone, Chester had escaped his public, and Frau Lindt was alone as well. She sat in an alcove that was done in an Oriental motif. There were chairs draped with lank fringes of bullion and silk, the thick wallpaper had bars of velvet, and tapestries hung voluminously from the window. The effect was to enclose whoever sat there as if in a bedouin's sumptuous tent. On the table next to Frau Lindt, where she had placed her wine, sat a ghostly white bust of an Ottoman sultan in a turban who, commanding silence, pressed a finger to his lips.

Chester paused a moment at the door, struck by Frau Lindt's appearance, by that brightness. The dress she wore was loose and blue with few petticoats. It probably was not bell-like enough to suit current style, and she wore no jewelry. This utilitarian disregard for fashion; her strong, composed features; her braided golden hair, all made Chester stop, practically breathless, in the door of the salon. In a few moments he would be talking with her alone for the first time since the night in the kitchen of Willing Mind.

He felt fevered; he actually believed he might faint. The activity of the room—the movement of waiters, the buzz of the gamblers, the talk, the laughter—had become languorous and distant to him. The sound seemed to part and open a silent passage that led directly to her. He stepped into this passage, crossing a carpet so thick that it was like sinking into a sedgy marsh, one he'd best hurry across lest he sink altogether, and finally he stood before her.

With her finger she traced the ridges of the knuckles on the upraised marble hand of the Turk. Chester wondered if she was purposely ignoring him. Perhaps seeing his form in the corner of her eye, she took him to be just another admirer come to make small talk and hopeful advances. Perhaps she took him to be one of the newly minted shareholders in the telegraph company who felt it was a perquisite of his investment that he be able to socialize with the beautiful female musician in the troupe.

But then she turned her head unprompted, magically, and looked directly at him. Seeing her face on, he thought he detected the last wisps of a distress, but that might have been a mirage, his imagination. What he saw without a doubt was a flicker of surprise—something so unusual on a face that he'd believed over the past weeks to be one of collected, knowing command. He saw surprise and, he thought, delight, which she instantly subdued to reveal a more proper, sociable pleasure at finding him standing before her.

"Frau Lindt, you are alone."

She smiled. "And you. So are you, Mr. Ludlow. Isn't that a bit unusual of late?"

"Such is the price of success—for both of us, I suppose." She motioned for him to draw up a chair and sit. He did, and when he turned on his seat to summon a waiter, she actually touched him on the knee and told him, with a playful look on her face, to wait.

"Watch this," she said and leaned over to the bust of the Turk and whispered in the statue's ear.

Chester had the sudden, unsettling image of her murmuring something salacious in the ear of the Ottoman. Chester imagined he felt her warm, moist breath in the folds and porches of his own ear.

In a moment a waiter arrived. Frau Lindt grinned at Chester's surprise. She patted the sultan's head. "He's a genie, you know. I whisper my wishes in his ear. I wished for a waiter for you."

Chester ordered wine.

"It's a pity your genie can't take our whispers across the Atlantic," he said to her. "Then we wouldn't have to vex ourselves trying to build a telegraph. The least you could do is whisper for our success."

"We are a success, you know," Frau Lindt said. "With our little show anyway. Mr. Spude tells me at this rate we shall be able to raise the needed capital in less than five weeks."

"That is if we can keep this rate up," Chester said.

"I think we shall," Frau Lindt said. "People love the spectacle of it. The smoke. The lights . . . *You.*"

Chester waved her away with a chuckle. "Well, I hope we *are* done in a couple of months. I need to attend to fitting the ships and inspecting the cable. The hoopla surrounding this show is a little too distracting sometimes. I have to remind myself that I am an engineer after all."

"Such is the price of success," said Frau Lindt. "Didn't I tell you I'd watch you succeed?"

The waiter brought Chester's wine. Chester took the glass and, leaning forward in his chair, took a long draft. He knew what he must do. He knew he must broach the subject of their encounter at Willing Mind, must explain his conduct, account for the kiss. It was absolutely necessary: for his own standing, for his future relations with her.

She seemed to sense something of moment about to come from him. She sat still. Chester took a breath, looked into the pinguid swirls of wine on the side of his glass, and lost his nerve.

"I don't see your husband about," he blurted. "He doesn't enjoy the fruit of his labors?" And with a forced smile, Chester grandly motioned to the room, its measured commotion. He felt they were caught for an instant in a quiet eddy beside a large, swiftly moving river that was the bustling club, the city beyond, the cable project, the Atlantic Ocean, the very century itself, all of which were flowing robustly, hastily onward. But here, here it was quiet.

"My husband prefers to–" and Frau Lindt paused, looking for a word–"withdraw from all this."

"He returns to the hotel?" Chester asked.

Frau Lindt shook her head. "No. He goes running."

Chester sat up straighter in his chair, his wineglass suspended before his lips. "Running? Good heavens, why? From what?"

"Just"–Frau Lindt waved her hand–"*running.*"

"*Where?* Where on earth does he go?"

"In parks. Along the river. Down roads. It's quite mad, really. Even he admits it. People stare, laugh. Children throw stones. Horses shy. He is cursed and mocked throughout London. But he can't stop. He's something of a physical culturist, you see. He thinks this will improve him."

"Running? *Running* will improve him?"

Frau Lindt nodded. There was a look of resignation on her face, but mixed with it was a covert glitter in her eye. She knew Chester was picturing Joachim dashing about the city, shoes slapping on the cobbles and the dirt, huffing and puffing, arms pumping, running. It was ludicrous.

A smile curled the very edges of her mouth. Chester caught it, and they both burst out laughing.

"Running!"

"Running!"

"Like a rabbit! Out from the hotel. Back to the hotel."

"That is truly mad!"

"He *is* mad!"

"Running!"

"And I am married to him."

The inertia behind that final statement, although uttered in mirth, was enough to deflate their gaiety. They stopped laughing and looked at each other over the top of their dissipated glee as if it were a capsized boat they now must cling to. They saw something more solemn in each other's eyes.

They sat a few moments in silence, acknowledging each other and the cumbrance of the weeks when they had worked together but had barely spoken.

"Frau Lindt," Chester said. His throat failed him. When he tried to continue, air merely hissed out of his throat as if he were a reedless oboe. He looked at her; she seemed so calm. He took a gulp of wine. It went down like naphtha.

"Frau Lindt," he began again, "it has been . . ."

She picked up the thought for him. "It has been a *long* time," she said. She found herself taking pleasure in seeing this handsome man struggle. He had been the winner of serial victories: the project was moving again, the success of the Phantasmagorium Show was all but assured, he was— she could see—creating a stir in London. He was not experienced enough to know that yet, but it was happening. Her husband's fantastical machine was the vehicle on which Chester Ludlow would ride to renown. The Phantasmagorium and then the Atlantic cable. The prospect thrilled her.

"Yes," Chester was saying. "A long time. And what I wanted to say . . . I feel I may have transgressed a certain decorum for which I have not asked your forgiveness. Back in Maine. At my home. With you. I perhaps should not have . . ."

He was crimson. Frau Lindt found herself wondering how this message would read if he were telegraphing it to her. Could it be any more halting or diffuse if it were coming through his cable on the bottom of the sea?

"Perhaps I shouldn't have . . ." he repeated.

"*Perhaps* you shouldn't have?" Frau Lindt asked. "That allows for the possibility that perhaps you *should* have."

Chester drew a breath, looked directly at her. "Please, don't indulge in casuistry with me. I want to set things right between us."

"Mr. Ludlow, things *are* right between us."

He looked startled. He didn't expect this direction, this directness.

She continued: "You kissed me. You have trouble saying it. Allow me: *you kissed me.*"

Frau Lindt leaned forward in her chair; Chester was unable to move. They now were both inclined toward each other.

"But let us not forget my part in the gesture," she almost whispered. "Did you not feel my part?"

He nodded.

"Well, there then," she said, and sat straight again, her eyes glittering. "That settles it."

"Settles what?"

"Transgressions. Decorum. If you were beyond the pale, then so was I. We were together. Were you not prepared for that possibility?"

"I—"

Frau Lindt laughed. "These are the wages of your sin, Mr. Ludlow: I kissed you in return. And I would do it again, right here, if it were not so public a place and if such conduct in a public place wouldn't seem unprofessional. After all, Mr. Ludlow, you, Mr. Spude, my husband, and I all have much to gain by my remaining strictly professional."

There was something slightly acidic in her tone as she said these last words, enough to place a barb on the otherwise intoxicating hook she had slid into Chester's breast.

Of course he'd known she'd kissed him in return. It was the thought he'd safeguarded and brought out from time to time during all those weeks since leaving Maine, crossing the ocean, rehearsing, opening and performing the show in London. She had kissed him in return.

"I am tired now, Mr. Ludlow. I think I should return to my hotel. Would you be so kind as to hail me a carriage?"

She stood and smiled down at him. Chester thought he saw patrons glancing their way, recognizing them from the performance perhaps. He rose and held his arm out for Frau Lindt's hand to rest upon as he escorted her toward the staircase. Passing a pier glass, he had a fleeting view of them as a couple: handsome, both blond, arresting, golden. Frau Lindt seemed to glide serenely next to him. It was no wonder, he thought, people were looking.

As soon as they left the upstairs lounge, they noticed louder than usual noise coming from the main part of the club. There was a crowd of some seventy or eighty people jammed onto the staircase: patrons primarily, but also actors from the show and, it appeared, not a few members of the house staff—waiters and dealers, even the majordomo had left his pulpit. There was cheering, laughter, a rising chorus of gasps and groans and then whoops and huzzahs that seemed to ebb and intensify in no particular tempo. At the fore, standing on the staircase landing, were two men pressed close to the tall casement window. They, and everyone else, were enthralled by something that was happening beyond the glass out in the rainy night.

Chester maneuvered Frau Lindt around some elderly gentlemen who were holding their drinks on high at the top of the stairs and serenading the otherwise occupied throng below. The elderly men made sadly wanting attempts at harmony:

> "Let school-masters puzzle their brain,
>   With grammar, and nonsense and learning:

Good liquor, I stoutly maintain,
Gives *genus* a better discerning. . . ."

Working around the singers, Chester could see that the cause of the
commotion below was wagering. Notes and bills were passing hands;
money was thrust over heads to grasping fingers. People were pointing at
the window, which was an impressive construction of two large, long panes
of glass that went from the landing, up the stairwell, to nearly the ceiling
of the second floor.

Two waiters made their way through the crowd, bearing long wooden
dowels and pairs of opera glasses. They gave the glasses and sticks to each
of the two men at the head of the crowd. The throng, even the singers,
grew quiet. The two men, using the binoculars, studied the highest reaches
of the window and after some consideration used their dowels to locate
points on the glass. The gentlemen then passed the glasses and sticks over
to the waiters, who, using the binoculars and dowels, traced the halting,
random, slow progress of something down the glass. Money began to pass
more furiously among the wagering crowd. The noise bounced around the
stairwell. The singers rejoined the battle:

"When Methodist preachers come down
A-preaching that drinking is sinful,
I'll wager the rascals a crown
They always preach best with a skinful. . . ."

"They're betting on raindrops!" Frau Lindt exclaimed over the noise.
Chester had come to the same conclusion—that the men were betting
on raindrops—but he was more concerned than excited, for he was just
then realizing that one of the two men in front of the crowd, the one betting
most heavily on the droplets, betting in a frenzy really, was his co-
electrician-projector for the Atlantic Telegraph Company, Dr. E. O. Wildman Whitehouse.

The wagering, for all its excitement, for all its near fever, had the
quality also of a familiar ritual. This must have been a common occurrence
of a rainy night at the Bardolph Club: two men betting each other on the

race of droplets down the long pane of the stairwell window. The waiters had been prompt about the glasses and pointers, the bettors seemed to know their places, and now the game was afoot. The two waiters, like efficient croupiers, used the opera glasses and the tips of the sticks to follow the progress of the drops selected by each of the bettors.

Whitehouse was flushed and sweating; his red face twitched with the rictus of a grin so extreme, it looked as if it might tear the skin. He was splitting his attention between his bets, his cheers for his raindrop, and a general boisterous camaraderie with the spectators and bettors around him. His rival, one of the admirals who had been talking to Spude, seemed able to match all of Whitehouse's frenetic wagering with aplomb. For a man accustomed to seventy-two-cannon broadsides on the high seas, this was nothing. He seemed to be enjoying Whitehouse's theatrics as if his own bets were merely the price of admission to the show.

Without speaking, because now talk was impossible, Frau Lindt pointed out Spude among the mass on the stairs. He was looking up at them as they stood trapped on the landing. Spude pointed toward White-house. Chester nodded yes, he saw who it was. Spude made a pantomime of bewilderment, confusion, abrogation, resignation, and disgust. The cause of his distress—Whitehouse—was upping the ante yet again, creating a greater stir. The Atlantic Telegraph Company's British electrician-projector was making a spectacle of himself. Chester nodded to Spude, then shrugged. There was nothing to be done. Spude shrugged, too, hung his head, shook it in a show of woe, then turned with everyone else to watch the race.

One drop would inch ahead and a cheer would burst from a portion of the crowd. A drop would lag and chants would spontaneously well up around the assemblage until the whole building shook with the noise.

The din, the consuming attention on the pointers, the progress of the tiny drops, all afforded both Chester and Frau Lindt a feeling of anonymity and seclusion.

Chester turned to her—he now was the one placing his lips nearly to her ear—and spoke, "Whom do you favor?"

She turned her head, and Chester purposely held his head close to her a moment too long so her face would be only inches away from his before he withdrew, inhaling the air redolent with her perfume.

"Favor?" she asked.

Chester nodded and pointed down to Whitehouse and the admiral.

Frau Lindt frowned and shook her head, then motioned for Chester to incline his head toward her.

"Neither," she said, "I'm in favor of the raindrops!"

Chester straightened and smiled and nodded. He and Frau Lindt stood side by side, their hands on the balustrade. The drops inched downward—they were at Chester and Frau Lindt's eye level now—and left a faint trail on the glass amid the other drops, moving and still. The city was black beyond the glass. Both Chester and Frau Lindt kept their eyes fixed on the window, no longer heeding the tumult all around them.

> "Let some cry up your woodcock or hare,
> Your bastards, your ducks, and your widgeons . . ."

They could feel nothing but the proximity of their arms—his right, her left—and how imperceptibly they had come to touch each other, first at the shoulder. The drops were below them now, Whitehouse's ahead, the crowd cheering and thumping. Then at the elbow. Whitehouse was flailing his hands as if he were lashing at the window with an invisible buggy whip. Their forearms were in contact now, Frau Lindt's pale golden arm hairs trilling along the wool of Chester's coat sleeve. The admiral now dropped his pose of tempered amusement and began bellowing at his raindrop as if it were a cabin boy quailing in the heat of battle.

> "But of all the birds in the air
>   Here's a health to the
>   Two Jolly Pigeons
>   Toroddle, toroddle,
>   TOROLLLLLL!"

Chester and Frau Lindt now were looking at their hands on the mahogany rail. As if responding to its commander's orders, the admiral's drop sprung downward. It raced faster as Whitehouse's took little left and right zigzags, a muddled beagle losing the scent. The crowd cheered wildly.

Their hands touched slightly. Or perhaps they didn't, and the two of them just felt with the outer edges of their fingers and palms a pulse arc across the infinitesimal space between them. They both looked down to see the hairs on the back of their hands prickling with stimulation.

"TORODDLE, TORODDLE,
TOROLLLLLL!!!!"

People were shrieking. Chester and Frau Lindt remained still, keeping their bodies motionless at the balustrade, their hands now definitely moving toward each other to close that minute space, the rest of them frozen in a seizure of incommunicable desire. It seemed as though their hands, almost separate from their bodies, would cross any distance, brave any danger, just to do something as simple, as grand, as touch. Then, as if wrenching their eyes away from their hands would bring them respite from their near swoon, they simultaneously looked up, not at each other, but to the window while their hands finally, unseen by them, finally clasped. The crowd was bellowing.

The drops had joined. They had slid down the glass and near the end of the race had veered left and right and collided. Bookmakers' tallies, even money, were flying above the crowd, thrown there by maddened bettors. Whitehouse was holding his head. The admiral shrugged and turned his back on the window. The two pointers touched, making an inverted V—a perfect pinnacle of two white lines against the black. Frau Lindt looked as if she were about to topple. The cheering around them turned to jeers and laughter and shrill whistling. Somewhere out in the city, in the rain, a man ran.

CHAPTER VI

BACK AT WILLING MIND

Maine, Spring 1858

A Ritual Interrupted

On fair days the sunlight was as soft as talcum. The air remained cold save at midday, when the sun was high and the rocks baked to give off a granite tang. It was barely spring at Willing Mind, but Franny Ludlow felt as if she were walking about in an August locust buzz. Otis had made it so.

Otis Ludlow had arrived at Willing Mind two days after his brother and the Phantasmagorium entourage sailed for London. He had approached like a vagabond tinker, shambling up the snow-packed drive from the Falmouth Road. Franny had been on the third floor, opening up rooms with Mrs. Tyler, a spring ritual she was performing unseasonably early.

Franny had been preparing to live alone in the house for whatever length of time her husband was away with the Phantasmagorium and the Atlantic cable, preparing, even desiring, to live as a recluse, to live hard by the excoriating Atlantic, pressed there by the fir trees and a self-enforced loneliness. Just the same, she had vowed to maintain a certain rigor and forward motion and had therefore instructed Mrs. Tyler to report the day after Chester left, to open every room. She knew this made no sense and would require unconscionable amounts of firewood, but she was not about to be cowed by winter, to live huddled in a corner of the mansion, waiting for spring. She would keep the entire house open, move freely as she chose. She most wanted, however, to rid the house of *their* presence, the Phantas-magorium entourage's. She was only too happy to purge the cigar smell from the chamber used by Spude and to sweep clean and air the room used by the Lindt couple.

So, Franny and Mrs. Tyler began with the topmost floor of the house, hauling with them brooms, dust mops, wet mops, water, sponges, and a wicker basket of linen, wool blankets, and bedspreads. They went from room to room cleaning as if it were spring, talking little but singing some under their breath. Franny flipped down each rolled-up horsehair mattress and swept up the remaining naphthalene flakes. She loved the musky smell that clung to the sheets as Mrs. Tyler snapped them open to reveal the crosshatched creases left over from being folded for months in the linen closet.

As they worked, first on the sea side, then on the landward side of the house, Mrs. Tyler kept a watchful eye on Franny. The old woman knew that the order to open the rooms so soon after the master had left was significant. She knew—or felt she knew—that Franny's condition was pre-carious, so in complying with the order, Mrs. Tyler arrived prepared to attend the young woman carefully, offer advice if asked, succor if peti-tioned, and extend a wing, as it were, over her chick. She had helped raise Franny every summer of the girl's life. She had stuck by the household after Franny's mother and then her father died. Mrs. Tyler had maintained the place while Franny's London theatrical career blossomed, remained steadfast during Franny's recuperation in Norway (even once traveling there to visit her: "The poor thing has no family now, no vocation, only her recovery"), and returned to watch over Willing Mind until Franny herself came home abloom with the promise of marriage to a bright young engineer.

Together the old Tylers had stood in as parents for Franny, giving the bride away at the wedding ceremony out on the bluffs and caretaking the estate as the newlyweds settled in. They watched with interest as Chester transformed the house from a summer estate into a year-round home. Mrs. Tyler looked askance while her husband, Gil, was amused by the inven-tions and contraptions with which Chester adorned and outfitted Willing Mind: the dumbwaiters, the hot-water plumbing system, the little funicular up from the beach to the top of the bluffs.

As a young bride, Franny seemed oblivious to anything other than her husband's devotion to her and hers to him. To Mrs. Tyler the devotion seemed real as long as the two of them were together; it carried through the birth of their daughter, Betty, and lasted the three and a half years until the little girl's death down on the bluffs with Otis Ludlow howling in the foreground and Mrs. Tyler watching from the house.

So it was with dread and regret that the old woman recognized the figure coming up the bluestone drive. He appeared as she flung open a sheet and the linen descended, wiping across her field of vision. One moment she was looking out onto the old snow in the estate's front meadow and the empty drive, then as a white cloud of percale floated downward, a dark figure materialized below.

Alerted by Mrs. Tyler's hesitation, Franny looked out the window, too, and saw Otis, who somehow was already staring right back at them as if he'd known all along where in the house she was and who was—and wasn't—with her.

"He's back," Mrs. Tyler said with a clipped voice that pretended to vagueness as the three of them stared at each other—the two women in the window, the man down in the drive—and from out on the shoals the buoy rang softly.

That was nearly two months ago.

Without a Compass

Otis Ludlow was the true genius of the family, or so some had said. He was the Ludlow with the widest-ranging mind, the most catholic knowledge, the true fire of superability.

But they also said he lacked a compass. His mother, the daughter of a lawyer in northern New Hampshire, died from a fall off a horse when Otis was eight. His father, Amos Bronson Ludlow, was hard on a course of self-absorption and artistic devotion as he sought to become a major landscape painter. He was not a devoted parent. He remarried and moved the family to Antwerp—"where the old masters learned to paint" and where Chester was born. The marriage floundered; the family returned to the White Mountains disparately. Chester and his mother lived in Conway. Otis and his father lived near Crawford Notch.

Instead of narrowing his considerable intellect on the mimetic problems of painting a range of mountains in New Hampshire as his father had done, instead of delving into mathematical problems and mechanical solutions as his younger brother, Chester, would do, Otis Ludlow began wandering.

At the age of fourteen, having outshone the beleaguered schoolmaster, Otis had taken over teaching in the one-room school south of Crawford Notch. For commencement day he had the students perform *Agamemnon* in his own translation. He began working in the first lumber camps west of Bartlett the summer after his fifteenth year because he was as tall, sinewy, and as able as half the French Canadians who came down to labor in the woods of New Hampshire. He single-handedly felled the tallest white pine ever cut south of the Ammonoosuc River. Riding with the tree by wagon to Boston at age sixteen, he saw the spar off at the Lapham and Pike Shipyard and then walked to Harvard College and began his studies in philosophy.

But, true to his ranging ways, the summer after his first year at Harvard he sailed on a merchantman carrying lumber to Le Havre and never looked back. He sailed on to North Africa, Asia, Alaska, and Australia.

He became much sought after as a mate in the merchant service and spent a decade and a half sailing the globe. He never, however, rose to captain. He was too peripatetic, switched ships and firms too frequently. For all his genius, Otis Ludlow was a poor risk to be the commander of a ship.

When he tired of the sea, he managed a lumber operation in the East Indies, supervising the cutting and shipment of teak. He drifted away from the mercantile aspects of his posting and turned himself to engineering better sluices and block-and-tackle systems to move the logs. He finally abandoned the lumbering operation altogether when the trio of a botanist, an ornithologist, and a geographer arrived from the American Museum needing a guide. They were astounded at Otis's autodidactic expertise in each of their fields. Otis, for his part, was astounded by the ornithologist and married her.

He and his wife remained on Celebes for three years after the other scientists left—the botanist leaving with a wealth of information that would ensure his preeminence in his field for the rest of his life, the geographer leaving only as a collection of effects in a teak box, the man having drowned by tumbling into a waterfall. Otis and Margaret remained and collaborated on ornithological papers and research until Margaret died five years later of diphtheria.

A fortnight after his wife's death, a grieving Otis received a letter from his younger brother. Chester was down in Cambridge at college. His mother had died of influenza, and their father was "faring poorly," as Chester put it.

Otis left the Pacific and returned to New Hampshire to find their father barely outrunning poverty. He was unable to sustain himself with intermittent work as an artist-in-residence in the luxury hotels. Chester had departed for the Lawrence Scientific School, so Otis and his father lived together in rented rooms in a frame house outside of Bartlett. Otis found work as a surveyor and crew boss for the construction of Horace Fabyan's bridle path up Mount Washington. For a time, his wandering ceased.

Tiny Lights

"If you say you can move about, is it your body or your mind that does the moving?"

They were sitting in the dining room, eating a lunch of sandwiches and chowder that Mrs. Tyler had prepared. All was silent save for the distant rattling of the housekeeper in the scullery. The sea glistened beyond the green bluffs. Another day of cloudless blue sky. Franny was thinking of the blueness stretching all the way to England, taut as a drumhead, a skin pulled tight over the world. If she could reach up and thrum it here, would Chester hear it there? And what would he be doing? She had received no word from him yet. He might as well not have existed. Could she live with that possibility? She didn't want to think about it. True, she wanted to be solitary, but she didn't want to think about the loss of her husband. Instead, she thought about what was here, her question.

Otis sat before her, across the table, eating chowder. He stopped to consider her query. He didn't look up. The forelock of his red hair, strangely lusterless since the last time she'd seen him—before he'd sailed again for the Pacific—hung down, half obscuring his face. Had the deprivations of his journey, of which he'd spoken only a little, drained him of vitality? He looked peaked, drawn, as if his insides were composed of dust and no amount of liquid—chowder now or the considerable quantities of ale and brandy he drank late each day—would suffice to quench that dryness. Strange, too, that he seemed *dried out,* for wasn't the jungle from which he came "steaming"? Wasn't everything wet? Weren't the humidity, the dankness, and the heat the controlling elements of the place? So she had read, at any rate, in the books he had given her and then in the letters and company reports he had sent to Chester. And his conversation had become parched as well. Formerly ebullient, effusive, by turns irate and irrepressible and funny, he now seemed pensive, abstract, detached.

"I don't know," he said, and took another sip of the chowder. "I don't mean to be coy." He looked up now, directly at her with those fiercely blue eyes. She didn't remember the blue being so concentrated. The uncanny thing was how well they matched—the glass eye and the real one. It was as if the blue of the artificial eye had instructed the real eye how to shine. She was tempted to turn quickly to see how closely the color matched that of the sky.

"But," he went on, "I have no witnesses."

"Wasn't the"—Franny searched for the word—"the witch doctor there? Didn't he guide you?"

"The *manang mansau,*" Otis said. "The shaman. Yes, he was. But I never asked him."

"That seems strange," Franny said. "I should think you would want to know. It seems part of the empirical evidence. You said you became interested in all this because of its scientific applications."

Otis nodded with eyes closed. It seemed both a gesture of contrition for a lapse in his investigative judgment and a show of respect for Franny, who was taking it all so seriously, who was showing her willingness to understand him on this prickly issue.

"Franny, the experience was so . . . so *moving . . .*" He laughed. "Excuse the pun. I mean to say so *profound* that I wasn't asking the proper questions. I had traveled, you see, I had traveled back here from over there."

"How do you know, though?" Franny asked. "Couldn't it have been a dream? Didn't you say he had given you something to drink first? Didn't you say he had talked to you for weeks before your 'journey'? Could not this have been the result of some kind of mesmeric suggestion?"

Otis nodded gravely as she spoke, his head sweeping up and down in greater and greater arcs until he brought it to an abrupt halt and looked at her again. He had talked of all this only twice before. Once vaguely, the first week he arrived as they walked on the gravel drive back from the barn after a ride to town, and once in greater detail some weeks later as they sat in the great room by a fire Otis had laid and lit, as it was a cold, clear night. He had approached the subject obliquely, had said each time he didn't know how to talk about it, that he would try to tell her the whole story, that it would take time, that he didn't have the words for it.

She had thought this might be the artifice of a mountebank, a trickster who doled out his hypocrisy by the spoonful to make it easier to swallow. But, she asked herself, why would he choose to trick *her?* And what was the trick? He clearly was tortured by what he knew, by what he had to tell. She had been an actress, after all, and she firmly believed Otis was not performing. He was in the thrall of something. He had come back to the Western Hemisphere with a cabalism. He called it "transetheric travel." Hearing of it by firelight on a dark night had given her chills. They both sat inclined toward the flames, the ruddy light illuminating their faces, as Otis spoke. He described his experience as if he were addressing the fire, or something in the flames, and Franny only happened to be an eavesdropper listening in.

She ventured to bring up the topic again here, at a midday lunch, because the force of Otis's story had stayed with her. The man believed he had traveled through time and space. He believed that this discipline, of which he'd only been instructed in the very rudiments by the Malayan *manang mansau*, enabled him to travel the globe, to exist in two places at once, to move in the spirit realm. His telling her of it that night by the fire had both frightened and possessed her. She had been afraid to ask questions by the fireside, but had listened in silence as his voice unspooled the tale of meeting the "medicine man"; of watching nocturnal ceremonies on the outskirts of the plantation; of the sound of the drum; the dancing; the allusions to the women; the shrunken heads; the conjunction of the spirit world and this world in special, "charged" places; the ordeal of the preparations; how his work slipped at the plantation; how he knew he was "going native"; how the Dutchmen and the Englishmen looked at him; how he had found a "special" native woman with whom he spent nights and who directed him to a distant cousin or uncle—the *manang mansau* who prepared him for the travels—how he wanted to quantify, codify, systematize what was happening to him; how the *manang mansau* found his notebooks and burned them and made him commit everything to memory so he still had all the ritual intact, learned, as he said, "by heart"; how he had been in Borneo *and* here; how he had lain in a Dayak ritual hut and simultaneously *walked on the slopes of Mount Washington only miles from where he'd been born.*

Then, after all this recitation with its details of the various odors of sweat and potions and heart-stopping trials by pain, of discursions into the local geography and waterfalls and food, of discreet references to the erotic practices of the Dayak women, Otis had said he was tired and left her and went to his bed in the back wing of the house. She had sat alone until dawn, watching through dry eyes as the firelight subsided to embers and thence ash. The darkness closed around her before the sun began to gray the east. In that realm of pitch, in that house of hers, she thought of herself as alone in the universe. No one could be in two places at once, not the way Otis described. All she knew was that she was alone. Her husband was gone across the ocean. Her daughter was dead and buried. The stars were inert in their sockets. But she had to ask Otis further questions. How could the mother of a dead little girl not want to know more?

"The only proof I have was the tiny lights on my boots." Otis smiled equably. This was the kind of manipulation of the narrative that irritated Franny. If she were going to grant him the benefit of the doubt, the least he could do was offer her directness as he told the story: no coyness, no withheld facts, no enigmatic phrases, no air of teacher and acolyte.

As if he sensed her displeasure, he apologized. "Forgive me my embellishments. Let me explain. . . . I had 'traveled' back here, to this side of the globe. As I said last night, I purposely chose to attempt a journey, a transportation, whatever you wish to call it, to a place familiar to me. I chose the mountains where I had grown up. I had walked the length and breadth of the White Mountains. I knew I could be placed blindfolded on any height of land there and, with the blindfold removed, in seconds pinpoint my exact location. So I chose the most prominent of the peaks to be my destination. I assumed that if I were to be traveling through space, if this was to be not unlike flying, I should look for a prominent landmark. I chose Mount Washington. I had climbed the peak from every possible direction and in all weathers. I had begun the surveys for Mr. Fabyan's bridle path to the summit. I had carried geological and botanical specimens off that old rock pile for professors from Harvard and Dartmouth and for scientists from the American Museum in New York. If the traveling was to be anything like my *manang mansau* described, then I should know its veracity by its accordance with my recollections. If it were possible to be simultaneously in Malaya and anywhere else on earth, then for me, Mount Washington was the best choice for that other place."

He pushed his soup bowl away, rippling the tablecloth a little, then smoothing it, then folding his hands before him.

"I did not tell my *manang mansau* where I was going. He had instructed me not to. We went through the preparatory rituals—I won't describe them now—but suffice it to say, when the trance or the transport or whatever you wish to call it was in effect, when I had come to my senses, heightened or warped or truly transported, I *knew*, Franny, I *absolutely knew* that I was standing on the slope of that mountain. It was mid-July in Malaya when I attempted this transetherian experiment, and there I was, on the slopes of the peak in mid-July weather if I'd ever seen it, perfectly rendered, not altered or warped or heightened the way we see things in dreams. I stood on the boulder field we call the Alpine Garden, near the upper reaches where we intended the road to go. Cumulus clouds were tearing across the summit from the north. The wind, the slight humidity in the July air, the headwalls of the nearby ravines, they were all there . . . and not as if in a dream, but tangibly, undeniably there. And the way that I knew this, Franny, the way I was sure I had not been lying in a thatched hut on the outer precincts of the gutta-percha plantation being manipulated by a Dayak 'witch doctor,' as you called him, the way I knew was when I was conscious again in that hut, when I lay there looking up at the palm leaf roof and heard the soft fuzz of the afternoon rain, I raised myself up to look at the length of my body. Was I still there? What had happened? Why did I feel so disoriented now when moments ago—or years ago or simultaneously, time was the slipperiest of entities—I was surer than I had been about anything theretofore in my life that I had stood and walked on that mountain?

"I had no answer. My *manang mansau* had disappeared. Before I tried to bestir myself to go out and see if anyone was about on the plantation, to see if I was still living in this world, to see if no time had passed or eons had, I looked down at my boots. They sparkled."

Franny, sitting now with the rest of her meal untouched and her soup bowl likewise pushed away from her place, her chin resting on her palm, her elbow on the tablecloth, tilted her head a little and frowned.

Otis leaned back in his chair, crossing his legs. "If you've ever climbed the higher peaks in the White Mountains, you would know the effect." He said this without pretense and with no implication that she was insufficiently experienced; it was a simple statement as he presented it.

"The rock there is schist and gneiss and there is a plenitude of mica flecks in it. Walk among those peaks, follow any footpath, and tiny bits of the glasslike mica will cling to your boots. There is nothing like it in the Atlantic Telegraph Company's gutta-percha plantation in Borneo, yet there they were—those tiny, sparkling flecks—on my boots. How else to account for it? I had been in a hut in Malaya and on the eastern slopes of Mount Washington. And if you ask, Does my body travel or exist simultaneously in two places at once, then I can only say, Yes. And if that answer means more than one thing, well then, so be it."

A Letter from London

March 19th

Dearest Franny,

I hope this letter finds you well. I was so concerned when I left you abed at Willing Mind. I had doubts as to the wisdom of my going on this venture of Spude's. It seemed utter folly: the Phantasmagorium, the idea we needed to go to England, where supposedly the financial picture is brighter than in America, that such a circus would actually help raise money for the cable. I felt I had been coerced into going. That the project's chief engineer was to be diverted into an endeavor for which he was so ill-equipped seemed a perversion of our hopes and true design. Clearly I had been delusional when I began to enjoy re-hearsing and thought the Phantasmagorium a cunning idea. The ill-advisedness of the whole enterprise left me despondent and morose for the entire crossing.

I longed for you, my dearest. I studied the gray Atlantic. I kept a solitary and mournful watch on the stern rail of the ship, looking not to where we were headed, the land Spude was certain we would con-quer; nor toward the sea itself, the realm we must conquer if the cable attempt this summer is to be a success; no, I looked instead toward the ever receding horizon behind us. I used my own charts and the ship's binnacle compass to pinpoint the exact spot each day where I should look to face toward Willing Mind, my home, my wife. Like a prostrate Muhummadan performing his daily prayers whilst facing toward his holy city, I stood my own watch, facing you, paying obeisance to our life together. I miss you, my sweetest.

And somehow I trust you are well. When I last sat with you in our room as the wagons were being loaded in the drive below, as I held your hand and bade farewell, I saw a weakened, troubled woman. How to name what befell you? And yet, sitting there with you, I saw in your eyes the strength and purpose I know so well. It is a resolve greater than any human illness. It is a strength to which I have turned innumerable times in our marriage. It is what I know has you up and about and walking the grounds of our home. I know this letter finds you well.

And so, arriving in London, I have set about joining the others in preparing the Phantasmagorium Show. We work in an old lumber warehouse not far from my hotel. Spude is out and about hiring supernumerary actors from the London stage to aid in our presentation. The Lindts work closely and feverishly preparing the technical equipage of the show: Herr Lindt spent much of the crossing perfecting his plans for new smoke engines that will use a form of atomized corn oil and water to provide a foglike effect that will, if it works, be far superior to the effect that now leaves us onstage and many of those in the first rows of the theater coughing. I am impressed with the ingenuity of his design. He works in the demesne of make-believe, but he has the brain of a great engineer. His wife continues to perfect her musical compositions.

I continue to "study my lines" as you were wont to instruct me to do. I employ your peripatetic method: I walk about carrying my manuscript, repeating the text aloud to myself. I do this by leaving my hotel early and walking in and near Hyde Park, incurring the quizzical looks of craftsmen and shopgirls bound for work as I mutter the hyperbole and the facts about our Atlantic cable.

That is my early morning regimen. Much of the rest of the day I spend time in my rooms, working on the problems that we will face this summer when we make the cable attempt. I have undone, I hope, the tangles—excuse the equivoque—in the paying-out mechanisms we will use on the ships. The machinery will be manufactured in Liverpool, and when Spude gives me time off from my thespian duties, I must travel to that city to supervise the production. When time permits, I also visit the cable-manufacturing plant in Greenwich to inspect the progress there. It is going well.

The logistics and production of the mechanisms are on schedule.

It is the financial prospects that look less encouraging. I am trying to stay out of it, but I know the cable manufactory is expecting more payments if it is to continue producing our order. Spude is running himself ragged trying to prepare the Phantasmagorium Show and address the fiscal problems of the syndicate. Cyrus Field wrote Spude that the New York office has done poorly in raising money. The collapse last year of the markets in America has made capital scarce. This puts even greater pressure on our "medicine show" here. Can we do it?

There is another matter that troubles me besides your own well-being, my dear. Whilst here in London I have had intercourse with the officers of our subsidiary, the Britannic East Indian Gutta-Percha Manufactory. They tell me they have had communications from their officers in Malaya that my brother Otis has abandoned his situation as plantation manager. They spoke vaguely of difficulties, of incapacitation on Otis's part from which I could infer either illness or dereliction of duty, perhaps both. They said he had left the island, perhaps the hemisphere, and had mentioned to some of the natives that he was returning to his brother's home. I tell you this to forestall any surprise should he arrive at Willing Mind but also as a request for information should you receive any.

I hear a knocking at my door. Most likely it is Spude's manservant Bailey coming to summon me for a rehearsal. Perhaps today we shall actually have actors.

Off I go to speak the speech trippingly on the tongue. I am awhirl in the world of theater. You must know the feeling. You must know, also, that for you I feel nothing but

Love,
Chester

P.S. I must tell you something of London. It has changed somewhat since you were here. I see some of it on my perambulations, script in hand. I wish instead I had you in hand.

As a whole, the letter did not please. She found herself resenting his supposition that she was well. She found herself, now that he was gone, left with a resentment that it was he and not she who was working on the stage. She found herself resenting that she had hidden herself away at Willing Mind, that it was she who was left to remain there with the ghost of their daughter and with her husband's brother, that she was left to curate the memory of that dreadful day, suspended as she was between the corporeal and the eidolic, between the man who saw it happen and the spirit of the child living now only in memory. She made no plans to answer the letter or to tell her husband about his brother's arrival. She resented her situation, and she resented the letter, but mostly she resented the simplicity and indirection of that one sentence: "His wife continues to perfect her musical compositions."

"We Do See Things"

For long minutes every day since he had arrived, he would stand in the front hall of Willing Mind meditating upon the painting. It was a form of calisthenics for his eye. Over the years he had devised a series of exercises to help him maintain depth perception. He would look at an object, look away, and quickly look back; the sudden shifts in his vision helped his brain compensate for the "eclipsed eye" and piece together a feel for distance.

The curious thing was, this painting—one of the last his father painted—seemed to do the work for him. It offered an almost disturbing sense of depth even for Otis's one eye. It was an ominous picture, large, forceful, a startling thing to place in the entrance of a home. Otis found himself admiring Chester and Franny for hanging the work there.

The painting, done in oils, was a large canvas, four by six feet, and showed a snowstorm just commencing to boil down through Crawford Notch. Otis thought the turbulence magnificent. He found himself looking at the picture for long minutes every day. He stood before it and felt a sense of pride that his father had been able to achieve the work before he died. Otis used to think his father had failed his talent in his final years. This picture, Otis now believed, showed otherwise. His father had been striking out for unknown territory.

Otis and Chester's father, Amos Bronson Ludlow, had been subject to fits and rages. His life was a series of passions, dark and light. Sometimes one seemed to grow from or confound another. His happiest moments were with his brushes and oils, his most ominous with hickory rods and fists. Both his boys and both his wives had felt the blows.

Amos Bronson Ludlow died from a fit—or a rage—in a tributary of the Saco. Otis had found him there. Turned away from the big hotels as being too insignificant a painter to be their artist-in-residence, he had worked at the smaller hostelries, offering classes and picture postcard reproductions of his paintings. But as the hotels and tourists in the mountains had become more numerous, Amos Bronson Ludlow's large, brooding depictions of the mountains became more problematic. People could see immediately upon disembarking from a train or coach and comparing the view around them with the postcard reproductions they held in their hands that the White Mountains *didn't look like that.* They just didn't have the hallucinatory couloirs, the precipitous defiles, the raging cataracts, or the gnarled trees all looking like an approach to Götterdämmerung. They were beautiful mountains, yes, even spectacular, but they were not manifestations of a primal nightmare.

Amos Ludlow had to subdue the wildness and grandeur of his canvases if he hoped to make any money. He painted *views* in his later years, Otis always thought, not true paintings. And he was not good at it. Finally, perhaps out of desperation or because he had nothing to lose, Amos Bronson Ludlow began a return to his original style. He had done a couple of scenes of Crawford Notch in his old, dark mode when he decided to take his equipment up into the mountains west of the Notch. Otis had been away working on the survey crew on the western slopes of Mount Washington for about two weeks and returned to Crawford Notch to check on the old man.

The railroad crew at Fourth Iron—the fourth iron railroad bridge west of Bartlett—told him as he approached Crawford Notch that they'd seen his father working furiously on a large canvas up near the cliffs where the Dry River flows into the Saco. He wasn't well, the crew boss told Otis. Earlier in the week, the old man had been found stiff, as if paralyzed, in the bed of his wagon, wrapped tight in a wool blanket.

"I thought maybe he'd been bound and robbed. He was lying there, staring at the sky, trembling," the crew boss said. "Making little sounds in the back of his throat. Then I could see he was having some kind of hysterics. I can't say how long he'd been there. We carried him back here. He slept on a pallet in the cook shack. When we awoke, he was gone. I saw him a few days later back up near the cliffs, painting again. He looked shook up. A logging crew up near Nancy Brook said they'd seen him walking west into the woods with his little packhorse and all his painting equipment."

Otis headed up Nancy Brook. He was familiar with the symptoms the crew boss described—the "some kind of hysterics"—he'd seen them before with his father; he'd known them himself. It was the way people described him when he had one of his fits. All the way into the unlogged forests west of the Notch, up to the height of land and on toward the Pemigewasset River, he thought about those fits, the "family curse," as his father had called them.

"But I think I see things," Otis once told his father when Otis was lying abed recovering from one of the spells that had stricken him in the schoolyard in his sixth year.

"We do," his father said. "We do see things."

And Otis, now looking at the painting on the wall at Willing Mind, realized that his father had put something of those spells, of those visions, whatever they were, into the paintings; the best paintings, Otis thought, not the tourist views. It wasn't anything he could point to. When he looked into those paintings, *this* painting, he was looking into something ineffable, into the world from which he returned every time he came around from one of those spells.

The story Otis always told was that two days after setting out from Crawford Notch to look for his father, he found him lying in Nancy Brook, up near the falls. The old man had drowned in about two feet of water. His horse was nearby, its lead rope ensnarled in dead hemlock branches. When he stepped into the water to lift up his father's corpse, Otis said, he noticed small gobbets of oil paint that had floated free from the pallet, which had fallen into the pool with the old man. The colors clung to Amos Bronson Ludlow's hair as Otis lifted the body up. When he laid the dead man in the coffin he'd fashioned at Fourth Iron, Otis made no effort to comb the colors out. He buried his father dressed in his best clothes with his paints around his head.

The Novitiates

For nearly two months now, they had each existed in their separate orbits at Willing Mind. Mrs. Tyler observed their comings and goings as she worked about the estate. Everything they did seemed to adhere to the utmost decorum. It was as if the house had come under the rule of a religious order and the two of them—brother and sister-in-law—were novitiates. They seemed to have taken a vow of near total silence. They rarely spoke by day. Mrs. Tyler would see them—never together—walking about the grounds or standing at the windows of the great room, looking out on the sea, or sitting alone, reading. Otis had taken up residence in the back wing of the house, what would have been the servants' quarters had Franny and Chester maintained a staff. Mrs. Tyler's responsibilities, which involved trafficking into the intimate precincts of household life, assured the housekeeper with reasonable certainty that there were no untoward intimacies budding between Otis and Franny.

And, in fact, Mrs. Tyler was right. The home *had* become chaste as a nunnery. The two novitiates were intent upon their paths. They spent their days apart and their evenings talking after supper by the fire or even, on the warmest nights, out on the moonlit seaward prospect. After these modest colloquies, they would retire to their separate rooms, their "cells."

Franny had had every intention of "righting herself," as she put it. She knew she was foundering; the feeling that she was about to sink was upon her every day. She had not been able to overcome it in the first year after Betty's death, and indeed everyone had told her that it would take at least that long before she might be able to feel she could breathe or look people in the eye. It took a year, then two, and now in her third she still felt helpless.

When Chester became absorbed in the cable project, when she watched him gird himself for the expedition, she envied him. His dream was perilous, true, but he set out with the certainty that enough attempts could bring success. She, however, was lost in the remembrance of her child and had no hope of the little girl's resurrection. She watched Chester float along upon the currents of work and the contagious energies of the other men in the syndicate. It was an admirable thing they were doing, something out in the world, something forward-looking, something to Advance the Age.

So, as Chester embarked on another attempt, as he left with the Phantasmagorium, she would make a stand against her sinking. The more absorbed Chester was, the more distracted by the cable and by that Lindt woman—and Franny knew there was distraction there—the more Franny needed to trim herself and become steady.

The trouble was, the arrival of Otis gave her a new direction. And the passion that adhered around this new direction felt so stirring, so compelling. Franny could have thought it sexual if she weren't so thoroughgoingly certain that it could only be spiritual.

"I want you to contact her," she told Otis one evening when they were standing on the small piazza just outside the great room's French doors. They had stepped outside with their tea. A mild, early spring breeze touched upon the flagstones that still held a vestige of the day's warmth. There'd been a thaw. There was no snow on the terrace, and only icy patches wrapped around the heather clumps like scarves. The earth was beginning to smell of mud. The dusk air was violet. The moon would be rising soon out of the sea.

"I can't do that," Otis said. "It's not what I do."

"You say you travel," Franny said. "You talk about moving beyond space and time or *through* space and time. Where is she if not beyond space and time?"

Otis looked down at the tea in his cup. It was discarded hotel china from his father's house. Chester had what belongings remained. The china. The painting. It was good, Otis thought digressively, that the possessions had been given a home.

"I haven't attempted anything since leaving Malaya," he said, still looking down. He saw a small insect flounder in the liquid in his cup.

"That's not true," said Franny.

Otis turned to her. The light was a perfect raiment for Franny's features, for her dark hair and pale skin.

"I've seen you," she said. "I've watched. You have gone out on the bluffs of a night—I don't know how often—and made your circles. I've seen the small scorched places in the side meadow where you built your ring fires. My room is right up there. I can look out. Do you think a bereaved mother would sleep her nights away? I spend hours looking out that window, longing for her. You must know that. You know it, and you perform your ceremonies nonetheless."

Otis looked up to Franny's bedroom window above them. He turned to see the rim of the moon poke above the eastern horizon out on the sea.

"I am willing to admit I may have been fooled," Otis said. "The *manang mansau* may have been more of a mountebank than a wise man. But I had a *vision*. This I know. I had moved in the spirit world but maybe only up here. . . ." And instead of touching his own head when he raised his hand, he reached across the space between them and lightly touched Franny's temple. She felt a shiver run down her spine.

"There are reports of spirit visitations," Franny said distractedly. "I mean, there always *have* been. But I've read . . ."

"Much of it is bunkum. The séances? The spirit rappings? You must beware, Franny. They're stagecraft. Catgut threads move curtains. Assistants closeted in chambers between walls tap out messages or play music."

"You told me you were administered potions. These led to your transetheric travel . . . or your visions," Franny said. "So wouldn't the potions possibly be like the stagecraft, as you call it? Couldn't they put the seeker in the proper state of mind to pass through the clouded veil or to have the spirits reach back through to this side?"

Franny was becoming agitated, urgent.

"Perhaps," Otis said.

"Reach back to *us*?"

"I only said perhaps."

"If the stagecraft is a lie, well, it may be a lie that leads to a truth. Just like your potions, your physics."

"Yes . . . Perhaps."

"Couldn't we try?"

"We?"

"We could experiment together. See if we could reach across the veil. . . ."

"Franny—"

"She was *my* daughter. You were there when it happened."

Otis had an urge to pace, to shake off her arguments. The piazza was like a moated cage. Looking toward the horizon offered a bit of relief from Franny's last words, a longer perspective: the moon was half risen, an orange globe pulling its way laboriously out of the sea. It was a sight he had seen from the shores of Celebes often during his years there in the compound with Margaret and again, alone, more recently working at the gutta-percha plantation. Otis found himself almost crumpling beneath the weight of the distances and years, of how far away he had been in his life: around to the other side of the globe; a courtship; a marriage consummated and ended there; a return home; the death of his father; then a return to a life with primitives, this time tumbling into their demonology, almost losing himself, leaving his own world and its attachments and encumbrances and aspirations. And the death of the child; leaving that.

Franny seemed to sense Otis's disturbance. Her voice became conciliatory, less ardent, as she said, "You've never talked to me about that day."

"I told Chester," Otis said, "He told you, did he not?"

"He said you were nowhere near her. He said you were by the heather thickets. She was by the cliff."

Otis lowered himself to sit on the fieldstone retaining wall that bordered the piazza. The knowledge that he must produce a narrative, uncomfortable as it might become, had an orienting, calming effect upon him. He was at the beginning of something. He must go back into the past and return with an answer for Franny. It involved space and time; it was a transetheric travel of a different sort. He thought of how to begin.

"The 'family fits,' " he said. "That's what Chester calls them. He calls them that because he never experienced them. They were—are—mine and Father's . . . and Betty's."

He heard a small intake of breath from Franny. He continued, "I don't call them 'fits.' I call them 'accesses.' True, they come upon us like grand or petit mals. True, they are debilitating. True, they can, if considered from the point of view of our everyday life, be serious maladies. Still, they are something else as well. They *offer* us something, too. I have spent my life trying to discern what that is, and I think my father sought it also. I don't think he could put a finger on it—or a brush to it. Still, I firmly believe he spent his life trying to do just that."

"Is it why you engaged the *manang mansau* when you were in Malaya?"

Otis nodded. Franny, still standing, looked down upon his head. A breeze riffled his red hair, still its newly dulled color, even duller in the twilight.

"It was my hope I could gain control of my accesses."

"Did you?"

"No. I gained transetheric movement, but not control."

"Wasn't it—*isn't* it—dangerous to experiment, knowing your condition?"

"Perhaps. But something about the accesses obviates that issue. It is more important to *learn*."

Franny's features had become lost to him in the purple light, as had his to her. Both of them were simply just shapes in the dusk.

"The day Betty died, I was right there," Otis said. He pointed to an area of grass amid the heather bushes. "Betty was over there." In the dim light it was difficult for Franny to be sure where Otis pointed, but she could tell it was farther out, almost to the edge of the bluffs.

"She was playing," Otis said. "Running through the little paths between the heather . . ."

"It will be three years ago this summer," Franny whispered.

"So it will," Otis answered quietly. He rose and stood next to her. They both looked out into the dusk that had given itself over to the moonrise. The lunar globe balanced above the sea, rust-colored and mottled by craters.

"She was laughing. Singing a little song," Otis said. "And then the song became a long, thin note. Frances, I can only tell you that it was like a silver thread. I mean to say the sound became instantaneously precious and delicate and piercing. I sat up. I knew what was happening. It is a lightness of anticipation I feel when an access comes upon me. The thing was . . . The thing about *this particular* access was . . . I knew, I just *knew*, little Betty was having one, too. Simultaneously. And I wondered, Is the sound I am hearing her cry, or is it *I* making that noise, crying out some demon wail to her? Even now I don't know. All I know is I felt at once unearthly and yet bound to that little girl. We were inheritors together of the fantod. We were in one together. I felt my father there. I saw him lying face up in the river. I saw myself inside one of his paintings. Then I saw Betty flying through the air. My first thought—*thought?* paroxysm, cognizance, I don't know . . . my first *inherence*—was that she was beautiful, soaring like that. Then, my God, I immediately knew she had fallen through the fence and was gone. I succumbed. Everything went black. That's how it went. That's all. You know the rest."

Franny's soft, clenched sobs were so subdued, so diminutive that Otis at first had no idea she was weeping. She was almost silent.

"We must try," she gasped. "Help me. You must try."

Otis touched her shoulder. She felt no chill this time. Only the weight of another human.

"When you're rested," he said.

"We'll try?"

"Yes."

Another Letter from London

April 18th

Dear Franny,

I have heard nothing from you. Dearest, are you well? Are you ill? I shall write to Mrs. Tyler to inquire as to your health, your situation. My days are exceedingly busy, but I spend much time fretting over your silence. Please send me some word.

I apologize for being so tardy with my own epistles. You know I am not famous for my letter writing, and as I said, I have been busy. You may be amused to know that I am becoming famous, though, for my part in the Phantasmagorium. We are doing quite well here in London. We have achieved our goal. We have raised the money needed for the cable project!

I would be happy to close the show down right now and attend solely to my engineering chores, but we are selling out every night, and Spude importunes us to keep performing, to enrich the coffers, to make the cable project more celebrated, and to keep him the toast of London society.

All our technical problems with the cable seem to be coming under control, although I am often in some sort of controversy with my British counterpart, Dr. Whitehouse. Never anything serious, just a different approach to matters electrical.

I often correspond with my former teacher, Professor Thomson in Glasgow, for solace and direction. He is wise and a comfort to me.

The British navy is favorably disposed to our project in ways the American navy and Congress are not, and our syndicate has nearly obtained from the Crown the ships we'll need to lay the cable. The other technical matters are falling into place nicely—cable manufacture, preparation for loading on, &c. Even London seems hospitable as I walk about. Spring is in the air, as I hope it is for you as well. Please, please, please, do write to your husband. I fret, and I send you all my

Love,
Chester

CHAPTER VII

THE GREAT STINK

London, Spring 1858

The News Hole

Sometimes of late, Jack Trace seemed to quail in the face of what he occasionally took to be a greater appetite than his own: the hunger of the News Hole.

This and other thoughts came again to Trace of a spring day as he stood before the *Great Eastern*. His story and especially his pictures of the ship's explosion had brought him renown, more money, and a good deal more work. The "Great Iron Cliff" was back at the Isle of Dogs, still undergoing repairs after its maiden voyage, docked now upriver from its birthplace. It had been such a fine morning, Jack had walked clear out to the Isle. He had been in a sort of reverie. Warm breezes had been blowing down from the north. Such trees as there were on his route were all leafed out and full of birds, their songs everywhere.

He walked with a spring in his step and wondered if maybe it was more than the weather that made him feel so light. Perhaps his new custom of being out and about as a strolling artist of the boulevard had taken a few pounds off his frame. He patted his waistcoat; he picked up his pace.

It wasn't until he saw the *Great Eastern*, though, its mass lying ahead like a mountain range, that his thoughts turned and began to darken with ideas of mortality and the News Hole.

It was what editors called the space they allotted for anything that wasn't an advertisement. The News Hole had to be stoked daily. Before his recent success, Trace's relationship with the News Hole was too abstract to be felt. He was concerned more with keeping out of debt, with making the rent, with just selling some*thing*. But now that editors were soliciting contributions from him, now that two or three popular novelists had made inquiries about his illustrating their serials, now that his byline was recognized beyond the select few drinking chums in the Dulcet Thrush, Trace felt a creeping and insatiable demand on his talents.

Sometimes he felt his spirit rise to the challenge. He had arrived at last; people needed him. At the same time, his audience stood across the chasm of the News Hole, a maw that struck a flutter of nausea in Trace's gorge. The News Hole would never be filled; the News Hole always wanted more. Jack Trace, a man of fifty, a man who could be a grandfather, realized that no matter how wonderful a story or how eye-catching an engraving, there would always be the question *What have you got coming for the News Hole tomorrow?*

And while the prospect didn't seem to be threatening today, the question nevertheless crept into his mind: *What if the day comes when I have nothing?*

Music—not the sound of steam fitting or riveting—drifted down from the deck of the giant ship. Bunting hung along the vessel's rails. The repair work had progressed haltingly because the beleaguered corporation that owned the ship had been nearly bankrupted and frequently had to stop operations while it scrabbled about for more money. Moored to land perhaps indefinitely, the *Great Eastern* was a tourist attraction now. People were queued up outside a striped pavilion tent at the foot of the gangway, waiting to board the vessel. They had come on this lovely afternoon to view the site and aftermath of the explosion. Trace walked past a sign:

THIS WAY TO . . .

The Site and Aftermath
of the Horrid
Explosion
Endured by the Steamship
Great Eastern

CHILDREN PROHIBITED
LADIES CAUTIONED
The magnitude of mechanical destruction
is likely to disturb the unprepared
and those of delicate constitution
SEVERAL PEOPLE
(mostly able-bodied seamen)
DIED
on the site
IN THE TRAGEDY

SEE THE DEVASTATION
PAY YOUR RESPECTS

Sir William Rathbone says:
"I wonder at the force it took to disable so mighty a vessel. I am humbled after visiting this ship."

Admiral Peter St. Leger of the Royal Navy says:
"Let us pray nothing like this should ever happen again. It is a blow to naval progress, nay, to our nation's calling. We pray too for the souls who departed this earth in the fiery blast that wracked this great ship."

Mister J. Baumol Spude of the Atlantic Telegraph Company and the Phantasmagorium Show says:
"A shade was pulled across a great vision of the future the day this tragedy occurred, but the shade will be lifted and the sun will shine once more on the future of mechanical and technological progress and on this ship, one—along with the subatlantic telegraph—of the great achievements of our age!"

ENTER TO THE
RIGHT
THROUGH THE STRIPED TENT

On the deck, velvet ropes kept the stream of onlookers back from the very edge of the hole. Under a small canopy in the V of the bow rails, the band—two coronets, a euphonium, a bass drum, and two concertinas—played. Banners fluttered from the foremast stays. As the sightseers filed across the deck toward and around the hole, several young gentlemen took their ladies' hands and swung their arms back and forth in time to the music. One couple even began to dance, to the delighted applause of the others in the queue. Trace stepped out of the procession. There might be something here for a sketch: the line of well-turned-out gentlefolk peering into the ragged crater, ladies pulling back from the lip of the maw while men edged forward.

Perhaps this was why he'd come to Millwall to the "Great Iron Cliff" again. Perhaps this damn ship, this bête noire of his, was really his muse. Perhaps he had to come back to see if being near the beast would set him on a new course. He had sworn, no more stories, no more pictures about this ridiculous folly. Yet this ponderous monster supplied him with the disaster that had given him a new lease on work and new success. It had nearly killed him, but it had saved his career.

He knew, too, that there was something about this preposterously large ship, all the structural and logistical genius and all the hubris that went into its construction, all of it had something to do with the damned image in his head. The one he couldn't shake, the one that crept back during idle moments: his mural of the future, *Progress*. The image was inextricably tied up with carnality and with the whore. (Maddy, who he was now convinced had died on the ship. Another reason he was drawn here.) The allure of the mural as well as his shame for the way he'd first come upon the vision—for that was now what he felt it was: a visitation or a vision—hopelessly confused him. He was too old, he thought, to be a visionary, artistic or otherwise. He should be respectable and accountable to his age and station. He was lucky to have achieved the success he'd so recently gained; that should be enough. And yet, he had aspirations. He wanted to fill something grander than the News Hole.

In exasperation he snapped his pencil in two and stepped farther away from the queue crossing the deck. Oh, he hated these thoughts. Especially on such a fine spring day.

As Trace stood at the rail on the Thames side of the ship, he noticed a singular odor. He glanced up at the flags. They hung limply. What breeze there'd been had stopped. The smell was back. All it took, now that the weather was warm, were a few moments of still air or a shift in the wind and it would be back—the river stench. The northerly breeze had ceased in a midday calm, the sun beat down, and instantly the odor was twisting up from the water.

Trace looked down at the Thames. From the height of the deck the flow of the river was barely discernible. It was merely a brown, septic plain stretching some three thousand feet across to the Surrey Docks.

On the deck of the ship, the gentlemen and ladies in the queue were now holding handkerchiefs and gloved hands over their noses and mouths. Some people were applying perfume to the cloths, and even to the cuffs of their sleeves. (All over London, street mongers had begun selling vials of scents for that very purpose.)

Trace, looking down from the ship's rail, suddenly realized that *this* should be his next drawing—the stink. It was testing the city's mettle, and there wasn't a neighborhood or precinct that hadn't been affected. The river was finally reaching its limit: the draining of cesspits, the dumping of night soil, the increase in sewerage and gully shoots, the discharging regardless of the tide, were all creating a foul smell that evinced a river taxed beyond its capacity to cleanse itself. People joked that nothing would be done until Parliament recognized that the odor was from the river just outside its windows and not from the politics inside.

And there were the diseases. Trace had already heard of a cholera outbreak east of the Tower.

The band had stopped playing. The smell had become too much. The musicians were packing their instruments with one hand while holding kerchiefs with the other. They shook their heads in disgust.

The smell was particularly bad on the ship, as the tide was out and mudflats were exposed. The poor ship was docked at the perfect place to receive the brunt of the stink. Debris and sewage had collected in piles on the flats. Trace could make out one or two "mud larks," a man and a woman, braving the stench to venture out onto the muck to scavenge for salvage.

The sightseers had left and were retreating down the gangway. The deck was deserted. Another day on the Thames had come to an end . . . and it was barely afternoon. Out in the central channel, a boat of corpse pickers was combing through a raft of flotsam that had made its way downriver and past the flats. The pickers had scarves and kerchiefs over their mouths and were pulling a body from the water.

Trace walked over to the shore side of the ship as he pondered an engraving for tomorrow's papers. Perhaps a boat with a skeleton at the oars. The corpse pickers had given him the idea. Remembering the burned-to-the-bone legs of the crewman he had seen the day of the explosion on this very deck had helped as well. And Maddy?

Trace shook off that last thought and looked down from the *Great Eastern* across the marshy expanse of the Isle of Dogs. He saw the carriages and cabs taking on the homebound sightseers. He saw a man running along the dike, flinging pieces of cloth into the river.

The Running Man

Joachim Lindt knew he was a cuckold once again. He carried the certainty high in his chest as if a stone had lodged there, shortening his breath. This he noticed whenever he ran, and he was running now nearly all the time. His life was a rondelle of changing paces: changes in footfalls as he ran uphill or down, along broad roads or gnarled alleys; changes in breathing rhythms as he ran or worked or slept, as he absorbed himself with his toil or watched Katerina and the American; changes of scenery as he ran through neighborhoods or as the scrim unscrolled in the Phantasmagorium Show each night; changes in the music tempos his wife played on the pianoforte and the organ; changes in mood: his, hers, everyone's.

Joachim Lindt had run throughout London. Many places more than once. Many places many times. He kept hearing the slap of his shoes on pavement, on cobbles, on dirt. The rhythm was soothing. But the stone in his chest made the running difficult.

He had spent the night alone. Katerina had not returned. He knew this because he lay in bed and heard no sounds coming from her room. They had moved to larger quarters in the hotel, to a higher floor—the fifth—and now occupied a corner suite. They could actually see the Thames from three of their windows. Joachim had requested the suite, and Spude had graciously acquiesced. It would have been miserly for him to begrudge two of his star artists finer accommodations. What surprised Joachim, though, was that Katerina proposed they each take separate rooms. "So I may practice," she'd said, adding that Spude was having a pianoforte moved into her room. "We'll have a connecting door," she'd said.

But Joachim knew, as sure as he lay there alone, that the connecting door was locked. All was quiet on the other side.

Joachim hated it when Katerina would creep into her room sometimes several hours after the evening's show had come down. He would hear her, and it would drive him to don his clothes and set out running. Katerina had been spending increasingly later nights out after performances, but last night was the first time she had not returned.

Sunlight poured through the east-facing window by the circular table in Joachim's room. He was surprised at first that he'd slept so late, but he knew it was because there'd been no noise of her arrival to wake him. Strangely, he felt no urge to run, no anger, none of that seething that had coursed through him when he lay next to her in their old room late at night. He felt instead still and hollow.

He slipped from the bed, took off his nightshirt, and stood naked in the sunlight. She was with Ludlow, he thought as he looked out on the rooftops. He despaired of having to confront her about it; they had talked so little of late. The moment had been coming, and yet he was not ready for it.

He cast his glance around the room and saw some of her underthings on the floor behind a chair, bathed in a corner of sunlight. Left there since when? Yesterday? A week ago? The silk heap lay like peaks of whipped cream or a snowy mountain range seen from miles above in a balloon.

The sun warmed him. He felt his genitals hang in the light. He felt the stirring as he stared at the silk.

He crouched and padded across the patch of light, a predator. He lowered his face to the small heap of clothes. The attraction and now the warmth of the almost glossy fabric was overpowering. He touched it and picked it up gently. He rubbed it against his cheeks, hearing the soft rasp of his whiskers. Then, unable to stop himself, he took the cloth and delicately swirled it around his chest as if he were dusting glass. Then lower— he began to stroke—to rub across his stomach now and lower still. Over in the corner of the room stood the dressing screen with its warring armies. He lay in a sun-warmed square of the Oriental rug in the middle of the hotel room; cuckolded, he began to move the silk on himself.

Afterward, he bounded up. He dressed hastily and fled the room, stuffing the silk underthings into the pocket of his Tyrolean jacket, the one he always wore when he ran, the one redolent with his own sweat.

He was delighted, as always, to sense his tangle of feelings instantly simplified when he reached the street. The air smelled so sweet and full of spring that he couldn't help but sprint almost immediately. He all but skipped above the cobbles as he headed east and south. The sensory flood and the burst of exertion had for a few moments suddenly and deeply washed him clean. He ran through the grit and grime of Whitechapel, barely noticing the catcalls and the slops that nearly hit him from an upper-story window as he ran. The movement, the feeling of his limbs pumping and his lungs filling with air, was intoxicating. He felt the tightness in his chest loosening a bit. As long as he ran, he felt this way.

His course—not planned but, as usual, improvised—took him parallel to Commercial Road and toward Millwall. He felt the small weight of the silk things inside his pocket.

For the first time he noticed something as he ran: people waved. Not many, but here and there, one or two. Had he been here before? He must have been. Had the people recognized him? They must have.

Out on the dike in Millwall, atop the long earthen mound, he ran south, as the river flowed, and saw the massive hulk of the *Great Eastern*, the largest steamship in the world, tied to its wharf. Condemned as a joke, there it was, disabled and bound to the land, kept from its destiny by petty circumstance.

Joachim knew how *that* felt. Didn't Katerina condemn him? He heard it in her voice, a deprecation that inched its way into her tone, even into the very music she played. Ever since she met the American. Joachim had seen it that first night in the warehouse in New York when Spude had summoned Ludlow to glimpse the Phantasmagorium, still then only a work in progress. And so this adultery had become a work in progress. Yet what had Joachim done to stop the progression? Precious little. He had been lost in his production, subsumed by the engineering and artistic obsessions of his invention.

He once thought Katerina had been attracted by his energy and per-sistence. He had courted her tirelessly, appearing at concert halls and prac-tice studios, spending his inheritance pursuing her on tour, presenting her with a music box he had fashioned himself: its top a relief map of Europe with her train running in miniature from city to city (Frankfurt, Paris, Milan, Vienna, Copenhagen—all the cities where he had followed her) and tinkling the opening strains of the first Schubert she had played for him.

But his compulsion to work, to perfect the Phantasmagorium, to delve deeper into the artifice of it until he could *live* there in the world of its scenes—the same feeling of being alive and inside the painted Japanese dressing screen of his childhood—all that had driven him away from her.

And yet, Katerina's own desires had driven her away, too. Her *appetites,* as she once called them. Joachim suspected they had led to other incidents: singers, a conductor in Vienna, a string of wealthy admirers. He had no proof, but he feared that these betrayals were the wages of an artistic, itinerant life. He told himself he could live with the compromises on his dignity. They formed part of the working partnership he had with his wife now that he had spent his inheritance. He had his secrets as well.

Joachim brooded as he ran. Then as he approached the monstrous ship, he noticed the smell. The odor of the river was back. He'd been a fool for coming down here so close to the water. He knew the day promised to be warm, and he knew what that portended of late. But the breeze had been so fresh when he started.

He was finding it increasingly difficult to get away from the stench. He thought it absurd that the English weren't doing something, engineering something, to solve their sanitation problem. He considered it bitterly ironic that this tour of Spude's, this wonderful Phantasmagorium Show, had cast him and Katerina upon the shores of a fetid river that befouled an entire city. And the more he ran, the more the stench followed him. He had awakened this morning into the certain knowledge that he was now a fool; he had run from the knowledge into a purged state of motion only now to find himself having difficulty breathing because the wind had died, the tide was out, and the entire metropolis smelled like the worst of sewers.

He had run past the *Great Eastern,* ducking under the hawsers in the very shadow of the behemoth. He saw ladies and gentlemen leaving in carriages, holding handkerchiefs to their faces.

Joachim would turn away from the river. He would cut across the Isle of Dogs and head inland again along the Lea, a small tributary. He would cover twenty or thirty miles before returning to the hotel room exhausted, with blistered feet and empty pockets because now, past the ship and running along the open dike, he was throwing Katerina's silk underthings into the river. They fluttered and tumbled downward, parts of them encrusted with his semen, and Joachim felt the stone high in his chest dissolve even as the stench threatened to choke him.

Conflicting Theories

The train guard told him they were about to cross one of Isambard Kingdom Brunel's bridges. From his coach window Chester Ludlow could see where the track curved on its approach to the span. He was able to make out the file of elegant stone arches crossing a vale at the bottom of which lay a small village. The train flew over the hamlet, and Chester pressed his face to the glass to look down onto the slate roofs and puffing chimneys. A boy, whey-faced and pointing, stood alone in a lane. Chester pictured the train as seen by the child: carriages flying on stone parabolas above the village, cinders and smoke sifting down after the clatter and roar had faded into the distance. Eventually all evidence of the train's passing would be gone, and the bridge would stand silently, the preeminent structure of the village, like a stone cathedral in a medieval town.

Seeing the bridge this way calmed Chester. He had to admire Brunel. That huge ship the Little Giant had built was very likely a monumental mistake, but these bridges, the railroads he'd constructed, the tunnels . . . they could capture the imagination. They were true monuments: elegant and functional.

Lately a new notion had stirred in Chester: he had begun to think of the cable as a monument. Strange to call a humble rope of copper, gutta-percha, hemp, and tar lying on the sea bottom a monument, but the thought persisted. Chester had often seen the cable as an engineering challenge, even as a means to wealth, but now—tentatively, for the thought might betoken hubris—he allowed as how the cable might confer upon him some great status. Unsure of what that greatness would be exactly, he cultivated it only as a feeling, a warm glow of optimism that he ought to ration carefully until he was more sure of the expedition's outcome.

He had plenty to do before they set sail. He was on a weeklong breakneck tour of the country to make the final preparations. Spude had objected to his departure; the Phantasmagorium Show was a complete sellout and he didn't want to shut it down, but Chester had to remind him that the Phantasmagorium was subordinate to the cable and that the month for sailing—June—would be fast upon them.

Chester had traveled from Plymouth, where the unused cable from last year's failed expedition was stored, to Birkenhead, across the Mersey from Liverpool, to visit the cable manufactory contracted to make the remainder of the wire. The new cable was ready and fit to specifications. It had been submerged in two-mile lengths in a canal near the works to test its insulation, then rolled on spools to await splicing and loading aboard the ships.

The syndicate had enlisted and outfitted the steam frigate *Niagara* from the American navy and an old British navy wooden wall, the *Agamemnon*. The *Niagara* was loading cable in Plymouth, and the *Agamemnon* was taking on its cargo at Birkenhead. All was on schedule. Chester had stayed a day at each port, watching mile after mile of the inch-thick black line snake from the wharf and warehouse into the half dozen tubs—cable "circuses"—built into each ship. Forty men at a time worked round the clock on the decks and down in the holds where they nestled the massive coils—each layer called a "flake"—around the conical hubs of the circuses, guarding against twists or snags or stray scraps of metal that might abrade or pierce the cable's cover. Chester crawled and climbed over every beam and strut as he examined each cog and rivet on the paying-out mechanisms he'd designed for the ships. On trains between ports, Chester went over the bills of lading, the supply manifests, the dispatches and schematics for the telegraph terminal stations in Ireland and Newfoundland. At each stop he would wire messages or post letters to keep the preparations moving along. The pace was invigorating. He fairly bounded on and off each train. On one leg of his journey, the railroad had arranged for him to have a private car hitched to what otherwise would have been an all-night freight to Glasgow. He felt incalculably important, and everything seemed to be coming together for him . . . rushed, but coming together.

Everything save the recollections of his meeting last evening with Professor Thomson in Glasgow. The meeting still bothered him. He found it flattering, almost disorienting, that circumstances of nationality had placed him in the role of chief American engineer on the cable project while Professor Thomson, his former teacher, had been retained only as an adviser on the British end.

Professor Thomson was an authority on submarine telegraphy, insofar as anyone could be in such a virgin field, but he seemed genuinely happy that his former student was supervising a project that in all likelihood would soon bind the continents. Thomson's only reservation concerned Dr. Edward Orange Wildman Whitehouse, who had so impressed the syndicate with his plans and apparatus that he was the choice for chief British engineer to work with Chester.

"I haven't finished the research yet to back it up," Thomson had said quietly. "I can't state it unequivocally, but he may be a boob."

Chester had kept his eyes on the gravel path along which they walked. The professor's Scottish burr reared up in his speech. The rattle of the older man's dialect had been comforting to Chester. It put him in mind of his student days and the thrill of leaving New England to work in the presence of some of the best minds in engineering. Then, too, there were the heady days in Glasgow of planning a life with Franny. He'd felt a knot form in his breast at that last thought while they walked along.

Because Chester said nothing, Professor Thomson had continued: "I am sometimes almost utterly convinced that the use of the high-voltage induction coils and the narrow-gauge core will be nothing but trouble." Then Thomson added with a chuckle, "Ah . . . *Sometimes almost utterly*. There's equivocation for you."

"But you wrote you were impressed by the papers I sent you," Chester said. "The ones Dr. Whitehouse had given me. I thought we agreed to approve," Chester said.

"We did," said Professor Thomson. "And I *was* impressed."

"Well, I just don't see how we can turn around now. We sail in the middle of June. The syndicate is pushing hard. We're using last year's cable for half the project, and that was built to Dr. Whitehouse's specifications.

Given your approval, I had the rest of the cable built to match the length we already had. I can't turn around and order larger-gauge cable. I barely have time to get my bags packed before sailing. . . ." The thoughts were tumbling out of Chester's mouth; a twinge of panic must have betrayed itself to the professor. He tried to calm Chester.

"Dr. Whitehouse has the field tests to prove his hypothesis," he said. "He's documented them well. You were wise to approve them. I was, too."

"But you said he might be a boob."

Chester had a sudden recollection of Dr. Whitehouse at the Bardolph, gambling with an almost licentious abandon. This was the man upon whose equipment the project depended, to whom Chester was yoked as co-engineer. Chester had a strong urge to tell Professor Thomson about that night at the club, but he refrained. The night was embroidered in his mind with Frau Lindt.

"A bluntness I should have avoided," Professor Thomson said. "I meant to say—or I *should* have meant to say—that I still wish for my theory, my Law of Squares, to prove true. I wish for *me* to be right. Doesn't any scientist?"

As he rode in the rail carriage and thought of the meeting, Chester was touched by this revelation of vanity coming from his mentor. He felt he now knew Professor Thomson as an equal: a brilliant man, yet capable of envy and avarice just like any other man. Just like him. Chester liked Thomson all the more for it; he liked himself more, too, for he was experienced and powerful enough now to recognize their similarity. A few years ago the subtlety would have evaded him.

He must have been smiling or looking wistfully out the window because when he turned his head away from the glass, he saw the banker's red-haired wife smiling at him.

He had been riding for the past three hours (ever since Leeds) with a couple on their way to the baptism of a niece. The husband, a Leeds banker, was a tall, robust man; his wife was comely with a blush of freckles across her nose and cheekbones. They had talked with Chester for the first hour pleasantly, the couple having heard of the Phantasmagorium, the wife saying her sister had seen the show in London and had written her glowingly of it. The woman's glances lingered on Chester, as his did on her, and he wondered what the sister might have written about him.

Soon the husband buried himself in the *Daily Journal*, the wife rested her head on her husband's shoulder, and conversation halted. Chester set to pondering the cable and his meeting with Professor Thomson, but occasionally he would look across the compartment, seeking a glance from the banker's wife. Unfailingly she rendered it.

These glances were a stimulant for Chester, and they charged the air around him. With his erotic humors aroused, his thoughts couldn't help but fix themselves on Katerina.

He had a handkerchief from her in his pocket. She had played with the thing when they were last together in bed in his rooms. She had tied it to his stiffened self, laughingly called it her standard, and saluted. She unfurled it from his erection and, after a couple of preliminary flourishes, withdrew the cloth beneath the covers, filled it with her scent, and gave it back to him to bring on the trip.

"Be home here before it loses its smell," she'd said. "I'll be waiting to freshen it for you."

Home, she'd said. The luxurious carnality of those few days, the intoxicating excitement of discovering their bodies, new as each was to the other; strangely enough, all that *did* feel like home to him.

Well, the bourns of the flesh were his habitat. Sensuality was his essence, and as long as circumstances permitted, it was something he would accept. He was an engineer, a man of theorems and intellect but also a man of pleasing physical attributes and growing renown.

The redheaded woman looked down, shyly, Chester thought. She inched a little away from her husband. Chester basked in the sinuous reverberations that were in the air between them. The carriage rocked. The banker husband rattled the paper, looked up, and smiled at them both. Chester looked back out the window and started to reach toward the woman with the toe of his boot, sliding his foot slowly across the coach's floor.

Oh, God, and what about Franny? There had been a letter. Chester had wanted to hear from her, and then when the letter arrived, it had the effect of only pushing him toward Frau Lindt. In every way, Chester thought, the letter was inadequate. It was terse, flat; it barely touched him.

She was well. The house was fine. Mrs. Tyler and she had opened the place up. *This is the third anniversary of Betty's death. I am happy you have the money to continue the project.* . . . A few more details about the weather and spring repairs. Then, *I love you, Franny.*

That had been the sum of her only letter. Its inadequacy had almost doubled him over when he'd first read it in London; then he was swept by bitterness. He deserved better. He didn't expect obeisance from a wife certainly, but he deserved something more than this. He deserved enthusiasm. Hope. Here he was, undertaking a crusade. Here he was, trying to unite continents. He was about to make a name for himself—and for Franny, too—and all she could muster was nothing more than a terse, neurasthenic missive. He didn't want a sick wife. He didn't want a child three years dead. He wanted something else. For himself. For the whole world.

The banker now dozed, his paper in his lap. Chester hadn't yet touched the red-haired wife with his boot toe when she suddenly let out a small gasp and bent forward with her gloved hand cupped to her eye.

"Cinder," she said.

The coach window was open at the top, for it was a warm day, and occasionally smoke and ash from the engine would be flung inside.

"Oh," she said. "It hurts."

Her husband snored and stirred but did not wake. The woman's head was still bowed. Chester leaned toward her, tilted over onto one haunch, pulled a handkerchief from his pocket, and offered it to her.

"Thank you," she said. "But I can't see. . . ."

"Perhaps we should wake your husband?"

"No," the woman said. "Let him sleep." She had a gentle roll to her voice.

"Well then," Chester said. "Allow me."

"Yes," she said. "Good. Thank you."

And Chester quickly touched the handkerchief to his tongue to wet a corner. He leaned even more toward her and gently pulled the lower lid down on the loveliest green eye he'd had the memory of seeing. There was the cinder, a black mote floating on a tear. As he daubed at it carefully, she held his hand to steady herself and to synchronize their movements with the coach's swaying. With his head held so close to hers, he caught the smell. He had pulled out the handkerchief that Katerina had given him. Her odor floated up between their faces. Chester blushed crimson.

"You got it," the banker's wife said. "Oh, good!"

Chester started to lean back, but the banker's wife, blinking her eye, held the handkerchief. "May I?" she asked, apprehending the cloth. She leaned back and patted her tears with the handkerchief. He could see she now smelled it. Her husband began to stir.

"Are we at Cambridge yet?" he grumbled.

"Mere minutes away, dearest," his wife said, and after a quick glance at her husband, she fixed her eyes on Chester. Her face had flushed, too, not nearly as badly as Chester's, but the color quickly receded, and now she regarded Chester with an imperious curiosity. He stared out the window, feeling some abashment, feeling devilish, feeling aroused. As the train began to slow down for the Cambridge stop, the banker awoke and began to pull the couple's things together. The train stopped, and the guard opened the door, placing small, portable wooden steps below the portal. Chester rose to bid the couple adieu.

When he sat back down and the train pulled out again, he saw the handkerchief on the seat opposite. It lay there partially twisted like the body of a broken gull, daubed in the corner with his saliva, the mote visible even at that distance. He picked the handkerchief up. It smelled now of both of them. Of Katerina and of the perfumed hand of the banker's wife. Chester held the handkerchief for the rest of the trip, and he thought more and more hungrily of seeing Katerina, of putting the burdens of the journey and the cable project and even his marriage aside for a few hours and of losing himself in her. The memory and smell of the flirtatious banker's wife only aroused him all the more.

Chester amused himself with these thoughts until, as they neared the city, the urban stench made its way into the train. He had forgotten about it during his week away. What a foul welcome. The smell from the Thames had drifted all the way out to the suburbs, well past Walthamstow. This was the sign he was back in London, back about to dive into its metropolitan entanglements before setting out to sea. Chester held the handkerchief to his face to obliterate the rank stench of waste.

A Matter of Grit and Wit

"I am a happy man," Spude said as he shook hands with the manager of the Egyptian Hall.

"I join you in that cheer," the manager said.

They had just signed a contract bringing the Phantasmagorium Show into the Egyptian for a two-week stand, with an option to extend if the cable expedition were delayed and Chester Ludlow remained in London. (Spude hadn't discussed this contract rider yet with Chester, but he wasn't worried.)

The Egyptian Hall was London's premier venue for dioramas, tableaux, and panoramas. A pageant about the lost Franklin Arctic expedition
was just finishing an engagement before heading to America. The manager
had a slot for the Phantasmagorium; he was eager to get Spude's state-of-
the-art show into his hall.

"I'll have to bump the Hottentot Venus that I'd booked for a return
stint," the manager told Spude. "But I'd much prefer you. It'll cost me a
little to buy out her contract, but it'll be worth it."

As for Spude, even a mere two weeks at the Egyptian would expose
the Phantasmagorium to an ever widening audience. The show's overwhelming popularity had done much to prevail over its handicap of being
first presented at a gambling club. At the Egyptian, however, patrons of all
stripes would feel comfortable about coming, about bringing their wives,
their children.

"We'll have matinees several days a week," Spude said. "An early
show and late show in the evenings. It will be true family entertainment."

The manager purred in concord and offered Spude a cigar, which
Spude smoked on his way from Piccadilly back to his hotel.

If only he could extend the show. Two weeks was nothing, but he
knew, as the schedule stood, Chester Ludlow could offer him no more
time. The show had been, after all, created to make the cable possible, and
now the cable expedition was on the verge of departing.

Spude had noticed the shift in the public's attention. A few weeks ago
the Phantasmagorium had been the toast of London; now, if one were to
study the newspapers, it was clear the tide of attention was turning—toward
the laying of the Atlantic cable. Sightseers would journey by rail from
London to Plymouth of a weekend to watch the cable being loaded into
the hull of the *Niagara*. Newspapers in their accounts of the preparations
would hyperventilate if their correspondents had had an audience with or
even made a sighting of the dashing chief American engineer Chester Ludlow. Cyrus Field and other members of the syndicate were heading to
London to be on hand for the launch. Editors were jockeying for exclusive
rights to send a reporter on the expedition. The cable had captivated the
nation.

Spude began to slow his pace. Maybe things weren't so great after all.
Maybe his Phantasmagorium was fast becoming a sideshow. Spude's mood
changed. He began to pass shops without looking in the windows, without
even checking his reflected figure in the glass. The warm, overcast sky now

seemed wadded like batting between the rooftops, and the air felt stuffy. He had booked the Egyptian, but maybe he *wasn't* such a happy man.

With Field and other board members from America arriving, Spude's position as senior American syndicate member would be eclipsed. He had been running the show in London—the Phantasmagorium Show and the cable; he'd been raising the money, signing the checks, meeting the donors. Now the inner circle was moving in, and he, the midwestern cattleman parvenu, would be on the outs again.

But they couldn't deny the Phantasmagorium. Spude had created something wonderful with it. Cyrus Field was a decent enough fellow, even if he was the center of the inner circle. He would credit Spude with the fine work he'd done.

Spude's step lightened again. He puffed harder on his cigar. Two weeks at the Egyptian. If that didn't confer glory upon his work, then nothing would. Still, the tide was turning. The Phantasmagorium could even become passé if Spude wasn't deft. Once the ships set out, the show as it now existed would be a goner. So Spude, ever the impresario, decided to revise the program. That would be the ticket. He would contract with Herr Lindt. He could continue with the story of the cable, which, if the project succeeded, would be a Modern Marvel and would need to be suitably immortalized. There would be lectures, books, songs, and statues. So why not an epic panorama as well? Some of the scenes they already had in the show would still be useful. All they needed would be to add a few new tableaux and more music, and Spude had no doubt Lindt would be able to come up with ever more dazzling effects.

There was the question of Ludlow, however. Through all the excitement over the Phantasmagorium and then the shift of focus onto the impending expedition, Ludlow was always the center, the polestar. The young man bore the idolatry with grace. He did well keeping his mind aimed on his true goal, the success of the cable. The crowds around his carriage, the admirers, the breathless prose about him in the papers, even what appeared to Spude to be a dalliance with Frau Lindt, did little to divert him from his tasks. *Admirable,* Spude thought. *If only I could bottle that quality and sell it.*

But he knew he would be losing Ludlow to the cable, so he began thinking about replacements. He'd send queries to the Booth brothers, Edwin and John Wilkes, back in America. Perhaps one of them could serve as the show's narrator. Spude gloated at the prospect of a Booth uttering the prose he'd written. And with a replacement for Ludlow, perhaps the tension now surrounding the Lindts would be moot.

It was all so entangled, Spude thought. But he'd work it out. Just a matter of grit and wit. He pitched his cigar stub into the gutter, and un-protected by the strong tobacco aroma, he smelled the river.

Even this made him smile. Only that morning on his way to meet the Egyptian's manager, he'd read in the papers how the gentry were heading off to their countryseats early this year to flee the stench and how the government, in order to remain in session so near the offensive Thames, had draped the windows of the Houses of Parliament with curtains soaked in chloride of lime.

Spude would do the same thing. He had already ordered the vats, the chemicals, and the curtains. The Phantasmagorium Show would go on despite the worst smell emanating from the Thames in the city's history.

And Spude would advertise it. The handbills and posters were already taking shape in his mind. Besides all the usual hoopla and hyperbole about the cable, the show, and Ludlow, Spude would include on the posters an item about the facilities—the great Egyptian Hall—and how, for the first time and for everyone's weal, the producers would

employ the same
OLFACTORY PROTECTIONS
as used by
THE LORDS OF THE REALM THEMSELVES
in the current
SESSION OF PARLIAMENT
to safeguard our audiences
and provide for their well-being
AND COMFORT.

That would keep the crowds coming.

Stations of the Cross

The smell was becoming too much for Frau Lindt. That she should have to endure this appalling stench was infuriating. It was everywhere, even in the nearby church where she'd been invited to practice on the pipe organ.

The hand-wringing, wheezing little rector was practically apoplectic with delight at the prospect of the Phantasmagorium's musical directress rehearsing on his parish organ. He'd promised that the smell inside the church was "minimal." The rector had attended a performance at the Bardolph, having so wanted to see the show over which even ladies of his church enthused. He had arrived just before curtain and, so as not to reflect poorly on his station as a clergyman, departed swiftly before the club had been converted back to a gambling hall. The show had been wonderful, and then, as luck would have it, he saw Frau Lindt herself, alone, outside the stage door after the performance. He rushed up to praise her and amid his effusions offered her the use of the pipe organ in his church. It had been built on a design by the German master Gottfried Silbermann. Perhaps she'd like to try it?

The rector had arrived too late to see Chester Ludlow and Frau Lindt steal a farewell kiss at the stage door. Frau Lindt was still feeling the tingle on her lips when the minister approached. Chester had rushed to catch a night train to Plymouth. The show was closing for a week while he traveled about the country making preparations for the cable expedition, and while the Phantasmagorium moved to the Egyptian Hall. Frau Lindt faced a week of nights alone—that is, if one were not to count the occasional presence of her increasingly abstracted husband.

She would have some free time, she said to the minister. She would come to his church.

Each day when she went there to practice, she found a cozied pot of tea and a tray of biscuits sitting on a small stool near the organ in the church's transept. The amenity was cloying, but the cleric kept out of sight, so Katerina was free to concentrate on her music. She rather appreciated sitting in the cool of the stone building, the light dappling through the stained-glass windows onto the keys. Although the rector was wrong about the stink, at least the smell from the river was less offensive in the church than outside, and the organ was serviceable. She could do worse than spend the week this way while she waited for Chester's return.

Perhaps that was what was truly annoying her: Chester's absence. She'd been down this road before. The flirtations with another artist (it was how things had begun with Joachim), the excitement, the absolutely delirious quenching of the lust. Then the first separation. It was always as if a part of her vitals had been torn away with the departure. But this was temporary, and it was worth it. He would be back.

And Chester Ludlow, her American engineer, seemed different. Usually her eye sought a man in the fullness of his reputation, but Chester Ludlow had something else about him. He seemed a man yet unmade, a man on the verge of something. Ludlow was attractive to her precisely because he was becoming something no one, not even he himself, had expected. And Frau Lindt had watched it happen from the beginning, from that first time she met him in the Manhattan warehouse. If she were deluding herself about her prescience, then it was surely a harmless indulgence. So what if she really hadn't seen his potential as a world-renowned engineer and unifier of continents? So what if she saw only a handsome young man who stirred her appetites? She'd been intrigued, and she'd acted upon that intrigue. Effects followed her causes, her actions led to equal and opposite reactions, and now he was her lover. Simple physical laws. So she was an engineer in her own right. A unifier. The thought made her almost chuckle aloud. She chose something energetic to play. She chose her reworking of the overture to Rossini's *William Tell*.

She had transcribed the overture for the organ, and when she played, the church filled with the music, although Frau Lindt's sense of it was only as a small, intense vortex of sound that swirled around the organ bench. She quickly lost all feeling for the size of the building that was reverberating with her playing. She was in a globe of her own music.

In the vestry, the rector, on his way out for a meditative walk, was trying to remember how many days until Whitsunday and what implications that might have on the sermon he should be writing. He stopped among the robes and vestments and listened. Such music! If the regular church organist was a substandard musician and ill-tempered drunk, at least during this week the building was filled with glorious melodies. True, it would cost him some to have the sexton on hand to act as calcant and crank the bellows for Frau Lindt's sessions, but it was worthwhile.

He smiled and went on through the vestry, quietly closing the door behind him, stepping out into the tiny churchyard, where the smell of the river nearly knocked him to the ground. Perhaps a sermon wouldn't come to him on a stroll through this stench. He stopped at the yard's iron gate long enough to grope for his handkerchief and to notice a man with a valise standing in the street listening to the music. It had a distant, melancholy quality out here, the rector thought, but it was making the man smile nonetheless.

The cleric went on his way and had gotten halfway down the block before he realized that the tall young man in front of the church was the narrator of the Phantasmagorium Show, the cable project's chief engineer. When the minister turned to look back toward his church, the young man was gone, so the cleric plunged onward into the city smell.

Frau Lindt stopped before a particularly difficult passage. She was about to back up and begin again when she decided to play something of her own. She had resumed composing. Only a little, spending a bit of each session here in the church or on the Phantasmagorium's pianoforte to work out her pieces. And that was all they were at this point: pieces. She wouldn't allow herself to consider them anything else. She carried the sheets around in her reticule, not collecting them in a folder or portfolio but leaving them as jumbled scraps of paper, mere notes to herself.

She took the music in parts, beginning with only her right hand. The towering pipes on the wall of the transept and above the narthex boomed the same eight-bar passage repeatedly.

As the music sunk into her muscles, freeing her mind, it occurred to her that these "pieces" could be useful in the new version of the Phantasmagorium Show she'd heard Spude discussing. She couldn't quite imagine herself playing for the Phantasmagorium much more. Perhaps she could sell the music to Spude. Make some money. Leave forever.

She didn't know what the future held for her. As if she were trying out chords or nudging her imagination toward a melody or song, she pushed her thoughts toward the idea that she would be with Chester. That he would be famous; that she would be as well; that they would live splendidly in their own bubble of renown. What would happen to Joachim, the cable, Chester's wife, Spude, everything that made up the complicated, annoying present, was of no consequence in these fantasies. She thought of Chester's body, the length of it, his golden hair. She thought of these "pieces" she was composing, of how their appearance in her imagination seemed to coincide with the manifestation of her appetite for Chester. He was her muse, she realized. Was she his?

She wanted him back. The mystery of what was about to happen to Chester could vex her as much as excite her. She considered that the praise was beginning to turn his head. A few nights ago he had as much as told Spude to lump it. *He* was the cable project, he'd said. Without him, the cable, the Phantasmagorium—all of them—were nothing. And Spude didn't contradict him. It was the first time she'd seen the bloviating ringmaster back down. There was satisfaction in that at least. She'd heard her husband curse under his breath backstage, and for a moment she even felt herself allied with the others against that overweening pride. *I am the project.*

She stopped playing the church organ and sat in the ringing silence, lost in thought. Then she sensed that someone had entered the building. It was as if the air pressure in the room had changed. Or perhaps the smell from the river had grown ever so slightly worse owing to an open door. Something had definitely changed. Perhaps the sexton in the bellows room had stopped cranking. No, she could still hear the air in the pipes. She pulled the little bell cord that would ring for the fellow to cease.

To see who might be there, Frau Lindt had to rise up from the organ bench, and when she did, she inadvertently stepped on one of the slatlike wooden foot pedals, sending an enormous last gush of air through a pipe and making a low note crash through the church. She cried out in surprise. As the echoing of the note faded, she heard his gentle laughter. She slid off the organ bench and could see him walking up the side aisle of the church, passing through the frames of colored light spilling from the stained glass above. His gold spectacles glinted in the wash of colors: red and purple and green, each a dominant hue from one of the stations of the cross depicted on the windows.

Later in bed, reveling that the stink of the river was powerless against the brine and loamy smells of their passion, she laughed and told him he had come through all the stations of the cross to get to her. He laughed, too, and said, "No. Only half." There were seven windows on that side of the church; the other seven with their stations of the cross were along the opposite wall.

"Ah," she said as she took him in her hands and guided him into her, glad beyond all expectation that she had him back. "Only half. You had it easy."

The Name Stuck

That everyone in the country now called it the Great Stink was attributable to Jack Trace. The name spread across the city in a day, across the kingdom within a week, and was now working its way over the oceans of the world as ships carried copies of the London papers abroad. *Punch* had featured a huge engraving by Jack of a skeletal monster in Death's hood and robes rising out of the Thames, looking to take the entire crosshatched and besmudged city in her embrace. She wore a tattered sash with the words *The Great Stink* upon it. The name stuck.

The city was caught in the grip of the "miasma of ordure," as a politician with a clothespin on his nose put it in one of Trace's cartoons (his less realistic drawings, the ones given more to caricature, were being given this semipejorative nickname, *cartoon*–especially by politicians).

In one week alone several buildings in the East End suffered methane explosions when gas backed up in cesspit drains. Five children were killed in the blasts.

Trace drew a lurid panorama that spread across the top of the *Despatch* one evening in early June, showing the miasmatic skeleton as a giant, sinister nursemaid. The panorama illustrated all the ways the fetid conditions were ravaging London's children: there were babies in cradles labeled "Typhus," "Cholera," and "Asphyxia"; babies blown up by gas explosions; children forced by the "nursemaid" to crawl into cesspits to harvest night soil for fertilizer. "And when you're done with that," said a speech balloon over the skeleton, "you can go back to sweeping chimneys!"

Across the top of the entire repulsive cityscape was the unfurled banner reading

MOTHER STINK TAKES CARE OF HER LITTLE ONES . . .

(In a nod to William Blake, Trace had written, " 'weep! 'weep!" in tiny letters over the children's heads.)

The worse the heat grew that spring, the more intolerable the conditions became. No wonder the gentry were fleeing, Trace thought. The upper classes were apathetic at best, willfully ignorant and hostile otherwise.

The Royal Commission of Sewers, in another of Trace's cartoons, was barricaded on Whitehall Street with an oppressed population all about in dissaray and distress. The Great Stink skeleton rose out of the Thames, towered over the bridges, blotted out Southwark, and loomed like the sinister clouds spewing from Vesuvius over a doomed Pompeii.

"Save us!" the citizenry called to the commissioners, who, like the caricatured politician, had clothespins on their noses.

The rector of the church where Frau Lindt had practiced found in the stench the topic he needed for Whitsunday and all his Trinitytide sermons.

"And it shall come to pass that instead of sweet smell there shall be stink!" he fairly bellowed from the pulpit.

His congregation sat up in shock.

"Noses have they, but they smell not!" he shouted.

And he preached as he never had preached before. The stench and Trace's illustrations had galvanized the little rector.

Other churches took up the cause. Playing to this, Trace drew an angel coming through a break in vapors over the city, bearing a tablet inscribed

> *Deut. 23:12–13*
> . . . Thou shalt have a place also
> without the camp, whither thou shalt
> go forth abroad: . . . and it shall be,
> when thou wilt ease thyself abroad,
> thou shalt dig therewith, and shalt
> turn back and cover that which
> cometh from thee. . . .

The Great Stink skeleton, adorned in this drawing with satanic tail and horns, cringed before the holy writ. The *Evening Despatch* was besieged by clergymen for reprints of the drawing. Trace, with his cartoon, was creating banners for the battle against city officials who, as the little rector said, "fiddle while London chokes!" Editors were dispatching messenger boys to Trace's rooms with requests for more drawings, more cartoons. They sent him to explosion sites, to scenes where entire families were carried out dead from buildings that had been shut tight against "the night air," to sites where sewer inspectors were dragged through furlongs of filth to reach fresh air after succumbing to chokedamp.

As he worked on the drawings, Trace found himself adding smaller and smaller details, little scenes within scenes, perhaps as a way to relieve the discomfort of the work at large. Even in the realistic illustrations he was unable to resist inserting faerielike figures—spirits, sprites, devils, imps—lurking between buildings, behind wagons, sitting on barrels. His drawings teemed with life, or more accurately, with depictions of squalor and suffering and death so that the effect was that the foulness of London permeated into every crack and cranny of the city in the pictures.

The engravers sent messages pleading with Trace to let up. They couldn't possibly reproduce such minuscule detail, and besides, there was something about duplicating all that foul minutiae. It made *them* feel filthy, hunched over the plates, etching the illustrated hells with their tiny, mephitic incubi.

He needed a break. Trace realized he needed to find some lighter topics for his subjects. The city's—indeed, the nation's—one diversion of late seemed to be the transatlantic telegraph. It was the topic that took people's minds off the smell around them. The expedition was only a couple of weeks from setting out.

He put down his pen. The thought of the telegraph drew his eyes to the wall opposite, above a roll of canvas, to where he'd pinned some sketches. The mural. His *Progress*. He had done a few preliminary drawings. He had let the pursuit go when the Great Stink began to make money for him and editors' demands picked up. But now, thinking about the cable expedition, he found himself wanting to look at the city in a different way, the way he imagined it in the mural of his mind: that gleaming, better world. The one he'd first seen beneath the Thames. The one he'd seen after hearing the ship's propeller.

His thoughts returned to the whore, her satiric eye, her wonder at the sounds of the propeller, her appearance and disappearance on the *Great Eastern*. Trace had been to the tunnel a dozen times looking for her, paying for information and coming up with nothing. Still, he hadn't been able to drop the idea of the picture, and she had always been inescapably bound to it.

He could barely entertain the thought, but perhaps if he could execute the mural, it would be, in a small way, a tribute to her. Oh, what rot. She was a whore. She had mocked him as an artist . . . as a *man*.

Curse it, he told himself. His were sentimentalized ravings borne out of desperation and loneliness, a mood that was the stuff of his orphanhood. He was past that.

At least now he had some success and income as an artist to ease the desperation, if not the loneliness.

He drummed the pencil on his drawing table. Perhaps he still *was* unworthy as a man. He was certainly still lonely.

It was probably folly to try to paint the mural, of course. He needed a new inspiration, a new topic.

The telegraph. He got up from his drawing table. He grabbed his hat. He would apply to get on the expedition.

Trace bounded down the stairs and rushed out onto the street so as not to lose the impulse, and there, as he stepped over some filth in the gutter, he was struck from behind by the running man.

Enlarged

Joachim Lindt had no idea he'd struck the artist and occasional writer for the *Evening Despatch*. He would have been hard-pressed to remember running into anyone at all. He had become accustomed to receiving blows; dodging tossed objects—food, bricks, excrement; colliding with pedestrians, horses, barrows, and street workers; hearing abuse and mockery hurled from windows and wagon seats, even carriage interiors. It was a matter of course that he would come back to the hotel or arrive at the Bardolph bruised and soiled and wild-eyed. That he had hit someone meant nothing. It was all part of his obsession.

For a while he had tried estimating how far he was running, but the circuitous streets of London and the improvisational routes he took defied measurement. Perhaps it was just as well he didn't know. He became interested only in the drained release he felt after racing through the city.

It was on an exceedingly warm, overcast afternoon, several days after he'd unknowingly collided with Jack Trace, when the Great Stink was sending its tendrils out through every alley and street down which Joachim Lindt ran, that he made his way back to the hotel and heard Katerina. It had been days—and certainly nights—since they'd crossed paths outside of work.

She was playing the pianoforte she'd had brought up to her rooms. Katerina was plunking desultorily with one hand, composing something, running a string of notes over and over. Joachim could hear her as he went up the stairs. He walked past her room as the piano stopped, started, then stopped again with a bang. He felt a twinge of satisfaction that something was bothering her.

For several moments there was no playing. Joachim leaned his ear closer to the door. He could hear the rustle of her skirts as she paced back and forth across the parquetry. He loosened his Tyrolean jacket and chuckled. He would leave her there to stew in her own juices. He went into the sitting room of the suite, from where he could see the Thames, a leaden trough between the buildings of the City and Southwark. He had turned into his room and begun sponging himself at the washstand before he noticed that the door to Katerina's room was open. The Japanese dressing screen had partially obscured the passage. Katerina was standing there, her sleeves rolled up to her elbows in the heat. She shone with perspiration.

Joachim smiled.

Katerina produced a handful of silken underthings from a tissue package.

"From you?" she asked.

"*Ja.*"

"So many," she said as she sorted through the silk. They moved liquidly, as if they could drain right through her fingers. "You barely let me wear the ones I have before you give me new ones."

Joachim shrugged, hoping he could handle the conversation with dispatch.

"I want . . ." he said. "I want you to have nice things. Now that we can afford it, now that the show is doing well, I want these things for you."

Katerina nodded, mumbling a thank-you. "We *are* doing well, aren't we?" she said.

Joachim dried himself with a towel and looked about for a fresh shirt. Katerina reached over to the bureau behind the screen and handed him one. He took it and snapped it open, the starched linen popping in the air between them.

"Herr Spude says the Egyptian Hall is sold out for our first night," Katerina said.

"Good."

"Herr Spude says you have been working hard to have the preparations ready."

Joachim shrugged.

"I should have thought he would have said you have been out running around in circles all week. 'Where *is* he when I *need* him?' " She mimicked Spude's broad Missouri drawl and hard consonants with surprising accuracy. "But he didn't. He said you have been working hard."

"And *I* should have thought," said Joachim, "that he would have said our musical director was too fatigued from the late hours she has been keeping. That he was concerned her performances might suffer, that perhaps she had another performance on her mind. Has our narrator, our electrician-projector, also been suffering from fatigue?"

Katerina's breath caught perceptibly in her throat, but she recovered and gave a slight nod and smile as if in gratitude for the entrée into this terrain. It was a grin, however, that hinted she might be obstinate.

She folded her arms across her bodice. "Running in circles, Joachim. What are you about, running in circles throughout the city? I'm curious; I thought that was something done by Greek warriors. And they did it in the nude, didn't they? Have you thought of that? I ought to commend you for the distances you must cover, though. Have you ever calculated them?"

Joachim fastened the studs up the front of his shirt.

"Our narrator-engineer-electrician-projector is young and strong," he said. "Perhaps if he is spending his after hours with you, he is in*vig*orated, he is *stim*ulated, he is in*spired*." Joachim paced away from the washstand and for emphasis grabbed each word from the air with his fists as if he were tearing fruit off branches hemming him in. "Perhaps he is en*light*ened, en*riched*. . . . Perhaps he is en*larged*. . . ."

And with that Joachim couldn't help but laugh as Katerina barked, "Stop it!"

Joachim spread his arms in mock surrender, his unfastened cuffs flapping, his shirttails still untucked.

"Stop," Katerina, suddenly breathless, admonished him with a finger. In spite of himself, Joachim couldn't help but be taken by the delicacy of her hand, the musculature of her bared forearm. She had strength there from her years of playing. He had always loved the sinews and veinous patterns of her forearms, a toughness begat of art. He let his own arms flop to his sides.

"So," he said quietly, "we have been here before, haven't we? Standing on this very brink."

Katerina looked down at her hand that still held the underthings. In her fury she had squeezed them into a tight ball. She let them fall to the seat of the chair like scraps of paper.

"There is no need, I suppose," Joachim went on, "to push each other over the brink, is there? What would be gained by that? Still . . . I am growing weary of the view. And it is always such a long, long trek to arrive here."

She said nothing, so he went on: "Long and arduous. Still, I once enjoyed it. The twists and turns. Your inventiveness."

"Joachim—"

"But what once seemed enlightened, what once made our marriage stand apart, now seems sordid, seems desperate—"

"I am not desperate," Katerina said curtly as she looked toward the windows. "*You* may be desperate, but I am not."

"Desperate." Joachim nodded, assuring himself he was on to something.

"I am not desperate!" Katerina repeated, whirling.

"Very well. You are not. But you have *appetites*. Am I correct?"

Katerina mumbled, "Don't *you* say that about me. Don't you—"

"*You* say it, dear. 'I have appetites.' 'I have appetites that need . . . assuaging.' I think that's the euphemism you last used when you were impugning my abilities. . . . *Assuaging* . . . How sordid."

In her anger, Katerina involuntarily hummed a quick two bars of something, as if to drown him out and provide herself with incidental music. Then Katerina said, "We *have* been here before, Joachim. Yes. You are right. We *have* done this before. But you're not worried about it becoming sordid."

"I do not want to be part of a sordid marriage, Katerina. I will not have it."

"You are worried about it becoming successful. You are worried that we are on a brink, yes, but on the brink of something big, something different. You have never known success like this."

"*You* are making me feel sordid."

"It's really quite funny, Joachim. One could say you are running from what I am doing, what you are failing to prevent me from doing. And one would be only partly right. You are running from something more. You are running from our success. You have built a mechanism, an entertainment, that people are calling a wonder. People are flocking to see what you have done, and you are running like a rabbit."

"Now *you* stop it."

"And you are afraid. The view from the brink is *not* the same, Joachim. It is all different, and you shrink at the sight of it. You pull back."

Joachim stared at her flatly.

"You are worried," Katerina said quietly, "that this time my appetite *will* be . . . assuaged.

"Before," she said, "it *was* always a trek, and before I *did* always share the twists and turns with you about . . . the men. But this time you are afraid, Joachim, because you don't know, because the terrain is new and because Ludlow is new and what we—you, me, him, even that stupid Spude—are doing is new and so fraught with possibilities that you don't know what will happen, and you are afraid."

For once Joachim didn't run. With Katerina's words in his head, he was walking. He had made his way deliberately out of the hotel and into the street. He was headed toward the theater, the Egyptian Hall near Piccadilly, when he saw the paper. It was the *Evening Despatch*, and there was a whimsical sketch in the upper left-hand corner.

Who Is the Running Man?

the heading asked. And the sketch showed a caricature, from the rear, of a man in a Tyrolean vest and flapping shoes dashing down a crowded London street, scattering pedestrians and horses and omnibuses before him.

There was a whimsical story beneath the sketch by a Jack Trace asking readers if they had ever seen the "ubiquitous galloper" about the city. It went on to say that with a few inquiries on the street, the reporter had been able to elicit reports of "our omnipresent Mercury" appearing throughout London, "sometimes, it would seem, *in several places at once!*"

"Is he a spirit or a sprite? Is he a goblin or a poltergeist? . . . The latter being a troublesome order of Teutonic faerie, and our 'London Hermes' seems to favor a garment of an alpine cut. Could he have blown our way on the 'mistral' from the Dolomites? Could he be the cause of our Great Stink? Or is he merely one more irritated soul, agitated by the smell, who can't find a place anywhere in our blighted city offering refuge from the Reek in the Streets?"

He let the paper fall to the cobbles as a wave of shame swept over him. No one knew the article was about him, but still the story made Joachim break into a thin sweat. It was something about the dissonance between that quiet in his head when he ran and the jangling mockery inherent in the words and picture he saw lying in the mud at his feet.

He began to run.

"Sail On!"

Chester's plan for the expedition was to send the *Niagara* and the *Agamemnon* each with twelve hundred miles of cable in their holds to the middle of the North Atlantic. There, sometime in late June, they would rendezvous, splice their sections of the cable together, and sail in opposite directions, the *Agamemnon* to Ireland, the *Niagara* to Newfoundland. They would stay in contact by means of the cable strung between them, and when they each landed, the ends of the cables would be spliced into the telegraphic networks of Europe and North America, thus connecting the continents.

A mid-Atlantic splice would save time and reduce risk. Chester sold the idea to Cyrus Field, the chairman of the British-American consortium that was financing the expedition.

"Instead of both ships sailing side by side at the slow pace of the one paying out the cable and then, when the first ship's cable runs out, splicing in the second ship's cable and sailing on," Chester said, "the ships can head quickly to the middle of the Atlantic, make the splice, then each work their way simultaneously in opposite directions. One to Newfoundland. One to Ireland. Quicker. Safer. More certain."

"But the syndicate back on land won't be able to know how it's going," Field said. "Last year the ships stayed in touch with Ireland at the shore end of the cable. This year, you'll be out of touch with us for the entire expedition until both ends are landed safely or the ships have returned in defeat."

"Mr. Field," Spude butted in, "with all due respect, sir . . . Defeat is not in our vocabulary."

Field pursed his delicate lips. "My apologies, Mr. Spude."

Chester couldn't tell if the patrician Field was annoyed at having to truck with Spude. Cyrus Field was always the model of civility. He had called them all together for a meeting shortly after he'd arrived in England from America. They were using the manager's upstairs office suite at the Egyptian Hall for their conference. A red banner emblazoned with PHANTASMAGORIUM TONIGHT!!! hung vertically from a pole outside the tall Palladian windows. The banner undulated in a breeze that, Chester noticed for the first time that day, carried none of the river's stench. For once, the wind was blowing in the right direction. This small aerological blessing relaxed him enough to take a deep breath and plunge in.

"If I may, sir," he said, smiling at Field. "In my brief experience in the theater, I have found that it is often best if the audience doesn't know precisely what is going on backstage. Aside from the practicality of the mid-ocean splice, I think it is of no great import that our 'audience' be kept abreast of our every move. Rest assured, we will be doing our best."

"Well put," Field said. A shadow from the Phantasmagorium banner crossed the room. "Having been in an audience for your show, Mr. Ludlow, I must say I am most impressed with what you do onstage. You are quite the thespian. And your engineering argument here seems sound. Very well, sail on to the middle, splice there."

Spude was beaming at the compliment on the show, while Field went on to inform Chester that in order to represent the investors, Field would be on the voyage, too.

"And as long as we're discussing passenger manifests," Field said, "I received a message from Dr. Whitehouse saying he fears he may be too ill to make the voyage. This is the first I knew he was indisposed. He didn't specify the nature of his malady. As we are using his induction coils and his receiving instruments at your recommendation, this concerns me. Half our engineering team will not be on the trip."

Chester burned under his clothes. This was not exactly a vote of confidence; it was a sign that the blustering Whitehouse had succeeded in casting himself as indispensable. Now Field was worried because *Whitehouse* might not be along on the trip. While Chester had been racing around England making preparations and being quite the thespian in that damned Phantasmagorium Show, what had Whitehouse been doing? Browning up the board members, no doubt, until they thought he was vital to the expedition.

"I will meet with him, sir," Chester said.

"Good. Now, as I said, sail on!"

CHAPTER VIII

THE OTHER WORLDS

Maine, Spring 1858

The Spirit Room

Otis Ludlow had given up attempting to follow the *manang mansau*'s techniques. He was unable to duplicate them with any sort of precision, and, it turned out, Franny was uncommonly adept on her own.

They had set up the Spirit Room in her father's old study. They had moved Chester's drafting table out and had hung heavy drapes over the windows even though they used the room only at night. Otis placed cloths over the oil paintings of seascapes and of the several Piermont forebears that hung on the walls. He told Franny there could be no views of other places, nor any viewers of their work, only their own eyes and the view—whatever it would be—into the Other World.

Always there was Betty's rag doll, a flatheaded, mangled, smiling, eyeless moppet in a calico frock. Franny had saved the child's plaything and kept it on the pillow in Betty's room at the far end of the second-floor hall. In the past year, Chester had begun to look askance at Franny's obsessive maintenance of the room, always swept, the bed meticulously made, the sheets sometimes changed, and the bedclothes aired—"to keep the place from getting musty," Franny had said. Chester had claimed he understood that Franny needed the room to hold her grief in check, but he soon became perturbed. "You *must* move on," he'd declared, and ordered Mrs. Tyler to remove the little girl's things, to box them up. It was exactly one day shy of seventeen months—Franny had been counting—after Betty's death. Franny was too stunned, too weighted with grief, to object and could only look at the floor when Mrs. Tyler silently appealed to her for a signal. So the doll and the room's furnishings were all packed away. Chester threw himself into the telegraph project; Franny brooded and could do nothing. Now, however, the doll was back, unpacked and with a new purpose. It was, Otis said, the "spirit lever" with which to pry open the Other World.

Mrs. Tyler pondered all this. She had never been around when her mistress and the brother-in-law had been trying their "spiritualisms," as she called the séances. The pair always waited until Mrs. Tyler had gone home for the day, but Franny was free enough about reporting what had happened.

"Otis is a firm believer in 'set and setting.' That's why we've made our little chapel in Father's study. It's quiet, dark. A place conducive to spirit visits," Franny said.

"And do they visit?" Mrs. Tyler asked. She was snapping peas, picked from the greenhouse, at the kitchen table.

"I think so, yes. I *think* they do," Franny said. "I'm not very good at it yet, although Otis says I have made progress."

"And he's an expert in these matters?" Mrs. Tyler didn't want to sound skeptical. She wanted to sound interested, because she was.

"Yes," Franny said. "He had experiences over in Asia. He had a guide. He said he may have even traveled through space. He had visions. And now he's training me."

"What do you see?"

"Nothing . . ." Franny said. "Yet. But I sense that they're near us."

"They?"

"The dead."

"You want to see the dead? In this house?"

Franny nodded. Mrs. Tyler had stopped snapping peas. She sat in a block of sunlight coming in the kitchen window, a brilliant straw-colored cube of luminescence, but she had a dark feeling in her breast. She wondered where her husband was at that moment. She felt a prickle of fear for him out in his boat on the calm midday sunny sea. She remembered what she'd seen on the bluffs the day Betty died. The child, in a frock;

yellow, Mrs. Tyler thought it was, maybe white. She *remembered* it as white, but that was memory. Not necessarily the same thing as fact. And where was the brother, Otis? He was howling, writhing in a clump of heather. Two of them, uncle and niece, separated by maybe fifty yards of grass and low evergreen shrubs, the ocean stretching all the way to Spain—as she used to tell little Betty—the ocean calm that day, like today, murmuring. And Franny asleep in her room, taking a summer nap before lunch. And she, Edwina Tyler, on the third floor, just happening to pass a window and looking out, as she always did in hopes she'd catch her husband, Gil, pulling up one of his lobster pots. Instead, she heard the screams. The man, the child. The child's were a high-pitched keen; strange how it almost sounded like a bug's whine in her ear. Did she raise her hand to bat the bug away only to realize the sound was coming from below, from the girl? And the grunting, horrid wheezing coming from the man. She had only a moment; it was as if she were granted that moment, as if bequeathed that moment, to compose the picture in her mind: the blue sky, the sea, the dark green heather, the pale slashes of granite at the cliff's edge; the man, supine and writhing; the girl, twirling and dropping off the cliff . . . and her own cry, a gasp, an uttered word—"No!"—so different from theirs; the two of them, their utterances uncontrolled, part of the seizures, she later learned from the doctor, but—and she never told anyone this—she felt as if they spoke to each other in a secret tongue and it was she with her one-word cry of alarm who made no sense.

"Actually, I can't say I've *seen* anything," Franny said. "And, you know, I really only want to see one thing."

Mrs. Tyler nodded.

"And I haven't," said Franny. "But I feel she is near."

Mrs. Tyler plunged her hand into the colander full of shelled peas, stirring the little green spheres. She said, "I hope you find her."

For several consecutive weeks Franny tried. She would sit with Otis in the shrouded room with the doll before her on a low table. She would stare into a candle flame. Otis would talk to her as he sat next to her and held her hand. He would begin by instructing her to relax, to feel the air in the room around her, to let her mind "unhitch itself."

"Is this what the witch doctor would have you do?" she asked.

"Not 'witch doctor.' 'Guide.' "

"Guide."

"He led me much like this," Otis said.

Then he would have Franny, along with him, stare into the candle flame and think of Betty. He would have her recall everything she could about the child.

"She's growing away from me," Franny lamented one night.

"That's what we're here for," Otis said. "To prevent that. We're here to let her know she's welcome back."

Twice, after nearly two hours of "spirit beckoning," Franny said she felt Betty near.

Otis seemed genuinely excited, almost relieved. She marveled at how devoted he was to this project of hers, but of course he had seen Betty die and had done nothing—*could have done* nothing—to prevent it. This was expiation as much as exploration for him. She felt a ripple of sympathy pass through her body, and the sensation vaguely troubled her. She tried to get back to the matter at hand.

"Did you sense Betty near?" she asked.

He shook his head. "But I am not the contact. Perhaps I am the magnet, but not the contact. That is you."

After three more attempts on three different nights in which Franny said she felt successively less, Otis said they might try something more drastic.

Something Happens

The next night, after Gil had picked up Mrs. Tyler in his wagon, after the sun had gone down and a waning moon was rising out of the ocean, Otis told Franny to meet him in the Spirit Room.

"I am going to employ a physic," he said once they were seated and the candles were lit.

He had a small, carved wooden box in his lap. The carvings were a series of slashes at right angles and diagonals. Otis opened the box and drew forth a pouch from which he pulled several flakes of something like leather.

"Alkaloids," he said. "A fungus from Celebes containing the compounds. It is what my *manang mansau* administers."

"Am I—?" whispered Franny.

He was already holding her hand, and she had the impulse to draw it away. She wasn't so certain about this.

"No," he said. "I am. I will take some of this compound in the hopes that it will make me a lightning rod. *Your* lightning rod."

He let go of her hand, produced a small mortar and pestle, and ground the flakes into a powder; then, placing the powder on the back of his hand, he raised it to his nose and inhaled.

"We must prepare quickly," he said, moving Franny's seat directly facing his, placing the doll and a candle on a small table between them. He blew out all the other candles around the room, and this time he took both her hands and held them.

"Look at my face," he said, "but tell yourself you are going to look *through* me. Tell your eyes to focus *beyond* me."

Franny tried to do as he commanded. Otis's features looked different in the candlelight coming up from below them. His cheeks seemed more sunken and his blue eyes more penetrating. The lock of hair that curled on his forehead seemed to have regained the luster she thought it had lost during his stay in the Pacific. She had the fleeting thought that he was handsome and that she was back onstage playing opposite him, down near the footlights, a fetching leading man with whom she was having a scandalous affair, with whom she was falling in love.

"Concentrate," he said quietly, and she flushed, worried that perhaps he'd read her thoughts.

"Concentrate beyond me. Try to imagine you can look through me to the space behind my head."

"All right."

"Pay no attention to what happens to my face."

She felt a twinge of dread as she wondered what he meant by that . . . unless it was the provocative image she'd just conjured up. Could he read her mind? What were alkaloids?

"What do you feel?" she whispered.

"I'll tell you later. Right now it's not important. Concentrate on seeing Betty."

And she felt a shudder go through his body and a tremble in his hands. She heard his breath quicken. The alkaloids—whatever they were—must be taking effect. She worried they might provoke one of his seizures. She didn't know what she should do. She had the sudden urge to pull out of his grasp, but as soon as the thought occurred to her, Otis uncannily tightened his grip. His eyes had taken on a strange combination of piercing stare and pleading look. She could almost imagine him hanging over a cliff or a parapet.

She made herself concentrate on looking through him. That was what he ordered. He was the guide. She willed her eyes to focus some three or four feet beyond him. The room's dim appointments began to arc and curve in the shadows as if they had been painted there and were reflected in a lenticular mirror with Otis's head at the center.

He began to hum. His grip was steady, and Franny allowed herself one moment to focus on his face. His eyes weren't closed, nor were they exactly open, either. The pupil was rolled back in his good eye, but the glass eye stayed low and peered out from beneath his half-closed lid like a prisoner looking out from under his cell door. It was frightening. She pulled back.

"Concentrate!" It was Otis's voice, but his mouth didn't seem to move; the sound seemed to come from some three or four feet behind her. She wanted to turn her head, but she didn't dare.

The candle guttered, and Franny jumped. Otis held her. She glanced downward at the table, the doll. . . . It sat slumped to one side, almost in a pose of insouciant ease, its eyeless face smiling up at her in a way that, with the flickering of the candle, seemed to restore its eyes, or the *idea* of its eyes, so that Franny could feel the doll looking at her, almost glowing there, urging her to concentrate. The convex forms and shadows of the room's paneled walls, the paintings in their shrouds, the manteled fireplace that seemed like a distorted cave mouth in her peripheral vision, all began to revolve as if part of a sprocketed gear wheel that moved several stops, then halted. Was the room tilted now?

Otis's humming was a soft monotone, almost soothing to her. His eyes were now closed. His breathing was fast but steady. She had the illusion that he was no longer hanging over a precipice but was beginning to float as a kite or a balloon might in a gentle updraft, and she was his tether. Their hands even rose a bit.

She told herself to look beyond him, to focus Out There, to concentrate. She told herself these things, but it seemed as if it were *his* voice commanding her inside her head.

And then the hum that filled her ears was joined by another, smaller, higher voice.

Franny concentrated, looking harder, trying to see through, around, over Otis.

Because she saw a light. Soft, undulant, shapeless at first but coalescing every time Franny relaxed her stare and cast her gaze slightly askance.

Something was there.

She found if she looked away a little, she could see it better—the way Chester had instructed her when he was teaching her the constellations during their courtship. Look directly at the Pleiades and they seem to disappear. Look to one side and the tiny Seven Sister stars twinkle in the heavens for you alone. Insight by indirection.

She looked away just a little from the glow behind Otis and could see the unmistakable countenance of her dead daughter. Betty's face was just beyond Otis's right shoulder. It hung, disembodied but for a faint, pale miasma that hovered below the face.

"My God," Franny whispered.

Otis kept humming.

The face floated a little to the left, then a little to the right. The ecto-plasmic light that could have been the child's body pulsed and rose and fell.

Otis was stiff in his chair. Franny dared not look directly at him for fear that the image of Betty—it was undeniably Betty—would disappear.

Soon—it was hopeless to guess how long—the child was fully formed, completely Betty, if translucent and luminous.

Franny desperately wanted to speak. Should she? Would utterances obliterate the illusion? But this *wasn't* an illusion. This was Betty.

"Betty!" Franny whispered.

Otis had stopped his hum. All was silent. Even the distant sea sound from beyond the bluffs—a noise so constant at Willing Mind that it was remarkable in its absence—had ceased. The world held still. Had the ship's clock on the mantel arrested its ticking? Franny would have sworn so. She had the thought that for a moment the entire world had halted all its motion, all its animations, and that she and this shape, this form of her daughter, were the only things alive in it.

But Betty was not alive. And this embodiment of her, whatever it was, now began to fade. In its last moments of visibility, it seemed—or so Franny thought—to fuse around the eyes enough to offer her a vision of childish recognition.

The look so moved Franny that she stood up, vaguely feeling Otis's hands drop away, and called to her daughter. But the effort, the sudden rising from her chair either drew the blood from her head or broke the spell or in some otherwise manner caused all that had been so delicately constructed in the moment to collapse, including Franny herself, and the next thing she knew she was crumpled on the floor, weeping uncontrollably, draped over the seat of her chair with Otis near her, shaking visibly because the glass of water he proffered for her was splashing above the rim and splattering his wrist, and he, still under the influence of the alkaloids, was barely able to form the words "We have done well."

CHAPTER IX

ASSIGNATIONS AND ENCOUNTERS

London, Spring 1858

Katerina Goes

The ships were ready by the first of June. The cable loading was nearly complete. And although the ships and the cable were the major items of preparation, Chester still felt overwhelmed by all he had to do. He had spread engineering files, provision lists, bills of lading, his own packing list, and received memos in separate piles on the round table in his hotel room. He would rise from his bed after a fitful sleep and, still in his nightshirt, make several revolutions around the table, going through each pile of papers, rearranging the order of the pages and shifting some from one pile to another. It was a meditative way of awakening, a way of testing the breeze before the day's whirlwind commenced. Several times Katerina had been there in his bed, watching.

But now, as of late, she was not, and Chester slept, if he slept at all, alone.

"There is no room for me," Katerina had mumbled her last morning there as she gathered her clothes from around the floor.

"Pardon?" said Chester. He was bending over a memo and ran his hands over his haunches, scratching.

"That is the way I left you last night," Katerina said, pointing at him.

She looked so pale, he thought, the sight waking him more completely than any of the paper shuffling he'd done since getting out of bed.

"The only difference is now you're bent over there looking at your work by daylight instead of by lamplight," she said.

"Well," Chester said, waving his hand at the papers, "there is so much to do. We sail in ten days."

Katerina did not answer this. She turned her back to him, head down as she fastened buttons on the front of her dress. Chester could feel air circulating under his nightshirt and a trickle of sweat running from an armpit down his ribs. He noticed she seemed to be trembling, perhaps she had begun to cry.

But she turned to face him, and he could see that her distress was one of vehemence, not woe, a passion of resolve. Her eyes blazed.

"Do you think I am nothing?" she asked in a voice that must have left a metallic taste in her mouth, it was so hard and brittle. "Do you think I risk nothing by coming here?"

Chester stood frozen, then slowly glanced from her to the pile of papers and back to her. Suddenly her eyes softened; she was imploring him for an answer, for a sign. Her quick switch to vulnerability shocked him. It was unlike anything he'd ever seen in her.

"I'm sorry," he said. He looked down at the carpet. His own feet were every bit as pale as Katerina's nakedness had been. He thought of their matching flesh, entangled.

"What are we going to do?" she whispered, just barely making herself heard across the half of the room that divided them. "I don't want to be without you."

"Nor I," Chester said, "without you."

"I said I would watch you succeed and enjoy it, but . . ." Her eyes had gone to the circle of papers on the table as her voice trailed off. "Are any of those from your wife?" she asked, nodding toward a pile of correspondence clearly not engineering papers.

"No," Chester said.

"We have never talked about her," said Katerina.

"Now is not the time," Chester said.

"When is?"

"I do not hear from her," Chester said. "This project, my separation from her . . . even before . . . We have fallen out of touch. I thought you might have noticed that when you visited our home."

Katerina nodded.

"So," said Chester, rubbing his hands across his face, then flicking them as if he had been washing and was now refreshed, "I am distant from my wife and close to you. Can't that be enough for now?"

Katerina said nothing.

"I mean," Chester said, "what else can I do?"

"Do you love me?"

"Katerina—"

"Do you?"

"Yes . . ."

But neither of them moved toward the other across the carpet.

"Yes . . . " Chester murmured again, and found himself surprised he might be choking back a sob. He was nearly panicked by the wrenching sensation that seized his chest. He felt naked, standing there in only a nightshirt. *What,* he wondered desperately, *have I said?*

Katerina looked calm, even bemused, as if she had initiated an experiment and knew she would be endlessly fascinated by the variety of its results.

"Do you want to work now?" she asked.

"No," Chester said. Then, "Yes. I mean, I'm afraid I must."

"And I must go," Katerina said.

Chester looked at her questioningly, and she responded, "I shan't come back tonight. Not to this. I know what you must do, and that is all right. But we needed to say something about these things."

"I shall . . ." Chester faltered. "*You* will . . . come back?"

Katerina smiled. She went over to the bedpost to get her cloak and reticule, and Chester met her at the door.

"You will succeed," she said, placing her palm against his cheek.

"*We* shall," he said.

"I shall see you tonight."

"Tonight?"

"The show," she said, and the door clicked closed.

"The *what?*"

But she'd left.

Dammit! Chester swung a fist in the air as he spun away from the door. He had forgotten. Spude had extended the Phantasmagorium Show yet another week at the Egyptian. Katerina had told him about it the night before, but he had barely paid attention, for they were falling into bed at the time. It had almost been a joke.

"Oh. Of course. Certainly."

He kissed the trenches between the tendons of her neck, and she laughed a low, soft laugh. She had her hands inside his trousers. She held him. And hummed.

"Oh. Of course. Certainly."

Their mocking tones somehow became a signal to each other to abandon the human delicacies of irony and to let their hungers go. Chester began to tug and almost tear at her clothing; Katerina did likewise to his. He kissed her frantically: her face, her neck, face, eyes. With her dress down to her waist, he pushed her back onto the bed, pinioned her arms, and buried himself into the blondness of her armpits. An earthy quirk he reveled in. A place on her body he thought of a hundred times a day.

She groaned and twisted under him. They were enacting a struggle here. She was almost growling, sometimes shaping the noises into the word "yes," mostly not. Their bodies were becoming slick.

This was nothing like anything Chester had done with Franny, with any woman. There was a recklessness about this cultured woman that made Chester all the more frantic.

He relaxed his hold on Katerina's arms and pulled her dress down farther, licking her nipples, her ribs, her navel. She took his head in her hands and, by raising up one leg and pushing against the mattress, rolled them both over. She was on top now and slid down so her breasts cupped his genitals. She moved around on him, making him now the one who groaned aloud. Perhaps she had her hand down below on herself. He couldn't tell, but the thought of it excited him even more. Her sounds might have been affirmative moans answering his or perhaps laughter, a delight in his agony. What he knew was he had but seconds left, so he repeated her very move, pushing and rolling them both over again. Katerina gasped at the alacrity with which Chester forced her legs open and had himself inside her. He felt he was burning himself alive. He began to thrust immediately, and she answered the rhythm.

His climax reddened the walls, the bed, the sun, all the stenchy air of London itself. He screamed, and so did she. A pulsing series of shouts burst from both of them as he shot into her and she seized at him, flinging aside any pretense of reserve.

Exhausted, later, just before sleep, he'd had a fleeting thought. Something about Spude. Another week? He forgot about it and slipped into dreamlessness.

Spude on Himself

"I will not do it!" Chester fairly shouted.

"Of course you shall," Spude said.

Spude was having lunch at the Bardolph; he was now an esteemed member there. He had half jokingly said he was considering giving up his American citizenship, he had been treated so well by England.

Chester had caught up with Spude and sat across from him at a table in a potted palm bower in the corner of the dining room. Other club gentlemen dined at tables nearby. The place was thick with the murmur and clink of jocose and well-fed satisfaction.

"We are barely over a week away from setting out," Chester said. "I can't afford to be still doing that . . . that *show*."

"You're doing fine," Spude said. "I heard you tell Field."

"Well, what the hell else do you tell the damned chairman of the company you're working for? Of *course* I told him I was doing fine. For Christ's sake, Spude, I need the time."

"One show a night. An hour a night."

"I have to go down and see Whitehouse tonight."

"He'll be here. I happen to know."

"In London?"

Spude nodded. "This very place."

"*Here?* Oh, Christ. Gambling?"

"Well, we know Whitehouse, don't we? I don't think he'll be dropping in to read the newspapers. He's taking one of the rooms."

Spude made eyes and poked his finger upward in the air. Chester knew Spude meant Whitehouse would be in one of the assignation rooms the Bardolph kept on its top floors for its better customers.

"Isn't he married?" Chester asked.

"I suppose," Spude said. "What do *you* as a married man suppose?"

Spude made himself laugh with that, and he was still chuckling when his chops arrived. He picked up a sprig of parsley from the meat and sneered at it as he twirled its little stem between his thumb and forefinger. The herb flew up out of his grasp and bounced on the carpet. Spude looked down at his plate.

"Mutton. I don't think I've had decent beef since I got over here. Listen, Ludlow, after you get the cable laid down, I want you to come up with a way to engineer a machine to keep sides of my beef preserved without ice, and we'll send these people some of the best steak west of the Mississippi."

"Spude, I can't do your show. You don't seem to understand. The Phantasmagorium is over. It's the cable now."

Spude's whole body shook as he vigorously worked his knife back and forth in the meat. His elbow bumped the fronds of a potted palm, and the plant moved as if a creature were stalking through the brush.

"Ludlow, my boy, I'm a successful man. I am thoroughly enjoying myself over here. Two years ago I was doing quite well shipping beef back East to folks like you. Then . . . well, then my dear wife died, and I was a widower. What to do? As it happened, when I was on a business trip back there in New York, the angels of coincidence introduced me to Mr. Field, and I found myself taken with his submarine telegraph idea. I was the first cattleman to use the land telegraph in my business to connect Chicago to the railhead in Omaha. Made me richer than Croesus. A line under the ocean? Good idea. Let's do it. Let's get the people together with the know-how. Let's get that fellow Ludlow up there in Maine. Need money? Uh-oh. Well, on that same business trip I was wandering down by the Bowery . . . Let's be discreet here and not say why I was on the Bowery, but I was a widower, I was alone. . . . At any rate, I chanced upon a theater showing a small panorama show—*Wild West Cattle Drive*. The Lindts had engineered it. I went in. Cleverest damn thing. Laughable what those Austrians had for notions of how to move cattle. They showed them crossing the stage all tied together with ropes! But the theatrical effects . . . I tell you, the damnedest realest thing you'd ever want to see. Almost made you walk out of the theater saddle sore. Anyway, I knew, I just *knew* I was to be the splice between these two great ideas: the telegraph, the panorama. When the first cable try failed and Field reported to the board they were low on money, I knew it was my time to step in. I don't mind saying it changed my life, Ludlow. I was a success in beef. I have become a success in show business. From beef to bullshit, you might say. But listen to me, Ludlow. I didn't become a success by letting my cattle stray off. I showed up at the market with the number of head I had promised. Now I'm going to do the same thing here with this show. You'll forgive me for equating you with cattle, but as I pointed out to that ever-so-proper back-East Yankee Mr. Field, I made the money that saved this enterprise, but we ain't out of the woods yet. We got another week in the Egyptian. When you're out there in the Atlantic splicing that cable together, getting ready to be famous, it'll be this week of shows that's paying for it. That's how bad you need this show. And I don't have to tell you how bad the show needs you. Tonight. At eight."

"Places, Please"

So Chester did it. And the theater was packed, as usual. Backstage, Katerina blushed when she saw him, and flashed him looks that were by turns imperious, coquettish, and longing.

Chester supposed he sent her the same variety of signals as well. He couldn't get her out of his mind. He *wanted* her, but at the same time he felt the quickening, inexorable pull of events: the details (thousands of them) of preparation that were joining together like tributaries flowing into the river that was the cable expedition. He was riding its current. He spent every waking hour dispatching and receiving messengers, letters, and telegrams; going over lists and specifications; assuring Field and the board that all was on schedule. There was no way he would be ready, he thought. Spude was right: the show took only an hour, but add to that the trip to the theater and the slow progress through the inevitable crowd of stage-door well-wishers afterward, and it totaled closer to two hours. Still, that wasn't so bad if it vouchsafed the success of the whole enterprise. And it did give him another week's proximity to Katerina, if only to see her.

He had no idea what they would do once he sailed. He would be on the *Niagara* and would continue on to Newfoundland with the American half of the cable. Whitehouse was supposed to be on the expedition on the Ireland-bound *Agamemnon*. Now even that was questionable. What Katerina's plans were or her husband's plans for her or Spude's plans for them

both were a mystery to Chester. There was so much he should have already discussed with her, and now the tide was pulling him out.

"We must talk," he whispered to her that night backstage. "More."

Katerina was at the organ console. The small whale oil lamp illuminating her sheet music glowed close by her face. Its flame was nearly the
color of her blond hair.

"Not now."

"When?"

"How should I know? What is there to say?"

"What is there to *do*?" Chester leaned over the keyboard. Katerina
glanced around, conscious that they could be seen by someone in the company.

"Marry me," she said in quick whisper.

"*What?*"

"Five minutes, please," the stage manager called.

"Leave your wife. Marry me."

"What are you saying?"

"*That's* what there is to do."

"*You're* married. *I'm* married. We can't just—"

"You love me."

"Yes."

"Marry me."

"Katerina, please—"

"Elope. We elope."

"That's absurd. Stop it. Right now. I won't hear it."

"I love you. You love me."

"*You* are the one who said you weren't coming back to my rooms
anymore. You are the one who said you would *watch* my success. *You*
walked away."

"And I thought about it. Marriage is the only solution."

"It's not a solution. It's insanity. Criminal insanity. It would be a crime,
you know. What about your husband?"

Katerina pushed out a scornful snort. "He's gone."

"No, he's not. I saw him over stage right, checking the Choctaw camp-
fire."

"He's gone from *me*."

"Not legally . . . I can't believe I'm even discussing this."

"Maybe even legally. He's the Runner, you know."

"What runner?"

"The London Runner. The madman. He's been in the papers. There were pictures of him in the newspapers. People follow him. He's a sensation and a laughingstock. How can a woman be married to *that?* Alienation of affection, I would plead."

"You could plead nothing. You're his *wife*."

"Ha!"

"Katerina, you can't be talking like this."

"Places, please." The stage manager's voice came through the tormentor curtains around the organ console. "Places."

"I have thought about it. Alienation of affection. Your wife. My husband."

"Places."

"Yes. Thank you . . . Listen, Katerina, we must think this through."

She leaned closer to him, smiling almost fiercely. "Tell me about thinking. I *think* what we did last night would be called 'fucking.' Isn't that the word? I keep *thinking* about it. I like the word. I like *thinking* I can do that with you. That we can do it together. Fucking."

"God . . . Katerina—"

"Places, *please*, Mr. Ludlow."

"Yes. Coming. Thank you."

"Fucking . . ."

"Oh, my Lord."

Katerina turned and struck the first chords of the Rossini overture she used as the prelude to the show.

"Fucking . . ."

Chester could read her lips over the din of the pipes. He staggered onto the stage thinking of the word. He loved it, too.

Sight Unseen

He didn't speak with her after the show. There was a crush at the stage door—"fans," Spude was calling them, his shortened form for "fanatics"— people who wanted to meet the cast (the hacks and bit players whom Spude practically had to commandeer from theater district alehouses a few weeks ago were now the toast of the West End); there were engineers both amateur and professional who begged for a look at the backstage works of the Phantasmagorium and a talk with Joachim Lindt, the London Runner, who'd designed it all; and there were stage-door johnnies who were smitten by Katerina. Spude had Joachim add a movable platform for the organ console so it would roll forward, thrusting Maestra Lindt downstage into the limelight, placing her angelic presence beside Chester's luminescence. And, of course, there were the women—and men—who wanted to speak or shake hands with Chester Ludlow, the man all London was coming to know as the dashing genius who would soon unite the Old and the New Worlds.

Chester could see Joachim, Katerina, and Spude all swamped by the crowd, so he ducked out the front of the theater. He had borrowed a cap from a stagehand, pulled it low over his brow, and was able to pass as a straggler leaving the auditorium.

Chester had to get over to the Bardolph. He'd left word he'd be there directly following the show. There was that problem with Whitehouse. Several streets away from Piccadilly, Chester was able to hail a hansom. He got the cab none too soon, because it looked as though someone from the audience had spotted him and was lumbering toward him. Chester jumped up the cab's steps and told the driver to hurry.

Soon he arrived before the brightly lamplit marble facade of the Bardolph. As he was paying the cabman, a costermonger's rattling donkey cart pulled up, and a large, huffing man in a bloom of sweat alighted from the cart, calling, almost gasping, Chester's name.

The man was in worn black trousers, an evening waistcoat, and dress jacket. He looked unkempt from all his exertions. He was thrusting coins into the hand of the costermonger and pushing away the donkey that was still agitated from all its running.

"Mr. Ludlow, I must speak with you, sir," the man called to Chester from over the top of the donkey's ears. "Stop it. *Please!*" and he smacked the beast that was nudging him and smearing his coat with saliva.

"Hallo, sir," said the costermonger. "I'll thank you to leave abusing my beast to me."

"Sorry," and the man thrust some more coins into the grizzled fellow's palm.

The cabman and costermonger, being paid, each drove off, the hansom gliding away, the donkey cart making a herky-jerky semicircle in the street and heading back toward Piccadilly. The two men were standing alone in the street before the Bardolph.

"Jack Trace," the heavy man said, extending his hand. "I caught your show tonight, Mr. Ludlow. I've seen it a couple of times, I enjoyed it so much. A truly excellent illusion."

Chester shook the man's hand. "Thank you," he said. There was something beguiling about this large fellow. His eyes, set somewhat too close together, his shock of chestnut hair that seemed piled like a bale of leaves upon his head, and his huffing and puffing gave him the manner of a plump child just come in from play. It was difficult to guess how old he was.

"A truly excellent evasion, too—leaving by the front of the theater the way you did. I was lucky to have spotted you."

"Yes," Chester said. "And how may I help you? I have business, you see . . . ," and he nodded toward the Bardolph.

"Oh, yes. Of course." Trace seemed even more short of breath now that he knew he was pressed for time. "I'm a . . . well, that is, I work for various newspapers, you see, and I have . . . I have a request. . . ."

Chester gestured to Trace to walk with him into the Bardolph. They proceeded up the steps to the club's ornately carved doors.

"You see," Trace said, "I am an artist, foremost. I execute engravings and drawings for the daily and weekly papers, plus I do the occasional story. And I know, or I happen to *think* I know, that is, that you are related to an artist as well."

Chester stopped at the front door. It was a warm night and the buzz of the club drifted through the open windows.

"How on earth do you know that?"

"Just a guess," Trace said, alert that he'd hit the nail perhaps spot on. "An art teacher, actually. He had a cousin who married quite well and sailed for America. She sent him picture cards from New England. The White Hills. He would pass them on to the class. Frankly, landscapes weren't my aspiration, but I could tell these were well executed. I recall the artist's signature was 'Ludlow.' When I read in the program you were from New Hampshire, I made a lucky guess."

"The artist was my father," Chester said.

"There you are," said Trace, beaming.

Chester opened the doors to the club. Trace seemed momentarily startled by the din and commotion and by the opulence before him. He blinked at the chandeliers, the stratifications of marble and velvet and mahogany, the fireplaces, the candles, the crowd of gentlemen flushed with risk and sport and ladies—or women—on their arms, at the croupiers and gliding waiters, at the whole bracing fever of chance.

Trace had to leap forward to match strides with Chester, who was nodding to the majordomo and walking across the marble floor toward the grand staircase. The majordomo met them and asked if they'd be gaming or wanting a meal, or both, and Chester said in a low voice he was there to see Dr. Whitehouse, whom he understood to be accommodated in the upper rooms. The majordomo nodded and gave him the room number. Chester motioned for Trace to come along with him.

"So what is it that you want, Mr. Trace?" he asked as they ascended the wide, curving staircase that gave Trace the feeling he was not climbing, but rather floating upward.

"Permission, sir. I have a good deal of it already, but I need yours to make it complete."

"What sort of permission?"

"To be the cable expedition's official documentarian."

As they went upward, Trace outlined his case, how he'd approached Spude and Field, both of whom were favorably disposed to the idea but each of whom thought he should check with Ludlow.

"Well," said Chester, stopping before one of the rooms. "I'll certainly give it consideration."

"Good, sir," said Trace. "I'll leave you some samples of my work." He thrust a packet toward Chester. "I hope you'll look favorably on them. Your expedition promises to be a singular moment for our age. I think its progress should be ably recorded. I believe I am the man to do it."

At that moment, Edward Orange Wildman Whitehouse opened the door before them. He was a broad expanse of undone collar, loosened cravat, flyaway hair, shirttails, and, most strikingly to the two men in the hall, no trousers.

"Oh. I say. You're not the champagne at all. I heard voices. I thought it was the boy with the champagne," Wildman Whitehouse said, looking over the pair. He began to laugh, and by directing his next words over his shoulder, he made it clear to the men at his door that he had someone else in the room. "It's Ludlow," he trumpeted in his shrill jay voice. "With a friend."

"I'm—I'm just leaving," said Trace, stepping back. "Beg your pardon."

"Leaving?" Whitehouse said.

"My fault, Whitehouse," Chester said. "We were discussing business on the way here."

"Business?" Whitehouse said. He rocked a little on his heels.

Trace glanced at Chester, trying to catch his eye and signal farewell when instead he caught a glimpse of someone moving behind Whitehouse in the room.

"Well, come in, Ludlow. No harm. Come in. Sorry you can't stay, sir," Whitehouse said to Trace. "We were hoping you were the champagne."

As Whitehouse stepped back enough to allow Chester to enter, he revealed that the other person in the room was a woman who was pulling on a robe and who, once she had its sash knotted, looked up to reveal the quizzical and delicately scarred face of Maddy.

Trace involuntarily raised his right arm, and whether it was to wave a greeting or to fend off the sight of the girl, he couldn't have said. Maddy looked as shocked as Trace and was perhaps about to say something or maybe signal Trace when Whitehouse slammed the door.

"Most unusual time to do business, my boy," Whitehouse said to Chester. "With that fellow or with me. You must be working round the clock. You'll excuse the young lady and me for being in somewhat of a state of dishabille. Better that than in flagrante, eh? Now, run along, pet."

The young woman smiled at Chester, who remained stiffly near the door. He reckoned he had blushed several colors since first stumbling upon this goatish tableau. Whitehouse, meanwhile, was gathering up clothes from around the sitting room, climbing into some trousers, and wrapping himself in a large, red silk robe.

"Business," he said, chuckling. "We were about business here as well, weren't we, little–," and as the young woman walked slowly past Whitehouse, he whacked her buttocks. "I said *run* along," he snarled. Her eyes flared at him, and in a surprisingly quick and vehement move, his hand shot out to grab her upper arm. He fairly hissed at her to "disappear," and she glided away toward the bedroom with a frozen expression on her face, a look of set, obdurate endurance. It was a moment that seemed to darken the otherwise farcical sequence of events. It left Chester uneasy and slow to respond when Whitehouse turned and asked what his business was.

"Well, sir," he said. "Well, sir, am I to infer from messages that I've received from Mr. Spude and Mr. Field that you are not planning to accompany us when we set out to lay the cable?"

"Ahhhh," said Whitehouse, nodding and sinking into a chair. "Ah, yes." His expression was one of a man about to break unavoidable bad news over which he has utterly no control. "I'm terribly sorry, but I'm afraid, you see, it's a matter of health."

Chester shifted the packet of Trace's drawings in his hands.

"You see," said Whitehouse, "I am suffering from several maladies, any one of which would seem insignificant unto itself but which in aggregation make a sea voyage perilous or at the very least so discomfiting as to make my abilities to attend to tasks nil."

"You are *ailing?*" Chester asked incredulously.

"In a word," said Whitehouse.

"With what, may I ask?"

"A bit of gout. A bit of dropsy. A predilection for debilitating seasickness . . ."

"And is this"—Chester gestured to the room and to the bedchamber where the young woman had gone—"treatment?"

Whitehouse shrugged, squirmed, ducked his head, and nodded contritely but with a sheepish smirk. It was clear he enjoyed being seen as a randy old satyr. "Treatment," he chuckled. "Well, I suppose it is. You see, *this* is not a sea voyage. Far from it. *This* is good for the humors. But the perils of a sea voyage . . . ," and Whitehouse gave a stagy shudder.

"So, you're not going."

"I'm dreadfully sorry."

"Dr. Whitehouse, we are using your receiving instruments. We will be employing your induction coils. It is well-nigh imperative that you be with us."

Chester had tried to keep his voice in check, but his temper was beginning to heat up. Whitehouse perceived this and met it with his own obstinacy.

"Oh, not so, my boy. You'll do just fine. Aren't *you* the finest engineer America has to offer?"

"I've never made that claim."

"You just have others make it for you?"

"What does *that* mean?"

"Don't you read your own press notices? Perhaps you should. It never hurts. I view reading my own press as akin to checking one's self in the mirror every morning. See yourself as others see you. In your case, your public self is most exalted."

It occurred to Chester that Whitehouse, amateur electrical engineer though he was, had gotten his nose out of joint because he resented being a co-electrician-projector on the expedition. He had the patents and the contracts for the equipment, but he also wanted the renown. The haughty doctor was feeling left out.

Well, let him be, thought Chester.

"Very well," Chester said. "You have my deepest sympathy for your acute and projected sufferings. You have my wish for a speedy recovery. You seem to be nursing yourself amply. I suppose I shall be finding myself another co-electrician-projector."

Whitehouse shook his head. "No. You won't. I retain that title along with my interest in the syndicate and my contract to have my equipment employed and remunerated for sending and receiving messages. I am still your partner. Just not on the high seas."

"How fortunate for us both," said Chester, heading for the door. As he grabbed his hat, he noticed the young woman floating out from the bedchamber. Whitehouse flicked his hand at her to retreat and remain invisible. She faded back into the room.

"Bon voyage," Whitehouse said as Chester went out the door.

In the hall, Chester threw the bundle of drawings onto the carpet in exasperation. Maybe it was for the best that the imperious and manipulative Whitehouse was staying ashore. Still, it meant the full brunt of engineering calculations and tasks would fall on Chester. Should anything go wrong out in the middle of the ocean, he would have no one with whom to hold council. He wasn't sure he was prepared for that. He needed time to think, and Whitehouse's truancy was just one more irritation in a line of problems that were piling up around him and making him less confident.

He bent down to pick up the bundle of drawings and saw the journalist Jack Trace watching him from an alcove halfway down the hall. Trace banged into the wall as he tried to back into a retreat.

"You're still here?" Chester said.

"Yes. And you?" Trace pointed at the bundle still on the floor.

"I'm terribly sorry about this," Chester said as he stood up and smoothed out the brown paper wrapping around the packet he'd flung. "Business pressures, you see. I forgot myself. I meant it as no judgment on your work. I haven't even had the pleasure of considering them."

"No doubt," Trace said. "Well, I must be going." His coat made a zinging sound as he brushed along the flocked wallpaper and headed toward the stairs.

It suddenly occurred to Chester that this man, this journalist, might have been listening in at the door.

"My good man," he said, "*why* are you still here?"

"Well, you see . . ." Trace looked abashed and almost stumbled in panic. "I'm—I'm afraid I may have already made the acquaintance of . . . ," and he nodded toward Whitehouse's door.

"Listen, Mr. Trace," Chester said, "perhaps the less said about this encounter—the one you had with all of us here at the door—the better. I don't know what you know now or what or whom you knew beforehand, but I think— Well, let me propose this: Suppose you *do* become our documentarian? Suppose I hire you herewith?" He extended his hand. "You are on our team. Fair enough?"

Trace was pulling himself together. The shock of seeing Maddy alive, of standing so close to her, the consternation at knowing she was with that muttonchopped man he'd first seen on the *Great Eastern*, the humiliation of being found in the hall, all those shocks and blows were tumbling backward in his brain as he realized he was being made an offer. He didn't know what Ludlow knew or what Ludlow thought *he* knew. Still, here was the chance to sail with the cable expedition. He'd sort out his feelings later.

"Fair enough," he said, and shook Chester's hand.

"Very well," Chester said. "I'll inform you of our sailing. You will have exclusive rights to illustrate our expedition."

Chester took Trace's card, which had been tucked in the twine binding the packet. He gave the drawings back to Trace.

"I've accepted you sight unseen, so to speak," he said as he handed the pictures over. "And you have done the same." He made a nod toward Whitehouse's room. "Understood?"

Trace looked toward the door. "Sight unseen," he said.

Both men descended the stairs, passed through the gambling tumult, and went out into the night, where they bade each other adieu and headed in opposite directions in the dark air, which, Chester noted, had once again regained its stench.

CHAPTER X

BETWEEN AMERICA AND THE INFINITE

Maine, Spring 1858

The Trail of Clarity

For Franny, the lecture couldn't have come at a more fortuitous time. She had stayed in her bed for two days after the incident in the Spirit Room. She had felt too weak to rise. She had an overpowering need for solitude and quiet, as if her psyche, like an eardrum subjected to too loud a noise, were ringing and needed time and silence to recover. She slept, and when she awoke she lay abed, numb.

Franny did ask once, when Mrs. Tyler brought in some food and the paper, hoping to rouse her, how Otis was; she said she hoped to speak with him.

"He's not about, dear," Mrs. Tyler had said. "I haven't seen him."

Franny raised herself off the pillow and looked around distractedly. Mrs. Tyler settled her back down.

"I'll find him. I'm sure he's around. Must be I've just been coming when he's been going. That often happens with me and him."

But Mrs. Tyler hadn't seen him, and she didn't find him. His room looked untouched. Mrs. Tyler suspected Otis's absence might have something to do with Franny's malaise. She began suspecting Franny and Otis of something very unspiritual.

The advertisement in the paper revived Franny. There was an engraving set amid the text. It showed a woman sitting at a small table, her hands poised in the air just above the table's surface; a wheel with counterweights and a circumferential etching of alphabet letters stood on a frame nearby. The wheel seemed to be attached to the table with a spindly system of articulated armatures, hinges, and springs. A needle on the wheel's hub pointed to the letters around the circle's rim, like a roulette wheel. The engraving's caption read:

THE SPIRITSCOPE

and below said,

> Dr. Hermes's Mechanism to Prove
> the Existence of
> Spirits

There would be a demonstration in two days at the Seamen's Hall in Portland. Dr. Zephaniah Hermes, spiritualist and inventor, would be in attendance. Additionally, the advertisement promised that the audience would witness contact with the "Other World"; that previous audiences, from Chicago to Charleston to Boston, had heard "direct proclamations from Benjamin Franklin, Emanuel Swedenborg, and Plato"; that Portland ("a city of easternmost situation and prime electrical positioning") would be a likely contact point

BETWEEN AMERICA AND THE INFINITE!!!

Franny was on her way to Portland the next morning. She felt compelled to see this exhibition, to compare it with whatever had happened to her in the Spirit Room. She had begun, as she lay in her room, to doubt her sanity. What *had* she seen? Had Otis induced the vision through mesmerism or some other manipulation of her psyche, or was that specter of the little girl really her daughter returned?

Franny hoped Otis was well. When she returned she would see him and report her findings to him, describe to him what she'd seen in the

Spirit Room and whatever she learned at Dr. Hermes's demonstration.

Mrs. Tyler was astonished by Franny's sudden recovery. Franny told her nothing about her purpose in going to Portland, just that she was going and would be needing Gil to drive her. She dressed quickly, packed a bag for a stay of a night or two, and had him bring the wagon around.

It was after Franny and Gil had disappeared down the drive and were well out on the Portland Road that Mrs. Tyler noticed the advertisement tucked into Franny's dresser mirror. She took it down and read it carefully. She was still fingering it in her apron pocket when later, out among the juniper bushes by the wash line near the cemetery plot with the small headstone, she found Otis Ludlow awakening.

Otis couldn't answer Mrs. Tyler's queries as to how long he'd been lying there. He had to ask her what day it was, and even then his mind was too fuzzy for him to calculate.

"Are you all right?" Mrs. Tyler asked.

Was he all right? His head throbbed. His mouth was dry. His saliva was the texture of mortar. His body ached from lying in the dew. Besides being thirsty, he was overpoweringly hungry. Was he all right?

"I'm all right," he mumbled.

"Well, I'll just leave you then," Mrs. Tyler said.

Otis was sitting upright now, his legs projecting out straight like a child sitting in beach sand. "Wait!" he called. "How is Mrs. Ludlow?"

"Gone," Mrs. Tyler said.

Otis twisted around to look at Mrs. Tyler, who had begun hanging laundry on the line. Sun crashed into his eyes. Mrs. Tyler was a round silhouette behind a damp sheet.

"She left for Portland this morning."

"Portland? Why?"

"Didn't say." Mrs. Tyler thought of the newspaper clipping in her pocket. She was tempted to tell Otis that she suspected Franny had left to see Dr. Hermes's lecture-demonstration; she was tempted to ask Otis what *he* knew about spirits, including the spirits of the drowned kin of a fisherman's wife, but she held her tongue. Forbearance was best, she thought, in light of what she intended to do.

"Was she well?" Otis asked.

"She recovered enough to rouse out of bed and be on her way by seven."

"She'd been ill?"

"She'd been bed-bound, if that's what you mean. As to ill, I couldn't say. Perhaps *you'd* know more about that. She said it was the heat. She looked pale. Pale as if she'd seen a ghost."

Mrs. Tyler ducked back behind the sheet she was hanging up. She'd surprised herself by that last remark. Otis had twisted around to look at her. She was pleased she'd managed to provoke him at the mention of ghosts. She felt for the torn edge of the newspaper advertisement again.

Otis turned back and rubbed his head, pulled his legs under himself, and slowly stood up. The gentle sea breeze was enough, he thought, to blow him over.

He left Mrs. Tyler at the laundry line and walked back to the house. He remembered he had walked Franny to the landing on the stairs outside her bedroom and had received her assurances that she would be all right. There was something about that moment, though, the two of them standing there, both of them having been through something: him still under the influence of the fungal compound, and she? . . . She had looked at him with a countenance of fear and some kind of longing and understanding so deep that it had frightened her. He remembered feeling that in looking at her face, he was staring into a chasm that bade him leap. But it was her sudden cry and her turning away into her room and locking the door that had snapped his intoxicated brain back, and he'd gone to the Spirit Room to see if he could find any traces of what Franny had witnessed.

He had walked slowly about the room, moving, stopping, moving again most tentatively, looking as if he were in a child's game and someone was about to spring out at him at any moment. The compounds in his bloodstream had made everything appear as if through poorly annealed glass. Parts of his vision seemed out of focus, other parts abnormally clear. He walked about, intrigued. He began to sense that the place he could see the clearest was behind the chair he'd sat in during the séance, the place Franny had become fixated upon when she'd had her vision. The very air there seemed to pulse with the utmost definition, even in the dim candle-light. It was as if the revenant had left a trail, and the drug now made it clear for him. The rest of the world seemed blurred and shadowy, but Otis could see the trail the spirit had left. It led to the French doors. He went there. It led out across the piazza. Otis opened the doors and followed. The path of whatever it was wended its way through the heather. Otis stepped up. He was barely aware that the waning moon was draped with clouds, that it was late, sometime in the early-morning hours. All was quiet but for the murmuring of the sea down on the rocks.

The strange, unblurred path of acuity went, he could see, some two hundred yards to the cliff's edge. The realization brought Otis up short; the shock caused him to laugh aloud.

"Oh, no," he'd said, shaking his head. "I'm not going there. Clever child. I'm not going there."

And he'd stridden back across the dew-soaked grass, hunched with his arms folded and clenched against his torso as if holding himself together. "Not there," he muttered.

He had walked the rest of the night and the better part of the next day inland, north and west, aimlessly following byways and farm lanes. He'd become so lost in thought, it was early afternoon before he realized that the intoxicant had worn off and that the whorled and swirling refractory his vision had become was settling back to its customary aspects. He asked a farmer for directions and found he had more than a twenty-mile return trip, even going by the most direct roads. The man gave him a wagon ride to the nearest highway and pointed Otis in the proper direction.

As he'd made his way back to Willing Mind, Otis realized that although he had only a scant perception of what Franny might have seen that night, he knew what *he* had seen. The trail of clarity, the spirit's path, had been leading him directly to the sea. Betty had been calling to him as she had the day she died. Otis began to see it as a pattern. There was a construct at work, a destiny: the Ludlows and the sea. His father had drowned, the old artist's spirit and his paints flowing downriver into the sea. Betty had plunged into the sea. Even Chester—the lucky one, the brother without the curse of the "accesses"—even Chester was engineering a way to uncoil his genius under the sea. And Otis himself . . . if Otis hadn't fled from that path of clarity placed there by Franny's vision of Betty, he might have pitched himself into the ocean.

Franny's vision. Another thing had come clear to Otis as he'd walked through the night: if he stayed too long at Willing Mind, he and Franny could very well become lovers.

He'd come to this conclusion as he'd trudged along the last moonlit path that worked up the sidelands of Willing Mind. The house had loomed darkly above him on the rise toward the sea bluffs. Moonlight glinted upon the upper windows. The clothesline showed against the sky and made Otis think of telegraph wires. He hadn't even contacted his brother to say that he was at Willing Mind. He wondered if Franny had. They'd been living in such austere proximity, truly like a pair of anchorites, that he'd had no knowledge of her day-to-day thoughts. He didn't know to what degree Franny felt the pull, perhaps not at all, but he felt it in himself. He was not about to let it win out. Flight was the only honorable recourse.

As he looked at Willing Mind, the idea of leaving it, of striking out alone again, of traveling without destination, weakened Otis so that he had to sit down. He was some fifty yards from the house. He'd begun to think of this monastery he'd created as a home. He'd thought he'd been on the verge of making peace with his niece's spirit. He thought when his brother's telegraph success was complete, he'd be able to live here, part of a family of engineers, adventurers, spiritualists. But he knew now it couldn't be. He knew what the path of clarity meant. He knew the stirrings he'd felt on the stair landing. He knew he had to leave. So he lay down in despair and resolve, curled like a snake, and fell asleep near Betty's grave, where Mrs. Tyler found him the next day.

He was fumbling around in the kitchen, looking for something to eat when he came across the advertisement with the headline

SIBERIA!!!

in the paper that Franny had left in the kindling box. The advertisement wanted men to report to Portland that week. Although the headline, the name of that distant Russian wasteland, had caught his eye, it was the text that truly set Otis to thinking.

Telegraphy

read the subheading. An entrepreneurial venture was proposing to construct an overland telegraph line from America to Europe via Alaska, Siberia, and western Asia. This would be the "shortest possible connection between America and the neighboring continents: across the Bering Strait. (Avoiding a long transatlantic crossing and relying on more proven overland technology.) *Help Us Achieve This Victory!!!*" The ad was a call for laborers, loggers, mule skinners, engineers, key operators, any able-bodied men. Over the course of his life Otis had answered scores of such jack-of-all-trades advertisements. This one, like all of them, promised hard work, high pay, and adventure in distant lands. This one, unlike all of them, was for work on a telegraph. But not on the ocean—a telegraph line dedicated to *avoiding* the ocean.

Otis tore out the ad and pocketed it, thowing the rest of the paper back into the wood box. He bathed, shaved, saddled a horse, and rode to Portland. He was in too much of a hurry to notice that he'd passed Mrs. Tyler south of Falmouth, riding to Portland herself in a neighbor's borrowed buggy.

The Spiritscope and the Bar Fight

The demonstration was not what Franny had expected. She had not expected the numbers in the audience. She thought perhaps only a few eccentric types would show (for she knew that what she was about was an eccentricity by any normal person's lights): a few lonely, elderly women perhaps and a handful of the more radical men from the Unitarians.

Instead, the hall was packed. As Franny had walked along Fore Street near the Customs House, she'd seen the carriages and horses converging; she'd heard the clatter of hoofs and wheels coming up the cobbles behind her. Inside, the gaslit hall was buzzing and ebullient.

The preponderance of the audience was women: eager, anticipatory, enthusiastic women. This surprised Franny and excited her. She had come here alone from Willing Mind, from her monastic term, from her solitary—or nearly solitary—search for her daughter, from the troubling but enthralling vision she'd had—or *thought* she'd had—from a bed wherein she'd lain numb for two days and nights and had even wondered about her sanity, and here she was confronted immediately with a roomful of people who *knew*.

They didn't know her (although Franny had recognized several faces from Portland and Falmouth society, wives of men Chester had done business with), and they certainly didn't know what she had experienced over the past several weeks. And yet, never had she felt such an understanding when among a gathering of people. She had been an actress; she had prided herself on being able to intuitively sense what mood an audience was in and being able to play, to manipulate, that mood. But here she was subject to the audience's disposition herself, had taken on its temperament almost the instant she stepped into the hall. These people were seekers, too. They were kindred souls. Franny found herself greeting people around the hall as if they were all her familiars. Eyes sparkled; smiles shone.

On the walls of the Seamen's Hall were floor-to-ceiling murals depicting a panorama of sea labors: men fishing, men reefing sails on stormy swells, lobstermen hauling traps, and along the shore that was depicted near the back of the hall, clammers digging in the flats, while on a bluff high above, a wife and two children stared into the wind and out to sea, looking for a husband's, a father's, sail. While the men toiled in the scenes along the side walls, the woman seemed to be staring straight out over the heads of the crowd to the stage. Below her gaze the heads of the audience moved, nodded, and chirruped in anticipation.

On the stage, sheets covered some kind of apparatus that must have been the Spiritscope. The white percale rose in peaks. It was draped and pulled taught over some crazy armature. There were large bouquets of flowers in floor vases on each side of the proscenium. And at center stage stood a lectern to which at precisely eight o'clock a large woman in a floral dress approached. The room grew quiet.

Down near the docks, Otis Ludlow walked toward Milk Street. He was cursing himself because he was late. He should never have stopped at the observatory. He had come into town around the Back Cove, rode up Munjoy Hill, and, seeing the observatory tower, couldn't resist a look toward the mountain.

As he was about to set off on another journey, perhaps to the other side of the globe, it made sense to check the pivot point of his life, to see if it was still secure. He climbed the stairs to the enclosed wooden tower's observation floor.

It was a clear, calm evening, and no harbor watchman was on duty in the tower. Otis had the little room to himself. Mount Washington was there to the west, reclined on a blanket of haze. It looked longer and lower than it had when he'd seen it covered with snow, the day he'd first returned to Maine from the Pacific. The sun, a large, red, westering disk, hung near the peaks. Otis pressed his forehead into the wood of one of the window muntins.

Looking to the west, he had begun again to ponder what Franny had seen during their séance. Something had happened to her. He ached to stay and learn what it was, but there was no home for him here.

The mountain began to fade in the twilight; a darker shade of purple than the sky, Mount Washington was becoming one with the air, disappearing like an apparition, a ghost fleeing at the cock's crow, cutting him loose.

He had to race down the observatory's narrow wooden steps—careful so his one eye's depthlessness wouldn't trip him—and hurriedly make his way toward the tavern—Barrett and Crane's—listed on the bottom of the advertisement.

He burst into the barroom. It appeared empty. The long, narrow pub was poorly lit and had a semicircular bar projecting from the side wall and resembling the blunted prow of a barge. The barkeep—Barrett or Crane—was a short man with black, spit-curled hair that twisted down onto his brow like two lobster claws. He was frowning as he carved with a penknife at a slender piece of wood about as long as his forearm. He told Otis that the gentleman looking for telegraph workers had left. He never looked up from the intricate lacework carving he was doing on the wood.

Otis asked him if there'd been many men signing up. The barkeep still didn't look at him. Not a one, was the reply. Would the man be back? The ad said today was the last day. Would you draw a man a beer? Coming right up. And the barkeep laid the club down on the bar and turned to the taps.

Otis noticed that the club was carved into the figure of a woman, naked, save for an entwining fishnet that draped around her nether parts. He was about to reach out and touch the carving when the barkeep clapped the beer down in front of him and again took up the piece of wood and his knife.

Standing at the curved bar, taking his first draft of the beer, Otis took a look at the advertisement that he'd spread on the bar. The paper put him in mind of all the other musters or shape-ups he'd endured over the years. He'd missed some, as he had today, and he'd always bounced to another crew, another job, another ship. His life was made of a multitude of such capricious events. The randomness used to intrigue him; now it left him with a hollow feeling. His optimism was leaking away as fast as he could pour beer down his gullet.

"You, sir."

It was a gruff voice from a table in the shadows at the back of the room. The tavern's front windows faced west, but the day's light had drained from the sky and Barrett or Crane had not yet lit the room's gaslights, so the pub's far wall with its tables and dark oak paneling was a grotto of shadows. The voice had come up from the depths. Otis had been in enough taverns to know the speaker had been there drinking for some time.

"You, sir," the voice repeated. Barrett or Crane had left his carving and the knife on the bar and had gone to the back room, where he was rumbling an empty keg out toward the alley. Otis was the only person to whom the voice could be addressed. He turned toward the dimness and touched the bill of his cap to the figure in the shadows.

"I know you," said the voice.

"It could be you do," said Otis, "but until I see you, I'm ignorant as to whether I know you."

"You know me." The voice had altered downward in register; it had a phlegmatic rumble.

"Well, friend, may I buy you a drink?"

"No, thank you. And I am no friend."

"Well . . . may I have the honor of knowing whom I am addressing?"

"Such honor as it may be, I wouldn't throw away on the likes of you."

The man stood up now and advanced. He was larger, if not taller, than Otis, and he moved side to side as if balancing in a dory or trying to trim the alcohol sloshing in his head. When he came into the light, Otis could see it was Gil Tyler.

"Why, Gil! What do you mean?"

"I mean," said Tyler, "you have put my wife, sir, and me as well in an untenable position." Tyler's barrel chest was heaving; his hands, at his sides, were flexing open and closed. He had worked up his agitation while sitting and watching Otis at the bar. Seeing the man's labored breathing made Otis's own breath come faster. A tingling itch ran up and down his arms.

"You had best explain yourself, Gil."

"No, sir. The explaining's all yours to do. You have played with the honor of your brother's wife. You have done it under his roof. Under our care. You have insulted us—my wife and me—to say nothing of casting a pall upon your family's honor."

Otis could see, could *smell*, the man was drunk. Gil's eyes were fixed on some spot in the air about a foot in front of Otis.

"Gil, I fear there's been a terrible misunderstanding."

"No, sir. There has not. I've seen what you're doing. Edwina has seen. We've *both* seen. And it is going to stop. It is unconscionable."

Tyler stepped closer to Otis, forcing Otis to edge backward until he felt the gentle pressure of the bar's mahogany gunwale in the small of his back.

"Just what is unconscionable, Gil?"

"Your meddling."

"What meddling?"

"*You* know." Tyler started to sway back and forth as if a motor had begun inside him, a pump churning up bile and pushing blood into his face. Otis felt his own skin prickle with nerves. The feeling made him edgy, almost exasperated.

"I *don't* know, Gil. Perhaps you'd better tell me and make yourself clear."

"*You* know."

Tyler stood there, heaving, swaying back and forth, flexing his hands. In the pause, Otis acted.

"Barkeep!" he called. "Another drink for my friend"—Otis turned away from Tyler to face the bar—"and one for me."

The bartender stuck his head out from the back room; Otis waggled his glass at him.

"I don't want your drink," Tyler said behind Otis. "I don't want his drink. Stay there, Barrett."

"It's Crane," the barkeep said.

"Don't trouble yourself to come out here," Tyler said.

Otis noticed Crane's stare turn dark at the very moment Otis heard a slap behind him. Otis turned slowly. Tyler had grabbed the piece of wood— the bartender's half-carved club—and was slapping it against his palm like a policeman with a nightstick. Otis thought quickly that the knife must still be on the bar.

"Back," Tyler barked to Crane, and Otis heard the barman slide away sideways like a crab scuttling beneath a rock.

"She is like a daughter to me," Tyler said. He began to wring the piece of wood in his hands.

"Franny," Otis said quietly.

Tyler nodded. His abstracted stare seemed even more distant as he focused on some point in the past.

"You are despicable."

"We've been over that, I believe," Otis said.

Tyler's eyes locked on Otis's now, tiny pinpoints of ire.

"Look, Gil, I think I know what's troubling you, and I can assure you it didn't happen."

"What didn't?"

"I have not compromised Franny in the least."

"What *else* are you going to say?"

"Gil, we've known each other on and off for years."

"Six. And I've never trusted you."

"Be that as it may—"

"I never knew why your brother trusted you. He was the one who was making something of his life. Still is. And what were you doing? He finds you a job to help you pull your life together—I heard him say it—and the thanks you give him is to run away and come home and work your charms on his wife. And *that's* after you was the one who killed their child!"

"Gil. Shut up!"

Tyler made a growling, expectorating noise.

"And then there's the spiritual swill you are spreading around. You've even got my wife stirred."

"Gil, I've had nothing to do with your wife."

"You've made a fine mess of Willing Mind."

"Gil, I've done nothing dishonorable. I stand by my actions."

The blow came from Otis's blind side, literally. Gil Tyler swung the stick at the right side of Otis's head. Otis had a sense of sudden movement, Tyler's left shoulder dipping abruptly, but the only thing he truly sensed was the flail-like blow of the stick across the side of his head and the flash of light he thought he saw with his blind, right eye.

The blow forced Otis nearly to his knees, with one hand up in the air. Tyler caught the hand across the knuckles with the backswing of the club, spinning Otis upward and into the bar. Otis could taste the blood in his mouth and thought he heard a crackling sound, something broken probably in his jaw or ear. His thoughts bifurcated into a fear that he'd be not only blind but deaf now on that side of his head and into a certainty that another blow was about to follow.

He pushed himself sideways, sweeping his hand along the bar, where he felt the knife handle smack into his palm. The blow meant for his head crashed against the bar, smashing the beer glass and making Gil Tyler grunt, then howl.

Otis spun around and dove for Gil Tyler's legs. The force of his dive sent both men sprawling out into the center of the room. Otis worked fast. He scrambled up Tyler's body, knife in hand. Tyler was gasping on his back, the wind knocked out of him.

Before Tyler could move, Otis had clawed his way up and had the knife at Gil's throat. Otis looked at the point of the small blade and held it carefully against the skin. All his focus was on that tiny knifepoint and the dimple it made in Gil's flesh. The point was perfectly still, and around it Otis could feel the pulsing of both their hearts, their lungs, their rage.

"Gil," Otis rasped, "I did *nothing*."

Tyler wheezed. His eyes rolled in his head, straining to see the knife.

Otis repeated what he said. Repeated it once more. Finally Gil's eyes stopped rolling. Otis could feel the old man's heaving chest settle into a more regular, if exercised, rhythm. A pair of blood droplets dripped from Otis's face into Tyler's beard.

"You," whispered Gil Tyler on a cloud of whiskey fumes. "You have made a mess."

"That may be, man, but I did nothing, *nothing*, dishonorable."

Tyler's eyes narrowed in defiance.

"I *saw* her," he said.

"What?" Otis said, and had to press his face closer to the old man's. Now Otis was looking into Gil's eyes, watery, blue puddles, made perpetually moist by the years on the sea and behind the bottle. *"Who?"*

"I saw her," Gil said quietly. He swallowed, and Otis felt the cartilage in Gil's throat move the knife. "I saw the girl. On the cliff. From my boat."

"When?"

"Three nights ago. She came out of the house. And fell again."

Otis looked away for a moment, distracted by the implications of what Tyler was telling him. Then, repenting his carelessness, he pressed back upon Gil. "You *saw* that?"

Gil nodded. "And you made it happen, didn't you?" Gil said.

"No," said Otis, and then saw Gil's eyes roll and open wide as if following the flight of birds overhead.

But it was Crane whom Gil was watching: Crane vaulting over the bar. He cracked down on Otis's head with a blackjack. Otis remembered a few flickering images: the bar ceiling, the sky, the cobbles. They popped out of the black and red whirlwind in his head before he had a sense of himself lying in a heap outside on a curb in the alley beside Barrett and Crane's. He lay there for a few moments, or perhaps several months, then felt the newspaper advertisement flutter down onto his chest, where he clutched at it as he passed into unconsciousness.

The bar fight had occurred not four streets away from where Franny was wondering whether the Spiritscope was a fraud. That Dr. Zephaniah Hermes was an attractive man obviously helped the illusion. When he strode onstage in his tails and red waistcoat after an introduction by the large woman in the floral dress, a voice from a seat near Franny—a woman's voice—exclaimed in a whispered gasp, "He's gorgeous!"

Dr. Hermes was near forty years old. He had black, almost shoulder-length hair with a streak or two of early gray at the temples. The soft, almost umber tone to his skin lent him a Sephardic or perhaps even a Polynesian aura. He could have come from anywhere on the globe—anywhere but the coast of Maine. His skin gave hints of something tropical or aboriginal or of a Romany tribesman. He looked exceedingly exotic to the audience of pale, northern New Englanders gathered in the Seamen's Hall. His hair swept back as he glided swiftly to center stage. His torso was long and his red waistcoat tight, accentuating his lynxlike movements. His voice was sonorous, entwining, almost droning. Within moments of his thanking the mistress of ceremonies and of his expression of gratitude for the fine turnout, he had the women in the audience palpably enthralled.

Franny thought how Chester, her own husband, must be exercising a similar spell over audiences in England. She had seen the beginnings of it before the Phantasmagorium Show had left for Britain. She sighed audibly.

But Dr. Hermes was most pleasant to listen to as he explained contact with the spirit world and how his machine could prove, by etheric sensitivity and ectoplasmic conductors, that a spirit from the Other World was near at hand.

Franny was comfortably lulled as the doctor—if in fact that's what he was—spoke and seemed to sympathize with each and every woman in the audience and to joke knowingly with each and every man. His stage presence impressed Franny—she felt she was considering him with the cool, appraising eye of a retired professional—but she was surprised when Hermes asked for help from the audience and her hand involuntarily went up and, from the sea of supplicants, he smiled and picked her.

She walked down the side aisle, past the mural of the lobstermen hauling traps, and stepped, light-headed, onto the stage, where Dr. Hermes met her with an outstretched hand.

"Thank you," he murmured.

She nodded, feeling strangely secluded and enclosed by the illumination from the gas footlights—a familiar feeling, one that sent a surprising thrill through her, a happiness that she was back on a stage.

"I chose you," Dr. Hermes was saying after he had led her to a chair near the shrouded Spiritscope, "because I felt you have had some experience with the spirit world. Is that right?"

Franny felt abashed and suddenly overwhelmed by shyness. But she whispered, "Yes."

"She says yes," Dr. Hermes announced to the audience. The house murmured its approval.

"Have you lost a loved one?" Dr. Hermes asked.

"Yes."

"A child? A husband?"

"A child."

"Your . . . ?"

"Daughter."

"She has lost a daughter."

Murmurs of sympathy and regret ruffled through the hall.

"And you have had a sign or signs from this daughter?"

"Yes."

The crowd muttered louder now, more excited.

"Well," said Dr. Hermes, his dark eyes revealing a softness Franny hadn't expected, "we may not witness a return so devoutly to be wished, but clearly you are a worthy subject and an attractor, as we say. You will be a wonderful operator for our Spiritscope. Please, allow me. . . ."

And with a flourish, he swept back the sheets, revealing the spindles, wheels, rods, and wires of the Spiritscope. It looked much as it had in the newspaper illustration. If anything, it was more ornate and complex, appearing as it did to be a congeries of parlor furniture, half-assembled bicycles, baby prams, and fishing gear. The audience shifted and shuffled in their seats to get a better view. A smattering of applause broke out.

Dr. Hermes had Franny place her hands on two palm-sized metal blocks—he called them lozenges—on the smooth surface of the round table before her. Beyond the table was the Spiritscope. Franny sat in profile to the audience as Dr. Hermes explained the mechanism and the operation they were about to undertake. Franny's receptive powers would, if all went well, draw spirits into the hall. The Spiritscope would detect their presence through registrations of the meters and needles. Dr. Hermes would interpret the results for the audience.

He had the house attendants turn down the gaslights. The hall grew dim. The crowd rustled in the darkness. The doctor requested silence. He achieved this almost instantly and to such a degree that Franny could hear the bell in the City Hall clock tolling three blocks away. A chair or two creaked; someone coughed; a horse and wagon clopped by outside.

Dr. Hermes stepped near her. She could smell a cologne on him as he passed his hands before her face. It was a pleasant, grassy scent. He told her to relax . . . relax, to focus on the candle he had lit on a pedestal that stood across the stage from her and the Spiritscope. Watch the flame . . . feel the light curl around your head, soothing your brain, entering through the portals of your eyes . . . watch it . . . see but do not heed the shadows of my hands as I pass them across your vision. . . . Are you feeling anything?

"Sleepy," Franny said. "A little sleepy."

"Good. Tell yourself you're sleepy but that you won't fall asleep. . . ."

Franny nodded. She did feel sleepy, but more than that she felt profoundly relaxed by Dr. Hermes's ministrations. When had she felt so at peace? Certainly not since Chester had left. Even before, not since Betty had died. Perhaps before that. She had a brief recollection of sitting with her infant daughter on the bluffs, the babe nursing, sunlight on the waves, Chester off happily building some project around Willing Mind. Domestic bliss. That was peace. Perhaps it had never happened?

There was a murmur in the audience. Pay no attention, Dr. Hermes whispered to her; someone out there had fallen asleep.

And it was true. Two or three women had succumbed to Dr. Hermes's suggestive voice. Gentlemen near them fanned the women with their programs. The rest of the audience, stirred by the doctor's provocative power, inclined forward in their seats.

But Franny knew nothing would happen. She knew because what Dr.

Hermes was conjuring here was nothing like what Otis had done back at Willing Mind. And *that* had worked. She was keyed up back then; she had felt her receptivity right in her skin as if she had become lucent herself and was beaming a signal to Betty as a lighthouse might to a ship at sea. If anything, here in the Seamen's Hall, she was settling into herself, signaling nothing, relaxing into a comfortable pliability.

Then she felt movement. Her hands were moving. Her hands that were on the metal lozenges on the round table were moving.

"You feel movement," Dr. Hermes was saying. He phrased it less as a question to her than as a bulletin to the audience.

"Yes," she said.

"In your hands."

"Yes."

"She feels movement in her hands."

The audience picked up the urgency in his voice. There were exclamations of excitement.

"You are not controlling these movements?"

"No."

"Do not resist them."

Franny nodded.

"Keep your eyes on the candle, please." Dr. Hermes had seen Franny's eyes waver. She had noticed something. His foot seemed to be manipulating a treadle or a wheel that was on the floor and that was shrouded by black cloth from the audience. His foot moved, and she felt the lozenges on the table move.

"The needle is moving," Dr. Hermes announced to the audience. "We are getting a reading! Please! We must have quiet."

The audience, straining to contain itself, watched, rapt.

"Is it your daughter?" Dr. Hermes asked.

"I don't know," Franny said.

Now a rapping sound came from under the stage. The audience gasped. Franny felt an excitement herself. Not from any belief that a spirit—Betty's or anyone else's—was at hand, but from an appreciation of the illusion and from Dr. Hermes's showmanship. The audience was in his power.

"I think . . ." Franny said.

Dr. Hermes leaned closer. "Yes?"

"I think it is she."

"Your daughter!"

Franny nodded. She couldn't resist seeing what would happen, couldn't resist joining the performance herself. The audience gasped audibly. A woman began to weep.

"The needle reads it is so!" Dr. Hermes said.

The rapping was louder now. A singing—a wordless intoning was more like it—a woman's voice or a man's high tenor, seemed to come from all around the hall, although Franny was nearly certain it was coming from beneath the stage.

"She wants you," Dr. Hermes said. "She or her attendant spirits have returned!"

The audience was nearly frantic with pent emotion. Several people applauded. A man yelled, "Hallelujah!" More than one woman wept, and several more fainted. Franny could feel the mood in the hall approach the breaking point. It was as if Dr. Hermes had conducted an orchestra to a crescendo and the instruments were about to fly out of the musicians' hands.

In the tumult, Franny saw the candle flame flutter in agitation as if from a breeze. In a quick glance she caught a look at Dr. Hermes's foot perceptibly pumping on a pedal. A gush of air tickled her neck, and the flame went out. The rapping stopped. The voice went silent. The needle on the dial dropped to zero. The lozenges under her hands grew inert. The crowd gasped, rose to its feet, and surged toward the stage.

"Lights, please!" Dr. Hermes was calling. "Lights! Lights!"

Franny fled from the hall. In the confusion she saw Dr. Hermes's dark eyes over the heads of several distraught women. He was looking for her, she knew. She avoided his glance and pushed out the doors. On the steps of the hall she ran into Mrs. Tyler.

"Frances, dear!" the old woman said.

"Were you in there?" Franny asked almost desperately. People were coming out of the hall, distracted, amazed.

"Yes!" said Mrs. Tyler. "I'm so proud of you!"

"Proud?"

Now people were bustling around them. Some were asking Franny questions, imploring her for attention, even pulling on her sleeve.

"Proud!" Mrs. Tyler exalted.

"How are you getting home?" Franny asked, almost having to shout.

"Home?"

The crowd was too much. Franny pulled Mrs. Tyler away, down the steps, and off toward a side street. It was dark enough now that they were able to escape. On the way, Mrs. Tyler, her arm wrapped through Franny's, exclaimed, "I *knew* what you and Mr. Otis were doing, and I must say I was doubtful at first, even dead against it, and I said as much to Gil, whose own opinions in the matter I best not bring up, but the more I thought about it, the more I wondered . . . and then the more I asked you, well, the more I wondered even *more*. I *know* you want to see that little child of yours. And I know she must want to see you. I thought of my own brother and Gil's father and the others that we've lost to the sea, all of them, and how they must want to come home, if only we could find a way to let them in."

"Mrs. Tyler—"

"So I began reading. I even found a newspaper. *The Spiritual Telegraph.* Now isn't that a coincidence? *Spiritual? Telegraph?* Something *had* to be guiding me. I wanted so bad to tell you that I was believing now. Then I saw the ad for Dr. Hermes on your dresser mirror and I knew I had to come and see for myself, and now I've run into you—"

"Mrs. Tyler," Franny said, holding the woman's hands in hers and confronting her directly, almost shouting in her face to get her to stop. "We must get home."

"Oh," said Mrs. Tyler as if snapping out of a trance herself. "Oh."

Gil wasn't supposed to pick Franny up until tomorrow at the hotel.

"How had you planned to get back, Mrs. Tyler?"

"I? . . . Oh. I . . . Well . . ." Mrs. Tyler was addled. "Well, I borrowed a buggy from the neighbors."

Franny gathered her things from the hotel and left word for Gil, should he arrive there the next day, that she'd returned home.

"Good Lord, don't tell him how," Mrs. Tyler said. "He's so against this spiritual stuff, I can't tell you."

It was dawn when they arrived back at Willing Mind, and Franny's head was spinning with new ideas. She had determined that Dr. Hermes's Spiritscope was a fraud, but she was sure she herself had stumbled onto some undeniable truths, truths bigger than she'd expected, truths that kept growing in her mind seemingly by the minute. The light of the new day stimulated her even more. Otis had helped her start on the path. He had brought her to Betty. She needed no gimcrack Spiritscope to verify Betty's presence in her life. Betty—and Mrs. Tyler's stories and Otis and even Dr.

Hermes, even Chester and his work and his absences and his dalliances: all the patchwork of serendipity and circumstance of the past weeks, the past months, perhaps even her whole past life—had brought her to the threshold of something terrifically new.

She embraced Mrs. Tyler with a fervor that surprised the old woman as they bade each other good night or good day. Franny insisted she carry her own bags into the house, and she did, humming, nearly singing, until she found, in the sun-filled main hall of Willing Mind, the packet of mail that had arrived in her absence. A packet that contained a terse letter from Chester giving her the date he expected to arrive in Newfoundland and requesting that, in due course, she proceed there to meet him.

CHAPTER XI

FINAL PREPARATIONS

London and Plymouth, Spring 1858

On the Pier

The hours Chester slept the entire last week of preparation could be counted on two hands. Katerina watched him during the last evenings of the Phantasmagorium Show and was by turns worried and awestruck. She knew he was driving himself mercilessly, and the fatigue showed in his eyes, but the excitement he exuded, the verve as he closed on his goal, were arousing in her a desperation she couldn't deny. She had put herself out of his daily—and nightly—life as a matter of necessity and pride, but she could not put him out of her mind.

Joachim had also become so distracted as to be almost nonexistent to her. Now that she was living in a self-imposed exile from Chester, she spent long hours in her room, looking out the window toward the river. She could hear Joachim's comings and goings.

He had abruptly stopped running. His notoriety as the London Runner, his caricatures in the papers, and now the crowds that had begun to follow him so revolted and offended his hermetic nature that he precipitously quit the mad dashing about the city. Katerina had heard him doing his exercises in his room, but now even that had begun to fall off. He seemed to be up pacing about at all hours of the night and holding meetings with men at all hours of the day. She could hear their rumbling voices and smell the cigar smoke coming into her room under the door.

It was after the final performance of the Phantasmagorium Show that a round Englishman wearing spectacles looking like two disks of isinglass pressed into the bulging dough of his face came up to her and instead of praising her music or her beauty—run-of-the-mill compliments for her of late—he praised her husband. This was a novelty. Katerina was surprised to learn that her very own Joachim Lindt had completely won over the Royal Commission of Sewers with his proposal for a central ordure-disposal system for the city: a complex of subterranean sluiceways and curved-wall ducts that would, in accord with the tides, flush London clean. The bespectacled man was an executive member of the commission, and he beamed with delight as he told Frau Lindt of her husband's accomplishment. She must be extremely proud, the commissioner said, to be married to such a man.

"He creates a marvel like your Phantasmagorium," the commissioner added, "a miracle of imaginative art that elevates our city's culture. Then he turns around and applies that genius to one of the lowliest and most base problems of our city's life. Of course, you know all about his plans, the marvelous schemes he's drawn up."

Katerina had no idea.

Still, she didn't let the commissioner know that. She barely heard the rest of what he was saying. It now seemed to her that all the men around her were on a ship pulling out of the harbor—in Chester's case this was almost literally true—and she was to be left standing alone on the pier. She, who had drawn these men—and others as well—to her. The thought sent a chill down her back. She excused herself and left the party.

The next day she took a train to Plymouth. Chester had moved to a hotel there to be closer to the final preparations. She hired a carriage to take her from the station to the navy docks, and it was there, late in the day, she saw the two ships: the *Niagara* and the *Agamemnon*. The American ship, the *Niagara*, with the Stars and Stripes popping from its highest yard-arm, had almost yachtlike lines and was the largest steam frigate in the world; the British *Agamemnon*, in the same dock but tied to an adjacent wharf, looked massive and dowdy by comparison.

It shocked her to see the size of the ships, the number of men swarming over them, the towering piles of crates and barrels and bales waiting on the wharves to be loaded. Here was a colossus of ambition and vision made manifest before her eyes. Chester, she thought, had been engineering all this, building his own navy, all while seducing her. She felt both gulled and aroused.

Soon a young man in a suit and spats came her way, bearing a sheaf of papers and making a kind of dance of stepping over coiled hawsers and debris on the wharf. He recognized her. He said he was a proctor with the law firm managing the cable syndicate's affairs, and he remembered her from the Phantasmagorium Show. How lovely to see her here. Could he be of help?

She said no, then demurely reconsidered and asked if he could answer a few questions about the ships. Which one has the cable? Where do the men live and work? When do they sail?

"Three days to the last one," he chirped. Then he said he had just come from the *Niagara* and a meeting with Mr. Ludlow. Would she like him to find her fellow *Phantasmagorian*? He delighted himself with his little neologism and was still giggling when she said, No, no. She wouldn't want to disturb Mr. Ludlow, busy as she knew he must be. But might the young proctor himself show her around?

"I have access to the *Agamemnon*, being British," he said. "I'll take you there."

"Wonderful."

And she was given a tour from stem to stern of the mighty old ship. To the young man, Frau Lindt seemed only slightly interested in the 1,300 tons of cable coiled in the specially built tubs in the hold and in the 250 tons wrapped on the deck. The complex paying-out mechanism her fellow Phantasmagorian had devised was only mildly more interesting. She seemed most attentive to the ship's appointments, its cabins and companionways, its galley stores, and its crew's quarters.

Shortly before leaving the ship and her young guide, Katerina caught a glimpse of Chester. He was across the dock on the quarterdeck of the *Niagara*. The evening sun, so close to the solstice, had just popped out from under a gray ledger of clouds near the horizon. The sun shone across the harbor and burnished the rippled water and the rigging of both ships. It made for a moment of luminescence that soothed Katerina's agitated mind. The light was one simple hue—gold—and it came across the world long and bright and straight. A steady breeze blowing in from the sea smelled clean and scrubbed. For the briefest moment nothing seemed complicated to her.

She looked at Chester standing in the light. The glint of his spectacles was visible even to her on the gangway of the *Agamemnon*. She had a strong urge to wave to him, to let him know she was there. Instead, she thanked the young proctor and went ashore to board her carriage.

Chester was on the *Niagara*'s quarterdeck reading a letter that had arrived in a packet of papers.

Willing Mind

My Husband,

Can you forgive my silence? I hope so. My thoughts have been of you often since I last wrote. Much has happened. I wonder how you are, how you occupy your mind, your heart.

I get word occasionally from Mr. Field's office in New York, and I know that you are sailing soon. I hope not before this reaches you. Godspeed, my dear.

Husband, I have news. For one, Otis is here. He returned from Malaya almost immediately after you left for England. He seems changed, but I suppose one would be hard-pressed to complete such an arduous adventure and not be transformed.

It is with some trepidation I essay to tell you that he has become my guide in matters spiritual. I do not mean he offers catechistic instruction or religious training. No, I should have said—and I know you are liable to bridle at this with your engineer's rational intellect—he has become my spiritualist guide.

He learned much while abroad about the art of contacting the Other World. There are levels or planes to our existence, much like rungs on a ladder. Shamanists in Malaya taught him to climb these rungs, my dearest; and now he teaches me. I tell you this because I have seen her. Our beloved little one. I have seen our Betty! And she is well. Even happy! No longer ours, but well nonetheless.

As you hope to send signals down an impossibly long wire under the sea between two worlds, know that I, too, have already received word from another world. Praise be! She is lost to us, though she is in love and light. How can that be bad?

May your mission reach the success mine has here. I eagerly await
your return home, where I remain your faithful and

Your loving wife,
Franny

If Chester hadn't looked out toward the gold-struck horizon and seen how still it was, he would have sworn the *Niagara* was rising on a massive groundswell, such was his reaction to the letter. He didn't know what to make of it. His brother had returned home unannounced, and his wife hadn't told him about it for weeks. His brother was home, and his wife had seen their dead daughter's spirit.

He read the letter again. It made no more sense to him. Reading it again made him more numb. He had sent Franny a brief note a couple of weeks ago telling her when he expected to arrive in Newfoundland, asking her to meet him there. That note and this confounding letter must have crossed in the middle of the ocean.

He looked up and stared at the wharf. His thoughts were a muddle. He could have sworn he saw a woman descending from the *Agamemnon*, a woman dressed much like Katerina.

He turned and looked back out at the western horizon. In three days they would set out to lay the cable to America. The distance they had to cover seemed farther than ever.

CHAPTER XII

WILLING MIND IS EMPTY

Maine, Spring 1858

Willing Mind Is Empty

Willing Mind is empty. It is another sparkling day on the coast of Maine. There is not a cloud in the sky; the ocean is a blue-green lea of furrows as far as the eye can see. A breeze not strong enough to stir whitecaps merely ruffles the water. Groundswells loll below the surface, making the ocean seem to suspire with lazy ease. Three gulls wheel over the rocks, occasionally calling.

Sunlight glints off the glass of the seaward windows of the house, glints off the water, even off the slime and kelp on the rocks below the cliffs. Before noon, Gil Tyler has pulled his traps and reset them for the day and, nursing a hangover, is out by the point, heading toward the harbor. His buoys bob amid the faint trail of bubbles his oars have left on the water's surface.

His wife has dropped off the mail in the main house at Willing Mind and straightened a few last things in the study as instructed by Mrs. Ludlow in her note:

> *Please, Mrs. Tyler, restore my father's study to its original state. Uncover the portraits, reestablish the furniture, &c., &c.*

I am sorry for the haste with which I must leave. Please keep the house in reasonable readiness for our return. As Mr. Ludlow predicts his expedition should be under way by now, I must depart immediately for St. John's even as he is making his way toward us with his cable under the sea.

Mrs. Tyler walks about the house thinking perhaps she will delay going home until the afternoon. Gil has been drinking of late; his mood is always sour. Willing Mind empty on a late spring noon is more peaceful for an old lady with a spiritual curiosity than a fisherman's cottage in the village with an inebriated husband snoring or, worse, ranting.

So Mrs. Tyler sits in a chair in the newly tidied Spirit Room, now returned to its former state as a study. Mrs. Tyler has put it back to rights, making it just as it had been even before Chester moved his things in, back to when Franny's father read and worked there. She sits and looks out at the sea. This was the room, she thinks, where Franny had a visitation from her daughter. Otis helped. He isn't around now; she has no idea where that strange man is. Still, if she looks out at the sea, tries to do what Dr. Zephaniah Hermes told Franny to do at the demonstration, perhaps something will happen.

Dr. Zephaniah Hermes. The name rings in Mrs. Tyler's head. He's her secret. She didn't even tell Franny about it on their night ride home. It is so special.

She had gone directly to the Seamen's Hall that day in hopes of getting a ticket for the evening's lecture-demonstration, and there in the foyer, setting up an easel with a program placard on it, was Dr. Hermes himself. He was so gracious and handsome. He came over and introduced himself. He said he was pleased she was coming to the program, and was she from the area? He asked if she'd had any contact with spirits herself. No? Well, perhaps she knew of a friend who had. And Mrs. Tyler told him all about Franny. Was Franny coming tonight? Well, Mrs. Tyler said she *thought* so, and Dr. Hermes said that would be wonderful and Mrs. Tyler could help the demonstration immeasurably if she would find Franny and point her out to one of the ushers, who would give Franny a choice seat. And for this help would Mrs. Tyler please accept a complimentary front-row seat?

Mrs. Tyler is so extraordinarily impressed and so protective of her special part in Dr. Hermes's program that she still doesn't know if she'll *ever* be able to tell anyone about it. It is her most wonderful secret right now.

Along with her little visits to the study. She has even brought the eyeless doll down because she suspects it has something to do with what Otis and Franny achieved. She sits with the doll in her lap and watches the sea and tries to empty her mind, to clear it for whatever signal may come.

Otis's room is empty, too. Completely empty. He has swept it out, stripped the bed, rolled the mattress up on the bedsprings, and left his dresser drawers to air by pulling them open like an ascending flight of stairs.

He, too, departed in a hurry, before Franny.

The hiring agent for the Siberian telegraph had happened back along Milk Street after visiting the docks and the seamen's bars along Commercial Street. He'd failed to find any candidates interested in travel, adventure, and high pay. Unfamiliar with Portland, he was retracing his evening's route as best he could back to his hotel. This took him past Barrett and Crane's again, where he found the comatose Otis Ludlow lying by the curb with the newspaper ad clutched in his fist. He awakened Otis with some handfuls of water from a nearby horse trough, helped him down the street to another tavern, and bought the headsore man some supper.

The agent needed to make his hiring quota and was desperate to sign Otis on. He was taken aback and moved almost to suspicion by the speed with which Otis took the pen and signed the memoranda of intent and all the necessary codicils.

"Are you *sure* you know what you're doing?" the agent asked, still trying to decipher Otis's skewed gaze.

"I am," said Otis, scanning the papers, signing, scanning and signing. "I've been situating myself in similar endeavors all my life. I only just this winter past returned from a gutta-percha plantation in Malaya."

"And your, ah, injury isn't bothering you?" the agent asked.

"Injury?"

"Or whatever it was that caused you to be indisposed. Out there? In the street?"

Otis laughed. "Not after that fine meal, sir." He was the picture of secretarial efficiency: signing, scanning, signing.

"You weren't, ah, suffering from inebriation when I chanced upon you in, ah . . ."

"The gutter?"

The agent shrugged. "Understand, it is important that there be no false pretenses or misconstructions in the agreement. It's to protect both parties."

Otis fixed him with a firm stare so that the agent at last could focus on the seeing eye. "I *told* you," said Otis. "I barely had one draft of ale when I was drawn into a fight to defend a lady's honor . . . and my own. I was bested, sir, but not belied. I am sober and compos mentis. My head aches and so do I to leave this city, this country, this hemisphere. Your advertisement was perfectly timed. It was Providence that led you back up that alley and perhaps Providence that had some cowardly barkeep smite me from behind and drag me into the street."

"Providence," the agent mumbled. "That's where I'm due next. Then Worcester. This town was a bust. You're my only hire."

"An honor, sir." Otis had finished signing.

The agent looked over the papers. "Ludlow," he mumbled. "There's a Ludlow trying to lay a cable across the Atlantic."

"My brother."

The agent frowned and tucked in his chin. "And you're not helping him?"

"We have led two very different lives. Although I have worked for him in the past, keeping a world between us is wisest. He will lay his cable, I shall string mine. May the best effort win."

The agent now studied Otis. "How do I know you aren't working for your brother still? How do I know you aren't going to work mischief on our telegraph line? That'd be a fine mess for me. My one Portland hire turns out to be a spy related to the competition."

"Tell your superiors to keep their eye on me. Tell them I'm a Ludlow, one of *those* Ludlows. Tell them whatever you want. But tell them you've got a man with a surveyor's license who ran a gutta-percha plantation in Celebes; who's worked railroad and logging crews since the age of sixteen; who survived the dengue fever twice; who lived a year with a Malayan witch doctor, as you no doubt would call him; whose one good eye can see better than any two of theirs; and who can take and send telegraph code upward of thirty words a minute."

The agent smiled faintly as he rested his hands on the papers on the table before him. He'd heard plenty of desperate and destitute men inflate their credentials. It was the agent's job to winnow them, or at least rec- ommend them for the lowest labor crews: "the expendables" was the company's sub-rosa term. But this fellow seemed neither desperate nor destitute. He seemed to be everything he said he was, maybe even more.

The agent considered what to say next as he looked at the back of his hands. "Of course," he began slowly, "perhaps we could look at this a whole *other* way. Perhaps we could look at your being a Ludlow brother as an asset. Perhaps you would use that birthright to *our* advantage. For suitable remuneration, of course."

Otis's hand had moved with such startling speed to the man's windpipe that the agent could have choked from fright as easily as from a lack of air. Otis's voice was steady, almost quiet. He was not about to be thrown out of two establishments in one night.

"All I want is a job, sir. I warrant no suspicion. I've given you my word. Nor will I turn against any other enterprise if I work for you, least of all my own brother's."

He released the agent, who, to his credit, composed himself quickly.

"Well," the agent said, "enough of that. All the papers seem to be in order. You are to report for sailing from Boston in three days' time. Can you make it?"

Otis made it. The note he wrote was still on the kitchen table, where Mrs. Tyler had placed it next to Franny's instructions. Franny had read Otis's note and left it lying about in her distraction. She left Chester's letter out, too. Mrs. Tyler has read them all, placed them side by side, weighing them down with the salt and pepper shakers and the sugar bowl.

Dear Franny—

Otis's note reads,

> *I regret I cannot talk to you further about our explorations, but it has become obvious to me I must leave. My being here, though of great benefit and restorative powers for me, was perhaps a breach of hospitality, if not decorum. We know we have wronged neither each other nor propriety. However, it is clear that others have not seen it so. I will not be a party to the traducement of your good name . . . or my brother's and, by extension, my own. I hope I will someday be able to hear from you about your experience, about your contact with your daughter. You are a woman of exceptional gifts.*

I must go now and employ such gifts as I have, though they seem to be at the moment no more than a talent for movement about this large globe.

Please give my regards to Chester. He has helped me so much of late. I regret I have not had the fitness to remain constantly in his service. He is an exceptional man, your husband, one who is about to make this large globe smaller.

I remain your affectionate

> brother-in-law and
> brother in seeking,
> Otis

The house is empty. The Ludlows, every one of them, are gone. Gil Tyler has rowed around the point, and Mrs. Tyler has roused herself after seeing nothing of her longed-for lost spirits, after falling asleep in her chair in the sun by the study window facing the sea; she has roused herself and trudged home to fix her husband his supper.

The sea sparkles. On the far side of the ocean, ships are weighing anchor and setting sail with tons of telegraph cable in their holds. On this shore, in this place, with no one watching now, a little girl in a white frock might dance through the heather paths and stare in the study windows to where the eyeless doll lies face up on a chair; she spins and twists across the ground and sings a high song that could be the cry of gulls but is not, and she whirls toward the bluffs and toward the precipice and hurls herself once again over the cliff, disappearing into the vacant light of day.

BOOK TWO

OTIS LUDLOW'S JOURNAL

Ireland, 1866

Foilhommerum Bay

Africa is the Dark Continent. America is the New World; Europe, the Old. But what of that quantity of land in Asia? What of Siberia?

It is a hole in the world. A nothingness. A mass so great, so blank, so stupendously absent as to be unattainable by thought or expedition.

For days there have been no comprehensible words from the cable. Meanings unattainable. A nothingness. I can wait. A design will come.

By 1861, I have been in Siberia something more than three years. I had journeyed to the country to devise a telegraph route for the Western Union Extension, also known as the Russo-American Telegraph Company. I was to scout and map a path through northeastern Asia, stringing an imaginary wire across the waste, drawing a transit through the void with the hope that someday the corporation might follow with more surveyors, pole cutters, spools of wire, and able manpower supplied by American money and the native peasantry, and then there would be a telegraph connecting the New World with the Old, America with Europe, coming the long way about, as it were, coming in through Asia by way of the Bering Strait, up from Russian America and British Columbia. It was a thirteen-thousand-mile gamble, a terrible wager, but it was a gamble on terra firma (excepting the short cable beneath the Bering Strait). It was the path of the greatest distance and the least resistance. The path I have always chosen.

For three years I stumped around the territory near the Amoor River mouth north of China and thence farther north to Okhotsk as we scouted the route for the proposed line. I traveled or visited with the main population groups of the Kamchatka Peninsula and the territories to its north and west: the Russians, many of them Cossacks; the Kamchadales of the peninsula; the Settled Koryaks of the Penzhina Gulf; and the Wandering Koryaks of the northern steppes. All these people would be allies in the project.

The climate of Siberia is a punishment and an exaltation. It would be a most exceptional challenge. The Siberian winters are corporeal entities. They envelop one, wear at one, humble one, and—upon occasion—elevate one unto ecstasy. I have seen the cold reach more than one hundred degrees below the freezing of water. It is a cold to which the Koryaks and other natives have learned to adapt but which proves daunting no matter what one's race. I have been buried by a blizzard as I huddled beside my dogsled, having every few minutes to struggle upward and dig myself out so as not to suffocate beneath the weight of the drift. I have been in cold so severe that a fire of "trailing cedar" (the flammable, low, bushlike, vinelike, treelike evergreen of the steppes) with flames towering ten feet into the air was ineffectual, and it was necessary to stand nearly in the conflagration to receive the slightest modicum of warmth. I have had to huddle for days in the yurt of a Settled Koryak while a "poorga"—a Siberian blizzard—blew across the steppes from the pole, a storm so brutal that to stick one's head out the chimney hole atop the yurt—a hole that doubles as the entrance in those peculiar structures—was to place one's head in a line of fire of snow and wind so severe, it was like enduring a continuous fusillade of buckshot.

But then there is the haunting blue snowblink of the Arctic winter, the howl of the wild Siberian wolves at night on the steppes, the aurora borealis, the transporting timelessness of the dark, the stars, the iron cold that rakes the soul like a scourge.

I had sailed during the early summer, once the ice had gone out, from Okhotsk to Petropavlovsk (the town of St. Peter and St. Paul—a small port village on the east coast of the peninsula) to meet with a representative of the Russo-American Telegraph Company who had arrived from San Francisco and was in Asia to receive my reports on the previous winter's route surveillance. I filed the report much to the satisfaction of the representative, Mr. Alden Wickenden, who was then to forward it to Mr. Collins, who was, Mr. Wickenden said, still beating the drum for the Russo-American line in Washington and at last making headway with Mr. Lincoln. My report would be a significant help, I was told. The United States government should be assisting our cause, the war notwithstanding, I was told. In the meantime, would I consider, he asked, continuing my exploratory ventures north of Kamchatka to the Bering Strait? He had authorization from Mr. Collins to requisition funds and supplies for me.

I agreed, with little consideration, but it was a letter from my brother, which Wickenden had brought, that complicated matters. In the letter—nearly two years old by the time I received it—Chester had made the usual inquiries into my health and well-being and had described his travails, in cursory terms, with the transatlantic cable.

"I confess, brother," he wrote, "that I was shocked when I first learned you had offered your surveying and exploratory services to an endeavor that was dead set on competing with and surpassing my own. But, with the way things are here, I can only wish you success."

His account of what happened was remarkable for its opacity. It inveighed against some fellow named Whitehouse but never explained what the fellow had done. He talked of the expedition's scandal and shame, as if knowledge of what he meant was a worldwide commonplace. (He had no idea, I suppose, of the remoteness of Siberia.) The letter was a frustratingly vague polemic on failure. His expedition had ended in defeat—or worse—from the sound of it. He had retreated home, he said. He sounded lost.

CHAPTER XIII

THE EXPEDITION

England and the Atlantic Ocean, June 1858

Irritants

In the final days before the expedition's departure, Chester Ludlow was often irritated. He'd worked almost a week without sleep, though it wasn't the work or fatigue that rankled him. As long as he could keep his mind on the preparations, as long as he could thrive on the pulse-quickening excitement he always felt at the critical stages of any project, he was fine. It was only in odd moments between tasks, when he was away from the fanfare and the banquets and their attendant hoopla; away from the absorbing calculations and messages and late-night paperwork; away from the grinding of the derricks, the sepulchral clanking of the massive yard chains, the shouts of men, and the screams of steam whistles; away from the nasal astringency of the creosote; away from all the filth and industry and intoxicating progress dockside; when he was away from the work and by himself, that was when he was irritated. He could manage the laws of physics and electricity and organization with aplomb; he could perhaps even defeat the Atlantic Ocean itself, but it was *people* who were confounding him.

That he had not seen Katerina for days was his prime irritant. He *should* have been able to relieve the pressure of his demanding work with assignations. It *should* have been their pleasure. At the very least, he wanted to see her before they cast off. But she was gone. Messages to her hotel went unanswered.

And then there was Franny. Any thoughts of Frau Lindt had their shadow thoughts of Franny. The frenzy of work and the obsession with the cable had kept any consideration of what he was doing to Franny at bay. He could tell himself, justifiably, that now was not the time for him to stop and ponder his marriage. Besides, his marriage, if he owned up to it, had been an arid landscape since long before he'd met Katerina . . . since, well, since Betty's death.

Chester knew men who had for years managed a marriage "arrangement" such as he was having with Frau Lindt. And Katerina, he would argue, was practically his muse. To have met such a sympathetic mind just as he was on the verge of his life's success had to have been a godsend. Katerina had infused him with an energy, a certainty about his prospects and purpose such as he'd never felt before.

But there was Franny, back at Willing Mind, troubling him, drawing him in with her weakness—or was it obtuseness that *looked* like weakness?—and their shared history pulling at him, just as Katerina pulled at him with her strength and hunger.

He had sent Franny word to depart for Newfoundland and, at the same time, had sent a dispatch in a courier packet bound for the cable offices in America. He instructed the cable office to contact Spude, who was returning to America ahead of the expedition, planning to be there, he'd said, to welcome them ashore and send the first telegram. Chester had asked Spude to check on Franny, to report on her health, her state of mind. Now he wished he could call the dispatch back. He probably shouldn't have been sowing such public doubt about his wife's mental stability; it was unseemly. Yet it might serve to explain, should people discover the affair, why Frau Lindt was so vital to him. Men would sympathize. A wife's neurasthenia was ample cause for a gentleman to seek solace elsewhere.

But such thinking also led him to the unavoidable possibility that Franny herself was seeking solace elsewhere. And thus Otis's return was another irritant. The letter Chester had received from Franny said he had been *teaching* her. He was, she'd said, "my *spiritualist* guide." Otis was always the puzzle. Always another irritant.

And then there was Whitehouse, the latest irritant. Chester was sure to see Cyrus Field at the farewell dinner, and Field was sure to trouble him about Whitehouse's intention to stay ashore.

As Chester rode in a brougham through Hyde Park, he felt alien to everything around him. The irritants held sway. They made a flat scrim of the smiling ladies and round gentlemen before him as he stepped from the carriage at Halberton Hall. Celebrants greeted him at the door, applauded him in the foyer, nodded to him at table, and listened attentively when he stood to address them in his prepared remarks. Cyrus Field and a dozen other board members were smiling generously over their sherbet glasses as Chester began to speak, but Chester still felt vexed. Fortunately, the speech was one he had performed at each dinner and fanfare he'd attended for the cable launching, and now as he stood before one last banquet of nobility, admiralty, industrialists, financiers, the helmsmen of the age, and their wives and mistresses, he felt his irritations gradually submerging. He was talking about work. Work at last. The cable. The task at hand. This was all it took. The irritants began to sink beneath the waves, and soon Chester lost himself in the work as he proceeded once more to deliver the speech.

The Speech

"Two ships will sail to the center of the ocean," he said. "Two ships will sail to the middle of the sea."

He always opened with this trope. The repetition, with its slight alteration, was an incantation for him.

"Each ship with more than twelve hundred miles of cable in its hold. Each cable weighing more than twelve hundred tons."

All the nights performing the Phantasmagorium Show had given Chester a confidence before audiences, an even greater confidence than he naturally possessed. His spectacles flashed gold and crystal in the eyes of his onlookers. He ran his hand once through his blond hair.

"There, far abroad in the Atlantic, with more than a thousand miles of ocean to their east and a thousand to their west and with two thousand fathoms of water below them, they will splice their cables together and begin sailing in opposite directions: one, the *Niagara*, flying the American flag, will proceed to Newfoundland; the other, your own frigate the *Aga-*

memnon, with the Union Jack atop its mast, will head east toward Ireland.

"They will slowly, carefully pay out the cable, which, in relation to the vastness of the ocean, would be as thin as a single strand of spider's silk running from here to Gravesend. Yet that strand—a gossamer fiber, if you will—shall, in a few weeks at most from the very moment I now speak to you, unite two mighty nations in a greater, and yet smaller, world."

Chester went on like this for half an hour, entertaining the audience, leaving the stuffed diners not fatigued but alert, ready to write bank drafts or pledges for one last hurrah before the sailing. He had wanted to make a hurried exit after the speech, but a throng of people pressed toward him. The Phantasmagorium had made him one of the most celebrated and widely recognized men in London. He'd even had his caricature appear that morning again in the *Mirror*: in it he was a curly-haired, strong-jawed giant with a little gleaming starburst of light on the rim of his spectacles. He was bestriding the ocean. The water came only to his knees, and he was tying two halves of the cable together with his bare hands.

As Chester greeted the swarm, thanking them for their good wishes and Godspeeds, Cyrus Field appeared out of the crowd. He looked grave and pale behind his beard. He gently tugged Chester over to an alcove near a portiere. His confident look during Chester's speech had obviously been a front.

"Any word?" Field asked.

"Not yet."

"Any other plans?"

"One: I do it myself."

"Impossible."

"It's the only other option I have."

"Well, if it's not impossible, then at the very least it's intemperate. How can I countenance such an action with all that's at stake? Do you propose *I* be the other engineer?"

"No, of course not, it's just that—"

"We sail in two days, Mr. Ludlow, *two days*."

A couple of officers from the Bengal Lancers lounging over by a potted palm observed the conference and gave Field and Chester knowing nods: one brace of strategists to another. Field smiled at them perfunctorily. He was exercised but, true to form, kept his voice in check and his manner decorous.

The problem was Whitehouse and his intention to stay home. It was a problem for which Chester had as yet no answer. Chester had been assuring Field he had the matter in hand, that the problem wasn't *really* a problem but was only . . . an irritation.

Yet it did more than irritate Chester. It infuriated him. He just couldn't show that to Field. The doctor had been so haughty, almost gloating, when he announced to Chester in the presence of that tart that he wouldn't be aboard the *Agamemnon* or anywhere near the expedition.

"I've sent three messages to Glasgow," Chester said.

"No response?"

"None yet. Perhaps Thomson is—"

"What? Sick? On holiday? What?"

"I don't know, Field. But see here, we could bring along a telegrapher from the London office, a good man with a key. I could train him on the outbound voyage about the payout and braking procedure. We could bring along a stevedore or two who supervised the loading, and we could each take a ship after the splice."

"No."

"Mr. Field—"

"No. A telegrapher is not an engineer. Stevedores are not electricians. Hundreds of thousands of dollars and pounds are riding on this. Get Thomson, or the expedition's off."

Chester had never seen Field so adamant. The pressure was straining him as well. The man had been fair—more than fair—to Chester. Field had been his champion through all the preparations, but now it looked as if he was turning on him. And all because of Whitehouse.

Chester watched Field disappear into the throng. Disconcerted and worried—and irritated—Chester made his way hastily to the door, ignoring, or not even noticing, the salutes of the Lancers as he passed.

June 10, 1858

It was grand this year, but it had been better before. Last year there were boats and packets and yachts and coracles flag-bedecked and full of cheering peasants and fisherfolk and sailors and nobility. The little harbor at Valentia on Ireland's west coast had been so choked with happy well-wishers that the expedition's shore-landing boat was barely able to make it to the beach to set the beginning of the cable.

Perhaps because this year they were sailing from a British port—Plymouth—and not an Irish fishing village; perhaps because all the cable was stowed away on the ships, the *Niagara* and the *Agamemnon* appeared to be merely two cargo vessels heading out to sea on a day in June; and perhaps because they'd failed once with two hundred miles of cable now lying useless on the ocean floor, there was an air of vincibility or furtiveness or, at the very least, the commonplace about the enterprise.

Nevertheless, it was a beautiful day, clear and sunny and boding well, and there were speeches and salutes and respectable, if subdued, cheers from the crowd. Then it was a volley of cannon salutes from the *Valorous* and the *Gorgon* at anchor in the roads, and at last the *Agamemnon* and the *Niagara* cast off.

A couple of hours later, Chester was standing on the leeward rail of the *Agamemnon,* looking down at the foam sliding away behind the ship. Soon land would be falling away below the horizon. He could hear the rigging buzz above him. Behind him the *Agamemnon*'s stack belched black smoke from the boiler that aided the sails in getting the ship well out into the Channel.

At the far end of the ship, on the foredeck, was a sight that made Chester almost gloat. Walking slowly around the curve of the massive storage drum, with one hand stroking the cable, was Professor William Thomson. Chester had succeeded in enlisting him.

The night of the final banquet, Chester left Halberton Hall after being upbraided by Field and returned to his hotel, where the concierge stopped him at the stairs with a telegram:

WOULD YOU BELIEVE IT? SPENT THREE DAYS IN LAB WORK-
ING ON CALCS. RE: LAW OF SQUARES. I STILL THINK WE'RE
RIGHT & THAT DOCTOR WRONG. YOUR TELEGRAMS ONLY
NOW CAUGHT ME. SHAME ON WHITEHOUSE. I'LL GO. SEE
YOU IN PLYMOUTH.
THOMSON.

When Thomson had met Chester at the dock in Plymouth, carrying his own bags to the wharf, the Scotsman announced preemptively that he would be volunteering without pay.

"It's for science, lad," he'd said. "And for some sea air."

Chester smiled now as he looked at the professor walking round the coil, and he began to relax. The sun baked his shoulders and face; the ship heeled as it caught the full breeze. The *Agamemnon* and the *Niagara* banked their boilers and went under full canvas. The flotilla leaned with the wind and proceeded on a broad reach into the Channel. Soon, beyond the Eddystone Rocks, they'd be tacking west. The cable expedition was truly under way.

"You look pleased, sir."

Chester turned to see the bulky figure of the sketch artist approaching him from the main deck.

"Jack Trace," the man said, extending his hand.

"Yes, of course," said Chester, feeling a twinge of embarrassment that his smug look had been observed. "I *am* pleased, Mr. Trace. I have rising expectations for our success."

"How can one not, with weather like this?" Trace said. The Channel water sparkled all about them.

Chester asked Trace if he'd ever sailed before.

"Only once, and it ended badly. It was the maiden voyage of the *Great Eastern*."

"Ah, yes."

Then Chester noticed Trace held a leather case.

"Have you some of your work there?" He pointed to the portfolio.

Trace pulled out a large tablet and propped it on the rail. He had a custom of first drawing on the last sheet of a tablet and working his way to the front. That way, when he flipped the pages, the pictures went in the order he drew them.

So Chester saw a magic lantern show of the cable's progress since he'd given the job of documentarian to Trace. The drawings were stunning. Sinewy, kinetic, viewed from precarious angles and minutely detailed, they actually made Chester's head snap back in surprise. He found himself edgy with excitement. Some were as precise as medical textbook studies, some were more sweeping; all were powerful portrayals of the industry and might of the cable endeavor. There were pictures of the ships' lading; of the cable snaking out of the storage vats filled with seawater to keep the wire supple; of stevedores' hands, arms, faces; sky studies; numerous nautical scenes; two gentlemen—Field and Ludlow—conferring near the riveted trusses of the braking mechanism on the *Niagara*'s stern.

"These are very good," Chester said as he began flipping through them again, this time catching a few pictures he'd missed on his first pass. "These renderings will do us and yourself credit. Do you have another portfolio with your—what are they called now?—cartoons? Men bestriding the ocean and whatnot?"

Trace blushed so pink, he looked as if Chester had slapped him on both cheeks.

"That is another, *separate* talent and occupation, sir. One I left onshore. I don't think it has any place here."

Chester smiled. "Actually, Mr. Trace, I think it might. You should continue in that exaggerated vein if your humors and our circumstances so move you."

"Really, sir, I—"

"No. I insist. We must have a massive, ocean-spanning egotism to set out on such an expedition, to even contemplate it. God willing, our egotism will be justified and eventually be seen only as foresight and boldness. But for now, it might lighten our spirits and sharpen our wits to have some of our qualities and intentions tweaked."

"Very well, sir. But I shan't consider it my prime responsibility. You hired me as a documentarian, sir, not as a jester."

"That I did, Trace."

The horizon rose and fell comfortably before them as the ship strode forward; the crew seemed to be gliding through its tasks, at ease now that the setting out was accomplished and only open water lay ahead; the helmsman, just forward of where Trace and Chester stood, moved the wheel, and the ship's heel increased ever so slightly to port as it took a more generous bite out of the wind.

"Mr. Trace," Chester said, "when I hired you, you remember the circumstances?"

"Yes, sir." Trace was uncomfortable with this turn in the conversation. He thought they'd been nearing the end of their chat.

"Well," Chester said, "at the time, as we stood before Dr. Whitehouse's door in the club, you said you knew him or had met him previously. I never asked you where or how."

Trace felt a flutter in his chest. "Well, you see, sir, it wasn't exactly *Dr. Whitehouse* to whom I was referring."

"It wasn't?" Chester said, then remembering: "Oh, I *see*. You meant . . . ," and Chester pictured the girl appearing and fading and being slapped by Whitehouse.

"Sir," Trace said, "you had said we would keep the circumstances of our *negotiations* that night private. I intend, in every way, to do so."

"I appreciate that, Mr. Trace. I didn't realize . . ."

"It's nothing," Trace said, and shifted the portfolio from under one arm to the other.

Chester regretted having embarrassed the artist. The man seemed kindly, almost innocent, and yet Chester couldn't help being amused by how abashed the big fellow was at having a randy episode from his past brought to light.

"Very good then," Chester said. "Well, good day, sir." He shook Trace's hand and proceeded toward the bow to see if he could find Professor Thomson. They had engineering matters to discuss.

Trace Thinks He Sees Something

After a few hours, unfamiliar though he was with seafaring, Trace began to think that an ocean crossing really could be tedious. He had been through one and a half of the ship's watches and precious little had happened. Things should change when the actual cable-laying operation began, he supposed. But for now, the wind was steady, the sails set. Even the helmsman hardly moved at the *Agamemnon*'s wheel.

He did a couple of quick sketches of the sailors holystoning the quarterdeck, and he gave them the pictures. He sketched the other three ships in the flotilla—the two British escorts were on the starboard horizon, the other cable ship, the American *Niagara*, was off the port beam. He wondered if it would be more interesting if he were aboard the Yank ship. His stomach growled, and he wondered when the next meal would be served. The *Great Eastern*'s maiden voyage, with its battalions of stewards and the feasting and celebration, prepared him poorly for the austerity of a cable-laying expedition aboard a British naval vessel.

He heard the skipper of the *Agamemnon*, Captain Preedy, mention to the first mate that the barometer was down to twenty-nine inches. But the sky, the first mate had said, still looked good. In less than three days they should be at the splicing point out in the middle of the Atlantic. A boatswain piped up a new watch. Trace rubbed his eyes and scratched his bale of hair. He needed a break. He closed his sketchbook and went below.

He was walking forward, feeling his way through the dimness of a port-side companionway. A blurred column of light came down through the thick blocks of glass in an iron-grated skylight implanted in the deck above. It was just enough illumination to give Trace a glimpse of what he thought was a pallid, oval face peeking out from one of the cabin doors at the far end of the passage.

The face flickered in the dim light. Trace had the simultaneous impression that it was real and that it was nothing more than memories of Maddy playing tricks on his tired eyes. Then a roll of the ship seemed to make the apparition disappear. Trace walked past his cabin, down to where he thought he'd seen the face. He found himself suddenly alert, keyed to the creaking of the timbers and the susurrations of the water gliding along the hull. He sniffed the air to see if there were any telltale signs of perfume. None. All the doors were closed. He couldn't very well go knocking on them, asking if anyone inside was a woman. Nevertheless, he stood still for a few moments, waiting, and when no one, or nothing, appeared again from any of the doors, he proceeded back to his room.

There he found Wilkins Moon lying on the lower bunk. Moon wrote for the London *Daily Journal* and was the sole newspaperman granted permission to be on the expedition.

"I hope you don't mind my resting on your rack," Moon said as soon as Trace opened the door. "It was easier just to flop down than to clamber up to that narrow shelf they have the effrontery to call my accommodations."

"I don't mind," Trace said, though he did. With Moon on his berth, Trace had nowhere to sit. He put his sketch pad in his sea chest; he fussed with his duffel.

Moon, a short young man with lank blond hair as pale as his namesake, went on: "One might think that if we are the only two men to be informing the world of this enterprise, then the cable syndicate would make some effort to offer us accommodations that would put us in a frame of mind favorably disposed toward the expedition."

"One might," Trace said, standing back up. He didn't think he liked Moon. Moon had a reputation on Fleet Street. He was a man known to be without scruples when it came to putting his name to a story. Trace suspected Moon had even stolen items from him. Certainly there were parts of Trace's story about the *Great Eastern* explosion that appeared, barely altered, in Moon's *Journal* account, and Trace wasn't even sure Moon had been aboard the ship that day. Moon had been one of the Fleet Street fellows who'd ignored Trace back in the days before the *Great Eastern;* now he was acting chummy and "delighted, de*light*ed" to have been assigned a berth with Trace, the "official *artiste d'expedition.*"

"I say, how did you get the position of expedition artist, Trace? If you don't mind my asking. Care for a smoke?"

Moon held a pocket humidor out from the bunk. Trace took one of the half dozen cigars and held it but did not light it. He resigned himself to conversing with the man, the necessary protocol of assigned shipmates.

"I applied for it," Trace said.

"Enterprising," said Moon. "And you were doing so well where you were, safe on land in London. A few humorous sketches a week, no need to risk life and limb and reputation out here."

Trace shifted from leaning against the bunk to leaning against the bulkhead. In quarters so cramped it involved hardly any movement at all. "But there are risks, Moon, inherent with staying in London and drawing, as you say, a few humorous sketches a week. Risks to reputation if not so much to life and limb."

"Such as?"

"I am here by virtue of timing. I was at the right place at the right time. I asked the right people at the right moment. I had the right stories to my credit at the right juncture. It all could have been otherwise. It all *could be* otherwise soon enough. The winds blow fickle in our business, Moon." Trace knew he was beginning to preach, to lean on the prerogatives of age, the only rank he had: the spurious authority of a bore. You're not at Miss Orford's Academy, he told himself. Moon is not a doe-eyed drawing-class maiden.

"And talent has nothing to do with it?" Moon said. "Surely you must think of yourself as talented."

"All right, something," Trace said, wanting to end this, to shut himself up as well as Moon. "But it's arrogant to credit it too much. As arrogant, I suppose, as thinking a ship out here is unsinkable."

"Well," Moon said, now rolling onto his side and propping his head on his hand, "Even *I* wouldn't think that. But I do seem to give my chances in the business better odds than you give yours."

"You know about Fate's caprices, Moon. You've been in combat."

Moon had an upturned nose and a wispy mustache that looked like a swatch of mold on his upper lip. He smiled languidly, but his eyes shuttled back and forth.

"Technically . . . no."

"No? The Crimea?" said Trace.

"The Crimea, yes. Combat, no."

"But your reporting . . ."

"An amalgam wrought from the dispatches and accounts of others and from a patchwork of sources. My secret. Served me quite well, don't you think?"

"It got you here," Trace said.

"Ah, yes. Here," said Moon, settling farther into the bunk, Trace's bunk. "Now that I've revealed this secret to you, I suppose we had all better sink and die at sea so my secret can die with us."

Because he couldn't think of any other way he could puncture Moon's indolence, Trace said, "What say you allow me to have a bit of lie-down myself, Moon? On my own bed?"

"Bed? *Bed?* You are too kind, Trace, to call this rack of pain to which you've been sentenced a *bed*." And he swung his feet to the deck. "Perhaps I shall go topside, take in some sea air. Sorry you didn't like your smoke."

And Moon left with a studiously casual nod toward the unlit cigar that Trace still rolled between his fingers.

Trace lowered himself onto his bunk. He knew Moon saw himself as a man on the way up. His ascendancy to the *Journal* before the age of thirty, his frequent contributions to the front page from the Crimea, his singular assignment to the cable expedition, gave him grounds for plenty of presumption. Trace would like to have strangled Moon, but the young man's eyes played tricks with Trace's repugnance. Moon had trained his face to assume a mask of insouciance and genteel disdain typical of one far above his station as a Fleet Street wretch. But his eyes betrayed him. They were nervous—not sparkling, but twitchy. They moved continuously, as if caged in the sallow face, as if longing to behold the world for someone more worthy than Wilkins Moon. The eyes made Trace feel sorry for Moon even as he wanted to throttle him.

Trace looked at his cigar. He could feel the ship turning, heeling at a slightly lesser angle as the helmsman adjusted to a shift in the wind. Maybe, Trace thought, he'd go up on deck, too, and have a smoke, free himself from the muddle he'd sunk into.

The companionway was empty, void of apparitions or anything else, save for a sailor on the stairs who was addressing Captain Preedy above him on deck.

"Twenty-eight five, sir."

"Falling still?"

"I tapped the glass, sir. She nicked down."

"Very well. Report to me again at the end of the watch."

"Aye, sir."

As the sailor edged past him, Trace asked if he was talking of the barometer. The sailor cast a quick glance back up the companionway through the opening to the deck. The captain was gone; only a trapezoid of hazy afternoon sky was visible.

"Aye, sir," the sailor said.

"And a dropping barometer means a storm?"

"A barometer dropping such as this one, aye, sir."

"How soon?"

The sailor shrugged. "Sky looks fine. Could be we'll skirt it, and the barometer is only telling us we're *near* a storm. Storms move, sir, but so do we."

Trace left the sailor and poked his head above deck. The blue sky and the mare's tails were gone now. The sky looked milky with whiter puffs of clouds superimposed upon it. Trace considered it as a painting problem for a moment: white on white, a gradation of pigments. Then he looked forward, where he saw Chester Ludlow talking to Professor Thomson, both men touching the cable spool coiled there on the massive drum. Moon was nearby, listening in, smiling, eyes darting, hands held behind his back. He wasn't taking a single note.

Trace climbed all the way out of the companionway and stood at the larboard rail. The *Niagara* was still out there, with the *Gorgon* and the *Valorous* on the other side, all looking less substantial, as they now were twice as far away from the *Agamemnon* as before.

The wind was fresher and had shifted from the west to the southeast. It would make enjoying the cigar difficult, so Trace went back below to his room, soon filling the tiny berth with an oily smoke. The cigar tasted good, but leave it to Moon to offer one with such buttery fumes.

In the thick cloud Trace leaned down to reach under his bunk and pull out a sketchbook. This was not the one he'd been using thus far on the voyage; this was something else, leather-bound with a brass hasp to secure the covers. Trace was feeling uneasy. Something about the weather, perhaps, or Moon's imperiousness or that trick of the light in the passage-way that had made him think he'd seen the pale face of a woman. The uneasiness, he hoped, might be dispelled by his special book. It was a risk, though, because looking at the book could be unsettling, too. He never knew what to expect, for inside the book were Trace's pictures of the future.

Whatever shameful or absurd feelings Maddy had engendered in Trace, that first encounter with her in the tunnel had given him this: studies for his mural. Trace could rarely look at them. He sometimes could barely draw them. He found the only way to approach what this sketchbook held, what it stood for, was to take it in small bits, to draw in it obliquely—a bit here, a bit there—with no eye yet to the final painting. The task kept beck-oning him, though. Although he couldn't completely imagine it in his mind, the finished product would be muscular and declarative; he knew that. Something invigorating, a vision robust and hopeful. Machines would fig-ure prominently, for machines were everywhere now and would be always. That was the future. Steam. Fire. Combustion. Cogs. Rails. Gantries. Scaf-folding. Rivets. Glass. Sunlight. Smoke. The telegraph should be part of this vision, too, but how to paint the sound of clicks flitting through a wire on the bottom of the sea? How to contain the marvel of the cable in a painting, no matter how grand? And it was more than just clicks, too. The clicks would cohere to form messages; the messages would have meanings; the meanings, information. It was all too abstract. You can't paint an ab-straction, Trace had always told his students at Miss Orford's, and they always looked at him . . . well, abstractedly.

But he was beginning to wonder. Maybe there *was* a way. Maybe that was what this mural was about: expressing the abstract, depicting the *feel* of the age, or the age to come. Somehow, though, he'd have to get the cable into the picture.

Then, as the ship rolled on a wave and the smoke swirled around his head, Trace experienced a strange inversion of thought. He imagined pic-tures in the cable. *That* would be a marvel. The very idea made his head ache. He puffed some more on his cigar. The room was rank with the smoke. He was anything but settled now.

Pictures in the wire? Well, there was a code to bring words across distances and, theoretically, across the sea. Why not a code to transmit pictures as well? It was an abstraction, if there ever was one. A scientific fiction. He laughed aloud at the notion.

His laughter hung in the weighted air. He looked up. He was enshrouded in the murk of his cigar smoke. It was thick enough nearly to extinguish the candle on the bulkhead shelf.

Then Trace heard a quick gagging cough come through the smoke.

"Hello?" Trace said. He stood up, alert.

The coughing stopped for several seconds, then explosively began again. It came through a small grate on the wall up near the top bunk. It came from the next room.

Trace stepped out into the passage. He moved lightly to the neighboring door aft. It was a narrow portal with a plaque tacked onto it: SPLICING EQUIP. LOCKER NO ADMITTANCE.

Trace tried the door. It gave but did not open. Someone was holding it. Trace clenched the cigar in his teeth and with his two hands tugged harder at the door. He could see, clutching the latch on the other side, a woman's hands and wrists.

His heart skipped, and with one redoubled pull, he yanked the door open and expelled a gushing cloud of cigar smoke directly into the face of Frau Lindt. She began to cough and sob instantly.

Trace threw down his cigar and reached out to comfort the woman. She shrunk back into the locker, where tools and wire and tightly lidded tar buckets were battened down onto shelves. She held her hands before her face. Trace touched her shoulder. She flinched.

"Madam," he said, "it is all right. I want to help you."

The closet had the stenchy closeness of a sickroom, and Trace realized that the woman had two chamber pots in there with her. There were several bottles of water and some bread and cheese on one of the shelves. Trace tried to fan away the smoke he'd exhaled. He stomped on the cigar.

"Please, madam . . ."

After two more sobs and a strangled cough, Frau Lindt tossed her head and composed herself as best she could.

"Sir," she rasped, her blue eyes rimmed in red as she clutched the sleeves of his coat. "You must help me."

"Madam—"

"You must bring to me Herr Ludlow, *Mister* Ludlow. Is he aboard?"

"Yes, of course, he's—"

"Then bring him. Please."

"Here?"

"Yes. Please."

Frau Lindt released him, and Trace stepped back from the door. He looked up and down the corridor. No one was coming.

"Please, sir. I beg you."

"Yes. Very well. I shall," Trace mumbled. "Madam," he said, "are you—?"

"Hiding? Yes. I am."

"No. I meant to say, are you all right?"

Frau Lindt stopped for a moment, muddled.

"Why, yes. I believe so," she said, straightening up. "I thank you."

Even in her unkempt, distracted state, her pale, golden hair seemed almost artfully arranged on her shoulders, and her eyes grew bluer and clearer as the smoke in the closet dissipated.

"I'll see what I can do," Trace said. He began to move toward the companionway. "You better go back in and . . . hide."

She nodded and started to pull the door closed. Then she stopped.

"Sir. I am sorry to ask. It will do nothing for my esteem in your eyes, but I am desperate. Could you. . . ?" And she reached down to pick up the two covered chamber pots, passing them to Trace through the door. They both were heavy, both full. Trace guessed she must have been in there for days.

He gingerly took the pots, and as the SPLICING EQUIP. LOCKER door closed, he proceeded with painstaking delicacy to the companionway and up the steps. Once on deck he strode with increasing speed toward the rail and, with a gasp of relief, hurled both pots into the sea.

"See here," a sailor called from the yardarm directly above him. "We aren't carrying a shipload of those. You're supposed to toss the slops and *keep* the pots."

"Sorry," Trace said. "They slipped."

"Better that than tossin' the pots and keepin' the slops, eh?"

"Yes," said Trace with a discomfited grin. "So it is."

"Had yourself quite a cargo there."

"Yes. So I did."

"We should be picking up speed now that you've jettisoned all that." The sailor chuckled to himself high on the spar. Trace went forward to look for Ludlow.

Chester Ludlow was still up at the foredeck spool with Professor

Thomson. Moon was still looking on. As he approached, Trace could hear them talking about coefficients, total cable resistance, capacitance, and something called the Law of Squares. Moon looked as if he were understanding every word.

Chester Ludlow had developed, Trace thought, an uncanny ability to know when eyes were upon him. He didn't preen exactly, but he seemed to stand a little straighter, set his jaw a little more firmly, to pose when he sensed onlookers. Had fame done this to the man? Trace wondered. Or was that particular ability a prerequisite to fame?

"Trace!" Chester said, turning toward him before Trace had even spoken or cleared his throat to announce his presence. "What can I do for you? You haven't come to sketch us, have you? I see you don't have your pens or your portfolio."

"No, I—"

"Professor," Chester went on, "I want you to meet our documentarian, Mr. Jack Trace. His drawings and engravings are some of the best I've seen in the London papers."

Behind Chester's back, Moon rolled his eyes.

"This is Professor William Thomson," Chester said, "my fellow electrician-projector on the expedition and, I am honored to say, my mentor."

Professor Thomson extended his hand. He wasn't much older than Ludlow, but he wore his status more gravely.

"And you know Mr. Moon?" Chester asked.

"I do," said Trace. "Honored, Professor."

Trace could feel the color rise to his face. He knew he was being brusque with his salutations. "Sir," he mumbled to Ludlow, "I wonder if I might speak with you briefly? And confidentially?"

"Of course, in an hour would be convenient."

"No, sir. I'm sorry, but now."

"Now?"

"Well, yes, now, if that would be possible."

"As you can see, I'm talking with the professor about the transmission—"

"*Please*, sir."

Trace looked so ill at ease, Chester acquiesced almost out of pity and excused himself from the professor and Moon.

Trace took Chester around to the other side of the massive cable drum.

Trace looked left, right, even above them, to be sure they weren't being observed by seamen or, worse, Moon.

"Sir, I come on behalf of a woman who would like to meet you."

Ludlow laughed heartily. "A woman! Well, I must be immodest and say that it isn't the first time. It's become one of the hazards of my duty. Where is she, in America where we're headed or England where we left?"

"Here, sir. Aboard the ship."

Chester's first, irrational thought was that it was Franny, that somehow Otis had transported her there telepathically or by some sort of spiritual conveyance, some Malayan shaman magic. Franny's spirit was there, aboard with him. He felt a wave of panic. But the fear passed with Trace's next words.

"She apparently is a stowaway."

Then Chester knew who it was.

"Take me to her," he said.

Swept Away

"I had to be with you."

"My God, Katerina."

"I said I would see you triumph."

"But this—"

"It was necessary. Do you understand now how serious I am?"

They were belowdecks, whispering feverishly. Katerina was in the locker still, Chester standing in the passage. Trace was on the companionway steps, half on deck. He was standing guard. He and Chester had gone down the passageway, knocking on doors to make sure no one was in any of their berths before Trace showed Chester to Frau Lindt.

Now that he had her before him, Chester didn't know whether to embrace her or rail at her. She was, after all, a stowaway. She had endangered herself by hiding. She could compromise the entire enterprise. He could hardly believe the predicament she'd created. Then again, it was all he could do to keep from hurling himself on her. She looked unkempt and beautiful, ethereal in her prison, an orchid locked in a box.

"Do you understand," she repeated, "how serious?"

"Yes."

"And you? Are you serious?"

"My God, Katerina—"

"And you?"

"Yes. Yes, I'm serious, but—"

"I know. I am illegal. And you have work to do. I won't interfere. Do you have a room alone?"

"Yes."

"Take me there."

"I can't. I mean, not now in broad daylight. We'd have to go on deck."

"At night then."

"At night, yes. Will you be all right? How long have you been in here?"

"An eternity. We'll be together at night."

"Yes."

Katerina was plucking at his clothes, his waistcoat, his sleeves, his trousers. It was a lascivious nervousness, and it stirred Chester to distraction. He looked toward Trace. He could see only the big fellow's legs on the companionway steps; the rest of him was above deck. Chester lunged toward Katerina, and she responded instantly. They fell back against the shelves, lips and hands all over each other.

"Oh, God, yes."

On the steps, Trace felt the first drops of rain; nothing much, just a few spits. The ship had begun a more pronounced roll as it cut through the waves. He looked up. The pale, white-on-white clouds had knit themselves into a dark gray mass. The wind had shifted again, now from the north, and had picked up. Spirited waves, wind-whipped, lashed spray frequently over the deck rails.

Coming along the port side, Moon was walking toward the companionway. Trace ducked down for a quick look below. The passage was empty, the locker door ajar. Ludlow must have stepped into the closet with Frau Lindt.

"I say, Trace, what *are* you doing?"

Trace banged his head on the companionway's frame.

"Might a fellow pass?" Moon stood with his arms akimbo, looking down at Trace.

"Yes, of course. Of course . . ." Trace said. Then added, "Oh, Moon, did you understand what the professor and Ludlow were talking about?"

"Talking about?"

"Up there, by the big roll of wire."

"Cable, Trace. It's on a *spool*, not a roll, and it's called the *cable*."

"By the cable. Did you understand?"

"Some. I suppose you want me to do your homework for you."

"I draw pictures, Moon, you write stories, so it's not as if you're doing my homework for me. I'm just curious. The Law of . . . something?"

"Squares. And you do write occasionally. I've read your stuff. Now I say, Trace, it's beginning to rain and the spray . . . What say I tell you all about the cable down below, where it's dry?"

"Dry?"

"Rain, Trace. Waves. Not to put too fine a point on it, Trace, but I'm getting wet. It's raining. There's a bit of storm here."

"So there is. They told me it might be so."

Hoping Moon wouldn't notice, Trace kicked the bulkhead twice near the ladder belowdecks as a signal.

"Trace, what is *wrong* with you?"

"Nothing. Well, actually I feel queasy. The waves."

"Oh, delightful. I'm billeted with a blighter who has a queasy stomach. Well, getting soaked to the skin won't help either of us, Trace. Now let me pass."

Trace gave another kick, but the sea was too heavy and the ship was rolling too much for the signal to be heard over the creak of the timbers and the thud of waves against the hull. Despairing of any way to delay Moon any longer, Trace stepped to one side of the steep companionway steps. Moon pursed his lips in impatience; his mustache wrinkled into a small patch of bristles.

At that moment, as Moon reached out to hold the rail with one hand and with the other hand either use Trace's shoulder for support or brush him aside in a final gesture of annoyance, the first of many waves that would break over the *Agamemnon* struck Moon from behind.

Trace had only a fleeting chance to see the water, looking like a giant, pale claw reaching up above the gunwale. Startled, Trace opened his mouth and had it filled with seawater, but Moon, struck from behind, pitched headlong down the companionway. He squealed a descending note of panic as he passed Trace, who managed to hold on to the companionway rail.

Chester had already made it to the foot of the stairs when the soaking, somersaulting Moon crashed into his feet. The wave had generally washed over the companionway hatch and shot across the deck to gush out the leeward scuppers. Very little water had reached Chester. He stepped over the tangled Moon, who was facedown at the bottom of the steps in a heap, sputtering from the seawater and his own bloody nose. Chester lithely hopped up the stairs before the reporter had even seen whose legs had stopped his tumble.

"Thanks for the signal, Trace."

"You heard my kicking then," Trace said, blinking and wiping his face with a soaked handkerchief. He pulled his clinging, wet shirt away from his chest.

"I did. I'm much obliged." Chester and Trace cast a look down at the weakly flailing Moon. The ship was heaving more seriously now, and Moon kept pitching into the bulkhead.

"I should see what I can do for him," Trace said.

"Good of you. It's probably best I disappear," Chester said. "The, ah, woman, Trace . . ."

Chester ducked down to make a quick check of the passageway doors. "Sir?"

"The woman is secure in the splicing equipment locker. It's a complicated story . . ."

"Indeed."

"I am going to assist her but, shall we say, I must do it *discreetly*. Once again I need your confidence. Much is at stake. Reputations. Hers. Mine. The expedition's."

"I understand."

"I appreciate it, Trace. More than I can say."

"He'p! He'p!" Moon's plaintive and broken-nose cries came from below.

"I'll take care of him."

"Thank you, Trace. And, Trace, what I said a while ago about tweaking?"

"Sir?"

"No cartoons."

The Storm

It was pitch-dark in the locker. Katerina had tried to relight the candle she'd brought, but the ship's rolling made the flame gutter so severely that the spilling wax kept extinguishing the flame. She was left in blackness to feel the yawing of the vessel and to hear the violent, thunderous crash of waves against the hull. She tried to take her mind off the noise by fingering a Mendelssohn passage on the shelving around her in the dark. She could hear the battened equipment in the locker shift and thump. She played all the more intensely. Once, a bucket slid against the railing and smashed her knuckles. She did not cry out but dropped to a crouch, sucking at her hand, her eyes shut tightly, making everything no darker than it already was, her fingers still moving to the music in her head.

She had not anticipated a storm. She had not anticipated being entombed in her closet for so long. Everything had gone so well. She'd used her charms and a generous remuneration on the young proctor who'd shown her around the ship to secrete her in the locker and to provision her. (The poor fellow probably thought she had designs on him.) She had assumed by now she'd be ensconced in Chester's stateroom, curled beneath an eiderdown, this annoying and risky stowaway endeavor over, her new life begun; she'd be there waiting for him to come belowdecks when he took a break from his glorious work. She was not supposed to be twisted here in pain in the crashing darkness.

She could feel the ship rise on each wave, then hover an awful moment before sliding down into another trough. The feeling was all in her stomach and lower. Up, up, up . . . then with a partial sideways slide, *down*; up, up, up . . . and *down*. The repetitions seemed to have been going on forever. She seemed to have been stowed away forever. The reasons she was here were slipping out of her mind: for a new life, to leave Joachim, to be with Chester. She whispered the phrases aloud; she spoke them aloud; she almost shouted them. It made no difference. The sound and motion of the storm swallowed every word. She played her fingers on the wood in the dark, over and over.

Chester Ludlow was on deck, near the helm. He needed to keep an eye on things. He had to make sure all the cable equipment was secure, and he had, with what attention he had left, to come up with a way to get Frau Lindt out of that locker.

He had seen storms like this before, but it was always from the bluffs of *Willing Mind*. It was something altogether different being on the deck of a ship that held the greatest gamble of his life.

The two small escort ships, the *Gorgon* and the *Valorous*, had disappeared, pulled far from the formation by the wind. The *Niagara* was still visible on the horizon, but just barely, a spindly little knot of masts and a plume of smoke.

Chester now noticed how much less canvas was aloft on the *Agamemnon* since the last time he'd been on deck. Captain Preedy had had the crew toiling above. The three spread sails were reefed. There was something skittish about the ship the way her stays and lines stood out now against the sky. Chester could only see the horizon and catch glimpses of the *Niagara* when the enlarging swells lifted the *Agamemnon* up to their heights. When the ship dropped into a trough, the sides of the swells rose above the *Agamemnon*'s deck nearly thirty feet. Spume blew off their tops like the cloud banners Chester remembered seeing as a child on the highest peaks in the White Mountains. The wind was beginning to whine in the rigging— no longer a hum—and had started to kick new waves out of the backs of the swells. More and more of the waves were slamming into the *Agamemnon* and sending fans of spray up over the decks.

Chester looked at the spool on the foredeck. There were 250 tons of cable wound up there; another 1,300 tons were in tanks in the hold below. The weight and the precariousness of the spool and the high center of gravity on the deck made the *Agamemnon* vulnerable. The helmsman now had a mate joining him, and together they held the ship's wheel. Captain Preedy gripped a lanyard that had been tied to the wheel post. He cast a quick glance at Chester, shook his head, and looked aloft. There seemed to be no encouraging sign in the heavens. Large, tumbling clouds raced one over the other from the northeast. Rain sprayed Chester's face intermittently and was joined by the more constant torrent of sea spray. What the ship's hull didn't crash against, the wind was driving into the air. It had all happened so quickly; coming upon the storm had been like stepping from a quiet garden party into the chaos of a riot.

Larger and larger piles of water rushed southwestward and pounded the *Agamemnon*'s starboard aft quarter. Chester held tightly to the quarterdeck rail as spray pushed against him.

Captain Preedy shouted something to his helmsmen and to his first mate below on the main deck. The men had to cup their ears in order to hear the command. Then the two men on the quarterdeck began to wrestle the wheel to starboard. The mate made his way forward, scuttling along between blasts of spray and holding fast to deck fittings or brightwork when the waves hit. He signaled and bellowed to men aloft and to those manning the halyards on deck.

"I'm coming up on her," Preedy shouted to Chester.

"Sir?" Chester shouted back.

"We can't keep running before these seas! We have to take them more head-on. I'm changing course."

"But we'll lose the *Niagara*," Chester shouted. "We'll be going the wrong direction."

"If it keeps us afloat, it's the right direction. We'll worry about our course and the rendezvous when this blow is over."

"Glass is still going down, sir. A tenth of an inch an hour." It was the sailor who'd been reporting the barometer readings to the captain.

"I could have told you that by the popping of my ears, Mr. Fenwick," the captain yelled. All the men were shouting now, no matter how close they were to one another.

"Off Madagascar I once had a stoppered carafe of Madeira explode, the pressure dropped so quickly," Preedy shouted to Chester. "*There* was a storm."

"Worse than this?" Chester yelled.

"Worse than this one is so far," the captain answered.

Chester did not pursue the captain's story. He was more concerned that the *Agamemnon*, in coming about, was going to turn broadside to the gale. Chester could see the crew was alert to the moment, too. Men held fast to their lines or hung from the yards, all squinting into the weather. This was the moment of maximum vulnerability for a ship: when she had to take the wind and waves abeam.

Chester kept his eyes aloft, watching the mastheads against the sky. He almost didn't want to know what was happening to the ship below. A blue and white cable syndicate pennant—designed by Spude, a lightning bolt connecting two interlocked circles (symbolizing the continents)—whipped from the highest point on the ship. Chester bit his lip and held his breath as the *Agamemnon* seemed to loiter on the seas and lose the will to move. It would be easiest for the storm to sink the ship right now.

A mercifully low wave rolled toward the ship, and the *Agamemnon*, as if sensing the reprieve, began to pull up into the wind.

They made it. The crew scurried and hauled lines with renewed vigor. Preedy looked relieved.

"I waited none too soon to do that, sir," he said to Chester. "Now we must bear down."

"Good work, Captain. A wise decision."

The waves, now slamming the ship nearly head-on, hit the *Agamemnon* with spray that reached as high as the bare feet of a sailor on the foresail yardarm.

A sailor clinging to the rail down on the main deck was shouting something to Chester: "The cable . . . in the hold, sir!" The sailor pointed at the deck.

"What?"

"Ca . . . ble . . . hold! She's . . . loose!" He was gesticulating and making twisted, tangled movements with his fingers. Gray waves and white spray were all about.

Chester nodded, and the sailor motioned for him to follow.

"Be . . . care . . . ful!" Preedy shouted after Chester, who was making his way between cannonades of spray to the main cargo hatch amidships.

Belowdecks in his cabin, Trace had given up his berth to Moon. The poor man was miserable; there was no point in trying to nurse him in the upper bunk, and there was no question that Moon needed nursing. The *Journal*man had broken his nose falling down the companionway. Trace had stanched the blood by tearing a pocket handkerchief and using the pieces as bungs for each of Moon's nostrils.

"Doddammbit," Moon cursed, supine on Trace's bunk, his arm flung over his forehead, a pose of recumbent misery. "Doddammbit to hell."

"Don't talk," Trace said.

The ship was rocking distressingly now. Timbers had begun to creak around the cabin, and the whole vessel would periodically shudder from a blow struck by the waves. One lurch of the ship sent Moon rolling against the bulkhead and Trace smashing into the berths.

Moon let out a howl: he'd struck his nose again. Blood and tears covered his face.

"Oh Dod, oh Dod, oh Dod."

Another lurch swiftly followed, and Trace grabbed Moon by the shirt and held him fast. Moon flinched and quivered, and for the first time Trace realized that Moon was mortally afraid. The man began to whimper.

"I'm doeing to be thsick."

"Pardon?" Trace said.

But Moon did not answer. He was racing out the door. He got only as far as the companionway before he vomited all over the bulkhead. Trace pulled back into his cabin and avoided the spew, but it instantly began to stink.

In her hideaway, Frau Lindt soon smelled it also. It was too much. If she stayed shut up in the locker any longer, she knew she also would become ill, again. She burst out the door.

On deck, on his way to the hold, grasping safety lines and trying, with the mate, to time his moves to come between waves, Chester had flashes of Katerina. He had tons of unwieldy cable to contend with, cable that could sink the ship at any moment; still he couldn't help picturing her disheveled, almost tawdry hauteur in her prison. Something thrilled him about having a woman of her power and beauty held captive, his captive.

"Sir!"

The mate was motioning to Chester. Water rose up and slammed down on them both.

"Take a look!"

The mate had led Chester through a small man hatch down into the main cargo hold.

"Don't go too far down," the mate said. Both he and Chester stopped on the ladder about ten feet above the cable circus containing the main bulk of the line. A small storm lantern swung crazily from a beam. The circus was thirty feet in diameter with black cable coiled, mile after mile, around the large, conical center post. The coil stood ten feet high. The end of the cable atop the coil had broken loose, and the upper layers of the coil were shifting with each considerable roll of the ship.

"Not good!" Chester shouted, thinking of how it would only increase the ship's instability if the cable's bulk kept moving with each wave. "Can we get some men down here to secure things?"

"We can try," the mate said.

With each roll, it seemed as if more cable was breaking out of its neat, flat flakes and piling up on the shifting sides of the tank.

While Chester was in the hold with the mate, Trace had made his way to the forecastle and was shouting into the dim and smoky crew's quarters for a bucket and a mop.

"You want to swab the decks at a time like this?" came a gruff voice from one of the hammocks. A round of laughter spilled out of the other hammocks.

"A passenger has been sick outside my cabin," Trace answered.

"And you want one of us to be swabbing it out?" asked the voice.

"No," Trace said, trying to make out to whom he was speaking. "I merely want you to tell me the whereabouts of a mop and bucket."

"Come with me," a sailor said, and slid from his hammock, the lowest of four stacked along the port bulkhead.

Trace followed the man, and both of them kept slamming their shoulders into the walls of the passageway as the ship pitched. When they came to a locker, the sailor grabbed a mop and bucket and said, "You won't have much trouble gathering water. Just hold this out in front of you . . . Ah, the hell. I'll help you."

As they passed a stairway, though, they ran into three sailors jammed into a hatch, almost plugging it like a cork. The sailor accompanying Trace pulled the trouser leg of one of the men on the steps.

"What is it?" Trace's companion called.

The man poked his head down from above.

"A bloody vision."

The man made way for Trace and the sailor to see on deck. The others squeezed aside.

There, in the last light of a stormy day, holding firmly to a ratline on the windward rail, was Frau Katerina Lindt, wrapped in a black cloak, her blond hair streaming out in spray-soaked tresses. She had her right hand up to her brow, shielding her eyes from the blast; her cloak snapped in the wind like Spude's lightning-bolt pennant on the masthead.

Trace could see that she must have just moments ago emerged from the hatch, for everyone—Frau Lindt, the sailors holding fast to the deck, even Captain Preedy—were all immobilized in a tableau of astonishment. Frau Lindt was shocked at the power and enormity of the storm, which she was seeing for the first time; the sailors, Captain Preedy, and Trace were shocked by the luminous beauty before them in the middle of the gray and white fury of the gale.

Chester Ludlow emerged from the main cargo hold's hatch into this frieze. He was able to shout, "Katerina!" just as the sailors were coming out of their transfixion. Captain Preedy was moving toward Frau Lindt.

Hearing Chester's voice, Katerina looked around. She saw men approaching her from all sides. They were coming carefully, trying to hold on to ropes, rails, anything to avoid being swept into the sea. But to Frau Lindt they looked as if they were creeping toward her about to pounce. She felt cornered. She let go of the ratline and made toward Chester, but just then a wave slapped over the side of the ship and sent her sprawling onto the deck. The ship pitched forward as it headed for a trough, and Frau Lindt slid on a cascade of deck water. She had a moment's panic that she would go shooting out one of the scuppers and into the sea.

Chester bent down and caught Katerina before she got past him and slammed into the forecastle bulkhead. Steadying his legs against the mainmast and cargo hatch, he scooped her up in his arms and held her there as another wave cracked over the rail, pouring more water down upon them. The crew broke into spontaneous cheers.

"Help me," Katerina cried into Chester's shoulder. In the din it sounded like a whispered intimacy.

"Of course," he said, not knowing if she heard.

He took her below. Captain Preedy snapped himself and the men into action by shouting for them to reef more sails.

As the night wore on, Jack Trace gave up any hope of sleep. Wilkins Moon's groaning alone would have been enough to keep him awake, but the violent tossing of the ship and increasing noise of the storm left Trace clutching the raised side walls of the upper bunk—Moon's berth. He may have dozed. He had no way of being sure. He saw images of his utopian mural, of each of his childhood beds in the orphanages and in the ragged schools he had attended, beds like small rafts adrift in large, dark, cold attic rooms. They may have been fleeting dreams; they may have been panicky, wide-awake hallucinations writ on the darkness of the tiny cabin as the *Agamemnon* crashed and rolled about. Trace lost all sense of being on a ship. His existence seemed to have shrunk into a lightless caisson that was his sole, flimsy protection from the chaotic and bottomless depths of black water that he knew to be the rest of the universe. He wished he'd never seen the storm on deck. He wished he was ignorant of what was going on out there. Now that it was dark, the night only dilated his terror. He tried to will away thoughts of the hull around him imploding, of what it would feel like to have his lungs fill with water, of clawing horror-struck in no useful direction, of being pushed down toward hell itself not by waves but by true mountains of seawater.

In one respect Moon's groans were a boon. They kept Trace's imagination from merging completely with the chaos of the storm and sending him into a screaming, weeping panic. His fear was there, flailing in his chest, but if he thought of the others on the ship, if he tried to imagine even Moon's pain—anything to keep from spiraling downward into his own dread—he could keep a tenuous grip on himself.

"Moon, are you all right?" he called into the darkness.

"No, doddambit! I'mb doeing to die, and thso are you!"

"Moon, this is just a storm."

"No!"

"The ship will make it."

"No, it won'dt. We're doeing to die!" And Moon began to howl in the darkness.

"Stop it, Moon!"

But Moon kept howling, making the only human sound Trace could hear above the screeching of the wind and the constant, astounding crash of waves against the hull. Trace gritted his teeth and held a grip on his fear. He'd be damned if he was going to go like Moon.

In Chester's cabin, Katerina clung to Chester in the berth. There really wasn't enough room for two people in the small bunk, but they had crawled in after he'd stripped her and himself of their soaked clothes. There had been the same impassioned speed about his disrobing as there had been the first time they'd made love, and in spite of her fear, Katerina couldn't help but feel aroused: he was ripping their clothes off, they were diving into a bed together at long last. She threw her arms around him.

Things crashed about the cabin. Chester had battened down his luggage and measuring devices, but a wall-locker door had flung open and drafting tools spilled onto the floor. He had kicked papers and instruments aside as he'd carried Katerina to the bunk.

"We are together," she said as she held him and they burrowed under the covers. "I've found you."

"We are," he said. "And you have."

He was surprised to feel a sense of calm as he held her like this. There was pandemonium raging everywhere, even there in his stateroom as the storm tossed things about, but closer in, there in the bed, was an atom of peace. It was in the touch of their two bodies. If he thought too much about it, he would be flooded with shame for feeling like this when others aboard were striving against peril to literally keep his expedition afloat. But he needed a moment or two with her. Katerina had been so audacious, so brave, to do this crazy thing for him, to be here, to fight so romantically for him. When had such a thing ever happened in his life? And what had he done to deserve it? He'd done his work. His work had seduced her. There was power in what he was doing, power enough to bring him here to a particle of tranquillity amid the bedlam; and the power would save them, he was certain. They would make it through the storm; the cable would be a success. The certainty of this aroused him further, and soon he was entering her and she was responding.

Katerina couldn't—wouldn't—bear to think of what lay beyond. All she knew was that she had him here, and she slid farther down under the covers to be more fully under him and to move.

With a sickly cracking sound that caused Captain Preedy to whip his head around in confusion to his helmsmen, a partitioning bulkhead broke belowdecks, and a wave of coal spilled loose. The fuel, several tons of it, tumbled against the newly constructed wall that formed the passageway outside Trace and Moon's stateroom. The wall began to buckle. With each roll of the ship, more coal spilled loose and more pressure went against the wall. Two stokers who'd seen what had happened were shouting from below for timbers, but no one could hear. All off-duty crewmen were confined to their hammocks. Moving about was too hazardous. In the galley the cook was trying to secure foodstuffs and utensils, but cutlery was flying about and the man fled.

Equipment and cargo were breaking loose throughout the ship but nowhere more ominously than in the forward cable tank in the main hold. While the spool on deck was miraculously holding against the pounding of the waves and wind, the loose end that Chester had seen earlier belowdecks was now shifting more, so that greater lengths of the cable were flailing about the tank; miles of the stuff were becoming entangled and snarled around the hold. Two crewmen had tried to reconnoiter the situation and had attempted to shine a lantern down into the cable tub. It was like watching a gigantic, blind serpent striking out at unseen tormentors.

The crewmen reported the problem to Captain Preedy, who had just heard from another sailor about the coal. Preedy had been staying up with the helmsmen through the night watch. He was constantly asking how the ship was responding, concerned about ballast, about strain on the rudder, concerned about the canvas aloft. He had ordered the boiler be kept fired and the propeller engaged to help the ship strain up the waves.

Preedy nodded to the man. He instructed the sailor to detail a crew to bolster the walls containing the coal with spare timbers from the carpenter's store. The cable they'd have to hope would not unravel too much. With cargo and fuel shifting about so radically, the ship's seaworthiness was in peril.

By the *Agamemnon*'s rise and fall in the pitchy night Preedy guessed the height of the waves to be gaining on forty feet. All he could do was pray there weren't greater waves out there in the dark. The wind shrieked through the rigging. Once or twice during the night the clouds had peeled back enough to reveal a moon that was like a dim, greasy blotch in the heavens. The ocean with all its foam was as white as driven snow. The ship might have been a sleigh careening across wild drifts, pulled by a panicked team.

At one of the partings of the clouds, Preedy got a look at the two sailors holding the helm. The men were pale and wide-eyed in the moon and binnacle light. They seemed, to Preedy, to be clutching the ship's wheel like two children clasping their mother's skirts.

"Steady as she goes!" Preedy shouted at them. An almost silly command, given the extremity of the weather and the near madness of the situation. But the men seemed to appreciate the order; one of the sailors even smiled a little before the clouds obscured the moon and all was darkness and howling once more.

Meanwhile, in his tiny stateroom, against all odds, Professor Thomson slept. He had rarely been to sea, had never encountered a storm like this, but was able to secure himself in his bunk by bolstering it with extra blankets rolled lengthwise and by fashioning a restraining net out of his belts and galluses. He had a physicist's eye and when last on deck had seen that as long as the waves were not breaking and the distance between troughs was greater than the height of the waves and as long as Captain Preedy kept the ship headed into the gale, the *Agamemnon* would ride out the storm. This was enough to satisfy Professor Thomson. He had commanded himself to attempt some calculations in his head and had even found his mind sliding over to visions of what life would be like if—or when—the cable was successfully in operation. Field had given him a dozen shares in the syndicate as compensation for sailing on this voyage. Perhaps they'd make him rich. Perhaps, he had laughed to himself while dozing off, he'd buy a yacht.

By morning a sense of resignation had taken over the *Agamemnon*. The storm still raged. There was so much water in the air and air in the water that at dawn it was difficult to discern where the sea began and the atmosphere ended. The ship still toiled up the rising slopes of the waves and skidded down the other side. The coming of daylight brought not terror but a premonitory fear that the storm wasn't about to give up. There would be another whole day of hanging on.

Captain Preedy had gone below for a little sleep, but by dawn he was back up by the helm. He'd sent a man aloft—only halfway up the mainmast—to see if he could spot any of the other ships.

Chester had come up, too, and was on the main deck. A seaman had knocked on Chester's door saying that the captain wanted to talk about the deck cable. Chester held fast to a belaying rail, taking spray and rain on his right shoulder, hunched over, watching the lookout to see if the man above reported any sightings. Katerina remained below; he had whispered to her that she must stay there. He had left her and with great difficulty managed to dress, smashing into the bulkhead with the ship's lurching as he pulled on his boots. He then proceded to the quarterdeck.

"I want to cut her loose!" Preedy shouted through the gale when Chester arrived. Preedy pointed to the foredeck cable. To Chester it looked fine, even through all the storm pounding.

"But it got through the night!" Chester shouted back.

"Your cable belowdecks is unraveling, shifting our ballast. I took the wheel. I could feel the effect it has up here. We could founder!"

"Captain, you're asking us to scrap the whole mission. We need all the cable. We can't lay a telegraph cable *partway* across the ocean. We need all the cable. We need the spool on the bow."

"That spool on the bow could be the marker on your grave, Mr. Ludlow. And on mine and everyone else's on this ship. I say send it overboard. We are discussing our survival here, sir."

Chester didn't know where Preedy's sudden trepidation came from. A few hours ago with his cracks about exploding carafes of Madeira, Preedy had seemed ready to sail into the teeth of any storm. Something had softened his resolve during the night. Fatigue perhaps. Darkness upon the face of the deep. Chester had the illogical thought that Preedy's failure of nerve was the curse exacted upon Chester for being with Frau Lindt.

"Give it some time, Captain," shouted Chester. "*Please.* Give me the morning."

Chester saw the helmsmen both cast quick sidelong glances at Preedy, who only looked aloft to where the lookout still clung to the mast.

"All right," he uttered, just barely audible above the gale. "Provided nothing gets worse. The morning."

"Good man!" Chester exclaimed, and made his way toward the main deck. He wanted to check the forward cable spool just to be sure it would hold for the morning, then he wanted to get back to Katerina.

The lookout above them had been turning in all directions, searching for a sign of a ship. It was obvious he could see nothing. He appeared confused, almost peeved, by the tormenting rain and wind. Then he looked off the port bow and froze. His left hand rose slowly, and he let out a long cry that grew into a keen: *"Wave!"*

The *Agamemnon* was rising on a large surge that would take it upward of forty feet. When the ship reached the crest, Chester, Captain Preedy, and all the crew on deck turned in the direction the lookout pointed.

"Two! Three! Four!" the man shouted.

On the horizon, or on what Chester and the others took to be the horizon, loomed a wave that mocked the vision of a headland whereupon wives and children might stand vigil for homecoming sailors. Instead of appearing to move toward the *Agamemnon*, this wave—this *mountain*, really— seemed rather to stand fast and be luring the ship toward it.

The wave was more than twice the height of anything the *Agamemnon* had ridden so far, and by the look of the foam crowns visible, it appeared there were more than one. That was why the lookout had been counting. There was a quartet of the freakish giants heading for the ship. The length of the waves was incalculable. They faded into the mist and rain. They could have gone on for a thousand leagues. The leading billow's face was gray and wrinkled with wind-driven ripples, making it look like a wall of curved, pebbled glass.

Then it disappeared. The *Agamemnon* had descended into another trough, and the crew could see nothing but the more local wave faces on either side of the ship.

Every sailor on deck immediately looked to one another in desperate need of confirmation of what they'd just witnessed out there. Hidden in the trough, they had a moment's shelter from the dreadful sight. It was out there, beyond these smaller, nearer waves, but for a moment they couldn't see the monster and therefore they must be safe.

Chester was grateful Katerina had not seen it. He was glad for all the ship's company belowdecks who hadn't seen it. They were perhaps troubled by their sleepless night and by the constant buffeting of the tempest, but they'd been spared the soulless vision of that approaching rupture in the very dimensions of the planet.

The *Agamemnon* rose again to another crest. It would be less, much less, than a minute before the ship would be contending with that first cliff of water. No time now for the lookout to scramble down, no time for anyone to go below and warn the passengers and crew, no time for the men on deck, from Captain Preedy on down to the least-ranking seaman, to do anything but hold on.

In another trough now, Chester looked around hastily for a firm hand-hold. He dropped to his knees and wrapped his arms through a pair of adjoining mainmast shrouds as if he were weaving reeds into a basket. In a few moments the *Agamemnon* had risen to the last crest. Soon the sea would fall away and the first of the monsters would gather the ship in.

Going down the back of the last storm wave was no different from anything the *Agamemnon* had been through already. It was the coming confrontation with the face of the giant that changed everything. Chester could feel the weight of his body pulling on his arms locked in the mainmast shrouds as his legs began to slide out from under him. He would soon be hanging from the lines. To walk forward now on the deck would be like ascending the roof of a steeply gabled house. Beyond the bowsprit, as if viewing the indifferent summit of an alp, Chester could see the crest of the wave with its whitecaps and spume blowing about like snow devils. The wave was so outsized that it was as if the billow were unmoving and the ship were some kind of toy cable car laboring up its slope.

For those belowdecks, the *Agamemnon* might as well have been standing on end. Stern bulkheads now seemed like deck flooring, forward bulkheads like ceilings. Belts and braces snapping, Professor Thomson was hurled from his berth. Katerina held on to the bed but felt the angle of the cabin incline so precipitously, she cried out. Throughout the ship, crewmen, who over the previous hours had adapted to the ship's tossing, were now dashed against bulkheads, flung to the deck, and dumped from their hammocks. Jack Trace, having just arisen, was shakily pulling on his breeches. He could hear Moon still groaning on his bunk. He was about to ask the journalist how he felt when there was an immense volley of cracking noise like artillery fire, and a rushing wall of coal burst from its bulkhead, crossed the passage, and smashed through the door of Trace's room.

Flour barrels in the galley burst their lids. Equipment, chains, buckets, ladders, tools—everything that had remained fast through the tortuous night now came loose in a cascade of debris. Katerina was crying out amid a tangle of bedclothes. As Professor Thomson clawed about for his spectacles, something heavy struck him on the head. Jack Trace was smashed against his berth by the crushing wall of coal that rose to his chest and kept pouring into the room. Seamen flailed at one another in vain attempts to right themselves and to fend off falling objects. The lookout on the mast was still howling.

The *Agamemnon* finally made the crest and stood there on the summit, level, as if it were a way station on a long, white ridge extending in either direction to the ends of the earth. Then came the inevitable descent and the relapse of all the havoc wreaked belowdecks.

Katerina was beyond crying now; she was endeavoring to wrap herself in the pillows and bedclothes to protect herself from injury. She had quelled her panic and went about the steely task of self-preservation.

Jack Trace, who had been buried up to his neck in coal, was amazed to see the stuff recede like a fast-ebbing black tide leaving swirls of jet dust in the air. He turned around to see a paralyzed Wilkins Moon, looking out from stunned, gibbous, white eyes. His face was as black as a minstrel's, his pink mouth working ineffectually. He couldn't utter a sound. He had been buried alive in his berth by the coal and now was disinterred by the rolling of the ship. Neither Moon nor Trace could know the same bituminous avalanche was about to hit them again.

The *Agamemnon* headed up the second wave, and Chester glanced at Captain Preedy and the helmsmen. All three men were embracing the wheel and the binnacle. Preedy looked excessively annoyed; one seaman was weeping; the other, laughing. They looked like a sculpture depicting three possible reactions to doom.

Chester turned forward again as the ship crested. He wanted to see how the bow cable spool was holding. It appeared to be intact. In a few moments, the ship began to nose once more down toward hell.

This time Chester noticed the cries of one of the helmsmen, the laughing one. Through his hysteria he was exclaiming that he'd lost control of the ship. She was slewing out from under him, he cried, and starting to slide abreast of the waves.

They reached the nadir of the trough and were ascending again before Captain Preedy himself let go of the binnacle and grabbed the wheel, but the ship was not responding. She was taking the wave three-quarters-on.

When the *Agamemnon* started down another decline, she was sliding nearly forty-five degrees to starboard. Heading up the third wave, the pitch was forty-five degrees to port. Chester could see the trouble they were in. Any seaman could. Captain Preedy was praying as he held the wheel.

The cable in the hold, the loose cable, was bunching and tangling and sliding in huge piles against the tub walls. The cable on deck, mercifully, was holding fast.

Belowdecks Katerina fixed her mind on Chester, on how she must hold on to be able to see him again. She prayed he hadn't been swept away by whatever was going on above.

Professor Thomson was unconscious on the floor of his cabin, having been struck by a falling clock. He had no personal effects, no furniture, and no amenities in his berth, save for the large nautical timepiece he'd brought that was now smashed on the floor next to him.

Two more waves sent the *Agamemnon* into a series of forty-five-degree rolls that forced the ends of the lowest yardarms into the sea. Not a man aboard was confident the ship would make it through. The crew on deck could see the astounding magnitude of the waves; they could feel the lashing of the spray and wind-driven rain. Belowdecks every sailor could feel the sickly sideways slide of the hull down the face of each giant. They knew that at these angles and these velocities, the *Agamemnon* could pitchpole, could capsize, could founder at any moment. More men than not rode the waves with eyes clamped shut in prayer.

The Incapacitated and a Job for Frau Lindt

Of all the ship's company, Wilkins Moon fared the worst. Days later, when he was finally able to write in his log about the storm, Captain Preedy listed Moon as "incapacitated by fright." Forty-five men were injured with broken limbs, cuts, abrasions, and dislocations. Six men had concussions (Professor Thomson was one of these, as was the ship's surgeon, Lieutenant Preston, who was too beset by dizziness and nausea from his skull fracture to minister to the injured), and there were two men scalded by steam. Yet no one was killed. No one was lost at sea.

Trace had reported Moon's malady to Captain Preedy even while the storm still blew, and the captain reassigned Trace to Professor Thomson's cabin. The professor, he said, might need some watching while he recovered from his injury. The crew would check on Moon. This was fine with Trace. He needed to get away from Moon, but mostly he was concerned with finding a place to work. He was trying to capture on paper what was happening all about the ship. The storm, though violent and frightening, was a vivid, almost intoxicating, inspiration for Trace. He wanted to get it all down.

Preedy had consented to keep the bow deck cable aboard, and the spool remained fast through all the pounding. It became impossible to jettison the cargo anyway, for on the second night after the big waves, the deck timbers below the spool gave with a deafening crack and the coil tilted into the deck, nestling there almost as if it were an egg in a giant nest. Sailors shored up the broken beams from below, and the *Agamemnon* blundered on.

Chester learned to move about the bucking and rearing ship with some skill. He made his rounds, checking with Preedy; visiting Thomson; keeping his eye on the cable and other cargo; trying his best, but mostly in vain, to prevent further damage. For Chester it was more than a week of hanging on, praying that the ship would hold together, hoping the other ships, long out of sight, were weathering the blow.

Chester knew during the storm he must proceed as if all were fine and the cable splicing would occur mid ocean just as planned. He had to meet with Thomson and continue to solve problems and go over details. Eventually, the professor was feeling well enough to work.

"That man's possessed, you know," Thomson said to Chester when they were alone.

"Who?" asked Chester.

The professor scratched under the bandage wrapped around his head. "The big fellow. He's up on deck every chance he gets. He can't draw up there, of course. The paper would be soaked in a second, but he goes up and 'absorbs the storm,' as he says. Then he runs back down here and draws like a madman. Even with the pitching and tossing. I almost think he enjoys this horrid weather. Likable enough fellow, though. And the drawings are quite good. Terrific, some of them, actually. Just something a little loose about the man."

Listening to Thomson's effusions, Chester had the thought that the professor's injury had addled him, all this going on about Trace. But Ches-

ter quickly realized the professor was working around to something: his
concern that Chester wasn't devoted to *his* work.

"I didn't see her, my man, but I know she's aboard," the professor
said abruptly, and Chester knew what was up.

The professor continued, "I don't think there's a seaman on the ship
who doesn't. Now, the issue isn't what you have done or what you are
doing. We are men among men, after all, and we are at sea. But the issue
is what are you *going* to do?"

Around them, the timbers creaked and the waves thudded against the
reverberating hull.

"Sir, I want you to know that I had nothing to do with her being here,"
Chester said. "I never encouraged her, and I most certainly never conspired
with her. She just . . . *appeared.*"

Hearing himself say this sent a wave of self-reproach through Chester.
Here he was reducing Katerina's daring, her risks for him, down to an
unseemly act of petulance from which he was trying to dissociate himself.

Thomson was sitting on the edge of his berth, leaning against the
bulkhead to steady himself from the rolling of the ship. He looked at Chester, who braced himself against a rack of Trace's artist supplies.

"I believe you, for what it's worth," Thomson said cooly, and Chester
felt himself shrinking in the man's estimation. "But you still must decide
what to do. Presuming we make it through this storm and get our cable
spliced and laid, you can't very well walk off the gangway with her on
your arm."

"Sir, she's not what you might think."

"She's the musician from your show, am I right?"

"Yes," Chester said dryly.

"Well, then she *is* what I might think. They say she is something to
behold, and her daring is a credit to you. But still, what are you going to
do?"

"I don't know," Chester said. "I've been trying to hold things together
during this damn storm."

"Maybe you should ask her," Thomson said.

"Ask her what?" said Chester.

"If you don't have a plan for her, maybe she has one for you."

"To be with you," Katerina said once Chester was back with her. "My
plan for you is to be with me. How nice of you to ask," she said.

She was sounding irritable. The storm had grown tedious for her.

Being confined had grown tedious for her. Chester's concern for all the wracked and smashed bits of equipment was tedious. This wasn't the out-come she'd expected from stowing away. Still, Chester hadn't asked for the storm; he hadn't wished for this outcome, either. Katerina tried to stifle her annoyance.

"I want you to be with me," she said again, much more sweetly. "Now . . . ," and she reached for him and tried to pull him into the berth, where she was sitting against the pillows.

"Katerina, we need a better plan than that. You can't, you must know, just walk off the ship with me when we get to Newfoundland."

"I accept that, dearest. I'm not incapable of discretion. Except for now," she added with a sigh of triumph as she pulled him under the covers with her.

"You will be transferring to the *Niagara* when we splice the cables," Thomson said to Chester when they met again. "She will stay here on the *Agamemnon*. You will go to America. She will go back to England and her husband. I can't believe, Ludlow, that I must outline this for you. It seems so painfully obvious."

"Of course," Chester said glumly. "I knew this all along."

"Of course," Katerina said darkly when Chester returned with the plan. "I suspected this might be what you'd suggest."

"Did you really think there could be any other way?" Chester asked. He had brought her some bread and, in a covered pail, some soup. She was having none of it or his plan. The cabin still pitched back and forth, and Chester had to keep his hand on the food so it wouldn't slide off the little table that folded down from the bulkhead.

"After all," Chester went on, "we're both *married*."

"You saw how I am married," Frau Lindt said. "I saw how you are married. I said I would watch as you triumphed. I meant that. If I must remind you, I have risked my life to be here. I don't have to walk off the ship alongside you, as you say, but I can be there in America, waiting."

"It's impossible, Katerina. How are you to transfer to the *Niagara*? In my seabag?"

Katerina slumped back against the bulkhead behind the bed, her face lost in shadows. The two of them sat alone in silence in the pounding gale.

"So, it's settled then?" Professor Thomson said. He now had the ban-dage off. There was a crystalline parabola of dried blood at his hairline where the clock had cut him.

"I suppose," Chester said.

"Now we can concentrate?" Thomson said.

"I suppose," said Chester.

Overnight the clouds, the wind, the rain, even the huge waves, dis-appeared. The *Agamemnon* was left almost becalmed on a gentle sea under a slightly hazy blue sky. It was weather befitting the summer solstice in mid-ocean.

The suddenness of the change added an extra measure of giddiness to the general relief and gratitude felt by the ship's company. The crew broke into song. Professor Thomson stood elated on the quarterdeck. Jack Trace laughed as he hung some of his dampened artwork out to dry on a line like laundry over the forecastle. Katerina, still in her berth, broke into tears, and Chester heard her as he passed by the stateroom on his repair rounds.

Captain Preedy set an immediate course for the rendezvous point and posted double lookouts on the masts in hopes of finding the other ships. He had the rest of the crew set about assessing and repairing the damage.

The ship was a shambles. Cables, lines, and shrouds lay tangled all over the decks. Sailors began shoveling and carting coal that had broken through bulkhead after bulkhead belowdecks. The fuel had seemingly wan-dered about the ship like a river that floods its banks and flows into what-ever cove or meadow it can find. Captain Preedy had his men clear an area in what was once the *Agamemnon*'s main gun deck and there set up a billet for the injured.

Three sailors had to bind and carry Moon, mattress and all, from his berth to this makeshift sick bay. Trace, busier than ever with sketching now that things had dried out, watched Moon go by. A stink emanated from the litter. Moon's eyes saw nothing. Trace followed the litter to the hospital deck, where the sailors set Moon among the groaning crewmen. They then stripped the reporter of his soiled trousers; swabbed his buttocks with a deck mop; threw the britches, the bedclothes, and mattress out a gunport; moved him to a pallet; and finally covered him with a blanket. Moon showed no sign that the indignities had made the slightest difference to him.

"Moon, old fellow," Trace said when the trio of sailors had gone back to tasks on deck.

No answer. Moon lay on his side, his fingers gently stroking his wool blanket. A pearl of drool formed at the corner of his mouth.

"Moon, speak to me."

Moon was silent.

"Moon, are you going to be all right?"

No answer.

"Moon?"

From above came the sound of dragging and thumping. Sailors were hauling broken timbers out of the way of the cable, long sections of which they were pulling up from the tub in the main hold to recoil.

"Moon, I say, you will be able to work, won't you?"

Moon's face showed no change. To see the man's eyes stall in their sockets—no more rattling nervously about—was most disturbing to Trace. Trace realized that Moon would not move, would not speak, would certainly not write a word for the rest of the voyage. Trace had no idea if Moon would *ever* be able to do these things.

"Were you afraid you would die?" Katerina asked Chester.

"When?" Chester said.

"In the storm."

She was lying next to him in the berth. He had stretched out there fully clothed after coming back from hours of supervising repairs. Her question was the first glimmer of a conversation she'd offered beyond perfunctory courtesies necessarily exchanged by two people living in tight quarters. In the days since he'd declared his intention of sending her back to England without him, he'd grown accustomed to the mood of resigned tension in the room. He'd held her through the storm; she'd held him. But after he announced his plan, there was only a dumb show of comfort in the storm-tossed cabin, a feeling that in such extremity you *must* hold each other.

"Yes," Chester said now, trying not to gulp down the chance to converse with her like a man starved for oxygen. "Yes," he said again more quietly. "Yes, I was."

"You did not act afraid."

"Acting unafraid was almost the easy part. There was so much to do, to keep the ship, the mission, together. Acting was easy."

"And it didn't take your mind off death? I thought action was supposed to do that."

"Anyone who wasn't afraid of death in that storm was a fool," Chester said.

Katerina said, "I was afraid."

Chester pulled her closer. He was glad she didn't resist. "I didn't want you to be," he said.

"I was afraid if death came, there I would be, without you," she said. "My only hope was we would both die together, but I don't know if that was because I knew we'd be together in death or because if I couldn't have you, then no one should. Then I hated myself for wishing for you to die."

Katerina shook her head and with a delicate finger picked at the grain in the wood of the bulkhead near their berth. She said, "Funny how we can think of such things, lying here, the sea so calm now. In the storm, I knew death was close by, but I didn't have the chance to ponder it. I was afraid. But still, I was numb, living in here, kept here by the storm and by you. I became used to having it close by, the fear, and death. It's not so bad, having death near."

"I had a child who died," Chester said. The words were out before he knew it.

"Her name was Betty," he said. "She was not well."

And Chester explained to Katerina about his father, about Otis, about other Ludlows who supposedly had the same "visitations." He explained to Katerina how Betty died.

"I wasn't there," he said. "I was up on the Gulf of St. Lawrence beginning work on the first cable."

"The one that failed."

"The one that failed," Chester said calmly, as if three years' preparation and work on that cable were nothing. And weren't they nothing, really, when compared to the loss of his child?

"I received word from Franny," he went on. "We'd established a line from the mainland to St. John's. Her message was so terse, so unlike the way Franny would have told me had I been there." He quoted the message exactly, as if it were before his eyes. He could see the telegrapher's handwriting: *"Accident. We lost our baby. Nothing Otis could do. Come home. She is at place."*

Katerina frowned.

"There was a misspelling, you see," Chester said. "I tried to believe Franny meant Betty had wandered off, that she was *lost*, that we still had a chance of finding her, and that simultaneously, against all logic, she was at *place*, at our place. I hoped that when I got back to Maine, there she'd be, but I knew what the message really meant. *Place* meant *peace*, and Franny had been circumspect because she couldn't bear to utter the word *dead* to the telegrapher. *We lost our baby . . . she is at place* instead of simply *Betty is dead.* I rushed home to find what I feared."

Katerina bit her lower lip, continuing to frown. Then as if she were speaking of an indictment handed down against Chester, she said indignantly, "All your work on these cables, and still all anyone can send is *signals* in a code no one can speak. And the code, is it good for anything but bad news?"

She tucked his arm closer to her body.

"I'm sorry," she said. "I do love you."

"That's all right."

"Do you think of her often?"

And Chester believed for a moment Katerina meant Franny. He felt his breath catch.

"Think?"

"Of Betty."

He shook his head. "I was spared seeing the accident. Franny had to go through that. She thinks of her constantly. To distraction, I'd say. Not seeing the end made things for me . . . less vivid, I suppose."

"Your brother was there?"

"But he didn't see it happen. He claims to have had a seizure, too. At the same time."

"You doubt it?"

"It makes no difference. She is dead. That is a fact beyond all doubt. I know he felt horribly guilty," Chester said. "Franny says we mustn't blame Otis. There was nothing he could do."

"And you do blame him."

"I don't know. I might as well blame myself for not being there, for being hundreds of miles away at work. Would it have saved her if I were there, back at our house?"

"You can't answer that," Katerina said. "No one can. You can only live with it."

"He is back there now. Otis. At my home. And they say they have seen Betty."

"*Seen* her?"

"In a vision or a visitation or a séance of some kind."

"Could that be true?

Chester shifted in the bed. "I have no idea," he whispered.

"So," Katerina murmured to herself. "Maybe we are together after death."

This was why, when Katerina was talking about her storm fear and an afterlife together, Chester had brought up Betty. The child, after death, was still in his life. Even if she wasn't a spirit, even if Franny and Otis were involved in some manner of humbug, Betty was still a presence for them all. But, he thought sadly, a presence that Katerina, his lover lying there beside him, his fellow survivor of the storm, a woman who dared death and shame for him, could never fully understand.

There was a knock at the door.

Chester sat up. "Who is it?"

"Preedy. A word with you, sir."

"Ah, one . . . moment . . . ," and Chester began to extricate himself from the berth.

"Actually," Preedy said, "a word with the *lady* would be more to the point."

"Let me . . . well, let me . . . uh, lady?"

There was a laugh from the other side of the door. "Yes. You remember saving a lady from sliding away with the deckwash in the storm? You brought her here for safekeeping. *That* lady?"

Chester looked at Katerina. She had thrown on his robe, tied it tightly, and signaled him to open the door.

Preedy stepped into the cabin, hat in hand, but with a small, slanting grin that betrayed some self-satisfied amusement.

"Captain," Katerina said with a nod. She stood regally, with one hand resting lightly on the table's edge.

"I've come to offer you a job, madame." He bowed. "How pleasant at last to meet you, by the way. I hope that you found our storage locker commodious and to your liking and that you have not suffered unduly here with these, your alternate accommodations."

"What job?" Katerina said flatly, almost cutting Preedy off.

"Nurse," Preedy said. "We have nearly fifty men in need of care. Every able man is detailed to putting the ship to rights. You would minister to the fallen."

"I'm not a nurse."

"Good. I knew you'd be amenable. For this, I and my injured men are grateful. You should report to what we call the hospital deck. Mr. Ludlow can show you the way. Lieutenant Preston, our ship's surgeon, was knocked unconscious. His eyesight is still bad. We had thought Mr. White-house would be with us as Mr. Ludlow's coengineer and could have also acted as an adjunct surgeon, but we have Professor Thomson in his stead; a fine man, an excellent scientist, I'm told, but no surgeon. We've had to fall back on our carpenter for medical treatment; a fine carpenter, I assure you, but very busy with repairs and also no surgeon. Therefore, whatever you do will be of help."

"But I know next to nothing," Katerina said.

"Perfect, because the carpenter knows *exactly* nothing. You are an improvement. Your stowing away turns out to be a boon. Thank you." He bowed and exited the cabin.

"I can't!" Katerina whispered desperately to Chester.

"You'll do fine," Chester said, but it was perfunctory encouragement, and she could sense it. He was thinking how, by the captain's demeanor, he could tell his status as chief engineer had been compromised by Katerina's presence and by his accommodating her in his cabin. He was a fool, and yet what else could he have done? Deny her? His choices were to be a fool or a cad. He would have to work all the harder to prove he was neither. He turned to her and held her face in his hands, staring hard into her blue eyes. "You'll do *fine*," he said. "We both shall."

Looking for a Sail

Repairs on the *Agamemnon* went round the clock. The ship looked as if a giant ill-tempered child had thrown a tantrum and broken or destroyed as much of the vessel as possible without actually sinking it. Chester and Professor Thomson devoted themselves to work on the telegraphy equipment. They supervised the cable recoiling in the main hold. They worked on testing and repairing all the sending and receiving mechanisms—both Thomson's delicate mirror galvanometers and Whitehouse's heavier magnetic devices—and they sorted through all the scrambled and shattered gear that had been battered by the storm. As they labored, they—and everyone else on the ship—kept an eye on the clear horizon or up to the lookouts to see if there were any signs of the other ships. It was as if, in waiting there at the rendezvous point, they hovered just outside a territory of apprehension and woe. Soon enough, waiting would become a vigil; if it went on long enough, it would eventually become a death watch, and that was a prospect no one wanted to entertain, so everyone worked all the harder to keep those thoughts at bay.

On the hospital deck, Katerina discovered she did have nursing skills, or at least the facility to learn some quickly. To the twenty or so men still not ambulatory, she was a vision of beauty walking among them. Though she wore the plain gray morning dress in which she'd stowed away and an apron that Chester had obtained from the galley, though she pulled her blond tresses back under a cap, her pale blue eyes set her countenance in bright contrast with the blandness of her costume. She walked the deck between the rows of pallets, with the carpenter stammering about each injury and his consequent treatment. The men on the pallets gaped. The carpenter had stitched wounds like a cobbler, salved burns like a mason, and reset bones as if every limb were a framing timber that needed sledging into place. Such treatment as they'd had from the carpenter was either irredeemable or barely sufficient. Katerina quickly saw that her job would be to offer the men comfort. She cleansed wounds, applied poultices, administered laudanum to the men in the most pain. But mostly she stayed with them, spoke with them, and even, in the softest tones, sang *lieder* for them. She began to spend as much time tending the hospital deck as Chester was racing about the rest of the ship tending to the cable equipment.

Late in the afternoon of the third day after the storm, a sail and a plume of smoke hove into view. Then two more. The *Niagara*, the *Gorgon*, and the *Valorous* had all survived. In a few hours all four ships floated near one another in mid ocean. Crews fired cannons in celebration and cheered one another from the ratlines. With semaphore flags the *Niagara* signaled the *Agamemnon* that Cyrus Field was coming over by boat.

Chester watched as the oars of the longboat flashed in the sunlight. Soon Field was visible in the bow, his eyes darting about, trying to assess the damage to the *Agamemnon* as he approached. Chester, Thomson, and Preedy all met Field at the main deck rail as he climbed the ladder.

"Good grief," Field muttered as he looked about at the wreckage still unrepaired.

"You should have been here four days ago, sir," Preedy said with bluff joviality. "Things are considerably quieter and neater now. None of those pesky waves washing all about."

"Your crew?"

"All alive, sir," Preedy said. "Some the worse for wear, but all eager to get to work now that our holiday is over. How are you?"

The relief coursing over Field's face as he heard this was palpable. It made Chester and Professor Thomson break into smiles.

"Oh, thank God," Field said. He held on to the ship's rail. "Thank God. Oh, I'm fine, yes. We're all fine. Thank God."

Field explained how the storm had gone for all the other ships. They were less burdened than the *Agamemnon* and with more freeboard, so they were better able to manage the waves. Once the *Agamemnon* was put to rights, he said with growing eagerness, they would be ready to begin the splice and connect the continents.

"Let's go to your quarters, Ludlow," Field said. "We'll make our plans final."

"My . . . quarters?" said Chester.

Field looked at him quizzically.

"His quarters," Professor Thomson interjected, "are a shambles. Much out of order. He's preparing to transfer to the *Niagara* for the trip to America. Correct, Ludlow? Besides, I have all the necessary specifications and papers in my berth. We can meet there."

"Very well," said Field. "But first let me have a look at the state of things. Can you take me to the injured men, Captain Preedy?"

Preedy nodded and gestured for them all to follow him toward the main companionway.

"After that, I want to see the cable," Field said.

As they headed aft, Chester leaned over to Thomson and whispered, "Thank you, sir."

"Nothing," muttered Thomson.

Chester caught Captain Preedy signaling something to a sailor, who sped on ahead of them.

Chester was relieved to see that Katerina was not on the hospital deck. The sailor whom Preedy had sent forward probably cleared her out. It gave him the queasy feeling that the whole ship was in on his duplicity.

Field stood near the companionway and addressed all the wounded men. He thanked them for their bravery and sacrifice. Then, when Field finished, the patients, led by a sailor with a broken shoulder, offered three cheers. Chester was surprised that it moved him so deeply. He thought

how it wasn't so much *what* Field said as it was the *sound* of it. For the first
time since they'd left England and sailed through the eternity of the storm,
Chester was hearing the cadences of American speech. He had been aboard
the *Agamemnon* with its British crew for what seemed like a lifetime, he'd
lain in intimacy with Katerina Lindt, but here he was listening to something
that conjured home. He thought of Franny and Otis, of all the complications there, but all the comforts, too. Would this wire they were about to
lay be able to convey such feeling? How could something as ineffable as
the emotions stirred by a New Englander's flat, broad inflections, sounds
that evinced a childhood and loved ones, be encoded and transmitted
across the ocean? Perhaps Katerina was right. They were doing so much,
and yet it could seem so meager in the presence of something as evanescent
as the sound of one man's voice.

Soon Chester realized he was standing alone. Field, Preedy, Thomson,
and the others had left to go inspect the cable and the paying-out device
on the stern of the ship.

"You all right, gov'nor?"

Chester looked down at a man on the nearest pallet. The fellow had
wispy blond hair, a dusting of a mustache and a blank gaze. His fingers
stroked the wool of his blanket. He seemed to be looking over Chester's
shoulder, through the deck above. The vacancy of his stare unsettled Chester. The man wasn't the fellow who had spoken.

"You all right?"

Chester didn't look to see who of the other sailors was asking the
question.

"Yes," he answered while still staring at the benumbed invalid at his
feet. "Yes, fine. Carry on, men. You're all needed. Get well quickly. We
all have great work to do."

His own voice sounded anemic—neither, he thought, British nor American. As if he spoke the dialect not of home but of some country lost in
between.

Trace Aloft

The word going around the ships was that if all went well, they'd have the cable laid in five days. It was a heady rumor for a company that had endured more than a week of a violent storm, several anxious days looking for the other ships, and several more days and nights in a frenzy of repairs. Now, though, they were ready to begin laying cable, and the prospect that it would all be accomplished in less than a week made the crews jittery with anticipation.

The *Agamemnon* and the *Niagara* were aligned stern to stern on the calm morning sea. The *Gorgon* and the *Valorous* hovered nearby, caparisoned in flags and banners befitting a naval revue. Cyrus Field and members of the *Niagara*'s cable crew came over to the *Agamemnon* in a longboat and three skiffs for the splicing ceremony.

Jack Trace sketched it all from the *Agamemnon*'s crow's nest. After the storm, the crew of the *Agamemnon* noted with amusement Trace's newfound surety aboard the ship. Scrambling up the ratlines to the masthead with a courier bag of art supplies slung over his shoulder was nothing now for him.

Trace could tell a prayer was in progress on the deck below. The ships' companies, lined in their uniformed ranks on the decks—and even so out on the circling *Gorgon* and *Valorous*—had their caps off and their heads bowed. Field appeared to be offering a benediction. The words were indecipherable on the breeze. Trace hoped messages on the cable would fare better.

Trace looked down at Chester Ludlow. The man had seemed subdued since the storm. Trace wondered about the woman. She wasn't anywhere to be seen. He had noticed her once working with the ailing men on the hospital deck, and he had sketched the scene. Actually, he sketched two versions. One picture had Frau Lindt ministering to the men, a figure of mercy bending over a bandaged sailor with a couple of battened sixty-pounder cannons in the background. The other version, less faithful to the truth, had the same injured sailors, the same lowering beams of the deck overhead, the same decommissioned cannons but without a woman at its center.

A cheer went up from the crew below. The prayer was over. Ludlow had apparently offered a remark that provoked the jollity. Field was clap-

ping the engineer on the back, and Thomson was applauding lustily. Trace
scanned the deck below. He looked to the foredeck companionway, where
he discerned movement in a portal unseen by all the sailors and officers
facing the ceremony. There, in her gray frock, peering discreetly out from
the hatch—watching Ludlow, no doubt—was Frau Lindt.

Trace thought he saw Ludlow's spectacles glint in the sunlight, but
when he looked more carefully, he saw that it was a shiny, polished coin,
a sixpence, bent to fit round the cable. Ludlow held the coin up and showed
it to all the assembled, then placed it on the cable, where a crewman
brought the final wraps of canvas around the coin and the cable and another crewman slathered tar on the splice. Ludlow stepped back, the men
worked smartly, and another cheer went up from the deck, a cheer picked
up by the crews on the other ships.

The crews stepped up to the splicing bench and, with men on each
side, lifted the spliced sections onto their shoulders and half-stepped it over
to the *Agamemnon*'s port rail. The outboard sailors ducked under the cable,
and on a count and command from Ludlow, the men tossed the cable over
the side. A rousing shout fluttered out over the bright water. The cable fell
into the sea with a serpentine splash. After a moment watching the great
gutta-percha eel begin to sink, the crew snapped back into action.

The *Niagara*'s emissaries clambered over the side and boarded their
longboat and skiffs, only this time along with Field and the American sailors went Chester Ludlow. His bags and instrument cases were lowered
and stowed. He stood bracing his legs on a midship bench as the longboat
pulled away, and he offered a salute to Professor Thomson, who stood at
the *Agamemnon*'s rail raising his hand in farewell.

Jack Trace put away his sketching supplies and made ready to descend
to the deck. He cast a quick glance forward. Frau Lindt was gone, the
hatch now just an open, black aperture.

Soon a puff of smoke and steam exhaled from the *Niagara*'s stern, and
one likewise from the *Agamemnon*'s, signaling that the paying-out engines
were commencing their labors. The delicate task had begun and all else
was secondary now to the cable. When the steam whistle from the donkey
engine on the *Agamemnon*'s stern sounded with one following almost immediately from the *Niagara*, Jack Trace finally quit the crow's nest and
worked his way down the ratlines.

Breaks

He had said he would telegraph her. Not, of course, while they were laying the cable, for then he must be in constant contact with Professor Thomson and everything must be strictly business. But later, after their victory, after the cable was set and working, he would send a telegram. Theirs, he'd said, would be the first message of intimates to cross under the Atlantic.

"How can you do it?" she'd asked.

"I'm the chief engineer," he'd said. "I can send whatever I wish."

"No. How can you put an ocean between us?"

He looked startled. It was so easy for him to get lost in the headiness of the project.

"I'm sorry," he'd mumbled, and clasped her to him. "I'm sorry."

"Send for me," she'd said, buried in his arms against his chest, feeling almost impaled there.

"I'll send you a telegram."

"Send for me."

"The first across the Atlantic from a man to his lover."

"His lover."

"*Yes*. His *lover*."

"But will you send for me?"

And even though she'd been looking into his eyes when she'd asked this, she later couldn't remember his answer. That he'd deftly avoided one, that he'd begged off, saying he had to get back to work, needed time to think of a plan, couldn't stay but wanted to, all smoldered inside her now. She lay on the bunk in his former cabin, which was now nearly bare since he and all his things were gone. All she had were the few effects she'd been able to smuggle aboard. She lay suspended between rage and grief and prostrate longing. She would not move.

Now that the cable work had begun, the cabin was beset by a new maddening noise. Before, it had been the relentless pounding of the storm; now it was the grinding of the outgoing cable. The noise rumbled down from everywhere. The rollers on the deck transporting the cable from the drum to the stern paying-out device rattled in their races. The donkey engine gave out percussive shudders with every piston stroke. She thought how somewhere on the ship Chester's messages to Professor Thomson were arriving through the wire. Somewhere on the ship his voice was here.

Not his voice really. His *signal*. His presence. His *mind* was here. His thoughts. But not him.

And they weren't thoughts of her. No doubt they were calculations or time notations or something wholly bound up in engineering matters.

She thumped her mattress in frustration. She was thinking about getting out of her berth and maybe returning to check on the poor journalist fellow still on the hospital deck—something to pull her out of these thoughts—when suddenly the grinding stopped. Katerina raised up onto her elbows. The donkey engine had shut down. There was no sound now but the gentle basso profundo rumble of the ship's main boiler. The cable was not paying out. Something must be wrong. Soon the little steam whistle shrieked.

On the deck the backup crew was scrambling to assist the men at the paying-out engine. Sailors were waving for Professor Thomson. Word came out of the telegraph cabin: no pulses from the *Niagara*—the signal might be dead.

The ships were nearly eighty miles apart. Preedy ordered the engine room to cut power. For the next three hours Professor Thomson tried in vain to raise Chester on the wire. On the *Niagara*, Chester was doing the same. Each man assumed the cable had broken on the other's ship. Each engineer ordered the cable cut, and the ships turned around to return to the rendezvous point.

When the ships met, the first message semaphored between them was "How did the cable part?"

In fact, it *hadn't* parted. At least not so anyone aboard either vessel could see. The break, the failure, whatever it was, occurred somewhere on the ocean bottom. Thomson had done some measurements before he'd ordered his end of the cable severed on the *Agamemnon*. He measured the signal resistance and calculated that the electrical impulses had trickled away into the sea somewhere between the two ships.

Immediately the engineers worried that perhaps the silty, sandy sea bottom they'd expected to be the resting place for their cable was not so benign after all. Had they dropped the wire on jagged rocks more than two miles down?

"Gentlemen, that we don't know what has happened must not deter us," Chester began. "This whole venture has always been a foray into the unknown."

The men around him looked stoic. No one wanted to admit to his worst fears, though the mystery of it gnawed at them all.

"But aren't we agreed we shall try again?" Chester said.

Although there was enough cable left aboard the two ships, the *Agamemnon* was low on coal, and the *Niagara*'s remaining food supply was mainly heavily salted meat that was nearly too old to eat.

"The coal we shall hope lasts. We'll transfer some victuals from the *Agamemnon* to help sustain the *Niagara*," Chester said. "As for the cable . . . Professor Thomson and I have done some calculations. Each ship can spare about two hundred and fifty miles of wire. Therefore, we propose this"— and here he read from a paper—" 'The ships shall splice again and proceed as before. Should any accident occur to part the cable before the ships have run a hundred statute miles from rendezvous, the ships shall return to rendezvous and wait eight days, when, if the other ships do not appear, they shall proceed back to England. Beyond a hundred miles, if a break occurs, the ships shall proceed directly back, dispensing with a rendezvous.' "

Chester looked up. Cyrus Field nodded gravely. The men—engineers, skippers, and Field, the president of the syndicate—all signed the document.

A day later, back on the hospital deck of the *Agamemnon,* Jack Trace was kneeling beside Wilkins Moon with a bowl of food. Trace had tried to talk with Moon, to no avail. The man just fingered his wool blanket, grinned, and stared. Trace was raising a spoonful of gruel to Moon's lips when the steam whistle shrieked.

A sailor's voice called out in the ringing air after the whistle stopped. He yelled the one word the entire company dreaded: "Break!"

Jack raced up to the main deck in time to see Captain Preedy throw his hat down and yell something into the engine-room pipe. Professor Thomson came out of the telegraph cabin and looked once toward the stern before he turned to the starboard rail and covered his face with his hands.

Katerina Lindt stepped out onto the deck, and Trace stopped near her. They looked toward the paying-out device on the stern deck. There, hanging like a dead eel from the chocks, was the broken end of the cable. The rest of it lay lost on the bottom.

"They've failed, haven't they?" Katerina whispered.

"We've paid out more than two hundred miles, last count I heard," Trace said. He told her about the signed agreement.

Already the engine room had responded to Preedy's orders, and billows of black smoke belched from the stack as the boilers fired up. The moment the cable had snapped, Captain Preedy had ordered the ship back to England. There was no need to consider any other option. In less than a second, with the split of the cable, the ship had become a vanquished man-of-war. A gloom swiftly fell upon the crew. Sailors despondently climbed the ratlines to set out more canvas. The crewmen who weren't working stood, like Trace and Katerina, looking dumbfounded at that sinister, dangling cord. Several sailors hid their faces. Of all on the ship, only Katerina felt an atom of gladness. For all that was terrible about the cable break, out there beyond the horizon before which the severed end danced, Chester's ship would be turning around, too, heading away from America and sailing back toward the same port as Katerina Lindt.

CHAPTER XIV

"WE LANDED HERE IN THE WOODS"

England and the Atlantic Ocean, July–August 1858

Maddy Above the Mezzanine

Well, she had come up a long way now, hadn't she? Literally up. Up from under the Thames to the top floor of this lovely gaming establishment, with its chandeliers and sweeping staircase and pretty pictures and enough potted palms to make it feel as if someone had set up chemin de fer tables and a dining room and a billiard parlor right in the middle of a jungle. No other Lady of the Tunnel had attained such a station—let alone lived in such a place. Usually it was the other way round. The Thames Tunnel was a late stop on the line that went directly to a kennel ditch in Whitechapel and death on a cold night, a death that, if you were lucky, was opium- or gin-benumbed and quick.

But Maddy had gone the other way: from the tunnel up. Her looks and youth had made all the difference. And her pluck. Her life often caromed like one of the billiard balls clicking in the gaslit parlor below her on the mezzanine of the Bardolph. Her skill was in knowing how to play those caroms.

She stood on the landing of the stairs coming down from the upper floors of the Bardolph. She sipped champagne. She looked down on the pomaded head of her E. O. Wildman Whitehouse—E.O. is what he, Edward Orange Wildman Whitehouse, wanted her to call him—as he played a hand of blind crumley with several corpulent, middle-aged fellows in evening dress.

E.O. was another carom in a new direction. And because of him, here she stood amid ease and dalliance. What luck. And she'd planned none of it. If all those men below could know what a game of chance her life was, they wouldn't exalt their acumen at cards and billiards so. From their seats of comfort, what did they know of risk?

During the past fifteen minutes, E.O. and his companions had gone from animated bonhomie to dour concentration. The cards must be getting serious. Maddy hoped E.O. wouldn't be lucky. She had begun to notice that when Whitehouse won handsomely, he would return to the rooms flushed and imperious. He would be roughest on those nights, and though she was imperturbable and could act out the roles he set for her and suffer the little cuts and cigar burns and beg quietly but desperately for him to stop, it was better when he lost. On those nights he came back empty and chastened, as if he'd been scooped out hollow and had nothing left to give or take and needed only to be held. Strange how winning did not make him happy. He seemed more pleased in the august presence of utter and uncompromising loss.

As Maddy sipped her drink, she turned to look down the broad staircase with its heavy marble balustrade and red carpet that swept out before her like some vast and luxuriant glacial moraine. It occurred to her that her own luck had turned about the time her father had died. He was killed working on that giant ship. It took ages for word to reach her in the tunnel. The drunken sot wasn't much of a dad. Probably wasn't much of a shipbuilder, either. She wondered if there was a connection, though: the old man dies and her luck changes. Oh, that was stupid. There wasn't any magic involved. She had shaped her fate whenever she saw an opening. Sometimes she caromed; sometimes she calculated. She was an opportunist and proud to be one. That was the way of things. There was no better world than this one, and you had better play your luck. Those who were sharpest were the ones who survived. Almost as if it were ordained. Almost as if God, if he cared about such things and wasn't off somewhere in a far corner of heaven ignoring this little globe, had set his creatures here to work out who was fittest to survive. That was what *she* believed, at any rate. Maybe she would discuss this theory with her E.O. He might be interested. The possibility made her feel superior to all the swollen men and bejeweled women gliding and gaming down there around the mezzanine and main floor of the club.

She didn't notice him right off, lost as she was in her musings. But her first thought when she did was *How long has he been looking at me?*

Standing down near the majordomo's podium, letting a footman take his hat, was the sketch artist, looking up at Maddy.

When the *Agamemnon* had arrived back in London, Jack Trace had taken Moon by carriage to Moon's two brothers, who lived together in a house near Cartwright Gardens.

"Why, I say, it's Wilkie," one of the brothers had called from the door to the other brother deeper in the house. "Wilkie and a friend."

The second brother came into the foyer, which was already crowded with Trace, Moon, the first brother, and a trove of objects that looked to Trace like aboriginal masks, shields, and spears.

"He's not well," Trace said, indicating Wilkins, who had his hand on Trace's sleeve and seemed not to understand where he was.

"Hello, Wilkie," the second brother said, to no response.

The three Moon brothers were various in height; otherwise, they could almost have passed for triplets. The two brought Trace and Wilkins into the parlor. Trace explained what had happened during the storm at sea.

"This will put off Egypt," the first brother said when Trace had finished.

"Oh, damn you, Wilkie," said the other. "You always find a way." Wilkins smiled.

Inheritors of a Manchester textile fortune, the brothers Moon—William and Walter—spent most of their time traveling and collecting objets d'art. Wilkins was the only one who made any pretense of working. The brothers intimated that Wilkie's writing might never have been published if the Moon family fortune had not been conveniently invested in certain newspapers.

"Wilkie is just not cut out for his aspirations. This kind of thing," William said to Trace, gesturing at Wilkins, who sat dumbly transfixed by the fireplace andirons, "is not unexpected. We always clean up after Wilkie. He is of a delicate constitution. Mentally more so than physically. He's returned to us this way before. There was the Crimea. The noise of the gunfire discomposed him. And a wandering tour of the Alps. The heights got to him on that one. It only takes time and our care."

"But that means no barge tour on the Nile," said Walter morosely.

"Not this season in any event," said William. "The Pyramids have waited this long for us. They can wait a little more."

"Oh damn," said Walter.

Trace left his disabled cabinmate with his siblings, politely refusing when they offered to sell him one—or two—passages to Egypt for a six-month tour. He had obligations, he said.

With his charity to Moon discharged, Trace decided upon a supper at the Bardolph while the cable syndicate's board grappled in private meetings about the future of the project. He was, he thought merrily, a sailor on shore leave with pockets a-bursting. And now, best of fortune, he was running right into Maddy, the very outcome he'd hoped for.

He ascended the stairs toward her. She was looking his way. She had been lost in thought, standing there on the landing, prettier than he remembered her, looking for all the world like a monarch staring down at the futile bustle of her subjects. But when she turned and saw him, she betrayed a surprise that he was sure—or *hoped,* at any rate—revealed an eagerness at his approach.

Then, however, up from adjoining stairs came Edward Orange Wildman Whitehouse. He was about to speak to her when he followed her gaze and saw a large, thatch-headed fellow whom he seemed to remember seeing somewhere.

"Ah, hello, my good man," Whitehouse said, now extending his hand to Trace. "E. O. Whitehouse. Forgive me, but I can't recall—"

"Jack Trace."

"And you are . . . ?"

"An artist!"

It was Maddy who'd answered for him. Even Whitehouse looked surprised.

"You know him?" Whitehouse asked.

"Why, *everyone* knows Jack Trace, E.O.," Maddy said with a giggle. She flushed, her scar a delicate pale line. "He's one of the finest sketch artists and portraitists around. Aren't you, Jack—Mr. Trace?"

Her audacity left Trace fumbling for words. She had smoothed out her Cheapside accent. And her use of his Christian name, was it a giveaway to Whitehouse? He felt his breath coming in whippy little bursts.

"Oh, modesty forbids his saying so," Maddy said, laughing. "But he is one of the finest."

"You *know* him?" Whitehouse asked again.

"No, no, no," Maddy said as if it were the evening's most ridiculous question. "Only his reputation. You must be dreadfully behind times if you don't know it yourself."

"Well," said Whitehouse, "I suppose I am. An old fogram like me. A penniless old fogram."

"Penniless?" Maddy said, turning to Whitehouse and, as Trace couldn't help noticing, angling her hips toward the fellow as she reached up to smooth a spit curl on his brow. "Did you lose tonight?"

"Dreadfully." Whitehouse briefly closed his eyes and sighed as Maddy stroked his brow. This gesture seemed to have been performed often before. Trace envied Whitehouse that touch from the girl.

"He's not really penniless," Maddy said.

"May as well be," said Whitehouse.

"He has pots of money back in Brighton."

"Ho-ho," said Whitehouse. "And a wife to watch over them." He winked at Trace.

"He need only wire for more," said Maddy.

"Wire," said Whitehouse derisively, and suddenly his face jumped with a revelation. He turned to Trace. "*That's* it. You were *here*, with Ludlow, the engineer for the Atlantic cable."

"Yes. I suppose," said Trace, "I am in his employ." Trace was wary about how much to reveal to Whitehouse—certainly about Maddy, but about Ludlow, too, or about himself.

"Then we have something in common. I don't know whether he mentioned it, but I am on the board of directors of the syndicate. It's my sending and receiving devices they'll be using any day now. In what exact way are you in Ludlow's employ?" Whitehouse had now turned full on toward Trace, positioning himself so Maddy was behind his shoulder, angled out of this, a gentlemen's conversation. Trace flicked a quick look her way and saw her large, gray-green eyes as she tilted her head to peep around Whitehouse's right flank.

"I am the expedition's documentarian," Trace said. "I am making a visual account of the cable laying."

"Wonderful," Whitehouse said. "But what, pray tell, are you doing *here*? Shouldn't you be somewhere in the middle of the Atlantic?"

Trace stared at Whitehouse a moment, unsure whether the man was gulling him. "Sir," he said, "you haven't heard?"

"Heard what?"

"We're back."

"Good lord!" Whitehouse gasped. "It's a *success?*"

Trace shook his head.

"The cable is *laid?*" Whitehouse barked, and Trace hastened to stop the man's growing agitation and his increasingly louder exclamations. "We've *succeeded? Have we?*"

"No!" Trace had to nearly shout it. "No, sir." And he saw Whitehouse's mouth gape.

There was nothing to do but recount for the man the story of the expedition, its trials and its defeat, and of the board's private meeting going on at that very moment. Whitehouse had calmed enough to hear Trace out, but now his perturbation rolled in again with even greater force than before.

"Why, they *never* told *me!*" he said.

His voice had a piercing rasp that made Trace wince.

"It must have been an oversight," Trace said. He suddenly felt obliged to make amends for being the bearer of bad news.

Instead of heeding him, Whitehouse wheeled around and snapped at Maddy to wait for him upstairs. She retreated, casting one look back at Trace. He wanted to wave to her, at the very least nod his head in a gentlemanly bid of adieu, but he realized that Whitehouse had never even introduced her, and now he was practically accosting Trace.

"They're meeting *now?*" he asked. "The board is meeting *now?*"

"Yes," Trace said, feeling a growing desire to rub it in. "A privy council, as it were."

"Why?" Whitehouse ran his hand furiously through his hair.

"Well, I suppose to decide whether to continue with the project."

"No! No, man. *Why* was I not informed?"

"I'm hardly the one to be asked that, sir. We returned only yesterday. I'm not on the board. Perhaps word was slow getting to you. You live in Brighton?"

Whitehouse had taken a step away from Trace and placed his two hands on the balustrade and leaned on his arms. He gazed down at the players at the tables. Trace could see Whitehouse's jaw working beneath his muttonchops, making the whiskers move in little waves the way a breeze stirs through the grasses of a dry marsh.

"So they're considering abandoning the project?" Whitehouse grumbled, not looking at Trace.

"I suppose," Trace said. "There may be enough cable for another try, as I understand it, but there's a considerable amount of money needed. . . ."

"Money," Whitehouse mumbled, then repeated it more forcefully.

"Sir?"

"My friend, I lost two hundred and fifty pounds down there in less than an hour tonight." Whitehouse pointed to the tables on the mezzanine. Waiters glided among the green felt circles, where heads inclined toward cards and blue clouds of cigar smoke rose among the palms.

"A considerable amount of money, wouldn't you say?"

"I would, sir."

"It's money I will make back probably in less than an hour if the cable is successfully completed and my patented receivers and senders are employed. So I know something about loss of money and the potential for recouping said loss. A potential forever unrealized if not for risk. I think I know something about risk, Mr. . . . ?"

"Trace."

"Trace. Those syndicate nambies have not yet stared into the hollow eyes of risk, Mr. Trace. They will find they must if they expect to get anywhere. They've failed twice? Damn it to hell. Let them fail again. Fail again and again. Fail until you succeed, Mr. Trace. Tell them that!"

Trace thought it outrageous that Whitehouse would accuse the cable expedition of cowardice. The hollow eyes of risk indeed. Trace thought he'd like to see those hollow eyes stare into some of the waves the expedition saw in the mid-Atlantic. Nevertheless, Trace reined in the impulse to say anything . . . almost.

"If I might venture to say, Mr. Whitehouse, I was on the expedition. I saw firsthand, unlike you, what this project is up against."

"It's up against a lack of nerve, my good man. That's what it's up against. Oh, I don't mean the sea doesn't have its attendant dangers. We all know that. I'm talking about a lack of nerve when it comes to risking wealth. On that count, I know something. You see that tonight. You see that I have risked money and my reputation on my sending and receiving devices. Why? Because I believe in them. I believe in them enough to bet you that they—and the cable—will succeed. And that I will be the instrument of that success. That's how much I believe. A wager, sir?"

Whitehouse had a gleam in his eye; Trace could see it even as he looked at the man in profile.

"I will bet," Whitehouse said, "a night with her that the cable and my devices will suceed."

"With?"

"Her." And Whitehouse nodded toward the upper gallery, toward the rooms where Trace had first met him and to where Trace knew Maddy had repaired. "Madeline. Her. A night with Maddy if the cable fails and my prediction is wrong."

"Sir," Trace blurted, not knowing what else to say, "you're asking me to bet against the cable? Against my employers? I hardly think—"

"Oh, good fellow, it's just a private little wager. You are not sure the cable will succeed. I *am* sure. You imply I don't know risk because I didn't sail with you. I say I do."

Trace did not know what to say.

"Have I offended your superior morals, Mr. Trace?" Whitehouse snickered. "Or just your taste? I can assure you a night with her would not be misery. Oh, no."

Trace knew he should tell this man to go to hell. Instead, he croaked, "What do I put up?"

"Let's see, what *could* you put up?" Whitehouse said, warming to the game and, like a true, shrewd wagerer, knowing this offer of Maddy was precisely the bait Trace would find irresistible. "If the cable succeeds you owe me—what?—a *portrait!* How about that? My girl said you're one of the finest."

My girl, he'd called her. It angered Trace, and so he said, "Deal," even before he knew what deal had been done.

Whitehouse was chuckling, seemingly relieved that he'd managed to construct a wager out of this encounter, as if going too long in the Bardolph without laying down a bet would be like going too long without oxygen.

"So, my good fellow," Whitehouse said. "The cable expedition has a new fascination for us both. Where did you say the board was meeting?"

"I didn't."

"Do you know?"

Trace hesitated, not because he was pondering that he might be able to obstruct Whitehouse and the cable by refusing to give any more information and thus win the bet but because he was awash in confusion about the possibility of winning. The prospect of a night with Maddy gleamed in his mind, but the notion that he'd been wagering for her threw a shadow over that gleam. And he'd been wagering against the cable.

"Oh, come now," Whitehouse was saying. "I'm on the board of directors. Fair's fair. I'm not asking for information I have no right to know. In fact, they probably did send word to my home in Brighton, and the message has yet to be forwarded here."

"I heard them say at a Mr. Brooking's house."

"One of the board. Very good. Thank you, sir. Well, I must repair upstairs. It's been a costly night for me."

Trace didn't watch Whitehouse ascend the stairs to the upper gallery. Instead, he turned to look at the people moving about below. He was numb, and he wanted only to leave.

He was waiting for his hat in the foyer when his attention was drawn by Whitehouse descending the stairs and hurrying, with hat and cane, out into the night. That meant Maddy was alone. He could go see her, he thought. He had an impulse to confess to her what he'd done: wagered for her. But how could he explain his confused feelings of titillation and regret?

"Your hat, sir. And this came for you." The footman handed Trace an envelope, which, he said, had come by a messenger who, the footman said, had been directed here by Trace's landlady.

Trace tore at the paper. He was about to mutter some deprecations about his landlady's meddlesomeness when his eyes caught the note's signature. It was Frau Lindt's.

The letter, its brevity heightening its implicit urgency, pleaded that Jack come to her hotel immediately—*tonight,* if possible.

"I hope," the letter said, "this message finds you willing once more to assist a woman in desperate need."

Trace looked up once toward the red-carpeted stairs. He probably couldn't find the room where Maddy was kept and probably would have his way obstructed by a steward who no doubt would be posted up there to keep the rooms and their occupants discreet. Trace, putting the letter in his breast pocket, decided to attend to the woman who'd requested his aid rather than seek the woman who'd requested nothing of him at all, least of all that he wager for her company.

Not long after Trace left the Bardolph, however, Maddy reappeared on the landing above the mezzanine. The place where Whitehouse had hit her before he'd departed was low on her cheek, and she'd covered it by wrapping herself with the fur stole he'd given her. He'd lost at cards, but he'd acted like a beast. She was confused. She was glad E.O. had stormed out.

She composed herself and looked about the club for the sketch artist. He was nowhere to be seen. She thought about walking down the stairs, into the night, and away forever. But that would surely lead her in due time back to a place in the tunnel under the Thames and eventually lower still. So she returned to the rooms above the games—as he'd ordered—to wait.

The Board Meets

"It *is* a gamble," Cyrus Field said. He was trying to suppress any hint of his desperation and was doing, Chester thought, tolerably well. Field had assembled all the British board members he could gather on twenty-four hours' notice at Mr. Brooking's home near Portman Square. Most of the cable's money had come from England, and most of the major backers lived about or near London. As soon as the *Niagara* had landed at Queens-town, the largest Irish port near Valentia, Field had wired the board members to arrange a secret summit in London and had spirited Chester away to the city even before the *Agamemnon* with Frau Lindt and Professor Thomson had landed.

Field had left word for the professor to proceed to London, but Chester was unable to get any word to Katerina. Once again she was lost to him. In the rail coach to London, Field kept Chester up most of the night planning strategy and discussing tactics to work before the board.

"Cyrus," Chester finally said in weariness, "I can convince them. If you'll let me."

"I believe you," Field said. "And I will."

Now, though, there in Brooking's study at twilight with the lamps just lit and shadows cast about the room with its ticking clock and books and specimen cases lurking in the background, while Field spoke, the board members shifted in their seats, coughed, sniffed, shuffled papers, and Chester Ludlow could see that Field was losing confidence.

The nine men—Messrs. Brooking, Balme, Runcer, Woodbury, Hindle, Brannen, Green, Tuxbard, and Clough—all looked peckish at best, dismissive at worst. The group, shrewd in the ways of enterprise, was almost to a man rotund, bewhiskered, and flush. They seemed to be sinking into their clothes, widening, gaining gravity, straining the very fabric of their suits. Hands clasped and unclasped on the polished table. Fingers drummed or picked at the quick of nails.

When Cyrus Field had finished, Mr. Brooking got up to read a telegram from Sir William Brown, the board's British chairman. Brown had been unable to answer Field's call to come to the meeting but had wired from Liverpool.

Chester doubted the telegram would bode well. Brooking had made it clear from the outset of the meeting, as the men had gathered in his study around the large oaken table from which had been cleared Brooking's butterfly and moth collection in its wood and glass cases, that he was in favor of abandoning the project. From the way Brooking brandished the telegram, which he had withdrawn from his breast pocket, Chester knew the tide had turned.

"I will cut to the point," Brooking said, unfolding the telegram. "And I quote our chairman . . . 'We must all deeply regret our misfortune in not being able to lay the cable. I think there is nothing to be done but dispose of what is left on the best terms we can. We could divide the proceeds equally among the shareholders; thereafter, the company should be abandoned.' "

Brooking laid the telegram on the table.

"Gentlemen," he said, "we have nays by proxy from all the other board members unable to attend. I am in agreement. So thoroughly in agreement that I see little need for further discussion. Therefore, as British vice chairman, I have determined to assume no further part in this undertaking, which has proved hopeless and to persist in which seems rashness and folly. I am therefore excusing myself from the meeting, as I am withdrawing from the board. I opened my home to you for this confabulation, and I earnestly desire you use it for as long as you need for your deliberations. I will be near enough at hand. I will repair to the garden." With that he pulled a delicate, long-handled net from a closet opposite the fireplace. All the men were watching him.

"The night moths are out," he said. "Specimens await."

His footsteps receded beyond the large dark oaken door.

Cyrus Field was pallid, almost visibly shaking, and speechless.

Romulus Balme, a large curly-headed man of twenty-nine, the youngest on the board but nonetheless a vice president of the Newell and Son Cableworks in Birkenhead, spoke first. "A bit of brinkmanship, wouldn't you say?" he asked. "Leaving us here alone like that."

"Leaving us in the lurch," said Mr. Hindle.

"Leaving us so that voting against him would look as if we were trusted to be alone in the nursery and mussed it up," mumbled Mr. Green.

Chester rose to his feet. He looked around the table. Field was still stunned and pale. Professor Thomson seemed preoccupied with calculations or scribbles on a pad of foolscap, but he looked up abruptly in the hush and, seeing Chester standing, smiled a small, confident grin. The other men had already turned their eyes to him.

"Brinkmanship, maybe," Chester said. "But nursery, definitely not."

Mr. Green shrugged, raised his hands in agreement, and nodded his head.

"And let me speak about brinkmanship, if I may, gentlemen," said Chester. "This expedition you have helped fund and put your good names to met with nearly two weeks of waves and storm seas more than half as high as the masts of the ships that bore it to the middle of the ocean. We sailed to the brink of foundering. We made it through. Sixty-some men were injured or disabled by the gale that lashed us for upward of two weeks. We made it through. Decks caved in. Tons of coal slid around the ship. We ran low on food and fuel. We had too little wind, and we had too much. We laid cable; it broke. We began again; it broke again. We— and I mean we, gentlemen; Professor Thomson here, Mr. Field next to him, and all the crew, down to the lowest man jack aboard—we went to the brink a score of times in the past weeks and we made it through. It *is* a gamble sending us back out there again, a gamble of *your* money. But every last man aboard the *Agamemnon* has volunteered to sail again if only you will allow it. The captains of the *Niagara*, the *Gorgon,* and the *Valorous* have wired similar expressions. We have enough surplus cable to complete the job. It will take three days to load it."

Professor Thomson nodded in assent; he tapped his pen on the calculations on his pad. The others, leaning back in their chairs, looked steadily at Chester.

"All we need is food and fuel. Give them to us. Please. Send us out again. Please. There is time. There is cable. There is the will. We can do it."

Chester sat down. Thomson subtly touched his sleeve in affirmation. Field looked relieved, grateful.

Across the table Mr. Runcer, the oldest of the board members, white-haired and stooped, turned in his chair to look out the windows facing the garden. A butterfly net swiped and dodged above the shrubbery in the gloaming and faded away. The room was silent, even absorbing, almost, the ticking of the mantel clock.

Mr. Runcer murmured at last, "As Mr. Ludlow was saying, I so move."

"I second," said Mr. Balme firmly.

"Call the question," said Mr. Hindle.

"All in favor . . ." said Mr. Clough.

"Aye" came from around the table.

"Opposed?"

There was a brief silence, out of which welled footsteps in the hall. The huge study door flew open, revealing Edward Orange Wildman Whitehouse, straining to full height while trying to catch his breath.

"Gentlemen!" he said. "I trust I am welcome." He stepped over the threshold. "I trust as well that I was invited?"

He looked directly at Chester, who turned to Cyrus Field, who stood up.

"Of course, Whitehouse. Of course, come in. Have a seat. We wired you. We hadn't heard, so we—"

"Went ahead," Whitehouse said. "Yes. Well. What is the question being called? I believe I heard a vote in progress."

"Whether or not to continue with the cable project," said Runcer.

"Ah!" said Whitehouse. "As profound as that, eh? Up or down? Yea or nay? Deal me in or deal me out? And what is the count thus far?"

Everyone at the table remained silent.

Cyrus Field spoke with a voice that was audibly trying to steady itself. "By my count, given the nays expressed here and by proxy, and now with your arrival, we need one more aye to carry it—according to the majority required by our bylaws."

"Bylaws be damned," Runcer grumbled.

"I'll second that," said Chester, and he felt Thomson's hand on his sleeve.

"Interesting," said Whitehouse. "So I have the deciding vote. How fortunate of me to stop by."

"Do you need an explication of the issue?" said Chester.

"No, my good man, I think I know the situation well enough."

"In spite of remaining ashore during the entire expedition?"

Again Chester felt Thomson's steadying hand, much firmer this time.

"In spite of that, yes," said Whitehouse. "Allow me to cast my vote posthaste. Why stop such an interesting enterprise at this juncture? Of course, it's not my money, but it is my reputation and my sending and receiving devices. I vote aye."

"You vote to continue?" said Field.

"Of course," said Whitehouse. "On with the show!"

The reference to the sending and receiving devices made Professor Thomson grit his teeth, but the success of the vote overrode his momentary annoyance, and it was he who proclaimed, "Gentlemen, the ayes have it!"

A relieved, almost incredulous grin pieced itself together on Field's face. The rest of the room broke into smiles, then jollity. Runcer, Green, and Woodbury even pulled out their checkbooks.

"Gentlemen," Chester said, rising from the table. "Thank you. *Thank* you. In three days . . . ," and he glanced at Whitehouse, who smiled so beneficently it almost looked like gloating, "we shall sail again."

Mr. Hindle moved for adjournment. Mr. Clough seconded. Mr. Brannen objected: "Not without first offering three hurrahs for Field, Thomson, Ludlow, and Whitehouse here to wish them Godspeed and success!"

The cheers, an amalgam of gruff, aristocratic formality and boyish exuberance, erupted, and the meeting adjourned.

Neither Chester nor Professor Thomson wanted to engage Whitehouse, who was almost immediately holding forth about his sending and receiving devices for several of the board members still at the table. They hurried from the room and asked the maid for their hats. Thomson caught Chester at the door and took his arm.

"Good show there with that exhortation," he said. "You turned the tide."

"Thank you, sir."

"Fortunately no one challenged you on that bit about the volunteers."

"Sir?"

"Our crew is all in the navy," Thomson said. "The men are under orders. If they don't go with us to lay the cable, they'd be deserting. And for that they could be shot."

Over and Under London

The model was a marvel. Forty by sixty feet: London from Hammersmith to East Ham, from Brixton to Highgate. The Royal Commission of Sewers had obtained a Naval Department warehouse in the confines of the East India Docks for Joachim Lindt to use. He had ten carpenters, two plasterers, two draftsmen (for the model alone; more draftsmen for the actual sewer lines would come later), several apprentices, and a messenger all at his beck and call. The commission had given him four weeks to work up his proposal, which was to construct an accurate model of London's topographic and man-made constructions—buildings, streets, greens, boulevards, alleys; but most important, its ditches, kennels, channels, sumps, and tidal creeks wherein the city's wastes backed up, stagnated, and festered, causing the Great Stink, which was Joachim's promise and commission to eradicate.

The model gave Joachim the information he needed to design the sewers. He had constructed the huge likeness of London on a vast, trestled platform that took up a whole corner of the dingy, vaulted warehouse. For all the model's usefulness, though, no one could deny it was Joachim Lindt's theatricalisms that made it more than merely practical. As a likeness of London, it was spectacular. Using materials borrowed from the docks, Joachim had his workers construct a cantilevered gantry that extended over the huge platform. With a series of ropes and pulleys, a man could move this rolling bridge the length of the miniature city, could lie on the gantry's deck and work on any part of the model he chose from above. Joachim had the men paint greenswards in the parks; he added tiny trees and shrubbery made from pieces of dyed sponges; he colored the river water a realistic brown with a tempera mix. He had the carpenters mill hundreds of rectangular blocks of wood of assorted sizes to represent the houses and buildings of all the city's neighborhoods. The men produced a mass of tiny ships to place along the river and in the docks. Granted these buildings and vessels were abstractions, just assorted blocks and dowels, but wherever possible, they matched the shape and placement of the real thing. There was a rounded block for St. Paul's, an upended oblong one for St. Stephen's Tower; Joachim even put an extra-large block with six masts at a berth on the Isle of Dogs to represent the *Great Eastern* . . . all familiar landmarks.

The model was so charming, members of the sewer commission would make trips to the warehouse to show it to their friends and families. They would point out where their homes were. They would ride on the gantry over the city—"It's like flying!"—as they extolled Joachim's artifice. Several visitors proposed the model be moved to the Crystal Palace for exhibition. Their distracting presence almost drove Joachim crazy.

But he held his temper, kept his purpose in view, and did not let the nattering praise divert him. He often calmed himself, now that the actual sewer project had moved on to the drafting stage, by remaining in the warehouse late at night, tinkering with his London.

At present he was lying on a dolly somewhere beneath the city, adjusting a length of slender lead tubing that supplied tidal flow to the model Thames. He loved being under the model. He knew by the configuration of the pipes where under London he lay. He had run over much of the surface of the real city during the previous months, but now he could lie on his back on the dolly and, with a slight push, roll beneath wide stretches of the metropolis, moving from suburb to city, from park to slum, from palaces to hovels, much the way he had run from one to another on the streets.

He felt as if he were under a being, a creature, a huge, sprawling female, he supposed. Thinking of it that way could actually excite him. Perhaps it was just the solitude and the chance to relax after a grueling day's work, lying under the model, his creation spread above him, the counterweighted propellers for the water pumps puttering softly away, the fluid in the pipes moving, duplicating the movement of the city's water, yes, but also her waste, the fetid, rank excretions. *That* product of the body—and specifically, a woman's body expelling it. He dreamed of it sometimes. A body. Its rich, degrading yield.

It was why he'd kept his wife's knickers, wasn't it? The smell of them. The parts they'd touched. To think of that and then bury his face in them, to lower himself with them. What else felt like this?

The shame of this perverse excitement had once caused him to work to distraction on the Phantasmagorium, to run madly about the city, to exert himself furiously, but it always came back, his need to feel that closeness to the most rank parts and product.

Footsteps.

Joachim Lindt froze under London. He could hear a creaking noise, a rattle. As the air rushed back into his lungs, he tried to stifle any gasping he might make that would give him away. There was an intruder in the warehouse. Joachim lay as still as possible. Quietly he buttoned up his trousers. He could tell that now someone was on the gantry, moving it. The iron wheels creaked and rattled on the grit of the warehouse floor.

Joachim slid off the dolly and silently on his hands and knees crept to the edge of the huge platform. He surfaced near St. John's Wood, rising only to eye level and peering over the edge of the world.

His wife stood poised above him and the city.

He couldn't believe it, but Katerina was on the gantry. There she was, pulling herself along by the ropes, flying slowly over London. He watched her as her eyes took in the spread of the city illuminated by the gas lamps that hung from the warehouse rafters. He slowly stood all the way up and spoke.

"You can see it much better in the daytime," he said, and pointed toward the windows and skylights above them. "But that would mean coming back."

Katerina hid any surprise she might have had at hearing his voice. She smiled. Now that he could see her better, she appeared harried. Her hair looked unkempt. The smile flashed, disappeared, flashed again.

"It is a marvel, Joachim." She gestured with her hand at the miniature city spread out beneath her. "You have done it again."

"You have done it again, too," he said.

"You mean come back?" she asked.

"Let's remember before that. To come back, you had to go away. You did that again."

"I did."

"And you are here to say you are sorry?"

"No."

Joachim was a little startled by the sting he felt.

"No?" he asked.

"No. I am here to say simply that I am leaving for good."

"How thoughtful, Katerina. You have been gone more than a month, and *now* you say you are leaving?"

"I returned unexpectedly. A visit to you . . . seemed fitting."

"And what about disappearing for five weeks? How fitting was that? And shall I tell you with whom you so fittingly disappeared? Or shall I play a game and guess for you? Or shall you tell me? What would be most *fitting*?"

"To simply tell you that I am leaving."

"You already have!" He pursed his lips. He did not want to shout.

"We both already have," Katerina said.

Joachim nodded.

"This time let us finish things," she said. "Let us not keep dallying with the idea of our separation. Let us do it. Will you . . . will you let me do it?"

She stood on the gantry over his London. She towered over the city. He thought of her above the real city outside. She would be miles tall, a colossus, her handsome face high in the clouds, her pale blue eyes looking down unable to see him, an ant crawling among the teeming masses. He was nothing.

"Go," he said.

"Thank you," whispered Katerina.

But neither of them moved.

"Where is your engineer?" Joachim finally asked. "Is his cable a success?"

"No. It failed. He has returned to London as well."

"You were with him? On the expedition?"

Katerina nodded. "I was a stowaway."

Joachim felt weak. The very idea of it—a stowaway. He was shocked at how utterly she had turned from him. She had *eloped*. Summarily left him behind. Traduced all the bonds of matrimony with a haughtiness befitting a heathen queen.

But there was something about his shock that held a twinge of relief to it. She had humiliated him. He could understand that; she would never understand it, but it was something he could accept and in the darkest part of his heart perhaps grow to relish.

"Where will you go?" Joachim asked.

"I don't know."

"You and your engineer haven't decided yet, or is it that you want to keep it a secret from me?"

"Neither. I am no longer in touch with him. I don't know where he is. I don't know where I shall go."

"But you are leaving?"

"Yes."

"On your own."

"Yes."

She saw his dark brows knit, and she spoke to forestall any criticism or, worse, patronizing advice he might offer.

"We must end it no matter what happens to me," she said. "I wanted that understood. I wanted us both to acknowledge it."

Joachim touched some of the block buildings near where he stood. His hand shaded an entire neighborhood in Notting Hill.

"Very well," he whispered. "It is understood."

"Thank you, Joachim. We are free of each other."

The gantry began to shudder gently as Katerina walked to its steps and descended. She was on the far side of the city from him, but he did not look at her. He only listened as her footsteps departed, and he heard her waiting carriage clatter away on the cobbles.

It was hours later when the watchman came by at dawn to make his final check before going home. He found Joachim Lindt sitting amid the wreckage of the model of London. The entire metropolis was smashed and scattered in a rough halo of shattered wood and glass and lead piping that covered half the warehouse floor. Even the gantry was toppled over, a twisted mess.

Herr Lindt was at the vortex of the destruction, lying in a fetal ball.

"You all right, sir?" the watchman asked, not sure if he'd get an answer or if he was addressing a corpse.

"Yes," Joachim said. His voice sounded thick, distant.

"What happened? Did someone do this?" the watchman asked. He was a short man, his long coat almost touching the floor. His face was a red hash from years of drink and Saint Anthony's fire.

"I did it."

"*You?*"

"It's . . . it's an old custom among model builders. When a project is done and no longer useful, you smash it."

"Do you? Must have taken a good bit of smashing."

"It did," Joachim said. "A good bit of smashing."

"You know," the watchman said in a lower, confiding voice, "a couple of times I came in here by myself and went up on the bridge you built." He pointed at the twisted wreck of the gantry. "I'd go out on it an' pull myself along over the city. Very nice. Could see everything. It was like flying."

He looked at the destruction.

"Please help me up," Joachim asked.

He extended a scratched and bleeding hand to the watchman, who stepped and crunched gingerly over the wood and plaster and then just gave up and plowed his way through it. He assisted Joachim to his feet and couldn't help noticing the man was sweaty and splattered with the brown water that had pooled here and there on the floor.

The two men hobbled across the mess to the giant warehouse door. The watchman opened a smaller, man-sized portal that was built into the larger one, and Joachim thanked him as he stepped out into the brightening, intact city.

"We Landed Here in the Woods"

Professor Thomson watched until the *Niagara* disappeared over the western horizon. He stayed until the coal smoke was a minute comma on the gray line of the Atlantic. He stayed on further, until even the smoke had disappeared and his eyes ached from all the watching. He thought perhaps young Ludlow was still on the stern deck of the *Niagara*, headed west toward Newfoundland, watching him as he stood on the stern deck of the *Agamemnon*, steaming east toward Ireland. The splicing had gone smoothly, and the cable was now on the ocean floor, fifteen hundred feet below them, and growing longer as each ship spun out wire, chugging away toward their respective destinations.

Thomson rubbed his eyes. Young Ludlow indeed. The man was only a dozen years, at the most, Thomson's junior. Yet the American made Thomson feel old. William Thomson had been the new lecturer in natural philosophy at the University of Glasgow ten years ago when Chester Ludlow arrived from Boston. Thomson had received the appointment through his father's maneuvering. James Thomson was a professor of mathematics at the university, so his good offices helped, but William Thomson was eminently qualified. He had never attended school—his father had tutored him—and he matriculated at the university at age fourteen. At fifteen he wrote "An Essay on the Figure of the Earth," which proposed the mathematical means for measuring the size of the planet. Once a professor, Thomson established the practical laboratory—he received the unheard-of sum from the university of £100 to procure equipment—for the study of natural philosophy. The lure of the laboratory—the only one of its kind in the world—had brought Ludlow to Scotland, and he'd immediately shone as one of Thomson's prize students. Thomson would tell himself that while he was busy pondering phenomena that generate force—electricity, magnetism, heat, gravity—he was encountering one right there in front of him: young Ludlow. The student's adroitness with formulae and theorems was equaled by his ability to apply the theoretical to the practical. In or out of the lab, it seemed he could build anything. Including a legion of followers. Ludlow was one of those fortunate men whose skills and achievements inspire not envy but allegiance. He guilelessly drew men (and women, too, apparently) to him. Even Professor Thomson felt the pull. A phenomenon generating force.

Thomson had not discussed the matter of the stowed-away woman with Ludlow, save for that one time on the ship. There were the pressures of the wavering board of directors and the rush to rejuvenate the expedition. It was, Thomson decided, none of his business. Anyway, it no longer seemed to be affecting the cable expedition. Thomson hadn't seen the woman around; Ludlow hadn't mentioned her; work proceeded apace. They were laying cable once again, well and good.

Besides, Professor Thomson didn't want to sit in judgment of young Ludlow. Though the two men had never discussed it, Thomson himself knew firsthand something of Ludlow's dilemma, for wasn't Margaret Thomson back in Glasgow, sick abed, her ailment growing to be an ever larger impediment and divide between them?

A year after they'd married, Margaret had taken ill, putatively from overexertion on their holiday trip to Gibraltar and Málaga. She had been suffering nearly five years now from what her physician sometimes referred to as dropsy, sometimes as a "feminine complaint," but most often just as "her condition," consigning its cause and its cure to something beyond human understanding.

Thomson knew Chester Ludlow had a wife back in America suffering some kind of malady as well. Ludlow had perhaps found respite from the burden of his wife's problem in the company of the beautiful musician. Thomson had taken no such route. Instead, he had thrown himself into his lecturing and now into telegraphy. He worried he had been too eager to sail on the *Agamemnon*. Perhaps he had only wanted to get away from Mag's infirmity. Still, he was always the faithful attendant when he was home. He cared for her. He carried her from room to room when her pains became too great for her to walk. He sat with her and read to her and transcribed her poems when she was too weak to write. But he often wanted to get away. And whenever he did, he had the feeling, as he did now, that he was being unfaithful after his fashion.

He looked at the cable slanting off the stern derrick and into the sea.

A steady clanking and burring issued from behind him. The coffee grinder laboring away. It was the name the sailors had given the small steam engine and cable paying-out device of Ludlow's design on the stern deck of the *Agamemnon*. The machinery rasped and bashed steadily and would do so, Thomson knew, round the clock, and he, the engineer in charge on the *Agamemnon*, would have an ear cocked to its sound through the voyage, day and night, until Ireland and success hove into view or until—God forfend—the cable broke and the expedition failed again.

Professor Thomson needed some rest, but he decided to make his rounds first. He gave one last look to the blank horizon, where the *Niagara* had disappeared beneath a distant stack of cumulus clouds. He nodded to Captain Preedy on the quarterdeck and went below to the telegraph room.

Professor Thomson wished they'd had more time to redesign the place. He pitied the poor graphers who had to work in there. The storm on the last voyage proved the cabin was a catchment for water showering down from the upper deck. The room was close and damp and constantly dark. (It had to be kept in gloom to make observation of the galvanometer possible.) The telegraph batteries were railed in on small shelves at one end of the space. A telegraph clerk sat at a table with the galvanometer. The *Niagara* and the *Agamemnon* were staying in constant contact, signaling every ten miles, as the cable was paying out; additionally, Thomson had his crew send a signal each minute and measure the resistance, so that a flaw would be detected the moment it occurred. Captain Preedy wouldn't let the ship's chronometer be brought into so wet and susceptible a place as the telegraph room, so a crewman had to shout from the clock in Preedy's cabin three seconds before an observation. "Look out!" went the warning call. The clerk at the galvanometer would fix his eye on the spot of light. "Now!" came the call, and the clerk would record the pulse. This went on once a minute, hour after hour.

Thomson patted the seated grapher on the shoulder. The galvanometer appeared to be working well, but the men on duty seemed edgy. The constant observations began to wear on a fellow near the end of a watch. This connecting of continents could become a form of torture.

Next, Thomson went to check the cable drum and the paying-out device. Things were working smoothly; they'd done a good job coiling and stowing the huge wire. The professor then went to lie down in his cabin. The percussive chugs of the coffee grinder were his lullaby. All was going well. He hoped it was the same over on the *Niagara*.

"They'll let me know if it's not," Thomson said, surprising himself, for he was not a man given to muttering aloud.

He thought about the strain on the clerks. Perhaps they should have been using Whitehouse's receiving devices. They'd be using them once— if—the cable was laid and put into operation. That was the agreement the cable board had with Whitehouse. But Whitehouse's induction coils were too large to fit aboard the *Agamemnon* or the *Niagara*. Thomson's mirror galvanometers were the only other option. Perhaps they were small and light, sometimes difficult to read, and—what was the word Whitehouse used?—"feminine," but they worked.

Thomson despaired of ever getting to sleep. He decided to try some calculations. . . . Steaming at five knots, he thought; paying out at six; average angle to the horizon that the cable enters water . . . fifteen degrees; average strain on dynamometer . . . 1,650 pounds. He pictured the catenary slope of the cable curving down into the increasing blackness of the sea. The curve glowed in his mind and was like a graph he might draw on the laboratory blackboard back in Glasgow. Sleep was coming on. A curve. A distribution of points. Indices of fatigue and frustration spread out through the day. An ocean. A vast fluid. Vortices in the ether. Material atoms.

Thomson's mind had slid away from Ludlow and Whitehouse, drifting down through theorems and hypotheses (more elegant, more specific, far more constant than men and mankind), down to images of force and matter. All to the rocking of the ship, the distant sibilations of the sea passing along the hull, the soft knocking of the engines. Until he slept.

At about ten o'clock a clerk pounded on his cabin door.

"We've lost contact, sir!"

Thomson was bolt awake and fairly shouting, "I'm coming!" as he pulled on his clothes.

When he stumbled into the telegraph cabin, Neely, the grapher at the galvanometer, was frozen, his eyes looking for the light to move on the scale. Neely's backup clerk was biting his nails and pacing, or more accurately, rocking in the small space of the cabin. Between gritted teeth, chomping on a cuticle, he said to Thomson in a whisper that they'd just signaled the *Niagara*, "Forty miles submerged," and she was beginning an acknowledgment when the line went dead.

Thomson slid into the seat as Neely moved out, neither man taking his eye from the spot of light. No movement. Thomson ordered a resistance test. He would have one of the clerks send a charge through the wire. They would record on the galvanometer how far the light spot swung up the scale and calculate, based on the known resistance of a mile of wire, how near the break was.

"Now," said Thomson, and Neely's partner touched a key, sending a pulse through the wire. The spot of reflected light traveled up and nearly off the scale. Thomson had the clerks send several more pulses and record the levels. He did some calculations on a scrap of paper in the light of the one small storm lantern that hung from a beam. The clerks kept repeating their tests, but there was no need. They all knew by the way the light moved that the break was nowhere near enough to pull a length of cable up and resplice the wire.

"Shall I send word to the captain to halt, sir?" Neely asked Thomson.

The professor had his head back close to the galvanometer.

"No," he said quietly. "We'll keep laying cable."

Without looking at them, Thomson knew the two clerks were glancing at each other in bewilderment.

"Because," he went on, "we will give this wire of ours every chance. We will have faith in our labors. Just as when a loved one lies ailing and comatose, we speak softly into her ear because we believe she can hear us and we must not desert her, we will stand by our patient here and keep speaking to her."

The two clerks shuffled in place, uneasy with the professor's metaphoric turn. Even Thomson wasn't sure what he was getting at.

"I mean," he said as much to himself as to the two young men, "guttapercha, as we've seen, has strange properties underwater. It grows more flexible, more elastic. Perhaps—I know this sounds wishful—but perhaps it could pull a fissured wire core back together."

The two men stared flatly through the gloom at Thomson.

"I don't know," Thomson said with a sigh. He pushed himself away from the table. "I just don't know. But I can't say we should give up. Not yet." He gave the seat back to Neely.

So the *Agamemnon* steamed on. Captain Preedy knocked on the door once, and Thomson told him, yes, they were having some trouble with the instruments but not to worry: steam on.

Thomson stayed in the room with the two clerks, taking the measurements as usual from the seaman calling, "Look out!" and "Now!" from the captain's chronometer, but they saw nothing register on the galvanometer. Thomson felt his body begin to tremble; a fluttering emanated outward from his sternum. He tried to adjust his monocle, but it kept falling off. He was sweating. He urged himself to note these physiological phenomena as if self-observation might calm him, but the prospect of disaster had crept up and took hold.

"Good Lord," he muttered to himself, and noted *that:* he was talking to himself again. He paced but kept bumping into the other clerk. Finally he went out on deck, placing his trembling hands on the ship's rail. He listened as the minute-by-minute testing went on, the clerks proceeding as if all were normal, but he knew no signal was coming through.

It was when Thomson finally looked away from the ocean that he noticed that the sailors and officers around the deck and on the spars were watching him. He realized with shock that the entire ship's company suspected something was wrong. They'd heard the call for him over an hour ago. The situation was general knowledge.

Thomson shrugged, held up his hands in a gesture of helplessness, and went back into the cabin. The clerks were still taking readings. Thomson did not speak. He walked to a forward corner of the room and stood in the apex of two bulkheads like a boy punished and sentenced to face the wall. He prayed that Ludlow had not yet cut his end of the cable; he prayed for clarity of thought; he prayed for an answer. He reviewed every possible thing he might have overlooked or done wrong and came up with nothing: neither a possible mistake nor a sign from God. Finally he prayed for something to say to the crew. He wished he had Ludlow's extemporaneous eloquence or even that damned Whitehouse's bluster. He was going to have to go back out on deck and announce that the expedition had failed.

Thomson was about to send for Preedy and begin procedures for cutting the cable when Neely, at the galvanometer, let out a grunt. Thomson turned. Neely was motioning abstractedly with his hand to come closer. He made several more soft, animal grunts. Thomson and the other clerk rushed over, bent down, and peered over Neely's shoulder at the dot of light. It moved . . . left, right, left. It moved! Neely's partner grabbed him by the neck and shook as if strangling the poor clerk. Both men began to make yelping noises. Thomson felt relief cascade through his body; it bottomed in some deep grotto of resolve that had kept him going and then bounced back as a loud, commodious laugh. All three men embraced and slapped one another on the shoulders. Thomson even tousled Neely's hair. There was nearly a minute of such exclamations before any one of the men uttered an actual word. That occurred as Captain Preedy, passing outside the telegraph cabin on his way to the quarterdeck, asked through the closed door if everything was all right in there.

"Yes!" Thomson cried from within. "We're fine. It's working fine!"

The other men laughed, and in a moment they heard three cheers roaring from the crew all around the ship.

In the hours that followed, it gave Thomson no small satisfaction that Chester Ludlow, his student and protégé, had not given up on the patient, either. He, too, had been steadfast through the silence. He hadn't cut the line. Thomson admired Chester's constancy and said so to the clerks, who had to remind him that he was every bit as steadfast, that if Ludlow deserved credit for his resolve, so did he.

Thomson stayed in or near the telegraph room for most of the voyage, sleeping in a chair a seaman had brought from Preedy's cabin, occasionally returning to his own quarters to change his shirt or relieve himself, then coming back to be near the galvanometer.

He had no answer as to why the cable had failed. He could offer only his first supposition: that once tension on the cable relaxed, the elasticity of the gutta-percha pulled the fractured wire together, restoring the contact.

Thomson spent the rest of the voyage either watching the cable pay out or attending to the dot of light. When he thought back upon it later, he realized he had become so fatigued that he couldn't keep the events of the voyage straight. There had been a storm. It passed. That brought some relief. The cable held. Signals continued. In all likelihood the fuel would last. Vigilance. Days, nights. The chair in the telegraph cabin had become his home. He began to hallucinate that he was hearing the gun that signaled a break in the cable and the failure of all his hopes, but it was only the normal creaking of the ship's timbers magnified by his exhaustion and his wavering on the precipice of sleep. One twilight he saw several icebergs off the port bow. Crenellated and with bowls scooped out of their midsections, they had flocks of birds circling their parapets and mists clinging to their highest promontories. Then there *was* a cannon report . . . from their escort ship, the *Valorous*, warning an American three-masted schooner, the *Chieftain*, that she was bearing down too close.

"It was a harsh greeting," Preedy said later, "but she nearly collided with us. When they saw what we were about, the fools saluted us, dipped their ensign, and gave us three cheers. They could have ended everything."

It seemed to Thomson's distorted sense of time only a few minutes later that on Tuesday morning, August 5, 1858, he was on deck, looking at the green and rocky mountains around Ireland's Dingle Bay. From across the ocean, the *Niagara* wired that they had spotted Newfoundland with 1,020 nautical miles of cable laid.

The sun was at his back and illuminating the mist that rose from the nooks and wrinkles on the mountains' sides. The sea was sparkling as it ran under the *Agamemnon*'s keel. The harbor of Valentia looked asleep until Captain Preedy ordered a gun fired, and soon people could be seen pouring from the cottages and houses and shops, their scurrying, antlike frenzy bringing laughter and cheers to the *Agamemnon*'s crew crowding the rail. They watched the townsfolk run down to the water and into boats—seemingly hundreds of them, with flags and bedsheets and handkerchiefs waving—to greet the *Agamemnon* as it slowly steamed into the harbor.

"Signal from the *Niagara*?" Thomson shouted from the deck into the telegraphy cabin, where the clerk sat in the dark before the speck of light. "Still coming in?"

"Still, sir."

It was afternoon when landing preparations were finally ready, and the *Valorous* sent over two paddle wheelers to transport the end of the cable to the shore. The boats beat in against a stiff breeze, and seamen, towns-people, Thomson, Preedy, the mayor of Valentia, the local Lord of the Isles, the Knight of Kerry, all splashed and pulled the metal-clad shore end of the line onto the beach and laid her in the trench that led up to the little white telegraph house on the bluff above the sea.

Neely sent word from the *Agamemnon* that the *Niagara* was landing in Newfoundland. Thomson ordered one of the boats to bring Neely and any clerk still on duty on the *Agamemnon* to the telegraph house so they could all be together for the first transmission. Soon all the clerks and Thomson and the mayor and Preedy and other dignitaries were crowded into the receiving room with shouts to dim the lights so the clerks could see the speck on the galvanometer that had been set up weeks ago and was waiting for this moment to be connected to North America.

When the message came, the clerks all read the letters as they became discernible from the silent wavering of the light. They arranged the flickers into words. It was like listening to a chorus of monks chanting, Thomson thought. A liturgy for a new era. He calculated that the world was about to be connected from the Missouri River in America to the Volga River in Russia.

Thomson stepped over to one of the windows and pulled the shade open a tiny crack. He could see out over the hats and bonnets and caps of the milling crowd below the window. He looked into the thin sliver of brilliant, reflected sunlight that shone in from the ocean. He thought of young Ludlow, across that ocean in a similar telegraph house, with his triumphant acolytes around him, dictating a message.

"We landed here in the woods," the clerks intoned behind Thomson as they read the message from America in unison. *"All well. The Atlantic telegraph successfully laid. By the blessing of Divine Providence we have succeeded."*

Thomson closed his eyes for the tears. It had all but blinded him, this huge light shining in from the surface of the sea. Someone ran outside with the news, and the crowd began to cheer.

CHAPTER XV

WAKING A NATION

New York and North America, August 1858

Dark New World

America loved hearing the story of how it had been caught napping. It seemed one minute the country was muddling along through the dog days of August, hearing nothing but its own somnolent grumblings about the economy's long struggle back from the panic of '57, grumblings about the southern states' increasing obstreperousness or the northern states' imperiousness, grumblings about politicians vacillating on the slave issue; muddling along hearing rumors of far-off Indian raids or gold strikes (some spurious, some actual), mumblings about the scandalous, bigamous, heathenish Mormons out in Utah finally submitting to federal authority; all the soporific, listless hum of late-summer news and tavern small talk came at once to a crashing halt when, in what was truly a single instant, the nation heard that the Atlantic cable was laid and electric signals—messages!—were traveling beneath the entire breadth of the northern ocean.

The country had not been paying attention to the fortunes of the cable syndicate. Word had trickled back to America that the expedition that had set out in June had turned back. Insofar as the country paid it any notice, this second cable failure had been consigned in the public mind to that category of harebrained, defunct schemes such as horseless, wind-driven Conestoga wagons or intercity pneumatic message tubes.

Then, however, out of nowhere came the news that the brilliant young engineer from Maine had stumbled in out of the night and onto the North American continent, pulling a magical wire behind him.

At least that was the cartoon as Jack Trace had sketched it and as it had been published along with the story in the New York *Sun*. Instantly the public was ravenous. Other papers picked up the piece or pirated it for their rewrite men to embellish, and in a matter of hours, the image was part of the American cognizance. There followed the ringing of church bells, firing of cannons, full-throated cheers, spontaneous village celebrations, ad hoc city parades, speeches, and wild revelry. The nation abashed itself with its own delirium.

"Are we mad?" one editorial asked. "Yes, in thunder! Let the world see how mad with joy we are that our sons—Ludlow and Field—have united two continents!"

ATLANTIC EVAPORATED! one Baltimore paper cried.

The American press gave short shrift to any British participation in the cable's success. To anyone reading an American newspaper, it appeared their countrymen had laid the cable solely themselves. Trace's caricatures of Field rowing ashore and Chester carrying the cable slung over his shoulder like a coiled hawser captured the populace's collective attention. They didn't notice the Union Jack on the horizon in the background. But Trace knew his audience. In the pictures Trace sent by ship to London, Field was replaced at the oars by a British sailor.

Nevertheless, there was a hint of truth to the picture of Chester coming ashore with the cable. While Professor Thomson and the *Agamemnon* were making an early-morning landfall on the Irish coast, the *Niagara* was still in the lees of night, sailing up the eighty-mile length of Trinity Bay, Newfoundland.

It was still dark on August fifth in Trinity Bay when the *Niagara*'s longboat scraped onto the stony beach with the shore end of the cable, and Chester realized he had no idea where the telegraph house was. On the beach there seemed to be nothing but a solid wall of black spruce, hemlock, and fir trees above the strand. The night sky was full of stars.

Chester commenced running along the rocks. "Look for a light!" he called back to the others. The men peered into the wall of darkness.

"Hallooo!" A cry came from the two crewmen who had gone the other direction. They were waving their lantern some five hundred yards down the beach. Chester and his cohort immediately tore off toward the pair, who pointed to a dim gap in the pines that revealed a tiny jewel of lantern light.

"That's it!" Chester said, and took off.

But what appeared to be an opening in the forest was no more than an interstice admitting a cranberry bog. Soon the whole group was flailing through thigh-deep water and slashing at thicket branches with their forearms.

It took them nearly half an hour to reach the telegraph house, and once there they couldn't find the door. Chester began running along the wall, banging on the unpainted clapboards and shouting to the inhabitants to wake up.

"I'm Ludlow!" Chester shouted. "This is Field. The *Niagara* has landed!"

Once they'd raised the graphers, once all the cheering and huzzahs had ceased, they dispatched crews to string wire and splice it quickly into the shore end down on the beach. Soon, as the men crowded into the telegraph room, Chester wrote a brief note to Professor Thomson back in Ireland. The first telegrapher began to tap out the message, passing the duty on after a few words to the other graphers so each could have his turn.

We landed here in the woods . . .

Then Chester handed the pad to Cyrus Field, who wrote a brief note to his wife, another to his father, another to the Associated Press, and a final one to President James Buchanan. He folded each paper and handed them to the telegrapher.

Field then turned to Chester, proffering him the pad. "You'll want to send something," he said.

"Oh, I—"

"At the very least, something to your wife?" Field said.

But Chester, now with the power to signal instantly halfway around the world, didn't know, for the life of him, where in that world his wife was. He'd sent her a letter from London to meet him in Newfoundland. He had no idea if she was here, or even if she'd received the message. And then, even if he had known where she was, what would he wish to say to her? He was at a loss. He could feel the men around him waiting, then

regarding him in puzzlement. So with a smile and a laugh, he bade the
telegrapher to hurry, go on, forget about him and his wife, wake up the
nation.

Trace's Message

During the whole trip across the Atlantic, there had been something Jack
Trace had wanted to say. It should have been simple, really; all it required
was that he find Chester Ludlow alone and tell him. But Jack Trace wasn't
sure he had leave to broach the subject.

Now that their victory was a fact and they lay at anchor in Newfoundland, word was coming to them that America was exploding with joy. The
news arrived mostly by landline telegraph but also by the increasingly
larger gatherings of well-wishers and curiosity seekers from St. John's and
smaller nearby towns who would make pilgrimages to the telegraph house
and sit outside in the meadows picnicking and just looking at the solitary
little structure, hoping for word that messages were flowing back and forth
between continents as if such electronic traffic might make the little building
glow or rise up off its foundation and levitate above the blowing grasses
and Queen Anne's lace.

But there were problems. Messages were taking hours to transmit and
receive. In Newfoundland they were using Professor Thomson's low-
voltage batteries and mirror galvanometer to send and receive signals, just
as they had on the voyage across on the *Niagara*, but they gathered from
garbled transmissions and snatches of phrases coming through from Ireland
that Whitehouse had arrived on the scene. Evidently, as soon as Thomson's galvanometer in Ireland detected a signal from Newfoundland,
Whitehouse would switch the cable to his patented automatic recorder.
Then, when Ireland sent signals, they did it with Whitehouse's spark coils.

"I know what he's doing!" Chester railed one evening to Field on the
deck of the *Niagara*. "He's overruling Professor Thomson."

"Well," said Field, trying to sound a note of equanimity, "he does have
the authority. He has the contract. Thomson is probably only letting him
try to prove the worth of his instruments."

"His instruments are blunderbusses. They can't read our signals, and our telegraphers here can tell the moment he's hooked up his spark coils. He's shooting something like two thousand volts through that wire. What we get are smeared globs of noise. No signal, just noise!"

"Well, that's not completely true."

"Very well. You're right," said Chester. "There are signals. Our own signals. Here."

Chester had a piece of paper in his hand. He showed it to Field. "One entire day's labor."

"I've seen it," Field said quietly.

"Well, perhaps Mr. Trace would like to take a gander." And he thrust the sheet at Trace, who had just walked up, hoping at last to speak with Chester but finding him instead in high dudgeon.

Trace looked at the sheet, written in a telegrapher's precise hand:

Repeat, please.
Please send slower for the present.
How?
How do you receive?
Send slower.
Please send slower.
How do you receive?
Please say if you can read this.
Can you read this?
How are signals?
Do you receive?
Please send something. Please send V's and B's.
How are signals?

"A whole day!" Chester said. "For that! And that's only what we were able to send them. Would you like to know how many complete words we received from Ireland today?"

Trace looked up from the sheet. Ludlow was flushed, standing with his fists clenched on his hips. His anger made him almost gleam.

"Not one," Chester said quietly and simply. "Not one word."

Cyrus Field let out a soft exhalation and looked at the purpling sky to the east over the bay. "We're all tired," he said. "They've gone to bed over in Ireland. They won't be attempting any more transmissions this evening. Let's retire and try again in the morning."

He walked away without saying good night.

As soon as Field had left the deck, Chester felt slack with embarrassment. He knew Field was every bit as hurt and frustrated as he. Chester stepped over to the ship's rail and looked down into the water.

Trace, standing nearby, still held the paper, unsure of what to do with it.

"I'll apologize to him in the morning," Chester said. "It's the apprehension. The feeling that we're so close but that we could still fail."

"I understand," Trace said.

"I apologize to you, too, Mr. Trace, for dragging you into this." He pointed at the paper Trace was holding.

"Well," Jack said, "I appreciate your keeping me informed."

Chester nodded and grinned ruefully, then frowned a little. "It might be good, Mr. Trace, if in your accounts you wait until we prove ourselves . . . one way or the other. Before you pass judgment."

"I'm not here to pass judgment, sir," Trace said. "I am here to document."

"True enough," Chester said. "But maybe you don't have to document our difficulties . . . yet. I'm trying to keep the world at arm's length while we work."

Both men stood at the rail, looking down into the clear bay water. On the hill, onshore, the day's last picnickers were heading home. The *world*, Jack Trace thought. My God, the world *was* waiting on them.

"I seem to be asking too often for your discretion or your temperance or your indulgence, Mr. Trace. I should not allow myself into positions for which I need such favors. It would make your life a little easier."

"Sir, I am not particularly concerned with the ease of my life right now. You have afforded me the opportunity to be here, on an expedition of great importance. The rewards of that far outweigh any consideration of ease."

"Good, Trace. I am glad. And grateful."

The two men watched a gull fly low through the twilit anchorage, a bit of food in its beak. Two other gulls were in pursuit. The birds cried a series of squeals and disappeared around the point.

"Sir, have you heard from your wife?"

"My wife, Mr. Trace?"

"Well, I couldn't help but notice you didn't telegraph news of our arrival to your wife when we first reached land. I wondered if you'd heard from her."

"In fact, I have, Mr. Trace. That's one telegraph signal that did get through today. All the way from St. John's." He pulled a piece of paper from his breast pocket. "She traveled there by packet from Maine to meet me."

"Ah. Good," said Trace. "Will she be joining us?"

"Tomorrow."

The word hung motionless between them in the dusk. When he gave up trying to discern which direction the pendulum of the conversation might swing, Trace cleared his throat and shifted uneasily on his feet.

"Sir," he said, "your previous reference to discretion puts me in mind of something I feel I should say."

Chester turned to Trace. He leaned his elbow on the rail. Trace kneaded his hands together and remained looking down into the water.

"Sometime before we left England," Trace said, "I received a message from a lady requesting my aid. She desired help preparing for a voyage. She needed someone, a gentleman, to book her passage, to assist with her belongings, to aid her in her departure. All this I did." Trace faltered here. He'd suddenly remembered he'd embarked on this conversation by first asking after Ludlow's wife. What had he been thinking?

"Yes?" Chester said.

"Well, sir, you are familiar with this lady. Professionally familiar, I mean to say, sir. . . ."

"Professionally?" Chester asked.

"She is an artist," Trace said. "A musician . . ."

"Frau Lindt," said Chester.

Trace nodded.

"Where is she?" Chester asked.

"She neither asked that I tell you nor enjoined me from mentioning it," Trace said. "So I am not sure what my duty is. Perhaps I never should have brought it up."

"But you did. And I value the disclosure. I am not blaming you, Mr. Trace. Not at all. Where is she?"

"I just thought—indeed, I have been thinking all the way across the

Atlantic—that you would want to know. It's just that I haven't been able
to find the time or the privacy to tell you—"

"Trace, where?"

"New York, sir."

Ludlow looked away, shielding his reaction from Trace.

"At least," said Trace, "that's the port for which she sailed from Southampton. What her plans were beyond New York, I'm certain I don't
know."

"Thank you, Trace."

Trace pursed his lips and nodded. He gave the telegraph log back to
Chester. Then Trace left, stumping down the deck to the companionway,
wondering if he'd breached some gentlemen's code that a worldlier man
would have navigated with greater ease. He was just too damned naive,
he thought. A naive, celibate, middle-aged bachelor bumbling his unavailing way through life. He was like the cable itself, sending out ineffectual
signals and wondering all the while, *How do you receive? How do you receive?*

The Center of the Universe

J. Beaumol Spude was happy. He had the world tied with a ribbon, and
that ribbon was a working telegraph cable beneath the Atlantic Ocean. He
had the world beating a path to his door, and that was because he'd been
designated by the syndicate to be the advance man for the American celebration when the cable expedition succeeded.

But J. Beaumol Spude hadn't always been happy. Back in June, when
Ludlow and Field, rather than having Spude aboard the *Niagara*, had sent
him ahead to prepare America for their arrival, Spude fumed.

"You're shutting me out," he'd protested. It was just another example
of these East Coast Brahmins spurning a frontier comer.

"Not at all," Field had said. "God willing, Ludlow and I—and you—*all*
of us will succeed at this enterprise, and when we do, we'll need the biggest
celebration the country's seen. It will be good for business. A big hoopla
will be an investment, draw attention to the cable, make people clamor to
buy stock and pay us to send their messages."

Spude regarded them through narrowed eyes. "I like your reasoning,"
he'd said grudgingly. Still, it had rankled him that yet again he'd been

shunted aside. Well, he'd already saved their Yankee hides once with the Phantasmagorium, now he'd just have to set them aback with an all-time blowout the moment they dropped anchor in New York.

So, he'd arranged for fireworks displays; he'd set up parades and booked bands, military detachments, and civic organizations; he'd talked to city officials and ward heelers about crowds and "spontaneous outpourings of joy" that by happenstance might be heavy on Irish laborers let off work for the day. Spude had done his job. There would be banquets and proclamations and plenty of attention paid to the cable. Business and stock purchases were sure to follow.

When word hit New York on August fifth that the cable was laid, the city acted as if God himself had placed Spude at the center of the universe. Business magnates, politicians, and civic leaders were on him in a flash, hounding him about Ludlow and Field's arrival in New York. Everyone wanted to toast, fete, lionize, practically canonize, anyone who had anything to do with the cable. Spude was indeed happy. It was enough to make him break into song, and that, one hot afternoon at the end of the first week of August, was exactly what he did.

"The cable lies under the ocean . . ."

he sang to the tune of "My Bonnie."

He called his manservant Agon Bailey into his office to take dictation. Bailey, who had been filing fireworks invoices in the other room, entered swiftly with his off-kilter stride, swung into a chair, and pulled out his stenographic pad.

"The cable lies under the sea . . ."

Spude paced from behind his desk and around the room, orbiting Bailey. It was a small office Spude had rented on Greenwich Street: two rooms on the third floor. He had all the ostentation he needed at his Amalgamated Beef headquarters in St. Louis and in the rooms he'd taken at his uptown hotel. This was an outpost. A line shack for the summer's work

on the cable. He was rather enjoying the austerity. He knew Bailey was
bridling under the cramped quarters and utilitarian decor—a desk, a chair,
a lamp, nothing else—but Spude thought it was fun, a role he was playing:
upstart entrepreneur, tiny office, one amanuensis, and a head full of ideas.
He could hear the usual clatter and shouts of street commerce coming in
through the open window on the broiling afternoon. But also in the air
was the more distant sound of a band playing, perhaps two bands or even
more . . . another spontaneous celebration. It was almost as if Spude just
had to get out of the way and let things happen.

Still, he couldn't help taking a moment to spin off new lyrics to some
popular tune, getting Bailey to transcribe the lyrics and run them down to
the printer, and sell the sheet music. They'll be singing Spudian ditties
about the cable around pianofortes and pump organs in parlors on both
sides of the Atlantic. Leaving no entrepreneurial stone unturned, Spude
had already sent word to the Newell & Son Cableworks in England to chop
him up ten thousand six-inch pieces of whatever spare or defective cable
they might have lying around—great for paperweights! He'd ordered the
telegraphers at the New York office to save every scrap of paper that had
anything to do with an overseas message (when they started coming). The
pieces would be framed and sold.

"The cable lies under the ocean . . . ,"

Spude boomed over by the window. He paused for inspiration, then waved
his finger, swordlike, at Bailey's pad and sang,

"Thus Ludlow brought England to me!"

Bailey looked at Spude a beat too long before lowering his eyes and
writing down the line. Bailey didn't like it, Spude could tell.

" '*Ludlow* brought England,' sir?" Bailey asked. "Isn't it Mr. Field actually who is the chairman of the syndicate?"

" 'Mr. Field' doesn't scan," Spude said. "Besides, Ludlow's the man
they're all going to fall for. Same as they did with the Phantasmagorium.

It was Ludlow. He has the look. The fair-haired son. The matinee idol. Write down 'Ludlow.' "

"Yes, sir."

And Bailey wrote down *Ludlow* as Spude continued,

"Lud-low . . .
Lud-low . . .
Ludlow brought England to me, to me . . ."

He was waltzing around the office to the chorus, affecting a slight operatic roll to his delivery, just to tweak the phlegmatic Bailey for not liking the song.

"Lud-low, Lud-low, Ludlow brought
England to me."

Spude abruptly stopped. It was too hot for this, and the street outside the open window was resounding with too much noise. It sounded as though a parade was approaching.

"I'll work on it more later," Spude said. "I'm going out."

"You'll be back at . . . ?" Bailey said.

"Won't," said Spude. "Not today. Rest of the day off for you, too. Join in the fun. If you can."

Bailey closed his notebook with a long-suffering sigh. Spude threw on his coat. It was too damned hot for a coat, even the linen one he had with him.

When he reached the street, the noise and the heat and the smell of the afternoon's horse droppings baked by the thick, buttery sunlight nearly pushed Spude back inside the building. Not one but two brass bands were heading north on Greenwich, each playing a different tune at different tempos. This kind of thing had been going on day and night throughout the city—throughout the country!—in the forty-eight hours since the news of the cable's success had broken.

A crowd of several hundred was moving along with the bands, many people cheering to their own rhythm:

> "The cay-bull!
> The cay-bull!"

Negro and Irish boys ran in circles and helixes around the front of the bandmasters as they marched. Dray horses shied and one cab horse reared over the heads of a drunken chorus of men in butcher's aprons whose song was unintelligible under the noise. If Chester Ludlow and Field wanted a celebration when they got to New York, well, look at this little warm-up.

"Herr Spude!"

Spude didn't hear the voice at first. Or if he did, he couldn't have picked it out of the general din. He realized when he finally *did* hear it—a voice both light and assertive, like a silver knife blade tapping against crystal—by then the woman had already hailed him several times and there was an edge of desperation to her cries.

"Herr Spude!"

Spude looked around. Directly across the bouncing, arm-waving, cheering throng that followed the bands was the carriage whose horse had reared. The cabman was down off his box, trying to calm his animal. Waving from the window of the lurching vehicle was Frau Katerina Lindt.

"Well, my God," Spude said aloud.

He waved mightily back to her as if she were far out at sea in a foundering dory instead of in a cab a mere twenty yards away. She made an exaggerated drooping sigh of relief that he'd finally heard her.

Getting across the street was no easy trick. The two bands had stopped up at the intersection of Greenwich and Fourteenth and had now joined forces and melodies with the crowd in one song, a most martial and heavy four-four rendition of "Old Hundredth," the Doxology:

> "Praise God from whom all blessings *flooooow!*
> Praise Him, all creatures here *belooooow!*"

The followers had jammed up behind the bands and were clogging the thoroughfare. Spude was swimming his way through the crowd, trying to keep his eye on Frau Lindt's carriage.

When Spude reached the carriage, he grasped the cab's windowsill as if it were a life buoy.

"Frau Lindt, what are you–?" He was shocked at how out-of-breath he was.

"I've been *looking* for you," Katerina said. She, too, clutched the cab's windowsill.

"Praise Him above ye Heavenly Host . . ."

"For *me?*"

"Yes!" She had to shout also. The parade had begun to move northward once more. People jostled Spude as he clung to the carriage. The cabman was shouting at marchers to move over, to give his jittery horse room.

"I must speak with you, if I may," Frau Lindt was calling practically right into his ear. He felt a pang of vanity when he realized it had been too long since he'd had a barber trim his thatches of ear hair. He flinched, turning his head quickly. She seemed unperturbed, concentrated as she was solely on speaking with him. She slid over on the leather seat and bade him join her in the cab.

"Praise Father, Son and Holy *Ghooooost!*"

"If we could just find a quiet place . . ." she said.

Frau Lindt's Case

A church garden wasn't the quiet place Katerina Lindt had anticipated. She had been forgoing her midday meals of late–an economizing measure–and the thought had occurred to her that perhaps Herr Spude would invite her to lunch. But it was midafternoon after all, and he was, he'd said, already late for an appointment down at St. Paul's with "a man of the cloth," so why didn't she accompany him there and they could talk on the way. Very well, she'd said, feeling her stomach tighten and her vision swirl a little. She'd be delighted.

When Spude had climbed into the cab and called out the new destination to the driver, Katerina realized it was the first time in weeks that she was not an unescorted woman. She had a gentleman giving orders on her behalf. The last time that had happened was back in Southampton when the kind sketch artist helped her with her escape—her *departure*. The sense of gratitude that she now felt almost made her swoon, and she had to check herself so as to keep her composure.

On the brief ride to the church, Spude talked steadily about the celebrations and the "sheer, blamed craziness, don't you know" of the reaction to Chester's success with the cable. And he made a point of saying *Chester's* success. A sign, she thought, that he wanted her to know he knew about her and Chester and about why she must be here in America.

It was when they finally reached the church in lower Manhattan that Spude stopped expounding. He even looked temporarily flurried over what to do with her when he went in to meet with the minister: leave her in the carriage? take her inside? introduce her to the clergyman?

"You said the meeting was to be brief?" she asked.

"Why, yes," he said. "I only have to swap remarks and ideas for a prayer for tonight with the reverend. Ten, fifteen minutes, tops."

"Why don't I walk in the garden?" Katerina said. "While you are busy."

"Excellent!" said Spude, and as his eyes sparkled, Katerina suddenly remembered the sheer fun she'd had working for this fellow, this American showman who was part millionaire and part mountebank, who'd dreamed up the idea of the Phantasmagorium and who, ultimately, had made it possible for her to meet Chester Ludlow.

"I'll be right back," Spude said.

He told the cabman to wait, and he left her in the shade of a maple tree in the garden. She strolled on a cobbled path. Nearby were some simple, brownstone grave markers. Her hunger made her think how they were the color of the dense, dark bread of the Kitzbühler Alpen where she had lived with Joachim in the early days of their marriage. She was surprised by the thought of those early days and by the sudden tenderness

she felt for Joachim. For his artistry. For his almost laughable idiosyncrasies. What a madman he was: sewers, running, the Phantasmagorium. But,
she thought, they were the quaint side of a character that also encompassed
something darker, something that had, if she admitted it, frightened her.

"I'm back!"

Spude was at her side. He told her the minister and he had discussed
the evening's ceremony "in nothing flat."

"And then if the son of a gun didn't ask me to pray with him. *Pray.*
We thanked God for the cable and for Ludlow and for Field and for good
weather and calm seas and for electricity and for I don't know what all
else." Spude shook his head in amusement. He looked out at the iron spears
of the picket fence that surrounded the churchyard's garden and separated
it from the brick commercial buildings and mansard-roofed brownstones
across the street. "Calmed me down, though. Got to say that for prayer.
Calms me down. Beyond that, frankly, I don't know what good it is in
this day and age, and I'd wager we'll see less and less of it as time goes
on. But"—and here he snapped himself up, shot his cuffs, turned on his
toes to face her, and came to attention as if she were a memsahib and he
her pukka boy—"my good Frau Lindt. What are you doing here? In New
York? In America? As if I didn't know."

They took several turns around the garden. Katerina wasn't sure if her
hunger would overcome her, but once she got talking, she became absorbed
in relating her story. As discreetly as she could, she tried to explain her
situation with—or more accurately, *without*—her husband; how she had
struck out on her own; how although she had the wherewithal, it wasn't
endless; how she was sure she could perform if she could find suitable
backing, perhaps a few recitals, a concert engagement, something to keep
her from stooping to offering lessons or pumping the pedals of some wheezing, moldy church organ until . . .

"Until Ludlow takes over?" Spude asked. The question could have
held a nasty bite meant to point up the wantonness of her situation, but
Spude asked it tenderly.

"Herr Spude," Katerina said. "I . . . cannot hide my feelings . . . nor my
history with Chester Ludlow from you. Nevertheless, I must remember,
must always remember, I am alone, I am as good now as unmarried. And
neither you nor I know what the future will bring for Chester Ludlow. I
have my hopes, but"—her throat caught in an involuntary gulp for air—"I
have my music and I must attend to it. At least for the time being."

"I think I get you," Spude said. "Hell, though. Chester arrives here, the hoopla over the cable dies down, we could start up the Phantasmagorium again. How about that?"

She must have looked startled, for Spude immediately laughed and said, "Just kidding. Just *kidding*. I know you don't want to go back there."

But the instant she heard him suggest reviving the show, she wanted it. Her heart wanted it desperately while her mind, almost as instantly, chased after and said it could never be done. Those days were over, impossible!

She forced a fluttery laugh and sat on a stone bench.

"I know," Spude said, sitting with her, "you meant your *serious* music."

"Of course," said Katerina.

"Well," Spude drawled, "it is a most interesting challenge. I tell you what . . .," and he proposed he escort her that night to the telegraph rally and welcome at City Hall, where they would be bound to meet fellow artistes of the first water and if not procure her an engagement outright, then certainly establish contacts that he would use to help her find the performance venue and occasion of her choice.

"Now don't you worry about a thing," Spude said. He raised his hand and brought it down. She was afraid it would be atop hers, and that would not be a precedent she wanted to set. But the hand landed on the stone seat between them like a gavel affirming a committee vote.

"Tonight, we're going to mix with all the right people!"

New York Lights Up the Sky

It was as if they were on the margins of a riot. First, she could see out her side of the carriage scattered groups of men and boys running. As they got closer to the neighborhood of St. Paul's Chapel, the running ceased and the flow of people and carriages thickened. Thousands of people were converging on the church.

When they rounded a corner, she spied a sea of hats and bonnets and caps, bobbing signs and flags, plumes of bandmasters' shakos and the flat crowns of the musicians' caps. Choking the street for several blocks ahead, the tide of people eddied around the scores of cabs and carriages. Spude finally convinced two policemen that he was actually J. Beaumol Spude, the field marshal of the evening's event, and that they should help his driver cut a path through the crowd.

At the church they took seats in the front pew. She had expected to participate in the events as Spude's companion for the evening, but it had not occurred to her that he—and she—would be so much the focus of the proceedings. Everywhere people were nodding and waving and smiling at them. There was a rollicking atmosphere almost unbecoming for the inside of a church. Men laughed loudly and slapped one another on the back. These were the men, Katerina realized, who were going to profit most from the cable's success . . . and profit literally: this was the top echelon of New York's merchant class. Katerina half expected to see them start lighting up cigars. The women with them twisted and turned in their pews to talk with their neighbors. Some threw their arms over the seats to chat and laugh with those behind them. The entire church was positively bursting with giddiness, and it occurred to Katerina that Chester Ludlow had caused all this. Although he was not present, none of them would be there were it not for him.

Katerina couldn't remember later what the minister had said. The crowd inside the church quieted enough for the blessing and benediction, but the distracting noise of the bands and firecrackers outside made attending the minister's text almost impossible. There were some prayers and some quotations from the Scriptures—from the Psalms ("Their line is gone out through the earth, and their words to the end of the world") and from Job ("Canst thou send forth the lightnings, that they may go and say unto thee, Here we are?")—and a hymn. Then it was back through the throng and outside.

"This is much bigger than we expected," Spude said to her as they were pressed down the steps by the tide of humanity. "We can't possibly take a carriage to City Hall. We'll have to walk if you want to go at all. What do you say?"

The spirit of the city's moment was infectious.

"They have laid a cable all the way across the ocean, mein Herr Beau. I can at least walk . . . how far?" Color rose in her face.

"Ten blocks."

"Ten blocks? Walk!"

And with that she hooked her arm through Spude's and walked at the

head of the crowd, behind a street-wide banner proclaiming THE CABLE IS
COMPLETE FOR NEW YORK AND THE REST OF THE WORLD! among the
dignitaries—Mayor Tiemann, members of the city council, borough presidents, bank presidents, clergy—all the way to City Hall.

Spude couldn't have been happier. He had planned all the marches to
gather revelers as they went, to take the celebration to the streets and sweep
up the city in the flow, to make their forces swell, their spirits soar. Like
clockwork, it was all coming to pass.

The weather cooperated. Hot, but cooling as dusk settled on the city.
Word had been coming by telegraph from the Long Island coast that the
Niagara was progressing steadily, if a little tardily, toward New York
Harbor, the ship still hoping to make the evening tide.

Outside City Hall Spude and Katerina were seated on a bunting-
swathed platform. The noise and the excitement were intoxicating. A general delirium had taken over the dignitaries. Happy, honored, and almost
woozy to be at the head of this outpouring, they all congratulated one
another profusely, senselessly, but they lauded Spude most of all.

There were several speeches, then a man in a frock coat, the mayor
perhaps, Katerina couldn't tell from her seat behind the podium, introduced
Spude to the crowd, and Spude sprung from his chair as if catapulted to
the rostrum. He waved his top hat. The crowd waved its hats and flags in
answer.

"Ladies and gentlemen!" Spude bellowed. He was red-faced and hoarse
already. It was going to be difficult to make himself heard. People weren't
settling down.

"Ladies and gentlemen!" Spude yelled again, and the crowd answered
with cheers.

"Cay-*bull!* . . . Cay-*bull!* . . . Cay-*bull!*" began to percolate above the
commotion from several places at once in the throng that spread across
three blocks in front of City Hall and stretched back perhaps twice that
far.

"Yes!" Spude yelled. "The cable is a success!"

Cheers. "Cay-*bull!* . . . Cay-*bull!* . . . Cay-*bull!*"

"And when," Spude yelled, "and when in future generations they look
back on this day, they may give thanks to the Lord God Almighty who
created the world in which this great feat could occur. They may thank
him, but they will be praising, too, the God-given grit and the ingenuity
and the perseverance of the men who did it! The men we shall welcome

home into our joyous bosoms tonight! For I have heard! By telegraph, no less! I have heard that the *Niagara* is sailing toward New York Harbor! At this very moment! Let us all go, then! Let us all go out to meet her when she comes!"

The crowd went mad with joy. At that moment, on a prearranged semaphoric wave from Spude, fireworks and skyrockets were launched from the rooftops of five nearby buildings. Arcs and cascades of lavishly colored phosphorous exploded against the night sky. All the bands—on the bandstand and spread throughout the crowd—began playing at once.

"I'd planned a longer speech," Spude shouted to the dignitaries behind him on the dais, "but I can see there's no holding them back!"

Acres of people were bouncing and dancing together in the streets before the platform. The mayor himself ran over to the edge of the dais and wrenched the American flag out of its stand. He swept across the stage with the flag streaming out behind him and presented the standard to Spude.

"Lead on, Spude! We'll follow you!" he shouted.

Spude held the swirling flag; it swept across his face and knocked off his top hat. He reached out for Frau Lindt's hand. He might have found it if someone—a groundling below the dais, a child in a window across the street, a woman far back in the mass—hadn't first let out a cry that spread swiftly through the crowd like an electric charge: instantaneous, alarming, a signal.

"My God!" someone screamed. "The roof is ablaze!"

Hands shot up pointing above and behind the dais to the top of City Hall. The crowd instinctively began to shy away and surge backward.

"The fireworks!" others began shouting. "Stop the fireworks!"

A green plume of incandescence spread above the lower end of Manhattan, then a yellow one, then a ball of blue-white with a delayed howitzerlike report that went off at its center.

"Stop the fireworks!"

One of the rockets had ignited the roof of City Hall. Others kept shooting toward the building. Flames were licking the parapets, and even the dignitaries on the platform could now plainly see the peril. The crowd was flowing away from the podium like an accelerating ebb tide, leaving behind on the cobbles a detritus of flags, banners, hats, even an occasional screaming child.

People began to wail. There were calls for firemen. Calls for help. Cries that City Hall, the city itself, was burning. The fireworks finally stopped, but now the night sky was illuminated by the undulant glow of the burning roof. Bells clanged in churches and soon in the streets, and the wild-eyed horses of the fire companies began to converge on the city's seat of government.

Katerina and Spude quickly became separated. They would not find each other for the rest of the night. Katerina would walk the entire distance, water-spattered and crowd-buffeted, back to her hotel on the edges of Gramercy. Spude would stay to aid the firefighters, who began battling one another for the right to quell the blaze before they got around to fighting the fire itself. Spude was too old and too corpulent to be of much help and ended up watching from the edge of the crowd, where policemen held him back, not recognizing that he was the field marshal of the evening.

The fire would not consume City Hall. Enough fire wagons would arrive and enough bucket brigades would form out of the roiling mass of bystanders so that the building would be saved with damage contained to only a portion of the roof.

But the evening was no longer about celebrating the transatlantic telegraph. When it was all over, Katerina was asleep, filthy and exhausted, in her hotel room, and J. Beaumol Spude, water-soaked, sooty, and utterly spent, had walked clear down to the Battery—the route of the parade that never happened—where he saw, illuminated by the first rays of dawn, the *Niagara*, at anchor, waiting in vain for her triumphal welcome.

CHAPTER XVI

THE ENGINEER ASCENDANT

New York, September 1858

Collapsing Space and Time

The poster was outdated; the performance had passed. The bill bore the rococo shell-and-scrollwork margins similar to the signs and leaflets for the extravaganzas of Mr. P. T. Barnum, but this was not a Barnum advertisement. The handsome, exotic profile of the man in the center of the poster looked Sephardic or Romany or perhaps some part Pacific Islander. The poster was the only one on a "post no bills" plank fence that enclosed an excavation on the eastern edge of Greenwich Village. A corner gas lamp illuminated the bill enough to make it visible from Broadway. The hackney cabman, who was sitting in the drizzle and looking at the poster, wondered what it was doing there. He'd seen no other like it, hadn't recognized the face, and had never heard of the theater listed on the bottom. The poster made no sense.

Nevertheless, the cabman did not know what else could have interested his fare. She'd called for him to stop so she could get a better look at the fence. *He* certainly couldn't see anything else of interest on this block of partially constructed brick buildings.

Franny Ludlow had called to the cabman when she'd seen Dr. Zephaniah Hermes's dark face floating out of the misty evening shadows. The suddenness with which the face sprang at her in its dim gaslight penumbra made her think the doctor had materialized right there on a wet, ill-lit street in lower Manhattan, and now that she considered it—and she had been considering it for some minutes, making her cabman restless—she was struck by how new the poster seemed. It was outdated, yes, for according to its legend, Dr. Zephaniah Hermes had appeared in New York some three weeks past. And yet the poster seemed eerily new, as if it had been placed there recently, for only Franny to notice.

It hailed the coming of Dr. Hermes and his miraculous Spiritscope. It extolled New York for being a metropolis "of central and eastern situation and prime electrical position." It had even more hyperbole and grand claims than the advertisement for the doctor's Portland appearance. (This was *New York*, after all.)

Seeing the poster there in the September dusk made Franny think she was caught in a tightening net of some kind. Of her own emotions, perhaps; or of time; or maybe even of space as well. She'd been hearing of such a tightening all week in Chester's speeches. "Space and time will tighten and collapse with the advent of the Atlantic telegraph," he'd said at every stop, at every dinner party, assembly, fete, or gathering that had become the rule of their days and nights since the cable's completion. He was probably getting ready that very minute to utter the words yet again at the Metropolitan Hotel. She'd spent the day in seclusion, avoiding the afternoon's parade, pleading an "indisposition," wanting really just to be alone, and Chester had gone on ahead without her. This evening was to be the capstone celebration for the Atlantic telegraph's success. And here she was, malingering, staring at an advertisement for Dr. Hermes that seemed to speak perhaps directly, perhaps *only*, to her.

Things had been uneasy for Chester and Franny ever since she stepped onto the deck of the *Niagara* in Bull's Arm. She'd obeyed Chester's letter instructing her to meet him in Newfoundland and had waited more than a month for his arrival, living in a drafty harbor hotel, watching the horizon each day like a good fisherman's wife.

She'd received word of the cable's break, the expedition's return to England, the second attempt. Finally, he'd arrived in triumph, and she'd gone by carriage from St. John's to Bull's Arm to meet him. He had been there at the *Niagara*'s rail to take her hand as the sailors helped her climb the wood-runged rope ladder up from the longboat.

He was there, gallant, smiling, hands outstretched. And yet she felt a woodenness in his touch, a coldness even through her gloves as he helped her aboard and embraced her to the crew's applause. She saw very quickly how everything Chester now did, from doffing his hat to strangers to waving to a child to embracing his wife, was scrutinized and approbated by the public. He was, after all, the engineer who designed and produced the Atlantic telegraph. His every move and gesture now had moment. It struck Franny as strange at first, this absolute attention, and it reminded her of her theatrical days: men asking for a lock of her hair, for her handkerchief. It wasn't long before this idolatry of her husband put her off. It wasn't a matter of jealousy. It was a matter of balance. It was disorienting. She and Chester seemed to exist in bubbles of air a little too thin to breathe. Also, it was changing Chester. Time and space were collapsing, as everywhere Franny went with Chester was becoming like everywhere else, his existence congealing into some foggy glass through which she tried to see him, as she had tried to see the spirit of little Betty, but finding that to her touch, to her sight, Chester had become abstracted or *dis*tracted. This was not like the Chester she had first known, the substantial man who could make and do anything, who burned with ambition and desire for her, who believed he could connect continents, but now that he had done so, seemed, well . . . *dis*connected.

When he wasn't occupied with the cable, he had been civil, solicitous even, during the week they'd spent anchored in Bull's Arm and then during the sail to New York, but those moments were rare. He was preoccupied, obsessed really, with the cable and its future.

That night of their arrival, she had stood on the deck in silence with him in the evening's last light and had looked at the flags fluttering on the Battery and around the squat turret of Castle Garden. The sketch artist, the shambling Britisher with the thick pile of hair and the cheeks quick to blush, was hovering nearby. She had grown to enjoy Jack Trace's company on that trip. It was a kind of chaste solace for the distance she was feeling from Chester. She had sat with Mr. Trace on the *Niagara*'s main hatch cover as he sketched her portrait and had watched one night with him as they passed the fir-cloaked point of land that was the seaward bourn of Willing Mind. There were no lights anywhere on the point. Chester had not even come on deck. He was below doing calculations. But Mr. Trace had sat there with her and listened most raptly as she talked of her home, describing it to him, trying to pin down for his artist's eye the fullness of summer light and the clarity she'd feel inflate her spirit when days were good. Then the kind Mr. Trace—she actually called him that once—sat in silence while she told the story of her daughter. Neither of them had moved when she lapsed into speechlessness, secretly trying to see or feel or somehow apprehend Betty's lost spirit as the ship sailed on in the dark.

Then, in New York Harbor, the three of them—she, Chester, and Mr. Trace—had been standing at the *Niagara*'s rail, looking at the city when they'd noticed the fireworks. The whole sky glowed orange.

"They've certainly set out a welcome for you," Mr. Trace had ventured.

But Chester had not answered. So the three of them stood there, wordlessly uneasy in triumph, and Franny thought she could hear, across the water, the faint clamor of alarm bells.

Now she sat in the carriage, looking at the poster, surer than ever that its presence bore her some particular significance. She had the odd certainty that the poster was directing her away from her evening's appointment. She had no idea where it was directing her, but she now knew unequivocally she was meant to be elsewhere. Then an image came to her, hovering before her in the cab's dark interior: an empty chair. On the dais. *Her* chair, at the celebration; the celebration beginning soon to which she should be hastening; the celebration beginning even as she sat there looking at the poster, the cabman confused, the horse shaking his halter; the celebration, Chester rising to speak, her chair, beside him, empty . . . She could see him.

Chester has entered the hall, making slow progress toward the stage, choked as the grand ballroom is with flowers, tables, scurrying waiters, and excited well-wishers rising to their feet to applaud and reach for him as he works his way toward the head table to join Cyrus Field, Mayor Tiemann, city dignitaries, Peter Cooper, the syndicate board members, and J. Beaumol Spude, who, as master of ceremonies, has just introduced him, saving him for last, the "Engineer Ascendant," as Spude has called him, the man "who convinced us it could be done, showed us how to do it, and, by gum, *did it!*"

Chester had been off in an adjoining room to the hall, a special telegraph room with instruments and a direct line to Trinity Bay and thence to Ireland and Europe. The telegraphers had been conferring worriedly with him. When the applause exploded from the grand ballroom, Chester had to go.

The ovation is thunderous, loud enough to make anyone who could possibly tear themselves out of the rapture of the moment wonder about the effect of the tumult on the ornate plaster ceiling and crystal chandeliers. Even the twenty-foot-long model of the *Niagara* sitting in the middle of the banquet hall seems to founder in the din.

Chester is working his way toward the dais alone, because Franny is not there. He makes it to his seat at the center of the bunting-festooned head table with its enormous cornucopia flower arrangements and lambent glass and silver. He cuts a dashing figure in his evening clothes; his face glows from the excitement but also from the days at sea, which have further bleached his blond hair, so its curls are the color of the palest flax. His spectacles flash as if to signal: look to this man, here is presence, here is brilliance. All eyes are upon him as he goes down the line of dignitaries, shaking hands or kissing the gloved ones of the wives. The ovation continues unabated. Chester thanks the mayor and grips Cyrus Field both by the hand and shoulder, and Field does the same to him. It is a moment Jack Trace, at a table below the dais, will capture in an engraving for the front page of tomorrow's *Sun*.

Chester is so caught up in the excitement, his shock at the note from his wife has been expelled for a moment from his mind. Shock is about to return, though, once Chester has finished shaking hands with J. Beaumol Spude, who has stepped toward him from the small rostrum at the center of the long table. Chester laughs at whatever Spude has uttered—no one can hear anything over the clamor; this is all a pantomime of congratulations and triumph. The shock comes when he releases Spude's hand and looks around the rotund toastmaster to see Frau Katerina Lindt offering her lovely hand up for him to kiss.

"Driver," Franny called from the cab. There was no response. Franny had to repeat the call.

"Ma'am?" He'd been dozing.

"Would you mind," she said, leaning toward the cab window, "would you mind bringing me the poster there from the fence? It looks to be fastened with tacks. It should come right off."

Franny could hear the man grumble, and she could feel the cab rock on its leaf springs as he descended from the box. The fellow delicately removed the bill after a quick look up and down the street. He handed the poster, loosely rolled, through the window.

"Begging your pardon, ma'am," the driver said. "But you requested to arrive at the Metropolitan by eight. It's now after nine."

"I know," Franny said softly.

"Shall I hurry along then?"

"No. Remain here," Franny said. "I'll tell you when."

The driver nodded, and raindrops that had collected on his hat brim dribbled off. He swung back up onto the box with a thud.

Franny wanted to stay a little longer. She knew she needed to hold the poster, touch it with her own hands. What had Otis called such a thing? A conductor? A receptor? A *spirit lever*, that was it. Like a lightning rod. Like Betty's doll. The poster would help.

Chester is speaking. He is at the rostrum now. The crowd is enthralled. Their presence here this night, they all know, will be to their everlasting distinction—an honor that they, and they alone, will possess even unto the end of their days.

But there are problems. The audience isn't aware of them yet, but Chester is. He is speaking graciously of the help and encouragement he had from Cyrus Field, the chairman of the syndicate, and from the other men who are sitting with him on the dais. It is all Chester can do to keep the problems from distracting him from the task at hand: being the celebrated—what was it Spude called him?—*engineer ascendant*. But the note in his pocket troubles him and has so ever since a cabman muscled his way into the crowd at the pre-banquet reception in the Metropolitan's lobby and gave him the message.

The note is from Franny. The cabman, gruff and with flecks of oat chaff on his coat sleeves, said he had express orders from Mrs. Ludlow to hand the note over to her husband personally.

The note says Franny won't be here tonight. She is leaving. She regrets her absence, and she doesn't expect him to understand. She wishes him well. She is all right, she assures him, but she must leave New York.

The note baffles Chester, is almost meaningless to him, and yet makes perfect sense, too. It's the logical culmination of the three weeks they've been together since they reunited on the *Niagara* in Bull's Arm. It wasn't a reunion, really; it wasn't a union of any kind; it was merely the placement of two bodies in close proximity.

Of course, she has every reason to depart. *He* left *her* months ago. The cable has consumed him. This is the culmination of it all: a celebration for him and an empty chair beside him at the table of honor.

And that's to say nothing of who is sitting a few chairs down from him, the person whom he can't help but see every time he gestures toward Spude; there, the person whose high-necked maroon gown elevates her countenance, who looks radiant, whose smile seems bliss itself but also subtly betrays the other feelings she has for him. He imagines—he *knows*, even as he stands at the podium—that her breasts are flushed as she looks at him; her breath, heated and quickening. He is feeling the same. To steady himself, he employs a gesture he has used onstage ever since he began addressing audiences with the Phantasmagorium. He thrusts his hands in his coat's side pockets. It's a small flourish of informality, almost a nervous tic. The problem is, however, he feels the note from Franny and knows he must say something about the empty chair behind him.

He winds up his encomium of Spude and waits as the crowd's applause subsides.

"I must now express my regret and convey my apologies for an absence," Chester says, and goes on to explain discreetly, with some dissembling, about what he calls Franny's "mild indisposition." He thanks her in absentia for her devotion and love and steadfastness and tells the people how the cable they've come to celebrate would never have happened without her. People—especially the ladies—smile up at him. One thousand faces nod in the candlelight.

Chester, however, glances over and sees one face looking patiently down at her own hands. Katerina is calm, seemingly content, letting this necessary, even admirable, moment pass. She is here, Chester realizes, to witness his victory as she said she would be. She is here. Franny is not.

Franny, excited, suddenly urgent, ordered the cabman to start back for her hotel. Then, when he nearly had the brougham turned around and back on Broadway, she said no . . . no, of course not; she must first go to the

Metropolitan as planned. So the driver, with a roll of his eyes and a muttered curse that went undetected by his passenger, turned the horse uptown and flicked the drizzled air with his whip.

It had been as if Franny could see into the banquet hall of the Metropolitan, as if she could hear what Chester would be saying, as if she knew what he would be thinking, and as if she conjured up the presence of the woman whom she remembered from the visit of the Phantasmagorium troupe last winter at Willing Mind.

So she had the cabman stop before the Corinthian colonnade of the hotel. A pair of policemen had tried to move them along, as Broadway was choked with several dozen other cabs and carriages and a mingling crowd of nearly two hundred well-wishers and gawkers. Franny pleaded with the officers to let her driver deliver a message to her husband, Mr. Chester Ludlow. The policemen were so impressed that one officer held the horse and the other brusquely directed traffic around the cab while the driver went inside.

While she waited, the picture of Dr. Hermes, the advertisement for the Spiritscope, whirled in her head, stirring up the force to impel her away from New York, her husband, maybe even her home. Things would be different, she told herself as she drummed her fingers on the poster.

"Done it, ma'am," the cabman said. "Where to now?"

"Back to my hotel," Franny said, rolling up the placard to cover her agitation.

The cabman touched the brim of his hat, and soon the brougham was rolling again. As they passed in front of the Metropolitan, Franny was able, between the parked carriages and cabs, to see glimpses through the windows of the main ballroom. She couldn't be sure because the images shuttered at her as her cab's horse began trotting along to flicks of the driver's whip, but she believed she saw through the long, parted drapes to the glow of the gaslight and to the heads of men and women; she thought she saw— improbably—the masts of a ship, the twinkle of cut glass and jewels. And finally as she looked back toward the last window, she believed she saw her husband—it couldn't be; maybe it was a spirit image—blond, aglow, standing at the rostrum, waving to the crowd, certainly to the crowd, certainly not to her.

*   *   *

The plan is for Chester to read a telegram sent from England to the assembly in the ballroom, a telegram that will be an answer to the message he dictated to a telegrapher joining him at the rostrum at the start of his speech.

This bit of showmanship is Spude's idea, and everyone loves it. Chester began his speech by summoning the telegrapher—resplendent in a maroon tunic and white linen trousers, a completely fictitious Atlantic Telegraph Company uniform invented by Spude for the occasion. The message Chester dictated was short: "Are we ready for the business of the world?" He then went on with the rest of his speech while he and the assembled—and the whole world—waited for the answer.

Chester has now thanked the dignitaries, apologized for his wife's absence, chronicled with becoming modesty and suitable diffidence the story of how they finally succeeded with the cable, and ended by predicting greatness for the investors in particular and humanity in general.

"And now, ladies and gentlemen," he says, "the message from Europe is here."

Chester has seen the telegrapher—a thin, twitchy, young man ill served by the maroon tunic, the sleeves of which are too short—waving to him from the wings of the ballroom stage. The fellow looks apprehensive.

Chester signals him on anyway. The young man walks across the stage dreadstruck to a rumble of excitement in the hall. People are craning their necks and leaning around flower displays; the sailors from the *Niagara* at the long tables toward the back of the hall are rising to their feet, as are some young men close to the dais whose coattails are pulled by seated companions hissing, "Down in front!"

The crowd thinks the telegrapher is congratulating Chester when he whispers into Chester's upstage ear as he hands over the paper.

"The line is dead," the man says through a forced smile.

"What?" Chester whispers, knowing instinctively also to counterfeit a smile.

"Dead, sir. This is all we received. I'm sorry."

Chester takes the paper and opens it. The telegrapher does a full turn as he backs away, looks once to the crowd, turns half around again, and hastens off the stage. There is some applause, some distracted laughter, but all eyes quickly go back to Chester.

Chester does not immediately focus on the words of the message. He can see instantly they are few . . . too few. He habitually dips his free hand into his jacket pocket, then pulls the hand out as if it were scorched. He's felt Franny's note.

He raises his hand high, signaling for silence, but the room is already waiting in a spellbound hush. He looks more carefully at the words now. . . .

Please inform . . . government
We are now in a position to do best
to forward

and that is all. There is nothing more, not on either side of the paper, for Chester has looked.

The crowd is beginning to shift in their seats, some surely thinking Chester has exploited the moment's suspense a little too shamelessly, others touched that the gallant engineer seems perhaps overcome by emotion. Chester clears his throat. He reads the words. He could have asked for pardon, saying that the cable was experiencing mechanical difficulties, but he reads the words instead. He reads every one.

And when he's finished he continues to speak, giving not the slightest hint that the signal was lost in the noise of the void. ". . . We are now in a position to do our best to forward any and all private and corporate cable traffic for the betterment of all our peoples as we endeavor to lead the march of humanity and to collapse space and time so we are all one people with a single vision, a single heart, a single soul!"

He looks up and smiles. The room explodes in cheering. Chester catches a quick glimpse of Katerina, exultant with all the others, rising to her feet to applaud. Chester quickly thrusts the paper into his pocket with Franny's note so no one will be able to see it. He balls both papers up tightly in his fist as he waves with his free hand to all the happy world.

"Fraud!"

Chester had never intended things to end like this. What his intentions were, he really couldn't have said. But not this, not exactly this, at any rate. Not Katerina unfastening his waistcoat in her hotel room: her eyes flashing, her teeth pulling impatiently at her lower lip as she worked the buttons. And she soon had the waistcoat and his shirt open—she'd given up patience altogether and popped the shirt studs right off—and now ran her hands, fingers spread, almost clawing at him, up from his stomach, across his chest to hold his face and bring it down to hers. As they kissed, her hands dropped down the front of his trousers to hold his erection. At first touch, she gasped aloud. Chester felt his vision cloud with a mist of desire. He had no intention . . . And yet neither did he have any intention of stopping. He wanted her. She had come to him. And so, engineer ascendant, he began removing her clothes.

They were in Katerina's rooms. Spude had left the two of them at the Metropolitan after Chester had told him about the notes in his pocket: the one from the absent Franny, the other being the incomplete telegram.

"You'll fix it!" Spude had said, and clapped him on the shoulder.

"Of course," Chester had said, not knowing whether he and Spude meant the trouble with Franny, the cable, or both.

A telegrapher had come up to Chester after the speech late in the evening and told him the news from St. John's was still utter silence from Ireland.

"Well, not silence really," the operator had said. "Noise. You know, sir, the gibberish we get from a broken cable."

Chester nodded and gave the order to dismantle the temporary telegraph room; the celebration was over.

In the main hall most of the guests had departed. Waiters were clearing tables. A couple of drunken crewmen from the *Niagara* had climbed into the model of their ship and were as sound asleep as babes in a cradle. The last of the guests were exiting toward the hall's front door, laughing and calling good night and tossing sprays of flowers at one another. At the head table on the dais, waiting alone for him, was Katerina.

She'd told Spude she wanted to have a word with Chester and that Chester would see her home. Spude had laughed and shook his head and said, "Of course!"

But there was no word between them. Neither Chester nor Katerina had spoken in the hall or on the entire way back to her hotel in Gramercy. They did not even touch in the carriage. They moved as in a trance. Like the cable, no words passed. But unlike the cable, a multitude of messages flashed between Chester and Katerina. For discretion's sake, Chester took a room in the hotel, though he never went to it.

Katerina fell back on her bed, half laughing, half groaning, pulling Chester with her. He had gotten her down to her light petticoat and chemise, and she wanted out of even those, too. Soon she was naked and on top of him, pinning his shoulders down and running her tongue everywhere.

Then they both began laughing. The laughter was unaccountable and unexpected—he'd had no intention. The laughter told them each of the other's desperation and guilt and exaltation, of their mutual excitement, their relief, and their pleasure that a long, indefinable, unutterable deprivation was now over.

With a deft move, she thrust herself down upon him and began to sway. He watched her breasts, with their pale pink aureoles, take on a blush from her throat to her nipples. He had imagined this blush from the podium; now he was witnessing it. He raised himself up to kiss her.

Katerina threw her head back, the tendons in her neck visible; the strength and musculature of her torso aroused him further. They were still laughing, but throatier now, with a sandier feel in their voices as they became more aware of their movements with each other, the frictions, the fluidities. She was raising and lowering herself on him, and he was moving in counterpoint. Her blond hair tumbled around her shoulders as she shook her head and her body shuddered.

He felt pleasurably tortured by every move. His whole nervous system was rampant. She was crying out now. Calling for him. And he answered with words at first, then with moans, and finally with silence.

He had no intention of being in Katerina's rooms for the next day and a half, sending a messenger out to check on the telegraph and always getting the answer back: all noise, no signal.

Certainly he hadn't intended to witness his life crashing so resoundingly down around him within a week. He even began to wonder if his affair with Katerina was somehow the cause. That the failure of everything was the wages of his infidelity. For things began to unravel furiously, as if a fell recompense had come due.

"The cable needs you," Katerina said the second morning they breakfasted in her rooms. For the first time Chester was noticing the threadbare carpet on the floor, thinking how he wanted to better her circumstances, saying so abstractly but not knowing how to go about it; still, taking pleasure in the impulse.

"Hm?" he said.

"The cable *needs* you," she said, and showed him the front page of the *Mirror*.

There was an article about the rumors that the cable was not, in fact, working, that since the banquet at the Metropolitan, there was no evidence that messages were crossing the Atlantic. Indeed, the newspaper itself had repeatedly tried to send a message to London and was continually rebuffed by telegraph officials.

No one knew what was going on. The syndicate wasn't speaking with reporters. Cyrus Field was "spending much needed time with his family." The chief engineer, Chester Ludlow, was in seclusion, according to J. Beaumol Spude, who himself always seemed to be just out or expected back at some indeterminate hour.

Finally, after a week, Cyrus Field had to announce that the cable was "inoperable" and that the engineers—and everyone knew that meant Chester Ludlow—had no explanation.

Within twenty-four hours newspaper headlines had evolved from somber announcements of the cable's demise to screeching imprecations like FRAUD! and HOAX! and HUMBUG!

Years of work and 2,500 tons of cable lay inert on the bottom of the Atlantic. Three hundred fifty thousand British pounds were submerged with it, along with thousands of American dollars belonging to Field, Spude, Peter Cooper, and the other American investors. The telegraphers kept transcribing the impulses that came through the cable, but there were no discernible messages. The cable was like an enormous receptor for the planet's electromagnetic currents. Thomson's mirror galvanometer registered the changes the ocean sent through the broken cable. It was the music of the sphere, one telegrapher quipped, but rhythmless, toneless, wordless music that made no sense.

Meanwhile, the noise in the newspapers became more direct, until it reached a rabid, accusatory crescendo when several reports hit the streets that the Atlantic cable was actually a stock market confidence scheme perpetrated by Cyrus Field and Chester Ludlow. In London, one article, purported to be by Wilkins Moon but actually ghostwritten by three Fleet

Street hacks one night at the Dulcet Thrush, claimed to demonstrate that the cable had, in fact, never been laid at all.

A telegrapher—probably a fellow in Newfoundland or in one of the mid-stations along the New England line—acknowledged that Chester had embellished the message he'd read from England the night of the Metropolitan banquet. The real message was the last transmitted by the cable, and it was only a fraction of what Chester had actually recited to the crowd.

Field and Ludlow, the stories went, had created this Atlantic cable sham to drive up stock prices for their phony venture, all as a prelude to a massive sell-off.

Cyrus Field was nearly frantic with indignation and wounded pride. He had records, he said to any reporter who would listen, proving he'd not made a penny from the venture. He'd sold but one share since July— and that to a relative and at a loss, to boot. Ludlow, too, was innocent, he protested. Or at least innocent of stock fraud. Admittedly, the engineer had "waxed poetic and extemporized upon that last broken message from Ireland."

But the press paid Field's expostulations little note. And as for Chester, he could not be found. Field received a message from Chester. He apologized for any calumny brought down upon Field because of the embellished telegram. He had meant no harm; he only wanted to buy them time. He told Field he could be reached in Maine. He must, he said, be with Franny.

The extremity of Chester's situation began to intrude on his preoccupations with Katerina. The focus of his concern went from her bed to the bottom of the Atlantic to, finally, Willing Mind. And with the press hounding him, demanding how much money he made from the putative stock swindle, Chester was desperate to leave New York.

"What will I do?" Katerina asked, not plaintively, not petulantly— merely a procedural question.

Chester tried to think of an answer. He had none.

And so he left New York. The cable was dead. The enterprise, an object of scorn and suspicion and worse, was becoming a laughingstock. In his letter to Cyrus Field, Chester also said that all his tests had led him to conclude that the cable failed because Edward Orange Wildman Whitehouse had refused to acquiesce to Professor Thomson's request he use the galvanometer. A letter from Thomson confirmed that the batteries and high-intensity induction coils had been attached to the cable on the Valentia end. They must have blown out the wire inside the cable.

"It was as if," Chester wrote Field, "we were sending high-pressure steam through a straw. Our cable couldn't stand the strain."

Thomson had written that he calculated the break to be someplace about three hundred miles off Valentia. "Perhaps other places, too," he'd said.

Chester brooded about this all the way to Willing Mind. When he arrived there on a cold, late September afternoon with sun reflecting off the house's west-facing windows and the sea a gray gash beyond the heather-topped cliffs, there was no one home. Chester had known this would be the way of his homecoming. He had sensed this moment was destined from as far away as the big banquet in New York when he'd read Franny's note. She'd left him. He had once supposed that, as troubling as this walk through his empty house would be, as he looked at the closets and wardrobes bare of his wife's belongings, at least he'd be arriving in the glory of the cable's success. Even if his marriage was a scandalous wreck, at least he could build a new life around the success of the telegraph.

Now, though, there was nothing. The cable had expired. Franny had disappeared. There wasn't even a note from Mrs. Tyler, although the old woman had obviously been keeping the place up. There was only a large, flat parcel wrapped in brown paper and tied with twine on the dining-room table. When he opened it, Chester saw that the parcel was Jack Trace's portfolio.

That evening Chester built a fire in Franny's father's study and leafed through the pictures, spending long minutes meditating upon each one. The drawings were of all sizes, some as large as three feet across, others only several inches square; some took up entire sheets, other pages had several small drawings, often variations on a theme or sketches for a later, larger piece. Every one, even the sketches, was accomplished, accurate, and true. Some of the bigger ones were stunning.

The pictures told the whole story of the expedition. Trace had caught details of the ships' fittings or of the crew's postures and attitudes in work; he'd caught facets of the waves—especially the waves—that Chester himself had never noticed. Chester went through the portfolio feeling a confusion of pride and bitterness, of longing and shame. They had failed. *He* had failed. But Trace had succeeded in making it all look so beautiful, so noble.

Chester paused over a drawing of himself, Professor Thomson, and

Field by the cable spool on the *Agamemnon* before sailing.

The Colossus Coiled, Trace had written under the drawing, *with Its Progenitors.*

And now the colossus was uncoiled and useless, and its progenitors scattered in disrepute. Field had retreated to his family home in Massachusetts. Professor Thomson had written that he would be returning to Glasgow. Chester had no idea where the knave Whitehouse was. Spude had gone to St. Louis or perhaps New Orleans "to check on other business opportunities." Was he there with Katerina? As for Franny, Franny had fled. Before he'd left, Spude had stopped by Chester's hotel and had given him a heartfelt embrace. That had surprised Chester. Spude, for all his bluff and bluster, seemed to understand something about Chester, had a faith in him, saw beyond the failure, saw beyond whatever it was that was going on with Katerina and Franny, saw perhaps to some essence that lay in the future, Chester's future.

"I'll see you again," Spude had said. "I know it." And he winked and laughed and called him "partner," and although he closed the door and walked to the curb to a waiting carriage, in Chester's memory, J. Beaumol Spude seemed to have vanished like a genie.

Chester jerked awake, not knowing why. Was someone else there? He looked at the black window. Empty. He sensed the ocean out there in the darkness; waves rattled on the rocks. The cable lay dead. He had no energy to move. He could only sit and stare into the night. The beautiful drawings made him want to weep, but he couldn't.

Out on the Atlantic, watching the dawn come up over the brigantine's forward quarter, Jack Trace thought of the cable below him. What a mess. The *Evening Despatch* had written requesting his return, offering him work and "remuneration of the first order." Jack had rather liked America. Of course, his whole stay until the very end had been a medley of parades and celebrations and fetes. Now that he'd turned in his portfolio, his official work was done. He worried for the cable's men: Field and Ludlow, Professor Thomson over in Ireland, the ships' crews who had toiled so steadfastly. It had all come to naught.

Jack supposed the editors would want all manner of cartoons about the cable's failure, about the outcry, and about the accusations of fraud, which Jack knew weren't true. He couldn't draw any of that. He wouldn't. The drawings in the portfolio were the only testament Trace wanted the world to remember. He hoped the best for Chester, though he'd heard the terrible news that his wife had left him. Such a beautiful woman, Jack thought. Loss all around.

Except for one thing. It had just occurred to him as he squinted into the sun peeking up above the horizon, above the ocean where the dead cable lay. The wager. His bet with Whitehouse. The cable failed. Everyone had lost, save him. The cable failed, and he, Jack Trace, had won a night with a Thames Tunnel whore.

BOOK THREE

OTIS LUDLOW'S JOURNAL

Ireland, 1866

Foilhommerum Bay

Forge ahead. If the cable will not speak, then I must.

I left Willing Mind so precipitously, I can say now, because I feared I was falling in love with Franny Ludlow. My feelings for her, the emotions binding me to the rest of our family—both living and dead—were too much. I fled.

The astringent quality of life in remotest northern Asia scoured away all but the simplest fond memories of her. This was a life lived through pure rigor and endurance. I did not pursue the spirit world, nor did it pursue me. My "accesses"—or seizures—vanished on the Arctic wind.

Still . . . reading about Franny in my brother's letter troubled me. Franny was lost, too. I knew this without a doubt even though all Chester wrote was that she was away on an "extended tour of the country." And now word had reached Siberia that the country was riven by war.

Blast it, I thought. A letter thirty months old. What did it mean now? If ever there was need for a telegraph . . .

When it was summer again, work beckoned and I had to take my own "extended tour of the country."

From Petropavlovsk, my intention was to proceed north, then across the Kamchatka Peninsula via the circuitous route dictated by the mountain ranges and rivers. Thence, from Tigil on the west coast of the peninsula, I would work my way up to Geezhega at the northern end of the Okhotsk Sea. From there, I was to organize a scouting crew—consisting of only myself and a dozen or so Wandering Koryaks—to make final a route to the Bering Strait.

The trek began in mid-July, and in my entire life I have never taken a more pleasant journey than the 275 versts I traveled through the flowery mountainsides and green valleys of the southern Kamchatka in high summer.

Owing to the variety of altitudes and climates, we experienced the pleasures and challenges of travel by whaleboat, horse, raft, canoe, dogsled, reindeer sledge, and snowshoe.

In early August we arrived in the village of Klyuchi, in every respect—save one—a picturesque mountain settlement of houses and yurts nestled amid stunning, isolated peaks on the Kamchatka River. The one qualification looms over the town and utterly dominates it: the Klyuchevskaya Volcano, a massive, towering cone that belches a constant plume of smoke and soot from its crater.

We were ahead of schedule and would need to defer travel north of Geezhega until the snows arrived, as nothing but sledges in winter could traverse the mossy, marshlike terrain of the tundra, which had to be frozen to be passable.

With time on our hands, we spent more than a week in Klyuchi observing the rumbling, threatening, beautiful peak. The temptation to scale the monster, which, for all I knew, had not been climbed, was too much for me. I set about preparing for an ascent of the Klyuchevskaya.

As I speak of my journey up one of the loftiest and imposing peaks of Siberia, I must also speak of one of the lowliest of fungi of the region, a toadstool—the "musk-a-moor," as the natives call it.

The musk-a-moor is a species of spotted mushroom that grows a small hood and resembles our own jack-in-the-pulpit. Its intoxicating powers are considerable, and its use is exceedingly popular among the natives, as there is not the means to produce any other intoxicant in this climate. Rare as well, one musk-a-moor can fetch three or four reindeer on the black market.

The scarcity of the fungus is mitigated by its ability to retain its potency even when filtered through human kidneys. One man may eat the mushroom and then, by means of his urinary tract, produce intoxicant for all the rest.

Habitual use of the musk-a-moor completely disorders the nervous system, and the Russian government has proscribed the brisk trade that flourishes around the plant. Moderate use can induce visions and feelings of well-being; so said the

Koryaks who spoke to me of the plant; so said the Koryak on my expedition, a man named Padarin, who was reputed to be a local shaman and who gave me a small morsel of the fungus.

We had been sitting together by an evening fire, and he was, I could tell, intrigued by my blind eye.

He asked me what I saw with my "different eye," as he called it.

Nothing in the outer world, I told him. Only things inside me.

He nodded.

Musk-a-moor is like his "different eye," he said.

Then he asked how the eye became different.

It was injured, I told him.

How? Why?

I could not tell him the story. I could only say that it was a punishment for seeing something I should not have seen.

Padarin nodded. Then he took a small morsel of fungus and presented it to me.

For your different eye, he said. When we go up the mountain. To help your eye see what it should see.

It was a three-day journey from the village to the summit. No one knew this would be the case; no one had ever made the ascent before; no one had any idea the weather would be so favorable or the mountain so hospitable. This is not to say it was easy, but the route was more an inclined plane up a cone of lava rubble than a precipitous mountaineering challenge.

We seemed to be ascending an endless ramp, sometimes in clouds, sometimes in bright sunlight, ever around the flank of the enormous conic massif, switching back and forth, each leg taking several hours before we turned about and worked upward in the opposite direction. From the crater a giant banner of steam and sulfurous smoke trailed across the sky several thousand feet over our heads. Occasionally— adding up to maybe a dozen occurrences during the three days—we heard the mountain groan. The loudest of the reverberations came as we were making camp on the evening of the second day at the edge of the snowfields that continued up to the summit some two thousand feet above us. Our group huddled near the edge of the ashen snowfield, which looked like an enormous, pale, dirty-nosed beast that had slunk down the mountain to sniff at us. The roar we heard halted us in our tracks. We could feel the noise reverberate in our chests as well as underfoot. The accompanying shock sprung our tent ropes and knocked teakettles into our fires. No Koryak had ever been this close to the crater, so no Koryak had ever heard the mountain speak so loudly. It induced them all to say they were leaving immediately.

The tremor receded after less than a minute, but the Koryaks were adamant. They were leaving. Even Padarin was unyielding.

The evening was surpassingly beautiful; one could see the green lowlands stretching seaward in a light haze. Some small clouds floated below us. The Pacific was a lavender plane scattered with a few tiny ice floes.

I looked upward at the indigo sky and the billows issuing from the crater. Perhaps the tremor had increased the outpouring of steam, but the smoke was less dark than before and less like the issuance of hellish coal fire and more like a column of cheerful summer clouds or a haystack of spun sugar. By climbing through the night, I calculated, I could be on the summit before dawn and back down out of the snowfields before the morrow's nightfall.

After much pleading, I dissuaded the Koryaks from their intent to flee. The tribesmen would be safe there, I assured them, and so would I upon my return, if only they would wait. They at last said they would, and so I set out.

My intention to climb by moonlight was, like everything else about the journey, happily realized. The moon was bright, the sky so star-filled as to be dazzling, and the temperature was moderate. What remained obdurately unclear, however, and to this day still troubles me, is why I was ascending the peak. It was a mountain of imposing beauty and height, and climbing it was simple enough. But this was an active volcano.

I believe it may have been the need to look down into its crater, to see what was there. I had climbed the mountain to see what I could see. Or perhaps to see, as the shaman said, what I should see.

It was near dawn when I approached the summit. The rumbling peak had been silent all night. Through the darkness I could smell the sulfurous exhalations, and in the moonlight I could see the towering steam cloud. Below me I could just make out the smoldering light of the Koryaks' little fire built from bricks of dried reindeer dung. All was peaceful.

I was approaching the peak from the east. The lightening sky was still cloudless, and a gentle breeze was blowing in at my back from the Pacific. I reached a promontory and inched up to its edge, mindful that the snow might be poorly supported beneath my feet and could crumble, plunging me down into . . . what? The earth's core?

As I looked over the edge, this is what I confronted: an amphitheater of volcanic rock, the columnar emptiness that was the inside of the mountain. A hole in the world. The crater was a void so magnificently large that the mountain itself seemed to shrink in bulk and become a mere arête, or dike, ringing the huge vacancy. Down inside the dark amphitheater were pinnacles and rock cornices, buttresses and crags, all beswirled in smoke and steam. I saw pools and seeps of lava leaking down from fissures and crevasses far below, their red, molten trails fading in and out of the steam and sulfurous fumes. A constant, almost smooth, roar emanated from the hole.

As I looked down into marvelous depths of the smoldering mountain, the billows of steam rose before me, pulling back occasionally to reveal the far rim of the crater. The parapets and crenellations of hardened lava over there were perhaps more than a mile away.

I sat on the brink of the chasm and ate some smoked reindeer meat the Koryaks had given me. I also swallowed the small bit of musk-a-moor from Padarin.

As I contemplated the mountain and my descent, as I savored the food and sucked on bits of ice for refreshment, eventually the rising sun that had cast a roseate glow on the higher pinnacles across the steam-beswirled void began to strike my back.

There is a phenomenon seen in the Harz Mountains of Germany, named for the highest of the peaks there, the Brocken. It is a play of light and shadow and cloud, and it occurs at sunrise—the hour at which I attained the summit of the Klyuchevskaya. In the Harz it is known as the Brockengespenstphanomen: the phenomenon of the Brocken specter.

As I sat on the volcano and felt the sun at my back, I saw thrown onto the vast, white curtain of steam an enormous figure of a seated human. It was I, and if my sense of scale was at all accurate, it was several miles high. Darker than the enveloping clouds, it nevertheless had a nimbus of spectral lights surrounding it, much as a halo surrounds the heads of the sainted or the divine in religious paintings.

I rose to my feet and saw the giant figure also stand. I looked in wonder at the ethereal quality of the sight: at once substantial and utterly evanescent. I raised my arm and watched the specter do the same. The gloriole—the rainbow corona that trailed and swirled around any movement of the shadow—made a many-hued, fluttering veil around the image.

I raised my other arm, raised a leg, hopped. I performed a dance on the top of the mouth of hell, and my projection joined me in the gambol. I heard myself laugh as the mountain rumbled.

The massive specter seemed to dominate the huge column of steam, to actually take it over, to mold the billows to fit its own contours, as if to sculpt itself out of the vapor. The figure spread across Kamchatka, perhaps across even all of Siberia.

I stopped my dance, and although I anticipated seeing the shadow begin to shrink and dissolve with the advance of day, I saw a new and unexpected sight. The billowing column continued to move upward. I stood—I swear—absolutely still, but then the specter began to move of its own accord.

Now, I understand that I might have mistaken a movement of the clouds for a movement of the figure, and this might have explained what I saw. But not when I sat down again, and the shadow remained standing. The figure did not follow.

The specter began to shift. It raised its arms. It began to run. The nimbus around it seemed to imbue it with a whiteness that began to bear the likeness of a frock. The upraised arms—though miles in length—seemed to have the proportions of a child's. And the head, the face . . . beautiful and horrible to me . . . the head and the face were soon discernible as those of little Betty. The figure, as I said, was running. Not away from me, nor laterally, either, but running directly toward me, arms outstretched; running but never progressing, never gaining ground. Her expression was one of fright or ecstasy—it was impossible to tell which; perhaps both, if that was conceivable—as she ran, suspended there over the crater, over the abyss. Running, and now I could see she was smiling, running and smiling; running for me, reaching for me and calling my name. Laughing now and running.

I began to feel faint. I had the flashing thought that I might be having a seizure, that I might pass out, that I might die there, alone on the crater of the Klyuchevskaya, that Betty would watch me die, as I had watched her. That she would be no more able to protect me than I was her. I could see the smoke rising toward me. I must have been looking down into the crater. Was I pitched over the edge? The lava floes were there, the spiny parapets within the abyss.

Then I felt myself fall backward, almost as if I had been pushed. As the sky rolled up, I feared I might tumble and, like a snowball, roll backward all the way down the mountain. But I stopped when I hit the snow, and I was able to catch one glimpse of the specter. She was disappearing. A tumescent wave of steam flung itself up from the crater, and as it convulsed upward, Betty disappeared with it. The sun had risen too high for her to be contained by the smoke from the innards of the earth. She was gone. Perhaps, I thought before I passed out, it was she who had pushed me back from the brink.

Anyone reading this will say it was the musk-a-moor, and I cannot discount that. Then again, perhaps it was a seizure; I must also concede that possibility. Perhaps a combination of the two. I saw what I saw, however, and I knew from that moment I must get off the mountain. I pulled myself up to my feet and began to stumble downward on the snowy slope of the volcano. I was disoriented. I very likely spent considerable time walking up the slope when I thought I was walking down. Images of the child kept coming back to me. Sometimes I thought of her as a blessed angel; sometimes, I'm sorry to say, I was certain she was a wraithlike demon. I wandered most of the day. I wandered until I was blind.

For all my preparations, I had not allowed for the intensity of the sun on the snow. Not even the Koryaks, in their agitation over the volcano, had thought to remind me, and so I had brought nothing to protect my eye from snow blindness. The omission seemed almost diabolical. As if it were part of my hallucination. Perhaps the whole climb, this whole sojourn in Siberia, was an hallucination.

My snow blindness, however, was real and excruciatingly painful. My one seeing eye burned as if filled with hot sand. The alacrity with which the malady beset me fed my panic. I began to run down the slope, blindly, weeping. It was my cries, no doubt, that luckily enabled the Koryaks to find me.

Darkness is the only thing that can help snow blindness. The Koryaks led me for two days as I groaned and wept, blindfolded, making my way off the mountain. I lay two more days in a yurt in Klyuchi. There, the dungeonlike interior without candles was as dark as any blindfold. I emerged on the second evening. Clouds obscured the volcano. Ash fell from the sky.

Padarin was standing outside the yurt, looking up at the clouds mixed, no doubt, with smoke and at the falling powder from the inner core of the world.

I told him I was leaving. No more trip. No more telegraph.

He nodded.

You saw what you should see, he said. And he walked away.

The next morning I was making my way toward Petropavlovsk and a long journey home.

CHAPTER XVII

THE LAUGHINGSTOCK
AND THE WAR

The Atlantic Ocean, April 1861

The Battlefield Artist

Ｔ he great ship was nearly empty. To Jack Trace, standing near the sternmost funnel and facing forward, this view of the ship resembled one of Kensett's seascapes: a mighty headland with a solitary walker or two inserted for scale, and the blue, rippled Atlantic in the far background, a minor presence.

The *Great Eastern* was steaming to America, as it had for nearly two years now, crossing the Atlantic with acres of empty space above and belowdecks and with only a third of its cabins occupied. Since its ill-fated maiden voyage, when the steam valve blew, the *Great Eastern* had gone on to tear an eighty-six-foot gash in its hull on a rock during a voyage to New York, and later, on a return trip to England, had lost its rudder in a storm off the Irish coast. The ship had foundered like a drunk, according to reports, and dozens of passengers had suffered cracked bones from flying furniture in the grand saloon. A steer had broken loose from the animal pens on deck and had crashed through the grand ballroom skylight, where the beast hung bellowing upside down above the screaming passengers. During the ensuing months, the ship had become the laughingstock of the sea-lanes and a financial abscess for its investors.

In the three years since he'd completed his assignment as the cable documentarian, Jack Trace had plunged into work as an artist and engraver for several London newspapers, had illustrated two novels published by Chapman and Hall, and had even been approached by Mr. Dickens himself to illustrate a work set in Paris and London, which the writer was then calling only *Two Cities*. (Trace had to decline Boz, as his editors were keeping his calendar full.) He was well remunerated, busy (keeping the News Hole stoked), and respected among his peers on Fleet Street. His life was becoming almost settled and flush.

Then one evening Mr. Selcome, the editor of the *Evening Despatch*, had taken Jack out to dinner.

"Trace," Selcome said. "We are going to war!"

"You and I?" Trace asked.

Selcome shook his head vigorously. "*America* is going to war," he said. "With itself. I know it. The new American president may not even know it. He is acting as if he believes it won't happen. But I, shall we say, have assurances from the other side that it will. And I want you there. For us. I shall pay over and above whatever you've earned as a freelancing artist heretofore in London. You are the best in the country. Dickens himself told me as much. You will be our correspondent artist."

"What would I do?" Trace asked.

"Send pictures. Battlefield pictures. Show us the war. Sell papers for us here."

"I shall go to the battlefields?"

Selcome nodded while he drank a draft of wine, nodded so forcefully that Trace saw a couple of red drops land on the white tablecloth near the editor's plump wrist.

Selcome's proposal was so radical—Trace, an artistic war correspondent, in America—and the money so generous that Jack knew he must accept. Though the turnabout in his professional life had begun when he'd covered the explosion of the *Great Eastern* and gone on to become the cable documentarian, there always remained inside him an all-too-familiar emptiness. It was the dark corner borne of his unknowable parentage; it was the void that inhered through everything. Even with his recent success, he knew it was still there. It occurred to Jack that perhaps the answer was that he must keep moving, must heighten the demands on his art, to some-how give himself substance. America's war could be the opportunity he needed.

He learned the following morning that Selcome's amenuensis had al-ready booked him on the next departing vessel for America, the *Great Eastern.*

The ship was more than halfway across the Atlantic, and Trace was having a late dinner when he heard the voice. He paid it no mind at first, other than to think offhandedly that whoever the man was, he was dom-inating the conversation at the table behind the palms. But when Trace heard the words "Washington" and "war," he lay down his menu and listened.

"Might be a good thing for a few of those Federal chaps I'm coming over. Eh, dear? They might need a surgeon. My goodness, if that gangly ape of a fellow they have for a President thinks he can hold his country together without a war, he's a fool."

There was general agreement from around the table. Trace tried un-successfully to peek through the foliage of potted ferns and palms. Then he noticed a waiter look his way questioningly. He picked up his menu and feigned studying it further.

Someone at the table asked a question.

"Yes!" the voice rasped. It was almost shrill, a squawk that seemed less substantial than any sound around but nonetheless managed to prevail over them all.

Trace knew the voice; he was certain. He'd heard it before, in the Bardolph, but he'd *first* heard it here on the *Great Eastern* the day the ship rained metal and steam down on its passengers.

"Yes! My niece and I are as eager as anyone to observe a battle. If it came to it. Could be rather exciting. Eh, Madeline?"

Hearing her full name, spoken by that voice, dealt Trace a blow to the chest. The pain radiated along his ribs. She was right there beyond the palms. He wondered if any of the other chortling dinner companions at the next table believed for a minute that Maddy was that ass's niece.

At the very least, thought Trace, perhaps he could just peek through the fronds and see her.

But he didn't. He wasn't ready. Besides, a steward was watching. Trace became too anxious. In a sweat, he pushed himself back from the table, rose to his feet, and strode quickly past his waiter.

"Very good meal," he said. "Bill it to cabin one-fourteen."

"Sir, you haven't even ordered."

But Trace was gone, practically running back to his stateroom.

The Ship's Artist

Beginning the next morning, Jack Trace walked the decks of the *Great Eastern* constantly. Twice Jack saw Whitehouse promenading with other passengers. Whitehouse was garrulous and self-aggrandizing as he regaled his acquaintants with repetitions and embellishments of the story—his version—of the transatlantic telegraph. Neither time did Trace see Maddy with Whitehouse; neither time did Whitehouse notice Trace.

The next evening Jack obtained Whitehouse's stateroom number by buying a copy of "*The Great Eastern* Polka" sheet music from a steward and tipping the man heavily. He checked the saloon. Whitehouse was there at his table, without Maddy. Jack went through the passageways to Whitehouse's room. He knocked on the door.

"Yes?" came a woman's voice from the other side.

"Ship's artist," Jack said.

"I beg your—?"

"Ship's artist," Jack repeated.

"I didn't . . . Did E.O.? . . . Did Mr. Whitehouse order—?"

Jack spoke into the angle of the door and the jamb. "No," he said. "Courtesy call."

Jack could hear a quizzical muttering and a rustling on the other side, then the door rattled and opened.

She was wearing a silk robe, which she held clasped to her throat with one hand.

"You!" she said, and managed to look surprised, affronted, and pleased all in quick succession. "Ship's artist!" She laughed. "Cheeky," she said.

She'd grown more firm of stature. Still, Maddy showed enough of her old skittish arrogance that he could not help but think of the night in the tunnel.

Jack had spent his store of courage and aplomb just getting her to open the door. Now, actually standing before her, he deflated into meekness.

"Hullo," he murmured.

"Come in," she said, "just for a minute."

Trace stepped in and closed the door.

"Mr. Whitehouse just began his dinner. I passed by the saloon on the way here. I saw him sitting down to eat."

Maddy nodded. She looked Trace over. A wry glimmer flashed across her face. "You didn't come to draw my picture. Where's your paper? Where's your pencil?"

Trace was too flustered to answer; he had no idea where he'd left his pad and pencil.

Maddy stepped backward toward the center of the room. Trace stayed by the door.

"How have you been?" he asked.

"Me?" Maddy said. She sat on one of the two large beds. The room was much better appointed than Trace's. Whitehouse, it seemed, was able to book passage in a stateroom suite with connecting rooms, adjoining w.c., bedspreads, two dressers bolted to the bulkhead, and curtains at each of the four portholes. Trace's room could have passed for a stoker's bunk.

"Oh," she said, "you can see . . ."

"It appears you're living well as Whitehouse's niece," Trace said.

"Going to see America," she said.

"I as well," said Trace.

"To do some sketching?" Maddy asked.

"Battlefield artist," Trace said. "My editor is convinced there's to be a war."

"You must be careful then."

"Yes. I shall. Thank you . . . I say . . . may I see you again?" he asked. "Somewhere else?"

Maddy seemed to be appraising him as she took this in.

"Just to talk," Jack said. "Privately."

"What could be more private than this?" Maddy asked.

"Oh, no," Jack said. "I mean to say, he might come walking in at any moment."

"He might, mightn't he?" Maddy said. "Exciting." She squirmed a little on the bed.

"No," Jack said. "Never mind."

"Ohhh," said Maddy. "I was only teasing. Partly. But of course I can see you. It will have to be, let's see, early, though. Early in the morning. On deck."

"Early it is."

"That way E.O. will still be asleep. He doesn't stir until nearly noon. I'll be up."

The next morning at seven, Trace was making his way along a companionway up to the main deck. He was carrying his portfolio. Maddy would probably think he'd want to draw her picture. That, in fact, was the idea.

He stepped out onto the deck and headed toward the sternmost of the *Great Eastern*'s five funnels. Maddy was waiting for him. The sun had risen but was behind a jumble of pink-tinged clouds low on the horizon. The rest of the sky was a pale, spotless blue.

"I hope you don't think this improper of me," Trace said.

"Now, if I did, wouldn't I have said so? Wouldn't I not have come?" Maddy gave him a gently teasing push on his chest with her gloved hand. She was nicely attired in a brown cotton walking dress and dark green embroidered mantilla with fringe that fluttered in the morning's westerly breeze.

"Of course," Trace mumbled. Then he held the portfolio up. "May I?"

"Me?"

Trace nodded.

"Why, Mr. Sketch-man, I'd be honored."

He responded by taking her arm, walking her around to the leeward side of the funnel, and posing her by the rail. There was a delicate fragrance about her, a perfume redolent of honeysuckle perhaps. He rested his sketch pad on the back of a deck chair and, in a near swoon, began to work.

Maddy fixed her gaze on the horizon, where the two blue elements moved with the barely discernible roll of the ship.

"So, tell me how you've been keeping yourself," Maddy said.

He wanted to tell her about the other drawing he hoped to do, the grand mural, the great picture he would draw, or paint, the one to define the age, the visitation he had when he first encountered her. But that all seemed too far-fetched. It was enough just to sketch her, he thought.

He did tell her about his newspaper work, how it was fine but had become, well, ordinary, and how on a flier he'd decided to take up his editor's offer.

"For a change," he said.

"Change can be good," Maddy said. "I think about change all the time."

They lapsed into silence while Trace worked. The roles of artist and model provided some comfort for them both. They settled into them.

Trace thought about how Maddy had changed. She was not all mercenary coquettishness and salacious provocation, as she had been. Had the rewards of being a mistress and the new social demands—demands, too, that might have included malefic uses in the bedchamber—matured her, given her a more worldly cynicism? Not completely, Trace thought, because looking at her here, he could swear he could still see a vulnerability. Maybe that was just a trick of the soft dawn light.

"Hello! What have we here?"

The voice. Trace flipped the cover of his pad closed.

It was Edward Orange Wildman Whitehouse, coming around the funnel. "Why it's the cable sketch artist. Hello, my dear."

After that quick acknowledgment of Maddy, Whitehouse trained his gimlet brown eyes on Trace. He must, Trace thought, have been watching us for some time. "Too rich a dinner last night. Couldn't sleep. Went for a walk. What a coincidence to find you here, at sea, Mr. . . . ah . . ."

"Trace."

"Yes. So. Heading to the United States?"

"I am," Trace said.

"And what, pray tell, for?"

"Work," Trace said. He tapped the closed corner of the portfolio.

"May I?" Whitehouse asked. He already had his hand on the portfolio cover. Maddy frowned as Trace let the volume slide into Whitehouse's grasp.

"My, my. Work indeed," Whitehouse said as he looked over the beginnings of the sketch. "Charming."

"Your . . . *niece* . . . kindly allowed me to—"

Whitehouse shook his head and held up a hand to stop Trace. "We both know, sir, who this woman is. Excuse me, my dear, for pursuing this, but I think it best to clear the air. We all three know that her life is incalculably better for her association with me, but we all understand the exigencies involved in the prevarication regarding my use of the word *niece*."

"We do," Trace said.

"I might have thought," Whitehouse went on, smiling, "that you would, upon realizing our presence together on the vessel, have approached me directly about our wager. You remember our wager? There was, you see, no need to go through this unnecessary preliminary rendezvous inasmuch as the wager was with *me*."

"Wager?" Maddy asked.

"Yes, dear. You are to spend a night with our friend the sketch artist. You see, Mr. Trace, I don't forget a bet. Win or lose. I don't forget."

"Wager?" Maddy asked again, but not in the least shocked, merely inquisitive, merely wanting facts.

"Yes, you—we—have the failure of the telegraph cable to thank," Whitehouse said. "Would tonight be convenient for you both?"

"See here, Mr. Whitehouse," Trace said. "If you think—"

"Tonight would be fine," Maddy interjected, and stepped forward. Her eyes bore into Trace, who was feeling as if the *Great Eastern* were pitching and rolling like a storm-tossed dory, not the greatest ship ever built plying a morning-smooth sea.

Jack's Progress

Maddy resolved to leave E. O. Wildman Whitehouse. That was the change she thought about. She resolved she wouldn't do it in America, but when she returned to England. She had a plan.

And Trace resolved to paint his great mural, his *Progress*. Also not in America. He'd do it when the war was over. *If* there was a war.

They both resolved these things during their night in Trace's cramped stateroom. Trace mustered the courage, after intimacies, to tell Maddy about his dream of the mural, describing it minutely, as best he could. The images, the sweep of the vision, and the fervor that she saw as he gestured with his hands in the dim lamplight so beguiled her that she felt she could almost see the picture there, too, floating above them in the near dark of the cabin. She kept asking Trace to tell her more about it, which he did, convinced as he spoke that he *would* find a way to make it come true, convinced of the worthiness of the idea, there in the dark insides of the *Great Eastern*.

"Did you see more of it when we did it just now?" Maddy asked. "If we keep doing it, will you keep seeing more of it?"

"More of it?"

"The picture, you silly man. You told me how you got the idea for it. Maybe you need more ideas." She reached for him.

"I need more of something down there," Trace said.

Maddy giggled. "That's all right. I can wait till you come up with it." And she snuggled next to him as he stared up at the ceiling, imagining his mural.

After a few minutes of silence, Maddy propped herself up on one arm to face Jack and asked, "So, if you won, why didn't you ever come for me? Why didn't you collect on your bet?"

"I thought about it," Trace said.

"Did you now?"

"Yes. I thought about *you*. I think about you every time I think about the picture."

"And you think about the picture a lot."

"I do."

"But you didn't ever come to collect your winnings."

"No." Jack frowned. He folded his arms, clenching his chest. "I just couldn't."

"Why?"

"It seemed so . . . It just seemed the wrong way to go about it." Trace turned so he was up on an arm, too, facing her.

"And so I couldn't," he said. "I wanted to. I thought about you. But finding you, finding Whitehouse and then saying to him . . ."

He dropped down with a sigh to lie on his back again. "All that time and I couldn't."

"But finally it happened," Maddy said. "Because here we are."

"You helped," Trace said.

Maddy giggled. "I did, didn't I?" She moved close to him again.

For her part, she was realizing how being handed from one man to another, the winnings in a wager, wasn't so bad. She liked her sketch artist. His ardor, though more uncertain at first than E.O.'s, was, in fine, kinder and more generous. It gave her room to think, to see beyond what shelter and comforts E.O. had provided, even with his demands and outbursts. She was able to imagine being on her own.

"What will you do when you leave him?" Trace asked.

Maddy shrugged.

"I have something saved," she said. "He doesn't know it, but I do. I could go into business for myself. Would you come patronize my establishment?"

"I just might."

"Ah, if you paint that picture, you won't be having time for me. You'll be the toast of London. Of Paris. Of America."

Trace couldn't say anything to that. He luxuriated in the notion of being the toast of all those places, but he didn't favor the idea he'd have no time for her. He liked lying there with her. Together they listened to the engines throbbing somewhere deep beneath them.

"You know," Maddy said after a while, "this ship killed my da. He worked building her. He got killed the day they launched her. Of course, I didn't hear about it for months."

"Good Lord," Trace murmured. He meant it in sympathy, but he was also putting together the connections, remembering the day, the flying corpse, the gory death.

"Oh, you don't have to feel bad. He wasn't much of a da. A right bastard, if you must know. Good riddance for the most part. Just funny is all. He begets me. He builds this ship. And here I am."

"Yes," Trace said, thinking now was not the time to say anything else. "Here you are."

"Oh, that's right. *We.* You and me, Mr. Sketch-man. Here *we* are." And she threw her leg across him.

The last time Trace saw Maddy on the ship was after their night together. They had gone back to their rendezvous place near the sternmost funnel. They had watched the sun rise out of the sea. Then Trace noticed Whitehouse stumping along the rail toward them as if he'd had foreknowledge of their whereabouts.

"Leave before he gets here," Maddy said.

Trace nodded. It was none too gallant of him, but at least he would avoid having to hand her over like chattel.

Trace squeezed her hand and walked away toward the stern. He looked back once and saw Maddy, her mantilla pulled tightly around her, looking at him as Whitehouse approached her. Whitehouse's cape fluttered in the wind, and he reached out to reef it toward himself. At that moment, a trick of the sea breezes sent a gust downward onto the deck, bringing with it a cloud of the sulfurous coal smoke from the funnels. Trace had to squint and turn away, holding his breath against the acrid smell. When he looked back, Whitehouse and Maddy were gone.

CHAPTER XVIII

THE LUDLOW GUN

Pittsburgh, Autumn 1862

At the Forge

ails suspended overhead, from which black chains hung like jungle vines that clattered through their blocks, making a tooth-rattling noise, a noise like the jabbering of a thousand jawbones in a thousand skulls. The huge reverberatory furnace emitting a churning sound of combustion and refraction; the coke, brought in by the cartload, burning; the steam-driven McKenzie bellows outside the four-story building pushing a quarter acre of flame over the molten metal inside the furnace; the smoke bounding up the chimneys in huge, endless clots to fill the valley's sky.

A man moved along a catwalk up by the clerestory, opening the sooty, hinged windows with a wooden pole. The black sky, upwind of the furnace stacks, was lustrous with stars. The man up on the gallery walk wore a protective leather mask across his nose and mouth. His head was swathed in rags wrapped in such a way as to resemble a turban. The rags had been soaked in water. The man lifted his leather curtain to take a drink from a ladle he'd pulled from a bucket. His tongue reached for the liquid. He drank his fill, then, for the hell of it, spat a mouthful of water out over the rail of the catwalk. Not a drop reached the foundry floor. It all evaporated in the rage of heat swirling in the air around the furnace.

They had been smelting for several days now and were likely to go until dawn, when they would open the sluice and pour the iron into the giant gun pit built into the floor.

That is what Chester Ludlow had told them—dawn—told vanderWees and Katerina. He figured he could last the night at the foundry, if the heat didn't get to him.

Chester was manufacturing, from this infernal noise and heat, the largest cannon ever made. A gun designed by Chester Ludlow, formerly chief engineer and electrician-projector of the Atlantic telegraph (may it rest in peace), now artillery specialist and engineer on retainer to the Army of the Potomac. He'd wanted to name the cannon the Monongahela, after the ironworks, but the cannon's nickname, the "Ludlow Gun," was what was sticking.

The weapon was to weigh ninety tons. It would be the shape of a gigantic bottle and, like an Armstrong cannon, with increasingly larger sections moving from the muzzle to the breech. This reinforcement would help prevent the gun from exploding and killing its firing crew. It would take nearly three hundred pounds of explosives, Chester calculated, to throw a half-ton projectile perhaps as far as ten miles.

The night shift crew was at its tasks. The stokers pushed carts of coke toward the hoppers and kicked open the furnace, where the white flames seemed to divert themselves from melting the iron to come rushing and tearing toward the door to lap up the fuel, only to be beaten back by the rotary bellows that blew the flames toward the molten ore.

It was a spectacle befitting hell—the furnace, the adamantine fuel, the overwhelming noise, the acrid smell, the vaulted roof pulsing with combustion light, the belching smoke, the men laboring in constant peril or sprawled, exhausted, on coal piles about the main floor—and it had a way of stimulating Chester. It shouldn't, he thought. This was the work of war; oh, but the Lord forgive him, it *did* stimulate him.

"It's your religion."

He did not say that aloud. Katerina Lindt had said it.

She was back in his life. The war brought her to him. The war and Russell vanderWees.

After the cable failure, Chester had become a man in hiding. Estranged from Franny, he lived alone at Willing Mind. He had no idea where Katerina was. He began to drink. There was a vapidity about his days that he didn't seem to notice after whiskey. He tried writing a narrative of the cable venture, but it kept coming out muddled and stillborn, too entangled with memories of his life breaking apart. He took on the occasional minor local engineering project: designing a new bridge for the Falmouth Road, supervising the reshoring of the village fishing wharf. But mostly the months unspooled dully. Three years went by while beyond the coast of Maine the country was falling apart.

Then one day in winter, a gentleman from Washington came to seek his help for the Union cause. So despondent and hungover was he that morning that Chester almost sent Undersecretary of War Russell vanderWees packing.

But Secretary vanderWees was a persistent man who marched past the flustered Mrs. Tyler, tracking snow into the front hall and halfway up the stairs to the second floor, where he rapped on Chester's door.

"Who is it?" Chester groaned.

VanderWees introduced himself, said he had attended the cable's celebratory dinner and ball all those months ago at the Metropolitan Hotel, and was here now, knocking on Chester's chamber door on the damn coldest day Maine could muster, at the behest of the President.

"President of what?" Chester asked from his bed, elevating himself to a sitting position, slowly so as not to cause his head to explode. Scalding white light poured in every window from the snow and sun reflected off the Atlantic.

"President of the United States of America."

"That would be Lincoln," Chester said.

"That would, God save him."

"What does he want?"

"The mightiest cannon ever built."

"And he needs an engineer?"

"That would be you. May I enter?"

The deal was proposed with the two men sitting on the bed in the harsh morning light, with Chester's head clearing as vanderWees allowed as how the President hadn't actually handpicked Chester, *he*—vanderWees—had. As U.S. Undersecretary of War, vanderWees was the President's emissary. He had been impressed with Chester. VanderWees praised Chester's engineering, declaring the absolute necessity that those abilities languish no longer—and vanderWees conspicuously eyed the empty whiskey glasses on the bedside table.

This man vanderWees, Chester began to realize, was privy to disturbingly complete intelligence. The undersecretary made oblique references to Franny's departure and Chester's melancholic interregnum at Willing Mind. More pointedly, he praised Chester's astute and wide-ranging capacities as an engineer.

Chester knew he was being flattered, so he was wary. But vanderWees was both obdurate and effusive. He took a room in Falmouth and visited Willing Mind daily, to drink and talk and tease an affirmative answer out of Chester. By the end of the week, Chester came to believe that here was an opportunity he had better seize, lest his ambition and his prospects be lost forever. VanderWees had convinced him. They shook on it.

Chester threw himself into the task, plunging back into his old metallurgy texts; corresponding with Thomas Rodman, the Union's ordnance specialist, and Sir Henry Bessemer, the esteemed English metallurgist; test-firing model cannons of his own design on the bluffs at Willing Mind (lobbing dummy shells over the buoys of Gil Tyler's lobster traps); forging a one-quarter-size prototype at the Wiscasset Foundry near Bath, using the hollow-core casting method he'd devised to cool the barrel from the inside out; and completing all work in seven months so that he was ready to travel to Pittsburgh by midsummer. VanderWees had telegraphed him to hurry to Washington. If Chester could be there by Friday, vanderWees had a surprise for him before they left for Pittsburgh.

Chester supposed it might be an audience with the President himself. And it was, in a way. Both Chester and the President, and several hundred others, were in the audience at the Richard Theater for a solo performance by Katerina Lindt.

"She's been taking the country by storm," vanderWees said to Chester during the applause, "or at least doing quite respectably out on the concert tour. Mrs. Lincoln supposedly requested her return to Washington, but I happen to know it was the President himself."

Chester struggled to remain composed and tried to take his mind off Katerina, who had yet to appear onstage, by looking up at the ponderously tall President and his button of a wife entering their box and acknowledging the applause of the audience. Chester was too distracted to indulge his old custom of looking around the house to see if any attractive women were about. He hadn't seen Katerina for nearly three years.

Then she made her entrance. The audience leapt to its feet—the President and Mrs. Lincoln included—and greeted Katerina with a rousing ovation. She was to play the piano that evening, selections by Schubert and Brahms and even—almost scandalously—one by Liszt.

Chester looked to the presidential box, where Mr. Lincoln was leaning over the rail, smiling and slamming his big hands together for Katerina, who was bowing, her blond ringlets framing her glowing face, her blue eyes casting a quick glance up to the presidential box, her hand resting on the piano's side, and her fingers tapping perhaps some run of notes she was about to play. And Chester thought how those same fingers had played on him and how long it had been.

VanderWees whispered to Chester, "I told her you'd be here."

They met after the performance. Chester and vanderWees worked their way through the narrow, gaslit backstage passage to Katerina's dressing room in time to see the towering frame and tall stovepipe of the President departing through the stage door to a waiting carriage in the alley.

Katerina demurely received Chester's kiss to her hand.

"I understand the President favors your playing," Chester said.

"He's grieving over the death of his son," she said. "Music helps. You understand."

And Chester was shocked because, for a moment, he did *not* understand, because he had forgotten about his own lost child, Betty, about Franny, about everything in his life, save that he was touching, at last, the hand of Katerina Lindt.

The Casting

Dawn. She was not pleased that cannon making had to be done at such an unreasonable hour. Even at the beginning of the day, it was a filthy, hot, noisy, utterly exciting place, that forge. She found herself almost stimulated to distraction by it and by the men working around, above, and beside the massive furnace. There were several Negroes among the forge crew; many of the men went shirtless, coal dust and perspiration tattooing their torsos and arms in wild, swirling patterns of filth. Undersecretary vanderWees had advised her to wear her darkest, oldest garments, and she had on a well-worn outfit of gray and black. She had tucked her hair under a broad-brimmed hat that though straw, nevertheless seemed to reflect the forge's heat back down upon her head and shower her in a swoon-inducing miasma. But she kept her composure, determined to admire Chester on the catwalk.

This was the recompense for coming to see the dawn casting: for the first time since resuming her affair with him, Katerina Lindt was seeing the old Chester Ludlow at work.

Katerina's route back to Chester began after they and the cable had parted and she had taken J. Beaumol Spude's offer of assistance to begin her career anew in America. Spude had moved her into a house on Fifth Avenue, not far from the Catholic cathedral under construction. It was a commodious home with a room on the third floor in which Spude installed a piano for Katerina's practice. Within two months he had arranged for her to play a concert at a salon near Cooper Union and at another in Boston. Several months after that, her name had spread—the "Prussian Euterpe" newspapers called her—and she was juggling requests for concerts and recitals around the country.

Throughout, Spude was precisely, and only, what he said he would be: a patron of her art. She had prepared herself for the eventuality that one night, after a concert, he would appear to—as her patron—discuss "artistic matters" and make his intentions clear at last. It never occurred. Spude was genuinely interested in her art. Uncouth though he could be, he knew something instinctively about her music.

She had other admirers, and of those, a railroad president and later a sculptor discreetly shared her bed. These were—even though the former affair lasted for over a year and the latter nearly two—more like serial assignations. They engaged Katerina, even inspired her playing, but her heart was not really in them.

It was after her first concert in Washington, at the reception at the President's mansion, that she met Undersecretary of War Russell vanderWees and heard again of Chester Ludlow.

From the catwalk, poised and in command, Chester signaled the man on the gate to let the molten metal flow. Looking up at the catwalk had put Katerina in mind of the gantry over Joachim's model of London: a world spread below.

A moving glow caught her attention. A gold and red trickle at first became a rich, flaring stream of iron coursing out of the furnace and down into the mold built into the foundry floor. A cheer went up from the stokers around the building. Chester acknowledged them, and with his spectacles reflecting the crimson of the incandescent metal, his shirtsleeves rolled up, his cravat loosened, he stood luminous in the flaming metal's light.

"Vulcan," said vanderWees as he stood looking up beside Katerina.

"Vulcan was lame and ugly," Katerina said.

"My mistake," said the undersecretary, and bowed, seeming to enjoy his error.

It was an unimpressive hole into which the metal poured, a small hatch in the floor. The matrix for the cannon was a vertical mold, extending downward some thirty feet below the furnace. Water was flowing into the cooling core that would shape the bore of the cannon as the hot metal oozed down the sluice. Below, stokers were shoveling burning coke into the jacket of the matrix to keep the outer layers of metal hot and thus cool the gun from the inside out so each layer of iron would contract and grip tighter around the layers within.

Katerina could hear the stoker bosses shouting orders on the galleries below them in the basement of the foundry. Chester came down from the furnace catwalk, smiled to her, shook hands with vanderWees, and said that he must continue down to see how the casting was proceeding.

"It's marvelous," she said. "You are doing wonderful work."

"It's for war," Chester said, looking surprised, almost as if it were a thought that was coming to him for the first time. "It's an instrument of war."

"It's to *end* a war," vanderWees piped in.

Katerina took both of Chester's hands and pulled him to her, placing her cheek against his and whispering, "You are wonderful," and then darted her tongue into his ear.

She felt Chester jump in her grip, and she laughed.

She and vanderWees left Chester to continue work. In the month since their reunion, Katerina had managed to spend most nights with Chester, arranging her concerts to be near him. She had booked a program in Pittsburgh and performed to a sold-out house that evening. VanderWees, who was making trips over to the foundry, sent notes to her hotel as to the progress of the cannon's molding. All was going well.

On the third day after the casting, she hired a carriage and rode through the early-morning streets toward the river and the foundry. Chester had stayed all night with the cannon. The day was already hot, and the sun was barely up. The paving stones were dusty, and the Monongahela appeared so listless that it might have been a broad swath of brown flannel lying between the hills.

It was Sunday. The foundry was empty. The watchman waved her through the gate. The carriage rolled down alleys between equipment sheds and piles of coke, the horse's hooves emitting little puffs of dust. Even the harness made only a stultified clinking, like the sound of prisoners chipping stone.

Katerina went past the buildings housing the two smaller cupola furnaces, then she rounded an ash pile to see the large reverberatory tower. It was smoking, but like all the other furnaces, its fires were banked. Nothing about the place pulsed or throbbed. It was a beast asleep, taking slow, slumbering breaths.

She got out of the carriage, told the driver not to wait, and walked toward the furnace building. On one side, two enormous bulkhead doors sat open. There on a ramp descending into the darkness of the basement sat the cannon on a set of six trucks. In the shadows, Katerina could see the dismantled mold: heaps of lumber, iron banding, and sand. The cannon had been lowered with block and tackle from the vertical and now lay on the wagons, angling out into the daylight. With its dark, sand-mottled surface, it looked like some blunt, armored lizard that had just hatched from the detritus that lay behind it in the shadows.

Katerina walked up quietly and touched the gun and ran her hands along its flank. Heat radiated from the metal. Its swell rose up over her head. She tried to imagine what the weapon would do, the largest cannon on earth. She tapped a little snatch of the "Battle Hymn" with her fingers on the warm iron. Then she heard a sigh and a rustling. She walked to the end of the gun, to its muzzle. There, lying inside the cannon, was Chester Ludlow, asleep. The opening was actually large enough for a man to climb inside. Chester's head was just inside the muzzle. Katerina ran her fingers through his blond curls, and he bolted awake.

"Oh, my God," he muttered, and twisted around to see who had touched him. He looked relieved it was she, but obviously abashed. "I was so exhausted. It was so warm in here. I fell asleep."

She went up on tiptoes and kissed him. He was awake enough now to smile at her.

"I know it's crazy, but I couldn't resist," he murmured. "I had to see if I could fit inside her."

"And so you do," she said.

CHAPTER XIX

LITTLE RENTS IN TIME

Boston, Washington, and the Union at Large,
Early September 1862

Her Mission Fields

T he dearly departed were everywhere.
America was a kingdom of dead brothers and sons, and little Willie Lincoln
was sitting on the throne. Although the President's child had succumbed
to bilious fever and was only eleven when he died, most of the nation's
dead were the creation of the war.

And so the dead were everywhere. They crowded in among the living
citizens. They moved among the pedestrians jostling on city streets. They
sat with their wives at night on the edge of their marriage beds. They
walked abroad through fields and passed among trees of the forest. Of this,
Franny Ludlow was certain. Looking out the window of her office, she
would see children stop suddenly amid their play and look at seemingly
nothing, then run on, laughing and squealing back into their games. But
those moments, those little rents in time, as she called them, those were
when Franny knew the living were in contact with the dead, even if the
children could never say exactly what it was that had diverted or distracted
them.

Perhaps the dead needed an infusion or inhalation, she thought. Some kind of a charge, something like what Chester had always talked about when he was fooling with Daniell batteries or fulminating about that Dr. Whitehouse and his pulses in the cable. The dead lacked a pulse; perhaps they came to us to be near one.

They came near, but never near enough. They couldn't return. No one could quicken the dead.

But there were mortals who could bring the living and the dead together, and Franny Ludlow had gained a reputation as just such a one. Professionally, she now went by her maiden name: Frances Piermont.

Her renown was deep, if not broad. She did not travel to famous halls and perform on large stages. She was not preceded by posters and placards tacked or plastered to fences, barn doors, or trees. Those were for the mystic lecturers and machine-laden conjurers who, more often than not, like the notorious Dr. Hermes, faked contact with the ectoplasmic realm.

Franny had left Willing Mind and Chester Ludlow as the telegraph was succeeding (then failing) and had gone to stay in Boston with an older second cousin, a woman who, though kin, was distant enough not to pry and close enough to be generous. She exerted influence to help Franny obtain a position at the Commonwealth Home for Little Wayfarers, a Boston orphanage. The position offered some remuneration while having the appearance of being volunteer work, thus lending it respectability in the eyes of anyone on Beacon Hill.

Franny had thought working near the children would keep her sympathies open to Betty, would enable her to see her daughter. She started attending séances. They were not hard to find. Notices were in every newspaper. She joined a group called the Organization of Primal Sympathy. Sometimes the members would hold their own impromptu séances. Quickly, members began to seek Franny out.

"You are a magnet, I can feel it when I'm near you," they would say. "I want to sit beside you next time."

Soon Franny was leading the séances, which she began calling "meetings," because there was something of the humbug about the other word. Franny used the methods she'd learned from Otis. She would sit with her companions and guide them back through their memories of the departed. Sometimes marvelous things happened. Sometimes her companions would weep through conversations with the dead, Franny hearing only one side of the dialogue. Eyes would brighten and focus on the departed, and the companion would reach out to touch thin air. Sometimes the bereaved would take up pencil and paper and begin transcribing dictations from the Other World. Afterward, they would leave the meetings drained and clutching the paper with its often incoherent or intermittently sensible writings as if it were the tablets from Sinai.

Whenever they left, they were satisfied. Whether they had talked with, seen, or listened to a beloved or had merely sat and thought about the dead, they were grateful. They would clutch Franny's hands, thank her, tell her she had a gift. She *was* a gift.

And it wasn't long before she had a reputation as a spiritual guide or "connector." She could bring people into contact with their lost loved ones. She was being offered payments and gratuities. She never took the money. This was, she said, her duty. But she thought of it privately as her mission field. Then, one afternoon, a telegram arrived. Mrs. Abraham Lincoln requested a meeting. She hoped to contact her lost Willie.

A Meeting at the Door

The Lincolns were spending the summer at a cottage on the grounds of the Soldiers' Home outside the capital. It was cooler there, by a little, and the risk of malaria was less. The President rode a carriage into the city each day, usually to spend long hours by the telegraph at the War Office next to the White House, waiting for news from the armies. On the peninsula, McClellan was stalled, or stalling; on the Mississippi, the Federals were stuck before Vicksburg; and in Tennessee, the Confederate cavalry was making raids with impunity. The war was going poorly for the Union.

On a hot evening in July, on a day that was ending in somber, gray light, a day that couldn't quite bring itself to disgorge its clouds of their rain but that hung turgid just over the treetops, Franny arrived at the Lincolns'. Her carriage crunched up the drive and pulled in behind another, from which was descending, unmistakably, the President.

Mr. Lincoln turned from going up the walk and stepped over to Franny's carriage door. He filled the window. His smile had a gentle quizzicality to it as he tried to peer into the interior gloom. He opened the door, extended a large hand, and introduced himself. Once on the ground, Franny did likewise, using her married name.

The President stood for a moment without saying anything. Then he said, "I somehow thought Mother had referred to you by a different name."

"Ludlow's my married name," Franny said. "I usually use Piermont as a surname. For reasons that are . . ." and she was unable to come up with a reason.

"Professional," the President said. His voice was high, nasal. Yet it was pleasant enough. He had a slow, loping way as he walked up the path with her. He seemed gentle in the main, but weary.

"Yes," she said. "Professional reasons. Although I am not here to, well, *profess* anything.".

They were approaching the front steps. Grackles were chortling in the trees around them, their songs sounding like the crushing of small seeds in a pestle.

"Then you're not here for the séance?" Mr. Lincoln asked.

"I am," Franny said. "I suppose I am. Mrs. Lincoln asked me down. Actually, insofar as I have any control over these matters, I prefer to call them 'meetings.' "

The President nodded and smiled warily. "They can be a great comfort to Mother," he said. "We lost our son, you see."

Franny knew. The whole nation knew. There had been a lying in state in the Green Room of the presidential mansion, a funeral in the East Room, a grieving procession to the mausoleum, and stories that the President's woe was so profuse as to be almost unseemly but was far surpassed by the displays of his wife. A woman on the train had gossiped that she had it on good authority that Mary Todd Lincoln, in three months, had bought three hundred pairs of gloves. "That's an average of a hundred a month!" the woman said. "Three a day . . . more!"

Franny addressed the President. "I'm dreadfully sorry. It's a terrible thing. I have lost a child, too. She was four."

They had stopped before the first step to the front door of the cottage. Franny heard the quick, high-pitched peal of a woman's laughter from inside. She caught the President casting a fleeting glance at the house. There was another burst of laughter from inside.

"Will you be attending the meeting?" Franny asked him.

"I'm afraid I must work," he said. "And, truth be told, such 'meetings' remind me of *my* meetings. From the little I've observed, séances are similar to my cabinet sessions. The spirits, like the members of my cabinet, usually give contradictory advice."

Franny didn't take this as an affront. The President's tone was too gentle, and perhaps he had a point. For all Franny's supposed success with the spirit world, where had Betty been all these months? She had refused every attempt Franny had made to reach her.

The cottage door flew open, and a plump, round-faced woman dressed in mourning wailed, "Look who's here!"

Seeing the tears streaming down the woman's cheeks, Franny realized that what she had taken for laughter coming from within the house had really been fits of weeping.

"Oh, Mother," said Mr. Lincoln softly.

A Meeting of Minds

The President's wife daubed the tears from her eyes and quickly composed herself as she greeted Franny with a surprising familiarity. Mrs. Lincoln said she had a "special attraction" waiting in the parlor. Her husband bent down to buss his wife on the cheek, then said he must find "some forage" before harnessing himself to his pen and spectacles for work in his study.

Mrs. Lincoln helped Franny off with her hat and took her parasol, prattling all the while at a pitch and pace that was higher and faster than Franny warranted as comfortable; still, the woman was so friendly, so eager to see Franny. How was the trip? Did she know her reputation as a spiritualist had reached Washington? (Franny hadn't known, had always thought of herself more as a "connector" than as a "spiritualist.") Well, no matter, no matter. Her reputation was of the first water, as was that of the "special attraction," and didn't she look lovely? Such a becoming color for a dress—a rose or a dawn, wasn't it? And was that color in fashion up in Boston this summer, or was she summering in Newport? And how lovely it would be if she—Mrs. Lincoln—could make it to Newport, a place she'd never seen, but there were obligations, *many* obligations, as she was more than just old Mrs. Lincoln, she was Mrs. President of the United States Which Was at War, which was besieged by grief for its lost sons, which was kin to the grief that so corrupted the tranquillity of her—Mrs. Lincoln's—life and made it a vale of tears, to borrow from Mr. Browning, and please excuse her for crying yet again. . . .

Franny was speechless. It made her uncomfortable, this outpouring, and she thought she understood the President's stiff haste in retreating to a kitchen supper and work.

"My Willie," Mrs. Lincoln was now struggling to say, "my Willie, we hope . . . *I* hope you can help me. . . . Oh, do come in and meet the others, especially . . ."

And she opened the door to the parlor, where several people stood near a table in the center of the room. Their attention seemed to be directed to a man with his back to Franny, a man with black, swept-back hair and an almost olive complexion.

"I wonder," said Mrs. Lincoln to Franny, "if you've heard of Dr. Zephaniah Hermes?"

Dr. Hermes took Franny's hand and bowed as Mrs. Lincoln introduced her as Frances Piermont. By the time he had straightened back up, Franny could see that he remembered her completely. And she stood confronting the face from the poster in New York and the presence that had both captivated and repelled her in Portland.

"More than hearing of me, I daresay we have met, Mrs. Lincoln," said Dr. Hermes. "Miss Piermont is conversant with the Other Side."

"Tonight is *your* night, though, Dr. Hermes." And Mrs. Lincoln explained that Dr. Hermes had consented to come out to the Soldiers' Home cottage to conduct a séance on the one free night he had in Washington. Mrs. Lincoln hoped Franny wouldn't mind being an attendee rather than a leader of the séance on this, her first night. As her invitation was for the entire weekend, they would have time for a séance led by Franny tomorrow.

"Actually, I call them 'meetings,' " Franny said.

"Wonderful!" Mrs. Lincoln fairly squealed. "Let me introduce you around." And she presented Mr. and Mrs. Cranston Laurie of Georgetown and several of the Lauries' neighbors.

"Mr. Laurie is chief clerk of my husband's post office," Mrs. Lincoln said, "and a spiritual adept himself. In the cooler months, we've been meeting at his house in town."

After the introductions, after the lemonade, Dr. Hermes had the group, nine in all, sit in chairs around the table.

"You won't have the advantage of the Spiritscope tonight, Doctor," Franny said as he held out the chair next to his for her. She could see a stiffening behind his smile.

"No, I won't, Miss Piermont," he said. "*We* won't have that advantage.

We shall have to do it ourselves. I have heard of your abilities. I am glad your powers have been enlisted to help us."

"Conscripted is more like it," Mrs. Lincoln burbled. "I drafted her!" And the others all chuckled.

Dr. Hermes then settled the group. He had them first all hold hands, then place them on the table. He rose to close a window, as the breeze was picking up outside; the curtains were rustling and would be, he said, a distracting noise.

"Please excuse me if the atmosphere becomes close," he said, "but we need things as quiet as possible. Spirits often communicate by knocking softly."

He followed procedures not unlike what Franny might have done had she been leading a meeting with the Organization of Primal Sympathy: having the participants think wholly, fully, and deeply of lost loved ones; suggesting that if someone felt a gust of chilly air about them, even on this hot night, not to be alarmed; it was a good sign that spirits were close. (Franny noticed, at this suggestion, Mrs. Laurie pulled her shawl up tighter around her shoulders.) Dr. Hermes told them all to relax. A dreamy susurrus settled in the room. Perhaps it was the trees rustling outside; a storm seemed to be coming up; perhaps the day's heaviness would be released at last. Franny felt by turns sleepy—from the long ride—and ecstatically alert. She had the feeling Dr. Hermes was manipulating the situation—"playing the audience," in the parlance of her stage days—but she also had a disquieting anticipation that she might, at last, once more see or hear or sense the presence of her daughter. She highly suspected Dr. Hermes of being a charlatan, began to resent Mrs. Lincoln for summoning her all the way to Washington for this; nevertheless, if there was a chance Betty might return . . .

But this séance was to contact Willie Lincoln, and this Dr. Hermes did. He quietly asked for all the participants to close their eyes and keep reaching out into the darkness to the Other Side.

"Does anyone feel cool?" Dr. Hermes murmured.

Silence. Then Mrs. Lincoln spoke. "Well . . . yes."

"Good," Dr. Hermes said gently. "All be still."

The wind rushed through the trees outside.

"Willie," Dr. Hermes murmured. "Willie Lincoln, are you near?"

Silence.

Then a knock. Or a tap, really, as if two hollow sticks had been struck together nearby.

Franny heard a startled intake of breath from someone at the table.

"Eyes closed," Dr. Hermes whispered. "Eyes closed." Then: "Willie?"

Another tap.

Franny felt the room become palpably still. The breeze blew robustly outside, but the parlor was in an apprehensive lull.

Another tap.

"Willie, tell us you are here," Dr. Hermes said.

Three taps. Almost like a trio of twigs snapping.

"Willie, can we see you?"

One tap.

"Does that mean yes?"

One tap.

"Does one tap mean yes?"

One tap.

"Does one tap mean no?"

Two taps.

There was shifting and a couple of sighs from around the table.

"Willie, let's have one tap for yes, two taps for no. Agreed?"

One tap.

"Willie, do you know how much your mother misses you?"

One tap.

Franny could hear Mrs. Lincoln's breath catch and the tiniest of moans vibrate in the woman's throat.

At that moment Franny felt pressure against her right leg. Dr. Hermes was to her right. He was pressing his leg against hers. She almost gasped from the effrontery.

"Do you know how much you are missed?" the doctor repeated.

One tap. But Franny felt, as she heard the popping sound, Dr. Hermes's leg move at the same moment. She realized the noise was coming from him, from his leg.

The doctor asked more questions of Willie—Is he well? (Yes.) Is he sad? (No.) Is it beautiful where he is? (Yes.) Will he return to visit again? (Yes.)—and every answer, every knocking sound, came with the simultaneous movement of Dr. Hermes's leg. He was making the noises, Franny realized, by some trick cartilaginous snapping of his limbs or an appendage as he moved his leg and rubbed his thigh lasciviously against Franny's. He was simultaneously disclosing his secret and trying to arouse her. She felt like leaping up from the table.

But at that moment, the wife of the President of the United States began to bawl and cry out her son's name.

"Ooooohhhhh, Willie, Willie, Willie!"

Franny was unable to keep her eyes closed any longer, nor were the others. Franny saw them all blinking in the dim light, hands held together in a chain around the table, except for Mrs. Lincoln, who was on her feet, her arms outstretched, her fingers clawing at the air, her voice reaching a tremolo.

"Willie, Willieeeeee, let me see you!"

"Madame President," Dr. Hermes said, raising his voice.

"Please, I beseech you . . ."

Mrs. Lincoln looked wildly around. "Go home," she fairly shrieked. "Everyone. I can't continue. Go home. This is too much. Oh, Cranston, did you see? . . . Oh, of course not! I can tell by your faces. No one saw. Go home. Now. Please."

And she ran from the room. There were footstops running away through the hall, up the stairs, a door slamming, a slower tread following up the stairs, a distant knock, a quiet voice murmuring indecipherable imprecations.

Mr. Laurie was the first at the table to speak.

"Sometimes," he said softly, "they end like this. Sometimes they end happily. You should not feel you have done anything wrong, Dr. Hermes."

Dr. Hermes nodded solemnly.

"Sometimes such a reaction is a sign of how right I have done," he said, and Franny was struck by the pomposity of his tone. "I have had experience with such outcomes," he said.

Mr. Laurie rose and said they had all best be going and leave the Lincolns to make of the night what they could. He offered to escort Franny back to her hotel, but Dr. Hermes intervened, saying he knew that would be far out of the Lauries' or any of the others' way—he had a carriage waiting; he would be honored to see her safely to her hotel. Franny gritted her teeth and nodded.

The Rest of the Night

In the carriage, once away from the grounds of the Soldiers' Home, Franny confronted Dr. Hermes.

"What was your trick tonight, Doctor?"

"Madame?"

"The knocks. You made it patently obvious to me—in a way I found broaching on the offensive—that there was no Willie Lincoln in the room with us."

"Offensive?" Dr. Hermes said. "I *never* meant to offend you, Miss Piermont." He turned in his seat to face her better, but it was too dark for either of them to see the other very well.

"I was hoping, Miss Piermont, to . . . to *attract* you. By that I mean to make you understand my methods, my means, hoping that as a fellow professional we two could *understand* each other, and perhaps at a later time, such as now, we could *confer* as comrades. I saw in you a magnetism, Miss Piermont. I saw it in Portland, when I first encountered you. You thought I might not remember, but I do. Vividly, Miss Piermont—"

"We may as well get something straight," Franny said. "I am more properly called *Mrs.* Chester Ludlow. Frances Piermont is my professional name. You, who *profess* to be a doctor, should understand what I mean. And if you remember so much and so vividly, then you will recall that I have a daughter—or I *had* one. I—we, my husband and I—lost her. And she, Dr. Hermes, is my reason for—" But here Franny broke off. Tears had leapt to her eyes. The darkness of the carriage was like a pond at night, Dr. Hermes a creature lurking in the depths. It was his hand that touched Franny's forearm. She jumped at the contact. Dr. Hermes, unphased by her shock, used a tone of gentle reprimand to steady her.

"Very well, Mrs. Ludlow, but it is now I who must be feeling offended. You are calling into question my credentials?"

Franny blinked her eyes clear.

"I am calling into question your propriety, sir."

"Mrs. Ludlow—"

"And your integrity."

"Please—"

"I know you remembered me from your . . . *show* in Portland—"

"Ah! See? There—"

"And I remember the subtle machinations you executed as operator of the Spiritscope. There were 'knockings' then, too, although I'd warrant they came from under the stage. Tonight's came from under the table. From your knee perhaps?"

"Ankle," Dr. Hermes said.

"Thank you for being so specific," said Franny.

"The joint. It pops. A riding accident when I was young. I used to delight my playmates. Now, I delight my audiences and my banker."

"Specific and frank," said Franny.

"I may as well be specific and frank with you, Mrs. Ludlow. I see no other way. I see I could never fool you. Your spiritualism is of a higher order. A mission perhaps?"

He paused for Franny to answer, but she sensed he could tell she wouldn't. She was wondering how he had come up with the word *mission*; she had never mentioned it to anyone.

"I only want you to understand that our . . . our missions are not that far apart. We have the same ends in sight."

"And what would those ends be, Dr. Hermes?"

"Confirmation," Dr. Hermes said. He leaned toward her in the carriage, elbows on knees. "Confirmation that we are not alone."

The carriage had made its way now to a gaslit street, and Franny could see Dr. Hermes's features: his tan-complected skin, his hair sweeping back off his ears and brushing the collar of his linen coat. And his eyes—not really visible in the shadows, but she knew them nonetheless—gray-green, long-lashed. His countenance, his forward-inclined posture, both beseeching and assertive, were contradictorily seductive, she knew, and calculated to be so.

"Confirmation?" she said. "I thought perhaps profit was your mission."

Dr. Hermes leaned back in his seat. He slapped his right hand down on his knee.

"So it is. So it is." He folded his arms across his chest, and Franny felt a pang of contrition for being so balky with him.

"What is it you are trying to confirm?" she asked.

Dr. Hermes didn't move, but for the rocking of the carriage. He addressed the night outside.

"That there is another world, Mrs. Ludlow. One where your daughter and my wife and this man's brother and that man's father and their forebears and all our loved ones still live on."

He hadn't mentioned a deceased wife before. It might be more artifice. It was mattering less to Franny that such might be the case.

"Mrs. Ludlow, you have read Darwin?"

"Not read, Dr. Hermes, but I have heard his ideas expounded."

"I shall not then," Dr. Hermes said, "bore you with what I understand to be his theories. Only the effects of his theories. We are beset by an Age of Science and Industry, Mrs. Ludlow. Men are building great ships, great bridges, great railroads, telegraphs everywhere. And now they—Mr. Darwin in the forefront—have taken science into the Garden and thrown Adam and Eve out. Or more accurately, they never let Adam and Eve in. They have uprooted the Garden, declared there *never was* a Garden, have said no first man, no first woman. Biological processes only! And you know, Mrs. Ludlow, I do not care whether Mr. Darwin is right or not. He may be. He may not be. But it is the longing that he has unleashed, Mrs. Ludlow, the *longing* that is my concern."

Dr. Hermes paused. He looked out the window again, and Franny looked, too. She thought she could see the unfinished dome of the Capitol through the shadows of the trees. Dr. Hermes spoke as they continued to look out the carriage window together. His words provided a narration for the passing scene of amorphous shades.

"We are more than mere biological processes, Mrs. Ludlow. I believe that, and I believe that *you* believe that as well. Darwin says otherwise—or is attempting to—but I know this is so: that we are more than mere biological processes. Life—or something beyond life—goes on. There is a spirit world. I *know* this in my heart. Now, I will forestall any accusations that my Spiritscope is fraudulent or that my use of 'knockings' are no more than biological processes themselves—the poorly healed joint of an ankle. I say to you that these are *means*, means to the end of confirmation. Not everyone can contact the spirit world. You know this. But everyone *longs* to. The country is at war." And here Dr. Hermes pointed out into the darkness, perhaps in the direction of Virginia. "How many families are touched by death? How many thousands devoutly wish to reach out and not feel they are merely stretching a hand into a void, but that there is a hand, loving arms, a soul, reaching back? Not everyone can find this satisfaction. But, I say to you, everyone deserves it. Everyone should know, should feel, in their heart of hearts, that we are not alone, that the dead are with us. And so if I must use a little stagecraft to bring the majority of

my subjects to this heightened state, I also serve them who are truly able
to reach beyond the veil. I would serve you, Mrs. Ludlow, if I thought
you needed me. For every sevenscore people who need the ruse of the
Spiritscope to feel the comfort and the confirmation, I can help one or two
who are truly adept at reaching from this world and touching the Beyond."

"You lost your wife?" Franny asked. The abruptness of the question
brought Dr. Hermes up short.

"No," he said. "I was never married."

Franny was amused. The man was a panoply of illusions and decep-
tions. They tumbled over one another as they were revealed, making him
by turns pathetic and noble, an altruist and a scamp. Underlying it all,
though, there was something earnest about him as well. He made Franny
think of her brother-in-law, Otis. Otis evinced the same longing.

But Dr. Hermes was closer to home, literally, and Dr. Hermes was
less perfect, and in that imperfection, more humane and more—Franny
couldn't think of any other word for it—familiar.

If Otis was a saint and Dr. Hermes was a scamp, then she was somewhere in between. She admired Otis's purity, was intrigued by Dr. Hermes's raffishness. But they were all three of them reaching out. She *was* on
a mission. She would go further into the world—maybe not as far as Otis—
and she would proselytize—maybe not with the theatrical fare-thee-well of
Dr. Hermes. But she would do it her own way. She was making up her
mind about her life, right there, in the carriage.

They were in front of the hotel. The jolting halt of the vehicle snapped
Franny back. She tried to remember what it was either she or Dr. Hermes
had last said. Ah, she thought, that he was never married. And at that
moment, his lips were touching hers.

She had not encouraged him. She was confident of that. She had not encouraged him, although she must admit that she did nothing to *dis*courage
him once he kissed her. She did not push him away. She did not call for
the driver. She did not slap Dr. Hermes. She merely waited. And when
the kiss was over, she opened the carriage door herself and calmly, purposefully—wordlessly—walked up the steps into the hotel.

Fitting, she thought later as she lay in the hotel bed. I am on my own
now. I am in the world, half as Miss Piermont—maybe more than half—

and the rest as Mrs. Ludlow. She would go forth, she decided. She would help people reach out to the Other Side, as Dr. Hermes would have it, but she would do it on her own terms.

There was a knock at the door. It was forceful and rapid, meant to wake the sleeping. Franny sat up. She wasn't sure she had slept at all. She fumbled for a lucifer, struck it, and lit her bedside candle. She threw on a robe, although with the heat it would have been more comfortable without it, and went to the door.

"Yes?" she whispered.

"Desk clerk, ma'am." A boy's voice.

"Yes?"

"An emergency." There was some mumbling, another voice, outside the door. "Mrs. Lincoln, ma'am. Wife of the President."

Franny opened the door, and Mrs. Lincoln burst in and embraced her. Franny had a fleeting image of the clerk, seen over Mrs. Lincoln's shoulder, looking sleepy and confused and gently closing the door to leave the two women alone.

"Oh, my dear, my dear, my dear," Mrs. Lincoln said, clasping Franny harder to her breast. "I am so, so, so sorry. I am so sorry. I threw you out of my home."

She pulled back but kept her hands on Franny's shoulders and looked her over as if she were inspecting a child for bruises or scars. Then Mrs. Lincoln threw her hands in the air, brought them back to cover her face, rocked on her feet as if buffeted by shame, huffed once, pulled at her shawl, and began to pace. Franny remained stunned.

"I didn't see Willie," Mrs. Lincoln said. "Oh, all right. I *did*. But it was a Willie of my imagination. Not a Willie walking up to me as a spirit. Not a *real* Willie, not a *ghost* of Willie. Just an *idea* of Willie."

She stopped before Franny with a look of abjection as if she expected an upbraiding.

"But it was a strong idea?" Franny ventured softly.

"It *was*," Mrs. Lincoln almost shouted back. "You know then. A *very* strong idea. I *knew* you would understand. I told Father you would understand. That's why I said I must come visit you *immédiatement*. Oh, I am terribly sorry for the intrusion."

Mrs. Lincoln began to walk around the room again. For all her distraction and emotion, she seemed to have enough presence of mind to be appraising the decor, the appointments, maybe even Franny's wardrobe that hung in the closet, the door of which was ajar.

"You must think I am, one, out of my mind and, two, unconscionably rude to come barging in like this at such an ungodly hour of the night, the morning—oh, whatever it is," Mrs. Lincoln said, looking nervously coquettish.

Franny shook her head. She was unsure what to say.

"But I felt I *had* to," Mrs. Lincoln said. "I had to come see you. To ask for your help. Do you think I am, one, crazy and, two, rude?"

"No," Franny managed to say. "No . . . Troubled, yes. But not crazy or rude."

"Good," said Mrs. Lincoln, throwing herself down on the chaise longue on which Franny had left a petticoat that now billowed out around Mrs. Lincoln's head, making Franny think of the portrait of Queen Elizabeth bedecked in ruffles.

"Mrs. Lincoln," Franny said, sitting on the end of the bed and facing the President's wife, "how can I be of help?"

"Sit with me. Now," Mrs. Lincoln said. "That is all I ask. Forgive me for banishing you from my home. The others I don't care about. Well, I *do*, but they will understand. Now, what do you think of Dr. Hermes?"

Franny took a breath and pursed her lips. "I thought," Franny said. "I thought how I might advise you to be careful with him."

"I, *too!*" Mrs. Lincoln said, leaping to her feet again. "I, too! I thought the *power* of that man is not to be trifled with."

"But, Mrs. Lincoln—"

"Mary. Call me Mary."

"What I mean to say is the knocks you heard—"

"Oh! The knocks. The *knocks!* What care I for the knocks? He could have been clapping two of Taddy's toy blocks together under the table for all I care. It was his power to put me in a *state* that counted. And you are right! I should be careful when near that power."

She sat back down on the foot of the chaise longue and clasped Franny's hands.

"But you. You lost a daughter. How is it with her? Do you see her?"

Franny shook her head. "No," she said.

"But you have a reputation. You are a spiritualist."

"Reputation or no, my Betty is not particularly sociable."

And Franny described to Mrs. Lincoln—Mary—how it was with Betty; how she died; how she returned; how Otis was there when she died and there when she returned; how scarce her husband Chester had been; how the telegraph and the war and his own ambition had pulled him away and how she, Franny, was now going away herself; how it was Dr. Hermes who had convinced her she could help others even though he'd had no idea that was what he'd done.

"But of course!" Mary said. "It's perfect. I can see by sitting here, listening to you, you *must* go forth. Allow me to help in any way. You have a power, Frances Piermont Ludlow. You must go. . . ." And she trailed off.

Thunder rumbled to the southwest, beyond the Potomac, out over Virginia. Franny suddenly felt weary. This woman was too much.

Mrs. Lincoln spun around and froze, looking in the direction of the noise.

"That could be cannon," she said.

"Do you think?" said Franny. "I believe the newspapers say—"

Mrs. Lincoln shook her head vigorously. "I meant it metaphorically," she said. "The war is so close to us all. It is as if it is right out there beyond the trees all the time, no matter where the battles are fought."

"Shall I see you tomorrow?" Franny asked.

Mrs. Lincoln said no. "You have done enough for me. Just by listening. You are an inspiration. I shall go now. I shall see Willy by and by. We all shall. Father. Willy. I. And you. And your Betty. By and by . . ."

And she left, a whirlwind exit. Franny sunk to the chaise longue herself. She felt as if she'd just witnessed a theatrical mad scene. A Lady Macbeth. An Ophelia. And she was the character left onstage afterward.

Another clap of thunder jolted her to her senses. In one quick gust of wind, rain began to fall on the capital. Franny leaned over in the chaise so she was able to see out the window. She was about to pull down the sash, for rain was beginning to splatter in, when she saw a carriage below in the street. The skirts of Mrs. Lincoln's dress were being pulled in the door. A tall man attended her. It was the President. There was no driver, no footman. The President had roused himself on behalf of his distracted wife and driven her through the streets of the slumbering capital. Mr. Lincoln swung his long body up onto the box. Lightning and thunder crashed out over Virginia. The President looked toward the storm as the thunder volley rolled in under the sound of the downpour. He clamped his stovepipe hat down harder onto his head. Then he snapped the reins and drove his wife away.

CHAPTER XX

JACK AT WAR

Carlisle, Pennsylvania, Late September 1862

After the Battle

One evening late in September, on a road he did not know was the Chambersburg Pike, Jack Trace walked as he always did after a battle. Coming out of combat, he would enter a dream state—a neurasthenic stupor—and wander.

He would begin, though, by sitting for long hours to draw the battle from memory. If the weather was good, he would sit near the battlefield while the burial details, with their white bandannas masking their faces from the stench, worked their way among the corpses, loading them onto wagons in silence. Often the only sound left would be the creak of the wagons or the mad laugh of a pileated woodpecker coming from a wood beyond a destroyed hayfield. Trace would sketch in silence, conjuring up a foregone pandemonium, as both Union and Confederate squads moved quietly among their dead.

If the weather was inclement, however, Trace would find a shelled house or a half-standing shed and seek shelter, sketching to the mild sound of rain dripping through the charred rafters. He would draw until he could stand it no more, then he would begin to wander, aimlessly, as he was now, heading north on the Chambersburg Pike, easily seventy miles from

413

the battle he'd recently witnessed, the worst he'd seen in his year of following the armies, the battle near Sharpsburg, Maryland, General Lee's farthest penetration north, the battle with more corpses piled behind it than any of the war: the Battle of Antietam.

The tramping about could go on for several days and nights. Mr. Selcome, in London, had employed a detachment of American couriers to find Jack Trace after a battle and then deliver his portfolios, first to engravers in Philadelphia, then onto a packet ship in New York or Boston bound immediately for England.

"Trace," Mr. Selcome had written some months previous, "would it not be more efficacious for all concerned if we established a rendezvous point? As it is now, we find your wanderings most difficult to accommodate and are concerned they will jeopardize our exclusivity as regards timely engravings of the battles. Please help."

But Trace could not. The tramping was as vital to his becoming a great battlefield artist as were the drawings themselves. That daze, that fugue state, was Trace's route back to humanity. A humanity that, on both sides of the Atlantic, was avid for his drawings.

The *Despatch* was flying out of newsboys' fists. To accommodate Trace's vision, Mr. Selcome would print portions of Trace's huge panoramas each day for a week, so that by Saturday, the thousands of eager readers and collectors could paste the daily, full-page panels into one long intricate frieze.

"Unmatched and positively Homeric!" Mr. Selcome wrote of the panoramas in a promotional story he'd placed on the *Despatch*'s Miscellany Page.

Some of the panoramas were elongated, single frozen moments, as if Trace had the power to command two entire warring armies to hold stockstill, defying gravity, momentum, and death, while he walked across miles of battlefield, rendering every detail on paper. Other panoramas were unfolding dramas, flowing from left to right, a temporal march—not unlike the Phantasmagorium's backdrop—displaying the progress of an engagement or a battle from the first approach of the combatants; through the heights of the frenzied fighting; to the denouement, the picking over of the corpses, the burial of the dead, the humble, numerous, and temporary wooden crosses scattered about the devastated landscape.

Trace worked his wondrous art for the Peninsular Campaign, the Seven Days' Battles and Second Bull Run. In addition, he had portrayed a dozen or more skirmishes and unfurled intricate paper tapestries of camp life. Soon papers in New York, Boston, and Washington had signed agreements with Mr. Selcome to engrave and print Trace's work in America.

Entering combat—and entering it so deeply that sometimes he would crawl on his belly as canisters and grapeshot sang overhead—was part of his work, necessary for it. And to recover from the extremity of the experience, Trace had to walk it off, mile upon mile, slowly, head down, the road passing beneath his feet, until some sound or smell stirred him and he began to wonder where he was and what he should be doing next. The rescuing odor could be a whiff of apples rotting beneath an orchard tree or the smell of honeysuckle recalling Maddy's perfume aboard the *Great Eastern*. The sound could be a birdsong that randomly rose above all the others as Trace walked through a wood, or it could be the snap of a whip as a cart tried to pass him on the road.

Just such a snap and just such a cart brought Trace back to awareness now on the Chambersburg Pike. A farmer was trying to work his small wagon, loaded with squash and other late-summer truck, past Trace. All day, farmers, riders, and walkers had hailed him, passed him, nearly jostled him, to no effect. They would look back at him as he walked along in his own fog, and mark him as someone to be avoided should he be encountered again down the road. Many camp followers or battlefield casualties wandered—or fled—along these roads, but Trace was clearly not one of them. He carried a bedroll and a large leather portfolio with straps so he could sling it onto his back; he had a musette bag with drawing implements, and his dress bore the signs of his origins. He wore a small-brimmed top hat and a wide, loose cravat. His one concession to his outdoor existence was a pair of knee-length, buttoned gaiters. These marked him as a foreigner, and once he spoke, his accent placed him precisely.

The whip snap prompted Trace to ask the flush-faced, toothless farmer which road they were on and if it was a wise way to proceed to Washington.

"A far ways from wise," said the farmer. "More a fool's way to proceed to Washington. Not meaning to offend, but you're headed *that* way. And Washington is *that* way." He held his arms up, like a scarecrow, pointing in opposite directions.

Trace blinked. This kind of confusion had happened before, after engagements, after other blind perambulations, after other returns to humanity.

"You just wake up?" the farmer asked Trace, who was rubbing his eyes.

"In a manner of speaking," Trace said. "Might I ride with you?"

"You might," the farmer said. "If you climb up."

And so Trace rode alongside the farmer, coming back into the world, piecing together the battle he'd seen, leafing through the portfolio and, by doing so, inadvertently forcing the farmer to stop his cart as the man looked over the drawings in amazement.

"Good Lord," the farmer said. "You *saw* that?"

Trace nodded.

"Well, I could do without *that* in my life," the farmer said, and started up the horses again.

They were rattling past a fingerpost: CARLISLE, 5 MILES; GETTYSBURG, 20.

Trace wondered if he could do without it in *his* life. He had begun to think something extraordinary flowed through him when the danger was nearest and at its utmost. It was like an elixir that stimulated him to experience colors and sounds with a vividness that made his times away from combat seem pallid by comparison. It was as if there were a thick scrim between who he was in his quotidian life and some truer, brighter existence, a scrim that in the extremity of battle was torn to pieces, so that for a brief time he, Jack Trace, was all there was to the universe. No London nor newspapers nor aspirations nor orphaned childhood; no whores, no cable. If there was a spirit world, say, or an afterlife; if there was an Essence or a Supreme Being, then Jack Trace knew It intimately—indeed, *might even be It*—during those times.

Without forethought, Jack was telling this all to the farmer.

"You hear the long guns first," Jack said, "the twelve-pounders, as you approach the field."

"I've heard 'em," the farmer grunted. "Sound like thunder."

"Precisely," Jack said.

And Jack related how a normal fellow would endeavor to keep his distance from such a menacing sound. But a soldier must march toward it, the sound coming out of the trees, forming itself into individual, percussive thuds rather than a solid rumble of low noise.

Then came the crack of rifle fire that follows muzzle flash and smoke. You see the shot long before you hear the report. It is in that interval, Jack said, when you know the fieldpiece or rifle might be pointed at you, that existence begins to glow with a spiky brighness. *What will happen?* is the only question. It's like a story, Jack said, the most important of all stories, a story all about you, only you, and you're desperate to know what will happen. *And then?* you ask. *And then?*

Jack was so exercised by his description that the farmer shifted over to the far edge of his seat.

"You from somewhere else?" the farmer interjected suddenly, almost in a bleat.

"Pardon?" Jack said. He was dazed, blinking again, as if he had come running into a dark barn from a brightly lit day.

"You from somewhere else?" the farmer repeated. "You sound like you ain't from around here."

"England," Jack said, realizing he must have been too worked up. "I'm from London, England."

"I thought you was," the farmer said. "Well, here's where you get off."

They were near the edge of a town. Stores and houses set on a grid around a main street; what appeared to be the gray limestone buildings of a small normal school or college clustered at the western limits of the settlement. It was a town like many of the others near the Mason-Dixon line, a town that, had it been set fourscore miles to the south, could have been in ruins in the wake of battle.

The cart clattered away up the main street, the farmer casting a furtive glance back at Jack, who was checking the hidden pocket in his musette bag for his cash supply. He had enough money to take a room.

If the whip snap of the squash farmer brought Trace partly back from Antietam on the road to Carlisle, seeing Franny Ludlow's picture on a poster in the hotel nearly brought Trace crashing to the floor. The bill heralded a "spiritual convocation." In the center of the poster was an oval engraving, meant to resemble a keepsake cameo, of a woman. Trace, casting a quick professional artist's eye at the poster as he made his way to the hotel lobby desk, dropped all his belongings and stifled an involuntary gasp of surprise when he realized the picture was of Franny Ludlow. He hastened across the lobby to read the placard. The meeting or performance or service—Trace wasn't sure what it was—was for that very night. The poster called for a "convocation of persons with connections to, or interest in, the spiritual world." It proclaimed Miss Frances Piermont as a "spiritual adept," as one who "has opened the way for the living to unite with the departed," "a still, small voice of calm."

Jack went to his room and cleaned up. He changed clothes and sorted his drawings. He began preparing them for transit to England by encasing them in tissue, cardboard, strips of lath, and finally oilcloth. He sent a telegram to Mr. Selcome's representatives in Philadelphia, informing them where he and his drawings could be found. He then sat in a stiff chair by a window in the lobby and held Franny's poster in his lap as he waited for the hour at which he would walk to the small college campus on the western end of town to the hall where Franny might open the way for the living to meet the dead.

The Convocation

It was not a séance. It involved no machinery or machinations. It was so effective, Trace later thought, because it was so simple. And also because it had Mrs. Ludlow—Frances Piermont. Trace hoped he could see her after the convocation and ask her about her name. But in the meantime, Trace, like every one of the three hundred other people in the hall, waited on benches and one-armed desk chairs brought from other buildings and classrooms around the campus. Curiosity and expectation rose in the room as the audience saw that on every seat in the hall had been placed a felt mask with ribbon ties—the kind used by sleepers sensitive to light—and a green leaf.

People fingered the masks and the leaves apprehensively or played with them as if they were appurtenances for a costume ball. Then, without introduction, Franny made her entrance. She wore a high-bodiced, black dress and came through the tall French doors on the side of the hall that faced the oak grove of the campus. She had on a broad-brimmed straw petasos, dyed lavender, that until she removed it at the doors made her resemble a female Mercury, floating up the steps on air through the twilight. The dark hues of her garment and the lightness of her movement gave not a somberness to her entrance, but rather a stateliness, a sort of majesty. No one applauded. People smiled and nodded and settled in to their seats as Franny made her way to the front of the hall with its planters of lilies and palms, its floral-pattern screen behind a small table with a water pitcher, and its black, spindle-backed, Windsor chair.

As she crossed the platform, she thanked everyone for coming. She praised the loveliness of the evening and commodiousness of the hall. She looked out the huge doors at the grove and said such tranquillity seemed so at odds with what they all knew had been occurring less than twenty leagues to the south. Heads nodded around the room at this, and Trace felt his heart bound in his chest. Did she know where he'd been? Did she know what he'd drawn?

Franny said she could make no promises that spirits would come or make a sign or sound. She hoped at the very least that she and the audience would have a few moments, a bit of a repose, with their departed ones. She had lost a daughter, she said, and many of them had suffered much harder griefs. Perhaps she could soften that ache; perhaps she could do more.

"Will you try with me, my brothers and sisters?" she asked, and the congregation nodded.

Franny told them this was not prayer.

"But I wish you to close your eyes," she said. "And to that end, please put on the masks I have left for you on each seat."

Everyone complied. As people tied the ribbons, men often assisting the women, there were some amused and apprehensive murmurings around the hall, and Franny assured everyone that there would be no tricks, no one had to say or do anything, no one would be forced to perform anything blindfolded. She, too, she said, would wear one, and she put hers on and sat on the chair on the stage.

Then, when everyone was blindfolded, she asked them to hold the leaf, to feel its outline. Trace felt his. It was an oak. Funny, he thought, he hadn't noticed that until he'd put on the blindfold.

Franny asked them all to feel the stem of their leaves, to feel the smaller veins running outward from the stem.

"Now, while you hold your leaf," she said, "I want you to picture yourself. Picture yourself standing alone.

"Now, picture yourself holding, with your left hand, the hand of your mother.

"Now, picture yourself, with your right hand, holding the hand of your father.

"Think of how they look on either side of you, holding your hands, you in the middle."

Trace wondered if everyone in the hall had, like him, gone from seeing themselves as an adult standing alone to seeing themselves as a child between two grown people. With a few words, Franny had transformed him into a little boy with a parent on each hand. He didn't know *who* these parents were, but he knew—Jack the boy knew—that they were his.

"Now," said Franny, "picture each of your parents' parents—your grandparents—standing behind them. If you can remember them, picture how they looked.

"Now, picture *their* mothers and fathers standing behind them. All of them standing there behind you. We now have fifteen people, including you, in our picture."

A picture, Trace thought. *What is she trying to paint here?*

"Now add *their* mothers and fathers," Franny said. "We've suddenly jumped up to thirty-one people. Twice what we just had. Do it again, we're over sixty. It's getting crowded, isn't it?"

The audience tittered.

"We're back to roughly the year the country was founded. Go back further, adding parents to stand behind each generation. By the time we reach the founding of the Plymouth Colony, we have over a thousand souls lined up behind you. Think of that: in just three hundred years, a *thousand* different people had to find each other, court, marry, and procreate to make it possible for you to be here tonight, to sit blindfolded, holding your leaf."

She paused to let the audience think. Trace could hear his fellow congregants breathing and shifting in their seats, and he felt as if the multitude—*his* multitude, in *his* picture, in his head—was crowded into the room, too. He resisted the impulse to pull off the mask.

"Now, if there are—let's be conservative—two hundred of us sitting here tonight," Franny said, "that's two hundred thousand people who had to match up to make this gathering possible. Keep going back . . . four hundred thousand have lined up, then eight hundred thousand . . . Now, we're over a million, and it's only the year of Shakespeare's birth. A million people had to take part in creating us."

Trace began to feel dizzy, pleasantly so, as he imagined a million people. He thought how he'd never seen a million anything. Oh, grains of sand certainly. Stars maybe. What else? His mind was wandering. Maybe that was Franny's point: letting his mind wander. Her voice seemed to fade away and return. There were more millions now, many more, all standing behind Trace, and Franny was saying that whether you believed in the

Book of Genesis or in the theories promulgated by Mr. Darwin, there were more people crowding behind everyone in the audience than had ever lived on earth.

"Which means," Franny said, "for us to be here tonight, we all have to be related."

The gathering murmured in assent.

"Now do you see why, at the beginning, I called you all brothers and sisters?"

More murmurs. Trace didn't bother to puzzle the mathematics or the logic of Franny's contention, but his feeling was that they made sense, and that sense was comforting. He stroked the veins of the leaf, felt the flesh of its blade. It was comforting, too, a talisman.

Franny asked the audience to picture a lost loved one. But to Trace it seemed Franny was speaking only to him.

"Have that person stand before you and before the multitude behind you," Franny said.

Maddy appeared. The teasing, smiling, haughty Maddy of the day of the *Great Eastern* explosion. The more somber, experienced Maddy on the deck of the same ship, but now at dawn, after their night together.

Trace felt a flash of alarm: *was* she a lost loved one? He hadn't heard from her or about her since he'd met her again on the *Great Eastern*. He had no idea if she was still in America with Whitehouse or back in England. So much had happened. Was she *lost?* And, good Lord, did he *love* her?

A black, fan-shaped form hurtled through these thoughts: a piece of the *Great Eastern*'s exploding funnel, a predatory specter. But Maddy *hadn't* died that day. He'd spent a night with her a little more than a year ago. He'd told her of his utopian painting, the one she'd inspired—or would inspire if he ever got to paint it. She'd said she would leave Whitehouse. She'd asked if he would ever come visit her.

Trace didn't know what to think. He *wasn't* thinking. It was a dream, and it was as if he floated on the sensation—not the actual sound—of Franny's voice in the hall. Was this some form of mesmerism? He'd heard about magicians and mountebanks who could hold audiences under a spell, make them do ridiculous things: cluck like chickens, bark like dogs. He'd been silent, hadn't he? No one in the hall was looking at him, were they?

The black winglike thing, that piece of the *Great Eastern* or whatever it was, came flying again through the darkness behind his blindfold, and he nearly jumped in his seat because the rushing wing made a huge cracking

sound in his head and he was lying down in the East Woods near Sharpsburg during the battle at Antietam Creek.

His throat grew raw because he was shouting at Federal troops—the
Tenth Maine Brigade, he thought—who were lying near him and firing on
their own men. Trace had intended to advance only with the rear guard
of the Tenth, to get as close to the action as he safely could, the better to
sketch the ground fighting, but in the predawn movement he'd gotten
turned around and swept too close to the front, and now he was pinned
down. The Federals had mistaken a group of figures in a clearing for rebels
in the confusion and smoke, but Trace recognized a boy carrying a tattered
guidon. He had seen him and his fellows the night before around a camp-
fire. The boy had been crying. Trace hadn't acknowledged the sound. No
one did. Everyone had heard it before. Other boys. Men. Other battles.
Both before and after. The quiet crying. The armies were aligned that night
for a terrible confrontation the next day, every soldier knew. Let a man,
let a boy, cry.

Now Trace was watching the boy run in panic, under fire coming from
a position he correctly thought he was meant to defend. Trace screamed
in vain for the soldiers to stop. The Tenth Maine had been ambushed in
the woods by Confederates. The Mainers plunged into immediate disarray
and panic. Trace thought a fellow near him had shouted he'd seen a Texas
banner. There was a circumference of chaos, screaming, and calls for help
around Trace, and it was impossible for him to tell how many Texans
were attacking. A swarm. A multitude. A legion from hell, out of the earth
risen like an exhalation, opening fire. He realized he could die. Bullets
whined in the air over his head. The colors of the woods grew sharper for
him, even through the smoke, and the smoke itself became particulate and
shimmering. This feeling of equipoise amid terror began to elevate his
spirit. *He would not be harmed.* He'd felt this before. It was his answer to
What will happen next?

He would not be harmed, he knew, but he also knew the boy and the
other stragglers were doomed. And then, as if on cue, the boy fell, shot
through the chest, his flag whipping in a quarter arc to the ground.

The next thing Trace saw—for he was watching this all under the
guidance of Franny in the college hall, watching it all behind the felt mask,
which he was vaguely aware had become sweat- and tear-soaked—the next
thing he saw was that he was beside the boy. Just as quickly as the Mainers
had opened fire on their own men, they had stopped, and Trace had made

his way through the smoke and the underbrush around the poplars and box elders to where the boy lay dead.

But this did not happen, Trace thought. *I did not do that. I saw the boy die. I moved back with the Tenth. I retreated up closer to a knoll near General Hooker's position and began sketching. I did not go down to that little clearing and see the boy.*

But that was what he was seeing.

This was not what happened. It was not the past.

It was something else. Franny.

Trace is by the boy. Amid the pandemonium, he turns the lad, who has fallen facedown, over. The boy has shaggy brown hair, gone uncut for months. The boy's features are fine, a surprisingly strong aquiline nose and chin; no whiskers, though. His open, blue eyes have gone soft in death and give him a preoccupied aspect, as if he is purposely ignoring Trace so he may look over his shoulder to something more interesting.

Trace lifts the boy up because his body is twisted, for it just doesn't seem meet to leave a boy, even a dead boy, in so uncomfortable a position. And while he is thinking perhaps he should see if the boy has about him some identification or a keepsake or the name of someone to whom Trace could write, the dead boy's head explodes.

An errant bullet strikes the corpse in the skull, and a storm of pink sleet lashes Trace's face and chest in one quick blast. He is soaked. He spits the salty, jellied grit out of his mouth. He wipes the sticky fluid from his eyes. Once he can see again, he looks down at the nearly headless corpse. He's seen them often after a battle, has placed them in numerous sketches and engravings. But this is the first one he can remember having seen beforehand, when there was a face to remember it by.

The boy's cranial matter is actually trickling down Trace's face. The sounds of battle are gone. *But this isn't the battle I saw, anyway,* Trace thinks. *I never saw this boy's head blow apart this way. I saw him fall, shot in the chest, then I ran back behind Union lines.*

Now he is trying to remember what the boy looked like. And when he looks down to see again the weight in his arms, he is looking at Maddy. He nearly cries aloud. Maybe he does. Oh God, has she died? No. She is alive, moving.

What is happening?

Maddy is with him on the battlefield.

Franny is doing this.

Trace looks again. And Maddy points. And Trace sees.

He sees as if again, repeated, but now slower in his mind's eye, a minié ball spinning toward Maddy cradled in his lap. The bullet spins slowly, floating in the air, a tiny bead revolving toward them. Trace can actually see sunlight glint off the rifling scores on the lead, making the minié ball glisten like a moistened gem. And in Trace's mind the projectile floats over the battlefield, hovering in the scorched air over the fire, the screaming, and the death. It floats and glistens and spins as if part of an invisible machine that gradually begins to reveal itself behind the smoke and dust. The bullet has become the key gear in a watchwork complexity of whirring governors, bearing races, and lubricated cogs; a sliding, spinning marvel of a device that is powering . . . something . . . a silent, alabaster railroad machine, perhaps, whisking people across a groomed and variegated farmland as they head toward white, pure white, cities shining between the hills on the horizon. . . . It is the utopia! . . . Trace realizes he is seeing his utopia— or a detail from it—all conjured by—whom? And how? By Maddy? Franny? His own fevered brain?

The minié ball is spinning, spinning, giving off sparks, not moving forward with its dole of mortality but just making a soft, humming sound as it floats, a soft humming as near to Trace as any rifle crack or bullet's scream, but soft; it's a part of Trace, this humming, and something celestial, too. And then Trace begins to come back to himself and the sound coheres into the gentle sobbing of someone nearby. . . .

There were people throughout the hall softly crying. Trace was coming back from the battle, from the battle as it had been at Antietam and from the altered version of it with Maddy and the glimpse of his utopian dream of the future.

Franny was speaking gently to the audience. Franny said now that they were all "back from our journey," it was time to remove the blindfolds.

"Reach up and untie them," she said. "Slowly take them off."

As Trace did this with the others, they were met with a sight that stunned them.

In a room now dark—for during the convocation, unbeknownst to the blindfolded audience, night had fallen across the campus, and the oak grove was black beyond the windows—there stood Franny Piermont bathed in lamplight and no longer wearing her solemn black dress, but now clad in a luminous white gown, her hair loose and garlanded, her smile beatific.

As one, the audience gasped. She'd been transformed. It was perfect:

to have journeyed inward so far as to see lost loved ones, dead sons and daughters, to have conjured up the chaos of war, to have communed with the departed, and then to return to be greeted by a vision of purity and peace, a woman in white, gently welcoming them back into the world. Joy swept through the hall.

People in the audience—even those still weeping—began to applaud.

It had been a simple trick. While everyone was blindfolded, Franny must have moved behind the floral screen upstage and changed gowns. Simple, really, but so artfully done. Tears sprang from Jack's eyes. He felt like laughing and crying all at once.

Everyone was out of their seats now. Some, the men in particular, were still applauding. People were smiling at one another, wordlessly acknowledging the rapture they'd felt and saw in others. And moving down the aisles, toward the stage, were still others, the ones with their arms raised, hands open, straining to feel, to reach for Franny; several score of them or more, grateful, ecstatic, enthralled, pressing toward Franny on the stage. Jack Trace was one of them.

He Meets Her

Jack surprised himself, approaching her that way, and once he was down near the stage, he came more to his senses. He lowered his arms and, blinking in abashment, chuckled self-consciously as if to say to anyone who might notice, he really was not normally like this, not nearly so . . . *emotional*. But no one noticed; the converts and acolytes were pressing ardently toward the stage.

Trace watched as Franny bent at the waist to touch the outstretched hands. She seemed aglow.

Trace turned and moved up the aisle to wait at the back of the hall. He came to stand near the last row of seats, where a handsome fellow with dark, swept-back hair leaned against the wall with his arms folded, seeming to watch with a pleased, proprietary air as the fervor wound down. Trace nodded at the man, and the fellow acknowledged him with a little, flicking salute but then, like Trace, quickly returned his attention to the stage.

After nearly half an hour, the noise in the hall had subsided from the thick hubbub of agitation down to the hollow rattle of a few departing voices and the rasp of chair legs scraping the wooden floor as a custodian began to sweep the aisles.

Trace walked alone toward the stage. Franny was listening to the last supplicant, a small, tremulous elderly woman.

"Kind Mr. Trace," Franny said, when the woman had shuffled away. "I'm so pleasantly surprised." She extended her hand.

"You remember me," Jack said, blushing and taking her hand and bowing all at once. Even with Franny on the platform, he was taller than she. They were almost eye to eye.

"Of course I remember you," Franny said. "I remember it all. Those days seem far away, though."

"They do," Jack said.

"You look fine," said Franny.

And Trace wondered how that could possibly be. He'd just been through a battle and had a boy's head explode all over him. No, he thought, that bit about Maddy *hadn't* happened. Good Lord, he actually had to remind himself of this. He *had* been in a battle, but that was days ago and miles away. He'd walked here. From the battle. No, from the hotel. He was so confused.

"You look," Trace heard himself say, "a good deal better than fine." And he reddened even more for having sounded so forward, so *American*.

But Franny seemed not the least affronted. The luminance that had graced her when the audience took off its blindfolds remained, but in a more delicate form. Reduced now and not needing to fill a whole hall, the radiance seemed to gather in little pleats at the corners of her lips and eyes.

"You go by the name Piermont," Jack said.

"My stage name. My maiden name," Franny answered. "I am, in a manner of speaking, no longer with Mr. Ludlow. We are still man and wife but have been a long time apart. My life has taken such a turn." And she pointed at the stage with its accoutrements. It was a forthright gesture, done without ruefulness or deprecation, but without joy, either.

Jack nodded. He still held the blindfold. He'd wrung the tears and sweat out of it. The leaf, he'd pulverized to a green dust that now clung to the black felt of the mask.

"I see your name a good deal," Franny said. "And I have seen your work. It is truly remarkable. Your reputation—"

"Oh," Jack said, shaking his head, even waving his hand to halt her.

The mask ribbons fluttered. He thrust the blindfold into his pocket, wiping his hands of the green dust.

"I still have the portrait you drew of me," Franny said. "Not here, but at my cousin's home in Boston. That's my home now. You drew the picture on the *Niagara* coming down the coast from Canada. On our way to New York. We were all on our way to great success."

And with this, her expression darkened a little.

Trace wondered what she had conjured up for her own mind's eye during the convocation.

"You told me of your daughter that night on the *Niagara*," Jack said. "Do you ever see her? I mean, with these evenings, these convocations. Do you ever see her? I should say, *I* saw so much. It was remarkable, really, what you invoked . . . the war . . . a–a loved one . . . a painting I hope to do . . ."

"Your vision of the future?"

Jack looked at her, startled.

"A guess," said Franny. "You told me about it on the ship."

"Well," said Jack, "you have a good memory."

"I do." She pressed her lips together and looked down demurely at the edge of the stage.

"Have you seen her?" he asked quietly. "With all this, does your daughter ever come back to you?"

Franny shook her head. Her eyes were still downcast.

" 'The kind Mr. Trace,' " Franny said, now looking at him. "Do you remember I called you that on our voyage to New York?"

"I do," Jack said.

"I am going west, kind Mr. Trace." Franny had pulled herself together to make that declaration, for it was a declaration, not an idle tidbit of news.

"The territories," she said. "There is work to be done. I have covered the East. I have become a success, too. It's almost embarrassing. I donate the monies to soldiers' hospitals, but the renown . . . Well, you saw . . . But I will return. For now, though, I will go. And you?"

"I?"

"Yes. What is next for you?"

"I–I have no idea. More of the war, I suppose," Jack said. "As you say, I have a reputation. I suppose I should uphold it."

"You won't forget what you saw here, tonight," Franny said, and Trace wasn't sure she meant his vision or just this encounter with her.

"No," he said. "I certainly shall not."

"Nor shall I, kind Mr. Trace." And Franny extended her hand. Jack took it and helped her down from the stage platform.

He asked her if she would be spending the night in Carlisle. No, she had arrangements to begin traveling west that very evening. She would be going.

"You were an immense help to me," Jack said.

"How so?" Franny asked.

"I don't know," Jack said, and then unaccountably laughed and felt light in his boots. "But I have the feeling that by seeing you, I saw tonight what I must do with my life."

But of course that wasn't true.

Franny could have told him that. Men will say anything when they're enthralled.

CHAPTER XXI

THE SECRET TRAIN

The Huron Frontier, October 1862

How It Traveled

The train moved only at night and sometimes not even then. Better to travel without moonlight was the idea, for the smoke from the engine would be a floating silver thread stitched through the pine forests when the moon shone. Best to travel in pitch-darkness, lanterns out, windows blackened, down the tracks through the pines during the season of lengthening nights. There would be sparks and smoke from the engine, to be sure, but the darker the night, the quicker it would swallow all evidence of the train's passage. Once, when the moon was full and the skies clear, the train forsook movement altogether. It stayed secreted for two days and two nights on a lonely siding somewhere between towns, its fires banked, its boiler chuffing softly, and its six sentries standing guard: four on the ground at each point of the compass, hidden just off the tracks in the woods, watching; two atop the cars, also watching.

The train was small. It consisted only of a Rogers locomotive, utilitarian and sooty, with its wide-topped smokestack; a tender loaded with cordwood; a boxcar for equipment and munitions; a caboose placed mid train as quarters for the soldiers; and then, following the caboose, the gilded, burnished, private railcar with the gold-leaf script emblazonry beneath the

windows that read VANDERWEES & SON LUMBER CO.; and finally, a flatcar
with its huge cargo shrouded by a black tarpaulin.

This was Undersecretary of War Russell vanderWees's train. Although history did not know it yet, it was to be the Republic's victory
train. The world's largest cannon was wrapped in canvas on that flatcar,
and even though it was called the Ludlow Gun, it was vanderWees's cannon. He may not have drawn up the plans or made the calculations, but
Russell vanderWees had made the cannon possible, for the engineer who
did draw the plans was vanderWees's engineer. The beautiful Prussian
musician who loved the engineer was vanderWees's, too—after a fashion.
She was there because vanderWees had ordained it and arranged it. If
there was to be a victory for the Union army, then victory's goddess would
lay her beautiful sword at young vanderWees's feet for drawing this together: the beautiful train; the beautiful, brilliant engineer; his beautiful
lover; the beautiful, deadly cannon; the soldiers; the beautiful victory;
beautiful moonless nights; beautiful dark.

The train moved through the night slowly, for the track from here
northward was not well maintained. The expedition had left the farmlands
along the Erie shore, had swung up into the forests, and now passed
through occasional logged-off regions that opened suddenly on all sides like
a magician's cape sweeping back to reveal . . . nothing really; a sensation
of just more space in the dark void. Then just as suddenly, the forest would
close in again around the tracks to push against the travelers with more
darkness.

Undersecretary vanderWees's plan was to test the gun in complete
secrecy. He was taking the weapon up to the limits of his family's lumber
holdings in the Huron frontier. He had spirited the cannon out of the
Monongahela Iron Works in Pittsburgh in a single night. One afternoon
the gun was there; the next morning it was gone. If any rebel spies had
word of its construction, they certainly had no word of its current
whereabouts.

As he was most nights, Undersecretary of War vanderWees was in
the engine with two of the soldiers. One soldier was acting as fireman, the
other the locomotive's engineer. VanderWees usurped each role at his pleasure, sometimes driving the train, sometimes kicking open the firebox door
and throwing in a few logs. The rest of the time he would regale the two
men with song and story and share liberally of his flask. This was a secret
expedition, but for God's sake, that didn't mean they had to be tiresome

dolts; they were safely far away from any rebs now. VanderWees's father owned the damned land the train was rolling through.

"All around us is the baron's lumber!" vanderWees crowed, and he saluted his compatriots with the flask, toasted the geography, and passed the spirits around the cab.

In the caboose, the other six soldiers slept. They would be on guard duty soon enough, for day was approaching though the sky was still all darkness, save for the stars and the slivered, waning moon.

In the private railcar, Chester Ludlow also slept, but not in the compartment he shared with Katerina Lindt. He was napping at the table with its bolted lamp and stained-glass shade, where he'd been working on calculations for the cannon. He'd laid his head down when the numbers had begun to swim about on the papers before him, and he'd dropped into a deep sleep. His cigar died in the ashtray. His whiskey rocked with the swaying of the train, the amber liquid marking ellipses up the sides of glass and once even slipping over the side to drip onto the cannon's trajectory charts and mingle with a small pool of saliva that had dribbled from Chester's lips.

And on the rear vestibule of the private car, outside, bundled against the night's chill, was Katerina Lindt, calculating with her imperfect navigational skills and her even more imperfect knowledge of the states of the Union where she might be in this New World.

Going north and past Ohio was all she could tell. Past Ohio because she'd heard Chester or vanderWees say as much one or two nights ago. And going north because if she carefully peeked around the side of the railcar to where she could look forward into the direction the train was traveling, she could see the Great Bear in the sky ahead. She couldn't look at it for long, as the wind blew back smoke and cinders from the engine's stack. But she remembered Joachim pointing out the Great Bear above the Baltic years ago, and she knew that above the Bear's back was Polaris, the North Star, and that was the direction the train was headed.

But that was only the terrestrial direction. In every other way, she had decided, this train was hell-bound. VanderWees was up in the engine cab, she knew, as he was most every night, and very likely drunk . . . as he was most every night. Chester had been back at the table in the car, working on calculations for the powder charges he would need for the tests, but Chester, too, had been drinking. VanderWees was drinking; the soldiers were drinking; *she* was drinking. They *all* were drinking. This war, this

damned cannon, drove them to it. The cannon was infernal, she told herself—infernal, depraved, and driving them all mad. There it was, huge,
pulled along behind them under its black shroud that, though well lashed
and dogged down, was still flapping here and there along its dark flank as
if it were waving to her to slow down, wait for me. By the shape of the
canvas, she guessed that under the tarpaulin, the cannon could be aimed
right at her. The thought made her shiver. It was the same feeling she got
sometimes when vanderWees stared at her.

She'd never met a man like vanderWees. He shouldn't have such
power, but he did, and he seemed to use it to bring anyone near him to
heel. He would toast Chester and light his cigar and lead him on until they
were crowing about their invention. (It was *Chester's* invention, Katerina
thought. Didn't that matter?) And soon they would be bellowing about
how it would turn to smoke and gaping holes the entire Confederacy.
Then, as would happen often after such roistering, they would fall into
sulks or quarrelsomeness or threats. Once the soldiers even had to pull
them apart, and later no one could even remember why.

Katerina Lindt was tipsy, but knew it. At least she knew how to drink.
She was learning that from the men. Both Chester and vanderWees could
measure their consumption so as to keep lucid enough to do their work
and, in Chester's case, be able to perform his amorous duties.

Amorous *duties?* Her thoughts were pitching about her brain like poorly
stowed luggage. *Duties?* No, Chester Ludlow still brought pleasure with
him when he put aside all this damned work, with its ballistics and gunnery
calculus, and came to her in the sleeping compartment. Yes, that was clear.
This journey might be mad, the way might be dark, but that one thing
was clear. Chester came to her.

Katerina leaned against the guardrail. Cold air swirled the tendrils of
her hair. The track's deadmen—the soldiers called the wooden crossties
"deadmen"; what a strange expression, horrid—flickered away beneath her
feet and under the cannon's flatcar. The forest closed in around them,
drawing up behind the train like a purse, sealing her up. She could feel the
brass railing press against her dress, against the layers of her petticoats. She
could feel the pleasurable tremble of the train shudder through her down
below.

And she laughed out loud. Good lord, she thought, how sinful can I
become? But she pressed herself into the bar again. To feel a little more.

She tapped on the railing with her fingers, tapped out not a melody but a meaningless run of notes. If it had been the keys of a pianoforte she'd been tapping, she would have made only noise. But this was a signal: she was in need of praise.

Such was her nickname for the little gifts from vanderWees, the yellow-tinted tincture. Actually it had been his nickname. He passed it on to her.

"A gift of Paracelsus," he'd said after she'd complained she was having trouble sleeping on the first night of the train ride.

It was a small, crystal bottle he'd handed her in a velvet pouch attached to a delicate silver chain.

"You may wear it around your neck," vanderWees had said, and she'd blushed, for she'd instinctively known he'd meant under all her clothes, next to her skin.

She didn't do that, however. Chester would have seen it, would have asked her about it. Instead, she kept it hidden in her belongings. She would go to it when the men were working, take a few drops—ten, in the beginning—for herself, and things would soon seem...better... smoother...except for the quick sidelong glances she'd detect from vanderWees, as if he were examining her, studying her for a reaction; then she would feel heated again and turn away in agitation, as if he had seen some or all of her naked, and she would need to run to the protection and attentions of Chester Ludlow.

The tincture—it was laudanum, she knew—would make her time alone with Chester all the more pleasurable, all the more luxurious, all the more *hers*, and all the more deserved.

They needed respite from the madness of this railroad, the cannon, the nights of slowly crashing and rattling north, the days spent sitting, shrouded in a railcar, in seclusion.

"Who was Paracelsus?" she'd asked vanderWees that first time. She'd whispered it even though Chester wasn't around. She knew they were doing something covert. They were sealing a pact.

"Was he a Roman?"

VanderWees chuckled and shook his head.

"Swiss. An alchemist. He lived three hundred years ago. This is his cure. He said it was made of gold dust and melted pearls, the scoundrel. It's merely opium in alcohol. Nevertheless, it *is* a cure. The name Paracelsus gave it comes from the Latin for 'to give praise.' "

"Laudanum," she'd whispered.

"Begin with ten drops," vanderWees had said, and placed the little bottle in her hand and, with his, closed her grip around it. "Accept my praise."

Katerina remembered all this as the train rattled and banged along in the frosty night. She looked forward again, around the corner of the car, to the head of the train. She had to squint into the wind. A tiny hot spark flicked her cheek. She let out a small cry and raised her hand to the pinprick of pain. VanderWees was up there in the engine. He was probably stoking the fire, sending back the sparks. She wanted Chester to touch the spot with his tongue, to lick the place, to soothe her. But he was unconscious at his table. So she took off her glove, licked her fingertips, and touched her cheek with her own saliva. Things would soon seem . . . better . . . smoother . . .

She thought how she was up to twenty drops now.

Then an even more profound darkness closed around her, as if a mountain had suddenly collapsed on top of the train. In a sense it had, for the brakes screeched, the cars lurched, and the train came to an abrupt halt. They were in a tunnel. And Katerina Lindt knew, with a sigh, that here they would stay all through the coming day, hidden until night fell again and, in the dark, they could move once more.

VanderWees's Theorems

It was not much of a town. It was more a lumber camp that had metastasized into a settlement. In the outlying acres some attempts at agriculture were under way, but most fields still bore the scars of logging, and what cultivation there was had to work its way around dozens of stumps. There were several businesses—dry goods, hardware, blacksmith—that were run from the front of homes or wall tents or cowsheds or converted camp buildings. There were maybe twenty wood-frame buildings on muddy side streets that, by dint of a laundry line out back or curtains in a window, gave themselves to be dwellings. The tavern was part of the hardware and grocery store. The bar was in a back room adjoining the firewood bin. It was a dark place, illuminated by lanterns even by day and slapped together with raw pine planks still oozing pitch globules.

Chester and vanderWees had taken a handcar ahead into the town to buy supplies. The train carried a two-man hand-pump car for just such purposes. The soldiers had helped them unload the car, and they'd set off. The train, with its sleeping engine poking out of the tunnel, its hidden cannon, its sentries, and the slumbering Katerina Lindt, disappeared around a wooded bend.

They traveled through thick forest pocked by numerous logged-over acres with the occasional rail siding, logging slash, and discarded timber lying about. There were the buildings of several empty lumber camps with the VDW & SON logotype stenciled on the side of a cookhouse or wooden railroad water tank. There were more miles of forest with dark pines and autumn yellow birches. And there were the small Indian settlements with bark and canvas wigwams that hunkered morose, numb, and seemingly abandoned in the still chilly blue mist.

"Who are they?" Chester asked.

"Oh, I don't know. Chippewa or Ottawa. This-a-wa or That-a-wa. One of those tribes. The company has agents to deal with them."

The predawn chill left Chester soon feeling giddy, newborn. The car was well geared, the pumping not too difficult, and the breeze they generated kept him from sweating. They went by turns through dashes of cool mist that stretched like dull bunting across the tracks and through warm zones of sunlight beneath holes of blue sky. Chester's spectacles would fog, then clear, then fog again. The day was opening up.

Chester and vanderWees purchased all the food and supplies for the train, had the boxes stacked by the bar's back door, where they could easily load the cargo onto the handcar that they'd pulled up on the siding behind the store, and had begun the day's drinking, all before noon.

Four Indians walked into the room just as Chester was losing track of what vanderWees was saying. Fatigue had finally caught up with him. Fatigue and drink. VanderWees was making some point about mongrels.

"Ah," said vanderWees, pointing his finger at the Indians and speaking in a voice calculated to be almost audible to anyone else around them. "As if on cue to illustrate my point. I submit to you yonder sample of inferiority as Exhibit A."

None of the other drinkers noticed. Chester glanced at the Indians. They were at the bar, ordering a bottle.

VanderWees's point was simple and not unpopular even among Unionists. He was quick to point out they weren't his ideas originally. He subscribed to Samuel Morton's studies of cranial capacity.

Even through his midday whiskey, vanderWees had a surprisingly thorough recall of Morton's points. The Teutonics—"The Dutch," vanderWees said, hooking a thumb at himself, "the English," jabbing his thumb at Chester—have the largest cranial capacity and thus "the highest intellectual endowments."

"Your Negro has the smallest," vanderWees said.

"Smallest what?" asked Chester.

"Cranial capacity," vanderWees said. "You know what I mean. We're not talking about any other organ here. Professor Morton studied over six hundred skulls from around the world."

"Go on," said Chester.

"Your American Indian, below the Caucasian and above the Negro, is—and here I quote—'averse to cultivation, slow in acquiring knowledge, restless, revengeful, and fond of war, and wholly destitute of maritime adventure.' *Voilà*."

The Indians, the four of them—three men and a woman—were shabbily dressed in, for the most part, grease and smoke-stained lumberjack clothing. All four had woolen hats pulled down low on their lank, black hair. The quartet made no impression on the dozen or so other patrons of the tavern, who themselves were similarly attired.

"You are a man of science," vanderWees said after he'd taken another drink.

"An engineer," Chester said. "Electricity. Metallurgy."

"But you are mindful of data. I submit them as data."

"See here, vanderWees, I don't think those fellows—"

"And woman," interjected the undersecretary with a smile.

"And woman," said Chester, "can be representative of anything. Four random people walk into a bar—"

VanderWees waved his hand to erase the notion. He lowered his voice and leaned toward Chester.

"*People?*" he said. "*Random?* You saw their villages. There are settlements all over out there."

"And this Caucasian metropolis is immeasurably better?" Chester asked. He didn't particularly like vanderWees's drift. He'd heard it before. Something about the reproving tone of vanderWees's voice made Chester think of Whitehouse and his theories. The more the evidence had tipped against Whitehouse, the more adamant he'd become. And still he'd managed to destroy the cable.

"I don't mean to offend vanderWees and Son's timber holdings," Chester said, "but unless I am mistaken, we are not sitting on Parnassus here."

VanderWees had to smile at that one. He'd gotten Ludlow's dander up. He could smell contention in the air. He liked that.

"They will go nowhere, Ludlow. They are underfoot, believe me. They lack the *capacity*." He leaned back confidently and tapped the side of his head. "It's a biological fact. Measurable. Verified." He nodded his head toward the bar, where the Indians now stood in a row, backs to Chester and vanderWees's table.

"Nevertheless," Chester said, "you are a war secretary in a government that is imperiling itself to free, as you would say, an inferior race."

"I am for the preservation of the Union, yes, and slavery I can do without, thank you," vanderWees said. "It is as degrading to the whites who practice it as to the coloreds who submit to it. It leads to interbreeding, and *that* is the worst degradation of all. I tell you this, interbreeding is the moral and biological equivalent of incest. There should be social division between the races. We must be separate, or the slide will be irreversible."

As vanderWees spoke, he sometimes stared at his hands as if they weren't even his own. Other times his eyes bore fiercely into Chester. Chester could feel the liquor's happy effects sublime inside him, leaving his head abraded and devoid of words except for those the undersecretary kept pouring in.

"This continent is manifestly ours. We are *winning* it. Beginning here, with this non-Parnassus, as you call it, which will someday grow into a fine metropolis perhaps. That is the Caucasian way. As for the hovels those savages live in, well . . . They have lived that way for centuries and will perforce be swept aside."

"That, vanderWees, is—"

"Do you want to live in a nation inhabited by the degraded progeny of mixed races? A nation half Negro, half Indian, with only a sprinkling of white blood? Answer honestly, Ludlow. Do *you* want to intermingle with the likes of them? Or with a *Negress?* Have you ever?"

VanderWees was chuckling, running a finger along his jawline.

"I asked the same question of Mr. Lincoln once," he said.

"You're joking," Chester said.

VanderWees shrugged. "As undersecretary I have had occasion to speak with him, to propound. He didn't answer me, either."

Chester drained his glass and started to rise from the table. VanderWees stopped him with a hand on his arm.

"Another round. I'll buy. Besides, I want to see if it's tavern policy to be serving spirits to such . . . data." He pointed at the Indians as he walked toward the bar.

Chester would think later that almost no time had elapsed before he was hearing shouts and breaking glass. He had been sitting, turned away, staring out the open rear door of the tavern, out to a coal pile and a privy; his head was swirling in the wake of vanderWees's fulmination; he wished he could settle into familiar, solitary drinking thoughts.

But then came the almost instantaneous commotion, and he turned to see vanderWees on the floor with one of the Indians, who had his boot on the undersecretary's chest, holding a knife to vanderWees's throat. The barkeep was coming around the barrel-and-plank counter, waving a club; the other two Indian men were pulling at their comrade; and the woman was wailing a long, single note of alarm. Many of the other patrons were rising to their feet in fear or to obtain a better view. Not even noon, and already a fight!

Chester was up in an instant and pulling vanderWees to his feet while backing him away from the Indians. VanderWees's rage made his entire body quiver, but he was covering the palpitations with a broad grin and upraised hands. He hissed at Chester to unhand him, and Chester did let one arm go. VanderWees reached into his pocket. The entire room jerked as the undersecretary pulled out not a pistol, but a calling card. He handed it to the barkeep.

"Until such time as this settlement is incorporated as a village or a town unto itself," vanderWees said to the Indians, his voice surprisingly smooth, barely hinting at his wrath, "it falls under the aegis of vanderWees Lumber. We will not be serving spirits henceforth to Indians. Please excuse yourselves."

Chester could not tell if the Indians understood the meaning or merely the intent of vanderWees's words. But after a nod from the bartender, who looked up dumbly from the calling card, the four Indians began to walk slowly toward the tavern's front door. They hadn't taken but a few steps when vanderWees barked, "Halt!"

The Indians stopped. VanderWees, free now from Chester's grip, stepped over to the quartet. The room tensed again, watching.

VanderWees stopped before the tallest, who was perhaps the youngest of the Indian men. The undersecretary extended his palm and waggled his fingers in a hand-it-over demand.

The Indian sullenly pulled a bottle from under his filthy wool mackinaw. The barkeep cast a quick glance back at the empty plank where the Indians had been standing. The man handed the stolen bottle to vanderWees, who took it and in one, quick, violent heave sent it sailing over three tables and out through the open rear door of the tavern. It smashed on the coal pile out by the siding, leaving a glistening black stain on the anthracite and shards of glass scattered in the cinders. VanderWees then tossed a coin—it looked like gold piece—to the barkeep and pointed to the back door to the Indians. They walked that way out of the tavern.

"Come," vanderWees said almost tenderly to Chester. "We have a cannon to test."

The Test

When they had returned to the tunnel on the handcar with the supplies for the train, vanderWees said to hell with night travel, they were too near their goal now and too far north in a wilderness to be troubled by rebel espionage, so he ordered the train to start up and move out.

Chester rode in the engine with vanderWees and the two soldiers manning the controls. They passed through the village with the tavern. Twice they stopped to throw switches and take the train up spur lines, moving deeper into the forest on rough roadbed over which the train had to creep.

Just before dark, they passed another Indian settlement, and Chester thought he saw the four Indians from the tavern walking along the right-of-way. VanderWees seemed to have seen them, too. He looked in their direction with a calculated flatness, then kicked open the firebox door and threw four split lengths of cordwood into the flames.

The train had moved slowly forward maybe another two miles when, just after crossing a small trestle bridge over a sandy wash, vanderWees called a halt. They moved the train to a siding in the wilderness.

"There are ten miles of cut timber ahead," vanderWees said, folding a company map back into his breast pocket. "We shall wait for daylight. Mr. Ludlow, I have brought us here to the most remote place to test this folly of ours. My guess is the Confederacy, if it ever heard about this cannon's existence, now must think it a chimera. Even the foundry workers in Pittsburgh probably don't really believe it was ever there, we got it out so quickly. But now the hour is at hand. If we fail tomorrow, no one will be the wiser. We shall just leave the gun here to rust. If we succeed, however, the war will be ours. Mr. Ludlow, you are the engineer. The mission is now yours. I shall see you at dawn."

He actually saluted Chester, did an about-face, and smartly leapt from the engine cab. There was such an abruptness to his gestures that it almost seemed as if he'd slapped Chester with a glove and challenged him to a duel.

VanderWees walked back to his small sleeping compartment at the opposite end of the private car from the large compartment Chester shared with Katerina. Still in the engine, Chester watched the lantern light go on in the small compartment, then go out.

Katerina did not awaken when Chester came in to lie beside her, nor did he make a move to rouse her. He could feel his body cleaved by the exhaustion of the carousing and sleeplessness of the past two days and by the excitement and dread he was feeling about the firing. If he slept that night, it was only for a few minutes. Soon gray dawn light was coming in the window. Chester pulled himself out of the bed and woke the crew for the test.

By late afternoon the cannon was ready. The rest of the train was removed a safe distance up the siding, and the outriggers had been set up to steady the cannon car. The gun crew had dug a shelter trench and bolstered it with timbers. They had rolled a thousand-pound round out from the boxcar and, using a special Ludlow-designed tripod with block and tackle, loaded the charge.

Chester ordered the tarpaulin pulled off the gun. No one had seen the cannon since its loading in Pittsburgh. Everyone was stunned anew. The enormous curve and thickness of the breech end of the monster were almost planetary, bending away to form a massive, curved iron horizon. The diminishing rings of the barrel extended out the length of the flatcar and up at an angle toward the gray sky. The iron of the gun's surface was dark and mottled, reflecting nothing, appearing colder than the overcast October day.

Chester looked downrange through his field glasses. The area to the west of the track ahead was the logged-over expanse. To the east, all was still forest. He ordered his ordnance sergeant to move the cannon's trajectory two degrees east. The men began cranking the wheels.

"What are you doing?" VanderWees was scrambling up the sandy embankment.

"We'll get a better idea of how our cannon and shells do if we have something to knock down. So, I'll aim for the trees. VanderWees and Son can absorb the loss of a few cords of timber, I hope."

VanderWees screwed his lips and tightened his gaze on Chester. "In this case I'm thinking the bigger loss, the better. All right. You're in charge."

"Thank you," Chester said. "Now," he added, "if you would be so good as to return to the train with Frau Lindt, we'll continue."

With a snort, vanderWees had already started sliding on his boots down the embankment, and Chester was unable to see from his face how angry the undersecretary was.

When Chester saw vanderWees climb up and wave from the vestibule of the private railcar (Katerina was beside him), Chester ordered the sergeant to ignite the fuse.

"Sir, aren't you coming down?" the sergeant asked.

"I'll take shelter here behind this rock," Chester said. There was a boulder near where he stood large enough to shield him from any blast. The sergeant lit the fuse.

Not one person—neither the soldiers in the trench, nor vanderWees and Katerina half a mile away, nor Chester crouched behind his rock—was ready for the double concussion that followed. First there was the magnificent blast from the cannon itself. A huge, enveloping blow that seemed to have a bipartite, iambic rhythm to it: *ba-BOOM.* After the instant it took everyone to comprehend that the cannon had not destroyed itself but had fired successfully, they all raised their heads—above the trench, above the rock, on tiptoe from the vestibule—to peer through the gunsmoke cloud to see what was happening downrange. The answer came soon enough in a fierce orange flash that rose higher than the trees and tore up into the gray sky about three miles down the line. Then, an upwelling of smoke, round, almost tuberous in its clotted unsightliness, bloomed from the space left by the flash. As bright and dazzling as the flash was, so the cloud was dark and ponderous. It was as if it contained the entire density of the overcast sky in one curved, horrid lump.

Then came the concussion. The sound of the blast rolled over the forest and came directly down the track on the rails. It thudded against all their faces, made everyone wince, flinch, or rock on their feet. Its force hurt their ears.

It wasn't until the ringing in his own ears subsided that Chester, who was still looking through his field glasses at the torched tops of the fir trees burning out near the shell's impact, realized the train whistle was blowing and that vanderWees was in the engine, already under way.

"We're going out there!" vanderWees shouted from the cab. "All aboard!" VanderWees was flush-faced, almost frantic.

"VanderWees, I want to fire another test round or two, for range, for accuracy," Chester called. "And we must inspect the breech."

"It'll be too dark," vanderWees hollered, and waved his hand distractedly at the sky. "I want to see! I want to see, goddamn it!"

Chester was about to object and invoke his authority as chief of the test when vanderWees preempted him. "I'm the undersecretary of war, Ludlow. Get on this train!"

The train had to stop at the edge of the devastated area, where a tree had fallen across the tracks. No one spoke. Smoke rose from around the blast field as if from tiny watch fires or fumaroles. The smell of the burned niter of the shell's charge hung in the air. It seemed much closer to nightfall now than Chester had remembered it being just before the firing.

He was checking his pocket watch—6:10—when he heard the first scream. It came from behind him, from the front of the train. It was a war whoop, really, like the shouts he'd heard in imitation of rebel yells or Comanche battle cries. It was vanderWees.

He had leapt from the engine, had run along the railroad bed, and was veering toward the crater, dodging the fallen trees and smoldering embers. He was hollering and laughing and kicking up earth.

Although he hadn't uttered a single intelligible word, everyone knew what his shouting meant: their gun, capable of this measure of destruction, was going to win the Civil War.

In a few moments, the entire company of soldiers was whooping and tossing their hats and jumping off the train to follow vanderWees toward the crater. Chester felt Katerina's hand lift from his, and he looked to see her smiling at the men's exaltation. She had stepped closer to the edge of the vestibule's platform. She would not venture down onto the ground— her way was blocked by downed and charred timber—but Chester knew she was there in spirit. The men disappeared with vanderWees down into the crater. Chester and Katerina couldn't see them, but Chester could picture them in there like beads rolling around in a pan, swirling about vanderWees. They came out of the earth only when Chester, after walking to the engine, sounded a long blast on the steam whistle, signaling that it was time to go.

The Revels

They woke the whole town. With vanderWees at the controls, the train—all cars and the unshrouded cannon—came into the settlement with whistle screaming and soldiers firing their carbines. Soon they had the train pulled up on the siding behind the hardware-grocery-tavern-depot, torches and lanterns and a bonfire were blazing, and the settlement's population was celebrating the certain end of the war. Citizens swarmed around the cannon. Children wanted to climb atop it. One blade, using a woman's parasol as a tightrope walker's prop, pranced up the length of the barrel to the cheers of the throng below.

An impromptu band began to play—the spinet had been pulled out onto the private car's vestibule. A coronet player and fiddler joined the local church organist, who was at the piano. People stomped and danced in the cinders. The soldiers, Katerina, and vanderWees joined in. Chester watched in the dark from inside the car. When the revelers had come in to lug out the piano, they hadn't even noticed him.

He couldn't explain his reticence. The whiskey was making illuminating thought unlikely, but Chester's mind groped toward a self-regarding light nevertheless. Why was he alone in here? Clearly his cannon was a success. The war's end was possible. Why not celebrate?

Because now vanderWees was on top. Chester was beginning to feel that vanderWees was the true engineer on this project. He felt a wave of self-pity rush through him, and it disgusted him all the more.

He was out of whiskey. He should go get another bottle. He stood and stopped when he saw in the door, eyes glittering, Russell vanderWees with a piece of paper.

"Telegram," vanderWees said. "Want to show it to you."

Chester frowned as much to squeeze vanderWees into focus as to sort out what it was he was saying.

"I wired Secretary Stanton," vanderWees said. "Here's his answer. Already. 'Congratulate Ludlow on success. Stop. Begin return immediately. Stop. Tell Ludlow have seen wife's convocation. Stop. Most impressed. Stop. Good work. Stop.'

"Whose good work do you suppose he means?" vanderWees asked as he folded up the telegram. "Your wife's or yours?"

"Ours," Chester said. The word felt thick. The whiskey. He needed more. "No doubt."

"Well now, I wouldn't be so sure," vanderWees said. "Your wife's reputation—"

"Let's not refer to my wife's reputation, Mr. vanderWees. At all."

"Very well. Care for a drink?"

VanderWees indicated the empty whiskey bottle Chester held in his right hand by the neck as if it were a club. Chester, in a show of gentle delicacy to defuse the clamped temper revealed in his white knuckles, placed the bottle on the table. "Yes," he murmured.

"Ludlow, are you all right?"

"Yes," Chester said with measured force now. "Very all right." And he proceeded with minimal weaving out of the car and toward the tavern.

In the bar, Chester endured backslapping and handshakes and allowed himself to be stood to drinks before he thought perhaps he should find Katerina. She was around. He thought. He had been watching out of the corner of his eye as vanderWees matched drinks with the soldiers and slapped them on their backs and shook their hands and made wild gestures that appeared to be a pantomime of an explosion. The lanterns hanging from the ceiling seemed to be swaying, but upon closer examination Chester could see they weren't. He thought again perhaps he should find Katerina. The piano on the railcar's vestibule kept hammering out a three-chord tune, which was the church oganist's sole grasp of dance music. It wasn't Katerina at the piano.

"You play like a goddamned Methodist dance band!" somebody shouted, and the crowd laughed and cheered and several shots were fired, and the music pounded louder and faster.

Chester would relieve himself. It was time for that, and that was what he would do. And he wanted Katerina. She *was* here. He thought. Somewhere.

He walked across a floor that suddenly seemed to have become a steeply raked stage and he, an actor making an exit in a drama he had never read, avoiding props placed to trip him up. But he made it safely to the door, where he saw a flash of something, a movement, back in the firewood bin. A glint of silver, up high. He looked. From a hand a silver chain twitched. The hand was raised in the dimness of the bin, caught in a slash of lantern light coming through a gap in the plank wall. The hand was attached to vanderWees's arm. Another hand shot up—this was all happening *very* fast—to grab at the chain. It was Katerina's hand. There was a man's laugh and a woman's whining, impetuous—what?—sob? laugh? guttural plea? gasp? She wanted the chain or what dangled from it. Then the two of them clicked into complete visibility, emerging out of the dark like a tangled snag rising from a pond bottom: he holding the prize high over her head, she vainly reaching for it with one hand, her other hand tugging at the front of his mussed trousers. They were a perverse dyad, twisting around each other and around their ravening.

He ran for them both, head down, and that was all he remembered, save for a scream, a thud, a brilliant electric flash that came from the back of his head and—he could have sworn—burst out his nostrils. . . .

Sometime later, he awoke with a horrible headache. He thought he heard the distant sound of a train whistle.

The wood bin where he lay was dark; no lantern light leaked through the gaps in the planks. The tavern, it appeared—or sounded—was empty. The revels now were ended, and Chester lay sprawled on the billets, sawdust adding grit to the dried blood on his scalp. His ribs hurt. And his eye. And his head, supremely his head.

He struggled to his feet and noticed there was a note pinned to his waistcoat. He tried to remove the paper, but his hands were like flails beating at it. After several attempts he regained his dexterity, unpinned the paper, and hobbled out of the wood bin into the adjoining tavern, where some feeble dawn light lay wounded on the floor.

The train was gone. Chester stood dumbfounded by the monumental emptiness of the tracks. He looked at the paper. It was Stanton's telegram, the one vanderWees had shown him. There was a penciled note on the opposite side:

No hard feelings.
I hope.
(No hard head either. Sorry.)
Join us

for success and
   Victory,
    vdW
Your country calls.
(So does she.)

Chester walked out to the tracks. By the way the switches were thrown, he could tell the train had headed north. He tried running between the rails, but realized you can't catch a train on foot. He trotted back to the town. No one was awake. The daylight was paltry, made more meager by the fog. He felt a panic rising in his chest that he might be facing entrapment in this wood-chip, mud-hole, antipodal sump forever. But then his eyes lit upon a handcar, very like the one he and vanderWees had used. After throwing the proper switches, Chester had the car on the mainline and was pumping north out of town.

There was no warning—or certainly not enough for Chester to do anything—when, about five miles up the track, the cannon train, now headed back south, came around a bend, out of the fog, and smashed into him.

Chester was able to jump free. He dove clear across the roadbed and landed, luckily, in a deep band of yellow ferns, then rolled farther into a hemlock thicket. The engine's drive wheels screamed as the soldiers locked them down to brake the train. A metallic wail cut through fog and forest like a giant scythe as the train's brakes strained against the rolling inertia of the locomotive, the cars, and—most ponderously—the thirty-ton cannon. Chester actually cried out during the prolonged noise, but no one could hear him.

When the screeching stopped and the train halted, he could hear the soldiers and vanderWees inquiring of one another what in the hell had happened, who was it, and where was he now?

Momentum had taken the train so far down the line, it had been swallowed by the fog. Chester could only hear them all running around, staring into the murkiness, kicking at the pieces of the handcar.

"Hello?"

"Hello?"

"Hello-o-o?"

Chester lay still. The scaly hemlock twigs prickled at his clothes. He could feel the burn of abrasions from the dive off the car start to flare here and there around his body, but nothing serious, or at least nothing more serious than the battering he'd already taken the night before in the tavern. The injuries and indignities and improprieties all blended together as he lay there feeling the fog bear down on him.

"Let it go." VanderWees's voice.

"Sir?"

"We're leaving."

"Sir?"

"On the train."

"Sir, there's a man out here somewheres."

"We'll tell them in town. They can send out a search party. The busted handcar marks the spot."

VanderWees sounded surly, his voice thick with annoyance. The fog thinned just enough for Chester to see the sergeant standing, hands out imploring, while vanderWees stumped back toward the train. The under-secretary was only half dressed—shirt thrown over trousers with galluses dangling. Obviously this crash had roused him from bed. Chester guessed from which berth vanderWees had emerged.

"Sergeant, the secretary of war wants us in Washington. We must go. Now."

"Yes, sir."

It was then that Chester caught the smells: smoke, niter, brimstone. But also, ominously, something else troubled his nostrils; whiffs of gristle; something fibrous, singed. He felt his heart sink, his bowels shudder. He lay breathing in the odor as he listened to the train leaving. When the sound of the engine had receded completely into the fog, the scent remained. Chester rose out of his hiding place and followed the smell.

What had once been the Indian settlement they'd passed yesterday on the way to the cannon test was now a burned-over waste. The crater and devastation looked much like yesterday's. But here, there were also a few traces of wigwams, some burning remains of blankets, and the clearly discernible smoldering carcass of a horse. Chester didn't want to look into the wreckage of the dwellings. There was no point. VanderWees had managed an amazingly accurate hit. Or hits. He might have destroyed it all with one exquisitely placed shell, or he might—like a good artilleryman—have walked the rounds toward the target, coldly proceeding toward the consummation of revenge for whatever grievance he thought he'd suffered at the tavern. Or coldly proceeding toward his desire to free his race from this . . . impediment. It was too foggy to tell how far the destruction spread, and it really didn't matter. Chester could hear the desultory crackle of small flames digesting bits of wood.

He stumbled off the tracks and through the blasted area. He wandered about the torn-up expanse until he came to a shell crater. The blast's striations fanned up the sides of the depression, streaking the dirt, inviting him to slide down. He stepped over the lip, and the dirt gave way under his boots. He half ran, half slid down into the center of the hole. At the bottom he dropped to his knees. He then began, slowly, methodically, to feel around in the soil. It was gritty with bits of wood and stone and a few tiny, pulverized metal shell fragments. As he worked, he sensed he was being watched by someone—a woman? a girl?—from the rim of the crater. But when he gasped and quickly turned to look, he could see that he was alone. Alone and digging.

He soon began to dig with increased concentration and vigor. Dig and sift. He wanted to find something of significance at the center of the blast. Not just pulverized bits of forest or the splinters of the artillery round. He wanted an artifact. A sign. The way soothsayers before battle dug through the entrails of birds to read signs. Maybe a token—a remnant from one of the four Indians' rank mackinaws or a charred bit of a woolen hat or a baby's primitive toy. Even a grotesque piece of flesh: a finger, a severed breast, a skull, mangled genitals. Something that might make him wretch or become ill, something horrid that would be an indication that he had no further to go. But even as he dug more and more frantically, he knew he would come up empty-handed. And he did. There was nothing at the bottom of the hole but earth.

CHAPTER XXII

FRANNY'S RECKONING

Ovid, Missouri, Autumn 1862

Her Night

Missouri was a mistake. They'd had nothing but trouble since St. Louis. They should have taken another route to the territories.

She'd thought that by heading west, there might be more openness for her work. Not that there hadn't already been openness and interest, even outright desperation, for her to make contact with lost loved ones. But she thought that perhaps out in the broader expanses, farther away from the battlefields, that the openness would be both physical—plains, deserts—and spiritual, that the connection would be more pure and volatile, the way she imagined the air and the sun would be out there: lighter, quicker to change. And thus, perhaps, Betty would reveal herself. Betty, who'd been lost to her on a clear day by the ocean, might return in the clarity and openness of the West.

Now Franny was having her doubts. There was no clarity out here, even if it was away from where the great battles were being fought. If anything, the war was more with the people here, tearing into their lives by way of raiding parties, partisan lynchings, ambushes, threats, attacks, and revenge. At least back East she could hold her convocations in reasonable safety, even if cannon fire was audible and whole armies were engaged in combat less than a day's ride to the south. There was tragedy and carnage and grief abroad in the land, but at least back East warfare was uniform, recognizable, and it followed some kind of code.

In Missouri there was no such order. A baleful lawlessness prevailed. Southern partisans would storm and pillage the homes of Union sympathizers. The raids would be met with reprisals. As she progressed westward upriver on the Missouri, Franny heard accounts of farms burned and towns attacked. From the boat, she had seen dead livestock, shot and gutted; a family sitting stunned and naked on the riverbank, staring at the boat as it passed, a chimney the only remnant of their home.

Few people in Missouri were interested in spiritual convocations. Some citizens even feared gathering in large groups lest they become a target for the raiders frequently being called a strange epithet that went back to Napoleon's struggles with the Spanish: guerrillas.

Franny hadn't held a convocation since a small session on Sunday evening two weeks ago in St. Louis. Now she was lying on the ground, alone, at night, wrapped in blankets on a bluff above Ovid, Missouri, and she could hear gunfire. They'd been warned.

She was traveling with Hermes. That she was thoroughgoingly collaborating with Hermes was more accurate. And although she'd been having misgivings about the arrangement almost from the start, now as she listened to the crackle of rifle fire down below, she feared for him. He was down there in the town, attempting to rescue his Spiritscope.

As she listened to the shooting, she tried to make out any human sounds that might float up on the night breeze from the river valley—shouts, wails, cheers. There was nothing—only gunshots, sporadic, popping in fell bursts then lapsing into silence. And in that silence, she lay listening for the sound of the wagon or footsteps, yearning for it to be him, mortally afraid it might be someone else.

She had been with Hermes—in one fashion or another—since late summer. There had been an intricate minuet between them when they met out on the Spirit Trail—his name for the circuit of assemblies, services, convocations, tent shows, and tabernacles where conjurers like Hermes with his Spiritscope and Franny with her guided, inward journeys would appear. She would see his posters and handbills as she had that night years ago in New York. And, no doubt, he saw hers.

He began appearing at her convocations. He came first as a congregant, then as if by some means of legerdemain that left her unsure how he had insinuated himself, he was assisting her. He still performed with his Spiritscope, but in towns where Franny wasn't appearing.

"No sense duplicating our efforts," he'd said in that low, tuned voice of his. "There are spirits around enough for the both of us."

Then, one night in Harrisburg as he was dropping her off at her hotel, she told him she was thinking of traveling west to the territories.

"It won't be easy or entirely proper," he said. "It may even be dangerous. You weren't planning on going alone, were you?"

"I hadn't really planned anything yet," she said. "It was merely an idea."

A strong one, but she knew that he was correct about the dangers and, most likely, the propriety.

"I will be your escort," he said.

He turned out to be more. They performed together. Crossing Ohio and Illinois, where the towns lay farther apart than in the East and where cities were even more scarce, they found there to be not enough spirits for the both of them. They had new bills printed for the appearance of Dr. Zephaniah Hermes's Spiritscope followed by a convocation with the Guide to the Other World, Dame Frances Piermont.

They did tolerably well, and Franny harbored the feeling that somewhere, out in the territories, things would get better, would open up, *her* spirit would release itself, Betty would find her.

But Missouri made things difficult.

She and Hermes had decided it was safest to travel west by steamboat on the Missouri River. But as space was limited and passage was dear, Hermes booked them as man and wife.

It was no affront to Franny. She knew, and accepted, that she was more than complicit in the arrangement. She could allow as how she had even *sought* it. He was desirable. He was attentive. He was proximate. She was a woman alone.

The gunfire had subsided some time ago. Franny was not sure how long. She was well hidden. She rolled quietly onto her back and looked up at the stars. She could tell herself that all the people she knew were seeing the same sky tonight, that she wasn't alone, and that they were all under the same firmament together, but it felt like folly to think so. The blackness between the stars bespoke more about her orphaned marriage to Chester than any constellated pattern of light. He was gone. She, too, had left. And Otis, where was he? And now Hermes?

She listened. Five low hoots. A great horned owl. Distant. Could it be a man's signal? Hermes had told her of such tricks: raiders whistling bird-calls to one another before an attack. Her heart was hammering in her breast. One call. Nothing more. It must have been an owl. Silence again.

The steamboat *Reuben Truthahn*, which they had taken up the Missouri, would have been, in other circumstances, comical. Its hull was low-slung and bargelike, and the vessel was almost as beamy as it was long: a floating square. Its stern wheel was missing paddles, its superstructure bore a sorry and blockish resemblance to the Parthenon; and the wheelhouse, as Hermes pointed out, looked like a privy.

But it was the safest means of travel. Franny and Hermes even held a performance at dusk in the saloon but could not illuminate the room after dark, as the pilot blacked out the boat to avoid making the *Reuben T.* an easy target for snipers.

"We heard Quantrill might be out there," the captain had said, and Franny wondered if he hadn't invoked the name of the dreaded bush-whacker just to scare the passengers and make them all the more grateful they were on a riverboat with a swivel gun on the bow and deckhands as sentinels, moving toward Kansas City.

The apprehension—or the confinement—on the small vessel brought the entire complement of a dozen traders, transient cavalry officers, homestead-ers, and a pair of professional gamblers to the saloon.

They were a skeptical lot and more interested in debunking the me-chanics of the Spiritscope than in actually making contact with the Other World. Franny noticed with perturbation that Hermes had tailored his performance so that it was not so much a reverent (if spurious) connection with the spirits as it was an occasion for patter and jocular asides that had the tone of a back-of-the-wagon medicine show. It appealed to the fron-tiersmen, but she was so put off by it that she pleaded illness and forwent her portion of the program.

"It was not worthy of you," she told Hermes later when they were in their quarters. The boat had tied up to the riverbank for the night. They could hear the crewman on guard walking the deck above their heads. The walls of the cabins were thin planks. One of the cavalry officers was playing a Jew's harp in the next room. She whispered her reprimand.

Hermes sighed in the dark.

"It wasn't," he said softly, then his voice grew brittle as he went on: "But what you also mean is it wasn't worthy of you. You suppose you know the order of things out here, that you know what is worthy of me and what is worthy of you. Well, Frances, this is not New York or Pennsylvania or Mrs. Lincoln's parlor in Washington. This is not the London stage. It is not the house your father built on the bluffs of Maine, and I am not your brother-in-law or your husband. Everything is different out here. I am quick enough to see that. I am surprised you are not."

The blood rushed to Franny's face. The feel of it made her sense of indignation all the more lofty and even made her take a flashing pride in it. How *dare* he.

And yet . . . He was right. It was obvious. Almost instantly her anger began to crumble, and she felt a shame sweep in: she had told him too much. He knew all about her, she thought, to be able to use those names and places against her. She turned away from him, her crinoline scraping the bed and the dresser, and she felt trapped by the clothing she wore, wedged in the cabin with this man. She stifled a sob of frustration.

"We are in none of those places," he was now saying quietly—he *always* spoke quietly. "And I am none of those men. I love you."

Was she to suppose none of those other men did? She didn't dare ask. And besides, his voice was so quiet, so soft.

He was moving toward her; she could hear him behind her as she was realizing he had never said those precise words to her before.

"What did you say?" she asked.

There had been no sounds—no gunfire, no horses, no footsteps, not even the distant hoot of the owl—for some time now. She needed to relieve herself, and she guessed it would be safe to move. She carefully pushed the blankets back and walked silently to the edge of the clearing. Before he left, Hermes had swept a path through the leaves away from her hideout.

"This way if you must get up at night," he'd said, "you won't be rustling about, making noise."

It occurred to her that such foresight was just another element of mystery about the man. Was he familiar with such stealth? She knew so little. That had become one of the precepts of their liaison. In the beginning she had used it to keep her own distance from the reality that they were growing closer. Now, although she might reasonably expect him to reveal more of himself, he remained closed about his past.

Once, in western New York State—that area of religious fervor and fomentation called the Burned-over District—Hermes had precipitously announced he would be taking a break from performing. He would meet her in a week's time when she reached Binghamton.

That night, in the audience, Franny saw what she took to be a family in the front row: a tall, swarthy man in a black suit flanked by four younger women in gray frocks. They appeared to be members of a religious community. The man had the same soft, gray-green eyes as Hermes; the near umber, polished skin; and similar collar-length hair—though more gray— swept back from his face. He could have been Hermes twenty years hence. The women, Franny thought, must have been the man's daughters. All of them had the same dark complexions and exotic, almost Gypsy, features of the man. But she found herself wondering, even as she looked out at the audience and at the man and the women in their blindfolds, holding their leaves, if perhaps they might be his wives.

After the performance, she was surprised to see the man standing before her at the head of the line of supplicants and well-wishers who sought her after every show. He stood tall, had the same lengthy frame as Hermes. His black suit was old but clean, and he wore a stiff white shirt. The women waited in a row along the wall on the left side of the hall.

"Have you seen Zephaniah?" the man asked in a worn version of Hermes's voice. "I expected him."

"Why no," she said.

"You travel with him," the man said.

"I . . . Well . . ." Franny was not sure how the man could possibly know this. "Well, no, I don't. That is, I'm not."

It was just dawning on her that she'd never heard anyone call Hermes by the name Zephaniah. To most people it was "Doctor" or "Dr. Hermes." Franny herself always called him Hermes, even at their most intimate.

"I will see him in— That is, I *might* see him," she said. "Do you have a message?"

"No," the man said. "I should have expected him not to show. He knows what's good for him."

Then he thrust out to Franny the mask he still held.

"You are tolerable good at what you do," he said, and turned on his heel and strode from the hall with only the slightest wave to the women to indicate they should follow.

When, after meeting him in Binghamton, Franny asked Hermes about the man, Hermes became occluded and mumbled only that he didn't know any such fellow, but Franny suspected otherwise.

She still suspected otherwise. There was much to suspect about Hermes, she was thinking as she stood now in the clearing. She knew before she helped him with the Spiritscope that he'd hired assistants to travel with him to maintain and move the machine, to scout the audience for likely "prospects." She even suspected that the helpers were not always hired men. She doubted she was his first female traveling companion.

Yet it was easier to live with these unknowns than to pick at the locks. Besides, she had her own, bigger mysteries to trip loose: the spirit world, Betty. The child was so close sometimes. Franny could feel it in her breast as if a stone were about to be riven, but then, always at the last instant before the blow was struck—a retreat. And the stone, the weight, remained. How long could she keep seeking? She surprised herself at how devoted she had become. And it wasn't only a devotion to finding Betty that was alight within her. Franny had found solace and rejuvenation in the aid and inspiration she gave to others who sought their own lost ones, to all those pilgrims she encountered in all those convocations that stretched from where she stood on the bluff above the Missouri back to the brink of the Atlantic Ocean at Willing Mind.

She shivered. The night had grown cold. She could feel the frost on the grass crunch beneath her shoes. The chill prickled her nostrils. A last-quarter moon was rising. Still no sound from the village. She wondered how long before dawn.

The *Reuben T.* had put in at Ovid to take on fuel, but two nights before, raiders had burned the log yard down by the river. Sawyers were cutting more wood, but it would be a day at least before the boat could sail again.

Franny and Hermes had made arrangements to perform in the village schoolhouse and had hired a wagon to transport the Spiritscope from the dock to the school. When they returned to the riverboat, however, they found on their cabin door the note:

You are Yankees and you must leave
or your lifes you forfeit.

There were several identical notes on other cabin doors. The captain was storming about the upper deck near the wheelhouse, demanding to know who had snuck aboard and tacked up the notes. Or, he raged at his crew standing at attention before him, maybe no one had *snuck* aboard. Maybe they were *ushered* on. Maybe they *work* here. The crew was silent.

"Perhaps it was just meant for the cavalry officers," Franny whispered to Hermes.

"Even so, don't forget we're Yankees as well," he said to her. "Pack your belongings."

There was no show that night. "Canceled Due to Illness." By dark, Hermes had secreted Franny on the hilltop, told her he'd be back for her, said he was going to get the Spiritscope before there was trouble.

"I'll purchase the wagon we used," he said. "I don't think we should be traveling on that boat."

"Where will we go?" Franny asked.

"We're only about a day from Kansas City. Once we cross into the Nebraska Territory, things will be different."

"We don't have to," she said. "We could go back East. Another way. Farther north. We don't need to go to the territories."

He told her not to think about that now, to bundle up in the blankets and sleep in the bushes, and to wait.

Now she was back in her bedroll, alone and shivering. The owl called again. Still distant, but somehow it was more comforting this time. The moon had risen and was a pale hook over the river plain. She slept.

There came a ringing, and her first thought was that it was the maid's bell in Willing Mind. A small silver bell that her parents had kept on the dining room table. She loved the sound. Betty must have as well, for she had taken to laughing and running about the house, ringing the bell, and Mrs. Tyler would groan happily and call, "I'm coming, Mistress! Where are you? Where is my Betty?" And the child's delight and laughter and the bell would ring throughout the house, ring as now.

She was awake, gasping, sitting bolt upright, flailing at the branches in her face. A horse's wagon traces were jingling. That was the bell she'd heard. A dream. Not Betty. Again, not Betty. The wagon crested the hilltop. Hermes was whispering her name, pushing apart the bushes, reaching for her.

He had made it back safely, the Spiritscope fine, damaged a little in the hasty flight but reparable. Gray light was gathering in the east. She had been dreaming. They must leave now, he said.

There had been a skirmish: local partisan differences plus revenge for the wood yard fire. It was mostly errant gunplay, Hermes said. Bad marksmanship between timid combatants.

"It could have been much worse," he told her. "They did sink the boat, though."

"Who did?"

"I'm not sure," said Hermes. "Unionists or reb supporters. I don't know which. I made out three men chopping holes in the hull with axes. She sank at the dock. Only the wheelhouse and the funnels are still above water."

He said again they should leave now.

"Not wait for light?" Franny asked.

"No. We must make time before light," Hermes said.

"Will it be safe?"

"I heard the telegraph is still working. None of the fighters down there had the presence of mind to cut the wire. A cavalry company is riding out from Kansas City already. The road will be quite safe."

"You purchased the wagon for us?"

"It wasn't necessary."

"What do you mean?"

"In a state of confusion, sometimes fortune falls to him who has the quickest grasp."

"You stole it."

He ignored her and began scooping up and shaking out her bedding, tossing it into the wagon.

"Were many people hurt down there?" she asked.

"No. I think hardly any. It was, I'd say, a petty feud notable for its ineptitude rather than for its connection to the larger issues of the day. But things in Missouri will get worse. Count on it. Are you ready?"

She had stepped over to a small rocky ledge at the limit of the clearing. It looked down on the river, out across the plain to the west. A few young oaks with their dead leaves still clinging to their branches stirred in a small breeze below the top of the hill.

This was the moment she should have said that she was leaving him; that she should not be—should never have been—a party to chicanery or theft; that her talent, however flawed it might be, was necessarily pledged to the pursuit of her daughter, to the aspirations of honest seekers; that she was a pilgrim and he was a mountebank; that this was a pilgrimage; that she should have made all these things clear from the start, before they ever joined together. But she had been alone and confused.

And so she still was: a woman alone on the edge of a bluff, amid confusion and menace.

She said nothing. She needed him.

There was enough light in the sky to see the river fog lying in a gray, twisted braid cast across the countryside. Wrapped beneath it lay the curving line of the river.

"We'll be fine if we move along smartly," Hermes said from over by the wagon. "Would you come here, please? I need your help."

"Pardon?"

"I need you," he said.

And so she said nothing.

She walked over to him. He was tying a loose armature down on the Spiritscope. The catgut had snapped. The gut was invisible in the weak light. She couldn't see what he was tying.

"Just hold your finger there while I make the knot," he murmured.

His hands moved in the air. She felt, but could not see, the cord he tightened on her fingertip. She pulled it free just as he cinched the knot.

CHAPTER XXIII

THIRTY DROPS

Pennsylvania, November 1862

Her Card

She was now truly lost. No Great Bear to guide her. No day. No night. Never even venturing out onto the vestibule. Just the pitching of the train, making forward progress, she surmised, because trains move forward, don't they? Forward because vanderWees was in a white heat to . . .

"To glory," she remembered him crowing at one point. "To glory, glory, hallelujah!"

It was just the two of them in the private car now. Chester was gone, folded inside the past for her. Enveloped there with Joachim. With so much else. Folded inside the word meaning "to give praise."

She had not protested enough about Chester. About their desertion of Chester. She knew this. It had been between three and five days, she guessed, since that night in the tavern when vanderWees had fought with Chester and she had fled to the train and vanderWees had found her and had ordered the train to leave. She did not know much of what followed. Too much of vanderWees's praise. It rang in her ears. Along with the cannon report. The huge sound. Driving out all music. Or was that the opium, driving out sound altogether?

Some of the soldiers had said they'd shot to hell an Indian village. They had told her this as if they were slipping her a note, a clandestine bit of news that even they did not fully comprehend.

If they had shot to hell an Indian village—with the cannon? to protect themselves?—she had been asleep when it happened. She slept so much now. It was easier that way. But her ears kept ringing, drowning out all other sound.

She had known for weeks that she was tilting away from Chester—and he from her. It wasn't Chester's devotion to the mission. It wasn't even his drinking. She had lived with and around men of such disposition before. It was something else. Chester had pulled away *first*. There had been an abstraction about him that had entered the picture. It had made him withdrawn, sometimes even petty. Petty! So unlike Chester Ludlow, cable engineer, Zeus of the Union, hurler of lightning bolts with his Ludlow Gun. Petty. He would criticize her breath in the morning, the heaviness of her tread while he tried to work, or even her playing. And all the while vanderWees was there with his facile geniality, offering her praise.

He had even offered her real praise once or twice, had said he had known "women of the Continent" who had been artists, musicians, but that she was "different." He had said the word declaratively, with force, as if it were a card he'd slapped on a table, but facedown, so she didn't really know what he meant by the word *different* or how its meaning—its face— might change the course of the game.

Perhaps he'd meant he had offered others praise, too, but that they had not taken to it as avidly as she. Was that the difference? Thirty drops she was up to now. She apportioned them over the course of a day, or what she supposed to be the course of a day. She was under the spell of this praise fairly continuously. She had become enraptured by the dreaming it afforded, the visions. In the early stages, the splendors of the dreams were musical. She would hear pieces she had played while she seemed to float just off the ground, suffused with delight and hope.

But occasionally the harmoniousness of her dreams transmogrified into visions of the sea, and she was put in mind of the storm and the near catastrophe of her voyage on the *Agamemnon*. Then the sea would turn into a sea of faces, imploring, wrathful, despairing, surging upward by the thousands. . . .

Or so she felt. These were opiated visions, after all, given and taken during a time of war. And now vanderWees would give the war its end: this gun.

"Where is Chester?" she asked vanderWees only once, soon after the train had begun its journey back East from the Huron frontier.

"He'll be following soon," vanderWees had said. "I wired for the next train leaving the outpost with a timber shipment to have him on board. I told him to meet us in Washington. No more specific than that. I didn't want to disclose our route exactly. You look lovely. Tousled, I'd say."

She turned away and pulled the shawl she was wearing tighter around her neck. She knew he was staring at her back and smiling. Damn him. He plunked five random notes on the piano. They sounded coarse and abrasive. It occurred to her in that dark moment that music had disappeared from her dreams of late. As the sea and the faces had crept into her visions, music had crept out. There was nothing but an occasional orchestral noise.

She felt acutely aware of her passage over the tracks, felt herself standing, legs obscenely apart to give her balance in the rocking car as it (and the engine and the other cars and the *gun*) made its way toward the war.

She could see, behind her closed eyes, the track leading as to a calamity waiting offstage. Ahead of her: the war. There was a word Chester had used. Something he'd learned from Professor Thomson, who took it from the German. She couldn't remember the word. *Heat death.* No, that was a phrase; there was a word. Came from the German. She should know it. She needed more praise. She needed to club these visions and feelings out of her head. A billet of stove wood. She wanted to hit vanderWees. But she was clubbing her own head with her fists, pounding her skull and crying, now sobbing, woefully missing Chester Ludlow and noticing that Russell vanderWees had taken hold of her arms. *Entropie* . . . Entropy! The word. The calamity waiting offstage. VanderWees held her by the wrists and, with her arms bent almost painfully behind her, forced her to fall backward into her compartment, with him atop her, she who now was letting him force himself inside her, she who was forever in this train of his, bound by entropy, bound by praise. Praise for the cannon, the end of the war, him thrusting into her. Praise for the card she'd been dealt, the card and its terrible face. The card with the face. VanderWees's lips, its grimace, his thrustings. How she'd played this terrible card, praise her for it. Look into its terrible face.

CHAPTER XXIV

CANNISTEO GORGE

Various Post Offices and Pennsylvania, November 1862

A Letter Undelivered

> *Taplin Rd.*
> *London, SW*
> *19 Sept. 1862*

My Dear Mr. Trace,

    As there is no way I can be sure this letter will find you until such time as you answer, I must hope for now that find you it does and that it finds you well. I inquired of your employer as to your whereabouts in America and your employer said that was a good question, one he often asks himself because it is your job to be in contact with him. Nevertheless, he said he would endeavor to help this letter get to you, so I hope he—we—were successful. In that hope, I do write you now.*

    Following my encounter with you on the Great Eastern*, the gentleman (whom discretion bids me to refer to only as "E.O.") and I proceeded to Boston. "E.O." had hoped to find some scientists to help*

---

*I should say Mr. Clapp writes. Mr. William Clapp being a law clerk living upstairs who takes copy work occasionally and is most generous and gentlemanly to assist me with this letter.

him defend himself against the men who said it was his machinery that destroyed the object which discretion also bids me not name. Finding few defenders—none, really—in Boston, we traveled to Washington.

We arrived about a month after the fort in the Carolinas had been attacked. You must know from that time, war was a certainty. You also may have been in Washington yourself then. I kept looking for you, but to no avail.

To come to the point, we were among the crowd of citizens at Bull Run.

It was a Sunday morning in July, and all the city could hear the cannons. Everyone became certain the rebels were being repulsed. "E.O." was among the many who thought it would be an opportunity to witness history, that we should see "the spectacle that is battle," as he said. He hired a carriage, ordered the hotel kitchen to make us a picnic hamper, and off we rode. Hundreds of other people had the same idea.

The problem came at a stone bridge. By the time we arrived, the northern army was in retreat. They reached the bridge to find a crowd from the city had come out to watch their victory, and they started attacking us to get across the bridge.

It was a hell unleashed there, Mr. Trace. I see similar things in your pictures in the newspapers, and I shudder because it puts me in mind of what I saw that day.

Our carriage tipped over, our driver fled. "E.O." disappeared in the confusion. I was unhurt, but frightened to distraction.

I found "E.O." many hours later in an infirmary that was set up in a house near the river that runs toward the capital. I'd walked there. Walked and cried.

I found "E.O." stitching a boy's chest back together while the lad lay on the kitchen table, legs draped over, him just moaning. He was too weak even to scream. Everyone was. Only "E.O." looked as if he had enough energy to go all night at a country dance. It was horrible to see such things.

For the next two months, "E.O." helped the Federal army surgeons in the hospitals. He became a wizard at taking limbs off bodies. Neat and clean. He was a big help to them in the hospitals. He said he felt like a new man. A new surgeon, really. He was full of himself. He said he no longer cared about electricity. His attentions to me began to *diminish as well, which I found to be satisfactory. I was only too glad when he announced we were returning to England, which is where I am now as I write.*

Do you remember the plan I told you of the night we talked on the ship to America? I have already begun. I can say no more for now. I am writing to you because I am, I admit, frightened for my prospects. But I am hopeful as well. I hope you are the same way about yours.

If this letter reaches you, know I hope to see you again. Know, too, I watch for your pictures in the papers, Mr. Sketch-man. That way I know you are there. When it is over or you are through with it, come find me. I remain your friend . . .

Maddy

A Bridge

It was late November when a rumor reached Jack Trace. He'd wandered away from the war after the evening of the convocation. He'd told Franny that he knew what he wanted to do, but the knowledge seemed to have evaded him. The war moved south; Trace wandered in other directions.

Now he was in Carthage Gap, a hill town in the Alleghenies where the mountains make their serious bend toward West Virginia. Teamsters frequented the town, as the gap, too steep for the railroad, provided a conduit for wagon traffic that was miles shorter than the railroad, which had to travel farther south around Evans Mountain and cross a trestle at the gorge over Cannisteo Creek.

The rumor that reached Jack Trace concerned a wreck in the gorge. More news of it came in with each wagon. East- or westbound, gossip was fluttering up and down the road: rebel sappers had blown a bridge; a train wreck; the trestle at Cannisteo Gorge; train went down; strangest thing; enormous fire and explosions; a military train; a man's and a woman's bodies pulled from the wreck; burned beyond recognition; soldiers died as well; a man and woman, though; two bodies.

The disparate, confusing elements of the news shouldn't have put Trace in mind of Maddy and Whitehouse. Logically, wherever they were, it couldn't have been on some military train in Pennsylvania. But he'd been left almost bereft of logic and sequence after his visions at Franny's convocation, so there didn't seem to be a need for a thought to make sense; the thought only had to exist. Two bodies: Maddy and Whitehouse. Beyond recognition. Or: Maddy and him, Jack Trace. A man and a woman. Two bodies.

He had to go see it.

He tied up his blanket roll and walked out of town. For the first time in weeks he moved with direction. He traveled a day and a night, all the time anxious—a man and woman.

Cannisteo Gorge was a geological surprise, a sudden dropping away of the piedmont into a slit carved by Cannisteo Creek that had eaten its way through the folded sandstone abutting Evans Mountain, a long, unpopulated, curving ridge, forests of oak and laurel, sumac and ferns on its slopes. All but the laurel were bare of their foliage now that it was November. The fallen leaves were brown and curled in the frost the morning Trace arrived at the trestle.

It had been a new wooden span across the gorge. Isolated from any town, it was about a quarter of a mile long and two hundred feet high at its tallest. Its timbers, the braces and piers, were still pale and unweathered. Where they hadn't been burned or blasted away, they were almost orange in the morning light.

It was Sunday, and about a score of curious sightseers had ridden or walked out to the wreck. Farmhands, youths tossing stones out into the chasm, men who appeared to be merchants from the nearest town who'd brought their families out after church.

From each side of the gorge, the broken span cantilevered into space. A bite, a hundred yards wide, had been taken out of the bridge. Crossties dangled from the severed ends of the track. The rails, twisted by the heat and force of the blast, stuck out into space like prongs.

It was obvious what had happened. The train had come out of the rock cut on the far side of the ravine. The curve through the ledges over there meant that the engineer couldn't have seen the dynamited span ahead in the dark, and the train went right into the hole that had once been the bridge. The way the rails bent downward, Trace could picture the locomotive steaming into space, drive wheels spinning, maybe never even braking, just plunging hard out into air, pulling all the other cars along, one by one. Then the explosions.

He had to see more.

Trace had become accustomed to heights back on the *Agamemnon*, so he didn't think twice about going out on the bridge. He just strode away from the sightseers and onto the tracks. But at sea, he always had lines or the masts to cling to. Here, there was nothing: no trusses above, no railing— just the tracks resting on towers. He had to walk out toward a void, making mincing steps to match the spacing of the crossties beneath his feet, and between the ties was the flickering sight of the long drop to the rock cliffs, the scrub brush clinging to ledges and the angry little creek churning so far below. It began to unnerve him.

"Scared of heights?"

Trace froze. He hadn't known anyone had come out on the bridge with him. He carefully looked around. One of the young men he'd taken to be a farmhand was loping along, striding over the ties two at a time. He came up to Trace and stopped.

"Me and my brother was on the gang built this thing. Last spring. Scared of heights? Nice bridge, hunh?"

"No," said Trace. "I mean, yes, it's nice. And, no, I'm not scared of heights."

"Just careful, right?"

"Quite. Just careful."

The fellow was probably still in his teens. He had a pimpled face, brown hair greased flat, and pale fuzz on his chin. He was in his Sunday church clothes, all wrists and ankles.

"Follow me. You got to go out almost to the end to see it best. But you don't want to go too far. I know when to stop. Call me Lucas."

"Very well," Trace said as the youth worked his way past Trace, who had to fight the urge to crouch and grab the rail, the ties, anything. They began walking forward, Lucas now going slowly for Trace's benefit.

"This is it," Lucas said after they'd walked another thirty yards. "Don't want to go no more."

Trace wouldn't have dared. He probably wouldn't have gone out that far had he not been with the boy, whom he'd foolishly trusted simply because he'd said he'd built the bridge.

They were so far above the ravine and so close to the blasted section,

Trace wondered if the tracks they were standing on might begin to sway and whip back and forth if a breeze were to pick up.

The air was calm, though, and Jack could look down directly onto the wreck.

"Something, hunh?" Lucas said quietly.

It was. Two hundred feet below, down at the bottom of the gorge was a locomotive, lying broken on its side, a small whorl of smoke still threading up from somewhere in the firebox or from the shattered boiler. The other cars lay broken and burned in a zigzag pattern in the creek: a firewood tender, the charred remains of blown-out boxcar, and a burned caboose. Then there was the cracked hulk of something that left Trace puzzled. Long, cylindrical, segmented, dull black in color, it resembled an enormous cannon snapped in two. The artillery piece, if that indeed was what it was, spanned the width of the creek and then some. And near it, with wisps of smoke spooling from the scorched and destroyed interior, were the remains of a richly appointed railcar. Even after the fall from the trestle, after the explosions and fire and two days lying on the gorge bottom, the car's brass brightwork and gilded adornments were catching a little of the weak but clear November sun.

"Did anyone survive?" Trace asked.

"Not a one."

"How did they get to them?"

"Half a day's slog up the creek from around there. Half a day back. My brother went. I didn't. My brother says everybody down there was deader than rocks."

"Soldiers?" Trace asked.

"All burned up."

Trace had to know: "Anyone else?"

"Man and a woman. Pulled them out of that car. The shiny one."

"Burned?"

"Nope. Crushed."

"I'd heard they'd been burned."

"Ain't true. Crushed. But you know what?" The boy was whispering now, and it felt strange to Trace to be straining to hear a boy whisper while they stood practically in midair above a ravine and a train wreck.

"They was in the same bed. And they was naked."

Trace swallowed. "Who were they?"

"Don't know. My brother says the woman was blond. He could tell on account of she was naked."

Trace became aware of his own breathing. Not Maddy, he thought. The creek's feathery rushing sound far below was the only noise up there on the bridge. Not Maddy.

Suddenly, the boy grabbed Trace's arm, jerked it left, jerked it right, then pulled it in close while he shouted, "Whoa! Whoa! Saved yer life!"

"*Goddamn you!*" Trace screamed.

The boy was laughing. He let go of Trace's arm.

"We did that all the time, my brother and me, when we was working out here on this thing. 'Saved yer life!' 'Saved yer life!' We'd always scare each other. Scare you?"

"Goddamn you!" Trace couldn't bring his voice under control. "*Yes!* You idiot! Go away. Don't touch me. Get off this bridge. Leave me alone. Goddamn it."

"Jeezum, mister."

"Please. Just. Go away." Trace was gulping, trying to rid the crying sound from his voice.

"Yeah, well. My ma is calling me anyhow."

He pointed back to the side of the gorge where the sightseers stood, tiny heads peeking over laurel bushes. A woman was waving, her voice a bleating call to her son.

The boy slipped by Trace.

"You was pretty brave to come out here. None of them others would," he said. "Be careful now. Sorry about 'Saved yer life.'"

"All right," Trace said. He could breathe again. He didn't dare shut his eyes, so he fixed his gaze on a white pine on the far cliff to steady himself. The boy left, hopping ties now three at a time, making his mother bleat all the more back there on solid ground.

Through the remainder of the day, for the whole time Trace sat out on the end of the trestle, he would occasionally turn around and check to be sure Lucas wasn't stealing up behind him to play tricks again. The distant sound of the creek was enough to mask any approaching footsteps. Someone *could* have stolen up on him.

But no one did. For reasons he couldn't at first explain, Trace stayed on. There were a few more sightseers who came to view the bridge and the wreck, but they remained back by the road. Perhaps it was too dangerous on the bridge. Perhaps only a knave and an Englishman were fool enough to venture out there.

Jack gingerly worked his way down to sit on one of the crossties, with his legs dangling out into space. It filled him with a soaring, hawklike sensation. But it was the magnitude and the strangeness of the destruction below that were even more compelling and what kept him there: the broken cannon, the sailing cantilever of the shattered trestle. The feeling of flight gave Trace a perspective of distance, a capacity to abstract what he saw below, to see shapes, geometries, curves, angles. There was a dynamism, reposing, fractured, rearranged. The cannon—curved, segmented . . . He'd imagined something similar when he thought of the mural, the one he dreamed of . . . *Progress.* He didn't know what those shapes were or what they meant, but they were part of the vision. Cylinders. Or pistons. Or something that would slip through the air . . . And the teetering, spindly, yet magnificent towerlike structure that the dynamited trestle had become, that was to be in the picture as well. If not directly represented, then, well, the *feel* of it. His suspension on the tracks out in space . . . he wanted that feel in his picture of the future, too. A look over all the land. Strange to think it was this destruction that brought him to this feeling.

Jack took out the one pocket notebook and the pencil that he'd saved on his wanderings, and sitting on the broken arm of the bridge, as if floating, he began to draw.

CHAPTER XXV

FAR TO THE WEST

Far to the West, November 1862

Far to the West

Far to the west, Chester Ludlow is walking along railroad tracks through a forest, heading east. He stops in the chill moonlight. His head is clear for the first time in months. He's had nothing to eat or drink for two days, save for some water from a spring he found near the tracks before nightfall. All he's done is walk.

Moonlight faintly limns the rails ahead of him. They make him think of a pair of wires, stretched taut and true, joining somewhere in the distance.

In his pocket, he carries a handbill. He saw it tacked to the clapboards of a dry-goods store in a town he'd walked through at dawn a week ago. The bill announces a "convocation of persons with connections to, or interest in, the spiritual world." Franny's picture, looking like a cameo portrait, is in the center of the flier. She has, the sheet says, "opened the way for the living to unite with the departed." The bill is outdated, Chester has noticed that. He doesn't even know the name of the town where he found the handbill. He just tore it off the building's siding and kept walking. He had wanted to keep the picture with him. Somehow that had seemed important at the time and has grown more so as he progresses on his journey.

It is good he has disappeared for a while, he thinks. He might stay this way for some time to come. Still, he is walking east, and he knows that will eventually lead him back into the war. He supposes that has to be.

But for now, he is resting a moment. Then he looks down the tracks to see her again. She is a small girl, dressed in white, balancing where the rails seem to join in the darkness. She is there only a moment, for when Chester begins walking toward her, she is gone. It is a little game they have been playing for a couple of days and nights now. He finds that it pleases him. He is grateful she is there, and he understands she must always vanish, leaving only him and the empty tracks ahead. And he must always keep walking anyway, he knows, so he begins again, continuing his progress toward, then through, then past, the war.

BOOK FOUR

OTIS LUDLOW'S JOURNAL

Ireland, 1866

Foilhommerum Bay

Forge ahead, but back in time.

I remember our rooms were in a neighborhood of marginal respectability near the Schipperskwartier in Antwerp. The sun must have shone at least once during the year and a half we were there, for I do recall seeing the fine old Hanseatic guild halls with their gables like rococo triangles all aglow. But mostly I remember the putty-gray skies and the piss-stained snow piled at the curbs and the creases of sooty ice between the cobbles. The low, ground-level vistas of a ten-year-old boy seeing with both his eyes back then: the small streets that twisted away from the larger Avenue de Commerce; the clumsy revolutions of the solid wooden wheels of the farmers' carts; the square-rigged masts that were a profusion of lacework and armatures in the Grand Bassin dock, while out on the Scheldt, lateen-rigged tenders sliced lightly through the brown chop. Antwerp was not a golden city for me. Antwerp was gray and dark and foreign. Antwerp was where my father took half my sight.

Father wanted to become a great painter. He wanted to live where the old masters had painted. So he brought his family to Antwerp.

My mother, Constance, lay in her family plot in Conway, New Hampshire, after a fall from a horse had taken her when I was eight.

Father had been a middling successful lawyer in Conway, but his true talent lay—and always had—with drawing and painting. His downfall lay—and always had—with his temper and his ambition. He longed to make a name for himself as an artist.

And he wanted to elope with the daughter of one of his clients—had to elope, if my calculations are correct.

"Because of Brueghel and Rubens!" I could imagine him bellowing about our decamping to Antwerp. "Because of Rembrandt! Because of the whole Flemish folderol!" And then he would have shaken his fist at me or anyone who dared question his purpose and, by extension, his destiny.

Funny to think of Chester as an immigrant. He was conceived in New Hampshire, born in Antwerp, only to arrive back in America two years later with just his mother. Father and I had to wait to leave for America while my wound healed. The marriage never healed, and when Father and I did return, Chester and his mother were living with her family in Conway. Father and I moved into a cottage north of Bartlett, the last town before the Great Notch in the White Mountains.

Father and Chester's mother avoided each other from then on, and so, by necessity, did Chester and I. Father and I lived on the edge of what was then mountain wilderness. I taught at the one-room Bartlett school—at fourteen, the school's youngest pedagogue. (I believe the eye patch I wore back then probably added to my authority.) I worked in the woods with logging crews in the summer. Father painted. A cold truce governed our life in the cottage.

Once, a shopkeeper had the temerity to ask Father what had happened in Antwerp between him and his wife. (Of course, I knew what had happened; I'd seen what had happened; I'd been half blinded because of what I'd seen.) I kept my mouth shut. Father grew steely, stared at the merchant, and replied: "We fell apart."

Wrong. He fell apart. Father would paint in fits of either inspiration or rage. Inspiration, rage, or something else altogether, something I understood and suffered myself.

I am speaking of the accesses. The family trait, visiting its tremors and visions only on us few. Chester avoided its touch, though his daughter did not. Neither did Father. Neither did I. Aside from the unconsciousness, or semiconsciousness, that the malady inflicts—the humiliation of being reduced in public to an uncontrolled and insensate invalid—the affliction also left us, upon recovery, with an ineffable longing, a desire to go further somehow. And that desire can become a ruling passion of one's life. I know that desire was behind Father's painting and behind my own long voyages around the world. The seizures and their concomitant effects were what bound me to Father. Little else did, especially after what happened in our family in the Low Countries in 1822.

I see our little family in Ostend, Belgium, on a seaside holiday from the heat of Antwerp. It is summer and sultry. We walk often during the month we stay by the sea. We walk along the Digue, the stone bulwark some half a mile in length and thirty feet in height that separates the town from the strand, protects the streets and buildings from the ocean's storm surges, and provides a promenade along which visitors and holiday throngs can take in the sea air. Mostly it is Germans who are there, and they are effusive, as the great majority of them have never seen the ocean before. Even on thick, listless days when the gray Noordzee heaves grudgingly against the shore and the haze hangs heavy and warm over all, still the Germans whoop and clap their hands from the Digue: "Der Zee! Der Zee!"

Father, with his leonine red hair and his robust, wide-shouldered stride, cuts a swath through the mingling and milling holiday crowd. We—his son, his new wife, their baby—follow in his wake as if drawn by some propulsive back current that he creates behind him. He walks along, nodding at the Germans, scanning the horizon, and emitting a fragrant trail of cigar smoke.

In the mornings, Father leaves the hotel and goes to the far western end of the strand, the section known as the Paradis, where gentlemen are permitted to bathe "sans costume." He takes me there occasionally. He seems even more robust and expansive when swimming among the men who slap the water with their overhand strokes and emerge on the beach with water dripping in sheets off their flaccid bellies with runic hair patterns plastered all over their pale hides and their generative organs hanging like wet velvet purses. In the bathhouse, he shows me something penciled in English on the tongue-and-groove boards of a locker door. A limerick:

> There was a young maid from Ostend,
>> Who swore she'd hold out to the end;
>> But, alas, halfway over
>> From Calais to Dover
>> She done what she didn't intend.

He has me read it aloud for the other men. The Englishmen among us join in before I am through. Father applauds. The Germans among us smile. In the sea, Father tosses me in the air by dunking me first, then pulling me sucking out of the water and hurling me upward to come crashing down in the marbly, hissing surf. Often he continues to smoke his morning cigar whilst swimming. Other men applaud our fun, the Germans especially.

At night we walk to the eastern end of the Digue to look across the harbor channel to the Bassin de Chasse with its massive iron gates built by Napoleon. The basin is filled with seawater at high tide, and the gates are closed to entrap the flow. Then, at low tide, the gates open and the torrent of water rushing out to sea sweeps the harbor clear of its daily accrual of ocean sand, thus dredging the port. When low tide comes of a summer's night, a crowd gathers to watch the rushing of the water and the resultant luminescence, which makes the harbor glow with an unearthly beautiful green light that moves the Germans—and everyone—to applaud. Father tells me one night that the glow is the result of millions—maybe billions—of tiny sea creatures that can flash luminously like glowworms, like stars.

Is it the pale coruscation of the watery light that brings on my first seizure? (Green emanations have been with me at moments of the affliction ever since.) When the attack first hits, I fall on the Digue. Father runs over and holds my head. I can discern enough to know what he is doing. And his wife lets out with her own long-drawn gasp and near shout, "Make the boy stop that! Make him stop!"

Later, when I'm resting in the hotel room, Father tells me about the affliction, his own experience with it, how other Ludlows have had it, and I listen silently. In the following days, I notice his wife increasingly isolates herself from me.

"Witnessing what happens to us is off-putting to some," Father tells me.

I rest in bed for a day. In my mind, I cling to how he said "us."

He does not paint on this holiday by the sea. He does sketch, though. He always brings his pad on our promenades and stops periodically to capture some traveler or merchant or sea bird. Everywhere he goes—the Digue, the strand, the town streets, the hotel, the market—he sketches.

"It is difficult to think of you as ever having been a lawyer," his wife says to him once, and I cannot tell if she is criticizing him or speaking wistfully. He ignores her.

So she sits quietly on a bench looking seaward. I stand near her. The Flemish nanny, Belinde, rocks Chester in his perambulator a few yards distant. Father is sketching us. Belinde watches him.

He often visits the daily auction at the Huâtrières, the oyster pens in their circular market pavilion, at the east end of the Digue. Oysters are not in season in the summer, but there are lobsters from Norway and plenty of turbot caught off Blankenberge up the coast. The fish are sold in lots mostly to women who later resell them from their stalls or carts or shops.

Father, I notice, is often sketching one monger, a young, handsome blond woman who laughs each day she sees us come into the Huîtrières.

The dealings at the Huîtrières are by Dutch auction in the central, open courtyard. The auctioneer, from his dais, begins by setting a high price for each lot, then gradually lowering the price until someone calls out, "Myn!" and thus a single bid closes the deal.

"Much simpler than the American way," Father says. "They should auction paintings like Belgian fish."

One day, I am there alone with him. His wife is resting; baby Chester and Belinde are also back at the hotel. Father is sketching. A crate of large, robust lobsters is up for bidding. Father smiles at the young blond woman. He is sketching her again. Her eyes widen with eagerness as the auctioneer lifts two large lobsters up from the pens for the approving crowd. I am struck by the armored legs scratching the air; the claws waving, biting at nothing; the strange submarine monstrousness of the creatures. But I am more drawn to whatever is going on between Father and the monger, whatever is in the intensity of his concentration on her, in the happy nervousness of her smile, whatever it is that when the auctioneer calls out fifty francs to start the bidding for the lot, Father immediately shouts, "Myn!" to the surprise and gasps of all the other mongers and the ardent blushing of the girl, who later puts the lot in her cart.

Perhaps I would think no more of this, were it not for the events of an evening that autumn back in Antwerp. There had been a row between Father and his wife. Perhaps over money, perhaps over her longing to return to America. These arguments were increasingly commonplace in our household. They often resulted in his wife retreating with Chester to her room on the floor above the studio at the back of the building—as far away from Father's atelier as possible. He would rage off to his paints to work, to drink, to brood.

The argument that night must have been particularly severe, for by the next evening, there was still no rapprochement. She was in her room; he was in the studio; I was at large in the rest of the apartment. Belinde had prepared me a meal, then had left for her evening off. I tiptoed to the closed door of the back bedroom. I thought perhaps I would knock, inquire as to Father's wife's well-being. But, of course, that would have been a pretense merely to afford me companionship, even if from a woman who was tolerant of me at best, cool or distracted or distraught otherwise. As I stood before the door, though, I heard her inside, singing to the baby. Singing a lullaby. The song paralyzed me. I could not embolden myself to knock. Sweet as her muffled voice sounded to me, I knew in there I would be a foreigner. Son of my father, I would be an interloper from the enemy camp. She had her Chester. I must, I thought, find someone else.

So I took a candle and stole down the stairs to the small room behind the studio. This was Belinde's closet, a tiny room with a bed and trunk for her belongings. On previous explorations, I had discovered this room had a small knothole in the wall through which I could observe much of Father's studio. By quietly sliding Belinde's trunk over to the wall, I could peek through the hole.

I saw the Ostend fishmonger, naked. Shielded by screens from the street windows, the fishmonger was modeling for Father. The wholly novel sight of an unclothed woman made me feel that I was about to be sucked through the knothole as my breath escaped my body. My chest constricted. My mind seemed to shrink me to nothing. I was stunned. How did she get here? Had they done this before? Did Father bring her here for this? Is this what always happens when he rages off to his studio?

I cannot say how long I watched. I must have witnessed the seduction, the abandonment of his painting for the other pursuit. I watched, I know, the entire act unfold on the draped chaise upon which the monger reclined.

When it was over, I slumped down on the nursemaid's bed. I was exhausted, heated, utterly confused, almost as if I'd had a visitation and, alas, determined to see more . . . if only I could gather my strength. I lay on Belinde's hard mattress and stared at the guttering candle. I could hear the voices on the other side of the wall: some laughter, a snatch of a song, more talk, a denial, some angry words from him, some from her, other more confusing sounds that were no longer recognizable as words. As the sounds dropped from language into something less intelligible, I found curiosity drawing me up once more. I climbed back upon the trunk and peered into the knothole. I was to see more of the same: our half-clad father from the rear, the fishmonger beneath him. But in a moment, they halted. He disappeared from my view; she remained, agitated, pulling the chaise's drape around her. It was too dark by the one lamp he had illuminating the studio to see any more particularly than that, to see what had caused their seeming alarm. Had I made a noise? No. Was someone coming from the outside? No. His wife? No.

The answer I learned in the next instant, as I heard Father curse, "Damn you, Belinde!" and I saw a flash of red explode inside my head, and I howled with pain as I leapt backward and fell off the trunk.

The candle I'd brought into the nursemaid's room had undone me. The fishmonger had noticed the speck of light that had shone through the knothole disappear when I rose to stare again into the atelier. She knew somebody was watching from the next room. Father, enraged that it was Belinde, stabbed through the hole with the shaft of one of his paintbrushes.

It was a wound that should not have been blinding but for the infection that ensued. When the fever had abated and I had regained consciousness, I learned that

Chester and his mother had gone, that Father was staying with me, that we would be returning to America when I was able to travel, and that now I was blind in one eye.

Everything before that night I recollect with the hindsight of two eyes. Everything since comes to me by way of one. A singular vision. A play on words, yes, but one that defines what I'd lost and what I'd gained. I would despise our father for what he'd done, and that was what drove me, as soon as I was able, out into the world. As a result of what happened, our father swore he would never paint another human figure, except in the smallest renderings, as tiny objects to show the scale in the great landscapes he would henceforth produce. That was how our father did penance for his injury to me: he transformed his painting, his art, his destiny. He bent my injury to suit his purpose. This singularity of attention, this self as measure of the world: I know it well. It is as much a part of being a Ludlow as the visitations that show me what neither eye—seeing nor blind—could ever apprehend.

CHAPTER XXVI

CABLEMEN

London and Maine, Winter–Spring 1865

Faeries by Day, Zob by Night

The letter lay opened near his jars of paints and mineral spirits on a shelf so color-splattered, it looked like a rookery for birds that had been fed nothing but pigments. He had read the letter, but he'd rather have forgotten it.

Caliban's View was what he was working on today. It was of Prospero's island, seen from the mouth of the cave of *The Tempest*'s mooncalf. The cave mouth. This was the dominant motif of all his paintings lately: the foreshortening, the sense that one was viewing the world through a keyhole or a telescope or through an opening in thick undergrowth or foliage.

And the subjects so viewed were always the same—scenes of elves and sprites and sylphs caught in moments of common faerie toil: building a tiny Yule bonfire, curing the wings of a slain butterfly to make a faerie king's robe, a nutshell mail coach drawn by crickets galloping down the high road on a mossy log. He hadn't lost his facility for exactitude and minutiae, only now he was compressing it into canvases less than a foot square. And unlike his drawings of the *Great Eastern* disaster, the cable expedition, or the war, his faerie paintings were not at all in demand. That was why the letter, opened and read, kept distracting him.

"It has taken us some while and effort to find you," the letter began, "and we hope that we have found you well and willing to return. . . . "

They had discovered his hiding place. Upon returning from America, Jack Trace had abandoned his rooms in the City and had moved to this retreat beyond the suburbs, a cottage on a lane off the road to Norwood. It was a sylvan hideaway with a little lawn and stile that opened onto a small flower garden. Here he could work in seclusion on his faerie paintings.

The faerie paintings were inspired by Trace's reading of *A Midsummer Night's Dream* while sitting alone on the porch of his cottage one spring evening. The paintings were going to be his way of biding his artistic time until he could create his mural, *Progress*. The subjects—faeries, pixies, sprites—were his anodyne for America and the war and, now, his night work.

He had begun by painting several whimsical studies of Titania and Bottom *en amour*. He decided to make one of them a gift to a reacquaintance he had made upon returning to England.

"I predict it will be very popular," Maddy had said from behind Trace as he hung the little picture at the top of the stairs of a certain house near Mayfair. "All the girls are going to like it."

The "girls" were Maddy's. The whole house where the picture now hung was Maddy's. It was a fashionable and most tasteful establishment patronized by if not the very summit of London's gentlemanly society, then at least by those on the upper slopes of it. Four floors, comfortable rooms, much brocade and damask, Moroccan carpets, glass fringe on the gas lamps, deep red velour, maroons and bright blues on the dresses that made the dozen or so "associates" who lodged—or worked—there with Maddy appear so vivacious in the gaslight, yet would, as Trace with his painter's eye could tell, make the girls look garish in daylight. But this was not a daylight establishment. Maddy ran it, having invested what she'd salted away from her years as Whitehouse's niece.

She'd made the down payment by means of a silent partnership with the majordomo of the Bardolph, who had managed over the years to find the odd bundle come his way when the house's nightly take was calculated. How fortunate, then, he'd become chummy with Mr. Whitehouse's niece, who'd spent so much time in the Bardolph's discreet lodgings on the top floor.

Theirs was a chaste partnership. The majordomo kept his distance from Maddy's (he was happily married with three lovely daughters and a comfortable cottage residence in Twickenham), only rarely stepping out from behind the fiduciary curtains when it was necessary for a male presence to effect negotiations with bankers, lawyers, suppliers, the constabulary, or municipal officials who had to be kept amenable to a pleasure house in their precinct. Maddy was the madam of the establishment, and her chastity in the partnership was manifested in her self-imposed disqualification from the nightly commerce of her place of trade. She was not for sale.

There was even a song about it, sung sometimes sotto voce at clubs over cards, or lustily in hansom cabs full of prowling gay blades, or whimsically in finer gentlemen's eating establishments around London when the question of what to do for postprandial amusement arose.

No laddy gets Maddy at Maddy's;
  No laddy gets Maddy alone.
  Though the selection is rare
  Of the bosoms so bare
  That to Heaven you'll think you have flown,
  Still . . . No laddy gets Maddy at Maddy's,
  No laddy gets Maddy alone.
  Though she's all that you long for,
  Her prize is a closed door,
  You'd sooner get blood from a stone.

Maddy's never lacked for clientele, and it may have been the unavailability of Maddy herself that was a chief attractor. Swains of all ages and stripes fancied they would be the one to win the woman with the alluring scar near her eye that gave her countenance a mysterious, haughty demeanor but also undercut it with a slight perpetual wince, as if this world through which she so comfortably glided was really all too much.

It was the fellow with the tall hair and the large frame who seemed to be the most successful with Maddy. Not that anyone ever saw Jack Trace and Maddy slipping up the stairs together.

Trace had found Maddy soon after he returned from America. Her letter had never found him, but he had visited the Bardolph, and the majordomo there knew just where to direct him. Trace would visit Maddy's occasionally but rarely went upstairs. Once in a while, when Maddy would insist, would worry that his melancholia looked too ponderous, would say that he needed a bit of relaxing, she would assign one of the associates to spend a little time with her "old friend." For that's what Maddy had become for Jack, that and a broker for his secret commerce.

One of Maddy's patrons had seen Trace's faerie paintings and sought to employ him. For more than a year now, Jack Trace had been making his chief income as a collaborator with a Mr. Zob. Every few weeks, Maddy would send a message to Trace's cottage that Mr. Zob had left a parcel for him. Trace would arrive at Maddy's to pick up the package. A few nights later, Trace would return with a portfolio of drawings for Mr. Zob. Jack Trace was Mr. Zob's personal pornographer.

Or *co*-pornographer, as Mr. Zob himself was writing the tale for which Trace was the illustrator. While Jack Trace was spending his daylight hours painting small, delicate windows into a faerie kingdom, by night he was receiving his assignments and executing his drawings for Mr. Zob's priapic story of liaisons and couplings and perversities that girdled the globe through "the fleshpots of Paris," "the seminal streams of the Nile," "the steamy loins of Araby," "the Nubian meat markets on the margins of the Sahara," and "the nymphomaniacal naughtiness of the opium dens of Shanghai," all as rendered in pen and ink by Jack Trace, who for the enterprise had picked his own nom de plume: Obz.

But this bipartition of his imagination was frazzling Jack. The more he worked on Zob's assignments—for which Zob was remunerating him most handsomely—the more he felt constrained to flee into his faerie world.

"You need a holiday," Maddy told Trace when he showed up at her place one evening. She had a package for him and invited him into the sitting room.

So, she thinks I need a holiday. Sweet of her, he mused. He sometimes—in the heated stews of his nighttime imagination stimulated by the wild eroticism of Zob's fantastical story—would imagine himself and Maddy as the subjects of the depravities and ecstasies he was so lavishly rendering on paper. Zob's narrative was a preposterous round-the-world quest by the dashing writer or inventor or ex-British army officer, Pit Rippons. The hero sought the mysterious Lady E, who was a world-traveling artiste, marchioness, or perhaps even a nonexistent phantom. The quest was really a pretext for the hero to be accosted, seduced, forced, or swept into sexual congress with great frequency, dispatch, and variety wherever he went.

"I would love a holiday," Trace said.

"Have you answered that letter yet?" Maddy asked. She knew about the letter that lay opened, and read, back at Trace's cottage. He had told her of its contents on his last visit, how it kept nagging at him.

One of the associates sat at the spinet and began to play something soft and lulling. Trace felt soothed for a moment, as if perhaps he could float away and not answer Maddy's question about the letter. A gentleman on a divan near the piano blew smoke rings from his cigar. The girl on his lap giggled languidly and poked each one with her index finger, swirling the clouds in the air.

"No," Trace said.

"Well, I think you should," said Maddy. She straightened the lace antimacassar on the lounge where Trace sat. He was up on the edge of the cushion. Mr. Zob's packet was on the floor between his boots.

Trace never had to ask Maddy directly about the identity of Mr. Zob. They both, in their own ways, knew.

"That's the last of it," Maddy said.

Trace looked up at her. She was surveying the room, a pleasant hostess's smile on her face, a true, glittering satisfaction in her eyes as she scrutinized the little world of pleasure and ease she had created. It was only her voice, as she spoke to Trace, that had sounded sad.

"There's to be no more packets," she said.

"How do you know? Do you read these as they come through here?" Trace had to ask. He was now holding up the parcel.

Maddy shook her head. "But I know the story. He tells me what happens. The story's over."

"He *tells* you?" Trace wasn't sure he wanted to hear this.

Maddy nodded.

"Has he told you the *whole* story, all along? The *details*?"

Again, a nod. She fussed with the lace some more, realized she'd just done that, patted it, and folded her hands in front of her dress.

Well, of all things, Trace thought, *Maddy is blushing.*

"He has," she said. "It's been his pleasure."

"That's what he comes here for?"

"They come here for all sorts of things, Mr. Sketch-man."

Now it was Trace who blushed, at the sound of her old nickname for him.

"Mr. Zob prefers to spend his time here in narration."

"With you?"

"Mostly, of late. In the beginning he would take one of the associates."

"And just talk?"

"Or read aloud. And then whoever heard the latest in the story would tell the rest of us, you know, after business. We'd sit down here, a little before dawn, when everyone had gone home or was fast asleep, and we'd all hear the latest from Mr. Zob as related by one of us, or me."

"So it was like a blooming story hour," Trace said.

"Pit Rippons never finds her, you know." Maddy was pointing at the packet in its brown paper wrapping bound with twine. "He never finds his Lady E. He's out on the sea somewhere in the Mediterranean in a boat he had to hire from a fisherman's daughter by performing on her— well, never mind, and he's chasing the pirate galleon that has Lady E captured—or maybe even is under the command of Lady E herself—and the pirate ship disappears into a storm up ahead, and so he puts on all the sail, but the storm sends out a waterspout, and it's coming right at him, and it sucks him up and he's gone and she's gone and there's nothing left of them at the end, just the sea, and his everlasting hunger for her."

Trace could see now it wasn't the pornographic details of the tale that had interested the girls. It was the bits of romance Zob had daubed in between the acts of sex; it was the romance of pursuit, of epic longing, of risking all to find an ideal on earth.

"They disappear?" Trace asked. "That's *it?*"

Maddy shrugged. "None of the girls was too happy about the ending, either. It didn't seem like Mr. Zob to end a story that way. But he did. Poof! Into thin air they went."

Trace was now frowning. He already was pondering what of this conclusion he might render in drawings. A blank ocean? A waterspout shaped like a woman's ——?

Maddy had stepped over to the girl at the spinet and whispered in her ear, and now the music changed to something a little livelier. The men and

women in the room began to laugh and converse more freely; as if refreshed from the quiet mood they'd just drifted through, they now seemed
more gay. Trace admired Maddy's grace as mistress of the house. She
knew just how to adjust an evening to keep her clientele happy. She nodded
and chatted with a couple of gentlemen who were looking at some pictures
in a stereopticon they passed back and forth. Maddy brought out a packet
of more pictures from a drawer in an end table and gave them to the men,
who raised their eyebrows and chuckled, "Oh ho!" in unison. Two girls
came over and began pawing at the gentlemen's waistcoats and lapels,
begging for a peek at the pictures, as if they had never seen them before.
Maddy returned to Trace.

"What did Zob say he is doing with all this?" Trace asked, again
hefting the packet.

Maddy shrugged; he had never told her.

"Do you suppose he's publishing it? In France perhaps?" Trace asked.

"I doubt it. For all I know, it's solely for his own amusement."

"My drawings, too?"

Maddy put her hand on Trace's shoulder.

"Why not?" she said. "It's the best of times for him and the worst of
times." Maddy's eyes flashed with mirth at her little joke. "He's a big
success, but his marriage is a disaster. His wife, he says, doesn't understand
him, and he's fallen in love with a beautiful actress named Ellen. He needs
a distraction, Mr. Sketch-man. That's where we come in. If he is amused
and refreshed by our work, then *he* will work all the better, and the rest
of England, and the world, will be amused and refreshed, too. The least
the likes of you and I can do is entertain him as he wishes."

Trace didn't like the sound of this: that he and Maddy were just there
to serve Mr. Zob, that Mr. Zob was artistic royalty to whom Trace was
just an indentured sketcher. He had a higher opinion of his art—and of
Maddy—than that.

But all of it was moot, Trace realized, because in his hands he held
the end of his employment and his connection with Zob. The story was
over.

"I think I'll say yes," Trace said.

"Say yes? To what?" Maddy asked.

"The letter." Trace could picture it lying there in the dark among his
paints back in his cottage.

*. . . We intend to conquer the Atlantic with our transoceanic telegraph
cable. We once again would be honored to have your services as documentarian among the Cablemen.*

    Please favor us with an answer at your earliest convenience.
I remain . . .

                                      Sincerely,
                                      Cyrus Field,
                                      Chmn., Atlantic
                                      Telegraph Co.

"I think that's good. I think they're going to make it this time," Maddy
said. "I can tell. Give the faeries a rest."

A flicker of darkness crossed Trace's brow.

"Jack, who bought the paintings besides me?" she said. "You're ahead
of your time. The world has to progress to catch up to you."

"Nice of you to say it, Maddy," Trace whispered, and he thought of
his mural, the one she had inspired: *Progress.*

"I'll do it," he said. "I'll sail with them."

Hearing this, she kissed him on the brow, much to the shock of the
several gentlemen and bevy of associates who witnessed it.

Jack Trace strode manfully into the cool London night. It wasn't until
he was more than halfway back to his cottage that he realized he'd left
Zob's manuscript at Maddy's.

"To hell with it," Trace said aloud as he strode along in the moonlight. Oh, he'd do one last drawing for Mr. Zob, he thought, and he
would do it from Maddy's description alone, without even going back for
the text.

Several days later, at his residence at Gad's Hill, Mr. Dickens received
in a brown packet a strange sketch signed by Mr. Obz. It was of a departing
storm at sea; the flotsam of a small sailboat was scattered in the foreground with swollen, fleshy-looking clouds crowding the horizon, and from
them there twisted a vortex, a waterspout, both as fierce and as alluring
as Trace could make it appear to an observer such as Zob. It swept
away over the finality of the nearly empty sea. It looked very much like a
woman's ——.

The Barge Soiree

Cyrus Field, progenitor and financial captain of the first Atlantic cable venture, had never, through the duration of the Civil War, given up hope of succeeding with his submarine telegraph. By 1864, according to his own count, he had crossed the Atlantic Ocean thirty-four times on behalf of the project. Now that the war was ending in America, his prospects for success looked excellent.

Field had managed to round up most of the original "Cablemen," as he was now calling them. He even had the original sketch artist agreeing to return.

Months ago, Professor Thomson, back in Glasgow, had written Field to say he'd be happy to join the ranks. It would be an invigorating and—who knew?—perhaps a profitable way for an old academic to spend his free time during Trinity term.

Edward Orange Wildman Whitehouse would not be among the company. It had been at least a year since the last of the doctor's tiresome protestations had appeared in *British Electrical Notes*. He had returned to Brighton and, it was rumored, was at work on a monograph entitled "Amputations Under Fire."

J. Beaumol Spude had disappeared into the Confederacy. He had written Field early in the war, saying he wanted to continue his relations with the cable, might even be able to offer some financial assistance—how would Field, in Massachusetts, feel about receiving money from a Confederate gunpowder manufacturer? Field wrote back that it would be best for all, and the cable, if they waited for the war to resolve itself before taking up that matter. He heard nothing more from Spude.

Joachim Lindt had spent the past several years enjoying his status as the "Great Eradicator" of London. The nickname was born—with a wink to Mr. Lincoln—in one of the newspaper accounts of Lindt's rise to prominence in social and scientific circles. It referred to his success emancipating London from its own odor. Lindt, with his marvelous sewer system, had eradicated the Great Stink.

Lindt did not hesitate to parlay his success into an entrée into the fashionable quality of London. Nor was he at a loss among the eminences of the engineering world. His former vocation as scenery designer for a rolling panorama that played nightly in a gaming club and his reputed identity as the comical Running Man were all but forgotten. He was an adulated addition to the technological circles, which held him up as an exemplary specimen of the new Age of Science and Industry. Plus, there were those titillating whispers of tragedy and scandal regarding his late wife.

In some of the more august academic precincts, where high theory and hypotheses reigned, Lindt was seen as an interloper and a mere technician. Wags in the scientific community were grumbling that the Austrian had "spent the past five years dining out on our sewage," but such aspersions were not the rule. Throughout Britain, in salons and lecture halls and around dining tables, Joachim Lindt was proclaimed a practical genius.

And for that reason the previous autumn, Cyrus Field had invited Joachim Lindt to the barge soiree. It was a nautical evening, a party afloat on the Thames to raise more British capital for the cable, and the voyagers were among the most influential men of finance and industry in the empire.

Late in the evening, as a little steam launch skippered by a one-armed pilot was towing the revelers' barge back upriver from Greenwich and Cyrus Field was flush with handshakes and promises, Joachim Lindt had several officers of the Telegraph Construction and Maintenance Company gathered around him near the stern. The Telegraph Construction and Maintenance Company was the new corporation that had been formed out of the old cable-manufacturing firms. It now held the controlling interest in the whole project.

The men of the Telegraph Construction and Maintenance Company had been praising Lindt for the refreshing atmosphere of London's river.

"I hope our cable can finally achieve the same success," one of the men said. The others agreed.

"Well, gentlemen, the answer to your cable's success is, I say, out there tonight on this very river," and the Austrian pointed above the string quartet that was in the bandbox near the taffrail.

The officers of the Telegraph Construction and Maintenance Company didn't know what Lindt was talking about. It was too dark to see beyond the gay Chinese lanterns hanging along the barge's gunwales.

"There's nothing out there but blackness," one of the officers complained.

"*Ja!* That is the whole point of what I am telling you," Lindt said. "You are looking at the solution. Only it is too big and too black to see. It is the Iron Cliff. It is the *Great Eastern*. She is there waiting for you!"

Lindt went on to propose it right there: the men of the Telegraph Construction and Maintenance Company should buy the *Great Eastern* and rip out the staterooms and saloons and whatever else was necessary to install the requisite drums to hold all the cable and equipment they needed to lay a line from Ireland to Newfoundland. Everything could go on one ship, he said.

"For instance, how many tons do you estimate this new cable of yours will weigh?" Lindt's eyes darted from man to man.

"Seven thousand," one of the officers of the company offered.

"What was the capacity of the boats you used in 1858?" Lindt snapped the question over the heads of the men like flicks of a buggy whip.

"Fifteen hundred tons" came a voice from over by the rail.

All the men turned. It was Professor Thomson. Field had invited him down from Glasgow for the soiree. In the group gathered around Lindt, he was the only one among them who had actually been on a telegraph expedition.

"Well, there you are," Lindt said. "The *Great Eastern* can do it. She has easily five times the capacity of those boats you used when you failed."

Thomson was about to say that they were *ships*, not boats, and that they hadn't really *failed* laying the cable. The cable was broken by too much electricity. But he checked himself. He was there to be cordial, to help Field.

The officers from the Telegraph Construction and Maintenance Company pressed closer to the Austrian. They wanted to hear more.

And soon it was done, just as Lindt had proposed: the *Great Eastern* would lay the cable for a partnership of the Telegraph Construction and Maintenance Company and Cyrus Field's Atlantic Telegraph Company. Actually, Field and company would hire the Telegraph Construction and Maintenance Company, which would charter the great ship and would lay the cable. Field and his syndicate would now be customers for a job they had originally created. It seemed backwards to Professor Thomson, but money was calling the tune.

It took all winter to overhaul the ship. The *Great Eastern* hadn't sailed for months. It had failed miserably as a luxury vessel, losing easily £1 million for its investors. The Telegraph Construction and Maintenance Company bought it for £25,000, a thirtieth of what it cost to build.

The outfitters built three massive tanks in the guts of the ship. This meant eviscerating most of the luxury appointments and accommodations.

They even removed one of the funnels and its boilers. Field had written glowing, excited reports all winter and spring to Thomson about how work was progressing, about how it seemed everything was finally coming together again, about the day they would sail, and about how surpassingly well all of the engineering was going under the stewardship of the Great Eradicator.

Joachim Lindt had virtually become the chief engineer on the cable project. As for the officers of the Telegraph Construction and Maintenance Company, he was their man. From his outpost in Glasgow, Professor Thomson mulled over this prospect. He wrote to Cyrus Field.

"I worry," his letter said, "that our 'Great Eradicator' has eradicated a most important person from our enterprise. We must address this."

Speakers' Corner

Wee Wilkie Moon liked to go hear the harangues in Hyde Park. On pleasant afternoons, he would walk from his big, lonely house near Cartwright Gardens every bit of the way to Speakers' Corner all by himself. Wee Wilkie Moon lived alone now. Brothers William and Walter Moon were dead. They died of typhoid, the doctor had told Wee Wilkie, contracted on their trip to the Nile. Wee Wilkie had not wanted to go on that trip, so he hadn't gone, and now didn't that make him glad? He was alive and brothers William and Walter were not.

He was alive, but he was alone. That was not so much fun. Walter and William had been such fussers and complainers sometimes, but they were company. Now Wee Wilkie had to go seek society elsewhere. So he went to Speakers' Corner. A nice place to hear a wealth of ideas expressed in a variety of ways, he always told Maid or Manservant whenever they asked where he might be going.

Wee Wilkie had given up trying to make his way in the world. He had dim memories of wanting to write for newspapers and of actually having done so, but now even trying to remember such pursuits, let alone *do* them, was beyond Wee Wilkie's capacity. He had folded in on himself, Maid told him. She had once worried about him, but no more, because now he seemed so happy.

"I am!" Wee Wilkie said. "I am, Maid."

He called her "Maid" because he could never remember her name. So he just called her Maid, and to deflect attention from his poor powers of recollection in this regard, he began calling his manservant "Manservant." They didn't object. He provided for them well. That is to say, the Manchester Woolen Fortune did.

Wee Wilkie liked thinking about how lucky he was to have a Manchester Woolen Fortune to support him. He wasn't too folded in on himself to forget his gratitude. Sometimes he would call on Banker—he called him that just to tease him—to discuss his finances and how they were holding up. "Surprisingly well," Banker would say, and tent his fingers. "You are amply provided for and will be in perpetuity. You are a most fortunate man. Now, if I might explain a few items . . ." But they were so troublesome, the figures Banker kept droning on and on about, such a bother that Wee Wilkie always wanted to just walk right away from there. And today, that was exactly what he was doing. Banker had been going on about investing in this and amortizing that, and Wee Wilkie just walked away, nodding at Banker's clerks and copyists as he went through the outer office with its globe lamps and low, wooden partitions that made the room look like a paddock for toiling scribblers. From behind, he could hear Banker calling from his chambers, "Mr. Moon . . . Mr. Moon? . . ." But that didn't stop Wee Wilkie. He had need of some air.

So, off to the park he went. It was a lovely spring afternoon. Maybe today he would blaspheme. Wee Wilkie had been thinking about it for some time now, ever since Maid told him the story of the man who lived seven thousand years because he'd said the Lord's Prayer backward.

Seven thousand years! Wee Wilkie had thought. That would show Walter and William. They'd only made it to forty-two and thirty-eight, but Wee Wilkie could go on for seven thousand. More perhaps. In perpetuity perhaps.

"Oh no!" Maid had cried when he'd told her. "Mr. Moon, that would be blasphemy. The man what did say his Our Father backward had to live in a *cellar* and never leave and had to stare at a pile of gold what he could never have. It were a *curse*, Mr. Moon. Don't do it. Please."

So Wee Wilkie had smiled and nodded, and although he'd said he wouldn't do it, he began learning the prayer backward anyway. He had yet to say the whole thing, but he was getting close. He almost had it. Perhaps today would be the day.

"Amen," Wee Wilkie whispered as he walked, now passing behind the big, gray museum on his way to the park. Robins darted through the iron pickets of the fence, heads twitching, listening for worms.

Or, thought Wee Wilkie, are they listening to me? To hear when I get the whole prayer backward? So then they will fly up to tell the cherubim, who will tell the seraphim, who will tell all the other orders of angels, passing the message along, one to another like a telegram, until it reaches the Lord, who will curse you, Wee Wilkie, to seven thousand years of life! All your Manchester Woolen Fortune, and you can't touch it! In perpetuity, Wee Wilkie Moon.

"Amen . . . ever for . . . ," whispered Wee Wilkie anyway. "Amen . . . ever for glory the and . . . power the and . . . kingdom the is . . . thine for . . ."

He looked uneasily up at the sky. Blue. Lovely little clouds. There was one shaped like a barouche, and over there many shaped like cobwebs. A sign of rain perhaps.

". . . evil from us deliver but . . ."

Wilkins Moon had folded in on himself completely when his brothers died. They had never come back from their grand tour of the Nile. Word arrived by telegram that they were dead of typhoid, and Wilkins had collapsed when he'd read the news.

". . . temptation into . . ."

He gave himself the name Wee Wilkie. He told Maid to call him that, but she refused. He supposed that was most proper and high-minded of her. He should be so decorous! But that wouldn't be Wee Wilkie, would it? That wouldn't be him. High-minded! Decorous!

". . . not us lead and . . ."

And now . . . now, he had a scheme to live seven thousand years. Would the heavens open? Would a pillar of fire rise before him? Would he be ready to live in a cellar, if it came to it? And how would he live in a cellar or anywhere if the Manchester Woolen Fortune did not last, which surely it wouldn't?

". . . debtors our forgive we as debts . . ."

This was bad. Wee Wilkie was having trouble. He was saying the Lord's Prayer—Prayer Lord's the—backward, and he didn't even want to! He wasn't sure he could stop.

Think of something else, he told himself. *Think!*

". . . our us forgive and bread daily our daily this us give . . . heaven in is it as earth in . . . done be will thy . . . come kingdom thy . . ."

His mind! His mind wouldn't stop! He only wanted to practice a little.
Now, it was as if a voice were shouting the blasphemy into his head and
he were compelled to keep the backward-reeling prayer muttering out of
his mouth. He marched toward the Marble Arch at the corner of Hyde
Park. Speakers' Corner was near the Marble Arch. Soon Wee Wilkie
would be at the Marble Arch, and soon Wee Wilkie would be at Speakers'
Corner.

The day's light had become a soft grayness sifting through the trees.
The cobweb clouds overhead had thickened. The temperature was still
pleasantly mild, and the air had the balmy smell of warm tea. A lovely
spring afternoon, Wee Wilkie told his mind. Pay attention to the lovely
spring afternoon. And to the speakers. He would be there soon. He hoped
there would be plenty of speakers today. A nice day. Plenty to distract
him.

". . . name thy be hallowed . . ."

And there were plenty of speakers today! All lined up along the walk.
He could pick and choose. Some had clutches of passersby stopped to
listen, others merely orated to open space or invisible auditors of their own
fancy. There was the fellow in the kilt and open-necked shirt denouncing
"Marxian causuistries." And the portly fellow with the face like raw meat
who shook his own fist inches in front of his own nose as he made a
connection between poor railway schedules and "Darwinist perfidy." There
were several men and one woman declaiming on various chapters and
verses from the Bible. (Wee Wilkie considered listening to them to divert
his mind from its blasphemous pitch.) There was a sepulchral, droning
man perspiring in a black frock coat who offered conclusive evidence, so
he said, of life on Mars. And then there was the man who stopped Wee
Wilkie's rebellious inner voices cold.

". . . heaven in art which—"

The man was tall, with long arms outstretched. He had lank, reddish
hair too long by half for current fashion, but this fellow seemed to be
beyond the reach of fashion; indeed, he seemed beyond the reach of civilization itself, his clothing and carriage were so singular and rough. He was
an American, that was obvious from his voice. One never saw Americans
speaking at Speakers' Corner. It was a voice that was strong with an undertone of weariness. It was a voice of calm authority and suasiveness, and
the man had gathered the largest crowd there.

The speaker's face was clean-shaved, his skin the color and seeming hardness of oak. His blue eyes were irregular in a way Wee Wilkie Moon couldn't quite discern. It was as if one eye was trained on what was before it—maybe thirty attentive men and women—and the other eye was sighted on . . . something else, somewhere else.

Wee Wilkie Moon felt himself drawn toward the gaze of the fellow who, Wilkie saw, stood on a small fish crate. He wore canvas breeches and boots so scuffed that they looked as if they'd been worked over by a carpenter's adze. A saffron scarf of silk served as a cravat, and his rough hide coat seemed to have been fashioned from the skin of a wild animal.

Wee Wilkie worked his way toward the front of the crowd, his little shoulders wedging their way between the bodies. Then he was there. The man's arms seemed to pass right over Wee Wilkie's head as if they were about to bestow a blessing upon him.

The fellow spoke of spirits and signs from the Beyond. He claimed to be a practitioner of something called "transetheric travel." A heckler from the back of the crowd shouted, "Travel, then! Travel through the ether for us!"

The man on the fish box smiled, almost demurely, and lowered his voice, though he could still be heard by all.

"I can't, friend. Not here," he said. "And I'm not asking you to even take my word for it. I'm only asking that you consider the *possibility*; that you—even just for a few minutes—entertain the *chance* that it could be done, that we could communicate with—"

"Heaven," blurted Wee Wilkie, then quieter: ". . . in art which—"

"Yes," said the man, also quietly, directly to Wee Wilkie, stopping him before he said more and leaving Wee Wilkie to wonder if the fellow had intended that.

Wee Wilkie felt restored by the small exchange. The fellow had heard him, spoken to him, stopped the rogue voice within him from uttering more blasphemy.

Now the man was telling a story.

It was about a little girl. A little girl the man had seen die. He had been unable to save this little girl, and he had spent his life seeking atonement. He had roamed the world—to run away, he admitted, out of shame but also for respite. For the little girl was his niece. She suffered from what he called "accesses." From fits. Just as he suffered from fits.

"Have a fit for us!" the heckler called, but a bristling wave of annoyance went through the crowd, and several men in the back told the fellow to hush, and the heckler, so nonplussed was he by the crowd's protective cordon around the speaker, actually muttered, "Sorry."

The red-haired fellow just kept relating the story of his life, all his travels, and how he returned to the scene of the little girl's death and to the pain of knowing his niece's spirit walks the earth and longs for her loved ones.

"Rest, rest, perturbèd spirit!" the man intoned, and a woman in the gathering let out a soft, short cry.

The man continued his tale of seeing his little niece again on the summit of a volcano. And it was as if Wee Wilkie and all the others saw her again, with him, as he saw her: huge, in the sky, her spirit as a pillar of smoke. And they went with him on his journey clear across the Russian wilderness, ever westward, traveling with herdsmen, brigands, soldiers, merchants' caravans, down through the Ottoman Empire, across into the Balkans, through satrapies and empires and duchies and kingdoms, until they came to rest here, together, in London, where he could finally tell his tale in his native tongue in this gentle park.

And that was not all. The man went on to make pronouncements and predictions. He was saying wild things—sweet things, too. And Wee Wilkie grew concerned. He wished the man would stop, so he raised a sympathetic, admonishing hand. Wee Wilkie knew when a mind was folding in on itself, and he would have said this man's mind was doing just that, if anyone had asked him. But no one did, and the man kept talking, and Wee Wilkie's hand dropped back down. The man was telling of a time when everyone might be able to travel through the ether. He said if that telegraph line for which he had been in Siberia were not constructed, then another one surely would be. And if one man does not lay a cable across the Atlantic Ocean, then another man surely will. For there will be wires and cables wrapping the globe, over land and under the sea. There will be conductivity everywhere; it will be as if the planet were coated uniformly with intelligence, not existing as now with little whorls and knots of civilization and knowledge and culture interspersed amid jungles and deserts and tundra and mountain ranges. And we shall live to see it, the man proclaimed. If a baby is born, anyone could know. If a president is elected, all will know. And we shall have our hands on the means to hear the music of the spheres and to speak with spirits, and I will tell my niece that all is well, and she may go to her rest at last with the angels and ministers of grace.

As Wee Wilkie listened to the man's peroration, he noticed that the fellow had begun to weep—but weep, Wilkie noticed, with tears flowing from only one eye. Wilkie also noticed something happening to the crowd behind him. He turned around and saw that people were parting for an approaching gentleman.

He was another tall fellow, like the man on the fish box. This new man was well dressed in a gray, light wool coat, suitable for the season. He was blond, wore gold-rimmed spectacles, and had an almost careworn erectness to his carriage similar to the fellow on the fish box. And by dint of this similarity, Wee Wilkie understood two things at once: that he knew this man who was parting the crowd before him and that the man he was approaching, the man on the fish box, was his brother.

Wee Wilkie watched with the crowd while the man on the fish box lapsed into silence and stood, hands hanging at his sides, as the other man came forward.

Wilkie knew the approaching man as the fellow who had been in charge during that terrible storm on the terrible sea voyage: the cable expedition. Wee Wilkie had been there. Wilkins Moon.

Wee Wilkie stepped back to allow the man to pass. The man now had his right hand extended. The man on the fish box raised his hand, too, and the two brothers clasped each other, and the brother on the ground drew the other brother down to him, gently, assuredly. The blond, younger man—for it was obvious he was younger—placed his left arm over the shoulders of his brother, and with his other hand serving as a fender, opened a furrow again through the hushed crowd. The assembled pulled back together after the brothers had passed. Men and women all exchanged looks of gratitude more than bafflement, looks of a shared relief that a lost man had been found.

And then the crowd dispersed. People ambled off to listen to other speakers at the Corner or to quicken their pace, to leave the park and get on with their day.

Wee Wilkie Moon stood alone. Drops began plopping on the pavement stones of the promenade, making marks like crushed flower petals strewn on the thoroughfare. The leaves overhead were beginning to rattle. It had started to rain.

Wee Wilkie looked right and left. The park was becoming a gray-green blur around him as the rain's vapors, the mist, and the day's dust rose into the air. Everyone was gone.

"Father Our," Wee Wilkie said.

An Embrace and News

There was rain on the coast of Maine, and there wasn't a room in the house that was away from the sound of it. The noise of the rain and the pounding of the surf below the cliff penetrated everywhere in Willing Mind. Water chortled down rainspouts; water splashed between the slates of the terrace walk, where the chamomile and clover were sending up spring shoots; water—as driven rain and a brackish mist—hummed across the lawns and hissed among the heather clumps; it sighed in the high fir boughs that flailed in the wind; it protested being forced, again and again, against the rocks below the bluffs. Water sent its moist, persistent suggestions into every room, down every staircase, into every closet, pantry, hall, and porch. And Franny Ludlow went everywhere that the sound of the water went. That is, she went everywhere in the house. She was touring her old home.

The show—even Franny called it "the show" now—had been a sellout in Portland for Franny's homecoming engagement. Mrs. Tyler had been there, eager in the front row and then effusive backstage after the program. Franny had been wonderful; Franny had been better than wonderful; Franny had been perfect; Franny had been like nothing ever seen before and sure to be like nothing to be seen evermore. Franny was beautiful, pure and perfect. Had Mrs. Tyler said perfect before? Well, no matter. It was *worth* repeating. Franny was perfect perfection.

Mrs. Tyler was so happy to see her that it surprised Franny when Mrs. Tyler seemed to balk at the idea of her visiting Willing Mind. Then again, maybe it was a curious request and lacking in respect, given Franny's current circumstances.

"*He's* not at home, is he?" Franny asked. They both knew whom she meant.

"Oh! Mercy. No," Mrs. Tyler said. "No."

"I would guess, from what I've read, he's back in England ready to depart with another cable," said Franny.

"Yes. Yes . . . that's what I've read, too."

"It's just that I've been away so long," Franny said. "So much has happened. . . ."

"Yes."

"And I'd like to go back. Only for a look."

"Goodness, my Franny, ma'am, it's *your* home. You don't need me to give you permission."

And Franny had laughed and admitted that, yes, that was true, but that Mrs. Tyler had been ever the faithful caretaker and that the house, though still Chester and Franny's by law, seemed more Mrs. Tyler's domain by rights.

"Well, it's pretty much shut up. Furniture covered and all. Mr. Tyler helped by boarding up the windows facing the storm side. But even closed down, it's in kept-up condition, I daresay."

And it was. The carriage let Franny off just after dawn, Mrs. Tyler waved good-bye, and Franny spent a good part of the morning walking from room to room. She had asked to be left alone. The omnipresent sound of rain softened her footfalls, which otherwise would have been hollow on the floors where the rugs had all been rolled up. The furniture was grouped together and covered in white muslin like misshapen bedouin tents pitched in the center of each room. The musty air that used to stay holed up in the farthest reaches of the house—the least-used guest rooms, the root cellar, up under the eaves of the back halls on the top floor—now had established itself comfortably throughout the whole place. It was this smell that signaled to Franny that the presence of Betty was diminishing here.

As she hadn't seen Betty in a single one of her spiritual convocations in the five years that she had been doing them in fourteen states and three territories, she could hardly expect to see her daughter here, today. She had opened up the spirit world—or the hope of it—to thousands of her countrywomen and -men. And she'd always felt steadfastly that someday, if she unfailingly trod the path she was on, Betty *would* come to her.

But not today, she concluded. Franny looked toward the sea-facing windows, the ones where Mr. Tyler had nailed the shutters closed. Slits of gray light shone between the slats, where occasionally water seeped through like suppurations trickling from a cave wall or tears forming at the corners of closed eyes.

Such grim, self-pitying images, Franny thought, and she tried to wipe them from her mind by turning about in the chill air. It was a girlish, almost dancelike movement, a pirouette practically, and she felt she might keep whirling, like a dervish, from room to room and perhaps she could spin Betty out of the air that way. She twirled down the hall, through a portal, across a floor, but when she saw another ghostly tent of furniture, belonging to Chester—she was in Chester's study—she stopped abruptly.

Franny and Chester had not been in contact with each other for more than four years. Lawyers had been their interlocutors, and Mrs. Tyler had been the keeper of whatever outward manifestation of the marriage still existed. Once they had established that the house would be closed—though not sold—that he was no longer responsible for debts incurred by her, then they were as good as unmarried. But not as good as divorced. Because, Franny thought as she walked now out of his study, down the stairs toward the parlor, because . . . why? *Why* hadn't they made the divorce final? Because, Franny had always maintained, they had *both* left each other, there was a mutual culpability for sundering the marriage, and neither wanted to admit it, so both did nothing to sever the final tie. And because Chester had all but fallen off the earth for most of those years and was beyond communication. But, no, those reasons never made ultimate sense.

Then it came to Franny . . . Betty. Betty had kept them bound, however insubstantially, however hopelessly, all these years. They were not married, but they were both still parents to their little girl. Maybe, thought Franny, *this* is how the child returns to me. Not by appearing as a walking spirit among the quick, but in reflections of my marriage to Chester. And maybe, Franny also thought, she appears to *him* the same way.

Franny now found herself in the great room, the parlor, near the clump of furniture clustered around the pianoforte. She remembered the night the troupe had arrived here at her home. The woman had played this very piano. Chester had been with the other men by the fire, but Franny had felt him watching. The question was, whom was he watching? With her fingers, she parted the gathering of two of the sheets covering the piano as if she were feeling between the folds of a garment. She found the keyboard.

Franny quietly struck a key. Under the cloth, the sound was muffled. She couldn't see what note it was. She struck it again, louder. And again, louder still. She kept striking it, steadily, unforgivingly. It tolled through the room, down the halls, upstairs, outside. It struck at the fabric of the rain's whispering, tearing holes in it that the rain stitched shut after each peal. She tapped out a steady, one-note cadence. Over and over.

Eventually, between the sounds she could hear footsteps. For the slightest moment, she thought it might be Betty, come at last to her, summoned by the tolling of the note. But no, the tread was too real, too much of this world and time. It was coming toward her. She kept striking the note as if it were a steeple bell, a storm buoy, a gong.

Then, suddenly, arms embraced her from behind. She could smell the sweet, earthy, grassy odor of him. The scent that, as much as anything else, had seduced her.

No, she thought, not now. Not here.

He had overseen the strike of the show's props and set, had sent their equipment on to Boston for the booking there in two days. He had said he would follow her up here to fetch her when he was done. She hadn't been sure she wanted him to come, especially when she hadn't been here herself for so many years. But he had maintained that she might need company and the support of someone dear.

Was that he?

Yes, it was. Franny kept striking the note. She did not want to feel his heat right now, but she did want the support of someone dear. She just did not want his embrace to turn into something more. Not now. Not here.

So she continued to strike the key.

Dr. Zephaniah Hermes loosened the embrace of his left hand and slid it down gently to cover her hand and cease the tolling of the single note. He held her trembling body firmly with his other arm until she settled. He held her, but not in a way that suggested a progression of lust. It was, she knew and appreciated, just to steady her.

Then he spoke as the rain hummed everywhere around the house, and he said something she, with all her powers of spirit and sympathy, would never have presaged.

"The President," he said from behind her, "was shot last night while at the theater. He died this morning."

CHAPTER XXVII

UNSPOOLING THE CABLE; UNRAVELING THE PAST

The Atlantic Ocean, July–August 1865

0 Miles Paid Out

Legend has it that Cromwell's Roundheads tossed Irish peasants off the fort above the bay just for fun. During Cyrus Field's address to his Cablemen and the crowd on the beach below the cliffs, a skyrocket sends its trail up and down from the highest battlement of the old ruin. The rocket interrupts Field just as he is introducing Chester Ludlow. It leaves only a pallid parabolic line against the light of the early-evening sky. July in western Ireland, and the heavens remain lustrous well into the night hours, so this one firework, shot to bid the Cablemen farewell, is only middling visible.

Better than tossing an Irish peasant off, thinks Jack Trace, and he goes back to sketching the scene. He has all the Cablemen before him. (All but one.) These are the engineers, the financiers, the ship captains, and the politicians lined up on the sand at the water's edge, with the thick-as-your-wrist shore end of the cable at their feet. They are Cyrus Field of the Atlantic Telegraph Company; Professor William Thomson, esteemed adviser to the enterprise; Captain James Anderson, commander of the *Great*

Eastern; the captains and first officers of the HMS *Caroline* and the escorting warships, the *Terrible* and the *Sphinx;* Sir Peter Fitzgerald, Knight of Kerry; Messrs. Hoyt, Rettig, and Skidmore, representative officers of the Telegraph Construction and Maintenance Company; and finally there is Chester Ludlow, who steps forward and nods when introduced as the associate chief engineer on the project, nods and waves perhaps in acknowledgment of the rocket or the crowd's applause (for, above all others, they remember his name best from 1858), or perhaps his wave is a gentle remonstrance to a tall red-haired man before him in the crowd who is applauding a little too loudly.

The only member of this cohort of engineers and commanders not present is out at sea, waiting aboard the *Great Eastern,* waiting by his own request so he can make final preparations. He is Herr Joachim Lindt, the *other* associate chief engineer and the technologist prince of the supervising Telegraph Construction and Maintenance Company.

Boats choke the normally secluded Foilhommerum Bay. There are hundreds of people on the beach and on the grassy hills above the cliffs around the little cove. Jugglers, hucksters, musicians, and entertainers are working the crowd. Cook fires send up their greasy threads of smoke. The weather is fine. Hopes are high.

The only disappointment for the crowd is that the main attraction, the giant *Great Eastern,* is not obviously present. The ship is too massive and cumbersome to negotiate the coastal skerries and shoals hereabouts, so Captain Anderson has left it at anchor several miles beyond the horizon to await the smaller, steam-powered brig *Caroline* to bring the shore end of the cable out to be spliced to the two thousand miles of submarine cable waiting in the *Great Eastern*'s hold. Spectators point to a small dark smudge on the horizon; the minute plume of smoke from the *Great Eastern*'s boilers is the only evidence that the grand vessel is out there.

After the ceremony (speech by the lord lieutenant, speech by Field, more introductions, huzzahs, hat doffing, hymn, prayer, cheers), the expedition boards longboats on the beach and makes its way out to the *Caroline,* which fires a salute that is answered by a rocket from the castle and by cheers from the crowd. Then the little ship begins paying out the heavy shore line and steams toward the smudge on the horizon.

For the first hour or so, all the Cablemen are at the *Caroline*'s stern watching the heavy line pay out. They wave to the armada that follows them out of the bay. One by one, the boats drop off to the stern, handkerchiefs and caps saluting farewell. Soon, though, each man makes his way to the bow to watch the *Great Eastern* heave into view. It is like witnessing an island rise out of the sea. First come the six masts, then the four smoke-belching funnels, and finally the black cliff of the hull. In profile the ship, with its low superstructure and perpendicular bow, is an almost perfect rectangle: a box with masts and smokestacks.

The sight moves everyone to silence, each Cableman alone with his thoughts.

Aloft in the rigging, though, above everyone else on the *Caroline,* is Otis Ludlow, whose head is so full of thoughts that they feel as though they will fly right out of his skull like startled birds. He looks up as if to check for those fluttering thoughts in the air above him. Stars are beginning to show through the indigo sky. He always liked this time of day—or is it night?—out on the ocean. It's a calming time. The time when Otis's thoughts can calm into inspiration. It's happened frequently since Chester found him. He has already helped Chester with matters of engineering as they prepared for the expedition. Otis will help more, if he can remain steady.

Below him now they are preparing to pass the cable by longboat from the *Caroline* to the *Great Eastern.* Light is slipping farther into the western ocean. Otis wants to see one shooting star before he leaves the masthead. Chester is calling for him to come down. It's time to board the *Great Eastern.* It's time to begin. One shooting star. A sign from the ether. The cables are about to be spliced. Otis keeps looking up. If he can keep steady. One is all he wants. For luck. The ships are about to part. He strains his eye as if it alone could draw a meteor out of the numb scattering of lights. One is all he wants.

50 Miles Paid Out

Dawn is still an hour or two from appearing on the horizon behind them. No one is sleeping tonight aboard the *Great Eastern.* Even crewmen off watch have stayed awake.

Things are going well. The joining of the thick shore line to the thinner transoceanic cable went smoothly. The splicing crew had rehearsed for days. They braided the ganglia of the copper filaments as if they were an infant's hair. They wrapped the core, painted on the gutta-percha, wove the armor cladding, all in minutes. The operation had the speed and cool purposefulness of well-performed surgery. The rest of the crew cheered when the jointure was done.

Now the line glides off the stern of the *Great Eastern*. The paying-out engines chug, the gears and ratchets clatter, and the flywheels spin in a blur. The black cable arcs over the stern drum and curves in the light of the lanterns strung along the deck to dip away into the froth of the *Great Eastern*'s wake. From the hatch that opens into the sternmost circus below-decks, the voices of the crew rise into the mild night air: sometimes a song, sometimes jibes between crewmen, but more often an exhortation or an affectionate entreaty to the cable itself to "keep bein' sweet," "keep runnin' along like a darlin' to the bottom of the sea," "keep lettin' us go straight on to Cana-day."

While the whole vessel hums with the determined activity and eager vigilance of cable laying, two men are standing stiffly at the leeward rail amidships. The men seem uneasy.

Joachim Lindt has paused after a light meal in the officers' mess to smoke his meerschaum at the rail. Out on the horizon are the lights of the *Terrible* and the *Sphinx*. Chester Ludlow, coming from an inspection of the cable tubs, has approached Herr Lindt.

Lindt nods and casts a quick eye about Oxford Street, the main deck that is so broad and so long that the nearest crewmen seem to be half an hour's walk away.

It appears that Chester Ludlow has something to say, but it is Lindt who, with a preemptive abruptness, speaks first.

"Herr Ludlow, I was pleased you approved of my changes to your paying-out device. Thank you."

Chester nods his head once. "It is a different-diameter cable this time out," he says. "Changes were necessary. Yours were well done."

"Yes, but you invented the mechanism. For me to make alterations in your machine without your approval was—"

"Was fine," Chester says. "I had not yet agreed to take part in the expedition at the time. You had. You made the necessary decisions and changes in the equipment. You made good ones."

"Again, thank you." Herr Lindt taps his pipe on the rail and makes to leave.

"Herr Lindt, if you please, before you go . . ."

"Yes?"

"We have not spoken of . . . things . . ."

"Of things? Of things other than engineering matters?" Lindt asks.

"Correct."

"Herr Ludlow, I think it has been quite a feat on your part to have been able to avoid such a conversation. We are *co*engineers here, and yet you . . . you do your work, and perforce I do mine. I receive your memoranda. I read your notes. We are—we *must* be—remarkable for our ability to accomplish so much with such an impediment between us. Everything we do, we must do around it. I have much to gain by succeeding with this expedition, Herr Ludlow. That is why I am here. That is why I shall work around this impediment before us. The humiliation of my enforced proximity to you is worth enduring for what I hope to gain by my—by *our*—success."

"I see," says Chester Ludlow, quietly, as he leans with both forearms on the rail. The sea hisses below them.

Herr Lindt faces him directly and continues, "No, I doubt you do see, Herr Ludlow. For I still wait for one thing. One thing that is not forthcoming, and I must say, it is unconscionable that it is not. I speak of an apology, sir."

It is a mild breeze that blows across the *Great Eastern*. There are animal pens belowdecks not far from where the two men are standing. Chester catches anomalous whiffs of manure and straw coming up from one of the portholes below, a most unnautical smell. *It is as disorienting as this conversation,* he thinks. *We should not have barnyard smells out here; we should not be discussing these matters out here.* But of course, he's known all along he would have to speak of these things once he joined the expedition. It is, he knows, part of why he is here. And Lindt is right: it was a feat to have avoided it for so long.

"I am," Chester says, "sorry."

Lindt stares at him, then slowly turns to fix his eyes on the lights of the escort ships.

"I was not there when she died," Chester says. He considers for a moment that this sounds like an excuse, but he presses on. "I wrote you that. Although how my not being there might expiate things between us now, I don't pretend to know. I feel constrained to tell you that she died, I am afraid, quite alone."

"Somehow I doubt that," says Lindt. His voice is brittle. He is biting the stem of his pipe.

"Well, perhaps I am being figurative. I was not with her. *You* were not with her. She was alone."

"Neither you nor I was with her," says Herr Lindt with an almost glittering bitterness. It is as if his controlled rage is escaping from his brow in sparks, and Chester imagines he can actually see them. "I might note for the record, Mr. Ludlow, she had done all this before. What she did with you? You weren't the first."

"I think we should stick to present cases, Herr Lindt. Out of respect."

"*Respect?* Respect for whom? *Her?* Respect for her?" He snorts. "How about respect for me? But then, I shouldn't think that you'd care about that. Not from what I saw during our original theatrical . . . *collaboration.* So, what about you? Respect for *you?* Is that what I am here for?"

Anger grips Chester. He knows there is truth to what Lindt says. Still, he has half a mind to hit him or, at the very least, walk away, to shed himself of this whole conversation. But he knows he must remain. He is calling himself to account here, as he has vowed for some time that he must—ever since recovering at Willing Mind, ever since lying delirious in the army hospital in Philadelphia, ever since walking half starved and hollowed out down the tracks through the frontier—so he cannot shirk this cauterizing moment that has come at last and that he sees as a bounden necessity.

Chester doesn't tell Herr Lindt that his wife was probably insensible on laudanum when she died and that she had forsaken her music, had forsaken Chester, was probably even sliding away from vanderWees as well. And for what? Chester has no answer for that. Three years and still no answer. He wonders if knowing would provide a key to what *he* had forsaken or lost or traduced in those years. Foolish though it may have been, he thinks that somehow reenlisting with the cable expedition, returning to the effort at which he once came close to success, might be the path to reconciliation with his better self.

Chester turns from the sea and looks up into the rigging. It's too dark to tell, but he thinks Otis might be up there in the first crow's nest, and Chester has a fleeting worry that it was a mistake to have brought his brother on the voyage.

Herr Lindt still stares out at the sea, trying to discern if that is dawn light insinuating its way into the eastern sky behind them. He glances over at Chester.

"Frankly, Herr Ludlow, I was surprised to hear you had consented to join this expedition. My first thought was that it was out of a proprietary interest. You couldn't let your cable fall into the hands of the likes of me. Now, I am not so sure. I am not so sure, because I can see in your face, Herr Ludlow, that *you* are not so sure. Nonetheless, you have come to join our happy band. We who picked up where you left off. You are thinking if we succeed, we shall do it standing on the shoulders of giants. On *your* shoulders. Such is science, yes? Such is progress. Your lust stood on the shoulders of my marriage. My success as a cable engineer will stand on the shoulders of your labor and failure of seven years ago."

"Lindt, you have said you expected an apology. I have given you mine. What recompense you may think is owed you is not for me to say. I can only say I am sorry. I am sorry for what I did to you, and I am sorry for Katerina's death."

This is the first time either of them has uttered her name aloud. It sends a shock between them that neither anticipated. *Katerina's death.* As they both have their eyes locked on each other now, each sees exactly the effects of the words.

65 Miles Paid Out

It was silence that had led Chester Ludlow back to this course across the ocean. A silence that began on his long march eastward from the shell crater. No words. No food or water. But the effect was a purgation and then an emptiness and then a pellucidity of the heart he hadn't felt in years, if ever. He began to suspect as he walked along the rails that he was walking out of some kind of crater more abstract and far larger than the one he had knelt in back in the remains of the Indian village. And he wasn't merely walking; something was leading him. It was the glimpses of the pale, little girl he saw ahead of him. That apparition, which Chester held close in his thoughts—guarded, never spoken of—that vision he knew was Betty. And he knew that following her might very well lead him deeper into other vales of darkness before he would be out of the crater.

And so he went to war.

After the soldiers had found him, fed him, and borne him to Washington, he had an audience with Secretary of War Edwin Stanton. In addition to learning that the train, its passengers, and the cannon had been destroyed by rebel sappers, he also learned that there would be no other attempt to build a gun so large. Russell vanderWees had been the champion of the Monongahela cannon—the Ludlow Gun—and now, well, with the undersecretary's untimely passing, the army would be purchasing a smaller if less mobile model, the twenty-inch Rodman Columbiad.

Secretary Stanton was concerned at how hard Chester seemed to be taking the news. The gaunt, haggard engineer, whom a military detachment had found walking toward Harrisburg, looked broken, stunned into silence.

Stanton never mentioned Katerina Lindt directly. Either he didn't know she was aboard the train or it was a discretionary omission. He'd only said, "There were no survivors."

But then he added, "There was evidence that a woman's corpse was in the wreckage. I realize I risk being imprudent, but I am constrained to ask. Would you know anything about her?"

Chester was seated, looking out the window of Stanton's office through the bare winter trees at the scaffolding around the still-unfinished Capitol dome.

"Yes," he said. His throat was abrasively dry.

Stanton thrust his hands into his pockets. He took a couple of strides before the window. "Undersecretary vanderWees had a reputation for . . . well . . . Shall I assume that he and this woman—"

"Yes! . . . Yes," Chester said, covering his face with his hands and sitting that way, motionless, for several minutes. The secretary went over to a sideboard and poured him a glass of water, but Chester refused it.

When he finally showed his face, he was flushed but composed. He caught the secretary off guard by announcing that there was nothing else to do. He wanted to join the Union army. Would the secretary help?

The secretary coughed, covering it by making as if to clear his throat. He smiled, nonplussed. Well, yes, the secretary supposed he could honor Chester's request. Probably. Yes. Certainly. After all, he was the secretary of war. And Chester was a man of great ability. But the secretary wondered if—

Good. Chester was grateful for the secretary's kindness. He would have that water now. And might he ask of the secretary one additional thing? Would the secretary extend his influence—only if it becomes necessary, that is—to see that Chester Ludlow could avoid service that might have anything to do with engineering?

The secretary could, would, of course, and yet still he couldn't help but wonder if . . .

But there was no dissuading Chester Ludlow. The secretary could see it in the man's eyes.

And so it was done. In a matter of weeks, Chester Ludlow was a commissioned second lieutenant in the Twentieth Maine Infantry. Most of the men and officers knew Chester by reputation as the hero and then one of the impugned of the failed 1858 cable expedition. It was a Maine regiment, after all, and Chester had been a famous state son. But there was a blank purposefulness to his bearing that made him seem unlike the Chester Ludlow of the cable whom they'd all heard about. There was supposed to be a spark about him, if those old newspaper reports were to be believed, but this was not such a fellow. This was a man of cool opacity and superior capabilities whom the other soldiers regarded warily.

Chester joined the regiment in time to be wounded at Chancellorsville. It was only a slight insult to the hand. Soon he was back in action, this time receiving a serious leg wound at Gettysburg. He was taken to a military hospital in Philadelphia. The leg began to heal badly; the surgeons feared gangrene, contemplated amputation; Chester escaped that, only to contract dysentery. When he was finally well enough to travel, when it appeared that the leg would eventually heal, it was fall. He was discharged from the army and sent to Willing Mind.

He had written Franny only one letter, informing her of his decision to enlist. He did not even tell her what unit he'd been assigned to or where he would muster. He heard nothing back from her. When he was to return to Willing Mind, he wrote to Mrs. Tyler, but not to his wife. Mrs. Tyler would open the house and receive him.

Shortly after arriving, Chester asked once if Mrs. Tyler knew Franny's whereabouts.

"I do," Mrs. Tyler said, and her housekeeper's instinct for family complications prompted her to ask, "Do you want to know?"

Chester shook his head, but then asked if Mrs. Tyler knew if Franny would be returning soon.

"No, she writes as not," Mrs. Tyler said. "She will be away traveling, touring, all winter."

"One last thing," Chester said. "Does Mrs. Ludlow sound well?"

"Oh, very well, sir."

"That's good."

And so Chester rested through the seasons. He lay or sat quietly many a day, looking out at the ocean. Mrs. Tyler mused that he seemed so incurious. He never asked again about his wife. Never spoke of his brother or wondered where he might have gone. He seemed incurious but calm, and Mrs. Tyler supposed that was all for the best. The man had been, after all, at war.

It wasn't until Cyrus Field's letter arrived, the one actually offering him a coengineer's position on the new expedition, the one declaring Joachim Lindt as now part of the endeavor, that Chester began to realize he would be sailing again with the cable and finishing work they had all left undone. He was feeling stronger. Mrs. Tyler had nursed him well. And so it was on a morning in late winter that Chester Ludlow broke his silence and wrote Field his assent. The light had changed in Willing Mind, as the sun had been rising higher in the sky each day. And the night before, Chester was sure he'd seen the pale little girl dancing out on the bluffs.

84 Miles Paid Out

Jack Trace has just finished a lovely, late breakfast of eggs, bacon, scones, tea, toast, honey, pheasant, more eggs, coffee, more toast, marmalade, a bit of ham, and more coffee. He is thinking how much he is enjoying this cable expedition; how glad he is that he answered Mr. Field's letter in the affirmative; how, if they offer him a chance to send a telegram when they finally reach Newfoundland, he will wire Maddy (and maybe sign it "Mr. Obz"); and how this unwieldy, self-destructive, bankrupting, purposeless, defeated mass of iron—this *Great Eastern*—seems to have found its calling at last as the bearer of the transatlantic telegraph cable. The line is paying out smoothly over the stern; the seas are calm; the ship cruises on like a happy, well-governed, island nation that serves, Jack Trace is pleased to note, lovely, late breakfasts, amply turned out.

But as Jack Trace is sunning himself, taking some preparatory relaxation before sketching the crewmen at work down in the cable tubs, he—and everyone aboard—hears the steam engines slow their thudding rumble. The ship with its almost planetary inertia keeps gliding along as before under the morning sun, but all aboard know that something is wrong. Jack grabs his sketching supplies and goes to the telegraph cabin.

There is already a crowd of off-duty sailors and graphers waiting around the door. Word is that the line is dead, has been for half an hour, no signals coming from Ireland. The men inside the cabin are right now running impedance tests, hoping to learn how far from the ship the trouble might be.

"Excuse me, documentarian. Please, excuse me, documentarian," Jack says as he works his way through the forty or so men before the door. The officer of the deck lets him in the small "light-lock" antechamber, and thence into the telegraph cabin itself, where Trace stands blind in the dark. He hears the grapher repeat, "Nothing ... nothing ... nothing ... nothing." He hears Chester Ludlow and Professor Thomson quietly conferring.

"My best estimate is ten miles back," says Professor Thomson.

"All right," Ludlow says in a louder voice, more to the room in general, "we'd better pull it up."

Trace still can't be sure how many men are in here with him.

"There seems to be no choice," says Professor Thomson.

"Shall I give the order, Mr. Ludlow?" It is Captain Anderson. He is standing right next to Trace, and Trace can hear the starched cloth of his tunic scrape like sandpaper even when the man breathes. Captain Anderson faithfully wears his operatic captain's uniform with its gold braid swirling around the collars and cuffs and shoulders. He is a reminder of the days, only recently gone by, when the *Great Eastern*'s owners had dreams of ruling the seven seas with the world's largest luxury ship, captained by the world's most splendidly dressed skipper.

A new voice jumps in: "No, not yet. No order yet. If you please."

Trace is now able to see enough by the tiny candle lantern to recognize Joachim Lindt.

"Mr. Ludlow must first confer with his coengineer before we *both* give the order to stop this ship. Am I correct? Is that not company policy?"

"It is," says Cyrus Field. His voice sounds a touch chagrined, probably as a way of letting Chester know that he, too, is not entirely happy with the new division of power on the ship.

"Very well then," says Joachim Lindt, and he makes a show of pausing and drawing a supercilious breath before uttering, "I agree with my coengineer, Mr. Ludlow. Stop the ship. Pull up the cable."

Orders are called down the decks. Bells ring. The ship begins to respond.

A new problem comes to light when Lindt, on the stern deck now with all the Cablemen, orders—with Chester's concurrence—the *Great Eastern* to reverse its engines, to reel in the cable, and Captain Anderson has to say, "She can't."

The Cablemen look at him. The captain holds both his hands out, palms up, sleeve cuffs strangled in gold braid.

"Well, I mean, she *can*. That is, she can reverse her engines. But what she can't do is *steer* in reverse. Well, I mean, she can. But not well. Not well enough to take up that bit of wire"—he nods toward the cable still slowly paying out as the ship glides sluggishly forward, waiting for her next command—"and then there's the screw . . ." (Trace notices the captain using the same circular hand sign that Maddy had used all those years ago.) "It's right under here," the captain says, stomping his foot twice on the stern deck planks, "and it could snap your cable like it was a dry straw."

The cohort of Cablemen squint at the receding line as it pays out into the sea.

"Then we'll have to pull it up over the bow. There's tackle below to do it."

It is Otis Ludlow addressing them all. Messrs. Hoyt, Rettig, and Skidmore, the triumvirate from the Telegraph Construction and Maintenance Company, look doubtful. Mr. Rettig even reaches to tap Joachim Lindt on the shoulder, to ask if this is wise, if they should be taking advice from—

Quickly, Chester forestalls any criticism or hesitation. "Yes," he says. "It must be done. Yes." And the Ludlows set the crew to work.

10 Miles Taken Up
(74 Miles Paid Out)

It is a long, tedious, and dangerous process. Dangerous for the men who must scramble and wrestle recalcitrant lines and hawsers under great strain as they hang out over the water, and dangerous for the cable, which runs the constant risk of snapping. They must turn the ship about and bring the cable up to the bow.

With the Ludlow brothers leading the operation, the crew has assembled a forward makeshift cable-take-up device: two small donkey engines and a set of pickup drums. In the stern, the crew cuts the cable after shackling it to an iron rope. The men then begin fastening safety lines to the iron rope and proceed to bowse the lines—along the bulwarks, around the shrouds, over the longboats, around the side-wheel paddle boxes, past mast stays and ratlines—working with block and tackle, clamps and bite knots, taking the cable seven hundred feet from the stern of the *Great Eastern* to the stem.

Now, eleven hours later, the cable is coming in over the bow as the *Great Eastern* creeps forward—eastward—reeling in the precious line to the clatter and chuffing of the take-up engines.

By evening, they have reached the ten-mile point back along the pulled-up cable, the point at which Professor Thomson estimates the problem to be. The Cablemen are queued up on either side of the line as it slides along a makeshift sluice fashioned out of boards and sawhorses. They are inspecting the cable themselves; they are not leaving this task to the crew. Their heads swivel as they try to make their eyes cover every inch of the passing line. Sometimes they touch it, appearing to pat it affectionately, but really they're feeling for imperfections or breaks.

Suddenly Joachim Lindt cries out, "Halt!"

The donkey engines screech, bells ring to signal the *Great Eastern*'s engine room to cut power.

"Something is here," Lindt says. He is licking his left forefinger, which has received a small, slashing cut. He is pointing with his other hand at a spot on the cable. His left hand has found what all eyes plainly see is the problem. Driven into the cable is a two-inch piece of wire. Its protruding end has sliced into Lindt's finger. As Professor Thomson explains to any of the assembled who don't understand electricity, the driven wire had been sending the tiny charges going through the cable down a shortcut, and instead of traveling to or from Ireland, the little bits of electricity had been trickling out this wire spike onto the bottom of the ocean.

Chester orders the cable severed and a test dispatch made to Ireland. He is not checking with Lindt as he gives the orders. If anything, Chester is checking with quick nods and glances to his brother and Professor Thomson.

The dispatch goes out. The Cablemen—all the ship's company—wait.

Ireland answers! A cheer goes up. Chester orders the wounded section removed, the ship brought about, the cable hauled around to the stern again and spliced into the line in the circuses, and the paying out to resume. The work begins again.

100 Miles Paid Out

Things go well. The crew is unspooling cable again. Chester is in his cabin preparing for bed when there is a knock at his door. He does not suspect trouble, as that always comes with steam whistle blasts, bells clanging, orders echoing down companionways, and the baleful tempo change of the engines driving the ship. This time there is only a knock.

In his trousers and his nightshirt, Chester goes to the door. Joachim Lindt is standing there.

"We must talk about this," Lindt says. He holds up the black two-foot piece of excised cable.

Chester can see lamplight glinting off the thin wire that pierces the cable section. Lindt holds the length in each fist and pings the wire fragment with his right thumb. He has a bandage on his forefinger where the wire cut him.

"No one said anything out there, but I could see it in everyone's faces and so could you, because I looked at you carefully. No one said it, but we all thought it." He raises the section of cable almost under Chester's nose.

"Sabotage," Lindt says.

With a sigh, Chester motions him into the cabin. It is true that this wire, driven clear through the cable, does not look like an accident.

Chester offers Lindt a chair at the small table fastened to the bulkhead. Lindt shakes his head. He remains standing.

"Yes," Chester says, "I thought about it. I was surprised. I admit this wire looks . . . suspicious. I wondered."

"You *wondered?*" Herr Lindt asks.

"Exactly," says Chester. "Should I jump to conclusions? I don't think so, Herr Lindt. We have here a ship of loyal, hardworking, brave men who are devoted to the success of our enterprise. I will not impeach them on a hunch."

"Good for you," says Lindt. "But, alas, I am not so high-minded. I am, shall we say, compelled to consider lower motives. Perhaps that is why we are so well paired, yes?"

"Tell me what you know," Chester says.

"I spoke with the crewmen who were in the cable tub when that section of line went out," Lindt says. "One of the men said he'd seen your brother belowdecks during that shift."

"Well, he was there on my orders."

"Ah. Good. And what were those orders?" Lindt bends the piece of cable into an O. "I am interested in the orders you give."

"To check the grappling equipment."

Joachim Lindt frowns, then brings the cable length up to his nose and sniffs it in a strangely tender gesture as he waits for Chester's explanation.

Chester says, "Having sailed previously on these expeditions, I have experienced too many snapped cables. I don't intend to leave this one on the bottom of the ocean should it, God forbid, break in two."

"And you would *grapple* for it? Drag the bottom? Two miles deep?"

"I would. We have the gear to do it. My brother and I made sure of that, but let us hope we never need it."

"Let us hope something else," Lindt says. "Let us hope no one of our loyal, brave company drove this wire into our cable on purpose. And let us hope that a man sent belowdecks to check on grappling equipment is doing nothing more."

"Good night, Herr Lindt." Chester is at the door, having swung it open so quickly that the candle on the table spits in the draft.

Soon Chester is lying in his berth, waiting for his anger at Lindt to subside. He is waiting and thinking about the wire. And about his brother.

The stateroom is dark, but he knows Herr Lindt left the length of cable on the chair. The stateroom is as black as the ocean floor. And the cable piece lies with Chester as it had once on the seabed, inert, bleeding signals out into the darkness.

210 Miles Paid Out

The *Great Eastern* is so large, with its crew of five hundred, its menagerie of barnyard animals, and its capacity to carry all the Atlantic cable in one go, that there's a new artistic problem for Jack Trace. There always seem to be two horizons he must contend with: the one of sky and sea, and the other of the *Great Eastern*'s vast deck.

Jack Trace is working on the horizon problem as he sketches one of the cooks slaughtering a hog. In the four days of the expedition so far, Trace has drawn plenty of studies of the cable work: the paying-out process, from a dozen angles; the men in the cable circuses, sunlight pouring its radiance down through the hatches; expansive views of the entire ship, drawn from aloft to render the full size of the vessel; the graphers in the telegraph cabin reading the galvanometer, done in "dark plate" style to simulate the feel of the lightless room where the men decode the signals from Ireland. But lately he has moved away from drawing tasks involving the cable, in part because it is all going so smoothly. Aside from that one, strange incident with the piece of wire piercing the line, things have been almost dull. So Jack finds himself here, amidships, on the leeward side, where one of the ship's cooks is butchering a hog. The cook has set up a kind of tryworks—a coal stove heating water in a pot large enough to contain the entire carcass of the hog.

As he watches and sketches the blank-eyed corpse being lowered into the kettle, and as a seaman uses a boat hook to shove the unusable entrails in their slurry of grease and blood out a scupper and into the sea, Trace thinks how while there are two horizons he must render, there are other things about the ship that need reckoning. The competing governances, for instance.

The patterns of power on this voyage are more byzantine, more crisscrossed, than the chain of command on the 1858 attempt. It has to do with the words Trace has heard more often than ever before on this cable expedition: the Incorporation. The Incorporation is the knot of financial entities that were tied together to raise the necessary capital. But Trace has the feeling that the Incorporation also has its own wants and needs and opinions. For one, it seems to have usurped the primacy of the first telegraph visionaries—Ludlow, Field, and Thomson. The Incorporation has brought aboard Messrs. Hoyt, Rettig, Skidmore, and, more troubling, Lindt. It seems almost absurd that the Incorporation has placed Ludlow, Field, and Thomson, officially at any rate, in the position of customers on this voyage. True, things are going along smoothly, but somehow the organization seems upside down. Just like, Trace thinks, that hog carcass being lowered into the vat.

Trace has created a quick, deft rendering of the ship's cook submerging the hog in the try-pot. The composition owes a little to Hogarth: some allegorical exaggeration, the cook and his apprentice looking a touch infernal, thus giving a bit of the "world, the flesh, and the devil" theme to the picture.

Trace is finishing up the reticulations on the side of the pot when, through the stench of sulfurous coal smoke, porcine excrement, offal, and boiled hide, Trace catches the sweet odor of pipe tobacco. He turns and sees Joachim Lindt looking over his shoulder. The Austrian nods, points with the stem of his pipe to the picture, and says, "Good." Then he walks away, being particularly careful not to slip on the slime on the deck.

575 Miles Paid Out

Heavy seas. Cable still paying out smoothly. Swells of fifteen feet and more roll toward the *Great Eastern,* which cuts through them and is able to maintain its six-knot headway. The escort ships, the *Terrible* and the *Sphinx,* are having difficulty keeping up and slowly drop off to the east. The *Great Eastern* pushes on alone.

650 Miles Paid Out

They are now six and a half days out from Foilhommerum Bay, less than fourteen hundred miles to Newfoundland. The men are feeling increasingly confident by the hour. Even with three-quarters of the task still to go, the crew begins to sense the obtainable outcome, that the ship—*they,* each and every one—will succeed.

725 Miles Paid Out

Even Joachim Lindt has caught the spirit of optimism. He walks the deck and nods to the crew back at the paying-out machinery as if he were a burgher out for a stroll along the Konigstrasse. He indulges himself by imagining his life after the cable is successfully laid. These are little mental pageants featuring a comfortable estate, perhaps in America. Or England. Why not both? he thinks. One on either end of the cable. He glows with the imagined approbation. The praise he won for vanquishing the Great Stink topped anything he'd achieved as a creator of the Phantasmagorium. A city lay at his feet. Now, with this cable, could come the plaudits of an entire globe.

And if these are grandiose imaginings, Joachim Lindt can admit of that. They are also a respite. They distract him from his noisome entanglement with Chester Ludlow.

But you have the upper hand, Lindt tells himself. Still, he can't help but also indulge suspicions of the other Ludlow.

Lindt knows he is the only man aboard who thinks of Otis in this light . . . for the present. But Otis Ludlow has no business being on the voyage. He is an affront to the enterprise. His presence is merely proof of favoritism shown to Chester Ludlow. True, the brother, Otis, clearly has an instinctive grasp of natural philosophy and engineering, including electricity, that rivals even Chester's. But he indulges forays into all that non-empirical claptrap. Joachim Lindt finds he must walk away, excuse himself from the table, whenever Otis launches into one of his disquisitions about spirits or the Universal Mind.

It is almost enough to make Joachim feel sorry for Chester, who, strangely, always looks earnest and almost wistful, if not altogether pleased or inspired, when his brother spins off into one of his speeches about the death of Lincoln, about the ether, about universality, about the "coating of knowledge" he says the planet will someday wear, whatever *that* means. It is as if Chester Ludlow understands—or desperately *wants* to understand—what his brother speaks of. It is as if Chester loves Otis for what he thinks Otis is doing on Chester's behalf, on *humanity's* behalf.

What claptrap, Lindt thinks.

Lindt shakes his pipe ashes into the sea and resolves to ask around about something he'd heard: that Otis Ludlow had worked on the Siberian cable.

782 Miles Paid Out

After luncheon, Messrs. Hoyt, Rettig, and Skidmore are at the piano in the saloon. This has become their chosen amusement after meals: one plays the piano, the other two play cards. Few aboard the ship can claim to know which one of them might be at the instrument making music and which ones at cards, their beards and comportment are so similar, and their society so insular from the ship's general company. They confer thrice daily with Joachim Lindt. The rest of the time, they keep, civilly but reservedly, to themselves.

The tune Mr. Rettig (or Hoyt or Skidmore) plays is "Away with Melancholy." Hoyt (or Rettig or Skidmore) beats Skidmore (or Hoyt or Rettig) at a hand of hearts.

800 Miles Paid Out

The uneventfulness of the paying out leaves Chester time to think about Otis. Chester realizes that he may have to care for his brother once they land in Newfoundland and make their way down to America. There are moments when Otis is as lucid and calm as anyone aboard, when he is capable of solving mechanical or logistical problems as well as any sailor or engineer, including Chester himself or even Professor Thomson. And then there are the other times, when he comes close to incoherence.

Yet for all the apprehension Chester feels about having Otis with him, he knows he had no other choice. His older brother was bereft without him, and there is something gratifying about that. Chester finds himself grateful that he is able to help his brother. He sometimes thinks they are, each for the other, the only person in the world.

840 Miles Paid Out

Afternoon, seventh day. Alarm bells. Engines stop. Ship glides. Paying out slows to minimum. No signals from Ireland. The cable is dead.

Professor Thomson runs an impedance test. The fault lies near the ship. They will pull up the cable again. More bells. All hands are roused for the job.

3 Miles Taken Up

Midmorning, eighth day and the seas are rough enough to hamper work. Nineteen hours pass. After the cable has been cut, brought fretfully the seven hundred feet around to the bow, and inched aboard again, the fault is found.

"The same damned thing," Cyrus Field says.

And it is easy for all to see. The trouble is another iron wire driven clear through the cable.

837 Miles Paid Out (Ship Not Moving)

"Where is he?" Joachim Lindt is demanding to know. He has pulled Chester Ludlow off to one side of the stern deck, as if for a private conference, but he is speaking too loudly for that.

"I don't know," Chester says, and he truly doesn't. Otis had not been present for the taking up, nor for the splicing, which is now almost done. Chester doesn't know where Otis is, and it makes him uneasy, but he's been too preoccupied with the repairs to go looking for him.

"I demand to know what he has been doing," Joachim Lindt spits out, drawing the attention of the men around the splicing bench. Suddenly all the Cablemen and the nearby crew know that one of the coengineers is angry with the other.

"Did you give him 'orders'?"

"Mr. Lindt," Chester says, "if you wish to talk—"

"I *wish* to find out what is being done to our cable!" Lindt exclaims this loudly enough to be heard by all on the stern deck.

"No one said it before me," Lindt continues. "No one said it, but everyone thought it when they looked at the cable"—and Lindt strides over to the bulwark, placing one hand on the rail, the other on his hip—"*someone* has done this!"

To Chester this would be an absurd display of coarse acting if the consequences for Otis—and for him—were not so serious. The other Cablemen are frowning. They are squinting in the bright sunlight, so it is difficult to tell at whom they are looking. Messrs. Hoyt, Rettig, and Skidmore stroke their beards. Professor Thomson and Field shift their weight from one foot to the other.

"Two wires are driven through the cable. Perfect for shortening the circuit, as our Professor Thomson here has said. How are these wires driven through the cable? By sprites? Did your brother or did your brother not work for the Siberian cable expedition?"

"Mr. Lindt!" Chester says, almost barking out the words. "If you wish—"

"*Did he?*"

"Yes! But that has—"

"Our *rival!*" Lindt exclaims. "The one company that, if we fail, stands to gain. The *only* company, for they will have the exclusive capacity to transmit telegraph messages from North America to Asia *and Europe. They* will span the globe! But if we succeed *first*, they might as well roll up their wire and go home. How interesting that a former employee of our rival has been invited aboard this ship."

"Is that true, Chester?" Field asks.

Chester is struck how Field, who always addresses him by his surname, has just now called him Chester.

"Is it true he worked for them?"

"Yes," Chester says. There seems to be no point protesting anymore. The best course seems to be to give Lindt what he wants. They go looking for Otis.

And they find him in his stateroom, on his back, on his bed. He is not asleep. He is in some sort of trance. His eyes are closed, his breathing rapid. A candle on the table has burned out. The room, though close and closed, has a strangely airy odor about it. Whatever it is, it is not the atmosphere of a cramped berth on a sea voyage. Only Chester—and probably Professor Thomson—is familiar with the odor, and that is by virtue of their experiments with electricity. If asked, Chester would have said the air had the quality of the aftermath of an electrical discharge—strangely purified and cleansed.

But there is no electrical equipment about—only Otis, lying on his bunk
with his brother whispering in his ear, gently chafing and patting his hand,
imploring him to wake up or come back or just to answer, to say something, *anything.*

And after a few moments, Otis turns his head and blinks his eyes,
surprised to see all the faces looking down on him, but calmed by the sight
of his brother.

"Otis, are you all right? Are you with us?" Chester asks.

"Yes," Otis says.

"Were you asleep?" Chester asks.

"No," says Otis.

"We need you to account for your whereabouts, Otis, if you weren't
asleep."

"My whereabouts?" Otis seems to be coming around to what is being
asked of him. If he hasn't been asleep, he nonetheless appears to be waking
up.

"Where have you been?" asks Joachim Lindt. "What have you been
doing the past twelve hours?"

Chester looks around with annoyance at Lindt for butting in. Otis, in
his dazed state, is staring at his boots and at the tiny flecks of light he sees
on them. Everyone else is waiting for his answer. He continues to look at
the lights.

"Where have you been?" Herr Lindt demands again.

"Mount Washington," Otis says.

1,100 Miles Paid Out

The Cablemen meet and elect to have an inspection team watch the tubs
at all times. The only crew allowed belowdecks near the tubs are the sixteen
men helping to keep the line feeding out smoothly. They will be under
constant watch by the inspectors. And the men in the tubs are to watch
the inspectors, thus ensuring there will be witnesses to anything that might
be going on.

Otis is not allowed to walk about the ship without being under the eye
of a seaman or one of the graphers. They are discreet and keep their

distance, allowing Otis free rein of the ship—except belowdecks near the circuses.

Just as the second mate is doing now: walking along the deck slowly in the moonlight, idly splicing a monkey's paw into the end of a length of hemp line, he follows the two Ludlow brothers. A waxing three-quarter moon lays down a silver path that bisects the *Great Eastern*'s wake. Boiler smoke from the four funnels flutters across the moonlight. The cable machinery chugs along and the ship's main engines rumble, but the crew on duty is neither singing nor chattering. It is a contemplative interlude aboard the giant vessel.

The second mate is too far away to hear what the Ludlow brothers are saying (and too absorbed in his splicing). Besides, eavesdropping is not his charge. His is only to be sure the taller, red-haired, older brother keeps away from the cable.

Chester is trying not to sound reproachful, but he is disturbed.

"What did you mean 'Mount Washington'?" he asks. "What am I supposed to make of that?"

Otis nods, runs his hands through his hair, purses his lips preparing for a response, but Chester continues:

"For that matter, what is *anybody* supposed to make of it? You know, they turn to me for explanation when it comes to your ... well, your idiosyncrasies. But that one was ... ," and Chester can only shrug, expel a gust of air to express his befuddlement.

Otis begins by explaining to Chester about transetheric travel. But Chester has heard all this before and stops him.

"Brother, it's not so important that I understand about this spiritualism of yours. It's not so important that I even *believe* in it. What's important is that the cable gets laid and that you have nothing to do with trying to stop it."

"Do you believe in it?"

"What?" Chester asks.

"Do you believe in transetheric travel?"

"Otis, that is not the issue."

"*Do* you?"

"Good Lord, Otis—"

"Do you?"

Chester wants to say no and put an end to it. But Otis sounds almost desperate.

Should he say yes? Chester wonders. Yes, he believes in transetheric travel? He can't do it, for it would be false, or would be riddled with a tentativeness that Otis would detect. And then, too, Chester remembers something. It comes to him when he tries to avoid Otis's piercing stare and looks out toward the trail of moonlight off the stern. The reflected light on the water out there puts him in mind of the figure of the little girl, dancing ahead of him on the tracks when he was walking, delirious or perhaps more clearheaded than ever in his life.

"I believe," Chester says, "in something like it."

And Otis smiles, faces his brother, lays a hand on each of Chester's shoulders, and flashes a look of almost paternal pride.

"That's all a man can ask," Otis says. "I'm glad of it."

He begins walking again, arm at Chester's elbow, encouraging him along. They round the bow deck and begin sternward. The second mate just stands by a longboat davit and watches—no need to follow them; they're working their way back toward him anyhow.

Otis is explaining that he had been in his berth, experimenting: leaving the ship and traveling through the ether. He *knew* he was under suspicion already. He could read the Lindt fellow like a book. Otis therefore decided to avoid any occasion for trouble and to isolate himself and use the time for what he calls "some spiritual work." He had his stateroom—his monk's cell—and he had some substances that, he says, help him "venture forth."

"And soon enough, there I was, on Mount Washington. Back practically at our old home," Otis says. "My old home."

He tries to explain how that mountain is his lodestone in these events, how, when he induces a trance and travels transetherically, he often finds himself back on that home peak, near where he—and Chester—grew up. He tries to explain about the flecks of light he saw on his boots when everyone was suspecting him of sabotage, those flecks that, strangely, aren't there now but that were a sign that he actually *had* been there on that rocky, almost alpine peak with the same waxing moon rising in the same black sky, the hulking summit cone rising above him, the lights of Conway and the hotels visible in the valley.

"Otis, did you teach Franny to do this . . . this travel you speak of?"

Otis stops. In all the time since Chester first came out of the crowd that rainy afternoon in Hyde Park, he has not mentioned Franny in Otis's presence.

"No," Otis says. "She had another gift."

Chester feels his throat suddenly constrict in the salt air. He coughs.

"What gift was that?" he asks.

They begin strolling again. To keep them in sight, the second mate, who also had stopped when they did, now begins strolling, too, tightening the monkey's paw splice.

"The gift of guidance," Otis says. "I could tell, however successful or unsuccessful she might be at contacting the spirit world, she would surely be a superlative guide there for others."

"She was," Chester says. "She *is*." And he explains what he's heard about Franny's life. It isn't much. Just what he's seen from a couple of newspaper notices, the flyer, and the little bits mentioned by Mrs. Tyler.

Otis smiles wanly.

"How is old Mrs. Tyler?" he asks.

"As ever," says Chester. "In some ways, to my earthbound life, she is the lodestone that Mount Washington is to you in your etheric wanderings."

"And her husband?"

"Holding on well enough for a lobsterman who drinks too much."

"He gave me a bit of a headache the night before I left Willing Mind," Otis says. "He had himself convinced I had been less than a gentleman with Franny while I was staying there. He expressed his conviction on my skull."

Even now Otis can remember where the blows struck, and he rubs the spots.

Chester has stopped walking again. The second mate down the deck must stop as well. He's finished the monkey's paw. He flips the end of the rope blunted by the splice. He wonders about all this stopping and starting the brothers are doing.

Otis steps toward Chester. "There was no truth to it. We were intimates only in our spiritual searchings. In our desire to reach out to Betty. In nothing else. I am as innocent of Tyler's suspicions as I am of trying to sabotage the cable. I had hoped you knew that."

Chester nods. "I know it."

They turn and walk the other way, back again toward the bow. They pass the second mate.

"You're my brother," Otis whispers to Chester. "He's my keeper."

Chester apologizes that he wasn't able to dissuade the other Cablemen from insisting on this surveillance.

"So you do believe me on that," Otis says.

"I believe you," Chester says, "on all things."

And Chester knows the rightness of saying this to Otis, knows that whatever darkness and demons flail at his brother, Otis is to be believed.

He wishes more than anything at this moment to tell Otis what has happened to his heart. Not, as with Lindt, to offer himself up for atonement, but to make a simple, brotherly accounting of how a life—*his* life—has passed, so Otis will know.

Otis listens as Chester tells of the 1858 cable, of his estrangement from Franny, of Frau Lindt, the cannon, the wreck, the war.

But strangely, to this brother so attuned to the spiritual world, so sensitive to visitations and specters and transmutative experience, Chester says nothing about the vision of the little girl. In this long unburdening of his heart, Chester owns to everything but that. He holds her a secret unto himself alone.

The second mate stands watching the two brothers. Then he notices sitting near the Ludlows, unbeknownst to them, another figure: a large, thick fellow, with a book or a pad in his lap. It is the sketch artist, leaning against the Tuesday mast, drawing the moonlight, listening to the brothers' tales. And the second mate stands, flipping and catching the monkey's paw. Flipping and catching, flipping and catching, wishing his watch would pass.

1,300 Miles Paid Out

It is Cyrus Field himself, president of the Atlantic Telegraph Company, who is on inspection duty in the cable circus midmorning August second when there is a harsh grating sound as the cable passes up through the iron bails guiding it out of the hold.

"That's a piece of wire!" a crewman shouts.

Field follows with a call to stop the ship, to stop feeding out the cable. The call must be relayed man to man up and out of the hold, forward all the way to the helm, where the officer of the deck must give the orders to the engine room (by calling down voice tubes) to halt the ship's way. By the time all that is done, the fault is long overboard and far astern.

But alarm bells are ringing, and the entire stern deck crew and Cablemen are rushing to the paying-out equipment.

"Halt the ship!" Joachim Lindt, still buttoning his waistcoat, shouts as he spills out on deck from his stateroom.

"Being done!" a seaman calls, and the *Great Eastern* trembles as the paddle wheels and propeller are thrown into reverse, beating against the forward progress of the ship. The paying-out machinery slows down as crewmen reduce steam and apply the brakes.

Meanwhile, Lindt and Chester have made their way to the telegraph cabin. Field has arrived from the hold; Professor Thomson is already inside, testing the signal. Trace is there. Even Messrs. Hoyt, Rettig, and Skidmore work their way in, having thrown down their cards and sheet music and bolted from the saloon.

"It's not dead," Professor Thomson informs them in the darkness. They can tell the professor is bent over the galvanometer, staring into the box, watching for indications of the little light's movement. Everyone is winded from sprinting from all parts of the ship. Panting sounds fill the shadowy, little room.

"It's not perfect, gentlemen, but it's not dead," Professor Thomson says.

Professor Thomson continues to watch the light. Chester shuffles through the bodies in the darkness for a look. There is conferring among the groups, all done in darkness—or nearly so, as their eyes are beginning to adjust to the minute illumination from the tiny red lantern.

"It appears," Chester says to the entire group after a few minutes, "and I think Professor Thomson will agree with me, that even with this flaw, the cable is still transmitting signals. Professor Thomson and I calculate that we are able to send and receive messages at approximately four words per minute. That is not perfect, but . . ."

"But it is enough for the cable to be profitable," says Otis.

"*What is* he *doing here?*" Joachim Lindt is practically shouting. He is twisting around in the dark, looking for Otis Ludlow.

"Out! I want him out of here!" Lindt is in a rage. He makes out Otis in the corner, standing behind an unwitting bulwark of Messrs. Hoyt, Rettig, and Skidmore.

"Mr. Lindt, *please!*" says Cyrus Field.

"Ludlow!" Lindt barks, wheeling around. "I hold you responsible. What is he doing here?"

"He came with me," Chester says. "We were breakfasting together. With Captain Anderson."

"I was interested in his travels in Siberia," says Anderson.

"Oh, shut up!" Lindt blurts. "Get him out of here. You're the captain. This is your ship. I demand you order him out!"

"Now see here, Lindt," Professor Thomson says.

"How can you countenance his presence?" Lindt demands. He seems to be asking the entire assembly in the room. It's too dark to tell whom he is addressing. "He is the man who very likely is destroying our cable."

"You have no proof," says Field.

"Even less than none," Chester says. "He's been under watch night and day for nearly a thousand miles."

"Gentlemen, we *all* have something that needs our attention," Professor Thomson says. The burr of his Scottish accent has a way of sounding like a reprimand to culprits in a schoolyard scuffle. "We have cable nearly three-quarters laid. What do we do with it?"

"I shall step outside," Otis says quietly. "If it will help."

"It will," says Lindt, and he orders one of the graphers to guard Otis. When they've gone, Chester speaks. "He's right, you know. At four words per minute, the cable can still handle enough traffic to be more than profitable."

"Bah! What does he know?" Lindt asks.

"Herr Lindt," Chester says, "he knows enough about telegraphy—"

"From working with our rival!"

"He knows enough about telegraphy to understand that even with the flaw, the cable is still functional and will more than make its money back."

Lindt snorts and says nothing. He stands next to Messrs. Hoyt, Rettig, and Skidmore with his arms folded across his chest.

Chester confers with Professor Thomson and Cyrus Field. "The seas are heavy today," he announces. "Captain Anderson, what do you know about the weather?"

"I know the glass is dropping last I looked," says the captain. "Not precipitous. But I can't say the seas will be getting any better."

"The most prudent course seems clear," says Chester. "Keep on as we are. We all know the risks of pulling up cable. A cable that works, if a little slower than we'd hoped, is still a success."

Field and Thomson are nodding in agreement. Chester can make that out in the dim obscurity of the cabin.

"No," Lindt says. "Absolutely not. I shall not allow it."

"Mr. Lindt—" Cyrus Field begins.

"No, Herr Field. This is not something I can sanction. With all due respect, sir, as the Incorporation is now constituted, you are our customer. We are to provide you with a satisfactorily constructed cable. This cable is now not up to my specifications. If it should fail, and you, our customer, should refuse to accept it, then, well . . ."—and he turns to appeal to the triumvirate of Messrs. Hoyt, Rettig, and Skidmore—"then *our* company would be ruined."

There is agreement from the three representatives of the Telegraph Construction and Maintenance Company, enough to make it clear that they side with Lindt.

And thus, given the constitution of the Incorporation and Lindt's obstinacy, the issue is settled: Chester is overruled; the cable comes up.

1,300 Miles Paid Out
(Ship Not Moving)

The cable has been cut, the ship turned, and the line brought around again to the bow. The sailors are becoming handy at the task, but the seas are showing a troublesome chop, and the wind is increasing.

It is as the men are preparing the take-up mechanism on the bow that Joachim Lindt notices there appears to be no one guarding the hatch to the cable circus. This should not be. A member of the inspection crew should always be there on duty, but no one is. The stern cable hold is unguarded.

Lindt says nothing but leaves the bow and walks swiftly down the deck, arms sawing the air. He doesn't want to draw attention to himself by running, but when he realizes how comical he must look scurrying along, arms scissoring like a semaphore, he breaks into his old Running Man gait.

His suspicion is confirmed. There is no one on duty. In the confusion of discovering the cable flaw, the changing of watches, the need for crewmen to transfer the line from stern to bow, the tubs have been left unguarded.

And someone is down there!

Lindt nearly jumps over the lip of the hatch and into the hold. A man is there, bent low, on his knees, hunched over the cable.

"Stop! You! Halt! Sabotage! I have him! Stop! Right now!" Joachim Lindt is screaming, pointing, practically dancing around the open hatch. He gestures wildly for nearby deckhands to come, and they begin rushing over.

"Sabotage!" Lindt wails.

Even with crewmen crowding around all sides of the hatch opening, plenty of daylight still shines down onto the orbital circles of cable lying in their tub, where the lone figure straightens up slowly on stiff legs and squints into the light. It is Professor William Thomson.

1,300 Miles Paid Out
(Ship Still Not Moving)

It is impossible not to take sides. Jack Trace has to admit there was legitimacy to Lindt's refusal to settle for laying a faulted cable. Still, there is pleasure to be found in seeing the abrasive Lindt make a fool of himself.

Trace had been one of the men gathered around the hatch when Professor Thomson looked up. The professor rose and turned slowly, and already there was a look of perturbation on his face: his brow furrowed, his lips pursed behind his beard. Lindt stopped his hopping about and stared, openmouthed but still pointing at the man in the hold. His shouts had turned to a stuttering series of grunts, his dance to a discomfited rocking back and forth.

The professor just looked up and said, "Oh hush, Lindt, and get down here with the others. I've found the problem."

Once the Cablemen are assembled in the hold, Professor Thomson explains that while the ship's company was bringing cable around to the bow take-up devices, he had quietly come down into the circus to inspect the cable.

"I paced off the distance of the cable lying here that would have been beneath the flaw that we estimate is three miles back. That puts it right about here." The professor walks around the large circular tub, pacing on top of the cable. The other Cablemen follow him. They, too, have climbed into the circus by ladders from the hold. The ship's officers, some of the crew, and Jack Trace are gathered around the hatch, looking down. Professor Thomson addresses them all as if he were in an amphitheater, lecturing a class.

"Now here," he says, tapping his toe on the cable, "you will notice something about the cable armor. It is cracked, split; and protruding from the fissure are pieces of wire. My guess is the weight of the cable in the flakes above destroyed this section of the armor, which split open like a bundle of sticks. The pieces of armoring wire penetrated the cable above it, which is now some three miles back toward Ireland."

The Cablemen in the tub squat down to inspect the cracked skin of the armor. Several pewter-colored iron wires poke through the tarred guttapercha like whiskers. Chester Ludlow breaks off a piece, shows it to Field and passes it on to Messrs. Hoyt, Rettig, and Skidmore. Lindt, arms folded, lower lip thrust out, will not touch the specimen.

"It would seem," Professor Thomson says, "that what we had been taking as a case of attempted murder was really an attempted suicide."

The engineers quickly decide that the best course is to be even more vigilant inspecting the cable as it goes out. The extra surveillance watches are detailed not to guard against sabotage, but to scrutinize the cable's sheathing for possible flaws.

Perhaps more opprobrium would befall Lindt were there time, but the cable must come up. Lindt remains stoic and tries to maintain a commanding mien by pacing the deck with his arms folded, chin jutting. Trace even considers sketching him surreptitiously with a small storm cloud over his head and devils poking him with bits of iron wire, but that seems a bit puerile under the circumstances, and besides, Ludlow has not given him authority to "cartoon" on this expedition. He settles for a picture of Professor Thomson, alone in the hold, making his discovery.

2 Miles Taken Up
(1,298 Miles Paid Out)

The retrieval has been going badly. Captain Anderson has trouble keeping the *Great Eastern* properly aligned with the cable as it is reeled in. Crosswinds and waves are tormenting the ship. The cable is refusing to come in smoothly over the bow and is abrading on the port side of the vessel, then riding over the sheaves crookedly. Crewmen are tense, scolding one another, as they fear losing the line.

And that is what happens. In a trice, men and machinery—the entire take-up operation—become like dupes in a magician's disappearing act. Suddenly, they stand useless and empty-handed. A piece of the cable catches the flange of a take-up sheave and snaps, and the weight of the ocean end of the cable yanks the severed end through the blocks and down into the sea. The winds and waves erase the splash in an instant. The men on deck stand staring at their empty hands.

Rescue Plan
(1,298 Miles Paid Out)

With Lindt still sulking, it falls to Chester to take sole command. It had been Otis's idea to design, build, and bring along a giant grappling iron to drag the ocean bottom in the event of a lost cable. It was a preposterous long shot—a folly, really—but back during the outfitting of the ship, Otis was so stirred by the idea of recovering a lost cable, so focused on its necessity and its possibility, that Chester, looking for a way to engage his distracted brother, had quietly assented to the idea. Now Chester will use it.

He instructs a detail to go below and bring up the equipment. He explains to the other Cablemen what he plans to do. Professor Thomson smiles with obvious admiration. Captain Anderson and Cyrus Field quickly build enthusiasm for the scheme, simple and audacious as it is. Messrs. Hoyt, Rettig, and Skidmore are reticent to align with the engineer they had increasingly seen as the opposition, but Chester's attention to their doubts and their position as the major voting bloc warm them and soon they are eager at the prospect.

Only Herr Lindt holds back. His defiant aspect has been reduced to a tactical neutrality. Trace, watching all this, has the feeling Lindt has withdrawn so far from contention that he is like a wraith, shifting about on the outskirts of the group.

And Otis. Chester wonders where his brother is. He should be here for this, to claim his vindication. For even if this plan fails, they will both be marked for cleverness, pluck, and valor. But Otis is nowhere to be found.

2 Miles East; Several Miles Upwind
(1,298 Miles Paid Out)

The *Great Eastern* has steamed a mile or two back eastward along the submerged cable's path and several miles upwind. The grapnel—a five-pronged claw, its shank taller than two men—is dropped overboard. It has been attached to every length of iron hauling line—five miles of it—that the ship has aboard. The crew has had to fasten six-hundred-foot sections together with shackles to reach the bottom. It takes nearly two hours for the descending line to show slack, indicating that the grapnel has hit the seabed.

It is midday, sunny, and the wind has eased some. Captain Anderson orders the engines shut down and just enough canvas raised to give the *Great Eastern* steerageway.

Drifting South, Dragging Bottom
(1,298 Miles Paid Out)

The ship is uncommonly quiet. The boilers are down to an idling murmur. The small waves on the sea's surface make their self-absorbed fussy noises. Occasionally there is a call from the helm to trim a sail, and the noise of it is startling even to the most seasoned crewman. Everyone able is on deck. There must be three hundred men topside. To Otis Ludlow, on crosstrees high up the Monday mast, it resembles a summer day on the Digue at Ostend with all the sightseers.

It is the helmsman who notices the change first. Early in the evening of August third, he reports to the officer of the deck, who reports to Captain Anderson that the ship is pulling forcefully to port. Something is weighing on the grappling line going out the bow of the *Great Eastern*.

No Longer Drifting
(1,298 Miles Paid Out)

It is long after dark, sometime in the middle of the night, when Chester orders the take-up engines to slow. He has calculated that they are within a few fathoms now of pulling up the grapnel and, he hopes, the cable.

Captain Anderson has to order men back from the bow. It has become too crowded there for the on-duty crew to work. Men have climbed the shrouds and ratlines of the Monday mast to get a better view, but there is nothing to see. A warm fog has settled in on the water, and the string of lanterns glows with yellow coronas, casting little light on the sea and on the line descending into it. But then the grapnel's shank, thicker than the iron line, appears, and after it, a slimy delineation stirs in the black water. It is the cable itself, caught in the claws of the grapnel.

There are cheers that begin with several yelps and shouts from men closest to the rails who recognize what has broken the surface. Soon jubilation and huzzahs roll down the deck and even up from below.

But the crew does not have enough securing lines tied onto the cable, and when the grappling line is released and the three hauling lines take over, they snap like a lute string and the cable flops back into the ocean. Gone again.

Two Days' Wait
(1,298 Miles Paid Out)

This time it is Joachim Lindt who says they must try again. The Cablemen look at him in surprise.

"No. We *must!*"

Lindt has dropped his pose as miffed and contravened coengineer. He blurts out his exhortation, giving voice to what everyone else feels, and they are grateful to him for it. Yes, yes, they all agree. We must try again.

But as dawn breaks, the fog remains, and Captain Anderson is unable to use his sextant to fix the ship's position and therefore unable to find the cable's.

They drift, fogbound, for two days.

Everyone who is not on watch sleeps.

Everyone, save Otis. He has not left the foremost masthead. He climbed up there sometime after the cable escaped back into the sea. Chester climbs up to speak with him. Otis reaches into a seaman's bag he has brought up to the platform and secured there. From it he pulls a sextant.

"Mine," he says. In clipped and abbreviated phrases he lets Chester know that the sextant is one he has kept with him for years, since his second sea voyage to the Pacific. He will use it to determine their position as soon as the sun shows itself. Then he will tell the ship where to go.

"They have one on the quarterdeck below," Chester says gently. "You needn't stay up here."

But Otis ignores him, so Chester descends.

Chester wonders later, down in his cabin, if Otis is perhaps some kind of receptor or relay for all the overwrought and strained emotions on the ship. As they flow downward toward the cable or out into time toward a future of success or failure, the emotions first pass through Otis. The intensity of it must be, Chester thinks, like Professor Thomson's delicate light galvanometer trying to cope with Whitehouse's ramrod voltages coming down the old cable.

It isn't long before the entire ship's company is nurturing an affection for the eccentric fellow on the foremast. His endurance, his fervid desire for the expedition's success, are marks of distinction to most sailors. His devotion at the expense of his own comfort and safety is admirable to others. They smile up at him, check to be sure he is aloft every time they come up on deck.

And when the sun does finally show its face after the third day of fog, Captain Anderson calls to Otis for the coordinates. When Otis shouts them down from the masthead, the first mate, who had been shooting the sun with his own sextant near the helm, whispers to Anderson, "He's right, sir."

The captain scowls at him.

"Just as we knew, sir, he would be, sir," the chastened mate stammers. "All along, right, sir."

With their position determined, Anderson tells Chester they are forty-six miles south of the cable. They steam full speed north.

Second Grappling
(1,298 Miles Paid Out)

They strike the cable after midnight August seventh. Captain Anderson calls general quarters; slowly they begin raising the cable.

But barely two hours into the raising, the grappling line snaps.

A shackle parted. Chester calculates they lost a mile of line and the ship's only grapnel.

A voice calls down from above.

Third Attempt
(1,298 Miles Paid Out)

"We loaded two!"

"What?"

Otis is shouting down from the masthead. Chester is shouting back. All hands are looking aloft.

"The gear locker just aft of the forward coalhold. Another grappling hook. You wouldn't go fishing with only one hook in your tackle box, would you? I had them build and stow a second grapnel."

It isn't even necessary for Captain Anderson to detail a gang to get the hook; already men are racing toward the hold.

Chester laughs and waves up to Otis, who, though grizzled and haggard, appears to be smiling as he waves back.

But with a mile of line lost on the bottom, it is necessary to fill out the grappling line with hemp hawser. No one is confident it will be strong enough to bear the weight of a rising cable, but there is no choice. The crew hauls every foot of line to the deck, carefully ties it into the iron grappling line while the *Great Eastern* steams into position.

For three days they drift and drag across the cable's coordinates, steam back, drift and drag, steam back, drift and drag. Finally, Chester orders the line hauled in. When the grapnel surfaces, they see the line had wrapped around one of the flukes. The ship had been dragging the hook backward, probably bumping the grapnel right over the cable every time they crossed it.

Fourth Try
(1,298 Miles Paid Out)

The wind has shifted and comes out of the north. The chill air meets the warm and suddenly it is raw and wet out. The seas are jumpy. The rain has an Arctic bite to it, even now in early August. Otis is still aloft. Messrs. Hoyt, Rettig, and Skidmore have joined with, each in their turn, Captain Anderson, Professor Thomson, Cyrus Field, and even Herr Lindt in entreating Otis to come down. He waves and refuses. He has tied himself to the lookout platform. The second mate has brought him dry clothes and an oilskin slicker. Chester had ordered the clothing taken up to his brother. Chester understands, in some inchoate way, Otis's need to stay aloft.

In the early afternoon, they hook the cable. The procedure begins, but few aboard can stand to witness it. For one, the rain is raw and the weather on deck is punishing. Almost no one but the sailors on duty—and Chester Ludlow—are watching the machinery.

In the saloon, Professor Thomson stares at the pages of a Dickens serial, the one about the interminable lawsuit, but he can't seem to move his eyes. Cyrus Field traces with his boot toe the vaguely floral and marine patterns of a Turkoman rug by the buffet table. The card-game-piano-playing pastime of Messrs. Hoyt, Rettig, and Skidmore does not work. None of them can concentrate, and time does not seem to pass. Herr Lindt is in his cabin, lying on his bunk, staring unseeingly at the Oriental silk dressing screen.

At dusk, with perhaps two miles of line carefully hauled up, somewhere below the surface, a shackle slips. The engines jerk with the lack of tension, then slow again when the weight once again takes hold. One of the sailors at the steam throttle makes a show of mopping his brow in exaggerated relief. Chester grins, nods. Hauling continues.

When the shackle finally does go, about two minutes later, the throttlemen and brakemen are so quick, the engines barely accelerate. But there is no doubt what happened. The line coming in is now slack.

A sailor runs over to pull the emergency whistle cord, but Chester stops him. There is nothing to be done. They have lost most of the hauling line. It is spiraling slowly through the black depths with the grapnel and the cable, headed toward the ocean floor. They don't have enough line aboard for another try. There is no point rousing the ship. They've lost the cable, this time for good.

Chester orders the men to continue hauling in the line, keeping the engines chugging at their usual speed, while he goes below to break the news quietly to the other Cablemen.

He finds them—all of them—in the grand saloon, having just picked their way through a dinner. The storm outside has lifted quite literally as the rain has stopped and the dark cloud bank in the west has parted from the horizon, allowing a fierce bronze light to slide through the crack, across the waves toward the ship. It burnishes everything in the saloon.

Jack Trace is marveling at the light and wishing there were a way to capture the color when he notices Chester Ludlow standing near the entrance to the deck. Even in the brazen light, Chester's face looks pale. As each man sees him, each knows what has happened. Without a word, all the Cablemen take their chairs and pull them into a circle near the piano and potted palms. It looks almost like a prayer meeting, Trace thinks, or a séance.

"Our last bolt is sped," Chester murmurs.

The others nod. They know the consequences. Trace looks out at the gash of amber sunlight between the clouds and the sea. A dark seabird makes a dive for prey.

The group sits in silence until shouts come fluttering in from the deck. Chester is perturbed. "Damn," he says, "I told the men not to—"

But it is not the lost cable the sailors are shouting for. It is something else. Otis Ludlow has hurled himself from the masthead into the sea.

CHAPTER XXVIII

THE HOTEL AMMONOOSUC

New Hampshire, Late Summer 1865

Into the Sublime

The railroads have threaded their way all through the White Mountains. They haul goods from the farms of northern New Hampshire, and even Vermont, down through the high country to Portsmouth, Boston, and the sea. Their tracks run through the mountain passes—the "notches"—and twist up into the valleys and plateaus to the spruce and fir forests, where new lumber camps are appearing. As timber and produce roll out of the White Mountains over precarious trestles and through sinuous cuts in the granite and pine, in return comes a new commodity, something infrequently seen in this frontier until recently—tourists.

From Boston mainly, but from Hartford, Providence, and even New York, they arrive in the "Chrystall Hills" to partake of what generations of Europeans have been flocking to the Alps to experience: the Sublime—that inspirational and restorative state to be found away from crowded cities, among high peaks and rocky alpine terrain, near roaring cataracts, in quiet forests proximate to precipices and defiles, a mix of serenity and intimations of awe. And waiting for the eager throngs to experience all this is J. Beaumol Spude.

His railroads are here—for he has come out of the Civil War with

considerable money invested in the Boston & Maine, the Grand Trunk,
and the St. Lawrence lines. And seeing that agriculture has moved west
and that the White Mountains are wilder and less settled now than they
were forty years ago, Spude is here with investments in hotels. Railroads
build the hotels, and Spude has his money in both. In particular, he has
invested handsomely in a fifty-room, white-clapboard lodge with wings and
ells, half a score of porches and verandas, and corner turrets topped with
red shingles and bright brass finials. The Hotel Ammonoosuc faces the
Crawford Notch road and extends lawns and a long, sweeping carriage
drive out to gather in the travelers. Behind the hotel, across more broad
lawns and beyond a dark montane forest, rise the granite-bouldered summits of the Presidential Range, the highest mountains in the Northeast;
pyramidal, treeless summits, the highest of all being Mount Washington.

It is late summer, and Spude has come to the Ammonoosuc for its
end-of-season splendor. The hotel is only two years old. It has done a good
business even through the last months of the war. For who wouldn't wish
to be relieved of the distress and cares of the conflict by the grandeur of
the mountains, by the croquet and badminton lawns, the pine grotto with
wishing well, the nearby stables, the meadows and rustic pasturage? The
Sublime has called, and the tourists have come.

This is the first year Spude has been able to visit the Ammonoosuc.
The incompatibility of his position as a Missouri-Louisiana financier and
gunpowder manufacturer and the hotel's location in that bastion of Yan-
keedom—New Hampshire—has made a stay at the Ammonoosuc impossible
until now.

But the war has reached its welcome, if grim, conclusion. The country
seems not to have toppled after the assassination of its president. (An *actor*
killed Abe Lincoln. . . . An *actor*. After his experience with the Phantasmagorium's dissolutes and misfits, Spude is not surprised.)

J. Beaumol Spude has come to the Ammonoosuc to inspect his holdings, but already his interests and his investments are heading west. These
New England railroads are flourishing, but the real railroad boom, now
that the war is over, is going to be out in the territories, all the way to the
Pacific Coast. J. Beaumol Spude dreams of the day when his money will
be part of the rail lines binding the oceans across the continent. The telegraph boys have tried—and failed—to get another cable across the Atlantic.
Shut out of their little club, Spude followed the adventures of the *Great
Eastern* in the papers. He could have been resentful, but what would

be the profit in that? There's room enough on this planet for all manner of enterprise. The war taught J. Beaumol Spude that. Or maybe it was the other way around: J. Beaumol Spude showed that your money could work either side of the battlements and picket lines. There's always room enough and need enough, especially during wartime.

Now, though, Spude is enjoying the returns of money well invested and the peace of late summer in the White Mountains. The air is crisp, there is the tang of woodsmoke in the mornings as the hotel fireplaces are lit to take away the night's chill. There is a hint of rust and yellow on some of the leaves higher up the mountainsides. And this morning, when the daylight on its far side became strong enough to illumine its features, Mount Washington showed a dusting of snow up on its rocky summit cone.

J. Beaumol Spude loves it. Early autumn up here is a world-beater. It makes J. Beaumol Spude glad to be alive. His health is holding up. He's a little stouter than before the war, walks a little stiffer owing to the gout, but still has the stature and demeanor of a well-stoked parlor stove. And life is good, if a little lonely sometimes for an aging widower.

But J. Beaumol Spude isn't dwelling on that. He's already looking forward to tonight's diversion. Someone he knows is here. It caught him by surprise. Tonight's entertainment for the guests is to be an evening of spiritualist virtuosities and wonders, a summoning of specters, a group séance with all willing patrons, an evening of amazement and connections with the Other World, featuring the Spiritscope of Dr. Zephaniah Hermes, thaumaturge, and the spiritual magnetism and prognostications of Dame Frances Piermont.

Spude might not have recognized her from the name, but the poster on the announcement board has the unmistakable cameo likeness of Franny Ludlow.

And "Dame" Frances, no less. Spude likes the appellation for its theatricality, but such a flourish doesn't seem to square with his recollection of the reserved yet sharp mistress of the handsome home on the coast of Maine he visited all those years ago.

The Show

J. Beaumol Spude is disappointed. Worse than disappointed, he is concerned. He *shouldn't* be disappointed, though, for Dr. Zephaniah Hermes is a consummate stage performer: handsome, commanding, smooth in his movements, supple of voice, manly. The ladies in the audience draw a simultaneous gasp when Hermes strides out onto the stage in the hotel's grand salon. Even the spinster from Pawtucket who had attached herself to Spude on the scenic horseback ride that afternoon clearly now has a new object for her infatuation. But to Spude's eye, at least, Hermes's stage presence notwithstanding, the act is the baldest of balderdash. If any of the fifty or so audience members can't tell that Hermes has kick levers and pulleys, catgut trip wires and diversionary mirrors as part of that scrap-heap contraption he calls a Spiritscope, well, then they deserved to be fleeced.

The more he watches, the more Spude realizes that Hermes is relying on his animal magnetism, which, though considerable, seems to Spude to be a cover for gimcrackery and humbug.

Still, the audience wants to go along. Spude watches the crowd as much as Hermes himself. The conjurer performs spirit summonses with a couple of people from the assembled. He keeps it light: no one with sons or brothers dead at Cold Harbor or Gettysburg, just a woman yearning to hear from her long-passed mother. Then there's a fellow wanting to hear from his late horse, and the Spiritscope produces hoofbeats to signal all is well in the Great Stable in the Sky. The audience is delighted.

Spude can dismiss this as the flânerie of a pleasing theatrical hack. Indeed, most of the audience seems to be taking it that way. Then Dr. Hermes introduces Dame Frances Piermont, and Spude perks up. It is fully dark outside now, and as it is still warm enough to leave the salon's four sets of tall French doors open, a balsam-scented breeze stirs in the room as Franny enters to applause and the extended hand and courtly bow of Dr. Zephaniah Hermes, who with a subtle sidelong glance to the audience and the faintest of smiles, is able to insinuate that he is on most intimate terms with Dame Frances.

This galls Spude. Here is Franny Ludlow, still elegant, still poised, if a little older, a little more square of figure, but still handsome in Spude's estimation. Yes, he remembers she had been a touch piquant with him, perhaps almost rude, that time at her home in Maine. But he could forgive her that. He was taking her husband away on the Phantasmagorium tour, and there was the intrusion of Frau Lindt, something that Franny must have foreseen as trouble, and something that Spude, in his way, may have even pandered—all to sell tickets, all to finance the cable. In the event, Frances comported herself well, Spude thinks. A woman of stature and dignity in a difficult situation. A woman deserving, Spude thinks, of better than this. Better than that Hermes fellow's lascivious silent aside to the audience and better than billing as—what?—a fortune-teller.

For that is what she is. Attired in a dark maroon, almost black, gown (almost mourning, almost royal purple), wearing her dark hair swept up with a small tiara of modest bejewelment, she invites audience members up to sit with her on the dais, to hold her hands, face her, and talk with her about their lives as she asks questions, then proceeds to answer some of them herself and to supply surprising embellishments, entwined with predictions for the future.

But really the facts and forecasts are nothing that a colluding desk clerk, bellhop, or chambermaid couldn't supply. At one point, Dame Frances is talking to a girl of fifteen about her grandfather. Franny—Dame Frances— lets go of the girl's hands and produces a chalkboard. She asks the girl to think about her grandfather, and Franny draws a likeness—bald, bearded, spectacles. It is sometimes difficult to see the telesthetic images, she says, but does this resemble the man? Yes! Yes! It does. Very much, the delighted girl tells Franny. The audience sighs, applauds. Spude guesses a chambermaid supplied Franny with a briefly purloined picture.

For her finale Franny says that she will, with the group's assistance, try to put them all in the presence of their fallen President.

"I knew him," Franny says. "And his wife. I shall try to bring his spirit closer to us."

She says the gathering should not expect to see President Lincoln walk among them. That is not likely within her ken or power. But perhaps— *perhaps*—she can bring them all to feel the presence of the great and departed man. She has them close their eyes. (Spude is in the back row, near the French doors.) She asks them all to think about Mr. Lincoln. (Spude keeps his eyes open. He wants to watch out for any tricks.) She says if they have ever seen a daguerreotype of Mr. Lincoln, then to fix their thoughts on it or on words they might have read of his. If they have ever seen Mr. Lincoln in person, remember that day. Spude notices that everyone seems to have their eyes closed. Whereas Hermes's stage presence has an erotic power,

Franny's is one of authority earned, gentle, sure, and compassionate. A calm pervades the room.

Then Spude thinks he hears some faint strains of music coming in on the breeze. He can feel the giant presence of the mountains looming in the dark out the doors and beyond the forest. But on the breeze coming down from the peaks, Spude is sure he hears a faint melody. He quietly gets up and tiptoes out through the French doors and stands on the long veranda with its rows of rocking chairs facing the darkened peaks. Out beyond the edge of the riding ring, he sees a lantern. A boy, a stable groom or bellhop no doubt, is holding up a light for a man playing a cello—one of the hotel's chamber players conscripted for the effect. He is playing a dirgelike rendition of the "Battle Hymn of the Republic." Spude looks back in the salon. Franny is on the stage with her arms outstretched in a benedictory pose. Men in the audience have tears coming down their cheeks. Women are softly sobbing. The melody just barely reaches into the room.

Then Spude notices shadows moving from a window down the porch to his left. He quietly walks there and sees, when he peeks through the glass, the hotel bursar's office. He does not have long to look, for in a moment, applause erupts from back in the salon. But Spude is at the window long enough to see the bursar counting out bills and passing them to Dr. Hermes. When the applause thrums through the walls, Hermes quickly pockets the money and darts out the office down the hallway back to the salon, where he will step up on the stage to take his bows with Dame Frances Piermont.

At the Picture

There is a pony staked out on the back lawn. In a semicircle around him, perched on stools, are three men and five ladies. The dew is still on the grass as the sun, though it is past midmorning, has only recently shone above the dome of Mount Pleasant, a lesser peak south of Mount Washington. The ladies and gentlemen, wearing shawls and capes against the nip of the morning air, are part of the drawing class offered by the hotel for the guests' edification. The staked pony is the model. The instructor is a stork of a fellow who goes from pupil to pupil, stoops over their sketch pads, points to the paper, then to the pony, sculpts the air to illustrate something about form or mass or foreshortening, then goes on to the next student, making high, trotting steps through the dewy grass. A bored stableboy holds the little horse in position. The pupils sketch intently. The sun is warming the grass and the forests on the western slopes of the mountains; steam is rising into the watery light from the ravines and brook gorges.

Franny Ludlow watches the art class from the Ammonoosuc's reading room. It is an east-facing chamber with large, draped windows that look out on the lawns and the mountains. The room has leather wing chairs and velvet settees, tables with newspapers, and three walls of floor-to-ceiling bookshelves with rolling ladders by which means gentlemen can fetch volumes for themselves or the ladies. A couple of the male guests are picketed behind the Boston papers. The men cough occasionally and rattle the pages. Two ladies are writing letters at the escritoires on the sunny side of the room. The rest of the hotel guests are on bird walks or horseback rides, shooting at archery targets, pitching horseshoes, or sitting on the porch, looking up at the high peaks through telescopes and field glasses.

Franny has left Hermes sleeping in their tight little room on the upper floor of the hotel. They are staying in the end of the hotel where the musicians, cooks, and itinerant entertainers are billeted. Their rooms face away from the peaks and look down on the tarred roof of the hotel storage sheds. Franny has put on a light wool morning dress, something not too travel worn, so she will blend in with the guests, to come down and look again at the painting.

The work is huge, five by eight feet, and is a mountain scene. It shows a misty, precipitous cataract plunging in the lower foreground; intricate, almost obsessively exact renderings of every fir bough and mossy rock making up the foothills and ledges in the middle distance; and, in the farthest reaches, a snowcapped peak, resembling Mount Washington out the window but appearing even more lofty and formidable. Then, up the slopes on the right side of the painting, a profusion of clouds and forest fog that seems to throb with light from within and that might enshroud a peak higher than the grand one visible on the canvas, a peak that, if the skies were to clear, would be a forbidding, maybe even frightfully imposing, pinnacle. It is a turbulent, disturbing picture. It is almost as if the mountains, the wilderness—the artist himself—are shaking a fist at the viewer. There is no plaque, nameplate, or signature on the work, but it is obvious the painting is of a provenance with the one that hangs in the foyer of Willing Mind. Similar in grand size and dynamism, the painting is calculated to shock.

Franny hears the reading room French doors rattle, open, and close. The drawing master bustles by her, removes his beret, and nods as he passes: fellow toilers in the vineyards of artistic and spiritual uplift for the recreative class. He goes, and Franny continues to study the painting. She stands before the towering and brooding work, but she is no longer seeing it. The painting has plunged her back to Willing Mind and her old life. Not that she hasn't thought of it before, but the combination of her weariness (lack of sleep, a long, relentless summer tour of theaters, tent shows, and hotels as the Spiritscope's costar) and her increasingly diminishing prospects makes her almost immobile before the painting. She feels herself in the presence of the Ludlows: Chester; Otis; their father, whom she never met; *herself*, for technically she is still a Ludlow, still carries the name, is still Chester's wife, though nothing about her life now would stand as proof of that. She wonders in what shape her old home, Willing Mind, might be. She thinks of Chester.

"Still admiring the Ludlow?" The drawing master is on his way back to his class, beret already squashed on his head, hand jittering up the front of his smock as he buttons it up. He smells of whiskey. Probably that was the reason for his dash back into the hotel. She musters a smile and nods.

"I enjoyed your show last night, by the way," the drawing master says. Franny thanks him. He points to the picture.

"Can you believe that was meant to entice tourists up here?" The drawing master shakes his head. "I mean to say, *really*. Does that look anything like what we have here?"

Franny looks outside. It is a scene of alpine tranquillity. Then she notices that the pony on the lawn is relieving himself. The ladies are turning away. The gentlemen seem to be nervously offering a diversionary conversation. She nearly bursts out in giggles. The art teacher misconstrues her suppressed laughter for something he has aroused in her. He goes on talking:

"I must admit old Ludlow strove for—and achieved—a modicum of power here, but there is something desperate and frantic about the gesture. For perhaps that is all it is, yes? A gesture? A grand *gesture*. But where are the people? Where is the humanity?"

"Well," says Franny, "I rather like it."

The drawing master blinks, not wanting to dispute her, expecting she would take his opinion as law.

"Ludlow had power," the drawing master says. "Amos Bronson. I never met him. He lived near here, though, I am told. Nice of the hotel to hang this one, I suppose. Except it bumps mine off to the side walls, between the windows there. See them? Small, I admit, but much easier to sell that way. Hope you'll take a walk by mine sometime. Back to work. Ciao."

And he slips out the door to stride toward the semicircle of artist manqués and their freshly relieved pony.

A gentleman's face peers around one of the papers. It is the florid, overheated, yet irrepressibly hale face of J. Beaumol Spude. He is on his feet, clasping and kissing her hand before she is able to catch her breath. He is saying he *thought* he recognized her voice speaking to the drawing master. He compliments her on her performance of the night before as she begins to realize that the last time she saw this man was during the celebrations for the cable seven years before. And he's hardly changed.

"You are as beautiful as ever," he says.

She knows that it's not true, that she's more worn, that her hair is coarser. She is feeling gravity and age pull at her, but she is so stirred by the sight of someone from her old life speaking a sweet bit of flattery to her that she almost bursts into tears.

Spude calls for a waiter to bring Mrs. Ludlow tea and some spring water. He senses he has shocked her. He invites her to sit with him. They take corner seats, windows on two sides. He arranges her chair so the sun is not in her face. She can see the drawing class.

"We must catch up," Spude says. And Franny, much too eagerly she knows, says, "Yes, yes! We must!" And she reaches for his hands.

Later she will think, it is the same way she reaches for the hands of marks from the audience when they sit with her onstage to hear their fortunes, the same way Spude will reach to lead her to safety as the hotel burns.

They Catch Up

The life of a textile and gunpowder manufacturer, former cattleman, current hotelier, and future railroad magnate surely must offer some touch of interest to a lady. Spude doesn't delineate too thoroughly his mixed investments on both sides of the War Between the States, but he does give a discrete accounting to Franny of his activities since they last met. The library gradually empties as guests wander off to tea or to prepare for lunch. The morning's fire has died on the hearth.

Inevitably the moment arrives when Spude turns in his seat to face her foursquare and ask, Now, what is it exactly that *she* has been doing?

"Well, not much. I'm afraid you saw it all last night, Mr. Spude."

"I did. I did," he says, and Franny expects him to remonstrate with her for being so self-deprecating, but he does not. He is looking most steadily at her. It is a look that tells her she is right to sell herself short. She has come down in his estimation. He has seen the show. He knows.

And that cracks her poise.

"Oh dear," she blurts, and looks away.

But J. Beaumol Spude does not move, does not say a thing, and with his silence, this usually garrulous man elicits her story.

She finds herself telling him about the years since she and Spude last saw each other at the cable celebrations in New York City from which she fled in confusion and hurt and hope and to answer, she thought, a calling. For what all this . . . this traveling; this living in sin with Hermes; all this life of leading people to the brink of believing whatever their hearts ache to believe about their deceased loved ones, about their prospects for happiness in the future; then, with a bit of chicanery, pushing them over that brink; whatever it may degrade into, it is, in fine, a calling. *That* she knows. She felt it when she sat with Otis and first saw Betty. The *only time* she saw her. She was called to do this, to reach out to the Other Side and to, one way or another, enable others to do so as well. This sundered nation that she has crisscrossed now for nigh seven years, leaving house and marriage behind, has been her mission field. This nation and the spirit world—her two mission fields.

But she doesn't tell Spude this—or at least not in so many words. She tells him of her travels, the cities in which she's performed. She tells him about Hermes, how they met. How they found themselves encountering each other on the road. How, though his act may *seem* to be humbug, he truly does believe in the spirit world. How he places his performance, his act, in service of her "higher power," as he calls it. How three years ago he proposed they join forces. How she had been on the road for so long. How she had grown lonely. How she said yes.

She becomes emotional during the telling, particularly at one point when she wonders aloud where her husband is. But they've been so out of touch, Franny says to Spude, she feels she's no longer a Ludlow. And she begins to cry because she *did* feel part of the family when she stood before the painting not long ago. She fights back the sobs, and in looking away from Spude, she notices the huge painting on the wall of the reading room behind him. The turbulence of the picture makes sense to her now. True, it is nothing like the mountain scenery out the windows around her that it purports to represent, but it makes sense nonetheless. It makes her think of her husband and of his brother. It is a window into something about both of them, something that takes different forms in each, something about appetite and turmoil and sheer will. And then she sees it.

She lets out a small cry. And J. Beaumol Spude is asking, Is she all right?

But she is on her feet, rushing over to the painting. She has seen something in the clouds that roil on the right side of the picture. A figure. It must be something you can see only when viewing the painting from a certain angle and distance, for surely she would have seen it earlier during her long inspection of the canvas. It seems to piece itself together from the swirls of gray and white pigments, and Franny can see it is a young girl, in the painting, in the sky, dressed in a white gown, a child.

But is it Spude's voice or Franny's movement closer to the picture or her own dread that makes the figure, so fleetingly seen, disappear? For when she stands before the canvas, the little girl is gone. Spude is asking still, Is she well? But she is moving left and right, forward, backward, almost in an antic dance, trying to bring the image back. She returns to her chair, sits, looks, pops up again. Nothing. The child is gone—or she was never there. What remains is the painting, as it was, the overly magnificent rendering of Mount Washington and the forested valleys, the roiled mists and clouds to the right that might enshroud a mountain higher than the highest peak we can see in the painting, a challenge to us, a taunt, a myth. But no figure in the clouds.

Franny weeps. She can't hold it back. Long, drawn-out sobs in Spude's arms. The letter writers and newspaper perusers have left, so Franny and Spude are alone in the sun-struck reading room. She cries and cries, and the old entrepreneur, the Phantasmagorium showman, gunpowder maker, and railroad baron-to-be, comforts her.

And when she is calm and has had a little more of the spring water (the tea has long since gone cold), Spude sits with her again, offers her his handkerchief, gives her all the time she needs to compose herself, and then asks her something very strange. He allows as how it is strange and apologizes if it is inappropriate, but he wants to know.

"Mrs. Ludlow, how much money do you make?"

What Spude Hates

He hates a double-cross. Of course, he had investments in both the North and the South, but he would tell that to anyone who thought to ask. He wasn't duplicitous about it, just discreet. He was only letting the money go where it needed to go. And both sides benefited from his investment. The Union soldiers had warm uniforms; the Rebs had gunpowder. Both armies had more of what they needed, thanks to J. Beaumol Spude.

But that is all history. What obtains now is Spude's understanding of the hotel's finances. He has summoned the manager and, as a shareholder and major investor, has inspected the books. It is clear from what Franny told him and from what he saw the night before through the window that the bursar and Hermes are in collusion, skimming a sum from the payments due the Spiritscope act, so that, all told, Franny was receiving less than half the amount she was due from Hermes. The cheating had gone on for weeks, maybe even months, before they came to Spude's hotel. And that is the sort of thing Spude hates.

That evening Spude and the manager wait on the veranda. A rainstorm has moved into the valley, and there is the covering noise of water dripping off the eaves all around them. It is the same time as last night when Spude was on the porch—during Franny's act. They see the bursar counting out money for Hermes, and they burst in the door.

The manager fires the bursar on the spot, and Spude informs Hermes that he will not be performing the rest of his run—another week—at the Ammonoosuc. In fact, Spude will be informing the other hotels in the White Mountains that Hermes is a fraud and bilker.

Hermes takes this information in with narrowed eyes and a slight nod of the head. He never seems to lose his poise, for it is Hermes who is first to notice the applause thrumming through the walls.

"As least, sir, allow me to take my last bow with Dame Piermont," he says. He looks and gestures with his empty hand toward the sound of the ovation, and both the bursar and the manager cast a glance in that direction. But Spude catches Hermes doing a one-handed bottom draw with the bills in his other hand, peeling a few off the wad he still holds, crumpling them up his sleeve.

"No, I think I shall not," Spude says, and grabs Hermes's arm. "She will be bowing alone tonight. And you will kindly unhand the bills, sir. And remove your jacket."

Hermes does, and the purloined money flutters to the floor.

"Now leave," says Spude. "Your equipment will be delivered to the edge of the hotel's property posthaste."

And beyond the wall, the applause dies.

The Fire

Franny awakes to shouts and the smell of smoke. Though she doesn't move at first, though she feels obliged to account for where she is (a different room alone), for what has happened (she's severed her ties to Hermes; he has cheated her, now she knows, out of hundreds of dollars), she finally realizes the hotel is on fire.

Some shouts come from the common hallways, some from outside on the lawn. The smell of smoke is growing more pungent. It is the sweet odor of incinerating pine planks and beams mixed with the slightly acrid smell of the oil in paint. It is beginning to fill her room. Light—orange, red, bouncing, coruscating light—is reflecting off the forest in the night outside her window. The ghoulish light out there makes Franny leap out of bed. She throws on a robe and runs to the window. She is on the third floor. Below, guests and hotel employees run about. The uneven pulses of the light make their movements jerky and infernal. Franny can see from the window that the fire seems to be largest in the wing with the little salon, the conservatory, and the reading room. It is headed toward the dining room and Franny's end of the hotel. She runs for the hall.

Mothers are dragging their children in their nightgowns. Men assist women. Everywhere is much wailing and crying. Whenever a door is ajar in the hall and windows in the room beyond are visible, there is the lurid, twitching light. It shines from either side of the hallway; the fire is on both sides of the hotel now. Pitch boles in the beams explode like gunshots.

And, once, Franny hears moisture in unseasoned planks escape in a wailing jet of steam that sounds like a child's shriek.

First Franny runs the wrong way. A bellhop who is dashing about in only a union suit, his cap, and unlaced boots stops her and turns her—hands scandalously on her hips—to run in the other direction. He takes off and passes her. She makes it to the stairs, looks back into the smoke, sees no one else, begins to descend. A little girl in a white gown comes out of the smoke behind her and races past. Franny gasps, reaches out; the child is gone. Franny looks back again, expecting to see the girl's mother or father following, but sees only a wall of smoke and a stratum of clear air right above the carpet runner on the floor. *Whose child was that?* she wonders. While turned back and still moving down the stairs, Franny slips and falls, tumbling only a step or two to stop on a stair landing, the one above the lobby. She can see through the banisters to the chairs and settees and potted plants and parquetry on the floor below. And there, amid the flow of people, is J. Beaumol Spude.

"Sir!" she cries through the balustrade, pressing her face against the spindles and reaching through with her hand as she swoons.

Spude is there in no time to deliver her to safety. He takes her hands as he had earlier that day in the reading room, raises her up, and leads her down the stairs, across the lobby, and out to the hotel's carriage drive. She was not hurt by the fall, only dazed; she only needed assistance. And J. Beaumol Spude provides that.

The hotel is not destroyed—almost, but not quite. The rain helps quell the blaze. J. Beaumol Spude, having experience in managing a powder mill, had ordered that if his investment dollars were going into a wooden hotel, said hotel would have at least two fire pumper wagons on the premises. So, with the pumpers, the rain, and water from the duck pond and the wishing well, the able-bodied guests and crews from three nearby hotels manage to save the Ammonoosuc's central structure—the lobby, the grand salon, and a portion of the dining room.

By dawn, there is nothing to show for the fire but white steam and smoke rising from the ashes and charred timbers that once made up better than half the structure. There is little sound other than the hiss of the rain on the embers, and the dripping of water off the pine boughs. The mountains are gone, completely obscured by the clouds. To Franny it is as if they existed—the whole vista, the whole beautiful hotel, with its lawns and views and art classes and cultivation and refinement amid grand nature—in another, sublime world.

And that is the way she is feeling about her life: everything up until sometime after midnight when she first heard the screams and saw the flame light, everything else existed in another world. This world, here and now, is small and burned and exhausted and closed in by low clouds and smoke obscuring every prospect.

She sees the drawing master, sooty, clothes singed, stepping over puddles in the drive. He is on his way over to the stables, where guests and staff are waiting for wagons to take them to nearby hotels. The drawing master has in his arms a bundle of small, framed canvases—his pictures.

He's saved them, Franny thinks, and she looks to where the reading room had stood. Gone now, burned, and with it the huge Amos Bronson Ludlow painting. It is the thought of that loss that hits Franny the hardest. Her room and all her things were destroyed. Hermes left without even speaking to her. (Spude had to tell her what happened.) But the loss of that huge picture now leaves her feeling truly cut loose. Too exhausted to cry, she sits on a log bench near the gentlemen's horseshoe pit, out in the rain.

Soon J. Beaumol Spude comes up to her with a blanket. It smells of smoke, but as she is beginning to feel chilled, she welcomes it and wraps it around herself. She knows she should probably go over to the stable, but for the moment, she wants only to sit.

"I think," Spude says, "it's safe to say who did this."

Franny looks at him. His suit is perforated with cinder burns. His skin is splotched from the heat. His hair sticks out in wings. His collar is sprung, and his aspect is so comical that Franny begins to laugh.

J. Beaumol Spude has seen enough in the past few hours that he takes her reaction in stride.

"The man was a cad, a crook, and, if you'll excuse my French, a real son of a bitch."

"He was!" Franny says.

Spude likes seeing her laugh. He chuckles, too. A couple of old warriors doing the only thing old warriors can do in the aftermath on a battlefield.

Soon, Franny is riding in a hay wagon with other exhausted and dazed guests. She sees the little girl from the burning hallway, wrapped in a blanket, asleep in her father's arms. The guests will all go to other hotels or to local homes. Dry clothes will be found for them. A special train will be coming up through Crawford Notch to speed them on their way, courtesy of the Hotel Ammonoosuc.

No one was killed. All injuries were minor. A miracle.

Franny looks back at the nearly destroyed hotel. The outer wings and annexes are gone, and the central, clapboard section looks exceedingly white against the gray rain clouds. Spude has said they will rebuild.

Then, as they pass through the gates, Franny sees the sprung, twisted metal wreckage of some kind of machine. No one pays it any mind, but as they pass it out by the road, Franny can see it is the Spiritscope. Hauled out here by Hermes perhaps. Or some porter or stable hand detailed to clear Hermes off the premises last night. And it was smashed by? . . . Hermes himself perhaps. Or the porter. Or maybe even Spude. Franny looks numbly at the ridiculous mess and closes her eyes.

She can hear J. Beaumol Spude bidding everyone farewell, promising them they will all be well cared for and encouraging everyone to make reservations, to come back to the mountains again next year.

CHAPTER XXIX

THE DISSOLUTION

London and Ireland, Winter 1865–66

A Christmas Visit

Night. The city of London is swaddled in snow. Chester Ludlow is swaddled in wool. Wrapped in blankets, overcoat, muffler, gloves, and hat, he feels he has become an infinitesimal atomy beneath layers of woven cloth and, beyond that, the carapace of leather, wood, and iron of the carriage, which in turn is wrapped by the storm— soft, persistent, embedding the entire city, probably the whole of the Isles unto the darkness of the seas. All of which he must cross: carriage to Paddington, train to Liverpool, packet to Dublin, train, coaches, donkey cart, and boot leather across Ireland all the way to the telegraph house at Foilhommerum Bay.

Infinitesimal and solitary, he feels. Wrapped, embedded, and buried, he feels. And not just by the conditions of weather and the solstitial darkness but by his circumstances as well: by his need to situate himself in his own history. He can feel tiny, alone, even naked, under all this embedment as above and around him whirl obligations, entanglements, achievements, and errors. Sometimes they are close to suffocating him.

In his lap he holds a package wrapped in brown paper, tied with twine, and adorned with a single ribbon to attest to its purpose. It is a Christmas gift. It is going with Chester all the way to the west coast of Ireland. It is for Otis.

The journey takes three days, and for every one of them it snows. The railroads persevere; the packet sails into the teeth of the storm across the Irish Sea, and the coaches slog their way right up to the last mile, which Chester walks from the high road to the telegraph house. By the time he can see the ocean from the cliff top, the sun is coming out through the gray sky. The snow on the ground burns white. It is Christmas Day.

Chester gave Otis the job at the telegraph house. There were no questions as to Otis's qualifications. He was faster at sending and receiving code than any of the graphers on the *Great Eastern* the previous summer. And so, after his great leap from the yardarm and after the crewmen had lowered the longboat and rowed out to where Otis was swimming—breakneck away from the *Great Eastern,* toward Greenland as near as anyone could tell—and after Chester himself had pulled his brother out of the water, taken him to his cabin, calmed him, talked to him, listened to him, it was Chester's idea that after some recuperation in London, with proper medicaments and a doctor's care, Otis might serve himself (and the cable) by spending the winter in quietude, exercising his skill at the telegraph house on the west coast of Ireland. It was to be a calming, focused, simple task. The cable syndicate needed someone to man the line all winter and to run the impedance tests that would account for the condition of the cable and ensure that the severed line was still in working order for as far as it went under the ocean and that there were no new breaks or flaws. Even Otis's physician agreed: a quiet life, a singular task, these could be beneficial and stabilizing. So, by early autumn, Otis had joined the other graphers detailed to the telegraph house at Foilhommerum Bay.

But everyone was mistaken about the nature of the work. Condemned to long hours in a darkened room, scrutinizing a tiny dot of light, watching it twitch in response to test charges or the magnetic disturbances of the ocean, of the planet itself, graphers would become querulous, then distraught, then combative. They drank heavily. They smashed furniture, sometimes over one another. They fought and then resigned precipitously. The syndicate would dispatch new graphers to replace the departed ones. The attrition by Christmas was nearly 100 percent. Every man had left, save one—Otis Ludlow.

Otis greets Chester by the front gate outside the telegraph house. Otis is alone in the house. Replacements won't arrive until after the holiday. He beckons Chester in.

He seems no worse for wear. In fact, Chester thinks, he seems invigorated. He welcomes Chester into the small kitchen, where he has a peat fire glowing on the hearth. The room is spare and utilitarian as befitting a household of men. It could be a garrison mess hall: whitewashed walls, swept floor, iron pots hung on pegs, tin utensils, a curtainless window facing the sea, raw planks on sawhorses for a counter. Otis has taken one sprig of heather and placed it in a cup on the table: a Yule appurtenance. The kettle simmers on the hob.

"How is the cable?" Chester asks after he's inquired into his brother's health and heard an almost overexuberant reply that Otis is well, thank you, yes, well, *very* well.

"And the cable is well, too," Otis says. "Intact all the way out. No new breaks anywhere along it. Been listening to it every day. Tests well. Still sends signals. Noise mostly but— Yes, it's doing well."

Chester thinks it's curious how Otis—other graphers, too—say they're "listening" to the cable when, in fact, they are *watching* it, really, recording the movements of a dot of light. But to those who can read and decode the movements with such facility, Chester supposes it feels as if they are listening.

Chester says he is glad to hear it, and then, over tea, he breaks the news of new plans to Otis. He tells him he has improved the brittle armoring of the cable, and Cyrus Field has decided to manufacture a whole new line. The *Great Eastern* is undergoing an overhaul so it can manage cable retrieval easily over the stern. Crews are scraping a layer of barnacles and seaweed off the hull, a layer *two feet thick*. All this is being done so that, sometime next summer, once the finances are in order, they will lay a completely new cable to Newfoundland.

Otis straightens up in his chair. He sounds enthused: "You mean, the old one, the one I'm listening to, will stay as it is?"

"No," Chester tells him. "Once we've laid the *new* cable, we'll go back out and grapple for the other end of this one, pull it up, splice it with more new wire, then finish it to Newfoundland. With a little extra effort and time, we'll have *two* cables between the continents. Won't that be something?"

Otis thinks hard about this. "Yes," he says, "something." He starts tapping his foot and rubbing his fingers together as if his thoughts are bodying forth as stray energy that needs escape through his limbs and digits.

He makes an odd show of being pleased about Chester's news by standing up suddenly and exclaiming, "Let's go for a walk!"

Chester doesn't have it in him to protest that he has just slogged a mile through snow down the lane from the high road, nor does he quite know what to do with the package. So he agrees to the walk and brings the parcel with him.

It is midday on the cliffs. The onshore breeze is resolute enough to throw the brothers' coattails back, ruffle their hair, and create a continual roar in their ears. Additionally, it freezes Chester's fingers as he holds the package. But he feels invigorated. Now the sky has cleared, the wind having picked apart the clouds and tossed the pieces back to the east. The bay and sea beyond are deep blue and fretted with whitecaps. The snow around the brothers is nearly up to their knees.

Maybe, Chester thinks, *I feel this way because I am with him. Otis can always do that,* Chester thinks, *make you feel large, larger than you thought you could be. It is his way of looking at you: a searing regard that, at the same time, seems to hold you in the highest esteem. It can almost throw you off balance. It's what always draws people to him.* Chester has some of it, too, he knows. It's the magnetism Spude saw in him. It's what helped get him where he is today.

"The snow makes me think of home," Otis says. "The Old Man would go out and paint in the snow. He designed a tent. A three-sided affair with a chimney hole. He had a little woodstove in there with reflectors to send the heat toward where he sat with his easel. He'd go out to paint his mountains in winter. He'd have me haul firewood and food up to him while he worked. Winter was hell on him. Not because of the cold. He could take that. But because of the dark. No light: no painting. Sometimes he'd come down from his tent and spend the night at home. Other times he'd just roll the flap down on the open side of the tent and sleep curled up in blankets. Be gone for days."

"Did he love us?"

The words just popped out of Chester. It must have been something about hearing of his father's obsession, his devotion, his willingness to endure hardship for his calling that made Chester wonder aloud how they— the sons—stood in relation to that distant, extreme man.

Otis looks baffled.

"I mean," Chester says, "did he hold us in any kind of affection? Did he think of us when we weren't around? I was around less than you. And I was younger. But I'm wondering, how did we stand with him? Did he love us? That *is* what I mean."

"No."

Otis says this in a small voice, a sound almost swallowed whole by the wind. It is as if he is addressing both himself and Chester as the boys they once were and must break the news gently.

"No," he repeats softly.

Or else he is speaking in the small voice of the boy he once was in that world. Alone.

"No," he says a third time. "He didn't love us."

It is as simple as that. Chester knows it is true, knows also that he can endure the knowledge—already has and will continue so—but that it is very likely that word, now uttered, will be Otis's undoing.

"I brought you this," Chester says suddenly, and offers the package to his brother. The ribbon has come untied, and it whips about in the wind, making a small, skeletal noise.

"Merry Christmas," he says.

Otis takes the package and opens it, carefully stuffing the ribbon, the twine, and the paper in various pockets on his person, then reaches into the box to pull out a new brass and porcelain sextant. Its radial arm and mirrors and lenses wink and gleam in the sun. He turns it over in his hands. Chester imagines the metal feels cold to the touch. Otis does not look up. He keeps turning the instrument.

"You lost yours on the ship," says Chester, "when you . . ."

Otis nods, still looking down.

"I thought," says Chester. "I thought that you might want another. New start, you know. Always know where you are, I suppose. It's a good one. I got it at a chandlery in Birkenhead. When I saw it, I thought of you right away. . . ."

Otis thanks him, and Chester is relieved because his brother seems genuinely moved.

"Oh, dear," he says, too obviously trying to laugh, "I didn't get you a thing."

Chester tells him it's nothing, not to think about it; besides, where would you get anything out here?

Otis does laugh now and nods and looks out to sea. His features are keener than Chester has ever seen them before. They look etched and as hard as the brass fittings on the sextant.

"Where would I get anything?" he asks of himself.

He turns to Chester.

"I am receiving messages," he says. And Otis explains they're from the Other Side. Not America, of course. The cable doesn't go that far.

"You mean—?" Chester asks, and Otis nods almost furiously.

"Come," he says, and bangs the sextant into Chester's shoulder as he urges him back, away from the cliff, toward the telegraph house.

Otis possesses reams of documents. He has been recording the wavering of the galvanometer light seemingly round the clock, whether he's been doing impedance tests or not. Chester begins to think this idea of a grapher job for Otis was a dreadful mistake, on a level with bringing Otis on the *Great Eastern*. How could he so misguide his brother?

"I know you can't leave this cable just lying there on the bottom of the sea to pick up signals for me *forever*," Otis says. "Too big an investment. But I won't make any trouble. I'll just be glad I have had time to listen in."

Otis has stored his notes in a dozen tagboard folders and filed them in the peat shed off the kitchen.

"They don't want to see all this," he says.

"Who?" Chester asks. He feels numb, insensitive now to the clarity of the brightening day on the cliff above the bay. It is as if he's being led into some dark cul-de-sac of Otis's devising. Only Otis doesn't see it as such. Otis thinks he's reached a new height.

"The other graphers," Otis says, "they think my notes are superfluous. They don't know that's how the Other Side reaches us now. Through me. Through the cable."

"Otis, it's the magnetism of the earth. The cable is just picking up noise from the earth's magnetism."

Otis shakes his head. "Sometimes, yes. *Most* times, yes. But then . . . look . . ."

He riffles through the pages and stabs his finger at circled words among the gibberish: *anatomy, wall, hunger lest I go, touché, blains, reach reach rea—, painting.*

"Otis, this is pure chance. Anyone who listens"—now Chester is calling it listening—"to the cable for as long as you have is bound to pick out some words."

Otis grits his teeth and shakes his head.

"It *seems* like chance, but when the words come through, there's a change." Otis says.

"A change in what? The apparatus?"

"No," says Otis, and takes a deep breath. "A change," he says, "in me. A—a vibration. There is something, I don't know, *bending* the earth's magnetism to reach me. I think sometimes it may even be *him*."

"Who?"

"The Old Man."

"Oh dear, Otis."

"No, listen, please." And Otis shifts around to stay in Chester's view, for Chester, in distraction, has looked away. The folder in his hands gains weight with every passing second. He looks for a place to put it down. Otis snatches it away.

"I've tried everything. You know that. It's what my life has always been about. And here, look, you've brought me to it. The cable . . ."

Otis is pacing now, folder under his arm. Papers stick out of the file. With his free hand he is raking his hair.

"The Old Man," he says. "And your daughter!"

"Otis!"

"What if I told you your daughter speaks through the cable?"

"Otis, I can't believe—"

"You can't? You *can't?* Very well. You're right. She doesn't. She hasn't. Not yet. But I tell you, she could. She *will*."

"How do you know that?"

"Because I can *feel* her."

"Goddamn it, Otis. Stop it!"

Otis does. He stands suddenly dumb before his brother. Stiff, holding the folder as if it were a schoolbook and he a captured truant.

"Otis," Chester says gently. "Otis, I am sorry."

"For what, pray?"

"Everything. I—" Chester shakes his head. "Otis, I want you to come with me."

"No."

"You've done fine work here. You don't need to do any more. There are new men coming after the holiday. They can take over."

"No."

"Otis, I am an officer of this company."

"And I will not leave my post."

"I can order you away."

"I won't go. I shall keep listening. Always." He closes his eyes.

That evening Chester sits in his room above the tavern in town. Stacked on the small table are the dozen folders and the transcriptions of every twitch of the galvanometer light for all the months that Otis has been at the telegraph house.

Otis is still out there. After his declaration to Chester, he stalked off and hoisted the white pennant signaling any passing horseman or cart on the high road to detour down to the telegraph house. A farmer came along soon and gave Chester a ride into town.

Chester has decided there is nothing he can do for now. He will leave Otis alone on the coast and hope for the best. Otis has given him all the records—the forms that document the impedance tests and the volumes of his own transcription, with all the cogent words circled.

Chester is too saddened to read any of them now and thinks how this heaviness was not part of his life in the grand days of the cable, in the grand days of so much of his life. It is something that is now permanently with him, something that has taken up lodging in his breast, something that he hates and yet, at the same time, because it is solely his, something that he can't help but hold and embrace.

He looks at the folders, full of randomness. Chester thinks of the ribbon on the gift fluttering in the wind that afternoon with all the same aimlessness.

On top of the pile of folders there is a hastily scrawled note from Otis. It was stuck in the topmost folder. Chester found it on the ride into the village. The two sentences seem as disconnected and as haphazard as anything circled in the stacks of papers.

"Thank you for the gift," says one.

"Find Franny," says the other.

One Secret Kept, One Disclosed

Jack Trace has asked for Maddy's hand in marriage. He's had to ask her directly, of course, because her father, as he knows, is dead. Jack has never told Maddy that he witnessed her father's death that day at the Millwall shipyard when the *Great Eastern* failed to move and a winch handle flung poor Thomas Donovan to his death. It is a secret that Jack, to his last day, will never disclose.

He has another secret, about another death, that he will reveal, if obliquely, and he will do it when he delivers his portfolio to Mr. Ludlow. He is on his way to the office of the Telegraph Construction and Maintenance Company now, working his way through the busy streets of the City, east of St. Paul's, trying to take his mind off Maddy's answer.

Or what her answer will be, for he does not know it yet. Two nights ago, at Maddy's, after all the clients had left or gone off to the upper rooms, after the associates had retired to their dormitory on the top floor or were down in the kitchen having a nightcap or a cup of tea, Maddy was surprised, when she turned around from straightening the faerie painting that had been knocked askew by a tipsy client on his way upstairs, to see the artist himself down on one knee at the bottom of the steps, casting a quick glance about to be sure they were alone, then asking her to marry him.

She raised her hand to her open mouth.

When he had finished the question, he clasped his hands together and held them over his heart. He looked directly at her.

She dodged her eyes right and left, as he had done and for the same reason—to be sure they were alone. And she had a powerful urge to say something like, "Oh, Jack, don't," or "Please, get up," or *something*. But her throat was paralyzed. *She* was paralyzed.

It was his appearance. He looked perfectly gallant down there. Better than gallant. He looked tall, brave, puissant—she'd heard that word somewhere in connection with knights. It sounded funny, but Jack Trace, bless him, looked like a knight kneeling there, hands over heart, head now bowed. He seemed aglow. Jack Trace. And so did she. Maddy Donovan.

Then something made her move. A noise from the kitchen? From upstairs? The turning of the globe itself as the city slid farther along under the stars and she with it? Something.

She raised her hand and actually said, "Arise."

Somehow that broke the spell, and the two of them were more themselves again. Maddy touched the picture frame unnecessarily, and Jack began to say in his deferential way that it would only be proper for him to wait for an answer and this he would do gladly at her convenience. And before she knew it, he was gone, having backed out the front door with a bow and still a touch of that . . . puissance. And she, she was found later by two of the associates as they went up to bed just before dawn. She was sitting on the stairs, seemingly in a daze, idly tracing the fleurs-de-lis on the wallpaper with her lacquered fingernails.

Jack Trace had gone back to his cottage and, in a burst of energy and a desire to distract himself, worked furiously to finish the *Great Eastern* cable portfolio that he is now bringing to Mr. Ludlow.

And something else has happened to Jack in his agitated state of the past two days. He's been pulling out his mural sketches and cartoons (not the humorous, topical kind, but the kind hewing to the older meaning of the word: preliminary studies and preparatory designs) for his utopian mural, *Progress,* the dream of which has stayed with him, in a variety of forms, through war and cable laying, employment and idleness, as if it has been with him always, from even before meeting Maddy in the tunnel, and has threaded through everything he has experienced and everything he has hoped to achieve.

And, he supposes, that is what led him to drop to his knee at Maddy's the other night and propose marriage. He must hazard a pledge of his heart. His has been a life of watching, of documenting, of depicting. And he has too little of it left.

Jack Trace can almost believe that he was placed on the cable expedition—twice—to learn that lesson. He remembers sketching the conclave of the Cablemen in the saloon of the *Great Eastern.* They were men, he realized, who had risked everything and were faced with yet another failure. Nevertheless, Trace knew, looking at them in the bronze light skidding in across the ocean waves, seeing them almost as a temple frieze that might be entitled *The Indomitables,* Trace knew for certain that they would go on. Even the lamentable attempt by Mr. Ludlow's brother to kill himself had impressed Trace with its fervor: not a shrinking from life, but a dive from a yardarm; a wild, mad swim toward oblivion.

Now it was Jack's time for fervor. Now or never, he went down on his knee, heart in hand, before Maddy. It wasn't unprecedented. Women of her ilk, as she once put it, often used marriage to leave the demimonde behind. Trace would do that for her.

He ascends the stairs to the Telegraph Construction and Maintenance Company's headquarters. The offices are in a former countinghouse near the Exchange. It is a place bustling with activity. Clerks in the outer room pour over charts and ledgers. Five ticket porters sit on a bench waiting dispatches. The porters all stand as Trace enters, and he mistakenly thinks it's for him until he sees Cyrus Field preparing to leave. Field meets Trace at the top of the stairs, shakes his hand, apologizes for being unable to stay.

"Going to see the *Great Eastern* launched again," he says. "She's all cleaned up. Sleek as the day she was born."

"Wonderful," says Trace. "And I hope she launches better than that day."

Field ignores the comment.

"So, Mr. Trace, you are here to see— Good Lord, I hope *I* haven't forgotten an appointment with you. Did I?"

"Not at all. I'm here to see Mr. Ludlow." Trace hefts the enormous portfolio.

"Oh! I'd love to see what you have," Field says. "I know I'll think it's surpassingly good. Only I must run. You will be sailing with us again, won't you? June. Talk to Mr. Ludlow." He was half down the stairs and calling back up. "*Two* cables this time! We're going for it this time! Yessir. Double or nothing. Be a part of it!" And he was gone.

The offices seem to reflect Field's optimism, for when Trace turns around, the porters smile at him. Clerks and messengers bustle about under an expanse of skylights that play a gibbous light over all, making the proceedings seem to be unfolding under a huge, airy canopy, as if this were a tent carnival.

Chester Ludlow is not of a spirit with the rest of the establishment, though. Although he appears hale enough, he moves with a tentativeness, as if a piece of furniture might slide over and strike him a blow or a windowsill might not be there when he leans against it.

"I apologize, sir," Trace says, "for being delayed getting these to you."

Chester smiles. "It's not a problem. As you can see, we're rolling right along here. And if these drawings are anything like the first series you did for us . . . Well, we probably should be requisitioning an art gallery along with all the other properties that go with cable laying."

He makes a sweeping gesture at the papers, forms—baskets full of them—charts, ledgers, folders, the things piled on every surface, tacked on every wall. He laughs. Paying a compliment seems to open him up. His smile ascends to a new, broader affability. It wrinkles his eyes beyond the gold rims of his spectacles. Trace notices Chester's blond hair is salted slightly with gray.

"May I?" Chester takes the portfolio from the chair where Trace has propped it, clears off a large drafting table, and unfastens the black cloth ties on the cover.

The first picture is a stunning lateral view of the *Great Eastern*.

"Good Lord," Chester murmurs. The picture's detail almost makes it rise off the paper. It is a moment before Chester realizes that Trace has drawn the ship on a map, an old nautical chart of the Atlantic Ocean. The *Great Eastern* truly stretches from continent to continent.

Chester is buoyed by the conceit. He even chuckles. He goes on to leaf through the other drawings and paintings, murmuring his approval as he goes, sometimes calling attention to a detail, sometimes exclaiming in wonder over a whole page. He hadn't intended to go through the entire portfolio, just take a polite look and save the rest for later. But he is pulled in by what he sees.

While Chester studies the work, Trace steps over to a window and waits.

"Mr. Trace . . ."

Jack, without even turning, knows what Ludlow has found among the sheaves. Jack planted it there.

"Mr. Trace, what is this . . .?"

What it is, is a large, detailed view of a ravine, spanned by a damaged railroad trestle, and at the bottom lies the wreckage of a train, a rather odd train, one with an enormous shattered cannon spilled off its flatcar, a toppled engine billowing steam, a boxcar spewing flames and smoke and the hulk of a luxury car in the course of being incinerated. Chester Ludlow's face is flushed, his jaw tight.

Trace tells Chester of being there, of seeing the wreckage. He tells Chester of overhearing him on the *Great Eastern* telling his brother about the cannon, its destruction, about Frau Lindt. And then, unable to stop himself, he tells about the battles he saw and that, true, whoever blew that bridge were killers but that a cannon was meant to kill also and that he, Jack Trace, couldn't escape being a part of it, he knows, responsible somehow, just for being there, just for drawing it. Witnessing makes you a part of it, and it part of you, and there, *that's* responsibility whether you like it or not. Just as overhearing a conversation makes you responsible. And he says that he couldn't think of any other way to acquit himself of that responsibility but to draw and there it is, and isn't it a funny angle, really? He means the perspective of it. See? Hovering above the ravine. To see the scene from that perspective, you'd have to be in a balloon or a flying machine of some sort. Flying—

The two men look at the drawing.

"What a strange thing to do," Chester says quietly. "To bring this here."

"I'm sorry," Trace says. "I wanted some way to tell you. I'm better at . . . at drawing than I am with words. I thought maybe I wouldn't be here when you saw this. Then I thought, Damn it to hell, *be* there."

Chester raises his hand to silence Trace, which he does, then places his hand on Trace's forearm and grips it firmly. It is at that moment they both hear Chester's name. Trace recognizes the accent even before he turns to see Herr Lindt.

"More papers for us to cosign," Lindt says.

He brings with him into the room some of the efficiency and purpose of the outer office.

"Why, Herr Trace, so good to see you again," he says flatly, and approaches to shake Trace's hand. Trace is desperate to keep him from seeing the portfolio and is inexpressibly relieved to see Chester slide around to block the drawings from Lindt's view.

"So," Lindt says as he pumps Trace's arm with a chopping motion, "you'll be with us when we sail in the spring? This time we'll do it. We all know it."

"Actually, no," Trace says. "I mean, I'm sure you'll succeed, but, no, I won't be with you. I'm getting married."

"You *are?*" says Chester.

"Yes," Trace says, flushing horribly.

"Well, congratulations. Anyone we know?" Chester asks.

"No," says Trace. "Well, not exactly. I know you've never met her, Mr. Lindt."

Lindt shrugs.

"But I have?" asks Chester.

"No. Well, I—I don't know. Oh, drat it. It's all supposed to be a secret, you see. Because we haven't talked it over with her family yet. Bit of a complication there."

"Well, sorry you won't be with us," says Lindt.

"Yes. And I, too," says Trace.

"I'll be leaving these on your desk then," Lindt says to Chester, and deposits the papers on Chester's blotter. Then it occurs to Lindt to ask:

"Have you brought the drawings from last year's expedition?"

"No, he hasn't," Chester says quickly. "We're having a bit of talk about that right now."

"Terribly sorry," says Trace. "Tardy, you know. Couldn't be helped."

"I'll iron it out, Lindt," Chester says.

"Very well," says Lindt. There is a pause as Chester and Trace hold their ground. Then, addressing the two of them really, Lindt says in a brittle voice, "Best of luck with your marriage."

And he leaves. Trace expels a long sigh. He wants to say something further, but he notices Chester has picked up the drawing and is walking over to the fire grate.

"Mr. Trace, in no way do I mean to impugn your artistry. Nor do I want to denigrate your need to draw this in the first place nor even to discredit your intentions in bringing it here, although I can't say I completely understand them. I can tell it has proved to have offered some relief for you. It may even have for me as well." He looks hard at the drawing. "But," he says, "I am going to burn it."

"That's fine, sir."

So Chester lays the drawing on the coals, and the two men watch as the heat discolors the paper, then blooms into flames seemingly all around the sheet at once.

"Your marriage," Chester says.

"Yes," says Trace.

"May it be happy."

"Thank you, sir."

The edges of the burning paper convulse inward, and it is like a fist clenching, then it transforms into black ash like a huge insect wing, then into nothing at all, and Chester and Trace are staring into glowing coals.

OTIS LUDLOW'S JOURNAL

Ireland, 1866

Foilhommerum Bay

One more thing must be told. I did not find him dead in shallow water in the brook west of the Notch.

He was alive.

I had returned to America, to home, alone, after my first years in Malaya. Chester was down in Cambridge, beginning his engineering studies. His mother had died the previous winter, of influenza. My Margaret had died on an island off Kalimantan of diphtheria. I journeyed home alone. The family was in disarray.

Not the Old Man, though. He was painting as never before.

I hired onto Horace Fabyan's crew building a bridle path for tourists to ride up the western slope of Mount Washington. I had heard from the foreman of the gandy dancers laying the track beyond Fourth Iron that my father had been seen painting near the cliffs east of the Notch. The foreman himself had found the Old Man a week before, senseless, in one of his fits. The foreman had nursed the Old Man, only to have him bolt and disappear, last seen driving his little packhorse hard up the Nancy Brook trail, this time west of the Notch. I went looking for him.

When I found him, I saw the horse first, tied—tangled really—in a thicket of hemlocks near a rockslide. The horse did not look properly tethered, something the Old Man would never allow.

Nancy Brook was rushing along nearby. The cascades were upstream a hundred yards, and I could hear their roar. My father's easel was there, on a mossy embankment. It was an overcast summer day. Nancy Cascades spill several hundred feet down rock ledges, and the forest thereabouts is filled with a mist from the waters.

First, I'd seen the horse, then I saw the painting. It was huge. Maybe six by eight feet. It wasn't of the cascades. It was of an entire forest and range of mountains. He'd evidently been moving it around the countryside to paint views and compose them into one vast whole. He'd brought the canvas up to the cascades to incorporate them into one corner. The rest of the painting was of towering peaks. There was a huge one in the distance, and a mysterious one, cloud-covered, loomed to the right, almost wholly invisible in some combination of fog, vapor, and storm clouds. A strange mix of turbulence and feathery softness. I remember thinking shapes were shifting in that painting.

Then I saw him in the water. He convulsed several times, and it drew my attention, the movement.

I could have run down then. He was only a dozen yards below me. He shuddered in the water.

I imagine he could see me. I know those fits.

I did not move. He made no sound. He shuddered. Water covered him.

With my one eye, I could look at him, but it was with my blind eye that I believe I finally, truly saw him.

Look at me, I thought.

But water covered him. He hid there. He shuddered. He would not see me.

And I did not move to help him. I watched him.

Until he was still.

That is the story. I did not find him dead.

It was not as it was to be with Betty, years later, when I, too, was helpless. This time I chose to do nothing. I would not help him.

I do not know what happened to the painting. I carried it, on the horse, with the Old Man's equipment and his body, down to the railroad camp at Fourth Iron. The painting went with all his possessions to an auctioneer in Fryeburg. I sent the money to Chester for his schooling. I returned to sea.

But first I buried the body. I built the coffin. It is true his paints were coloring *his hair as his palette had fallen into the pool with him, and the colors stained the water. But blood did, too. He'd struck his head when he fell. It didn't kill him. I did.*

The blood washed away. His paints, they did not.

I am sorry for this.

CHAPTER XXX

TO HEART'S CONTENT

Ireland and America; Summer–Fall 1866

He Stays Behind

Chester sits on the coast of Ireland for more
than a month, waiting for the body to wash ashore.

Late winter and spring had been seasons when everything was pulled
in two directions at once: the London weather tugging between cold North
Sea blasts and warmer winds blowing in from the Canaries. And then there
was his own attention being torn between the exigencies of cable work and
the increasingly disturbing messages from Foilhommerum Bay.

The messages had not been from Otis. Otis never spoke with Chester
again. They were from the other graphers stationed at the telegraph
house. . . . His brother was acting strangely. His brother was talking to
himself. His brother was sending messages down the cable–the *broken* cable.
His brother sat as if expecting an answer in return. His brother was telegraphing a place called Mount Washington; did Chester know of it? His
brother would refuse to yield his post to the next watch. His brother would
sometimes drop from exhaustion at the galvanometer and collapse at the
table, head thunking on the wood. His brother was becoming a hazard to
the smooth functioning of the telegraph house and to himself.

Graphers were resigning. Soon there was only one grapher left besides
Otis. Then, evidently, none.

It was a fisherman who sent word to the publican, who sent word to the constable, who sent word to the London office that Otis had drowned by his own hand. The fisherman had seen him do it: jumped from a dory with rocks tied to his neck. He did it out at sea, just beyond the protection of Foilhommerum Bay early one morning.

No one had been there at the telegraph house. Otis, and the maddening job of watching the dot of light, had driven all of the other graphers away. He was alone to "listen" to the strange noise and random signals that came down the severed cable, alone to send his own signals out into the sea . . . or the ether.

Chester left his London office as soon as he heard the news. He followed the same route he'd taken for his Christmas visit to Otis. This time there was no storm. England and Ireland were verdant with high summer. The seas were calm.

When he arrived at Valentia Harbor, Chester found the fisherman and asked him to take him to the spot and help him drag for the body. They used grapnels and line much like the ones Chester and Otis had used the year before to drag the sea bottom for the cable. After three days, though, they had found nothing.

"Sometimes, the sea will find it for you," the fisherman said. "All you can do is wait."

"I shall wait," said Chester, pointing to the shore. "Right there."

And that is where he is when the cable expedition arrives in early July to set off again across the Atlantic. Both Cyrus Field and Professor Thomson come looking for him.

The *Great Eastern* is offshore, reconditioned, improved according to Chester's specifications, with new take-up machinery and paddle wheels that operate independently so the ship can turn within its own length.

Chester wired London of his decision to stay ashore. He knows Professor Thomson will once again be aboard, and Joachim Lindt, for all his faults, at least now is experienced. Plus, the Telegraph Construction and Maintenance Company has assigned other engineers to assist the project. Men who have laid Channel and Black Sea cables. Though all the improvements and new engineers are likely to help, they nonetheless mean the Incorporation has encroached further into the Cablemen's dream.

But Chester doesn't tell that to Field or Professor Thomson. It really isn't important to him. To wait for his brother; that is the reason Chester cannot go.

And Field sees the resolve in those eyes behind the gold and glass spectacles. A resolve, Field thinks, he could wear down, given the time. Field is nothing if not persistent; he has worn down all the impediments to laying a transatlantic cable. This time he is sure they are going to make it. With or without Chester Ludlow.

But the sadness. There is a sadness and a confusion in Chester, too. And that, Field thinks, would be beyond him. Reckoning with that is for Chester alone.

Professor Thomson sees the same thing. He comes to visit Chester in the telegraph house. The Incorporation has sent several new graphers to man the shore end of the new cable and to stay in touch with the *Great Eastern* as it unspools the line. Chester keeps to himself and stays out of their way. They will have their work; he will have his. He has cleaned the place up. Among Otis's things, Chester has found a leather-bound journal that Otis had been keeping—not the log of the cable's gibberish, but of his own thoughts, an accounting. Chester has read it over and over. He has made a small bundle of Otis's effects, placing the journal and the sextant atop the pile in the spare room where he sleeps when darkness forecloses his vigil on the cliffs.

"Your staying here or sailing with us really won't matter whether the sea gives up his body or no," Professor Thomson says.

"That's unprovable," Chester tells Professor Thomson.

Thomson nods. "My boy," he says, "when this is all over, I shall call for you. We still have work to do."

"Telegraph me," Chester says.

Thomson smiles, says he will do precisely that, and goes.

The whole expedition goes. On Friday, July 13, 1866, the *Great Eastern* sails for Newfoundland. There is a small, somber ceremony on the beach, nothing like the celebration of the year before, only a few fishing boats to help take the shore end out to the *Great Eastern*. Chester Ludlow is among the handful of locals on the cliffs watching the progress of the boats, watching later the plume of smoke from the *Great Eastern* disappear from the horizon.

Chester is there, still watching, still walking the cliffs and beaches when, two weeks later, the constable finds him to say that the *Great Eastern* has succeeded. It is the twenty-seventh of July, and there is a working cable spanning the Atlantic Ocean.

"The whole village is celebrating," the constable says. "I believe the whole country is. Likely your country, too."

When Chester returns to the telegraph house at dusk, one of the graphers hands him the message that came in earlier that day:

> Heart's Content, July 27. We arrived here at 9 o'clock this morning. All well. Thank God, the cable is laid and in perfect working order. Cyrus Field.

"We've passed the message on to the rest of Britain," says the grapher.

Heart's Content is the name of the new, deeper harbor the Incorporation found for its North American landing.

"Nice name," says one of the off-duty graphers, handing Chester a whiskey for a toast. "Nice bit of work," the grapher says, raising his glass. "Hear! Hear!" All the graphers cheer. Even Chester takes a drink, then goes to his room to rest so he can be up early on the bluffs tomorrow.

By the same hour the following day, the new cable has done £1,000 of commercial business.

"The sea is giving up some of the fortune it has swallowed," one of the graphers says.

Within another twenty-four hours, Otis's corpse washes ashore, gnawed by fish, battered by the rocks. There is no efficacious way to preserve the body. Otis hadn't intended there to be. His body he had intended to commit everlastingly to the sea.

So, with the help of the off-duty graphers and the fisherman, Chester gives his brother a proper ocean burial. Enshrouded and weighted, carried well out beyond the bay, the corpse slides quickly over the gunwales of the fisherman's dory as Chester gives it a push and whispers a prayer. He has chosen a place he hopes is near where the cable lies. He imagines Otis drifting down to rest by the line, to listen to its signals.

Reunion

Clearly, there has been a fire. The center of the hotel—its portico, central rooms, a turret, the southern wing—still stands. The building's white paint is scorched and smudged here and there, and the red roof has pale shake patches where cinders burned through. Off to the north side, there are piles of ashes—old and gray, pounded flat by last winter's snow, this spring's thaw, and now by a midday, late August sun. Charred beams and posts still stand—or nearly so, as many are toppled, leaning against one another in diagonal disarray—their surfaces shining like anthracite and heat-scored in patterns like alligator hide.

Nevertheless, framing is under way; a new wing will soon be taking shape. Scaffolding made from fresh-cut pine the color of buttermilk grows out from the standing building. Timbers, barked and notched and fragrant, lie stacked along the hotel's drive. It is Sunday, so the carpenters are off.

Chester is alone on horseback, having ridden all morning through the Notch up from Bartlett. The Hotel Ammonoosuc is on his way to the Fabyan bridle path up Mount Washington. He and his horse are standing at the end of the hotel's drive. A white-throated sparrow pipes its up-and-down, six-note song in the pine bough over his head. It is a sound so familiar in this country. Chester knows he will hear more of it on the mountain when he gets up closer to the tree line.

He could have taken the train here, but he wanted to arrive more slowly, alone, to study his home terrain. The day before, he'd paused in North Conway to walk by the frame house on Seavey Street where he'd lived with his mother. Then he rode to Bartlett and stood in the cemetery where Otis had buried the Old Man.

The grave marker is a rock cairn. It is completely out of keeping with the rest of the headstones in the cemetery, but it is fitting, knowing, as Chester does, that Otis was responsible for it. A rock in the center of the pyramidal pile has been smoothed and Amos Bronson Ludlow's name and dates—1789–1841—had been chiseled in. The rocks, the sexton told Chester, were brought down by the deceased's son from the summit of Mount Washington. The deceased was a painter. Big on painting these mountains. There are piles of rocks like that—cairns—up there above the tree line to mark the way for travelers.

This cairn, though, Chester thought, could just as easily have been built to weigh down what lies beneath it. Chester has read Otis's journal. He knows what happened.

The sexton told Chester that if he looks on his way up the Notch, he'll be able to see Mount Washington. The day will be clear enough. The sexton also told Chester about the Hotel Ammonoosuc, how some railroad fellow who's now out west is rebuilding it after the fire last season. Chester doesn't plan to stay at the hotel, although he knows he will be visiting there. He has seen the posters.

The mountains, in the high early-afternoon sun of August, look bleached above the tree line and flat as stage scenery. It was Otis's wish that Chester go up there. Chester had found a note scrawled to him in Otis's journal: instructions for the disposition of his effects. Chester has Otis's few worldly possessions: some relics brought back from the Pacific (rocks, shells, a bit of some sort of fungus) and the sextant. The note asks for the objects to be taken "somewhere near home ... possibly high up Mount Washington and placed under a cairn there, please. The journal is for you." That was his last request. Chester is honoring it. He will ride up the bridle path tomorrow or the next day. But for now the posters have diverted him here.

His horse shuffles and paws at the gravel in the drive. Chester can see hotel guests out playing badminton and horseshoes. Children squeal down in a meadow as they try to get a kite aloft. Three or four cloud shadows pass along the upper slopes of the peaks. Before him, a woman is stepping gingerly among the burned beams and framing in the part of the hotel that is being reclaimed from the fire.

Years later Franny Ludlow will tell her boys of how she saw their father that day for the first time after their "years apart." ("Our years apart," she will call the time, roughly, of the cable expeditions and the Civil War; the time when Chester Ludlow made his name in the world; the time, she will say, when they *both* made their names in the world.) She will say that she was there, staying at the hotel. (But she will not go into details as to why; that she was employed as a house fortune-teller for the guests, a parlor amusement; that the posters and bills heralding the Hotel Ammonoosuc, "rising like a Phoenix from the ashes of last year's fire!" will feature "all the usual amusements and attractions!" including, "Dame Frances Piermont, soothsayer"; that despite Spude's bombast, her prospects were diminished; that it was one of those posters that brought Chester there; that if he hadn't arrived, well, things might have ended very differently for her. None of this will she go into.) She will say that she was walking among the ruins of a fire that had consumed a great part of the hotel the year before, the part that contained the library. Dandelions and even the tiny seedlings of birch trees had sprung up here and there in the ashes. Always the first plants to sprout after a house fire, they were pushing their way through the rubble where once Turkish carpets and mahogany writing desks had been.

She will say that she looked up to guess where, approximately, their grandfather's greatest painting had hung in that library, for she had seen the painting the year before. She has seen many of Amos Bronson Ludlow's paintings, she will say, but that one was the greatest of them all. And it had been destroyed in the fire. She was trying to remember it, she will say. And then she saw before her, framed by the burned posts and beams where the picture once hung, her husband, astride a horse.

Chester looks at his wife from a distance of nearly fifty yards, waiting to see when—or if—she will recognize him. He is thinking how, in ways he may never work out, Otis—manifested now only as a bundle of personal effects and written obligations—may have been the true agent of their coming together like this.

And then Franny Ludlow steps through the frame of the burned building and walks toward her husband as he dismounts and walks toward her.

Two Weeks Later

Two weeks later they are back at Willing Mind. It is the day they have buried Otis—his belongings—in the family plot on the bluffs. There is no fence around the plot, only heather to form the border of the little cemetery. It is just below the crest of one of the bluffs, in a spot the wind can't reach, so it always seems calm there. Franny's parents lie in one corner; Betty lies on the other side. Otis—Chester and Franny are already thinking of the effects as *him*—lies closest to the ocean. There is a small cairn for his headstone. Chester built the cairn from rocks he brought back from Mount Washington. Otis is not next to Betty's grave, for that is where Chester and Franny will lie, one on either side, when their time comes. But Otis is nearby.

Chester and Franny decided together, late at night on the porch of the Hotel Ammonoosuc, to bring Otis back to Willing Mind. They had read his last request and his journal, reflected, and decided he would have found it acceptable, maybe even preferable, to be laid to rest on the bluffs.

"He only said 'near home,' " Chester pointed out. "He only *suggested* his things be taken up on Mount Washington."

"Willing Mind was his home," said Franny, knowing that years ago she had once told Otis this was not so, but knowing so much more now, about home, about returning, about laying things—and lives—to rest.

There are two telegraph cables working under the Atlantic Ocean. After successfully laying the first line in late July, the *Great Eastern* steamed back out to sea and began dragging for the twelve hundred miles of line it had laid out the year before. It took nearly four weeks of hauling it up, having it break, dragging for it again; dragging, hauling, breaking, and searching some thirty times until finally they were able to retrieve it. They spliced in new cable, sailed to Heart's Content a second time and completed Cyrus Field's dream.

Chester had been able to keep abreast of the cable's progress. Professor Thomson sent him several messages, once they found the second cable, by telegraphing from the *Great Eastern* back to Ireland on the old line (real signals coming through the old line, not the delirious mutterings of the sea), then having the message sent back from Ireland to Newfoundland to America and finally Willing Mind.

"You have high claim to what we have achieved," Professor Thomson wired to Chester. "And remember. We still have work to do."

The thought comforts Chester. As he toils about the estate, putting the neglected house back to rights, he thinks of that work as a store of something he will draw upon as his future unfolds. But he knows, for now, where his foremost attention must be applied.

He and Franny had spent that whole night talking together on the porch of the Hotel Ammonoosuc. They decided about Otis's interment, but they couldn't have come to that decision without deciding something else first. Or perhaps the decision about Otis was what led to the other decision. It is impossible for them to remember the exact sequence, as thoughts and feelings eddied and pooled around them while they sat in the dark, side by side, on rocking chairs facing that huge wall of mountains. It was the same experience as that night years before on the packet from Bergen to Newcastle when they watched Orion slowly dip into the sea, spent the night talking and never realizing precisely when their lives together had begun. It's not something you realize, Franny once said, but it's something you know.

And it is the same way about their return to Willing Mind.

Franny supposes the moment came closest to definition when she asked

Chester, "Do you think we can do this?" (But then, she thinks: *See? We already knew.*)

And he said, "I know I cannot live if I do not at least try."

"And I," she said. "I, too."

So, they are living at Willing Mind, repairing it and preparing it for winter. Gil and Edwina Tyler are about during the days to add such help as two old retainers can. No task is performed too quickly even though Chester and Franny could work faster. There is something ceremonial about the pace of their labor. There is a kind of genuflection before each task, a hold, then a reengagement with the overall design.

Chester and Franny do not sleep together. Nothing too soon. Nothing too quickly. And yet they know they do not want to let the opportunity miss them for want of attention. So they are constantly mindful of each other. It is all so tricky.

One night they are sitting in the study, the room Franny and Otis had once used as the Spirit Room. The nights have grown cold, frost has already shown up on the grass several mornings running, but the study is a room small enough for a fireplace to heat efficiently. Franny has fallen asleep on one end of the sofa, and Chester, at the other end, has been doing some calculations, figuring out the board feet he will need to repair the walkway and guardrail out by the bluffs.

He must have dozed off, too, because he notices that the fire, when he is aware of it, has died down considerably and the lantern's wick needs trimming. He does not check his watch, but he knows it is late, the small hours. Perhaps it was the fluttering, sooty light of the lamp that roused him.

Perhaps it was the presence of what he sees before him out the window.

He reaches over and snuffs out the lamp, thinking this will help him determine what it is out there. The room is dark, save for the small dot of light in the embers in the fireplace.

Something is moving out on the bluffs.

Chester finds himself worrying, wishing he were not seeing this, but at the same time he's stirred by not knowing what it is. He rises quietly and slips toward the window.

The night is a tangle of dark shapes. What could be clouds could also be clumps of heather or spume from the breakers below the cliffs, or dim reflections of the room behind him. It is as if the wind and cold are sculpting forms or have bodied forth themselves as visible, changing objects.

But there is something cohering. A human figure. Their daughter. Chester almost murmurs the word. He is close enough to the glass of the window to fog it with his breath, a white halo.

He will never be sure of what he saw that night, if anything. Maybe it was only his wishes, shaping themselves out of the jumble of the world at night, or maybe it was only his breath on the glass. Nevertheless, he will tell Franny he saw her, their daughter, Betty.

But she is not as they remember her.

It is plain to Chester that she has grown. She is a girl now, not a child, almost a young woman. She does not dance the way she once had over the railroad tracks through his long, horrible journey during the war, dancing and drawing him onward. Nor does she hover, just beyond perception, the way he thought she had during those years soon after her death, during the time of the cable laying, when he was trying to connect continents.

She is right there, but this time she turns away at the very moment he comprehends it is her, so he never can know exactly how she looks. He is not allowed to gaze in her eyes or see her face. And in that turn of hers, timed to come at the very instant of his knowing, she leaves him. She walks away, calmly, assuredly, toward the sea, and rather than fall over the edge, she simply vanishes.

At the window, he's enthralled and calmed by her poise, how she's grown. Whereas she once drew him on, now she leaves him.

Franny awakens with a start and a cry. She calls his name. "I've had a dream," she says in the dark. Chester knows without asking what it was.

"Where are you?" she says.

"Here," he says. "Follow my voice."

And she rises to come toward him.

EPILOGUE

ranny did not accompany Chester on the trip across the Atlantic to see Professor Thomson. She stayed behind because the theater she was managing was about to begin rehearsals for its first production of the season, *The Tempest.* Chester would be back in time for the opening. The theater was in the barn at Willing Mind—the barn where the Phantasmagorium Show had once had its first performance. The Ludlows had converted it into an auditorium complete with seats (not benches), proscenium stage with flies, traps, and a scenery turntable. Chester had thrown himself into engineering the place. The summer tourist trade was poised to sell out the shows. (J. Beaumol Spude, east from San Francisco, would see *The Tempest* and make arrangements to book Franny's shows in a theater he would later construct at the Hotel Ammonoosuc.) Life at Willing Mind had become, at least during the summer theater season, full, almost rollicking.

And there were the boys. Augustus, named for Franny's father, and Otis. Chester brought the boys with him, their first big trip away from Willing Mind, for a look at the wider world.

A steward had told Augustus about the *Great Eastern* amusement park on the Thames and had cataloged all the attractions in vivid detail, thus giving Augustus, who was eleven, the data he needed to prevail upon Chester to take them out to the Isle of Dogs.

"Also, the captain says the winds are fair and we look to be arriving early," Augustus said. "We should have the time before our train to Glasgow."

"Should we?" asked Chester. Augustus had clearly done his homework.

"It's the Wonders of the Age," said Otis.

"What is?" asked Chester.

"The ship!" said Otis. "The fair!"

"That's what they call it," Augustus informed his father soberly. "Mr. James the steward told us."

"Can we go?"

The morning after their arrival in London, they took a carriage out to the great ship. Chester half expected to be saddened to see the vessel gussied up as a carnival attraction, and he was. But its magnitude was still of an order that no amount of tawdriness could wholly belittle. Though it would never sail again, though it had been reduced to being an advertisement for a department store, it was nonetheless majestic and still the largest ship afloat.

"Criminy!" said Augustus when he first saw it. Otis could only reach for his father's hand, speechless, almost frightened by the enormity before him.

"You sailed on that, Papa?" asked Augustus.

"I did," said Chester. Even he was speaking in a low voice.

"With the cable?"

"Was it fast?"

"With the cable. It was fast enough," said Chester. "And big enough."

"It's big!" said Otis.

"But you weren't on it when they did the cable that worked, were you?" said Augustus. "You weren't on it the last time."

"No."

"He wanted to be with Mama," said Otis.

Chester looked at both his boys. "Is that what Mama said?" he asked.

"Yes," said Otis, sensing something about the question that needed a somber answer. He spoke the word slowly and nodded his head.

"Well," said Chester, "she's right."

The boys went on to urge their father to let them run ahead with the other fairgoers who were making their way along the boulevard down to the ship. Chester told the boys to mind the horses and go ahead. He paid the cabdriver and walked quickly, keeping them in sight.

After its 1866 success laying the cable, the *Great Eastern* went on to lay five more transatlantic cables and a three-thousand-mile line from Bombay to Suez. It then lost hundreds of thousands of francs for the government of Napoleon III when it failed, yet again, to make a go as a luxury liner. It sat rusting for years until Lewis's Department Store, a Liverpool emporium, bought it and transformed it into the "World's Largest Floating Amusement Park Replete with the Wonders of the Age."

Lewis's *Great Eastern* Floating Exposition, Amusement Park, and Fancy Fair was berthed below Limehouse Reach, just beyond the yard where the ship was built, on the Isle of Dogs. Flags and banners and a newly cobbled boulevard ushered the throngs toward the giant attraction. By tearing out bulkheads and coal bunkers, Lewis's created a thousand-seat musical auditorium on the ship where Swiss yodelers and lady boxers performed. In the rigging, up where Otis Ludlow had once kept vigil and whence he had leapt, trapeze artists swung and flung themselves across the vacancies between the masts. Bob the Missing Link, a slightly hydrocephalic Negro from the Belgian colonies in Africa, dressed in furs and rawhide, gamboled and roared for the patrons in the forward cable circus. A Gypsy tribe bivouacked on the quarterdeck. Footraces were held around the promenade. There was an aquarium in the aft circus, a Riding School for the Millions to teach the equestrian arts to all comers on the former livestock deck, a Gutta-Percha Man contortionist in a tent on the bow, moored balloon rides that ascended from amidships ("Look Down with Great Amusement on the Greatest Amusement!"), food vendors and cafés on every deck, games of chance, a casino in the grand saloon, orchestras and musical ensembles from each continent (excepting the uninhabited and tuneless wastes of Antarctica), even a telegraph line running from one end of the ship to the other (an idea stolen from Cyrus Field's barge fete years ago, when Joachim Lindt thought of the *Great Eastern*'s first transformation: from failed luxury liner to cable ship).

But perhaps the greatest attraction of all was Jack Trace's mural. It certainly held the most people entranced for longer than any other act on display. The painting hung from the side of the hull. A catwalk enabled customers to stroll along before the canvas that covered nearly the full length of the vessel. Throngs would stand before the work, spellbound, almost as if they were lost in a reverie inside the painting.

From where Chester walked, the painting's details were indistinct—land and sky—but he could see the crowd on the viewing platform. So, the shy, shambling artist who had done those beautiful cable portfolios had painted a popular masterpiece. Visionary, the critics said it was. Chester was glad he had come to see it, glad Trace had lived to see its glory, even if only briefly.

Chester had heard of Jack Trace's accident. Professor Thomson had sent him the obituary two years before. While he was putting the finishing touches on the work, Trace had fallen from the scaffolding. He must have stepped back too far for a better look—a simple workman's error, a momentary human lapse—and he fell thirty feet to the Thames shore, breaking his neck.

Close enough now, as he walked, to make out the sweep of sky and earth in the painting, Chester noticed the breeze occasionally sent long ripples down the canvas. It was then that he thought the landmass of the painting looked very much like a reclining woman. An artist's joke perhaps, thought Chester, as he wondered what woman it might be.

The obituary said Trace had never married, but Professor Thomson had written that he'd heard Trace had a long-standing "friendship" with a fancy woman who owned a house in Mayfair, so Trace hadn't exactly died alone.

The boys were running ahead, Augustus turning to check on his father, both boys waving and beckoning him to hurry when they saw him out of the cab and on foot, too.

He could distinctly hear the shipboard bands now, a march from one, bagpipes from another. Other fairgoers walked along with him, chatting and laughing. The noise lifted his spirits.

He would enjoy seeing the ship again, no matter how tarted up it had become. He would enjoy seeing Professor Thomson again and introducing him to his sons. They would all go for a sail on his yacht, the *Lalla Rookh*, and Chester would let him show them a thing or two about sailing, let him tell them some stories of storms at sea and the perils the Cablemen faced while laying a line beneath the ocean to send a tiny spark and then another and another down thousands of miles of cable until someone on the other side knew what you were saying. He could hear old Professor Thomson telling them that in his hard, rolling Scottish burr and telling them to take the tiller and to try steering the boat themselves.

"Steer her true," the professor would say. "Straight and true."

And Augustus and Otis would try, and Thomson would shake his head and laugh and point sternward and say, "Look at the wake, Mr. Ludlow. Your boys are trying to write their names on the ocean!"

And Augustus and Otis would try all the harder to lay a straight wake on the waves.

Chester could picture all this as he walked.

Almost before he knew it, he was at the viewing platform for the mural. It cost nothing to go up the steps and see the work. The promoters had used the painting to lure in customers, and it was wildly successful. People crowded the rails and looked across the open wharf to the side of the ship where *Progress* hung.

At this distance, the details of the painting were manifest. People ogled and pointed and talked to one another about what they saw and what they thought they saw.

The mural showed a vast, fantastical landscape awhirl with the complexities of futuristic transportation—silvery trains that seemed to run on one track, lozengelike carriages with no visible means of propulsion that looked to be gliding over velvet roads, airships afloat with opulent gondolas dangling from the netted balloons that held them aloft. There were cities with clean, broad boulevards; buildings so tall that Trace had misty clouds bisecting their many-windowed facades. Fields neatly under cultivation, hedgerows, cottages (with the little transport lozenges sitting outside each one), all reminded viewers that this future, this wondrous whirligig utopia, could someday be right here, right in the England they knew; London itself could be transformed, the countryside remade—bettered!—all the wealth and resources of the empire brought to bear upon the Sceptered Isle's improvement.

Chester wondered, as he found himself enchanted by the details of the painting, if that was what had killed Jack—that he had lost himself inside the work and then lost his footing and fell from the scaffold. It would be nice to think he just disappeared inside that world and never even knew he'd died in this one.

Chester began pondering if such manners of flight and propulsion and communication could ever be built. He wondered if he could ever build any of them. Already, over in America, a Scotsman named Bell was sending not just flickers of light or clicks of a key but his own voice and music down a wire. Progress was everywhere. How could a man keep up?

The boys had had enough of the painting. They ran back along the length of the viewing platform to the gangway that reached into the ship. A banner that proclaimed THE WONDERS OF THE AGE! arched over the ascending ramp. Chester knew his sons would be calling for him any minute.

He would go, but first he paused because he noticed something when the breezes, coming up Limehouse Reach, caught the edge of the canvas. The line holding one corner grommet of Trace's painting had slipped loose, and the edge of the picture flipped up when a gust strong enough took hold of it. Chester had to wait for several gusts to come and go to be sure of what he was seeing.

There was something painted on the backside of Trace's canvas. Eventually, Chester recognized the palette and brush strokes of the Phantasmagorium's scenery. Chester looked up at the whole of *Progress*. The stitched-together canvas Trace had used had come from the Phantasmagorium Show's backdrop scroll. On the other side of Trace's painting was the whole rearranged pictorial history of the cable. The story Chester had narrated to raise capital for the real story that he had come to live, the laying of the real cable. And they had done it, he told himself. Raised the money. Built the line. Joined the continents. Painted the picture.

The boys were calling him. He saw them now up on the deck of the huge ship, looking down, tiny dots emitting small noises, waving from the rail.

He had better follow them up there. He started making his way toward the gangplank.

"Papa!" It was Augustus waving his cap from high up on the deck.

"Hurry!" cried Otis.

"Look where we are! You come, too. That way."

And Augustus pointed down from the great height to the route Chester should take.

"I'm coming," Chester called.

"It's wonderful up here, Papa!" called Augustus. "They have flags from every country!"

The boys are so full of enthusiasm, thought Chester. *I shall wire their mother what we did today.*

"We need money to get in!" called one of the boys.

"Hurry, Papa!"

In the wind, it was hard to tell one voice from the other.

"I'm coming," Chester called, and quickened his step for his sons.

"It's the Wonders of the Age!"

"It is?"

"Yes! I can read it!"

That must have been Otis, proud he could con the words.

Chester was about to board the huge old ship once again. He strode across the gangway over the water. There was music and cheerful noise and the flags of all the nations snapping in the breeze.

"It's the Wonders of the Age!" he heard one of his sons call.

"Hurry!"